P9-DCD-886

**Theo Vilmos' life is about to take
a real turn for the worse.**

A thirty-year-old lead singer in a not-terribly-successful rock band, Theo once had enormous charisma both onstage and off—but now, life has taken its toll on him. He finds himself alone, heartbroken, and plagued by a recurring nightmare—and Theo can't shake the feeling that bad things are happening to him for a reason. Seeking solace and escape in a cabin in the woods, he begins to read a old handwritten memoir by his great-uncle, a man named Eamonn Dowd, and quickly becomes mesmerized. Dowd writes of another world—the world of Faerie—but it is nothing like the familiar fairyland of childhood stories.

But before Theo can disregard the account as the writings of a madman, a horrifying *thing* tries to break through his front door—a terrible hunting-spirit in the body of a dead man. Terrified and trapped, Theo is saved only by the intervention of a tiny, foul-mouthed, winged sprite named Applecore, who transports him into the realm of Faerie. But *this* fairyland is even darker and more bizarrely modern than Eamonn Dowd had described, similar to the mortal world and yet dangerously different, and although he can't imagine why, there are creatures in it that intend Theo Vilmos serious harm. With only the reluctant sprite Applecore for a guide, Theo must search for the true meaning of his life—before those who seek him can cut it mercilessly short.

Raves for
The War of the Flowers

"Darkly satirizes every sort and condition and politics, ideology, religion, and other human foibles . . . Williams has a supremely powerful imagination."   —*Booklist*

"Fascinating . . . A sort of land of Faerie, but one unlike anything you've ever encountered before. A very elaborate and fully realized setting for adventure, intrigue, and more than an occasional chill."   —*Science Fiction Chronicle*

"While the subject of changelings has been explored numerous times, Williams keeps the theme fresh by incorporating his trademarks of wonderfully complex plot twists, masterful character development, and expeditious pacing. Highly recommended."   —*Barnes and Noble*

"An intense urban fantasy of fairies, changelings, and the end of the world . . . a richly detailed, fully developed world of mortal vs. fairy."   —*Romantic Times* (top pick)

"Tad Williams is one of America's better and more versatile writers, notable for his extravagant and varied world-building. Williams has shown himself a master storyteller, equally adept at whatever genre chosen, and often on a grand scale. *The War of the Flowers* is no exception, showcasing his talents in a fictional realm that until now has been dominated by the likes of de Lint."   —*Interzone*

"I welcomed the chance to read *The War of the Flowers*, because it clocks in at only (!) 675 pages and is a self-contained story. In a way I'm sorry I did, because now I'm a fan, so now I have to figure out some way to take the next year off to get through his back catalog."   —*SF Site*

"The plight of the modern American male from a master of fantasy. Williams displays a deft hand, creating an addictive world with its own history, mythology, and internal rules, and rich, intricate culture. He definitely knows his way around the magic kingdom. When I found myself reading *The War of the Flowers* while standing at the stove stirring some ramen noodles, I knew I was hooked. The world of Faerie turns out to have everything a fantasy fan could desire. But there's a delicious twist, one that elevates *The War of the Flowers* above the vast majority of sword-and-sorcery schlock swamping your local bookstore. For the world of Faerie is plagued by problems, that, whoops, are plenty recognizable. Urban decay, power failures, class warfare, prejudice . . . this land of make-believe is in big trouble, and there isn't going to be an easy talismanic cure. Heck, the fairy lords even have magic cellphones, which is a kind of evil I really wasn't expecting. In other words, in this epitome of an escape genre offering, there is no way out from mundane afflictions. It would be a mean trick to play on readers if it weren't so well done. Even as he weaves his 'make-believe' world, afflicted by rank bigotry, blackouts and even magic e-mail, Williams simultaneously delivers moments of grandeur and potency that fit snugly into a Tolkienesque tradition. But he does it with a modern sensibility—imagine a Tolkien who listened to Metallica—and he has more up his sleeve than thwarting the legions of doom. *The War of the Flowers* isn't just about magic, it's about the struggle to be human when that seems too hard. So, while readers will relish a fantasy novel that belongs in the top tier of those currently being produced, that masterfully plays with all the tropes and traditions of generations of fantasy writers, they will also become absorbed in Theo's real quest, which has nothing to do with sword wielding or inner powers or 'greatness' by any commonly understood definition. His real quest is to become, basically, a good guy and a stand-up mensch.   —*Salon*

DAW BOOKS PRESENTS
THE FINEST IN IMAGINATIVE FICTION BY

TAD WILLIAMS

Tailchaser's Song

The War of the Flowers

Shadowmarch
Shadowplay

MEMORY, SORROW AND THORN
The Dragonbone Chair
Stone of Farewell
To Green Angel Tower

OTHERLAND
City of Golden Shadow
River of Blue Fire
Mountain of Black Glass
Sea of Silver Light

THE WAR
OF THE
FLOWERS

Tad Williams

DAW BOOKS, INC.

DONALD A. WOLLHEIM, FOUNDER
375 Hudson Street, New York, NY 10014

ELIZABETH R. WOLLHEIM
SHEILA E. GILBERT
PUBLISHERS
http://www.dawbooks.com

Copyright © 2003 by Tad Williams.
All Rights Reserved.

Cover art by Michael Whelan.
For color prints of Michael Whelan's paintings, please contact:
Glass Onion Graphics
P.O. Box 88
Brookfield, CT 06804
www.michaelwhelan.com

DAW Book Collectors No. 1225

DAW Books are distributed by the Penguin Group (USA) Inc.

Book designed by Stanley S. Drate/Folio Graphics Co., Inc.

All characters and events in this book are fictitious.
Any resemblance to persons living or dead is strictly coincidental.

The scanning, uploading and distribution of this book via the Internet or any other
means without the permission of the publisher is illegal, and punishable by law. Please
purchase only authorized electronic editions, and do not participate in or encourage the
electronic piracy of copyrighted materials. Your support of the author's rights is appreciated.

First printing, May 2004
7   8   9

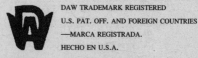

DAW TRADEMARK REGISTERED
U.S. PAT. OFF. AND FOREIGN COUNTRIES
—MARCA REGISTRADA.
HECHO EN U.S.A.
PRINTED IN THE U.S.A.

This book is dedicated with great love to my wife, Deborah Beale, who makes my life worth living in more ways than I can count, let alone list here.

A good marriage and a loving family may not be the easiest things in the world to create, but I find it hard to believe there is anything more worth the effort. It is a Great Adventure, and I share mine with a wonderful woman.

Deb, you are my personal fairytale ending.

This book didn't have quite as many midwives as some of my others, but it still wouldn't have made it into the world without a lot of help.

I have again received support and useful feedback in too many ways to list from my wonderful agent Matt Bialer and my British editor Tim Holman, and my German editor Ulrike Killler. My brilliant wife Deborah Beale as always provided words of wisdom at many stages, both as a reader full of useful comments and because of her literary and publishing acumen. My thanks to all of them—I'm a very lucky writer. And of course, profound gratitude to my most excellent American publishers (and primary editors of this book) Betsey Wollheim and Sheila Gilbert, along with all the folks at DAW Books, for helping me to see another wild idea from conception to its emergence into the world, and for their constant exercise of creative patience. I couldn't do it without them.

Blessings on you all.

AUTHOR'S NOTE

Readers may notice a certain uncomfortable resonance in parts of this book to events around the terrorist attacks on New York and Washington, D.C., of September 11, 2001. The part of the story that most closely parallels things that happened on that horrible day was actually part of the planned book since the beginning—while preparing to write this note I found it mentioned prominently in an outline written in January of 2000.

I have modified those sections slightly so that they echo the real events a little less closely, but it was too central an event in the story to take out entirely. I hope anyone disturbed by the similarity will accept my apology for discomfort caused, and understand that this was a case of leaving in something already planned and important to the story rather than adding something after the fact to try to gain some cheap thrills out of a tragedy that was international in scope but also personal for very many people.

CONTENTS

🌸 Part Three
FLOWER WAR

PROLOGUE

A single flower, a hellebore, stood in a vase of volcanic glass in the middle of the huge desk, glowing almost radioactively white in the pool of a small, artful spotlight. In other great houses the image of such a deceptively fragile-looking bloom would have been embroidered on a banner covering most of the wall behind the seat of power, but there was need for such things here. No one could reach the innermost chambers of this monstrous bone-colored building and not know where they were and who ruled in this place.

In the mortal world the hellebore is sometimes called the Christmas Rose because of an old tale that says it sprouted where a little girl who had no gift for the Christ Child wept into the snow outside the stable in Bethlehem. Both snow and the flower itself were unlikely to have been found in the Holy Land in those days, but that has never hurt the story's popularity.

In Greece of the old myths, Melampus of Pylos used hellebore to save the daughters of the king of Argos from a Dionysian madness that had set them running naked through the city, weeping and screaming and laughing.

There are many stories about hellebore. Most of them have tears in them.

The Remover of Inconvenient Obstacles was no stranger

to silence—in fact, he swam in it like a fish. He stared at the
spotlit flower, letting his thoughts wander down some of the
darker tracks of his labyrinthine mind, and waited, patient as
stone, for the figure behind the desk to speak. The pause was
a long one.

The person on the other side of the desk, who had apparently been pursuing some internal quarry of his own, stirred
at last. Slowly, almost lazily, he extended an arm to touch
the flower on his desk. His spidersilk suit whispered so
faintly only a bat or the creature sitting across from him
could hear. His long finger, only a little less white than the
flower, touched a petal and made it quiver.

There were no windows here in the heart of the building,
but the Remover of Inconvenient Obstacles knew that it was
raining hard outside, the drops spattering and hissing on the
pavement, coach tires spitting. Here the air was as still as if
he and his host sat inside a velvet-lined jewel casket.

The shape in the beautiful, shimmering blue-black suit
gently prodded the flower again. "War is coming," he said at
last. His voice was deep and musical. Mortal women who
had only heard him speak, waking to discover him warm and
invisible in their rooms in the middle of the night, had fallen
so deeply in love with that voice that they had forsworn all
human suitors, giving up the chance of sunlit happiness forever in the futile hope he would return to them, would let
them live again that one delirious midnight hour.

"War is coming," agreed the Remover.

"The child of whom we spoke before. It must not live."

A long breath—was it a sigh? "It will not."

"You will receive the usual fee."

The Remover nodded, distracted by his own thoughts. He
had very little fear that anyone, even this most powerful personage, would neglect to pay him. With war coming they
would need him again. He was the specialist of specialists,
totally discreet and terrifyingly effective. He also made a
very bad enemy.

"Now?" he asked.

"As soon as you can. If you wait too long, someone might notice. Also we don't want the risk. The Clover Effect is still not perfectly understood. You might not get a second chance."

The Remover stood. "I have never yet needed such a thing."

He was gone from the inner room so quickly he might have been a shadow flitting across the dark walls. The master of the House of Hellebore could see much that others could not, but even he had trouble marking the exact progress of the Remover's self-deletion.

It would not be good to have to guard against that one, he thought to himself. *He must be kept sweet, or he must become ashes in the Well of Forgetting. Either way, he must never again work for one of the other houses.* The master of the house stroked the pale flower on his desk again, considering.

Another curiosity of the hellebore is that its bloom can be frozen solid in the deepest winter snows, but when the ice melts away, dripping from the petals like tears, the flower beneath is still alive, still supple. Hellebore is strong and patient.

The tall, lean figure in the spidersilk suit pressed a button on the side of his desk and spoke into the air. The winds of Faerie carried his words to all those who needed to hear them, throughout the great city and all across the troubled land, summoning his allies and tributaries to the first council of the next war of the Flowers.

Part One

GOODNIGHT NOBODY

1

CLOUDS

Theo felt a small flutter of guilt as he turned the cell phone back on, especially when he noticed he'd left it off for more than two hours, and was relieved to see that there were no messages. He'd only meant to flick it off for a few minutes, just to make sure there were no interruptions while they were tuning—the young guys, especially Kris, the guitarist, got really pissy about that—but things had started happening and he'd forgotten.

Johnny stepped over the guitar cases spread across the living room rug like discarded cocoons and slid open the door to join him outside. The fog had come down the hill while they had been practicing; the fenced patio seemed an island in a cold, misty sea.

Jesus, San Francisco in March. He should have brought his jacket out. *Might as well be in Minnesota.* "Hey," he asked Johnny, "got a smoke?"

The drummer made a face and patted his shirt pocket, then his pants pockets. He was small but he had long, strong arms. With his paunch and his shaggy but balding head, the chest hair climbing out of his T-shirt collars, he always made Theo think of the soulful chimpanzees in that English-woman's documentaries.

When Johnny found the pack at last, he shook out one for

Theo, then one for himself and lit it. "Man, you never have your own."

"Never buy any. I only smoke when I'm playing."

Johnny shook his head. "That's so typical, Vilmos—you always get the easy road. I'm an addict, you only smoke when you want to—like, when you're around me. I'll probably be the one who gets cancer, too."

"Probably." Theo considered calling home, but he was going to be leaving in a few minutes anyway. Still, Cat was very deep into *I'm-pregnant-and-I-want-to-know-where-you-are* mode . . . He felt another ripple of guilt and couldn't decide what to do. He stared at the phone, as perplexed as if it were an artifact of a vanished civilization.

"Your old lady leave a message?" Johnny was the only one in the band who was Theo's age but he talked like he was even older, unashamedly using words like "chicks" and "hip." Theo had actually heard him say "out of sight" once, but he had sworn later he was being ironic. Johnny was also the only one who'd even understand something as archaic as phoning home. Kris and Dano and Morgan were in that early-twenties stage where they just paged their girlfriends to announce when they were dropping by after practice to have sex.

"Nah. I gotta get going, anyway."

Johnny flipped his cigarette over the fence and out into the street, a tiny shooting star. "Just listen to the playback on 'Feast,' first. You don't want Kris's asshole to get any more puckered than it already is, do you?" He smiled deep in his beard and started peeling off the athletic tape he wrapped around his knuckles before playing because he bashed them against the rims so hard. Theo thought that he'd rather have scars than the pink, hairless patches that striped Johnny's hairy hands, but Johnny was a seemingly permanently single guy who hadn't had a date in months, so he didn't worry much about things like that.

Theo did. He was seriously considering whether it was time to cut his moderately long brown hair. It was bad enough to have turned thirty and still be singing in garage bands without looking like an aging stoner, too.

As it turned out, Theo spent at least another half an hour listening to the demo tracks they had recorded for "Feast of Fools," a sort of high-Goth processional that Kris had written, and over which the guitarist fussed like a neurotic chef preparing for an important dinner party. He had more than a few irritating things to say about Theo's vocal, wanting more rasp in it, more of an air of menace, the kind of melodrama that Theo didn't much like.

On their last listen, as Kris bobbed his close-cropped head to his own music, his expression oddly combining pleasure and pain, Theo had a sudden flash of insight: *He's going to want to do the vocal on this himself—that's where this is going. And even though I'm a hundred times better, eventually he's going to get his confidence and want to do all the lead vocals himself. And that'll be it for me with this band.*

He wasn't certain how he felt about that. On the one hand, much as he admired the young guys' playing and Kris Rolle's musical ideas, it wasn't anything like his ideal band. For a start, he hated the name—The Mighty Clouds of Angst. It was clumsy. Worse, it was a joke name, playing off a famous gospel group, The Mighty Clouds of Joy. Theo believed firmly that joke names equaled joke bands, the Beatles notwithstanding. Plus, it just irritated him. Kris, Morgan, and Dano weren't even old enough to remember The Mighty Clouds of Joy, so why pick that as a name to parody? It smacked a little of white suburban boys making fun of earnest, religious black people, and that made Theo uncomfortable. But if he ever mentioned it, he knew they'd just show him that fishlike stare they had perfected, the all-purpose defense against hopelessly uncool parents and teachers, and he would feel even older than he did.

So when did I wind up on the wrong side of that particular line?

He eased on his ancient leather jacket and bummed another smoke off John for the road—or for home, rather,
since it was pretty hard to smoke while wearing a motorcycle helmet. He looked around, feeling like he was leaving
something behind. Lead singers didn't carry much in the
way of equipment. The mikes and PA belonged to Morgan
and Kris. Theo could walk away from the Clouds as easily
as he was strolling out the door tonight. If he was good at
anything, it was leaving when things got too weird.

If he did get forced out, would Johnny quit too? Theo
wasn't sure how he felt about that. This was the third band
he'd played in with Johnny Battistini, following the obliga-
tory should-have-made-it-big disaster in which they'd met
and the horrible cover band in which they'd marked time
until hooking up with Kris and company. Theo wouldn't
mind the downtime of looking for another gig, and God
knew Catherine would be happy to have him home some
nights, especially with the baby coming, but ol' Johnny B.
didn't have a lot else going on in his life. Besides his record
store job and the Clouds, in fact, John was pretty much the
kind of guy advertisers made fun of but who kept their
clients in business—an amiable lump who lived on take-out
food, rented porn movies in bunches, and watched wrestling
by himself.

Kris looked up from yet another playing of "Feast of
Fools" as Theo reached the door. "You going?" He sounded
irritated. Kris had gray eyes like a sky before a storm, the
kind of eyes in which teenage girls probably saw things that
weren't really there at all.

No, Theo wanted to say. *No, I'm going to hang around
here and stay up all night smoking dope and marveling at
my own brilliance, just like you guys, because I've got nothing better to do and nobody on my ass about when I come
home.*

"Can't stay," he said instead. "I've got a pregnant girlfriend, remember?" And for a self-righteous moment he almost forgot he had left the phone off for two hours.

Kris rolled his eyes, dismissing the entire unimaginably boring subject, then punched the buttons on the DAT deck with his long fingers, rewinding the tape to listen to his feedback-heavy solo again. Morgan and Dano bobbed their heads once each in Theo's direction, which he assumed was to save the energy of waving. John smiled at him, sharing the joke, although unlike Theo he was going to stay and hang out with these kids a decade younger than himself, sharing bong hits and loose talk about a hypothetical first album until one or two in the morning. "Stay loose, Thee," he called.

Theo's ancient Yamaha started on the first kick. It seemed like a good sign.

The bedroom light was out but the television was flickering behind the blinds, which meant Catherine was probably still up. Even though she hadn't tried to call him, he had a feeling she wouldn't be too happy with him coming in after midnight. Theo hesitated, then sat down on the porch steps to smoke the cigarette Johnny had given him. The streetlamps made little pools of light down the sidewalk that ran in front of the dark houses. It was a quiet neighborhood in the Western Addition, a working neighborhood, full of people who watched Letterman or Leno through the opening monologue and then switched off because they had to be up early. A wind sent leaves rattling and rolling up the street.

I'm dying here, he thought suddenly. *I don't belong here.*

He had surprised himself. If not here, then where? What was he going to find that was any better? It was true that he never felt quite alive except when he was singing, making music—he often had the disturbing feeling that in his job, his conversations, even sometimes being with Cat, he was just going through the motions—but he felt sure he was past the childish dreams of being a rock star. He would be happy just to play club dates in front of live human beings every few weeks. No, this was what he wanted, wasn't it—a house, a grown-up life? It was certainly what Catherine Lillard wanted, and he wanted her. He'd been with her for almost two years. That was nearly forever, wasn't it? Practically married, even before they'd received the test results.

Theo walked across the tiny lawn to the sidewalk and flicked his cigarette into the gutter, then went inside. The television was on, but there was only a tangled blanket in Cat's usual curling-up spot on the couch.

"Hey, honey? Cat?" The kitchen was dark, but it smelled like she'd been cooking: there was a weird, spicy scent in the air, something both sweet and a little sickening. The windows were open and it was a nice March night, but the air inside the small house felt as close as if a thunderstorm were moving in.

"Cat? It's me." He shrugged. Maybe she'd gone to bed and left the television on. He wandered down the hall and saw that the light was on in the bathroom, but that was nothing unusual—Cat hated fumbling for the switch when she was half-awake or barking her shin in the dark on something left in the hall. He took little notice of the bundle on the floor against the far bathroom wall. It was the red smears on the side of the tub that caught his eye instead, weirdly vivid against the porcelain. He pushed the door all the way open.

It took perhaps two full seconds to realize what he was seeing, the longest two seconds he had ever experienced, a sideways lurch of reality as disorienting as a hallucination. Blood was smeared across the bathroom floor behind the door, too, screamingly scarlet under the fluorescents. Cat's terrycloth bathrobe, rolled somehow into a huge lump and flung against the wall near the toilet, was soaked in it as well.

"Oh my God . . ." he said.

The bathrobe shuddered and rolled over, revealing Catherine's pale face. Her skin was like a white paper mask except for the bloody fingerprints on both cheeks—her own, as he found out later. But for a moment he could only stare, his chest clamped in crushing shock, his brain shrilling *murder murder murder* over and over.

He was right. But he didn't find that out until later, either. Much later.

Cat's eyes found his face, struggled to focus. A parched whisper: "Theo . . . ?"

"My God, my God, what happened? Are you . . . ?"

Her throat convulsed so powerfully he thought she was going to vomit—he had a terrible image of blood gushing out of her mouth like a fountain. The ragged sound that leaped from her instead was so horribly raw and ragged that he could not at first understand the words.

"IlostitIlostitIlostit . . . !"

He was down on his knees in the sopping fingerpainted mess of the bathroom floor, the slick, sticky scarlet—where had it all come from, all this red wetness? He was trying to help her up, panicking, an idiot voice telling him *Don't move her, she's an accident victim,* but he didn't know what had happened, what could have possibly have happened, did someone get in . . . ? Then suddenly he understood.

"I lost it!" she moaned, more clear now that there was almost no air left in the cry. "Oh, Jesus, I lost the baby!"

He was halfway across the house to the phone when he realized his own cell phone was in his pocket. He called 911 and gave them the address while simultaneously trying to wrap towels around the outside of her bathrobe, as though she were some immense wound that needed to be held together. She was crying, but it made almost no sound.

When he had finished he held her tightly against him, waiting to hear the sound of the paramedics at the door.

"Where were you?" Her eyes were shut and she was shivering. "Where were you?"

Hospitals were like T. S. Eliot poems, somehow—well-lit wastelands, places of quiet talk that could not quite hide the terrible things going on behind the doors. Even when he went out to the lobby to stretch his legs, to walk off some of the horrible, helpless tension, he felt like he was pacing through a mausoleum.

Cat's blood loss had not been as mortal as Theo had felt it must be. Some of the mess had been amniotic fluid and splashed water from the hot bath she had taken when the cramps first started becoming painful. The doctors talked calmly to him of premature rupture of membranes, of possible uterine abnormalities, but it might have been Byzantine religious ritual for all his poleaxed brain could make of it. Catherine Lillard slept most of the first ten hours, face pale as a picture-book princess, IVs jacked into both arms. When she opened her eyes at last, she seemed like a stranger.

"Honey, I'm so sorry," he said. "It wasn't your fault. These things happen."

She did not even waste her strength responding to such vacuities. She turned her face away and stared toward the dark television screen angled out from the wall.

He went through Cat's phone book. Her mother was there by breakfast, unhappy that Theo hadn't called earlier; her best friend Laney showed up just after. Both women wore jeans and work shirts, as though they were planning to roll up their sleeves and cook a church dinner or help build a barn. They seemed to draw a sort of curtain around his pale, silent girlfriend, an exclusionary barrier Theo could not cross. After an hour of manufacturing errands for himself, fetching coffee and magazines from downstairs, he told Catherine that he was going to go home and try to get a little sleep. Cat didn't say anything, but her mother agreed that was probably a good idea.

He was only able to sleep three hours, tired as he was. When he got up, he realized he hadn't called anyone in his own circle of friends and family. It was hard to imagine who to call. Johnny? Theo knew what his friend's response would be, could even imagine the exact tone: "Oh, Thee, wow. That's such a bummer, man." He would run out of things to say in moments and then the inadequate guy-talk would hang, lame and awkward. Johnny would be sincere in his sorrow, of course—he really was a good guy—but calling him just seemed so pointless. And the idea of telling any of the other guys in the band was ludicrous. In fact, he needed to pass the news to Johnny at some point just so the drummer would do that for him, so that Theo didn't have to watch Kris and the other two pretend like they gave a shit, if they even bothered.

Who else should he call? How could you lose a baby—his baby, too, he had to keep reminding himself, half his, not just Catherine's—and not tell anyone? Had it really come down to this, thirty years old and nobody in his life who he needed or wanted to talk to about the miscarriage?

Where are my friends? I used to have people around me all the time. But who were they, those people? It had seemed exciting at the time—the girls who had flocked to his gigs, the guys who had wanted to manage him—but now he could hardly remember any of them. Friends? No, just people, and people didn't seem as interested in him these days.

He wound up calling his mother, although he hadn't spoken to her since just after the beginning of February. It seemed unfair, to wait four weeks or so and then call up to deliver this sort of news, but he didn't know what else to do.

She answered before the second ring, as usual. It was unnerving, the way she always did that—as though she was never out of arm's reach of the phone. Surely her life wasn't that empty since Dad had died? It wasn't like the two of them had been party monsters or anything in the first place.

"Hi, Mom."

"Hello, Theo." Nothing else, no *"It's been a long time,"* or *"How are you?"*

"I just . . . I've got some bad news, Mom. Catherine lost the baby."

The pause was long even by Anna Vilmos standards. "That's very sad, Theo. I'm sorry to hear it."

"She had a miscarriage. I came home and found her on the bathroom floor. It was pretty awful. Blood everywhere."

He realized he was telling it already like a story, not like something that had really happened to him. "She's okay, but I think she's pretty depressed."

"What was the cause, Theo? They must know."

They. Mom always talked about the people in power, any kind of power, as if they were a single all-knowing, all-powerful group. "No, actually they don't. It was just kind of . . . kind of a spontaneous thing. They're doing tests, but they don't know yet."

"So sad." And that seemed to be the end of the conversation. Theo tried to recall what he'd thought when he called, what he had expected, if it had been anything more than a sort of filial duty—*look, Mom, here's what's gone wrong in my life this month.*

It would have been a real baby, he thought suddenly. *As real as me. As real as you, Mom. It's not just a "so sad."* But he didn't say it.

"Your uncle Harold is going to be in town next month." His father's younger brother was a retail executive who lived in Southern California. He had taken on himself the role of family patriarch when Theo's dad died, which meant that he called Theo's mom on Christmas Eve, and once or twice a year when he flew up to San Francisco on some other business he took her out to dinner at the Sizzler. "He would like to see you."

"Yeah, well, I'll call you about that, maybe we can set something up." How quickly it had turned into the kind of interaction they always had, dry, faintly guilt-ridden. Theo wanted to say something different, wanted to stop the whole thing and ask her what she really felt, no, what *he* was supposed to feel about the terrible thing that had happened to him, but it was useless. It was as though they had to force their words across some medium less rich than normal air, so that only the simplest, most mundane things could pass from side to side without disappearing into the empty stillness.

A quick and unclinging good-bye from his mother and

Theo was alone with himself again. He called the hospital, wondering if Catherine was by herself and needed company. Laney picked up the phone and told him in a fairly cool manner that Cat was sleeping, that he didn't need to hurry over.

"I took the day off work tomorrow, too," she said. "I'll be here." It sounded more like a threat to him than a favor to Cat.

"How is she?"

"How do you think?"

"Hey, Jesus, Laney, you're acting like I pushed her down the stairs or something. This was my child, too."

"I know that, Theo."

"Don't you think I wish I was there when it happened? But I still couldn't have done anything about it. The doctor said so."

"Nobody's blaming you, Theo."

But it sure didn't sound like that.

He stood in the living room after he had hung up, staring at the clutter untouched since the night before, the residue of normal lives suddenly interrupted by disaster and entombed like Pompeii. She had been sitting just there, watching television when the really bad cramps came. She had bumped the table getting up—a glass was still lying on the floor, a ghost-stain of spilled diet cola visible on the shaggy, seen-better-days carpet. Was there blood before she reached the bathroom? He started to follow her track, then caught himself. It was too sick, too horrible. Like examining a murder scene.

Only three hours of sleep, but he was buzzing like he was full of bad speed. He turned the television on. The images were meaningless.

Where did my life go? How could something so small—it wasn't even really a baby yet, whatever she says—how could it change everything so much? But what kind of life was it, really, when you were only alive playing music, but you couldn't ever seem to find the right place to do that, the right people to do it with?

Things came too easy for you, his mother had told him in a resigned way a few years back. *You were so good at things when you were a little boy, the teachers made so much of you. That's why you never developed any ambition.*

Right now he needed to find something, anything, to keep himself busy. He wished Johnny were around so he could bum a cigarette off him, several of them, sit and smoke and drink cold beers and talk about bullshit that didn't matter. But he couldn't bear to call him and have to explain this weird, miserable thing, not right now.

Cat's face was so pale . . . ! Like it was her heart that came out of her, not a little dead baby.

He stood up and moved into their bedroom. They had boxes of things stacked there, waiting until he cleared out the spare bedroom—his practice room, as he sometimes called it, although he could count on one hand the times he'd actually spent in there with his guitar. The practice room was going to be the baby's room, and all those things would be the baby's things. Would have been. Now she wouldn't want to see them when she came back, the first few symbolic baby-clothes purchases, the books and stuffed toys she had picked up at a garage sale.

"It doesn't count if you buy it used," she had told him, only half-joking. Or maybe not joking at all. *"It doesn't jinx the baby."*

But it had. Or something had—Theo felt like he had been the jinx, somehow, although he couldn't say why, was drenched in guilt that he couldn't explain, like a mysterious stain on his clothes. In any case, here he was and there stood three big grocery-store boxes full of things that would make her cry when she got home. He could do something with them—that would be something useful he could manage. He could put them in the garage where she wouldn't have to see them right away, wouldn't have to walk in on her first day

home and find a cute little stuffed dog looking back at her
with button eyes.

It wasn't all that easy to find a place for the baby things
in the garage, where Theo's boxes of secondhand science-
fiction books and other miscellaneous crap stood in tottering
piles like the ruins of an ancient city, where unused exercise
equipment and unbuilt packaged bookshelves left so little
room for Cat's car that once the warm weather came for
good she wouldn't even attempt the difficult task of parking
in there again until late autumn, at which point all the new
crap that had found its way in during the summer would
have to be relocated so the car would fit in the garage again.

As he was trying to squeeze the last box onto the narrow
shelf above the workbench it toppled over and caught him a
good shot on the temple; when he reached up, he came away
with a spot of blood on his finger. The children's books had
spilled out onto the steps leading down from the kitchen.
Theo's head hurt. He lowered himself onto the bottom of the
short stairway like a geriatric case so he wouldn't have to
bend as he picked them up from the floor—old, well-
thumbed and clearly loved copies of the Pooh stories, of Dr.
Seuss and *Where the Wild Things Are,* all bought secondhand
to fall within Cat's exemption. He picked up his own contri-
bution, one that he'd bought new in a store just because he
couldn't imagine raising a baby without it, and because even
though he never made it up early enough Saturday mornings
for Cat's garage-sale runs, he had wanted to contribute.

Was I the one who jinxed it? In his bleak state, he couldn't
even laugh the thought away. He flicked the book open. The
strange, flat images, crude and almost childish at first glance,
caught him up as they always did. Had his mom really read
this to him? It seemed impossible to believe now that he'd
had a mother who held her child in her lap and read him
Goodnight Moon, but the words were as familiar as a catechism, the little rabbit in his great green room saying goodnight to all the familiar nursery objects, to the mittens and

kittens, the comb and the brush, and of course, strangest of all, to "nobody."

Goodnight nobody. He had never understood that—in one way it was the most magical part of the book, and in another, the most frightening. All the other pictures, the rabbit-child in pajamas, the fire, the old lady rabbit reading, all made sense. The catalog of items, chairs and cats and socks, goodnight, goodnight, then just that blank page and "goodnight nobody." But who was Nobody? It was childhood zen. Sometimes he had thought in his little-boy way that he might be the book's Nobody, Theo himself, an anonymous presence—that the book knew he was out there watching the bunny get ready for bed, looking into the warm, cozy room from outside, as through a window. His mother had contributed to that: whenever they reached that part of the book, she had always said, *"Goodnight, nobody. Say goodnight."* And Theo had done so. Perhaps she had only meant for him to say goodnight to the little someone known as Nobody. But he had always believed she was calling *him* Nobody, telling him it was his turn to say goodnight now, and so he had dutifully obeyed.

In this last winter, since the pregnancy test had come back, Theo had sometimes imagined a little girl sitting on his lap—Cat had been certain from the first that it was a little girl, even though they hadn't had an ultrasound exam yet—her head against his chest as they leafed through the book together. In his offhand dreams he had never quite been able to imagine what she looked like, had pictured only a head of soft curly hair, a warm little body pressed against him. Nobody. She had looked like Nobody. And that was who she had turned out to be.

He flicked through the pages, the drawings with their strange, dreamlike perspective. Then at the end, the final little catechism, saying goodnight to the last things—the stars, the air, and to noises everywhere.

That should go on the baby's gravestone, except there would be no stone, no grave. Cat was going to have a D & C,

as the doctors so artlessly called it, to remove anything that
hadn't already come out. Any thing. There would be nothing
to bury. Polly, Rose, all the names they had played with, taking their time because after all there had been no hurry,
months to wait, and now she wouldn't be any of them. She
was Nobody.

Goodnight Nobody.

Sitting on the stairs with a box of books on his lap, he
cried.

H er face was still pale, framed by the straight lines of her
uncombed, unstyled, dark red hair. She had told him
that the D & C had been all right, not too bad—she had insisted he go back to his delivery job that day, that she didn't
need any hand-holding—but it looked like something more
than just now-useless flesh had been scraped out of her.

"How's the pain?"

She shrugged. Her skin seemed paper-dry, as though she
had lost some essential vitality. Her mother handed her a cup
of ice.

Laney was gone, but both of Cat's parents had arrived for
a postoperative visit. Earlier her dad had made chitchat with
Theo in the hall while the nurse helped Cat with the bedpan,
Mr. Lillard doing his comradely best in the current air of
circle-the-wagons emergency to obscure the fact that he had
never been that thrilled with his semi-son-in-law. Theo appreciated the gesture, but Cat's dad and his yachting sweater
had never been a real stumbling block, anyway: his wife and
only daughter treated Tom Lillard as though he were a
graceless but acceptably familiar sundial in the middle of a
flower bed they were gardening. When Cat had wanted him
to approve of Theo, or at least pretend to, she had enlisted
her mother's help and there had been dinners, family out-
ings. He was a figurehead—an aging CEO of his own family

who only showed up for the board meetings and wondered how so much got done without him.

"Can I talk to Theo for a minute, Mom?"

Her mother rose and drew her father by the hand to the door. "We'll just go down and look at some magazines in the gift shop," she said. "I'll bring you back a *People.*"

"Thanks." When they had left, Cat closed her eyes for a long moment and let her head slump back against the pillow.

"I . . . I didn't think it would hurt so much," Theo said. He suddenly wanted her to know that he was grieving too, although other than the tears on the garage stairs, he wasn't completely certain that was true. "When you get home, we . . . did they say when we can try again?" Was that an insensitive thing to say? Maybe she would think he was talking about sex. "I mean, when you're ready inside, too. In your head, I mean."

Her eyes came open in her dry white face, slowly, like something in a horror movie. She took a deep breath. "I'm not coming home, Theo. Not like that. It's not going to be like . . . like that."

He stared, puzzled, but he could already feel the tide sucking away what he had thought was firm sand beneath his feet. "Not . . . ?"

"I'm going to stay with my parents for a few weeks. Mom wants to cook for me, you know, fuss over me."

"Well, that's . . . that's fine . . ."

"And when I come back . . ." She sighed, someone bravely picking up a heavy burden. "When I come back, I want to live by myself."

It felt like the time he had been hit in the back of the head with a pool cue, the innocent victim of a violent argument that he didn't even know had started behind him. For a long stupid moment after the world exploded he could only stare. "You mean . . . you want us to . . . to separate?"

Her mouth was firm, almost pinched shut, but her eyes were suddenly wet. "Yes. No. More than that. I think . . . it's time we went our own ways."

"Own ways? What kind of bullshit is that?"

She blinked, the sad resolve suddenly agitated by anger. "It's not bullshit, Theo. We lost the baby and it opened up my eyes. I can see now that the baby was the only reason I was staying with you—to give our child a fighting chance to have two parents who were together. But it wouldn't have fixed things between us. I can't believe how stupid I was— like I was under some kind of spell, believing that somehow we would have this rosy little family life. But in real life you would have been just the same, doing just enough to get by, a smile, a joke, oh yeah, lots of cute stuff but nothing real. Eventually we would have broken up, and then you'd have been a weekend dad, doing the bare minimum, no plan, no organization, no commitment, take the kid out and buy her an ice cream cone, drop her back off with me afterward."

He could only shake his head at this torrent of fury, judged guilty of neglecting a child who didn't even exist.

"Don't pretend it would be different." The anger had finally brought color back to her bloodless face, coarse little patches of red like sunburn. "It's always the same with you. You're a grown man, Theo, but you act like a teenager. *'Where are you going?' 'Out.' 'When are you coming back?' 'I don't know.'* I can't believe I was going to have a kid with you."

"Is this all about me coming back late that night . . . ?"

"No, Theo. But it's all about a hundred, a thousand other things like that. The shit you start and never finish. Your going-nowhere job. Coming home late smelling like the . . . the Fillmore West or something, hanging around with your teenage musician friends. You've probably got little teenage groupies, too. *'Wow, Theo, do you really, like, remember the Eighties?'* "

"That's bullshit." His fists were clenched. "Bullshit."

"Maybe. Maybe I'm being unfair, Theo. I'm sorry—I've just lost a baby, remember? But I've hit the end of the road and that isn't bullshit."

"Look, I know that women and motherhood is like this

sacred thing, but you're not the only goddamned person who lost a baby here, Cat! I was going to be a father."

She stared at him for a moment without speaking. "When I first met you, Theo," she finally said, "I thought you were the most amazing man I'd ever known. Beautiful—you really were beautiful, even my friends agreed on that. And you had that voice, and that . . . charm. Like you were someone out of a movie, with perfect lighting and choreography and good writers. You charmed me, all right, but I don't see it any more. Either it's fading or I just woke up."

Anger made him feel like his skin was tight, like he was the Incredible Hulk or something, growing muscles. But he was standing over a woman who'd just gone through a miscarriage, a woman in a hospital bed. He opened his fists, made himself take a deep breath. "So not only are you breaking up with me, you're telling me I'm shit, too? Just, what, as a going-away present? A parting gift for the losing player? You thought you should just let me know I'm a big fake and I'm not worth anything?"

"No, Theo. But I *am* saying that something about you has changed, and what's left isn't enough, at least for me. I don't want to spend the rest of my life hoping that things will get better, that you'll stop being a good-looking, footloose guy with potential and start being a real man. Okay, you sang 'The Way You Look Tonight' to me on our first date and I fell for you, but it's not enough to last a lifetime. I don't know why I couldn't see that until the miscarriage, but I sure see it now. I'd rather be single. I'd rather have a baby by myself, if I can even get pregnant again. So why don't you take the time while I'm at my parents' and get your stuff and find an apartment or something."

"You're throwing me out of my own house? I pay half the rent!"

"Barely. But it was my house first, anyway, remember? I only let you move in because Laney was getting a place with Brian and it was easier than putting an ad in the paper."

He stood, full of diffuse rage and with a hole in the center of him that seemed like it could never be filled. "Is that all it was, huh? Easier than putting in an ad?"

It took a moment, but her expression softened. "No, that wasn't all it was. Of course not. I loved you, Theo."

"Loved." He closed his eyes. Everything had just liquified and swirled away from him, his entire life gurgling down the drain.

"I probably still love you, if that's what you're asking. But I can't live with you any more. It's too much work, trying to believe in us. I'm too old for fairy tales."

When he passed her parents in the hallway, their embarrassed expressions showing that they knew damn well what their daughter had just told him, he wanted to say something cutting to them, something bitter and clever, but he was too empty, too angry, too sad. The only thing he could think of was "It's not fair!" and that was not the kind of thing thirty-year-old men were supposed to say.

THE SILENT PRIMROSE MAIDEN

Half a day's drive outside the great city, far enough away to intrude only lightly on the consciences of families and friends—consciences underdeveloped by both habit and breeding in many of the leading clans—the mansion stood. It had once belonged to a scion of the upstart Zinnia House, but the fortunes of that family had fallen as swiftly as they had earlier risen, and although it still bore their name and crest above the door, the former inhabitants had sold the huge house long ago and moved to more modest digs in the city, a collection of family apartments near the waterfront where they could keep a close watch on their shipping interests and dream of better days gone—and, they hoped, better days still to come.

But Zinnia Manor remained, nestled in a fold of the forested hills of True Arden, surrounded by grounds that although less carefully cultivated than in its happiest days were still green and sumptuous and, most important of all, large enough to create privacy.

The manor had three or four times as many inhabitants now as when the family still owned it; the administrator, Mr. Lungwort, a small, dapper fellow whose rudimentary wings had resisted all attempts at cosmetic removal, growing back several times and thus forcing him to try to hide them with carefully padded suits, claimed it was more like managing a village than a house. Besides the regular residents there were several dozen staff, including cooks, maids, janitors, and gardeners, not to mention the nurses and orderlies. Two alienists and a certified chirurgeon were on duty at all times, and other practitioners were kept on call for when things got busy, as they often did during full moons.

In such a large facility, with an impressive catalog of patients whose conditions were vivid and even occasionally dangerous—inverted shadows, spontaneous creation, infectious hallucination, and several variants of uncontrollable shapeshifting—it was strange that the most noteworthy resident should be so quiet and inoffensive. She had her own suite of rooms on the south side of the manor, courtesy of her famous and powerful family (which, except for occasional visits from one brother, wanted nothing to do with her anymore) but she might as well have been living in a ditch beside the highway for all the notice or advantage she took of her surroundings. Day after day the morning sun splashed into her room, but she never raised her eyes to the windows. Day after day attendants came and got her out of the bed where they had placed her the night before, then washed and dressed her, manipulating her slack body as though she were a corpse being readied for burial. Day after day, at least when the weather was fair, they set her in a sedan chair—not an easy task, even for some of the larger, stronger creatures on the staff, for although the patient was slender, she was tall and long of limb, and always as limp as a sack—and rolled her out to the manor's garden.

There she would remain, eyes staring straight out at nothing, the hands her attendants had folded still lying neatly in her lap, her handsome, fine-boned face as hollowly purposeless as a bell with no clapper, until someone came and took her away again.

Once, during one of the power outages, which were occurring in the city and its outskirts with worrying frequency these days, a muddled staff had neglected to bring her in.

The night nurse, seeing her empty bed, had gone looking for her and found her still sitting in her chair in the garden, staring at nothing, her dress soaked with dew and her milk-white skin goose-pimpled with cold.

Mr. Lungwort had been very upset about that, not so much out of pity—it was hard for anyone with the administrator's somewhat narrow personality to pity something that showed no more liveliness than a lump of wax—but out of fear that her wealthy family might discover the mistake and remove her from Zinnia Manor, along with her sizable endowment. Two nurses were sacked and a night orderly was severely reprimanded, but the patient herself gave no sign that her night outdoors had made any difference.

Lungwort's records showed that her name was Erephine, but he did not encourage conversational familiarity between his staff and their charges—the "guests," as Lungwort called them—and especially not toward members of the highest Houses, however intimate the staff's interactions with them might be, however unprepossessing the patient. To her blank face, a face that animation might have made beautiful, they addressed her only as "Lady Primrose," or simply, "my lady." The sound of their voices and the touch of their careful hands seemed to mean no more to her than had the night dew. If she had been a mortal woman, and her caretakers mortal too, the word "soulless" might have been whispered, but fairies do not pretend to have souls, and if they do have such things, they are not aware of them.

To the nurses and orderlies of Zinnia Manor, many of them unabashed wearers of wings and unrepentant believers in the old tales and ways, it was clear that their unmoving, unspeaking charge, so pretty, so utterly lifeless, must have a story, something darkly romantic and grandly tragic, but if the administrator or anyone else knew it, the secret remained closely held. When the staff drank betony tea together and gossiped about Mr. Lungwort's padded suits and the disgusting proclivities of the Feverfew twins, they called her the Silent Primrose Maiden and tried to imagine what had happened to bring her to this terrible condition. Not even the most extravagant guesses came anywhere near the truth.

After all, it was possible to imagine that lives might once have been lost and reputations sacrificed for the light in her eyes, those eyes that were now so terribly, terribly empty, but none of the gossiping staff of Zinnia Manor could have guessed that soon an entire world might pass into eternal shadow for the sake of that same, dead stare.

3

DESCENT

It was a good day, one of very few in the two months since
Cat's miscarriage—since the night his old life ended, as
he sometimes thought of it, never considering how he might
be tempting fate. A decent night's sleep and for once no bad
dreams gave him a looseness in his heart and his step he
hadn't felt for a while. (He had been having the same nightmare a lot lately, eerie and claustrophobic, where he was
trapped in something like a room full of mist or smoke, staring out at the unreachable world through a thick window.)
But today bad dreams seemed to have evaporated in the sunshine. Walking through a building lobby carrying a combination of flowers clearly chosen over the phone by someone,
but guiltily displayed in an expensive vase to make up for it,
he even found himself singing an old Smokey Robinson
song. A pretty young receptionist (too young to be more than
a momentary fancy for him, but that made it all the more satisfying in a way) told him he had a beautiful voice.

"Thanks," he said. "I'm a singer. That's my other job."

She didn't inquire further, but that was all right. It was
enough just to be reminded that there was more to his life
than this delivery job. The band hadn't practiced for at least
three weeks—all kinds of weirdness going on there, but for
once nothing to do with him, since Kris and Morgan were

having some kind of feud. He was still a singer, though. He could pick up his guitar and go stand on a street corner and earn almost as much as he did dragging potted plants up elevators to overworked secretaries and retiring data clerks. Of course, almost as much as "very little" equaled "nearly nothing," so for the moment he'd keep driving the van, thank you very much.

As the bit of Second-That-Emotion falsetto and the receptionist's smile had reminded him, there was more to him than just an aging adolescent with longish hair and a *Khasigian—the Florist* patch sewn on the breast of his shirt. But the problem was, if his old life really had ended that night, where was the new one? It was one thing to have your girlfriend throw you out—even in such miserable circumstances there could still be something liberating in that kind of forced change. But not when you had to move back in with your mother.

It was only for a few months, of course, only until he had saved a little money for first and last on a decent apartment. He could have moved in with Johnny Battistini, who had invited him, but although he loved the man like a brother, the idea of living with him again was a bit much. Theo could never be called fastidious, as Catherine herself had often pointed out, but you didn't have to be a neat-freak to be uncomfortable with six-month-old fast food hardening to stone under the couch. He had shared an apartment with Johnny once, years before he'd met Cat, and he still hadn't shaken the memory of stepping on bugs in the dark.

Besides, it wasn't like his mother forced him to talk with her, or even to interact much at all. He had his own key. If he was home at dinnertime, which he rarely was, she would heat him up the same leftovers she was eating, or put a frozen meal in the microwave for him. If he wanted to watch a different program than she was watching, she didn't seem to mind; she would silently hand him the remote, take a book, and go to bed. She didn't make a mess, she didn't play loud music, she didn't force him to have

long, boring conversations: if she had been a male roommate she would have been damn near ideal. As a mother,
though, she was a little spooky.

When he had tried to explain her to Cat back when they
were first dating he had stated, a bit archly, "Mom's flame of
life doesn't burn all that bright." But, faint as it was, it had
burned brighter once than it did now. He was surprised at
how little she seemed to care about anything these days. Was
it some kind of delayed reaction to his father's death almost
six years ago? Or was it Theo who had changed—had living
with Cat made him more used to how normal people behaved? He had no idea. Anna Vilmos was a hard woman to
figure out.

She came to all his school plays, he remembered. *Showed
up every night when I had the lead in the musical—it must
have meant something to her. But she never had much to say
about it. "Very nice, Theo, you did well. I enjoyed it." That
was about all, like she was talking about a piece of corned
beef she'd got from the butcher.* And his father had been too
tired most of the time to say anything either except that the
show or recital in question had been "pretty good," all the
time making it clear that what he really wanted was to get
home to bed because he had to get up early the next morning. *See, Cat? Who can turn into a normal grown-up when
his role models are polite strangers?*

But today, driving the delivery van, even the bleakness of
living back at his mother's house could not dim his feeling
that a change was coming, that a sort of dormancy was over.
He had been surprised how powerfully the twin blows of
losing Catherine and the baby had struck him. It was more
than just the weird bad dreams: for weeks he had found himself bursting into mortified tears while listening to old songs
on the van radio—songs he had never liked that much in the
first place. Anthems of lost love, Fifties car accident weepies
and horrible, saccharine tunes about dead girlfriends and
children, even things that seemed to have nothing to do with
his own upside-down life could catch him like a sharp nee-

dle in the heart. Once an old chestnut from the Seventies about a drowning sheepdog (as far as he could tell, since he had never listened to the lyrics very intently) made him pull over because he was crying too hard to see. But not today. Spring had actually arrived a month ago, but for the first time he could feel himself respond to it, as though he too were full of sap being warmed by the sun, as if he were about to bud.

Don't know about budding, he thought as he pulled the van into the slot behind the store. *But maybe I could go out and catch a few beers with Johnny, go listen to some music.* An Irish band he had heard about was playing at a club in the Mission. He considered inviting his mother—she was Irish by birth, after all, and she had a kind of weird soft spot for Johnny B., soft for her anyway. And Johnny in turn kind of flirted with her. He had actually once said, "Your mom must have been at least a semi-babe when she was young." The whole thing had been far too bizarre for Theo to deal with, but now he found himself liking the idea of taking her out with him and Johnny. Might do her good, and he would feel a little less guilty about sharing the house with her as though he were an itinerant stranger.

"You're singing," Khasigian said as Theo hung the keys on the hook board. "Is that a good thing?"

"Guess that's for the people listening to decide."

Khasigian squinted at him, gnawed his pencil. He had a shiny bald head like an ancient tortoise, but the rest of him was surprisingly fit for his sixty-something years. He jogged, sometimes coming into the shop on hot days in running shorts and allowing the employees to make respectful jokes about his thin brown legs. "It could be worse. You sing okay. But I don't like it when my employees are happy. I think when they are not afraid they don't work so hard."

"A priceless example of your nineteenth-century management style." Theo plucked his faithful leather jacket off the rack. "That's why you win the Ebenezer Scrooge Award year after year, Mr. K. They're going to have to retire that trophy, you know."

"Go home, Singing Boy. Go annoy someone with less to do."

Khasigian could be an unalloyed bastard occasionally, and he certainly wasn't going to drown his employees in money and benefits, but he was at least middling honest and did a pretty good imitation of the Gruff But Lovable Boss when he wanted to. Too good, really—that's how you could tell it was only an act.

Theo rode back to the Sunset district with the visor of his helmet open. The wind was damp and warm and the smell of blossoming things filled the air, stronger even than the auto exhaust.

Mrs. Kraley was out in the yard next door, watering her garden. Theo waved to her. She did not wave back, although she was only using one hand to operate the hose. Mrs. Kraley was another thing that made staying at his mother's such a warm, satisfying experience.

His mother did not respond to his call when he came in. After the terrible night when he had found Cat, he had a reflexive need to know where everyone was, so he checked and found her in her bedroom, napping fully dressed, propped on three pillows, her chest moving up and down just like it was supposed to. It was strange to see her sleeping in the middle of the day, but then again he seldom came home right after work ended.

He wandered back to the kitchen, took a bottle of beer out of the refrigerator, then made his way out to the tidy emptiness of the living room. He found himself wishing that if he had to be stuck in his parents' house, it was at least the house in San Mateo in which he had grown up, a place with memories, where he would have something to react to, even if only depressive nostalgia. But his mother and father had bought this house less than ten years ago, a year after Theo had moved out for good and his father had retired—a retire-

ment Peter Vilmos had only a few years to appreciate before
the massive stroke had killed him. His picture stood by itself
on the mantel, a setting too stark to be any kind of a shrine.
There were moments when Theo thought he saw his own
features in his father's, when the jaw or cheekbones seemed
inarguably his own, but most of the time the man seemed as
remote genetically as he had been paternally, a decent guy
who had simply worked too many hours to have much
strength left for dad-stuff.

There were no other pictures of Pete Vilmos anywhere on
display, which had more to do with Theo's mother than any
fault of his father. She had only one of Theo as well, a school
picture from when he was in second or third grade that sat
on her dresser, still in its original little cardboard frame.
There were no other photographs visible in the house, and
very few pictures of any kind. The large framed print of a
bridge over the River Liffey in Dublin on the living room
wall was the exception, and Theo believed it was mostly
there because the wall would look too bare without it. Anna
Dowd Vilmos was not sentimental.

In an uncharacteristic bit of disorganization, his mother
had left her coat over one of the chairs and her purse lying
on its side on the dining room table; a small scatter of objects had fallen out of the open top. He found himself wondering what exactly it was she did all day. She volunteered
at the library, but that was only once a week. Most of her
working years had been spent cooking and cleaning for her
child and her fairly old-fashioned husband. What did she
do with her time? A pang of guilt struck him, that he was
only thinking about this now, with his own life in tatters.
Dad had been dead for a long stretch. Had Theo, her only
child, ever gone to her and asked her if there was something he could do to help? Had he tried to make time for
her, take her out, get to know her? Sure, she wasn't the
most responsive person in the world, but he hadn't done
much to try to overcome that, had he?

He left the silent television, the muted scenes of car accidents and school district protests on the early evening news, and hung his mother's coat up in the closet. He could make her dinner. That would be something nice to wake up to, wouldn't it? He wasn't a great cook, but he wasn't hopeless, and even grilled cheese sandwiches and canned tomato soup would be better than her having to get up and do the cooking. Or maybe he should just take her out to a proper dinner. Call John from a restaurant, then they could all go out and see that Irish band.

He was halfway through scooping the fallen objects back into her purse when he realized he was holding a pill bottle, that he had been looking at it for some moments without quite understanding why he had paused.

Fentanyl Citrate, the label read. It also had a bright orange warning label.

It took long seconds reading through the many cautionary notations on the label before he understood that what he was looking at was some kind of morphine derivative—serious, serious pain medication. His insides went cold, as though he himself were being numbed. He stared at it a moment longer, then, not entirely conscious of what he was doing or why, dumped his mother's purse out onto the table. A lipstick rolled off and clicked onto the floor but he did not bend to pick it up. The glossy pamphlet, folded and unfolded so many times that the creases were white, had a bar across the top that identified it as a publication of the California Pacific Medical Center. The words on the cover, the typeface careful, almost respectful, read *"Pancreatic Cancer: Questions and Answers."*

"Why didn't you tell me?"
           She gave him a look that was like something he'd expect from Kris Rolle, almost teenage in its sullenness. "I didn't know for sure. They're still not one hundred percent certain until they do a biopsy, but the what-do-you-call-it, the endoscope, showed there was a big tumor." She

shrugged. "It wasn't nice, that endoscope. I didn't want to go in for it—I hoped it was nothing."

"This is bad, Mom. We have to get serious about this. This is important!"

For a moment her expression seemed to lighten, but there was an abyss behind her crooked smile. "Yes, Theo. I know."

"Sorry. Jesus. Sorry." He took a deep, shuddering breath. "What did they tell you?"

What they had told her was not good. If the biopsy confirmed it was malignant, as seemed very likely, it was probably Stage Three or Four, she said. He found out the next day, when he used the computer at the library to go online, that they were usually spelled "Stage III" and "Stage IV," as though putting the ugliness in Roman numerals made it distant, somehow, less fearful, a mere historical footnote. It seemed to have gone undetected for a long time already, the doctor had told her, which was often the way with pancreatic cancer since it was seldom noticed until the tumor began to press on the other organs, and the chances were high that it had spread into her lymphatic system, rogue cells sowing the seeds of chaos throughout her body.

"Six months," she said. "A year if the radiation and chemotherapy help."

"Jesus." He stood staring at her awful composure. "Are you telling me it's incurable?"

She shrugged again. "There are some, what do they call them, some temporary remissions. Sometimes with the chemotherapy and all that, people survive longer. It's not usual."

He couldn't understand how she could sit here talking about death, her own death, as though discussing an appliance warranty. "But there's a chance, right?"

"There is always a chance, Theo." She did not have to add what was in her voice. *But probably not for me.*

"Has this . . . oh, God, has it been hurting you a lot, Mom?"

She thought about it before answering. She was not in a

hurry. He had a sudden insight into how that part must feel, anyway: there was no point in hurrying anything now. "For a while. At first, it wasn't so bad. I thought it was just aching muscles—my back, you know. Sometimes I get that when I carry things around, move the furniture to vacuum."

Another stab of guilt—no, of something closer to pure misery—at the thought of his mother dragging heavy sofas around so she could vacuum a house empty but for him and herself. But what did it matter now? He wanted to laugh at the horror of it all, but even with his mother's strange, detached mood, it didn't seem like the right thing to do. But he had a feeling that she'd like it better than if he started crying. He looked around the empty house, at the clean carpets and unprepossessing furniture, at the small dark-haired woman sitting on a chair in front of him, and tried to think of something to say.

"I wasn't very hungry either," she said abruptly. "But I've never been someone who wanted to eat a lot. Not like your father. He always had a can of nuts next to him, or something like that. . . ." She stopped as suddenly as she had begun, finished with the thought.

"Do you . . . do you want to come out with me? Tonight? There's an Irish band at the Kennel Club. They're supposed to be good—real Irish music, all acoustic instruments."

She actually smiled, and because it was a real smile, for the first time he could see the pain and weariness. "That would be nice, Theo. Yes, let's go out."

After that, the descent began. What had happened with Cat and the baby had been so sudden that it had seemed more like a brutal mugging—one moment walking down the street thinking about what you were going to have for dinner, the next lying in the gutter wondering if you could manage to crawl to where someone would find you. Watching his mother die was like something else entirely, a sort of ter-

rible, slow-motion accident that went on and on and seemed
to have no ending. But there would be an ending, of course.

They spoke a different language in the land of death, he
discovered. If he had thought Cat's miscarriage was wrapped
around with strange arcana, he had not even begun to
glimpse the possibilities. First off, it wasn't just cancer or a
tumor they were dealing with, it was *adenocarcinoma*. They
didn't examine his mother, they performed *laparoscopic
staging* or *endoscopic retrograde cholangiopancreatography*—that last word something you couldn't even fit on a
Scrabble board. And there seemed to be no real treatments,
just mysteries of which even druid priests would be proud,
things like *Gemcitabine* or *Fluorouracil, palliative bypass* or
even *chemical splanchnicectomy*. Sometimes the smoke
would rise, the curtain part, and someone in a white coat
would lean out and breathe, *"percutaneous radiologic biliary
stent,"* before disappearing again. It was like someone had
opened a hole into Theo's life—his life and his mother's, but
she was daily growing more and more distant in her haze of
pain-deadeners—and backed up a dump truck full of spiky
Greco-Latin terms, then poured them over everything in an
avalanche of meaningless but still terrifying syllables.

Unresectable. That was one of the worst.

Metastasized. That was the worst.

He had to quit his job, of course, although Khasigian
was kind enough to tell him he could have it back
when he wanted it. His mother, frugal by nature, had stashed
a bit away out of her husband's pension and Social Security
over the years, enough to pay the tiny mortgage payments
and put food on the table, especially as Anna Vilmos seldom
ate anything now, no matter how much Theo begged her. He
was so worried about her not eating that he even got Johnny
to bring over a few buds of high-grade weed, which after a
great deal of argument they convinced Theo's mother to
smoke.

"You're trying to turn me into a dope addict like you," she

said, wearily amused, clutching John Battistini's furry arm. It would have been comical, the kind of thing Theo and Johnny would have marveled over forever—"the night we got your mom stoned!"—except that there was nothing funny about the circumstances, about Anna Dowd Vilmos' yellowish skin, the bruised circles under her eyes, the headscarf that she always wore now because the chemotherapy was making her hair come out of her scalp in patches. She had just discontinued the Gemcitabine, declaring in a moment of stubborn determination, "It's not going to help anything and I'm not going to die without my hair."

Marijuana didn't have the effect Theo hoped. In fact, Anna had a sort of bad trip, the kind of thing he had rarely seen even in the most paranoid of first-time smokers. She moaned and cried and began to babble about "the night they took the baby," something that made no sense to Theo unless she was talking about Cat's miscarriage. As he held her, patting her awkwardly and trying not to think about how thin she had become, whispering reassuring nothings, he wondered if something in her own family history had triggered it. It was shocking how little he knew about the events of his mother's life before she had given birth to him.

Even when the worst had passed, she was too distraught to do anything more that night, and certainly had no interest in eating. He put her to bed at last. Johnny went home full of apologies, promising that he would find "some mellower weed" so they could try another time. But Theo knew, as he looked down at his mother whimpering in her shallow sleep, that this would be the last experiment. It was hard to say whether her remoteness in the last weeks had been denial or courage, but whatever it was, he didn't want to take it away from her again.

"I want you to sell the house," she told him one morning, a morning like every other morning of late, on their way to the clinic with hours of treatments ahead for her, tattered waiting room magazines and mediocre coffee for him.

"What do you mean, sell the house? What, are we just going to move down to the clinic full-time?"

She still had the strength to give him an annoyed look. It was one of the few pleasures she had left. "I mean after I'm dead."

"Mom, don't talk like that . . ."

"If I don't talk like that now, when do I do it?" She pulled down the scarf where it had begun to creep above her ears. "When? No, you just listen. That's not your house—you don't want to live there after I'm gone. You'll never keep it clean anyway."

"I don't want to think about it right now."

"You never want to think about things like that. That's why you're still doing what you're doing, Theo. That's why you're living with me."

"I could have moved out if . . . if you hadn't got sick."

She made a face. "Maybe. But you listen to me. You sell it, get yourself a nice apartment, then you'll have a little money. You can go back to school, get a degree. You could have done well in school if you'd ever tried—the teachers always said you were bright, but you wanted to spend all your time in those rock and roll bands. The house is almost paid off—there's the second mortgage for the kitchen remodeling, of course, but you'll still get enough to go to school."

The thought of how it would happen was ghastly, but it kindled something inside him all the same, something that might have been an idea of eventual freedom. "We'll talk about it . . . we'll talk about it later, Mom. You're going to beat this thing."

"You are a very bad liar, Theo." She paused for a long beat. "It's a lucky thing you're musical."

He flicked a glance at her. Yes, she was—she was smiling. It was all just weird beyond belief. *Did my mother have to get cancer to develop a sense of humor? That's a fairly shitty trade-off, isn't it?*

But there are no trade-offs. The universe isn't a machine

*for fairness. There's no Complaints Department. There's no
court of higher appeal.*

   Pretty well sucks, doesn't it?

T he descent went on throughout the spring and early sum-
      mer, a free fall both agonizingly swift and yet somehow
as thrashingly, stickily slow as a nightmare. Johnny Battistini
quit coming over, unable to face the scarecrow figure that
Anna Vilmos had become, although he still called from time
to time to ask after her and to urge Theo to get out, just for
an evening.

   "Come on," he said the last time. "It would do you a lot
of good, man. Just for a couple of hours . . ."

   "Right. Right. And what if she falls down in the bathroom
while I'm out?" Theo heard the hysterical edge in his own
voice as though he were eavesdropping on someone else's
conversation. "I'm supposed to just sit there drinking beers
and scoping chicks and hope that doesn't happen? Easy for
you to say. If it was your mom, you probably would."

   "Hey, man . . ." John's voice faltered. They were lurching
across a line they had never crossed before.

   "Look, I can't do it, right? I'm sorry, man, but I can't. So
just stop bugging me."

   "But what about the band, Thee? The guys are asking me
when you're coming back."

   "Tell them as soon as my mother dies . . ." Even in his
fury, he realized he was getting too loud—he was only assuming Anna was still asleep in the other room. "Tell them
once this whole . . . inconvenience is over, I'll be back,
cheerful and ready to play power-chord music with a bunch
of twenty-year-olds. Yeah, with bells on. No need to worry
about it."

   "Theo . . ."

   "I don't care. Tell them I quit. Now leave me alone."

   Putting the phone down felt like slamming a door. He

wanted to cry but he wouldn't let himself. *Stupid, stupid, stupid.*

Catherine's call a day later was a different kind of misery. Someone had told her about what was happening—Theo had resisted the urge to phone her up himself a dozen times, resisted it like a drunk fighting a late-night run to the liquor store, but now there she was, that familiar voice. But there was something different in it, a careful distance as though she had scrubbed up like one of his mother's doctors before calling him, pulled on surgical gloves and a mask.

"I'm really, really sorry to hear about your mom, Theo."

"It's pretty tough. On her, I mean."

Catherine asked how he was doing, listened while he talked a little about the icy horror of the daily routine, even made a little small talk of her own—a promotion at work, a movie she'd liked—but there was an unmistakable subtext to the entire conversation. *This call is about loyalty and human decency, but nothing more than that. Don't get ideas.*

No problem there. His ideas were gone.

When the careful pas de deux with Catherine was over, he walked into the living room feeling entirely empty, as though something had eaten him away from the inside out, removing all the essential Theoness, leaving only the skin. He found his mother sitting on the couch, her head back but her eyes open. The television was off. She was so far gone most afternoons, wandering far off the map in the realms of her own pain, that she didn't even bother to turn it on anymore.

"I think it's time for me to go to the hospital," she said when she heard him.

"You had your appointment this morning, remember?"

She shook her head, but just barely, as though if she turned it too far it might simply fall off. She was having a very bad day, he could tell. "No, I mean it's time for me to move into the hospital."

Something had a grip on his innards—something chilly

that squeezed. "You don't need to do that, Mom. We're doing all right here, aren't we?"

She closed her eyes. "You're doing fine, Theo. You're a good son. But the doctor thinks so, too. I can't do it any longer."

"Do what?"

"Hold up my side of the bargain. I'm too tired. I hurt too much. I want to rest."

"But you can do that here . . ."

She raised her fingers to quiet him. "I don't want you carrying me around, Theo. You've had to do that a few times already. And I don't want to have my own son wiping my bottom. I couldn't stand that. It's time."

"But . . . !"

"It's time."

And so the last, pitched phase of the descent began, a voyage into the depths as bad in its way as anything Dante had imagined. But there would be no beatific vision at the end, Theo felt blankly certain. No shining city. Only the endless white corridors of the hospital ward.

She was letting go, he could feel it, spinning away from him like a moon that had broken the tethers of its orbit and would soon disappear into the empty dark spaces. He spent part of every day at her side, trying to concentrate on books he had been planning to read for months or even years. There was no point being with her all the time, but what else was there to do? He was afraid to return to his job, as if somehow that would be tempting fate, would ensure the receipt of the dreaded phone call while he was away from her more surely than if he were simply sitting around the house. The boys in the band had taken him at his own grief-maddened word and had made the split official—John had left him a halting, apologetic message making it clear without ever quite saying it, and Theo had not bothered to call him back. A sympathy call from a friend of his and Cat's, really more acquaintance than friend, had also gifted him with the unwanted information that Catherine was dating someone. When he hung up, he put on an old Smiths record and walked through the house from room to room to room trying to remember what a person was supposed to feel like inside.

It sometimes seemed to Theo that he was letting go too, cutting all ties, following his mother on his own journey into the void. Only the knowledge that she had no one else kept him connected to the Earth. Uncle Harold had come to visit once, in the early days, but he was even less gifted with sickbed chat than Johnny Battistini, and Theo knew they would not see him again.

There were still a few good days, though, days when the pain was not too bad, her mind not too fogged by painkillers. He wished he had more news of his own to offer her as distraction, but he was as barren as a stone. It didn't seem to matter, though: when she felt well enough to focus, she talked. It was as though during its destructive course the cancer had also eaten away a wall inside her, the partition that had kept in all the normal chitchat and reminiscence, so that he had only realized when she became sick what a stranger she was to him. She talked about Theo himself at first, about his childhood, his school days, his inordinate love of Hallowe'en and the work of trying to make the costumes he wanted, but then, increasingly, she began to talk about her girlhood in Chicago. She told him stories he had never heard about the large Irish family of which she was the youngest child, of all those aunts, uncles, cousins, brothers, and sisters from whom she had become estranged when her mother did the unforgivable—in a Catholic family, anyway—and divorced Anna's abusive, drunkard father. Theo knew little of this history, but it explained why he had met almost none of his relatives on his mother's side of the family, and it also explained why Theo's Grandma Dowd, a woman with seven children in Illinois, should have wound up living with her youngest out in California.

Hearing his mother talk now, he missed his maternal grandmother all over again. Grandma Dowd had been much

more loving than her daughter, so much so that Theo had
sometimes felt that he and his grandmother had a sort of secret treaty. Most of the childhood things he remembered
fondly had her in them somewhere—trips to the drugstore
that stretched to the candy counter as well, little gifts of
money when his parents weren't looking, and of course all
her wonderful, quirky Old Country stories about fairies and
giants that made his mother roll her eyes and actively irritated his aerospace technician father, who thought his
mother-in-law was filling the boy with what he called "simple-
minded nonsense."

Grandma Dowd had died when Theo was twelve. At the
time he had thought it didn't bother him much, had been
surprised and impressed at his own *sangfroid*. He realized he
had simply been too young to know how much it truly hurt.

And now, as though in dying her daughter was somehow
assuming her essence, he almost felt he was at his grandmother's bedside, something he had been denied the first
time as she lay dying from pneumonia, since his parents had
thought it would give him nightmares.

This is my whole family, he thought, staring down at his
mother's wasted, sleeping form. *My whole family is dying.
I'm the last one left.*

"I want to tell you something," his mother said.

Theo sat up in the chair, startled out of a half-sleep
and another of those persistent, disturbingly vivid dreams in
which he was looking out through fogged glass as though
he were a shut-in or a captive animal in a terrarium. He had
definitely felt himself to be someone else this time—not
Theo, not Theo at all, but instead something old and cold
and amused. It had been terrifying, and his heart was still
hammering.

At first, before he saw his mother's open eyes, he thought
the whisper might have been part of the dream. She slept so
much now—sometimes through the whole of his morning or
afternoon visits. He had almost begun to think of her as

something motionless, as an effigy, although there were also the times she moaned in pain, even after the nurse had come to give her more medication, and he found himself wishing frantically for the return of that absent, dismal quietude.

And there were still moments of lucidity, as this seemed to be.

"What is it, Mom? Do you need more meds?"

"No." It was a sound made only by the least amount of air, a sip. Deep breath pained her, made smaller the space in which the cancer grew like a dark conqueror. "I want to tell you something."

He pulled his chair over close to the bed, took her dry cold hand in his. "I'm listening."

"I'm . . . I'm sorry."

"For what?"

"That I didn't . . . didn't love you like I should have, Theo." Through the haze she was trying to see him properly; her eyes rolled a little, trying to focus. "It wasn't your fault."

"I don't know what you mean, Mom." He inched closer so he could hear her better. "You did fine . . ."

"No. I didn't do what I should have. It was just . . . something happened. When you were a little baby, practically a newborn. I suppose it was that, what do they call it . . . ?" She paused to get her breath, laboring in a way that made his stomach lurch. "Post-natal depression? I don't know. We didn't know about those things, really. But it just happened one day. I went to your bassinet—you were crying and crying and you wouldn't stop. Gas, maybe." She showed the ghost of a smile. "But I suddenly just felt like I didn't care, that you weren't really my baby." She frowned and closed her eyes, trying to summon the right words. "No, it must have been different than that. I didn't even understand what a baby was anymore. Just a little screaming thing. Not a part of me." She screwed her eyes more tightly shut against a wave of pain. "Not a part of me."

"You can't beat yourself up about things like that, Mom."

"I should have got help. I tried to tell your father. He

didn't understand—told me I just needed more rest. But I didn't love you the way I should have. I never did. I'm so sorry, Theo."

He felt his eyes sting. "You did all right. You did your best."

"That's a terrible thing, isn't it?" Now her eyes came open, fully open, and for the first time in days he thought she really saw him, complete and true, with a terrible clarity that would make normal, everyday life a nightmare. He tried hard to hold that awful stare.

"What is, Mom? What's a terrible thing?"

"When you die, and the only thing anyone can say about you is, 'She did her best.'" She took a shaky breath, then waited so long to take another one that his heart began to race again. When she finally spoke, it was in a whispery quaver like a frightened child. "Could you sing me a song, Theo?"

"A song?"

"I haven't heard you sing . . . in so long. You always had such a nice voice."

"What would you like to hear, Mom?"

But she only closed her eyes and gave a little wave of her hand.

He recalled the day he had found out about her illness, when they had gone out to hear the band play. An old one, then, an old Irish tune. She liked those.

> *"I wish I was in Carrickfergus,"*

he began quietly,

> *"Only for nights in Ballygrand.*
> *I would swim over the deepest ocean,*
> *The deepest ocean, my love to find."*

She smiled a bit so he kept going. A nurse stuck her head in the room, curious about the sound, but then backed out again, staying near the doorway to listen but trying not to intrude. Theo ignored her, struggling to remember the words, the tale of some nameless poet's regret.

> *"But the sea is wide and I can't swim over*
> *And neither have I the wings to fly.*
> *If I could find me a handsome boatman*
> *To ferry me over, my love and I."*

> *"My childhood days bring back sweet reflections,*
> *The happy times I spent so long ago.*
> *My boyhood friends and kind relations*
> *Have all passed on now like melting snow."*

The words were coming back to him, which was a relief, since he didn't want to break the spell: this felt more like being called upon to perform a ritual than just singing an old song. He sang it as simply as he could, avoiding the reflexive mannerisms of pop music. Only as he finished the last verse and began the final chorus did he remember what it was really about, the poet's regrets in the face of imminent death. He faltered for a moment but saw that his mother was asleep, the smile still on her lips, faint as starlight on a still lake.

> *". . . For I'm drunk today and I'm rarely sober,*
> *A handsome rover from town to town.*
> *Ah, but I am sick now, and my days are numbered;*
> *So come all ye young men and lay me down."*

He left her there sleeping. The nurse, a young Asian woman, smiled and started to say something to him as he came out of the room, but saw the look on his face and decided not to speak.

In the end, Anna Vilmos did not get even half a year. She died in the middle of the night, August 8th. It seemed to be a good death, given the circumstances. A nurse saw that she didn't appear to be breathing, took her pulse, then began the list of procedures that would ultimately free up the bed for another patient. Someone from the hospital called Theo at home and, after giving him the news, told him there was no point in coming in before the morning, but he roused himself anyway and got into his mother's old car, feeling that it would be safer to drive in his somnambulant condition than to ride his motorcycle. They had drawn the curtain around the bed, covered her face with a sheet. He pulled it back, his thoughts fractured into such tiny, whirling pieces he felt like a snow globe, felt he had been shaken and shaken and then set down.

She did not look peaceful, particularly. She didn't look like anything.

She looks like where someone used to be, but isn't anymore.

He kissed her cold cheek, then went to find the night administrator to make arrangements.

THE HUNGRY
THING

The warehouse district sweltered in heat unusual even for the season. A work gang of nixies, lounging on a break in the shade of one of the tall old buildings, were reluctant to move back out of the black coach's path until one of them recognized the flower-glyph on the license plate. A name passed between the lean, hard-muscled creatures, a murmur like the sea that was denied to them until their indenture had been paid, and they quickly flattened themselves against the wall to let the limousine past.

The pixies talked of it that evening in the tavern called Tide's End, but not much, and only in nervous, rippling whispers.

The coach pulled to a silent stop in front of the last building in the row, a large, windowless, ramshackle structure perched at the end of the wharf like an ancient animal sleeping in the sun. The coach shimmered in the heat-haze; when the first two figures got out the distortion made them seem even more monstrous than they were. Both wore long black overcoats which did little to hide the immensity underneath. The pair stood for long moments, motionless except for eyes constantly moving in the shadows of their wide-brimmed hats. Then, at some unspoken signal, one of them leaned and opened the coach door.

Three more figures stepped out, all in fine suits of dark, understated weave. The tallest of these newcomers looked up and down the now-abandoned wharfside road—the nixies had ended their break early and made themselves extremely scarce—then turned and led the rest into the building, pausing only to allow one of the gigantic bodyguards to pass through the door first.

The inside of the building was quite different than the rust-flecked, peeling exterior suggested. The five visitors made their way down a long hallway, through pools of light angling down from what seemed to be ragged holes in the high ceiling but on closer inspection proved to be oddly shaped skylights, each one carefully fitted. The hall itself was featureless, the walls painted a uniform smooth black, the floor carpeted in some dark, velvety material that suggested its owner had no need to be warned by the sound of approaching footsteps, no fear of anyone piercing his sanctum without him knowing about it long before they reached the door at the end of the hall.

The door had a brass plate, but the plate was blank. One of the bodyguards reached for the handle, but the tallest of the well-dressed figures shook his head. He pushed it open himself and led his two slightly smaller companions inside, leaving the bodyguards to shuffle their feet nervously, making sparks crackle in the velvety corridor.

The huge room inside was lit by more of the high, strange sky-windows, so that the distant ceiling seemed to be held up by columns of angled light. The air was hot and close and the smells that mingled there would have been unpleasant to a mortal, perhaps even maddening. The newcomers, despite superior senses, did not seem taken aback by the odor of the place, but as their catlike eyes became accustomed to the strange striping of light and dark the tall man's two companions slowed and then stopped, seemingly astonished by the jumble that surrounded them.

The vast space was a warehouse of sorts, but even in this most ancient and mysterious of cities it was unlikely there were any other warehouses like this. Although the down-stabbing light from the ceiling picked out much, it illuminated little, but what could be seen was very strange: manlike shapes, statues perhaps, frozen in a thousand different attitudes, filled the room like a crowd of silent watchers, most standing but many tumbled onto their sides, arms that once reached toward some heavenly object now seeming to grapple at the legs of their upright fellows. The silent figures were only part of the room's catalog, and many other objects were less immediately familiar: fantastic animals stuffed or reduced to rolled skins and piled bones; open crates overflowing with rusting weapons or lengths of fabric whose colors seemed inconstant; urns; caskets; and overturned cases that had spilled a wild variety of trinkets, from silver and gold jewelry to things that looked like children's toys formed from purest black carbon. Raw gems were even scattered carelessly about the floor like wildflower seeds. Shelf after shelf along the walls held jars in which things floated that did not encourage close study, things with eyes and even facial expressions, although in no other way manlike. Other jars were opaque, many extensively and carefully sealed, but some with the lids propped against the containers as though whatever was inside had been sampled in haste (or had perhaps escaped on its own). None of these containers appeared to be labeled, and even the small traces of powder sprinkled on the shelving around them in what were obviously careful patterns gave no clue as to what the contents might be.

Other mysterious objects hung from the ceiling on wires—kites made of skin, lamps that seemed to burn but gave no light; there was even a cloud of feathers that swirled continuously in one high spot near the ceiling as though caught in a whirlwind, gleaming white tufts cycling in and out of one of the columns of light but never scattering no matter how violently they blew.

The tallest of the three figures continued on until he had reached the far corner of the warehouse, a place where no direct light fell. His two companions, their first curiosity sated—or perhaps curdled into something else—moved forward with a speed that in less graceful creatures might have been mistaken for hurry, and when they stopped they stood close to their leader.

A seated shape stirred in the darkness of the corner. "Ah," it said. "Welcome, Lord Hellebore."

The tall one nodded. "I received your message."

The thing in the chair moved again, but did not rise, and—to the unspoken but obvious relief of Hellebore's companions—did not come out of the shadows. The Remover of Inconvenient Obstacles was not pleasant to look upon at the best of times and far less so at home. "And you have come. That is very kind of you, very . . . obliging. I do not believe either of your companions have previously visited me here."

Hellebore nodded and gestured to his fair-haired companion and to the stern-faced fellow whose hair was even darker than Hellebore's own, a black so pure it suggested artifice. "These are the lords Foxglove and Thornapple."

"Yes, I know them." There was a strange wheezing creak as the Remover stirred again. "You will pardon me, Lords, if I do not offer you my hand in greeting."

"Think nothing of it," said bearded Foxglove, perhaps a little too quickly.

"So, then." This was Thornapple, the First Councillor of Parliament—after Hellebore, the second most powerful man in Faerie. His ancient, chilly eyes were as black as his hair, but his shaggy eyebrows were snowy white, as if they were the only things on him that had aged past indeterminate middle years. "Is it time?"

"I believe so," said the Remover. "As you specified, Lord Hellebore—and as you paid for—I have kept careful watch. If we wait longer, we may miss our moment."

"Are you certain we have not missed it already?" There was no trace of impatience on Hellebore's pale face or in his silky voice, although it would have been madness to suppose he was not impatient, even eager.

"I am certain of nothing. But I think it is very unlikely."

Hellebore waved away the distinction. "Then let us begin. Tell us how to reach him."

"It is not so simple. I found him for you. You will also need me to accomplish the rest of what you wish to do."

Thornapple frowned. "Then who will we send for him? One of us? You?"

"Not *who*," said the Remover, and laughed his papery laugh again. "You and your companions have used up your exemption from the Clover Effect, and you must take my word that travel to that world is no longer possible for me, either. In fact, I very much doubt you can find any willing tool on our side with both the power and self-reliance needed to make the crossing and find your quarry—brute force without wit or wit-without sufficient strength would both fail, and with things changing so quickly you won't get a second chance, I think."

"So there is no one we can send?" Foxglove seemed relieved.

"I did not say that—I simply said it was not a 'who.' " With a strange, wet sound the Remover settled farther back into the darkness. "Bring me what I need, please. I will describe the objects to you. . . ."

While Thornapple and Foxglove searched for the mirrors, Hellebore stood with his hands thrust casually into the pockets of his trousers. He did not look directly at the place where the Remover sat, but that might have been courtesy, although Hellebore was not known for it. He had not seen this most honest of the Remover's various appearances before, but he had seen many things that even his most venerable colleagues could not imagine and was not in the least squeamish. "You realize that we will be crossing a line," Hellebore said at last, watching the angular Thornapple picking fastidiously through a pile of dusty framed pictures. "This will not be like what happened with the unborn child. If we fail, we may all be fed to Forgetting—you included."

"That is not much of a threat to me, my lord."

For a moment Hellebore looked troubled, but was distracted when the invisible figure stirred and even seemed for a moment about to rise and step out into the light.

"Don't touch that!" the Remover shouted, voice ragged but startlingly loud. "Put it down!"

Across the large room, Lord Foxglove, startled and a bit afraid, hastily put down the carved box he had been handling.

"The mirror is not there," the Remover said, more quietly now. "The next pile over. Do not touch that box again."

Hellebore had noticed something like pain in the Remover's words; he cocked a thin black eyebrow but said nothing.

At last the two powerful fairy lords came back, staggering like overloaded servants, each carrying a large mirror framed in ugly, coarse black wood. At the Remover's instruction they propped them facing each other on the floor with perhaps an arm's span between them.

"Here," the Remover said, and for a moment his hand appeared from the shadow holding a black candle in a dish. The two other lords quickly looked away, but Hellebore stepped forward and took the candle.

"Put it down on the floor midway between the mirrors," the Remover said. "Then light it and step back."

Hellebore touched index finger to thumb and made a flame. At the moment it ignited, the apertures in the ceiling above narrowed, or something else happened to block their light; within a few seconds the warehouse was dark except for the candle's flame.

"Silence now," said the Remover of Inconvenient Obstacles. "And I'm sure it does not need saying, but I will say it anyway—do not reach between the mirrors or in any way interfere with the light passing back and forth between them until I have finished."

He began to chant quietly, a sound only barely distinguishable from raspy breath. It seemed to take a long time.

The flame above the candle shrank until it was scarcely larger or brighter than a firefly's lamp, a tiny point that nevertheless became the focus of all the darkness around it.

Something began to form in the space between the mirrors, a faintly glowing cloud, as though the original light of the candle had spread into something watery and diffuse. The cloud grew more distinct without becoming more solid, flowing from one side to the other of the light that bounced between the mirrors. It seemed constantly about to take shape, but although it never quite did so, there were shifting suggestions of a face, a dark hole of a mouth and pitted, empty eyes. It was hard to look at it for more than a few moments, even for the three gathered lords of Faerie. As the Remover's tuneless singing grew louder the thing began to move more violently, writhing and snapping within the empty space between the mirrors like something trying to find its way out of a cage. The room grew piercingly cold. The thing's mouth opened wide, then even wider, as though it could swallow even itself if it wished.

"What is it?" Hellebore's voice was perfectly modulated, not too fearfully loud, not too overawed and quiet.

The Remover fell silent. When he spoke at last, his weary voice seemed to come from far away. "An *irrha*—a ghost from one of the older darknesses, a spirit of pestilence unknown in the mortal world since the stones of Babylon were leveled."

"And it will . . . will do what we need? You said that force without wit would be useless. Are you telling me this . . . *thing* has wit?" Hellebore looked to his companions, perhaps for support, but they were staring at the shape between the mirrors with sickened fascination.

"It does not need wit. What one of you would have to do by craft, it will do by instinct, for lack of a better word. It is terrible in its implacability. It will follow its quarry wherever he goes, in whatever world, without pausing to rest and without a single qualm or hesitation. It does not think, not as you and I do, but it does not need to. It will take new bodies as it needs them to pursue its quarry, so it will never grow weary. Eventually—inevitably—it will find him and cleave to him, and then it will bring him to us. Clutched in its grip, the one you want will tell you anything, do anything, give up anything he has, just to be free of this hungry, gnawing thing."

"Ah. I see." Hellebore nodded. "It is very good."

"It is . . . horrible," said Lord Foxglove.

"It is both," said the Remover. "In all the spheres there are only a few perfect things. This is one of them."

When the three lords left the warehouse room, they found the two ogre bodyguards halfway down the corridor, staring up at the ceiling with mouths slack and arms dangling uselessly. Their legs worked just well enough for them to plod after their masters, but it was only when the black coach's doors had thumped shut and the horse-faced chauffeur had laboriously turned it around and driven it back out of the narrow street toward the freeway that the bodyguards began to blink their eyes and mumble. By the time the long black limousine passed out of the waterfront district they could talk again, but the huge gray creatures still could not remember anything that had happened to them while they waited in the hall.

5

BOOK

"But, hey, you'll be getting some money from the house, right? You could buy your own PA system."

"I don't know. I don't think so—not right now."

"I'm serious, man. What they did sucked. I'd quit tomorrow if you wanted me to. We could find some other musicians, no problem. Guitar players, man, they grow on trees. The world is full of skinny guys who sat in their rooms all through high school learning to play every Van Halen solo."

Theo couldn't help smiling, even though Johnny couldn't see him. "Yeah, just what I need. Hook up with another worshiper of the extended guitar break."

"Whatever, man. Hell, we could get a keyboard guy, instead. We could play anything. You used to write some cool tunes, Theo. And lyrics, too—remember that thing you wrote about your father was a storm, or lightning, something like that? You should start writing again—you were wasted with the Clouds, anyway. You need to get back to your roots, dude. When I first met you, I used to think, 'Man, this guy's definitely going somewhere,' and I just wanted to hang onto you 'til you got there. You could be that guy again."

"What is this, National Theo's-Over-the-Hill-Month or something?" Cat had said something like it, too. *Potential.*

A great word for people to use about you when you were twenty, an embarrassment when you hit thirty.

"What are you talking about, man? I'm just saying that you got tons of talent, Thee. You need to use it."

It was hard to talk. It had been good to hear Johnny's voice, to get past the stumbling apologies and into areas in which they were both comfortable (like what an asshole Kris Rolle was), but now he was tired. He hadn't been talking much lately and he was out of practice.

"I don't know, John-O. Maybe. Maybe later on. Right now I don't feel much like playing music, anything like that. You keep playing with the Clouds boys. Kris is pretty talented, really, even though I can't stand the skinny little bastard. Maybe you really will get a record deal. Don't give that up for me."

"But you're my friend, man!"

That caught him short. It took a moment to move forward, to continue letting go. "Thanks. Really. You're my friend too, John, don't ever doubt it. I'm just not going to be very good at friendship stuff for a little while. I'm . . . I don't know, I'm just out of juice. My batteries are empty."

"So what are you going to do, now that . . . ? I mean, you gonna go back to Khasigian's?"

"Not right now. I'm going to sell the house, take a little time. You know that old joke—'Death is life's way of telling you to slow down'? Well, it works best when you're the one that dies, but I found out it pretty much works no matter what." He hesitated, unwilling to wander too far out into the things he had been thinking about. It wasn't really the kind of shit his friend wanted to hear, or would even understand. "I'm just not ready to be in the world right now, Johnny. Give me some time, I'll be back."

"You better, or I'll come over and kick your ass."

When he was off the phone he took a deep breath, stared hard at the pile of real estate forms on the dining room table, and decided that it really wasn't too early for a second beer after all. You could pour things into an emptiness like this all day but it would never fill up.

Hey, I'm doing paperwork, selling property, right? That means I'm employed. I'm just lucky enough to have a boss who allows me to drink in the afternoon.

He emptied half the beer in the first few swallows, then rubbed the cool bottle against his forehead, wanting everything to soften up, to get smooth and simple. Sure, he was drinking too much, but give a guy a break. He'd lost his girlfriend, their baby, and now his mother, all in a few months. Not a therapist in the world would fault him. And if he bumped into one who would, well, he'd smack him in the mouth.

Shit. He stared bleakly at the forms, at the boxes of his mother's carefully ordered papers. The house was oppressing him, everything staying just where he left it each day because no one else lived there. All the clean, desolate surfaces, the empty rooms, his mother's things already stuffed into boxes and moved out to the garage because it was just too damn depressing to look at them any more. But yesterday the real estate lady had been in two or three times with clients, and seemed in her horrifyingly chipper way to think that she had a few serious buyers already.

Thank God for a strong housing market. The faster it sold, the less time he'd have to live there.

He finished off the beer, contemplated briefly getting two or three more out of the fridge and just cashing in the afternoon in front of some stupid television movie—not that he'd find anything decent, because his mom had never bothered to get cable, but that wasn't the point, was it? The point was to blot out the long hours, to smear the transition into evening, when he would have the excuse of going out to get dinner somewhere; then he could come back and safely, responsibly drink a few more beers like any normal householder, fall asleep watching the late news, and not have to think until the morning sun was blazing through the windows again.

Something gurgled in his throat. It took a moment before

he realized it was a scream bottled in his innards, a blast of
misery trying to force its way out. He felt a chill across his
hot skin, like the first signs of a bad flu.

What am I doing? I don't belong here.

He forced himself to get up and go to the table, staggering a little as he went—had it been four beers already, or
just three? He sat in front of the boxes and spread papers,
the tidy big blue envelopes from the realtor, his mother's
address book and card files, but he found he couldn't move.
The light suddenly seemed wrong even with all the drapes
pulled, as though the entire house had been lifted out of the
warm but unexceptional Northern California sunshine and
dropped down onto the boiling surface of the planet Mercury. Worst of all, he felt something else staring out through
his eyes, as though like a television image gone out of sync
there was suddenly more than one Theo. It was the dream,
the terrible dream that came to him so often, but he was
awake. The alien presence was just ... *there,* no thoughts
he could share, nothing but a vague, oppressive sense of
connection.

Whatever the other Theo was, though, he didn't like it at
all. It felt horribly cold, this phantom self, even in the midst
of the heat that scorched his brain, cold as a nugget of ice
dancing in the tail of a comet.

*What, am I having a ... a stroke or something? Oh, God,
please, no ...*

His thoughts fizzed for a moment like a string of dud fire-
crackers, then the twist of strangeness suddenly loosened,
leaving only the normal bleak light of a warm, shuttered living room and a single thought that remained echoing in his
brain.

Dead. They're all dead.

He put his head down and waited until he felt like himself again, one single self. It was just a sort of fainting spell,
coupled with depression. They weren't all dead, of course.
Catherine was still very much alive, alive and dating someone else. And Johnny—shit, Johnny was immortal.

Don't even think it. Don't jinx him like you jinxed the baby . . .

Theo pushed the beer and also that terrible thought away, but when he tried to concentrate on the real estate papers again it was hopeless, like trying to read the grain of a piece of wood. Lender's details, fire insurance, contents insurance, title insurance. Hours of research. No way he was going to manage it with his head in this kind of shape. He looked at his mother's box of personal papers, saw the edge of an envelope with blue and yellow flowers stenciled on it, and pulled it out.

It was a card, a kitschy illustration of a kitten playing with a ball of string while the mother cat watched contentedly. The printed verse inside read,

> *Someone who helps me, someone who*
> *Keeps me safe and happy, too*
> *Someone who'll guide me my whole life through*
> *And that someone, dearest Mom, is you.*

Scrawled under it, ragged as a killer's confession,

> *Hapy Birthday Love From Theo*

And here came the damn tears again.

He couldn't even remember giving it to her. From the writing he must have been about six or seven. What was surprising was that she had saved it—his mother, the queen of unsentimental pragmatism. What else was in there?

He took the box back to the couch and tipped it over. Most of what fell out were the kind of things he had expected to find in the carton, insurance policies, old bankbooks for saving accounts long closed—so why the hell was she hanging onto them, then?—and a few marginally weird things like a handbook for breast self-examination, hidden in its own little manila envelope as though it were pornography. But there were also a few letters to her from his father, one of which seemed to have been written in the Fifties, before they were married, while Peter Vilmos was still stationed in the Philippines and she was still in Chicago. Any hope that it might reveal his father's lusty, romantic younger self—the self a younger Theo had wanted to believe had been there before normal life had crushed it, but had never quite been able to believe in—disappeared quickly as he read it.

> *Dear Anna,*
> *Well, it's been a few weeks so I thought I should write*
> *you again, since you said you wanted me to write. Life*
> *is pretty much the same. Jenrette, the guy in the next*
> *bunk, still snores like crazy. The food is pretty bad, but*
> *at least there's not much of it! (Joke) I hope you and*
> *your Morn and Dad are good, and that your Dad isn't*
> *still having so much trouble with being sick and missing work, like you wrote. We had to put together a supply hut the other day and I was in charge, which was*
> *harder than if sounds because it is really windy here,*
> *"blowing up a gale" most of the time, and the sheet*
> *metal wants to blow away and it is really heavy! But*
> *we got the hut built OK . . .*

There was another page just as inconsequential, and it was signed, not "Love," not "Passionately yours," but "Sincerely."

Had they slept together yet? Theo wondered. A stolen night or two at a motel, or in a school friend's room before he shipped out? It was frighteningly close to what he'd believed of his father at the worst moments—that he really was the kind of man who would send a letter signed, "Sincerely, Cpl. Peter Vilmos" to someone he'd seen naked.

His mother had kept a few other letters from his father, and some anniversary and birthday cards, but the old man hadn't gotten any more Casanova-ish as the years went by, although he did at least abandon "Sincerely" as the years went on, and even signed some of the later ones "Love, Pete."

Other than that, there was very little to show for a lifetime. More birthday cards from Theo, but notably absent once he had turned twelve or so, some letters from relatives and, to his surprise, more than a few clippings from local papers about his own youthful career. Here was one from the *Peninsula Times-Tribune* about his high-school production of *Guys and Dolls,* one paragraph marked with a highlighting pen:

> *"If some of the other leads were a little shaky in both vocal range and Runyonesque accents, the same cannot be said of Theodore Vilmos, who brought verve and energy and an astonishing strength of voice to the role of Sky Masterson, the big-time gambler with the heart of gold. Young Vilmos commanded the stage, and this reviewer would not be surprised some years up the road to hear that he is playing this role and others on Broadway . . ."*

She had saved other things, too, more local write-ups about other plays and choral concerts where he had soloed, and even a review of a performance by his first band from *Shredder,* a semi-punky Eighties fanzine. He had wondered once or twice where that review had got to, and here it was.

> *"The lead singer is fucking hot, man, and I don't usually say that about boys, if you know what I mean. I haven't heard anyone sing like that since Bono and U2 broke, pretty angry and angry-pretty. I mean, if Eaten Young hang onto their singer, these guys are seriously commercial. I don't know if that's good or bad, but it's the truth . . ."*

The fact that his mother had carefully censored the f-word with a black felt-tip, the fact that she would even have a magazine called *Shredder* hidden away in her drawer just because it mentioned his singing, almost made him start crying all over again. Who knew?

But the story's clear, isn't it? Johnny, Cat, even these reviews—I didn't take it where I should have. When did it all go sideways?

He was depressed now in a way he hadn't expected to be, not just about his mother's insignificant life, but his own. He put the reviews aside and riffled through the rest of the papers. His mother had saved a few random recipes, a couple of notes from Grandma Dowd—no letters, but then she had lived with Mom and Dad the last fifteen years of her life, so why would she send her daughter letters? The notes from his grandmother were so uninteresting on the surface—one seemed to be a request for Anna to pick up a prescription, the other a page torn off an insurance company letterhead notepad that said only, *"Im sorry I forgot. Please remind me to look for it tomorrow. Mama."*—that for a little while Theo wondered if they might, given some momentarily absent context, actually be important, might be revealed as clues to some larger family story. It was only as he leafed through the rest of the unedifying pile of paid bills and statements that he realized the reason Anna Dowd Vilmos had hung onto those meaningless notes was because she had nothing else of her own mother's to keep.

Goodnight Nobody.

For a moment the chill seemed about to return, but it was only a shiver of despair at the thought of two people, both dead now—three people, counting his father with his quonset-hut news bulletins—who had left so little behind to mark their existence, who had disappeared into death like stones thrown into a river, the ripples gone within moments.

Everybody starts out as somebody. Then it slips away.

He wanted another beer, now. He really wanted another beer.

As he piled the papers back into the box, something he had missed the first time tumbled out of the large brown envelope of holiday recipes into which it had fallen. It was another small greeting-card envelope, but strangely heavy. His mother's name and address were written on it in old-fashioned, somewhat cramped handwriting.

What slid out of the envelope was not a card but a folded letter. The surprising weight came from a bankbook and a small key taped to the bottom of the last page of the letter with yellowed cellophane tape. Theo's eye flicked to the ornate signature, which took him a moment to puzzle out.

Your obedient servant,
Eamonn Dowd

He was pretty certain that Eamonn Dowd was one of Grandma Dowd's brothers, although he couldn't remember much of what she'd said about any of them, since she'd left them all behind when she'd moved out to California.

It was a longish letter, at least by comparison to the others his mother had saved. The postmark gave its date as January of 1971, only a couple of years after Theo's own birth. He considered another beer, then changed his mind and made himself a cup of instant coffee as he worked his way through the somewhat spiky handwriting.

My dear niece,
You will doubtless have trouble remembering me, since we have not met since you were a very young girl, but now that your mother is gone you are the only family that I have left—the only true family, that is. Your mother, my sister Margaret, was the only one of that quarrelsome, blighted brood into which I was born for whom I felt fondness. If I saw little of her over the years, and even less of you, it is because my travels did not permit it, rather than any lack of good feeling.
Having known so little of me, you will doubtless find it strange when I say I owe you and the rest of your family a debt of shame that cannot be reduced

or put right. I will not explain it—I could not do so in
a letter, in any case—but I will say that it weighs
heavily on me now, when I am about to set out on a
journey from which there will be no returning. As a
small gesture of good will and regret at having been
such a poor uncle, I give to you and your husband
and infant son what little I have left in the way of
worldly property.

Sadly, there is no family manor or chest of jeweled
heirlooms. There is instead a small bank account and
a few personal papers and other odds and ends. The
money is yours—it is not much, but it will perhaps one
day help pay for an education for your son, or tide you
over some of the lean times through which most lives
pass.

Again, I am sorry, even though it means nothing to
you now, and most likely never will. Among my effects
you will find a book. Should you be so surfeited with
leisure time that you decide to read it, please do not
take it as the ravings of a disordered mind. It was an
attempt at fiction of sorts, although not a successful
one, I fear—a type of modern fairy tale that I hoped
might find some small readership. But I could think of
no effective ending. Now all endings seem one to me.

I wish you and your young family healthy and
happy lives.

Theo narrowed his eyes, shook his head, then read the letter again. It did not seem to fit into the rest of his mother's
keepsakes any better than it had the first time. In the midst
of stultifying normality, it made an odd little space for itself—like something out of an O. Henry story.

The small key had to be for a safe-deposit box: that much
seemed clear. The bankbook, its ruled lines full of careful little handwritten notations, was from something called Traveler's Bank, with an address on Duende Street here in San
Francisco. He'd never heard of the street, but the smudgy,

carbon-paper directions to the place suggested it must be somewhere in the area of Russian Hill. The account had totaled something near five thousand dollars—not a small amount thirty years ago, but not quite the life-changing bequest from a rich uncle that people dreamed about. It had all been withdrawn a week or so after the date on the letter, and the emptied account seemed not to have been touched since. It was funny that his mother had never mentioned it, but not really out of character.

Theo now remembered that he had heard his grandmother talk about her brother Eamonn at least once or twice: she had described him as "the handsome one in the family," but also said that he "never did put down roots," or words to that effect. But she had seemed fond of him, as his letter suggested. He also recalled her saying something like, "If only he'd put all that cleverness to work," about some close relative of hers, which he guessed now might be this Eamonn, "he'd have been a millionaire. But all that reading and such is no substitute for a bit of elbow grease."

Theo stared at the bankbook. What had happened to the man? Had he been sick when he wrote this? That "a journey from which there will be no returning" didn't sound very good. And what had he done to the family that he felt he had to apologize to Theo's mother, someone he seemed scarcely to have known?

The bank account was long empty, but where were the other papers the letter had mentioned? Theo knew he had more pertinent matters waiting for him, but this letter from his great-uncle was the first thing he had come across in ordering his mother's estate that wasn't simply depressing. After that weird turn he'd just taken, he very much wanted to be doing something, anything, that might take him outside into the fresh air.

And why is this key still here, anyway? It has to be a safe-deposit box. But even if it's at this whatever-it-is bank, this Traveler's place, it won't do me any good unless I know the box number. I suppose I could do it the legal way, show them

*it's part of my mom's estate and ask them to tell me the num-
ber, but that means I have to wait until it all goes through
probate or some damn thing, doesn't it?*

Irritated and weary at the thought, he picked at the edge
of the stiff, ocher-tinted strip of tape that secured the key to
the letter. The ancient cellophane parted from the paper on
one side and the key swung out like a hinge, giving him a
glimpse of ink. Behind it, so small that it had been hidden by
the key itself, was the number "612" written in his great-
uncle Eamonn's cramped, careful hand.

He found it on a strange little cross street halfway up a
steep hill; it was one of those San Francisco Victorian
houses so narrow that it was easy to walk past it without
noticing the Traveler's Bank sign beside the doorbell. His
first thought was that it was pretty strange to have a bank in
a house, his second that someone must have kept the name
but turned it into something else—one of those bijou restaurants people don't find unless a friend tells them about it, or
a graphic arts studio. It was too small to be a modern bank,
and on a street like this the walk-in business must be nonexistent.

There was a glass panel in the front door, but the lights
seemed to be out inside and he could see nothing of what lay
beyond. There was a speaker grille with a small button next
to the bank's name, so he pushed it.

"Krrawk murrkagl mornt?" The small, nervous voice
that gurgled back out of the grille might possibly have been
human.

"Hello? I have a safe-deposit box here, I think?"

After a few moments, the door buzzed. He popped it
open, found himself in a dark stair-lobby, and walked up the
steps. The door on the first floor landing was open. A plump
young woman with pale, straight hair stood there, waiting
nervously. "Did you say you have safe-deposit?" She had a
bit of an accent, perhaps Eastern European.

"Yes. It was part of my mother's estate, given to her by

her uncle, a man named Dowd." He handed her the letter and
the passbook. "You can see for yourself. He had a regular
savings account here, too." He held up the key. "The box
number is 612."

"Oh." She said it as though he had just informed her nuclear war would begin at any moment. "Oh, no."

"What?"

She shook her head. "Mr. Root, he is not here." But she
turned and led him through the door.

If it was a bank lobby, it was the strangest, smallest one
he'd ever seen. The whole room was about the size of a
Victorian parlor, and similarly decorated. Pictures of stern-
looking men in antique black suits hung on the wall, surrounded by dusty baroque frames; in such a cramped room
they seemed almost to be leaning in on top of visitors. Four
clocks showing different times were displayed in a row on
the wall, but instead of the usual London, Tokyo, and other
financial centers, the plaques beneath the old-fashioned
faces read *Glastonbury, Carcassone, Alexandria,* and *Perse-
polis.* Was it a musty old joke of some kind? He'd heard of
most of them, but he wasn't sure why anyone would care
what time it was in any of those places. There were a few
other pieces of office equipment, but none of them appeared
to be a great deal more recent than the Age of Steam, except
for some kind of huge teletype machine with a table all to itself near the back of the room, which looked like it might
have been state of the art during the Second World War.

"Do you still have the safe-deposit boxes?"

She nodded eagerly. "Oh, yes. In back rooms." She gestured at the rear wall and the door there, flanked by portraits
of two frowning patriarchs.

"And when will this Mr. Rude be back?"

"No, Root—like tree, yes? But I don't know." Her pleasure at being able to confirm the existence of the boxes had
dissolved, plunging her into anxiety once more. "He comes
in not very much. Maybe Friday? Maybe Monday?"

Theo looked around again. A stuffed crow stood in a glass

case just behind the room's front door. "And you're just here by yourself the rest of the time?"

Now her slightly bovine features took on a look of alarm. "Not alone. There are other people in other offices—next door, there is Pan-Pacific Novelties."

"I don't mean any harm, I just . . . it seems weird. I mean, this is a bank, right? I've never seen a bank that looked like this."

She shrugged. "Most of customers very old, I think. They don't come here. Used to be very busy, this place, but years are gone. Now most of banking done by telephone, by fax." She pointed first at the rotary-dial phone, then at the massive piece of machinery Theo had noticed earlier. "Mostly I just answer questions."

"Questions? Like . . . ?"

She flushed, and was suddenly a much prettier girl. "Like, is fax machine on?"

He felt guilty for giving her the third degree. It wasn't her fault she was working for a company that was probably a front for some bizarre offshore money-laundering scheme. "Sorry. Let me just get into the box and I'll let you get back to your work."

"Get into box?"

"Yes. You said they're in the back, right? The safety-deposit boxes?"

"But Mr. Root not here."

"I don't need a loan or anything. There's a box in there that originally belonged to my mother's uncle. It's mine now. I've got the letter where he gave it to her, and I've got a photocopy of her letter making me executor of her estate, and I've got the key to the box. That's how these things work." He started toward the door at the back of the cramped room. "Back here, right?"

She flapped her hands a little and looked at the heavy old dial phone as if considering calling her absent boss to come save her from this madman who actually wanted to use the Traveler's Bank as a bank.

Or maybe she's thinking about stunning me with that ten-pound bakelite receiver if I get any farther out of line.

If the front room was dark and old-fashioned, Theo thought that the back room made it look like a pop-art painting by comparison. The only light came from a nest of wires which had once underpinned a spherical paper shade, the naked bulb now exposed in their midst like a glowing sun at the center of a medieval orrery. There were shelves and shelves of long, narrow boxes, but most of them seemed to be the bank's records, cartons stuffed with three-by-five cards lettered by hand.

"Mr. Root, he wants to get someone to put all this in computer," the girl said apologetically.

Theo tried hard not to laugh at the thought of some poor bastard having to do the data entry for what looked like a perfectly preserved nineteenth-century fiscal institution. If this was not the back room for Scrooge and Marley, it was a damn good imitation. "Just show me the safe-deposit boxes, please."

The metal boxes had several shelves of their own near the back, with a strip of carpet and a very old swivel chair set up for the convenience of whatever Bob Cratchit had to work with them. Theo found 612, sat down with it in his lap, and wiggled the key back and forth several times without success. The problem was an old lock, not the wrong key: after a few more tries the key scraped past whatever grit had impeded it and the lock opened. Theo would not have been surprised to see a cloud of dust billow up out of the box, as though he had unsealed Tutankhamen's tomb.

Instead of gold or jewels—not that he'd been counting on either—he found only a leather-bound notebook.

He said good-bye to the flustered young woman and walked down the stairs, the fairy-tale reader in him half-expecting to discover that his dozen minutes inside had really been a dozen hours, that he would find the moon high in the sky and the nighttime neighborhood deserted, but outside the front door it was still prosaic afternoon. He stepped out of tiny

Duende Street and headed back toward his motorcycle, the
sun glaring flatly and the wind curling up the steep road, carrying the scent of the bay to him as it tugged at his hair and
clothes.

He went to a Denny's to get an early dinner, and while
he waited for his turkey sandwich he sugared his coffee and opened the notebook.

Eamonn Dowd's cramped script was easier to read now,
either because Theo was becoming used to it or because the
piece of writing he had labeled an attempt at fiction had
been produced in less hurried circumstances than the letter
he had sent to his niece. From the opening lines it read more
like autobiography than a novel, but that was well within
the eighteenth- and nineteenth-century tradition that
seemed to have been more comfortable for Dowd than
something closer to his own era. Theo wondered when his
great-uncle had been born, working back from Grandmother Dowd's death in the early 1980s. If he was one of
her older brothers, especially by as much as fifteen years—
not impossible in such a large family—he could have been
born in the late 1890s, which would make his literary influ-
ences fairly reasonable.

*The 1890s. By the time he read Hemingway for the first
time, he would already have been at least as old as me.*

It also meant that the "journey from which there would be
no returning" he was referring to in 1971 probably meant his
own natural death.

The sandwich and its little nest of french fries almost
dropped out of the sky in front of him as the waiter hurried
on to another table. Theo ate slowly, using only one hand so
he could read.

    I have always been restless,

the story began.

In an earlier century, in the country of my ances-
tors, I would have perhaps been one of the fishermen
who ventured far down the coast into the strange, for-
eign lands of Wales and Cornwall, or perhaps, given a
slightly different cast of mind, a priest carrying the
Gospel out into the small, scattered islands of the Irish
Sea. Instead, I was born into a world where even the
farthest reaches of Asia seemed nearer and more
available to me than County Cork would have been to
one of my great-great-great grandfathers. I valued the
advantages of this smaller world, but even as a child I
did not love what the growth of knowledge and the
shrinking of distance had done to banish Mystery.

Books were the sailing vessels of my childhood,
taking me out of the wind-scraped streets of Chicago
and carrying me away to Baghdad and Broceliande,
to Sparta and Sherwood Forest. At times—for my
childhood was not a particularly happy one, and not
only because of poverty—it seemed to me that such
places were far more real than the dull world of
cobblestone and cement that surrounded me.

There must be finer worlds, I decided, and set my
own course in life without realizing it. There must be
more than the chilly shadows of our home on Calumet
Avenue and the rattling of trains overhead, twice an
hour.

Eamonn Dowd, or at least this perhaps entirely fictional
version, ran away for the first time at age twelve, riding the
hobo road as far as Denver before being caught by railroad
police and sent back to Chicago, where his father beat him
soundly but otherwise seemed to have little reaction to his
eldest son's three-month escape.

When he was fifteen he got away again, this time making
it all the way out to San Francisco where, by lying about his
age, he connived his way onto a cargo ship heading for
China. The First World War had not begun and the ports of

the Pacific were dangerous, exciting places; the young Eamonn eventually decided that, happily, Mystery was not entirely dead. He watched as a Japanese sailor who had
knocked down an old woman was beaten to death by a mob
in Hangchow, and had his first sexual experience with a pros-
titute in Kowloon who was only a little older than himself, a
girl named First Rain who had run away from her farming
village in Shensi. Dowd (or in any case the book's identically
named protagonist) lived with her for some months, but
eventually his wanderlust claimed him again and he took
passage back to the States by way of a ship that stopped in
Hawaii.

By the time Dowd was marveling at his first hula
dance—a much more sexually inspiring experience to a
young man in the early part of the century than at its end—
Theo had finished his sandwich and was on his second re-
fill of coffee. Outside the restaurant, the cars had turned
their lights on as the long summer afternoon dropped into
evening.

He riffled through the close-filled pages, skimming. The
narrator had joined the navy when the United States entered
the war in 1916. A year later he wound up as a cook on the
USS *Oregon,* but since it was primarily a training ship he
didn't see combat—he didn't seem sorry to have missed it,
either. Afterward he had tried to settle in San Francisco
where the *Oregon* was based, was even briefly engaged to
marry a girl named Lizzie O'Shaughnessy, a dockworker's
daughter, but his urge to travel was not so easily stifled.
After leaving the navy he also left town in the mid-1920s.
Several of Lizzie's brothers threatened to kill him if he ever
returned, but presumably only for disappointing her: Theo
didn't think Dowd would have gotten away safely if he'd
impregnated a nice Irish Catholic girl and refused to marry
her. He joined the merchant marine, traveling to Europe and
Africa and the Middle East, always with an eye open for the
sort of intrigue that in his childhood had fired his romantic
sensibilities, and having adventures of which Theo could not

help envying even the least interesting, if they were actually real incidents.

Theo had finished his piece of coconut cream pie and was distractedly putting money onto the shiny tabletop, just about to close the notebook and head home, when the sentence at the end of one of the book's unnumbered chapters jumped out at him.

> *It was while I was on shore leave in India, my pockets rather more full than usual, that I stumbled across the book and the secrets that would forever change my life.*

Theo wanted to keep reading, but had a nagging feeling he'd left the house's back door unlocked. He hadn't planned to be out so long. The lights were certainly off, since he had left in midafternoon—an invitation to thieves or vandals. Regretfully, he closed the notebook and walked out to his motorcycle in the parking lot.

Drinking himself to sleep with three or four beers was no longer as compelling an idea as it had been earlier in the day: he was enjoying, or at least interested by, his great-uncle's story. Theo propped himself up on the couch in a pool of light from a table lamp and left the rest of the lights off. For the first time he could appreciate the silence of the small house.

The narrative—which despite its picaresque incidents had been to this point so realistic that he had begun to consider the book clearly autobiographical, despite its author's assertions—now took a turn toward the decidedly strange. Eamonn Dowd wrote of finding a copy of an infamous but unnamed book in a flyblown bazaar in Harappa, a discovery he described as "so lucky as to make one think more than luck was involved." Whatever the book was, it awakened in the narrator an interest in unspecified places that, like the book, he knew by rumor but had never thought possible to achieve—"magic names," as he put it, reached only by "lost tracks and highways which have mostly faded from the memory of mankind."

As the story in the notebook got stranger, its descriptions also became more vague, so full of unspecific references to Eamonn's new fascination with "experiments" and "studies," as well as his growing interest in what he called "the Outer Lands" or "the Fields Beyond," that Theo found it increasingly difficult to maintain his interest in the rows and rows of close-set writing.

He yawned and looked up from a passage about "the Gate, beyond which is the antechamber of the City and its fields," and saw to his shock that it was after midnight. Despite the purposeful obscurity of the narrative, he had been reading on the couch for over three hours. No wonder he was tired.

He looked at the page where he had stopped, reading again the description of "a city beyond anything known, more alive than any metropolis of West or East, and more frightening."

> *And now, at last I had found the way, or thought I had. At the next darkness of the moon I would find out whether my years of study had been in vain. I would realize my heart's desire or I would find my hopes dashed to pieces . . .*

Something moaned outside the house. Startled, Theo dropped the book. For a moment he thought it was a child crying, then relaxed at the realization that it must be a cat on the back fence, some neighborhood tom singing a song of territory disputed or love proclaimed.

Those noises they make, sometimes—creepy little bastards . . .

But as he found his place again and slipped an unopened

utility bill into it as a bookmark, the noise continued, even grew louder. Theo's skin goose-pimpled and the hairs on the back of his neck seemed to stand up and quiver. It was the strangest sound he could remember hearing, a moan like something in terrible pain, but oddly detached, too, with an eerily keening edge—the sound of something that knows it is terribly, irremediably lost. It unnerved him, and when he discovered that the patio light had burned out, it was all he could do to fumble the flashlight out of the kitchen drawer and step out the back door, wishing for one of the only times in his life that he had a gun.

By the time he got outside the noise had stopped. He stood for a moment, holding his breath, wondering why what was almost certainly the yowl of a horny tomcat had his heart thumping like a rave-track drum machine. There was nothing but silence now—even the crickets had gone still—but he could not shake off the irrational feeling that something had reached out for him, something even more alien than the cold presence which had touched him earlier in the day.

Theo slid the beam of the flashlight along the back fence, across the dying flower beds he had again forgotten to water, and probed the undergrowth beneath the elm tree in the corner of the yard. No cat eyes reflecting. No sign of anything at all. He must be overreacting, he told himself, and it certainly seemed logical, even though he couldn't entirely make himself believe it. Whatever had made the noise had heard him coming and run away, simple as that.

But the memory of that hungry, mournful sound had not left him even half an hour later. Tired as he was, he could not fall asleep until he had got back out of bed and turned on the little light in the hallway bathroom, so that the door of his bedroom became a faintly glowing rectangle in the darkness, a gateway to some shining country beyond dream.

6

A CORRUPTION OF MOONLIGHT

"My name ain't no goddamn Stumpy" the lost man said, even though no one was listening.

He scooted even farther back into the corner, trying to get a little more of the Dumpster between himself and the wind that was scratching around the mouth of the alley like a dog trying to dig under a fence.

"Ain't Stumpy. That ain't no proper name." He patted his pocket, hoping that he had just imagined finishing the bottle, but of course he hadn't imagined it. "Goddamn."

It wasn't right to take away a man's name. Bad enough when they sent him away to Viet goddamn Nam and took away both his legs and part of his arm, but at least back then they had called him by his right and true name, even put a rank in front of it, as if to stick him even more firmly into the world—Marine Private First Class James Macomber Eggles. The fellows in his platoon had also called him "Eagles" before a short round blew him back all the way from An Hoa to Stateside. "Eagles" may not have been written in his grandmama's Bible like his real name and all his brothers' and sisters' names, but he had still liked the sound of it. Even when he had first rolled back onto the street in his wheelchair, and some of the kids down by the courthouse lawn had started calling him Stumpy Jim just to see him get upset, at least they had still partly called him by his right name. Now they just called him Stumpy, and that made him angry, real angry. You could take away a man's legs and his arm, but you didn't take away his name. That wasn't right.

"Where's that cat?" He had made a friend, of a sort, a scrawny thing that happily gnawed on his leftovers and huddled next to him for warmth, but he hadn't seen it for two days. "Damn cat run off." It had been nice to have some companionship. He hoped it would come back.

It wasn't like he wanted so much. His cat back. A second sock to roll over the stub of his forearm, because it was going to get so goddamn cold when the winter came back and the stump always pained him so when the Hawk was blowing in from the lake. Someone to fix the skateboard wheels on his cart so he could roll himself up and down the sidewalk again properly and not have to drag himself around on a sliding mat of old cardboard. That was humiliating. He was a veteran—a goddamn Marine! He ought to at least have some goddamn wheels. It wasn't like he wanted much. And a bottle of brandy. Didn't have to be expensive, just a bottle of brandy that would go down his throat smooth and easy and make the other things stop hurting. He hadn't had any brandy since that man in the nice coat had given him half a bottle two Christmases ago, but he hadn't stopped thinking about it since. That stuff beat your bullshit cheapjack cough-syrup wine all to shit.

He scrabbled through his pile of possessions, looking for the new plastic sack he had found, nice thick plastic from some uptown clothing store, not some raggedy-ass grocery store bag already splitting at the seams before he'd even found it. He was going to chew a hole in this nice new bag to put his head through, wear it high on his neck to keep the cold off at night. He thought it might look like one of those collar-things the astronauts had, the rings that their helmets screwed into, and he wondered briefly what it would feel like to sleep winter nights in an astronaut suit, with a little window over his face he could close and keep in the warmth until the morning sun began to put a little heat back into the sidewalks.

Cat, sock, skateboard wheels, a bottle of brandy, and a goddamn astronaut suit . . .

Something moaned quietly deep in the clutter piled at the end of the alley. The man who had once been Private First Class James M. Eggles flinched.

"Cat? That you?" But it didn't sound like any cat. The noise was too big, too rough.

They threw a body in there, but the poor bastard ain't dead yet, was his next thought. The pile of rubbish rippled, bulged, then settled. The moan became louder.

Shit, no, it's just some goddamn junkie fall asleep puking in my alley. No respect.

He pushed himself upright with his good arm and waved his stump at the quivering pile of cardboard and shredded plastic packing. "You get out of there." His voice was a little more shaky than he would have liked. "This is where a decent person sleeps. This is my place." But what if it wasn't a shriveled, bony little junkie? What if it was something worse, some kid waking up crazy with a head full of angel dust, his arms and face scratched bloody from his own fingernails, his muscles knotted up like live snakes? Or what if it wasn't even a person? Maybe a big old dog, one of those pit bulls, got bit by a rat with rabies or something. *Maybe it's going to come up out of that pile of junk with its mouth all foamy and its eyes all red . . .*

"I got a knife, you know," he lied. Frightened, he still took a moment to add that to his mental list, right after the astronaut suit. "Don't make me cut you, hear? I don't want no trouble, but I'll give it to you free if you come looking!"

The thing stood up slowly, a corruption of moonlight, a tattered, flapping shadow come to life. At first he thought that he must be more sheltered by the Dumpster than he realized, that the lakeshore wind must be blowing real hard to plaster paper bags and fast-food wrappers all over the other man that way, so that you couldn't see even a bit of his skin or clothing.

The figure lurched a little and staggered a step toward him.

"Goddamn it!" he said shrilly. "Now, I told you about my knife! You stay back!"

But when it turned toward him—slowly, strangely, as though it had not heard a thing he had said, but had only now sensed him somehow, felt him or smelled him—he suddenly realized that it looked so strange because there was no body beneath the wrinkled, flapping assortment of bags and torn newspapers, no confused junkie face hidden behind the ragged clot of papers. The crumpled, grease-smeared mask was its face, the last face he was ever going to see.

His heart climbed right up his throat like an Otis elevator, choking off his air. He turned away to drag himself away up the alley toward the sidewalk, scrabbling toward the people who must be only a few dozen yards away on the warm summer-night streets, the corner-hangers, the would-be pimps. Even the worst of his tormentors surely wouldn't leave him to this! He tried to scream, but a weight heavy as cubic yards of graveyard dirt fell on him and shoved him down, then something smelling of rendered fat and old bones wrapped itself around his mouth and nose, clamping tighter and tighter until James Macomber Eggles at last gave up his own tired, reduced body and went shrieking soundlessly into the void.

*I*t had waited so long to feel this strange but pleasurable sensation again. Aeons in that cold dark place, in that nothingness inhabited only by other presences like itself, battening on the flickering heat of its unfortunate neighbors (while avoiding those few whose emptiness was deeper and more powerful than its own) had all but wiped away what little consciousness it had once had. Now it was free once more.

But the freedom was not complete. A compulsion ran through it like a red scar: all its hunger, its chilly hatred of that which was warm and free, was centered around a dot of life that it could sense but not immediately reach—the theovilmos *thing, the quarry. For a moment as it traveled to this plane, that quarry had almost seemed in reach, although the bodiless hunter had not been prepared to engage it. But such was the fierce fire of its hunger that for a moment the two of them had almost touched across incomprehensible distance. Then the* irrha *had been forced to let go, swept on to another point where the planes pressed closer together and it could more easily make its transition to the physical reality in which its quarry moved.*

The disease spirit flexed its new limbs, extended its new senses. Warm life surrounded it—warm life and cold geometries of stone, mixed together. So long, it had been so long since it had touched this material plane, felt these particular and exquisite pains. The irrha *tried to look out the eyes of the stolen body, but could not at first make them focus. Its own peculiar senses were still sharp, though. It could taste other living presences close by, things much like the creature whose body it now wore: they were moving and making noises just beyond the mouth of this enclosure, innocent as birds flying past a branch on which a leopard pretends to sleep.*

It was time to begin the hunt, but the irrha *hesitated. Something was wrong with this form it had usurped: it was somehow incomplete, the limbs foreshortened and unbalanced. The* irrha *had chosen this body because its owner had been close to the place where the* irrha's *crossing had ended, and because it had sensed the owner would not fight hard for it—the* irrha *had been depleted by its journey and in need of conserving strength, but it had turned out to be a pointless economy.*

The hungry thing paused to make repairs. There was much hard, physical travel to do now that it had become a part of this plane of existence, and the body must hold up for a long journey. This stolen vehicle must also be strong enough to capture the theovilmos *thing and to carry it away to the dark places, as had been ordained.*

But perhaps, it thought in its wordless way, when the ones who had summoned the disease spirit were done with the theovilmos, *they would let the* irrha *feed on it. That would be a very pleasurable hour, when hunger was at last filled.*

7 WOODS

After such exhausting researches (and after so many failed attempts!) to behold at last that fabled metropolis standing before me, the teeming streets and the shining towers that so few men have seen, and fewer still have returned from, was to understand once and for all that Science is a sham and what we call "human knowledge" a compendium of evasions and half-truths. As I stared at this breathtaking vista, even without knowing what would happen to me—and perhaps the gods or Fate blessed me by that ignorance—I understood that my life had now changed so completely that all of the experience I had so eagerly sought, in so many unusual corners of the world and among so many odd people and situations, had served only as a brief, shadowy prelude to this moment . . .

It seemed like a good place to pause. Theo wrapped the book in a towel and then placed it carefully in his backpack, having decided it would be better to take it in the car than to risk it getting smashed up in a box among the rest of his things. Of the small stock of possessions he was moving to the cabin, it was the only thing that could not be replaced.

While his great-uncle's story had grown more and more unlikely, Theo's respect for it as a tale well-told had grown too. While it would never be classed as a great work of fiction, or even a particularly good one—the rhetoric tended toward the florid, for one thing, heavily influenced by the pulps Eamonn Dowd had read in his youth, and it also seemed far more like a travelogue than a novel, unimportant incidents often given the same weight and detail as far more meaningful events—he had to admit that it was a pretty good book of its sort. Despite the purposeful obfuscations (the "but of that I will not speak more" bullshit, as Theo thought of it) picked up from too much Lovecraft or whoever, the protagonist's unrelenting search for some way to reach the mysterious, magical city had been genuinely entertaining. Theo was interested to see whether the fictional city, now that the protagonist had found the arcane wisdom to make his way there, would live up to the buildup—in other words, would Great-Uncle Eamonn turn out to be a real writer or just an amateur trying to spice up his own interesting but unmagical recollections with things stolen from *Weird Tales?*

In fact, since he now had about two hundred thousand dollars from the sale of his mother's house stashed in the bank—a reassuringly boring bank on a main street, with lots of tellers inside and ATMs on the outside walls, nothing at all like Eamonn Dowd's choice of a financial institution— Theo could afford not only to finish reading the book at leisure, but also to toy with the idea of having it published. Even living in as expensive a place as the Bay Area, two hundred thousand would keep him going for a few years. He supposed he might use the money instead as a down payment on a house of his own, but then he'd need another source of income to get a home loan, and by itself the money left over after his mother's mortgages and other debts were paid off wasn't enough to buy anything bigger than a Boy Scout tent within driving distance of the city. No, better to rent, to live off at least some of the proceeds while he figured out how he was going to get his train wreck life off the siding and back onto the tracks again.

So since he had a little money, why not publish his great-uncle's book? It was unlikely a real publisher would want it, but surely a thousand dollars or so could get him a nice little print run from a vanity press. He could even dedicate it to his mother, give a few copies to local libraries. It wouldn't exactly rescue Anna Vilmos from obscurity, but it would be something.

He looked around her tidy, anonymous living room for the last time—her truest legacy, now about to pass into the hands of some young couple she'd never met. He owed her something, didn't he?

She said she never loved me properly. But did that mean he should feel bad, or be proud of her because she'd done as well as she could, proud of himself because he'd still turned out halfway decent? Maybe not a success, but not a criminal or a wife-beater, either. Mom had done her best. *Maybe some people just shouldn't be parents,* he thought.

That beckoned him down some unpleasant paths. He picked up the backpack instead and carried it out to his car and the rented trailer that held his motorcycle.

Good-bye, house. Can't say I'll miss you much. Now another family would move in—the Marshalls, or whatever their name had been—and begin their own lives here. It wasn't anything to do with him any more. It should feel different than this, shouldn't it? But then again, if there had been any real memories left here—any good ones, that was—it would. He had enough of his mother's final weeks to last a lifetime. It had been another excellent reason to sell the place, more compelling even than the money.

I never really felt at home even in the old house, he thought. *Or when I lived with Cat. So what's wrong with me?* He climbed behind the wheel and began to back the trailer down the driveway and out into the street, turning the wheel hard to avoid taking the fender off a pickup truck that some idiot had parked a full yard and a half away from the curb.

Mrs. Kraley had come out to her fence to watch him go, the hose's spray making a rainbow in the air next to her impassive face. He waved to her cheerfully, just for old time's sake. She didn't disappoint him by waving back.

Theo drove slowly down Highway 280, and not only because of the awkwardness of the trailer behind his mother's small, underpowered car. It was a beautiful late summer day at the end of the millennium, after all, and he was tired of listening to himself bitch. It might be nice to savor the moment a bit, instead. Things were a bit bleak, sure, but if he looked at it the right way, he could decide he had finally reached that oh-so-elusive bottom and was about to start climbing back up. He would have felt more certain about it with an attractive, intelligent woman in the passenger seat, sharing his new start, but as Mick and Keith had so accurately stated, you couldn't always get what you wanted.

Fifteen miles south of San Francisco he saw the first watch-out-for-deer sign, a leaping black silhouette of a stag blazoned on the yellow diamond like a medieval coat of arms. It gave him a genuinely good feeling, even though he knew from friends that most of the people who lived in the Santa Cruz Mountains thought of their local deer as something like big rats, destroying gardens and trampling newly sodded lawns.

Theo didn't care. The idea of living somewhere that wild deer lived was exciting, and he certainly wasn't going to be planting a lawn. He turned up the car radio and punched buttons until he found something loud and thumpingly exultant, some piece of jolly stupidity from AC/DC. On his right, combs of fog curled across the mountaintop like white claws, wet air from the ocean turning to mist as it passed over the cold crest, but the sky above the freeway was cloudless and the road was vivid with sunshine.

*   *   *

It was funny how the day seemed to wither away as you drove up into the hills, as though the time was somehow different here in the grip of the mountains. The clock in the dashboard of his mother's Toyota said it was still only 3:30, and there were stretches of road where the sky flared bright blue overhead, but in the shadows of the trees it seemed almost twilight.

He had only been to the cabin once before, on the day the real estate agent had shown it to him, and the smaller roads on either side of Skyline were often poorly marked. He made the exact same mistake he had made coming for the first visit, mistaking one winding road for another, but recovered much more quickly this time—the first error had left him completely lost and he had been forced to call the agent and let her guide him back to the right road by cell phone, a process apparently as difficult as remote brain surgery.

He was over the top and onto the coast side of the mountains before four o'clock, although he was still far removed from any views of the ocean as he turned off a narrow, meandering road named Mariposa and onto the unmarked strip of alligatored asphalt that served as a private driveway for the cabin and two or three other houses scattered back in the woods among the redwoods, firs, and red-skinned manzanita. The sun was still above the tree line, but as he reached the end of the drive it was blocked by a tall stand of evergreens behind the cabin that left it and the bumpy, weed-cluttered yard plunged in shadow and for a moment made Theo regret his decision. He stopped the car and got out, stood listening to the silence, the flat, unanswered echo of the car door closing.

It's what you wanted, right? No distractions. A place to think about things, to put things back together.

The key was hung on a nail as the realtor had promised, tucked out of sight on the rickety fence that pointlessly separated the overgrown chaos of the cabin's front yard from the overgrown chaos of the back, a tangle of weeds and grasses on all sides that flowed smoothly away into the trees and continued largely unabated to the hillcrest and beyond—right out to the ocean, for all he knew. It was weird to have left his mother's trim, orderly neighborhood a short while ago and find himself here, with no neighbors he could see or even hear unless they took it on themselves to start shooting off machine guns in their backyards.

He'd heard there actually were people like that up here in the mountains. Theo could only hope it was more the exception than the rule. It had taken him nearly half an hour to drive from Skyline, the main road. How long would it take police or an ambulance to get here?

You wanted it, man. He could almost hear Johnny's voice. *Shit, stop whining.*

The inside of the cabin raised his spirits a little. It was small, really just one room plus a small bathroom and smaller closet, but as nicely appointed as he remembered it, with an efficient little kitchen area, a stone fireplace, and polished wood floors everywhere except the sunken, carpeted area in the center of the room. No television, and he doubted that the small one he had brought from his mother's would get much in the way of reception out here with its tiny little aerial, but if he really started to get desperate he could always get a satellite dish. He had a one-year lease, which meant he had plenty of time to figure out what he did and did not need, in lots of different ways.

The bed was on a platform raised more than head-high in one corner of the room, almost a little separate loft with its own built-in ladder, leaving room underneath it for a bookcase and a comfortable-looking armchair, both of which the absentee owner had preferred to leave in the cabin. Theo had been happy to accept. One of the large windows displayed a tangle of trees just outside and looked like it would get good sunshine during the middle of the day. He had a brief, cheerful vision of himself sitting there, reading *Moby-Dick* or something else he'd been promising himself he'd get to for years—what was that Pynchon book that Cat had kept bug-

ging him about? *Crying in Lot 49,* something like that? Hell,
why not? He'd read that too. A couple of trips a week down
to the flats to get groceries, occasional stops at the bookstore. He'd read, play guitar, maybe get back to writing
songs again like Johnny had suggested. Take long motorcycle rides through the hills, cruise down to the beach now
and then or even up the coast all the way to San Francisco,
just to fill up the culture tanks a bit. Take it all real slow.
Think about what he'd lost over the last few years and where
he might find it again.

Feeling better, he started carrying boxes in from the car.

*It has many names, this fabled metropolis—Aval-
lone, Cibola, Tir na nOg, to mention but a few, and
doubtless dozens more I never heard, because I spoke
only the common language of the place (of which I
shall say more later) although there are many other
tongues also spoken there. I myself named it New
Erewhon, after Samuel Butler's famous creation, but
that was only a human conceit (as I suspect is true
with the other names as well). Its inhabitants, and
those who live in the vast countryside that surrounds
it, call it only "the City," because it is the only one,
and dominates all around it as no earthly city ever
could . . .*

Theo was intrigued. This was the first direct admission in
Eamonn Dowd's story that the mythical land of which he
had said so much, and in such glowing but guarded terms,
was not to be found in some removed but still terrestrial lo-
cation, like Shangri La or El Dorado, but was all the way . . .
out there.

*Avallone. That's King Arthur or something, isn't it? But
Arthur only went there after he died, sort of. So is that Road
that Uncle Eamonn's always going on about supposed to be,
like, just a metaphor or something? And the Last Gate, too?*

*Some kind of magical passage to fairyland? I suppose I
should have guessed, since they were always capitalized.*

Before I speak of the inhabitants, I should tell more
of New Erewhon itself, although no words—at least no
words of mine—can ever truly describe its strangeness
and beauty. It rises out of a ring of thickly wooded
hills, a forest that surrounds the city like a moat. That
great wood, which despite its spread can be circum-
navigated far more quickly than it can be crossed, so
deceptive are the distances beneath the trees, is called
True Arden by some, but I have heard it called the
Forest Sauvage and Oldheart and the Murkwood as
well.

I did not know at first whether this meant that the
multiplicity of names came from the different types
of magical folk that inhabit the City and its surroundings, or whether the names came originally
from earthly dreamers, who somehow influenced the
land's true residents. In fact, the mechanism that allowed me to speak the common language is itself
quite mysterious. After having spent much time there,
and learned more than most thought I would, I suspect I know the answer, but will not spend the time
here to publish my speculations because they are
complicated and strange.

The City itself is formed in a huge spiral like a
monstrous nautilus shell, but this makes it sound simpler than it really is. The coil is crisscrossed by thousands of alleys and side streets, and all the unplanned
building over the years—for instance, all through the
outer rings, especially in the Morning Sky and Sunrise
districts, the goblins have simply affixed their crude
houses and shops like termite nests to the walls of
older and more refined structures, creating a maze of
tiny alleys and one-way streets—has long since broken
up any chance of an uninterrupted spiral passage

*from the outermost rim of the City to its innermost
point, which was off-limits to one such as I, in any
case. But the shape still exerts an influence: the most
ordinary parts of the City (or at least, what to my mortal eyes were the most familiar-seeming) are on the
outskirts. As one moves closer to the center, not only
do wealth and power create an increasingly intense
atmosphere of their own, but there is also a more subtle alteration, as though each step toward the heart of
the metropolis is also a step into something not quite
definable—a magical pressure, for lack of a better
word. Inside the innermost districts the families are
rich and mad, but even that does not explain the
volatility of experience there. And in the City's
shrouded heart (a piece of remaining forest referred to
as the Grove or sometimes the Cathedral, where almost no one goes, and certainly an outsider like me is
not welcome) it is reported that the warping of earthly
time, which begins from the moment one passes the
Last Gate, is at its most powerful, and is no longer
simply different than earthly time, but becomes a more
plastic medium altogether . . .*

Theo shut the book. As though himself affected by his
great-uncle's time-warpage idea, he was reading more
slowly as the story grew stranger and stranger. A week in the
cabin and he still hadn't looked at any other books, caught
up in the puzzles and fascinating invention of Eamonn
Dowd's creation. He hadn't spent as much time as he'd
promised himself playing his guitar either. The days had
been unexpectedly full, for one thing—despite the guaran-
tees of the real estate agents that everything would be ready
for him, it had taken him half the week and several calls to
the owner's management company just to get the cabin's
plumbing and electricity working properly, so the long
leisurely stretches of nothing to do but read and think were
still largely theoretical.

He also wasn't sleeping that well. The creepy dreams, especially the ones in which he felt he was someone other than himself, or rather that he was somehow *sharing* himself against his will, still kept coming back like a foul odor. They didn't show up every night, thank God, but often enough to make him wonder if he needed to think about Prozac or something.

All the luckier, then, that he had the matter of his great-uncle's book to help occupy his thoughts.

As far as he could make sense of it, the story's protagonist was definitely supposed to have traveled not just to some backwater place in the real world, but through some sort of magical barrier—a process described at great but unenlightening length, with even the few grudging bits of specificity couched in terms Theo did not understand, full of references to books or other writings and their authors which might be completely fictional as far as he could tell. Eamonn Dowd's invented world itself seemed to be in some ways a standard Fairyland, but it was neither the butterflies-and-flowers place of children's tales nor even the glamorous, perilous land of Celtic and Scandinavian mythology. Instead, from what Theo had read so far, it seemed like a bizarre mirror-version of the real world, albeit in a slightly old-fashioned way. Already there had been references to office buildings and railway lines. What kind of fairyland had railroads, for God's sake?

It was original, at least—he had to give his great-uncle credit for that. Maybe he really could find a legitimate publisher.

In some ways the City's organization is unsurprising. The powerful families tend to draw their less powerful supporters close, so that a given neighborhood might belong almost exclusively to the adherents of the Starwort or Marigold clans (to name just two of

the lesser High Houses). These neighborhoods have become virtually self-sufficient towns within the greater city, centered around the towers of the leading families. In a way, I suppose, it is a bit like Florence of the Quattrocento, where nearly everyone found his or her allegiance with one of the leading family tribes, the Pazzi, Albizzi, or Medici.

New Erewhon is by its very nature a dangerous place for a mortal, but oddly, I was able to find a niche for myself. The citizens are surprisingly tolerant, perhaps because they are themselves so various in form and constitution. (Although the leading families seem to have almost completely adopted the appearance of human beings—assuming that I have the process right-way-round!) Mortals have always found their way to that place, either by themselves or as fairy-pets, but travel between there and here has become much less frequent in recent years, almost nonexistent, so I was treated as a bit of a welcome rarity—even invited to the homes of many of the leading families.

When I was not a guest of the Flower Houses themselves, I found it possible to make a living in another unusual way. Because of the present rarity of mortal visitors and the infrequency of fairy-folk traveling to our world, things that once were in common supply within the City and its environs are now very hard to find—tears, for instance, since although the fairy-folk themselves do cry occasionally, they find the tears of a human being far more useful in many of their preparations (including those that we would think magical, although everything in that place is magical just by dint of where it takes place). In fact, when I learned about this specialty trade, I found myself regretting for the first time in my adult life that I was not a woman and, especially, not a virgin, because the tears and other excreta, hair, even the fingernails and dried skin of a mortal maiden fetch a very high price all over

New Erewhon, either in barter or fairy-gold. Still, I did well enough: with the whiskers I trimmed from my beard and the tears I was able to wring from my eyes with the aid of onions obtained at the weekly market in Fernwater Row, I managed to secure myself a small but pleasant dwelling on carefully chosen neutral ground in a neighborhood near New Mound House, which is the site of the Fairies' Parliament and has long been a kind of sacred place, secure from the contendings of even the most rebellious houses. Later I moved to a larger place in the Forenoon district, but often missed the bustle of the City center.

I mentioned that the leading families all closely resemble human beings (although a man would have to be almost deaf and blind to mistake them for real humans). This may give my reader the idea that a walk through the winding streets of New Erewhon would be almost indistinguishable from a tour through one of the great cities of our own world. I will take a moment here to tell you why that is not the case.

First, the Flower families, with their semblance of humanity, are but a small part of the population. Even their house servants do not, except in the richest or most fashion-obsessed houses, look much like us. For one thing, the wings that the great families have somehow discarded or at least completely hidden are still to be seen on their servitors, shining behind their shoulders, translucent as the wings of dragonflies and shot with subtle color. (They are working appendages, too, although the larger fairies seldom fly.) And these servants are among the most apparently human of the other fairy classes—one of the reasons they are allowed into service. The population of the great city is staggeringly diverse, and a journey down Fernwater Row at twilight is more like entering a Hieronymous Bosch painting than any earthly stroll: on every side tiny sprites, boggarts, pookas, elegant wisp-maidens, even beetling goblins jostle one another, argue, shout their wares, and conduct the first steps of the dance of romantic attraction—and these are but a few out of hundreds of types, thousands of strange sights. Every time I believed I had seen the strangest, I was almost instantly proved wrong.

A single anecdote will illustrate this supremely well.

I was on my way back from a moon-brandy party in the fortress-house of the Stock clan, where I had been the guest of one of the young women of the family, who had introduced herself to me on a dare from some of her friends. Moon-brandy is a distillate of dew, taken at a certain phase of the moon, and from what I can remember is highly potent, creating a surplus of both amusement and lust in even the most staid creature. Here I might note that the sun and moon, as far as I could ever be certain, are the same sun and moon that climb above our mortal world, although as with everything else beyond the Last Gate, they seem more potent in that place, more present and more magical—especially the moon. Whether they truly are the same celestial orbs that mortals see, now reduced in our present day to a giant gas furnace in the one case, and in the other a cold round stone where men in diver's costumes may swing golf clubs and erect stiffened American flags, I cannot say. I am not sure I want to know. In the city I call New Erewhon, and in all of Faerie, sun and moon are what we humans so long thought them, the heavenly brother and sister who watch over us.

In any case, I was on my way home from Stock House by way of Weavers' Row, a place that seems perpetually under cloud, although that might merely be caused by the shadows of the much taller buildings that surround it. (In any case, the darkness is healthful for the spiders in their strange artificial forests, where they spin and spin so that the city's gentry may have this most elegant of silks for their clothing.) As I lingered for a moment to look in the illuminated front window of one of the shops, I was surprised by a cry from behind me, and turned to see young Caradenus Primrose staggering toward me. He was generally a serious young fellow as befitted the importance of his family, which was one of the Seven, but at that moment he was clearly suffering from the effects of moon-brandy. Two saucer-eyed kobolds were propping him up, one at each elbow. The squat little creatures seemed a bit worse for drink themselves, but evidently had a greater capacity than the youthful laird of Primrose House, who was having trouble explaining to me where he was going and why he so wanted me to go with him because he kept interrupting himself with snatches of song . . .

Something went *snap* outside the window. Theo flinched and turned to look out. Something dark was just disappearing around the corner of the cabin—the haunch of a deer, he was almost certain. He turned back to the book, but his concentration was broken. He leafed ahead a page or two. In his wordy, roundabout style, Great-Uncle Eamonn appeared to be working his way up to some kind of brothel scene, which might be interesting, but Theo had been reading for an hour already and he was feeling restless. He put the book down, not just out of impatience with his great-uncle's old-fashioned prose, but also because the tale, however fantastical, had given him a sudden pang of dissatisfaction with his own situation.

I mean, I'm obviously not going to make it to Fairyland, but think of all the other places he saw, real places—China, Africa. I've got some money now, I could really do something, but here I am sitting by myself in a little cabin, twenty miles from where I was born.

He took his helmet off the chair by the door and headed out for a ride.

*   *   *

Battered by wind, buoyed somewhat by the two beers he had drunk in a roadside tavern down near the bottom of the hills, and also by a conversation with the bartender about the man's boat and the problems he was having with it—it hadn't been particularly interesting, but at least he had been talking to a live human being, something he hadn't been doing much in the last few days—Theo low-geared up the steep driveway and found an unfamiliar car parked in front of the cabin. For a moment he thought that it might be Johnny come to visit in some borrowed ride, but the dark-haired man in a short-sleeved blue shirt and a tie was a stranger. He looked to be in his forties, and also like he might spend regular time at the gym.

"Are you Theo Vilmos?"

Theo nodded. "Can I help you?"

"Maybe so. I'd like to ask you a few questions, anyway." He pulled out his wallet and displayed a badge, a gesture so familiar from television and movies that for a long second Theo did not entirely take it in. "I'm Detective Kohler, from the San Francisco Police Department. Do you have a minute?"

"Sure." The two beers suddenly felt like more. He hoped he was standing up straight. "Come on in. You're a little out of your way, aren't you?"

"Didn't mind the ride. I have books on tape in the car." The police detective said it lightly, but he was watching Theo's face as the motorcycle helmet came off. Theo had a brief moment of paranoia as he led the man inside, wondering if that eighth of an ounce of weed Johnny had given him the last time at his mother's house was out in plain view, somewhere—he had run across it the other day, unpacking.

C'mon, he told himself. *Don't be stupid. I'm a solid citizen now. I've got two hundred thousand dollars in the bank. Nobody's going to send some plain-clothes guy all the way up here to look for a little dope.*

What the hell was this about?

"Can I offer you anything? I'd say a beer, but you guys can't drink on duty, right? That's what they always say on

TV. But maybe that's bullshit, too, like most of the other stuff on TV." He felt himself flush a little. He was babbling. "But I think I have a Coke or something. Coca-Cola." He moved his Gibson acoustic off one of the chairs and into its case. "Please, sit down."

The man shook his head. His smile didn't quite seem genuine. "No, thanks. I won't keep you long. Looks like you're pretty well moved in. How long have you been here?"

The cramp of paranoia returned. Why did this guy know anything about him? "About three weeks. Well, if you're sure you don't want anything to drink . . ."

"Bear with me, I'll make this as quick as possible. Just out of curiosity, Mr. Vilmos, where were you the night before last?"

Theo went through a moment of panic—where *had* he been?—before remembering. "I drove down to the coast for the evening. Wandered around on Pacific Avenue in Santa Cruz. Had some dinner. I thought about seeing a movie, but I was tired." He had a sudden idea, pulled out his wallet. "I think I've probably got the receipt in here." He found it—a yellow credit card slip for an upscale diner called Jimmy Brazil—and handed it to the cop, who surveyed it briefly. "What's this about?"

"What time did you get home?"

Theo shrugged. "Not sure—probably sometime between eleven and twelve. Nobody saw me come in, if that's what you're asking." He tried a casual laugh, wondering how he could feel so guilty with nothing concrete to feel guilty about. "You can see that it's a little tough around here to know what your neighbors are doing."

The policeman nodded slowly, as if what Theo was saying had answered a question he had nursed for a long time. "I see."

"Look, I know you're just doing your job, but this is kind of freaking me out a little. Did someone get robbed around here or something?"

Detective Kohler held his eye for a long time. He had the

sharp, unhurried gaze and thin mouth of an Old West gun-fighter. The shirt and cheap slacks began to seem like a dis-guise. "How well do you know Dennis and Stephanie Marsh?"

Theo shook his head. "Sorry, can't help you. Who?"

"They bought your mother's house."

"Oh, Jesus, them! The name didn't ring a bell. How well do I know them? Not at all, really." He tried to remember if he'd ever actually seen them. It would have had to have been at one of the viewings at the house—all the sale papers had been signed at various real estate and title company offices, and buyers and seller had never been in at the same time. "Are they . . . is she kind of tall?" He vaguely remembered a woman with dark hair and long legs, the skirt on her busi-ness suit surprisingly short. If that was the right couple, he had thought Stephanie Marsh was a bit sexy, but he couldn't remember her husband at all.

"You didn't meet them?"

"Only if I was there when they came to see the house. The real estate agents took care of everything. I wasn't real sentimental about the house—my mother just died there, but I had never lived in the place before that, so it wasn't like I was all worried about making sure it was going to nice peo-ple or something, like they were adopting some puppies from me or something . . ." He stopped. Babbling again.

"And you haven't been back to the house since?"

"No, no. Like I said, it wasn't a real happy place for me. Why?"

The detective nodded, apparently lost in thoughts of his own. "They're dead," he said at last.

"What?"

"Dead. Murdered, maybe as part of a robbery that got out of control, maybe for some other reason."

"Jesus!" He stood for a moment, overwhelmed. "Jesus. In the house? In my mother's house?"

"Yes. Did you . . . did anything happen while you were still there that seemed suspicious to you? Prowlers?

Strange people coming to the door, or hanging around the neighborhood?"

Theo could not help a moment's flashback to the moaning sound that had brought him out into the backyard, heart thumping. But what could a randy tomcat have to do with people getting killed? "No, nothing I can remember. Christ, is that when it happened? Night before last?"

"Yes, and fairly early in the evening, as far as we can tell, so if this receipt checks out you don't have anything to worry about. Do you mind if I keep it?"

Theo waved his hand, anxious to get rid of it, as though merely by being from the same night it was somehow tainted. "But why would you think I might have anything to do with . . . with that? Jesus."

"We don't think anything, Mr. Vilmos. We just have to ask questions, get ideas, try to get a feeling for what happened." The detective shuffled his feet a little, looked around. "I'll get going, let you get back to what you were doing."

"Doing? I wasn't doing anything, really . . ." Theo frowned. "Have you talked to the lady next door? To my mom's house?"

"Why?"

"Because she's the kind of, excuse the expression, nosy old bitch who was probably watching the new neighbors like a hawk. Mrs. Kraley, that's her name. She could probably tell you everybody who went in or out of there, to the minute. She probably writes it all down."

"The neighbors haven't had anything very useful to say so far, but I'll check with her again, based on your . . . characterization." His smile was a grim thing; Theo suddenly wondered how you could have a job like that without it burning away parts of you.

"Can you . . . what happened? I mean, how were they killed?"

Detective Kohler examined him again. "We're keeping the details to ourselves as long as we can. It makes it a lot easier to sort through the good and bad information as it comes to us. But I can tell you this—it wasn't pretty."

For long minutes after the policeman's car had rumbled away down the driveway, Theo could only pace back and forth across the cabin, unable to settle, his thoughts tumbling like windblown leaves. Why should the deaths of two people he didn't know bother him so much, people less real to him than the fictional characters of a daytime soap opera, connected to his own life only by one thread of coincidence—two people out of the thousands that died somewhere every hour? Why should these two distant deaths, however awful, give him such a feeling of morbid, fearful helplessness? Was it something to do with his mother's death, with his own lost, miserable hours in the house?

Whatever it was, he didn't like it. But that didn't make it go away.

8

RUNAWAY CAPACITOR

Findus Dogwood always thought of himself as a decent chap, unlike some of the other supervisors—that Barberry, just to name one, was sour as curdled milk—so when he was told that one of the capacitors from the day shift was feeling poorly and wouldn't work, he didn't send Saltgrass or one of the other foremen to beat the slacker out of the dormitory and onto the line, but put down his cup of saxifrage tea and went to go see for himself. He walked across the station briskly, just as if Lord Thornapple himself were sitting in the big main office looking down at him. It was actually possible he could be, although it would be the first time in several years the owner had made an appearance on the premises: Aulus Thornapple was one of the most important people in all Faerie, after all.

"What's the problem's name?" Dogwood asked Snowbell, the wizened block captain.

The old fellow, who had long since given up on a promotion to management, but still harbored hopes of a little something better in the way of his eventual pension, bobbed his woolly white head up and down. "Kind of you to ask, Mr. Dogwood, very kind. Nettle comma Streedy is what the boy's called."

"Metal Comets Greedy? What sort of name is that? Is he a goblin or somesuch?"

Snowbell's rheumy eyes grew wide. "No, sir. Sorry, sir. His name is Streedy Nettle, out of some farming village in Hazel."

"What's wrong with him?"

"Couldn't say, sir." Snowbell managed to make it clear that he didn't think anything much was wrong with the shirker at all. "He didn't sleep well—his bunkmates say he moaned and groaned all through the night. Then he didn't get up for breakfast." Snowbell sucked one of his remaining teeth. He was an urisk; like many cold-climate fairies, he had aged rapidly in the warmth of the City and looked two or three centuries older than he actually was. "Lovely bit of porridge, it was, too. Fool boy."

Dogwood nodded. "Yes, yes, I see. Well, then, you can go join your line . . . er . . ." He couldn't for the life of him remember the old urisk's name, so he substituted a quick, insincere compliment, which always seemed to work. "Good job, by the way. Appreciate your help."

Old Snowbell bobbed his head so quickly as he backed away that Dogwood feared it might fall off. "Thank you, sir. Always a pleasure, sir."

To Dogwood's irritation, the boy's pallet was at the room's far end, one of two hundred beds in this dormitory alone. The pallets lay lengthwise on the floor all across the barnlike dormitory, like a mouth too full of teeth.

"Here now, young fellow." Dogwood tried to put a comforting, cheery tone in his voice as he crossed the vast, echoing room—that kind of thing always made the little chaps feel better. Perhaps the fellow was just homesick. Nettle—a farm-country name, common as mustard. There must be half a hundred working in the station.

His first surprise was that this Nettle was not in the least a "little chap": the youth stretched out on the pallet was so slender his knees seemed wider than the rest of his legs, but he was also quite startlingly tall. Dogwood's second surprise was the look of something like pure fear in the pale boy's eyes.

"I hear you're feeling a bit under the weather this morning, eh?" Dogwood smiled to show he was not that other kind of foreman, the Barberry kind. "Out with some of the other young fellows, eh? A little trip to Madame Gentian's, perhaps, and a bit too much to drink? I've been there, lad. I wasn't always what you see now, with responsibility and all." Dogwood paused, narrowing his eyes. The boy was not responding as well as he'd hoped, which was a bit irksome. "Come now, lad, you know you can't stay in bed all day, right? We've a job to do, a very important job. The City needs us—all of Faerie needs us."

The boy stared at him, not aggressively, but as though he was having trouble focusing. "I . . . I don't feel well." It was a mumble, and the rustic Hazel accent made it almost unintelligible. "I think I should . . ." His sweaty, pale face became sweatier still as he realized he had almost made an unsolicited suggestion to a foreman.

"You'd be surprised how much better you'll feel if you just get up and do your job, lad. What are you? Bulk storage? Is this the storage dormitory?" The vast sleeping rooms all looked just the same, after all, which was as it should be. Wouldn't do to have rivalries inside the machinery.

"Capacitor, sir." A whisper. The boy really was extraordinarily pale, but some of the outland fellows were like that. There were other forests besides the ancient one that surrounded the City and in which this power plant nested, and some of the country lads hadn't ever been out of the trees and into the sun properly before they came to town.

"Ah, a capacitor! So you're a bit of a specialist, eh?" Findus Dogwood laughed encouragingly at his own joke, but the boy was too dense or distracted to join in. Dogwood frowned. "Come, now, you don't want to let your mates down, do you? If we're short a capacitor, there'll be just that much more work for the others."

The boy groaned. "But . . . truly I'm sorry, sir, but . . ."

"Here, do you know how much time I've spent with you already, son?" Supervisor Dogwood leaned close. It was time to show the boy a bit of hardwood. "A capacitor? There are others out there who'd spin sunwise twice and widdershins thrice to have your job, you know. And you'd still have to work off your indenture on the power line. Or perhaps you'd rather wind up laboring in Lord Thornapple's sewage filtration plant instead?"

The boy actually sat up, although he had to struggle to do so; for the first time his oversized wings uncurled behind him—they were big as sails! Dogwood looked away. No wonder his parents had been in a hurry to get rid of him. "But . . . that's a nixie job, sir . . . !" the young fellow began to protest, but a cough interrupted him. It continued for some time.

"You'd be surprised, Myrtle." He hesitated—the name didn't sound quite right—but the boy was still wheezing and hadn't heard him. "You'd be surprised what kind of work can be found for someone who's failed at a perfectly good position like this one." It was time to give him another flick of the thorns. A boy like this could go one way or the other, and Dogwood prided himself on having saved a number of young fellows from their own worst instincts. "Or what kind of treatment someone earns when they try to back out on their indenture. I'm going to head back to my office, now. When I get there, I expect to get a call from your foreman telling me that you're on the line. You tell him I said so. And if I don't . . . well, there are even worse places than the filtration plant, Myrtle. Lord Thornapple's quicksilver mines get a bit close, I'm told. Not the best place for someone with a cough like that."

He turned and strode out of the room with back straight and head high, as always. As he expected, the foreman called him soon after he returned, saying the boy had staggered out to take his place on the line. Findus Dogwood enjoyed a quiet moment's pleasure at this further proof that his velvet glove had again proved more efficacious than the old-fashioned, heavy-handed approach.

He had just started sketching out the short article on friendly discipline he had decided to write for the Darkwood Generation LPB management newsletter when he got another call from the same foreman. Then the lights went out.

Foxfire lanterns had been kindled everywhere, but they cast only a thin light and smelled like rotting wood, which didn't improve Dogwood's temper. He had begged upper management for the newer, cleaner emergency witchlights, but had they done anything about it? Without the huge overhead lighting fixtures, the floor of the station looked like a will-o'-the-wisp's Midsummer dance. In the flickering near-darkness Dogwood barked his knee on a wiring stool that someone had left in the middle of an aisle, and by the time he reached the site of the accident he was in an even fouler state of mind, if such a thing were possible.

"Why haven't we gone to backup power?" he shouted. "Why are all these workers standing about?"

"We'll be back on line in a moment, sir." Saltgrass turned and slapped a resistor, who was standing over the body with wide eyes and gaping mouth. "Get out of here, you—back to your group! We don't feed you and house you so you can stand around gawking."

The other line workers now began to drift back to their own spots, some shaking their heads. Certain that they were all in some absurd way holding him responsible, Dogwood did his best not to let it bother him. "What happened?"

"Hard to say, sir." Saltgrass was heavier and more muscular than most of his kind, which suggested there might be more than a bit of human blood in him somewhere—a "mayfly in the hive," as one crude phrase had it. "We powered up and took over for Unit Three. Everything was right where it was supposed to be, then all of a sudden the impedance went wild. It was Nettle, sir. I've never seen anything quite like it. For a moment, he looked like he'd taken fire—all green and blue, sparks flying around, like that. Then he just fell down. We hauled him out and I called you. That should have been the end of it—fourteen other capacitors just in this section, and they were all working fine—but a few minutes later all the circuit breakers tripped and Ob's your uncle, everything shuts down!"

Dogwood suppressed a scowl. Bloody Saltgrass seemed awfully cheerful about all this, as if the whole thing were no more than a schoolboy lark, the excuse for an afternoon off. Instead, there would be messages flying about this for weeks, and not a few of them would be coming right through Findus Dogwood's office like hornets.

Barberry. Why couldn't this have happened on that cursed Barberry's shift?

The supervisor looked down at young Streedy Nettle. The boy's limbs were still jerking, but they had slowed a little. His eyes were open, his strawlike hair curled tight to his head by the force of the generative magics that had briefly been contained within him, like a dammed river. Nettle's once-huge wings had curled and shriveled against his back like melted glass.

"What happened?" Dogwood asked him. "What did you do, you fool?"

The boy stared at him, eyelids fluttering, teeth chattering.

"He can't talk, sir," Saltgrass pointed out. "I've seen 'em taken like this. Lucky he wasn't turned into a cinder, or a frog, or worse."

One of the company doctors, a Bitterroot who had once been in private practice but had for some reason fallen on hard times, crouched down beside the boy and dangled a pendulum above his paper-white brow. "Not good," the doctor said, shaking his head. "I think we'll have to tell his parents to prepare themselves."

Dogwood grunted. The cursed boy had not only brought down the whole line, but now he was apparently going to die and thus create hours of tedious paperwork as well. "Get him out of here. And somebody find out why we're not back on line yet!"

It was three hours before the power was restored, and many if not most of Lord Thornapple's customers were affected. Offices went dark all over the Gloaming and Eventide districts. The trolleys did not run. Factories shut down. Delicate silk-spinning spiders died by the thousands when the heating charms in their artificial grottoes failed. It was fortunate, as it turned out, that the lord himself had not been visiting, as Dogwood had half-hoped that morning, but was instead far away on a hunting holiday in Birch. There would be time enough to blur the facts before he returned, and all of middle management would work at that assiduously. It wasn't as if there hadn't been other outages lately, for reasons having nothing to do with the power plant's native functions: they could make this incident look like another of those. With luck, no foremen or supervisors would be executed this time.

Still, Findus Dogwood no longer felt the moment was propitious for his planned article, and in fact the week might have gone down as one of his worst since he had accepted the supervisorial badge from Lord Thornapple's factor, but he was a little cheered the day after the failure when the block captain Snowbell informed him through the foreman Saltgrass that not only had the Nettle boy apparently survived the night, but he had recovered enough to run away. At first Dogwood suspected that the foremen themselves had arranged the disappearance—Saltgrass' lightheartedness had faded during the extra hours they were all forced to work by the blackout—but a little questioning convinced the supervisor that Saltgrass and his comrades were just as puzzled by Nettle's departure as everyone else.

The paperwork was much easier for *Indentured Worker, Escape Of* than for *Indentured Worker, Death Of,* and no crusading society matrons or charity organizations would be asking difficult questions, either. Instead of dealing with all the rigamarole of a fact-finding emissary from New Mound House, affixing blame and computing compensation before sending Saddened Letter #4 to the family, he could turn everything over to Lord Constable Monkshood's Runaways Office and let them deal with the problem.

Enlightened management styles certainly had their place, Dogwood decided as things finally began to return to normal around the plant, but next time he had a shirker on the line he thought he might just let Saltgrass beat the creature bloody and save his own precious time for more useful and elevated pursuits.

9

VISITORS

It was a beautiful day outside, sunlight streaming down through the redwoods and pooling on the ground, but the peace Theo had begun to find here had suddenly dissolved. He had awakened several times in the silent mountain night, once from the now-familiar dream of being a helpless prisoner in his own body, another time from an equally terrible dream of being chased across a muddy sea floor by some relentless thing like a huge lamprey, all idiot mouth and muscular tail. His sheets and underwear had been so sweat-soaked that for a shameful moment he thought the nightmare had made him piss himself.

Now, as he nursed a cup of coffee in the overgrown front yard, sitting in the weathered wooden folding chair he had found in his mother's garage which now served as his de facto porch, Theo still felt exposed, almost hunted. The deaths in his mother's house had somehow corrupted everything. He had planned to spend the day working on some songs, playing the guitar, but that didn't seem even slightly appealing now. He had to get out, that was all there was to it. He had been wanting to go down to the flats and use the library, look some things up. That would certainly be better than sitting by himself all day, jumping at noises.

He found his wallet and keys, then pulled on his leather

jacket and checked to make sure the windows were latched. As he stood in the doorway, something seemed to flare just above the sink, a tiny point of light like a miniature nova. Theo stared, but it was already gone. He walked back into the cabin to make sure there wasn't an electrical fire starting, but all seemed normal.

Light coming through the glass and bouncing off the faucet or something. Like what those pilots used to see and thought were UFOs. Sundog, that's what it's called, right?

He shook his head and climbed onto his motorcycle. It took a couple of kicks to get the cold engine to rattle into life.

At the bottom of Mariposa, just before turning onto the main road, he saw something move in the undergrowth—not the velvet-brown of a deer, but something green, like a military duffel coat. He slowed a little but was already past it. When he looked back he couldn't see anything except branches and dappled light.

A hunter? But they wear orange, don't they? In any case, he didn't imagine that you were allowed to hunt around here, not legally. Maybe it was some kind of paramilitary weirdo, some antitax crusader stalking the hills in his fantasy uniform. There might even be a whole platoon of them in the area, out on maneuvers. The Santa Cruz Mountains were home to all kinds of odd sorts, folks who had come up in the Seventies to take a lot of acid and live with nature and had never found their way back down, folks who just didn't like cities, not to mention people who had scarily legitimate reasons not to be too high profile. Who could say—there were probably several generations of different kinds of weirdo living up here by now . . .

Come on, man. All this because you saw what? Some green? In the middle of the forest? You're losing it, baby.

He was lonely, he realized. There were more problems with solitude than just being horny and bored. If you didn't have anyone to talk to for days on end, you didn't have anyone to let you know whether you were going nuts or not.

*   *   *

The woman working behind the reference counter was pretty in a quiet, glasses-on-a-cord kind of way. She smiled at his nervous jokes while she showed him where the back issues of the *Chronicle* were, and how to work the microfiche machine. It was all he could do not to ask her out on the spot.

Why not try it? The worst she can say is no.

But it seemed for some reason as though it would be very difficult to be turned down today. Maybe he could come back later in the week, let her see that he was a quiet, serious sort of guy, then ask her. Still, he felt better just for being interested, for having something like that to think about.

He wanted to do some research on his great-uncle, but found himself drawn first to the murders at his mother's house. It wasn't hard to find information in the *San Francisco Chronicle,* since it was a scary and so far inexplicable murder in a quiet neighborhood. It had even made the front page the first day, although only a couple of paragraphs actually showed up below the fold, with most of the article buried deep in the front section.

The pictures of the unfortunate Marsh couple jogged his memory. They were younger than he had remembered, in their late twenties. She *had* been the pretty one with the short skirt, and now he remembered her husband, too, although the man hadn't said much, had mostly checked messages on his cell phone while the agent led them around. In fact, the only thing he really remembered anyone saying was the real estate agent talking about what a lovely "starter house" it would be. And apparently they had agreed, since he had their money in the bank right now.

Starter house. Ending house.

He pushed away the unpleasant thought, suddenly struck by something else. Was there some way the deal could be rescinded, by their parents or something? Who would own it now? They couldn't make him pay the money back, could they? It was a petty thought, perhaps, but the two hundred thousand wasn't petty to him, and it was already less than that because he'd put down the first and last on the cabin, not to mention other living expenses.

Nothing he could do now. Maybe he'd call the real estate company later, check with them.

The articles talked a lot about what the neighbors thought—Mrs. Kraley was even quoted as saying, "This neighborhood is going downhill. You just don't know what kind of people are around," which Theo took with a sort of sour pride as referring almost as much to himself as to the actual murderers. Of the killings themselves very little was said, except that they were characterized as "brutal" and "senseless." Mrs. Kraley, with a keen eye for what was really important, also complained that the murderer had apparently thrown garbage all over the lawn and front porch. The police had not offered any possible motive beyond robbery, but it didn't say in the article if anything had been stolen.

The newspapers had nothing more to offer, and Theo was beginning to feel like a bit of a ghoul. He moved over to the microfiche machine and decided he might as well see if they had anything about his great-uncle.

He found two newspaper articles, which was more success than he'd really expected. One seemed to be a character piece from the *Examiner*, written in the early Seventies, the other was Dowd's obituary. As Theo browsed through the longer piece, struggling a bit with the machine's white-on-black text, he was surprised by how sad he was to know that Eamonn Dowd was really dead. It would have been very surprising if he hadn't been—the article confirmed his earlier guess that Dowd had been born at the end of the nineteenth century, so he would have been over a hundred by now—but in the past weeks Theo had come to feel very closely connected to him. The article, which seemed to be little more than one of those interesting-local-old-person puff pieces, was accompanied by a picture of his great-uncle in what the caption called his "study," but because of the microfiche it was essentially a photographic negative and Theo

could make out little of it. Eamonn Dowd seemed to have
been slender and dapper at the time the picture was taken,
and perhaps a bit younger-looking than his seventy years of
age would have suggested, but it was impossible to be sure
about any of it.

The obituary had no photograph—Great-Uncle Eamonn
hadn't been important enough for that. It was also terse.
Theo wondered who'd written it, and why. Had it been a
kind of guilt-gesture from his mother after receiving the
money? She was mentioned.

Eamonn A. Dowd, 76
adventurer and world traveler

Eamonn Albert Dowd, who spent much of his early life
traveling the world, and much of his later life sharing
his stories with others, died April 30th at his home in
San Francisco. He was 76.

Mr. Dowd, who contributed to travel magazines and
the travel section of this newspaper, and also spoke at
libraries and schools, first went to sea at age 15 and
never lost his love of exotic places.

The obituary continued with an abbreviated version of
what Great-Uncle Eamonn had described in the notebook,
and ended with the information that he was survived by *"his*
niece Anna Dowd Vilmos of San Francisco, and other fam-
ily in the Chicago area."

Theo sat back, staring at the screen without really seeing
it any more. "Anna Dowd Vilmos of San Francisco"—it
made his mother sound like someone from a famous family,
like one of the old Nob Hill socialite crowd or something.

So old Uncle Eamonn was definitely dead. The obituary
didn't specify, but since he'd died at his home it must have
been a stroke or heart attack or something.

Feeling a bit unsatisfied, although he should have been

delighted to find anything at all—it wasn't like they really were a famous family or anything—Theo located an open computer and did some searching on the Internet. He wasn't hunting more information on his great-uncle, since there wasn't any, but on some of the more obscure things and places mentioned in the notebook. He lost himself for a while in the realm of online fairy information, land of both the scholarly and the stunningly credulous, but mostly just of dippy unicorn-poets with too much time on their hands.

When he pulled himself away from the computer at last he discovered that the woman at the reference desk had gone to lunch or gone home; in either case, she'd been replaced by a glowering man with a hearing aid, so asking her out was going to have to be a long-term process whether he wanted it to be or not.

He stopped for lunch at a café near a bookstore on the El Camino, purchased copies of Graves' *The White Goddess, Grimm's Fairy Tales,* and a book about the Beatles, then stopped at a mall and prowled around the L. L. Bean store. He bought himself a Coleman lantern and a good flashlight in case the power went out up on the hill, and briefly considered an expensive parka—it would get cold up there when the winter came—but it was impossible to manufacture enthusiasm in summery early September for buying an expensive, heavy parka. After all, he had his trusty leather jacket, companion on many an adventure. Well, on many an excursion, anyway, some of them embarrassingly stupid when you'd reached thirty and thought back on things.

Theo realized he was stalling. He stopped at a liquor store and bought a six-pack of Heineken, then rode back up the hill in a slanting afternoon glare.

He sat with the book across his lap and three beers under his belt, tired and still heavy with the sense of impending . . . not doom, that was too strong a word, but impending *something*. It was cold in the cabin, but he didn't have the energy to get up and turn on the heater. He lifted his motorcycle jacket off the floor and pulled it on.

He was losing patience with his great-uncle's book. The descriptions were interesting, even fascinating: whatever other faults Dowd might have had as a writer, he definitely had an imagination. But the tales of his life in the fairy-city were just as anecdotal and, ultimately, pointless as his stories of real-life adventure. The book was a strange and probably hopelessly uncommercial mixture of fantasy-without-adventure (not *real* adventure anyway, the kind the *Dungeons-and-Dragons* kids wanted) and authoritative traveler's guide to a place no one could ever actually visit.

He was only fifty or sixty close-written pages from the ending now, and found himself skipping ahead, distracted by thoughts of what other people would be doing on a beautiful Thursday night like this—getting ready to go out, see a movie, go to a bar. What if he had just asked out the woman at the library? She hadn't had a name tag, so he couldn't even construct an imaginary dialogue. What would someone like her be called? Eleanor? Elizabeth?

Just my luck, it's probably Catherine.

That stung. He turned his attention back to his great-uncle's neat handwriting. Not a tremor to be seen—it didn't seem like an old man's handwriting at all. He must have written it years before he died. It was hard to focus on it, though, with the afternoon dying and the world turning dark outside.

A thick, ragged line of ink ran right across the middle of a page. It followed a seemingly inconsequential sentence about a party at a gambling club where he had again met the young lord named Caradenus Something-or-Other, who had featured in the brothel story. There was nothing beneath the black line, although there were many pages left in the book, all of them blank.

No. Here, several pages from the end, leaping out at him from all that emptiness like black paint spilled on snow, was a last addition, also in his great-uncle's handwriting, but

much less steady, the lines uneven on the page, the words
large and hurried.

> *I have come to the end. I will never finish my story,
> because the ending is something I cannot face. I hoped
> where I should have had no hope and fell into shame
> and darkness because of it. I was sent forth and the
> way back is forever barred to me, beyond even des-
> peration.*
>
> *I thought I could tell it but it is too bleak. I have lost
> what few men could even dream of having because of
> my own hubris—that courage that even the gods abhor.*

It had the stark look of a confession, or a hurried last will
and testament.

Puzzled and disappointed, Theo leafed back over the
pages that had led up to Dowd's abrupt abandonment of the
notebook, but could see no suggestion of what might have
stopped him. He decided to go back to where he had begun
skipping and read more carefully, but it was a less enchanting process now that he knew the story would have no resolution. He tried as always to keep up with the minutiae of
invented names and places, the intricacy of invention, but he
was finishing the fourth beer now and his eyes were getting
heavy. The sky had gone slate blue, the trees were shadows.

I really ought to get up and turn on a light . . . was his last
conscious thought.

Apparently he *had* got up and managed to turn on the
light before dozing off, because although the sky outside the window was black he could see the lines of the
countertop in front of the sink and the curve of the faucet
and the white face of the little microwave quite clearly, all
bathed in a sort of shuddering yellow light. He felt stupid,
like he'd been partying seriously, and not just with a few
beers, either.

Gotta change that bulb, he thought.

But the glow was coming from the shelves beside the sink, not from any of the lamps in the room, an unsteady glare that grew brighter even as he stared.

Fire . . . ?

Even that thought could not spring him out of his chair—he felt as though someone had draped an invisible, weighted net over him. He stared at the gleam on the bottom shelf as it wriggled and pulsed, then died. Then, in the moment before the shining spot faded and the room dropped into darkness, he saw something that finally made him lurch up out of his seat. By the time he reached the light switch he had decided it had to have been a remnant of dream, and that four beers had been a few too many.

Oh, man, what have we learned here? Maybe that depressed people shouldn't drink . . .

But when the light came on, the woman was still sitting on the shelf. She was still about half a foot tall. She had wings.

"Shite and onions," she said, hugging herself, then dropped lightly down to the countertop beside the sink, translucent wings beating gently to slow her descent. Her feet and legs and arms were bare, the rest of her covered by a red dress that shimmered like butterfly scales. "That damn well hurt."

"Oh, Christ," Theo moaned. "What now?"

The tiny woman stared at him, frowning. She was terrifyingly solid, not a blur, not shadow. She had short carrot-colored hair—a bad color to go with a deep-red minidress, a heretofore unsuspected part of his own mind noted—and a heart-shaped face that was somehow a little too wide across the eyes and cheeks. She looked like the type who would have freckles, but if she did they were far too small to see. She didn't look happy, although he didn't know why she should be. He wasn't all that happy himself.

"This is a dream, isn't it?" he asked hopefully.

She bent to rub her knees, then straightened up. He could not get over how small she was. It was sort of like looking

at a cute girl at the end of the block, except this one was in
perfect focus and only a yard and a half away. "Well, if it's
a dream, then I'm dreaming too, and I'm going to put in a
request for a better one next time, 'cause this one is desperate. Now are you going to sit there staring like a gobshite or
are you going to offer me a thimble of tea or something? I
ache all bloody over from getting here."

"You . . . you're a fairy."

"That's one to you. And you're a mortal, so that's sorted.
Now, I'm tired and I'm hurting and I'm afraid I'm in a bitch
of a mood, so how about that tea?"

If this was a dream, what did it mean? *It's one thing to
fantasize about women, but women half a foot high? What
does that say about your sense of self-esteem, Vilmos?*

"Look," she said, and suddenly he could see that imaginary or not, she was definitely exhausted. "That tea? I'm not
shy. I'd get it meself, but I'm not big enough to turn the
knobs on your whatchamacallit here, your stove."

"Sorry." He walked toward the countertop, turned on the
burner and put the kettle on it. She still didn't disappear.
When the ring began to heat up she even extended her hands
toward it, warming them. "So you really . . . really are a
fairy," he said at last. "I'm not imagining it."

"I am. You're not."

"But . . . why do you talk like . . . like you're Irish?"

She rolled her eyes and blew a minute strand of hair off
her face. "Thick, you are. We don't talk like the Irish—the
Irish talk like us, more or less. Get it?"

"Oh."

The unreality of the situation began to seem a little less
glaring, but no more explicable. The water boiled. The fairy
fluttered her wings and lifted herself back half a foot to get
out of the way of the steam. He fumbled two teabags and
two cups out of the cupboard.

"By the Trees, fella, I'm not going to drink that much.
Just pour me a bit of yours."

"Oh. Right." He put one cup and one teabag away, then

set the tea to steeping. He didn't have a thimble, so he re-trieved one of the Heineken caps from the pile on the book-shelf. "Is this okay?"

She sprang up and hovered beside him, wings beating swift as a hummingbird's. She sniffed the cap. "If you wash it out. I've nothing against beer, but I don't want it in me tea, thank you very much."

He sat down with his mug, lost in a roaring internal silence of utter dumbfoundment. The fairy kneeled on the counter, blowing on her capful of tea to cool it.

"I'm sorry if I haven't . . . haven't been a very polite host," he began.

"Don't worry," she said between sips. "They often get taken that way, your kind. It's the glamour, I expect."

"Are you . . . do you . . . What's your name?"

She gave him a look that did not seem entirely friendly. "What's yours?"

"You don't know?"

"Of course I bloody well know, you great eejit. But you have to tell me first, then I can tell you."

"Oh." He realized he'd been saying that a lot. "I'm Theo Vilmos."

"Fair play to you. My name is Applecore."

"Applecore?"

"Don't start."

"But I just . . ."

"Don't start, fella, or you'll be wearing the rest of this tea."

He stared at her, alarmed but also amused at the thought of being attacked by an angry fairy. Then again, maybe it wasn't funny—maybe she could turn him into something unpleasant, a toad or a pea under a mattress. At the very least, wouldn't she sour the milk or something?

Of course, the milk in my refrigerator's probably sour already.

"I didn't mean to offend you," he said out loud. "I was only surprised because . . . well, because I don't know anyone with a name like that."

She gave him a stern look, then softened somewhat. "It's not my fault. I was the last born."

"What do you mean?"

"We're a big family, the Apples. Got twenty-seven brothers and sisters, I have. Seed, Skin, Pie, Pip, Doll, Tart, Tree, Wood, Bark, Blossom, even Butter, just to name a few—all the good names were taken by the time I came along. 'The mistake,' Ma and Da always called me, but it was in good fun. But there was bugger all choice left for names."

"Ah." It wasn't very clever, but it was better than "Oh." A little. "So . . . so what brings you here? Not that you aren't welcome," he added hastily. "But we don't get many fairies around here."

"And with these prices, I'm not surprised." She showed him a weary smile, the first from her he'd seen. "Sorry. Old joke, that." She tilted her little head to look at him carefully. "You really don't know?"

"Is it something to do with my great-uncle's book?"

"Not that I've heard. The old fella who sent me didn't tell me much. Apparently he's not the only one interested, but . . . Someone's keeping an eye on you."

"Someone? Someone like who?"

"Shite, man, I don't know! But the old fella's worried about it, so he sent me to fetch you. Don't ask me, ask him."

"Old fella . . . ?"

She put down her tea and cocked her head as though listening for something.

"You said 'old fella.' What 'old fella'?"

"Tansy, his name is. He's a sort of doctor-fella from one of the important families."

"But who is he? Where is he?"

Applecore shook her head slowly, distracted. Suddenly, he thought he knew what she was noticing—a sharp stench, sourly rotten. "God, what is that?" he asked. "A skunk?"

"Something's outside."

He stared at her, slow to catch on, but his nervous system knew it before he did: his heart was already going triple-speed. "Outside . . . ?" The smell was painfully strong now. His eyes were beginning to water.

She was up and hovering, her wings blurred almost to invisibility, making the air hum like the propeller of a toy plane. She shouted something in a high clear voice, words in a language he did not recognize, then turned to him, clearly frightened despite the attempt to keep her tiny features hard and expressionless. "It'll take a little time to open again— who knew we'd need it so fast?"

"Open . . . ?" It seemed like he hadn't finished a sentence in hours.

Something bumped the front door, one, two, three times. Theo was so bewildered that he actually reached for the knob.

"By the Trees!" she shouted, buzzing up close to his face, fists clenched. "Are you completely thick? Don't open that!"

"But there's somebody there . . ." Something shoved the door again, hard enough to make it creak, as though a huge animal had leaned against it. The stink was even more powerful. He reached out and flicked on the outside light, then put his eye to the peephole.

He was actually relieved to see the green duffel coat in the glare of the porch bulb, the slouched but obviously human shape huddled against the door. He could see a matted tangle of curly hair, a sheen of dark-skinned scalp and forehead. *Some old black guy, a transient . . .*

"It's all right," he called to the fairy. "It's just . . ."

Then the figure's head lolled back. Its jaw was broken, dangling flat against its chest. The blind eyes were not just milky-white, but like poached eggs were beginning to collapse and run out of the sockets. Theo staggered away from the door, his heart frightened straight up into his mouth so that for a moment he could not even draw a breath.

Applecore buzzed to the peephole, then swam backward in the air. "Bad," she shrilled. "This is bad!"

"Wh . . . what . . . ?"

"You don't want to know. Where is that double-cursed door?"

He didn't know what she meant. It was pretty obvious the door was right there, and hell was on the other side of it. But this had to be another nightmare, all of it, however real it seemed—that was the only explanation. He was locked in sleep—maybe he was even comatose, dying, limp on the cabin floor with his mind showing weird movies like a projector running in an empty theater. There couldn't be anything in the real world like any of this . . .

But if she was part of a dream, Applecore did not know it. She sped around the room like a fly in a bottle, her tiny shape little more than a shadow. "It will get in the easiest way it can. If it has to break in, we may have time. Are there any other doors, man?"

She was on about doors again and Theo couldn't stand it anymore. He sank to a crouch on the floor and clutched his splitting head. The stench was terrible, as though the thing were right in the room with them . . .

"The bathroom," he said, dragging himself upright again. "Oh, Christ, I think the window's open. There's just a screen . . ." He lurched across the room and pulled the bathroom door open. His nostrils were scorched by a blast of ammonia and sulfur.

The thing in the duffel coat was pushing at the screen. Even as Theo watched in stunned disbelief, it began to come through, the rotting meat of its hand forced through the netting like hamburger through a grinder. It stopped, impeded by bone. The wormy strands of the fingers writhed and groped a little farther forward, then the screen ripped out of the frame.

Theo shrieked and stumbled back into the main room. The bulky shape came through the high bathroom window and fell to the floor with a complicated, wet noise, then dragged itself upright. Theo snatched up his guitar and held it by the neck, trying to keep his legs under him as the stinking thing shambled out into the light.

It wasn't even a rotting corpse. Nothing that simple.

It stood, swaying, a thing of stinking tatters. Bits of bone and rags and greasy flesh and even curls of newspaper protruded from the torn pants and coat. The left foot was bloody-ragged and moldering, but where its right foot should be two smaller feet seemed to have been smashed together as a makeshift, one of them still wearing a filthy woman's shoe. One of its hands had been mangled by the screen, but was already growing back together. The other arm, raised now beside the collapsed face, did not end in a hand at all, but in the mummified corpse of a cat. Its skeletal jaws opened and closed like clutching fingers as it extended toward him.

Theo screamed and swung his Gibson as hard as he could. Part of the thing's mouth and nose flew off and it staggered but it did not fall. Air rattled in the hole of its throat. The gaping, crooked jaw twitched, tried to close, but most of the muscles were gone. As the duffel coat gaped open he saw that a suppurating hole in its chest had been bandaged over with a shredded mask of flesh—something that had once been a human face. Theo felt himself growing dizzy, saw blackness close in on him.

Suddenly the fairy was there, a winged glimmer between him and the monstrosity. The room grew brighter, until it was full of flickering light. He could even see Applecore's face, hard as a cameo brooch.

"Go on!" she shrilled, then flew at the thing's head like an angry sparrow. It leaned away from her, hissing, and swung its arm. The cat-hand clacked, the teeth just failing to close on her. "It's open, the door's open! Go through!"

A smoldering glow hung just before the kitchen sink, a seam of dripping light like a zipper in the fabric of reality. He stared at it for a stupefied moment, then flung aside his broken guitar.

"*Hurry up!*" Applecore screamed, but Theo hesitated. Where did it lead? Anywhere would be better than here, now . . . but . . .

Suddenly, he knew. He bent to snatch up his great-uncle's book. "Come on!" he shouted at the fairy.

"Don't be daft—the passage's about to close," she cried, although she had little breath to spare. "Just go! I'll keep it busy!" For a moment she wheeled up above the thing's head, into the full glare of the phantom doorway or whatever it was, and he saw that the fairy magic she was wielding against the undead beast was Theo's own corkscrew, as big in her arms as a painter's ladder. She spun again and dove, jabbing the sharp point at the thing's ruined face. It flinched back, perhaps out of some forgotten reflex—there was not much there worth saving—but did not seem very alarmed.

Theo's heart felt as though it were about to explode out of the top of his head like a Polaris missile. He leaped toward the glowing seam and scrabbled at the opening with his fingers. It tingled strangely but did not burn. He turned for one last look. A rotting paw just missed grabbing Applecore, but tipped her wing and sent her spinning. She landed on the floor and crouched there for a moment with her head down, clearly stunned. The thing gave a kind of squelchy huff of triumph and staggered toward her. Theo threw himself onto his knees, scooped up the fairy just ahead of the reaching cat jaws, then turned and clambered across the floor toward the door made of light.

He fell through in a most ungraceful way, into nothingness, into a colorless void that crashed like ocean waves and sparkled like stars.

Part Two

LAST EXIT
TO FAIRYLAND

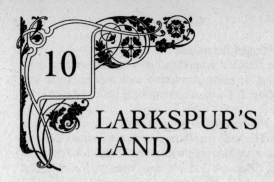

10

LARKSPUR'S LAND

He was not simply traveling, he was *stretching,* somehow—as though a part of him were still rooted deep in the reality he had just left while an increasingly attenuated Theo-ness was being drawn out through thousands of miles of noise and light. All that he was seemed to be getting thinner and more insubstantial, until he felt himself to be a near-infinite, near-invisible line of consciousness, each mote of thought touching nothing but the single beads of comprehension directly on either side, and all of them pulling farther and farther apart. He was like a rubber band in the hands of God, and God was spreading His mighty arms as wide as they would go . . .

And then the rubber band snapped.

When he came back to himself, half his vision was filled with what at first seemed to be a smeary abstract painting of green lines. *Grass.* He was lying on his side in long grass, and something was moving.

He regained his focus in time to see Applecore, who was kneeling a few inches from his nose, bend at the waist and decorously throw up. Despite her appearance and proximity, watching didn't trigger his own reflex as it might have with another human being. He sat up.

That *did* trigger the reflex.

As Theo finished emptying his stomach, spitting over and over into the grass, Applecore took a deep breath and groaned. "Oog. It's worse coming here than going to your side."

"Glad . . . to hear that." He wiped his chin with the back of his hand. His head was thumping like a timpani solo and he would have sold his soul without hesitation for a bottle of mouthwash. "Because I don't ever want to feel like that again." He raised his head and looked around. "Oh, God."

It wasn't so much that anything looked expressly different, or wrong—in fact, it all looked very right in a sort of romantic, pre-Raphaelite kind of way: close-standing trees and shadowy grassy dales, beams of midday sunlight diving straight down through the forest roof like glowing plumb lines, sparked with dust and the bright flicker of flying insects. His nausea had faded, but still the colors around him were almost too strong, the edges too crisp; it made his eyes water to look at anything for more than a few moments. It reminded him of the way a dose of psilocybin made the colors of everyday objects leap out like neon.

"Where are we?"

Applecore bent again and spat an almost invisible streak of light. "Home. Well, home for me. What would you call it? I was never up with all that book-learning shower of shite, and Faerie can't translate what you can't say." She frowned, then brightened. " 'Course. Faerie. That's what it's called."

"So I was right. No, *Uncle Eamonn* was right." Theo stretched his legs out in front of him, listened to the almost subliminal fluting of birds. His headache and nausea had all but disappeared. He could almost forget that he had just been through the weirdest and worst half hour of his life. "It's . . . it's beautiful here."

"That's why they saved this piece," the little fairy told him. "Don't think this is the whole story, boyo."

He nodded slowly, although he had no idea what she meant. It was hard to think, almost exhausting: spending time in the midst of such overwhelmingly powerful scenery was hard on mortal senses. So strange, all so strange . . .

He turned back to Applecore. "What the hell was that . . . *thing* that came after us?" The unearthly scenery suddenly felt different, even threatening, especially the shadowy depths behind the closest trees. "Will it come here? Is it coming now?"

"Will it come? Likely." Applecore sniffed. "Now? Couldn't say, but I doubt it'll find you again so fast. Eventually, though. So is it a good idea to laze around in the woods like a fat gobshite? Likely not."

"What was it?" It took a moment. "Hold on, find *me*? What do you mean, find *me*?"

"Start walking first." She was up and away, quick as a dragonfly, twenty yards in a couple of seconds, then back just as swiftly to hang in midair before him, a grim little half smile on her face. "Just curious. You standing there with your mouth open—do you have to do that for a bit before your legs start workin'?"

He shut his jaw and let her lead him through the psychedelic forest.

"I'm not being difficult," she said as they came out of a stand of trees and into an open dell. "I just don't know much. I'm a messenger, me—strictly hired help. All I can tell you is that just like Tansy sent me after you, someone else must have sent that falling-apart thing. Doesn't take much in the brains department to figure that out. You said you've never seen anyone like me before, not in real life. Ever seen anything like *that*?"

"God, no!"

"There you are, then. It came from one of the in-between places, must have. If I could find you, then it could too."

He shook his head. He was tired of the adventure already. He wanted to lie down and sleep, but instead all he did was put one foot in front of the other, following this irritating little flying woman, on and on through what had changed from a magical landscape into a fatiguing nightmare, as though he were being forced to do a survival trek through a Disney film. The sheer visual intensity of the forest, the glittering motes of dust, the bumblebees bright as spun coins, the snaking, tangled roots and colorful toadstools in all their profusion, even the vivid green of the grass, was hallucinatory, and it was getting to be like an acid trip that wouldn't end. It made his head ache. "But why me? I'm nobody! I'm . . . boring!"

"Am I arguing? Just save some of the questions for the old fella—he'll probably be able to tell you a good whack more than I can."

"Tell me about him. You said his name was . . . Tansy?"

"Count Tansy, yes. One of the Daisy clan, but a good bit less stupid than most of your landowning shower." She pursed her mouth in distaste. "Still, I don't owe him nothing and I wouldn't have done this for him if he weren't paying me, even if he did say it was important."

Theo shook his head again. "Me? You're talking about me again. Important."

"Important to someone, yeah, or they wouldn't have sent ol' Bag-of-Bones to suck your brains out through your nostrils, would they?"

"Speaking of sending, why did this Tansy send you? Why didn't he come himself?"

"He's used his exemption already, I guess."

"He's used . . . what?"

She stopped, hovering, and held a finger to her lips. At first he thought she just wanted him to stop asking so many questions, but then he realized she was listening to something. His skin suddenly seemed to fit poorly, his heart to grow a little too big and violent for his chest.

"Is it . . . that thing?" he whispered. She shook her head, but did not seem very happy. He did his best to stay still so she could hear whatever it was she was straining her tiny ears after.

"Follow me," she whispered at last. "Quick but as quiet

as you can. That means pick up those great clumping feet!"
She zigzagged away toward the edge of the clearing and
he half-ran, half-pranced on tiptoe after her through the
wildflower-sprinkled grass. "Down here." She pointed to a
gully shielded by undergrowth. Theo scrambled down into
it, pressed himself into a mat of fallen leaves that glimmered
silver and gold and smelled like something that came in expensive bags from a posh gardening store, then cautiously
raised his head to look back at the clearing. It was empty.
"Didn't expect I'd have to spend my last charm so soon,"
Applecore muttered.

"What . . . ?" Theo began, but Applecore flew up beside
him and gave him a surprisingly solid kick on the jaw.

"Shut it!" she hissed.

Long seconds crept by, then what looked like a horizon-
tal flash of sunlight burst from the trees and streaked
halfway across the clearing in a heartbeat, then stopped,
changing from blur to solid shape so abruptly that he almost
gasped in surprise.

It was a deer, a huge white buck, with a spreading rack of
antlers like two leafless trees carved out of ivory. It stared at
the spot where Theo was hidden. The dark liquidity of its
gaze seemed to mark him easily despite his held breath and
tight-clenched muscles.

Beautiful, beautiful . . . was all he could think as it stood
frozen in an angled stab of sun like a statue made of burning
phosphor. It blinked, then leaped away into the trees on the
far side of the clearing, a movement so swift and effortless
that Theo could not at first entirely understand what had
happened.

His mouth worked as he tried to express even a halting
appreciation for the vision he had just been given, but
Applecore's wings were buzzing beside his ear. She prodded
him with her foot, more gently this time.

"Ssshhhh." Her whisper was so close he thought he
could even feel the tiny puff of her breath inside his ear. To
his surprise, she began to sing. Her voice was scratchy but

tuneful. He could not make out the words, but the repetitive melody was oddly compelling, so much so that he did not at first notice that another noise was growing all around him, a sound that even at its loudest never became more than a flutter like rain on hard-packed earth.

The riders stormed into the clearing.

Again, he found himself dumbstruck, but it was a less simple awe than that which had pierced him at the sight of the stag. There were close to two dozen of the newcomers, male and female, dressed in costumes that seemed to come from completely random times and places, both modern and ancient; even the colors of the cloth were elusively inconstant, changing like mother-of-pearl, like sunlight on the water of a moving stream. The riders' faces were fine and proud and strangely ageless—every one of the hunting party could have been twenty or forty in human age, or neither. He found it was as hard to look at them as it had been to look at the land around him when he had first come through. His brain searched desperately for measurements, categories, ways to make these creatures into mere humans, but could not find the mechanism: they confused his familiar ways of judging people just as surely as the stag had turned him into mud and stone by the mere fact of its lightning-swift loveliness.

Even their horses were strange, although he could not say what was different about them—they had four legs, manes, eyes, flashing teeth. But that did not make them horses, at least not the sort of horses he knew, any more than elaborately curled and arranged hair, jewelry, and quiet conversations made people out of these frighteningly beautiful riders.

The hunt party paused in the clearing for only a few moments, riding around the spot where the stag had stopped, staring down raptly as though something were written there that they had never seen before. One of them, a tall man with long golden hair, dressed in something like modern riding gear (if riding clothes were ever made from millions of pearlescent scales) and carrying what appeared to be a rifle

Dear Christy,

Thank you!!!

Love,

Mom

6/4/09

with a bright silver barrel and a bone-white stock, stood in his stirrups and pulled his mount around to face the quarter in which the stag had vanished. He spurred out of the clearing and the others followed him, swift as the crack of a whip, but so quiet that by the time the last of them had passed between the nearest trees Theo could not hear them anymore.

"That was Lord Larkspur," said Applecore after half a minute of silence. "The one in the lizardy suit. Seen him in the mirror-shows. He's better lookin' in real life, I have to admit, if you like that sort."

Theo wasn't sure what sort that was, but he wasn't even too sure of his own name at the moment. "Those were . . . fairies?"

Applecore snorted and drifted down to the ground a foot from Theo's face. "Damn few who aren't around here, 'cepting you. Flowerfolk, those were. You might call them the local gentry. Oh, they think they're fine, but."

"They . . . they *were* fine."

For a moment Applecore only looked at him, something almost like hurt on her little face. "You've never seen them before, 'course," she said at last, then scowled. "Larkspur, right on top of us, and cursed lucky we were not to be noticed. By the Trees! I told you not to come back for me!"

Still overwhelmed, it took him a long moment to make sense of that. "Wait a minute, you mean back . . . back at the cabin? Are you saying I should have left you there, with that ugly dead thing?"

"I could have made a door for meself. I made that one just for you—I was planning to keep Old Ugly busy for a bit. But you dragged me through with you and buggered up the landing, so we've come down in the wrong spot." She shook her head. "Right in the middle of Delphinion. Shite and double shite. Even if we're near the edge of the forest we're half a day's walk from Daisy lands, the rate you waddle, and we don't dare go out from under the trees in daylight."

"We can't go out from under the trees . . . ?"

"Because this is Larkspur's land, ya thick. It belongs to

him, and so does almost everything on it and a lot above it, including some of the birds. If we come out of the trees, chances are he'll know about it before an hour's passed."

"Hey, damn it, quit calling me thick. You may have saved my life, but that doesn't give you a license to kick my ass for the rest of it."

"Ooh, he's gettin' snappy."

"Look, a couple of hours ago I was back in my own world thinking about nothing more earthshaking than hopping on my bike and picking up a burrito to go, then suddenly I'm in the middle of Storybook Land being led through the enchanted frigging forest by Thumbelina—and Thumbelina's kind of bitchy, just between you and me. Anyway, I'd like to see anyone else do any better, so back off!"

He walked on in silence for a little while. Applecore didn't desert him, or even seem to have taken much offense, so at last he hazarded a question. "What the hell difference does it make whether this guy knows we're on his land or not?"

"'Cause Larkspur's a Chokeweed, see? It would be one thing if he were a Creeper, or even a middle-of-the-road fella like Tansy, but I'm guessing every one of them Chokeweeds would be just as happy to slit your throat as look at you."

Theo was completely baffled. "Larkspur? Chokeweed? Aren't those plants?"

Applecore gave out a quite expressive noise of disgust. "Ah, well, I s'pose it's not your fault you don't know anything. Keep walking and I'll try to tell you a wee bit about things. But pay attention! Even if you do think I've been givin' you too much stick—and maybe I have, but then again maybe it's what you need—if I tell you to shut up, stop where you are and shut right up. This world is dangerous for you, boyo, and not just because the way you walk you're liable to trip over a branch and break your nose. Dangerous. Got it?"

He nodded.

"Right then," she said, rising into the warm afternoon air. "Get those feet movin'."

It would have been hard to absorb so many details of Faerie history and culture if he had been sitting in a quiet classroom listening to a professor or reading it in a textbook. Hearing it from Applecore while staggering through the bizarre and distracting forest landscape was a bit like trying to take a complex course in political science from an immigrant taxi driver during the first half hour in a new city. And his instructor's style was not the most helpful, either: every time he felt he was beginning to see the light, Applecore would suddenly decide to fly ahead and scout the terrain, or would buzz up in front of his face to comment adversely on his pace or attention.

What he did manage to grasp went something like this:

Fairies here came in all shapes and sizes, but the most powerful caste—the nobility, in a sense, or at least the upper class—seemed to favor roughly human shape and size, like the hunting party he had just seen. Like humans of a similar social position, they generally maintained residences in both the country and the City. (There seemed to be only one big city, as far as he could tell, apparently the same strange metropolis as described in his great-uncle's book.) The noble houses were all named after flowers, and these clans seemed to wield most of the control in Faerie.

"They own the powerhouses, don't they?" was Applecore's slightly cryptic explanation of why that should be.

The Flower-clans moved through a shifting and bewildering set of political alliances and conflicts, but the one that seemed most important for Theo to understand was the struggle between the Creepers and the Chokeweeds, since the subject of dispute was mortals. Applecore did not have a firm grasp on the entire history of the conflict, but as best Theo could make out, the Creepers believed in coexistence with human beings but the Chokeweeds were opposed.

"Opposed?" he asked. "What does that mean?"

"I suppose it means they want to kill them."

"Kill them?" A chill ran through him. "Sweet Jesus, how many mortals have you got around here, anyway?"

She wrinkled her little brow for a moment, thinking. "None that I know of, these days. 'Cept you."

He swallowed. It wasn't easy. "But . . . but why would there be such a big deal made about killing mortals if there aren't any here?"

"'Cause it isn't just the ones here they're talking about killing, ya thick."

It didn't sink in for a moment or two, but when it did, he stopped walking. "Hang on. Damn it, stop flying! Are you telling me there's a bunch of . . . of fairies who want to kill all the people in the world? The people where I live? *Real* people?"

Applecore scowled. "What does that mean, 'real'? Amn't I real, you? If you cut me, do I not bleed? If you piss me off, will I not kick you up the arse?"

"I'm not trying to offend you, I'm trying to make sense out of this. What exactly does that mean, they want to kill mortals?"

She shrugged, still angry. "Like I said, it's a big political thing. If you want to know more, ask your man Tansy. I'm just the laboring class."

"Jesus." He started walking again. The magical forest was beginning to seem even less attractive. "How many of these . . . Chokeweeds are there?"

"Not that many. Maybe a quarter of the Flowers, tops."

"A quarter . . . ? Jesus Christ!"

"Would you quit saying that?" Applecore buzzed around his head three times. "It doesn't do me any damage personally, but there's plenty here as don't like it, not to mention that if we meet up with a stranger you'll give yourself away throwin' that name around sure as winter brings frost. Wouldn't go shoutin' 'Mohammed' or 'Buddha,' either, now you come to it."

"What, are you telling me the other fairies wouldn't notice I didn't belong here if I just kept my mouth shut?"

"You'd be surprised." She smirked. "There's some stupid fairies, but. Now, far as the Chokeweeds go, you've got to remember there's at least that many Creepers, and they like your sort well enough. The question is how many of the in-betweeners get pulled one way or the other. Don't worry so much, boyo—it's all been going on for a long, long time." She paused, hovering. "Hang on a bit, I hear something strange." She raised her head, tilted it. "Smell something, too . . ."

"What do you think . . ."

"Just stand here and do nothing, will you?"

"But . . ."

"By the Trees, I'm ready to start reading Chokeweed pamphlets meself after putting up with you, and I don't even have a vote! Now just shut it and wait for me." And she swung wide around him and then shot off like a bullet, a blur of red dress disappearing among the trees.

Theo sank to the grassy ground, then put his head in his hands to rest his eyes. It was all just bizarre past any grasping. A few hours ago he had been living a normal life in his normal cabin in the mountains of normal northern California. Not a great life, maybe—in fact lately a pretty pathetic-loser sort of life—but one almost completely empty of shambling, corpse-limbed monstrosities and smart-assed fairies.

How did Uncle Eamonn deal with this shit without going crazy? Of course, his great-uncle had gone looking for it. It had been his life's dream.

Reminded, he pulled the notebook out of the pocket of the leather jacket, which was tied around his waist. The book had been bumping against his legs so long as he walked that he had actually considered pulling it out and throwing it away, just to keep from going mad—Theo was not a great hiker, he was the first to admit—but it was pretty much his only connection to anything resembling the world he knew.

But I read almost all of it, he thought. *I sort of remember some of the families being named after flowers, but why*

*don't I remember anything about this Chokers and Creeps
stuff?*

He began to leaf through the pages as he waited for
Applecore to return, wondering what else he might have
missed that could save him from being eaten by big bad
wolves or some other godawful thing. It was just so hard to
believe that he was actually here—that everything in the
book had been true . . .

Applecore buzzed back into view. "Trouble," she said.
"We're right at the edge of one of Larkspur's farms. We
could go around it, but it'd take us days longer."

"Days longer . . . ?"

"To get to Tansy's. Larkspur won't be anywhere near the
farmholding—too busy chasin' that corpsey hart—but if one
of his factors gets wind of you, his lordship'll come quick
enough."

Theo shrugged. "So what are we supposed to do? You can
fly, but I sure as hell can't."

She stared at him for a moment, perhaps about to say
something rude, but instead she brightened and pointed a
finger at him. "Disguise, boyo. That's how we'll save your
mortal hide."

He waggled his arm. A shower of twigs fell out of the
sleeve of his leather jacket. "What am I supposed to
be, a scarecrow?"

"Quit messing about with the branches—they're supposed to stick out. Same with the leaves in your hair. No,
you're not a scarecrow, you're a woodwight. A *leshy,* some
call 'em. Bit big, but if you hunch over . . ."

"You mean I have to *walk* with this jacket on? I'll get
heatstroke."

"You'll get worse than that if Larkspur and his mates get
hold of you. Put you in the wicker man, roast you like a Hy
Breasil potato, they will. Now quit squirming till I put this
mud on your face."

"Mddd? Whnnuhhll?"

"So you'll look like a little old thing that lives in the woods and hardly ever comes out in the daytime." She buzzed backward a foot or so and hovered, surveying her handiwork. "A few more leaves in your hair would have helped. Ah, well. Keep the collar of that jacket up. Now follow me. No, I told you, walk slow. Like you've got crookedy legs."

"It's hard to remember."

"Tell you what, boyo, I'm trying to save your life and you're not helping. Maybe I should take one of these sticks and lodge it up your back passage. That'd make you walk slow enough."

"You know, on a per-inch basis, you may be the most unpleasant person I've ever met."

He followed her out through the thinning forest fringe. The mud on his face was itching already, but not half so badly as the twigs and dried leaves in his jacket and trouser legs. Theo did his best to keep up the shambling, arm-swinging walk Applecore had shown him, something like a chimpanzee with a broken neck, but it was hard to feel very confident about imitating something he'd never seen. "Are there a lot of these slushies around here?" He saw flat, green-gold land past the trees now. "The thing I'm supposed to be?"

"Hardly any," she said. "And leshies don't come out of the forest much, anyway. Maybe one day a year."

"What?" He pulled up short, rubbing at his face in irritation. "Then how is this going to fool anyone?"

Applecore flew so close to his ear that he winced at the pressure change. "I didn't say it *would* fool anyone," she hissed. "I said we had to hope it might because, first off, it's the only thing around here big and stupid enough for you to pass yourself off as, and second, on that single day when one of them woodwight fellas does come out of the forest, he walks around honking and whistling and acting mad as an old stick. Don't ask me why because I don't spend much time in the leshy taverns. But when they've got their spring fever on 'em nobody much goes near 'em, so if people think you're one, chances are they'll leave you alone. But just in case anyone does come up looking to pass the time of day, I advise you to start squealing and honking and whatnot, real grumpy-like. Got it? Because I'd say it beats the jabbers out of being roasted like an old spud."

Properly chastened, Theo fell back into his shambling, uncomfortable walk.

The great ocean of trees through which they had been traveling had thinned now to a few small copses dotted along the hillside. As they made their way from one cluster of trees to another, Theo saw that they were descending into a disconcertingly wide plain. It was hemmed on either side by rows of green hills, lush as something in the background of a Maxfield Parrish painting, but those were far away—the nearest at least a couple of hours' walk, Theo decided, and probably more. At the base of the hill they were descending the land had been leveled and plowed, the soil dark as ground coffee, but mostly obscured by a sea of waving, shimmering fronds. Here and there figures moved among the stalks, bending and straightening.

"What . . . what is all that?"

"Wheat. Bend over more, you're starting to look human."

He crouched, conscious of a nagging pain starting in his back. "But . . . but it looks like gold. Like real gold!"

"You don't think we make fairy-bread out of the same stuff you mortal fellas grow, do you? Keep walking."

Even as they descended the hillside Applecore led him in a wide swing to one side so they could cross the broad field closer to its edge. After a few minutes she lit on his shoulder—"If they see me flying around they'll wonder why a sprite's keeping company with a leshy," she explained—and nestled in among the twigs and leaves, but continued to issue instructions from her new perch. "Root and Bough, man, can't you remember to gibber a bit? And wave those arms around!"

Theo did not want to die in a wicker man or by any other quaint methods the locals might have devised. He did his best to make appropriate noises and movements. He could see that some of the nearer farmworkers had stopped to watch him over the tops of the rows, but was relieved to see that none of them seemed inclined to do anything but look.

He stumbled along, gratefully aware that the sun was beginning to dip toward the horizon. He had never thought of fairyland as a place where you could get a sunburn, although he supposed the mud and twigs would protect him from that, but it was certainly warm enough to make the leaves down his neck itch like sin and the hot leather jacket feel like a very cruel punishment. There was a tiny bit of solace in the smell of the wheat itself, a rich, heady aroma like freshly unkegged beer, as though there was drunkenness in the grain of Faerie even before any distilling took place.

As he reached the edge of the field and stepped between two rows of golden stalks, a trio of heads popped up only a couple of rows away. Theo let out a gasp of surprise and stopped. As astonishingly small as she was, Applecore still looked quite human, and the fairy-gentry he had seen earlier could also have passed for human at a distance, but the three faces staring at him were not so easy to mistake. All three had huge eyes, faces as wrinkled as a thousand-year-old mummy, and instead of noses just two round nostrils opening straight into their faces.

Something sharp jabbed his earlobe. "Make some noise, you eejit," Applecore whispered.

Theo began to wave his arms and moan. The strange faces regarded him expressionlessly for a moment. He lunged into the wheat as though heading toward them and they vanished down behind the row.

"What the hell were those?" he asked when he could hear them rattling away in the other direction.

"Dobbies," said Applecore. "Not too bright, those lads. But they'll not come back."

"Ugly." Theo shivered.

Applecore laughed sharply. "Ah, if you find those a bit

homely, I'd hate to be in your shoes when you meet a kill-moulis or one of them fachan. Or old Peg Powler herself!"

"Don't want to meet any of them," Theo said wearily. "Want to go home."

Applecore frowned. "Yes. Well."

It was a long trip across Lord Larkspur's wheatfields, but although they saw many other creatures tending the crops, brownies and hodkins and hogboons and other domestic fairies who, according to Applecore, did most of the rural manual labor, most of them seemed quite willing to keep their distance from Theo the Woodwight. The sun continued to sink lower until it seemed to be sitting atop the hilly meadows to the west. Once, when Theo looked back, he could see the forest stretching behind them all the way back to a line of distant mountains whose peaks were as faint as wind-tattered clouds in the southern distance.

"The forest . . ." he said. "It's huge!"

"The Silverwood? One of the biggest," Applecore said. "Inside the borders of Faerie, only True Arden and Old Brocéliande are bigger, or that's what they taught me."

"And it all belongs to this Larkspur guy?"

"No, no, he's not that important. Delphinion, the bit his family owns, only runs into one edge of the forest—just happened to be the place we ended up. It mostly belongs to the Six Families, like everything bloody else." She pondered for a moment, then darted ahead and out of sight. Theo slogged on. He could see the end of the wheatfield, now. It was very close.

Applecore was back within a minute. "We're in luck," she said. "The border is near—just the other side of the river, only a couple of hops. And there's a bit of woodland there, too, so we won't have to worry so much about being seen."

"Does that mean I can pull these damn leaves out of my hair?" He sighed. "Border with what, exactly?"

"With the Sun's Gaze Commune—the Daisy House

lands, where Tansy lives. As for those leaves, just wait until we're across the river, boyo."

"Commune . . . ?"

"They're big on old-fashioned names for things, the Daisy clan. You really don't want to be wasting time discussing this now, do you?"

Theo staggered out of the last of the wheat like an exhausted distance runner breaking the tape, only to find that Applecore's idea of "a couple of hops" seemed to be derived from some kind of mutant-kangaroo scale. The river was wide and active, dark water and sparkling foam intermingled like some kind of living crystal, but it wasn't very near at all, not the way he felt. He groaned and sank down onto the grass at the edge of the field. "I'm not going to make it." He lowered his head, felt sweat and dirt and scratchy leaves on the back of his neck. "I'm dying of thirst, too."

"The river, Theo." She said it almost kindly.

As he got up and began to limp down the long hillside, he realized it was the first time she'd used his name.

He was only a hundred yards or so from the water, could feel the spray in his mouth and breathe the ozone tingle into his lungs, when Applecore, hovering beside his ear, said something he didn't want to hear.

"Oh, shite, we're in trouble now," was the way she put it.

"What?"

"Don't turn around! Riders on the far side of the field, back where we started. Some of Larkspur's march wardens, most likely. They look like they're talking to someone up there."

"Probably those Dob-thingies," Theo said miserably. "I never trusted the no-nose bastards."

"Just hurry. They're a long way away, and they don't look like . . . Whoops."

" 'Whoops?' What the hell does *that* mean?"

"It means they're riding across the field. Don't look back! But see if you can sort of hurry your bony arse toward that river, will you?"

Theo did not waste breath on more talking. He sped to a stumbling lope. Although he had abandoned any pretense at leshy-hood, preferring to concentrate on running rather than gibbering and throwing his arms around, he was pretty sure his fatigue and uncomfortable costume kept him from looking entirely human: a few of the leafy branches that had started under his collar had worked their way down past the small of his back until they threatened to become the stick-up-the-arse Applecore had mentioned earlier.

The sun had dipped behind the low western hills, and although it brought a measure of blessed coolness to the air, it also made Theo think about what it would be like to be chased through unfamiliar lands in the dark. He galloped awkwardly down to the edge of the river and stood there, staring at the current. He almost thought he could see faces in the eddying water, shapes like fingers in the froth.

"I'm . . . I'm not that good . . . a swimmer," he panted.

"Any nymphs owe you favors?" Applecore didn't seem to be joking.

"What's a nymph?"

She scowled. "I think you'd better just jump and swim hard and hope for the best. Because in about the time it's going to take me to explain, those horseback fellows are going to be here."

Theo turned to see half a dozen tall, mounted figures riding through the wheatfield, trampling the stalks as they came—not at full gallop, but not going slowly, either. "Oh, shit," he said, and jumped into the river.

It was stunningly wet—like ordinary water that had undergone some kind of molecular shift: in the moment of submersion he could almost feel it trying to force its way in through his pores like an invading force. He came up thrashing and spluttering, an electrical thrill of cold running along his spine and squeezing his skull. Trying to paddle, he dug at the water with tingling, clumsy hands, and for a moment he actually made some forward progress, but the current seemed to reach up and grab him, a cold fist that squeezed him hard and then turned him over and over like a toy; within heartbeats he had lost any sense of up or down. He tried to call out to Applecore, but there was only the ravishing chill and a view of sun and sky like something seen through the wrong end of a telescope—in fact, the coin of bright air rotating above him was getting smaller very rapidly indeed.

He was sinking, his last breath burning in his lungs.

Just as the blackness began to extinguish his thoughts, he thought he saw pale shapes floating toward him through the swirling, muddied waters. They surrounded him, their faces green as pale jade, hard and unsympathetic as masks. Their staring eyes were like bottomless holes, like abandoned wells forgotten in a field, but it didn't matter because he was sinking, sinking, drowning, dying. . . .

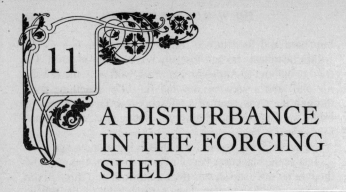

11

A DISTURBANCE
IN THE FORCING
SHED

Because she was by birth a loireag—a type of water fairy—Mary Mosspink had a patience with humidity that other, dryer folk did not possess. Even so, the hot damp evening depressed her, and she could sense that the mood of The Forcing Shed's patrons was not a good one. In fact, several decades' experience as an alewife told her it was the sort of night when it would be a good idea to prepare for trouble. She was already regretting that she hadn't found a replacement for Shortspan the half-troll, her other bartender and unofficial bouncer, who had called in sick.

The clientele was no different than usual, a few serious drinkers who always stopped in on their way home (but never actually seemed to go home), some Twilight District office workers who really would go home after a drink or two—the Eastwater-Merrowtown train station was just across the street—and a table full of young Flower bloods on the first stop of what looked like a long night's revel. These last were loud and a bit rude, but they'd already been in almost an hour and hadn't caused any serious trouble. In fact, nothing looked much different from normal, but Mary still couldn't shake the feeling of unease.

Thus, when she left old Juniper in charge for a moment and went back into the tavern office to get change for a gold

Oonagh out of the safe, she took a package out as well. She unwrapped the Cuckoo automatic briefly to make sure there was a bronze-jacketed iron egg in the chamber, but also to check that the safety was on, then folded the cloth around it again and slipped it into the pocket of her capacious smock. When she had given the waiting customer his change and released the old greencoat back to the kitchen, she slid the gun into the shelf underneath the register, far enough back that Juniper or someone else wouldn't come upon it by accident. Just as she withdrew her hand, the front door opened with a bang that made her jump and set her small wings flexing.

Her initial apprehension seemed misplaced. The little brown figure backlit by the newly kindled streetlamps attracted the eyes of several patrons but did not hold them long. It was only a goblin, and not a very healthy- or happy-looking one, either. Mary scowled and stepped around the counter, meaning to head him off before he put the touch on any of her customers, but the little fellow walked straight toward her, bony-legged and awkward as a stork.

"Shake the Trees, who dragged that in?" laughed one of the young gentry as the goblin limped past, and a few of the office workers muttered or chuckled behind their hands, but that was all the attention anyone paid to the new arrival.

And I'll wager he's used to that, Mary thought.

"You are . . . *hem* . . . the proprietor? Of this drinking place?" He had the whining goblin voice, but he spoke with a certain cockeyed dignity. She wondered if he'd been drinking—goblins had a legendary fondness for strong spirits. Of course, she'd been in the business a long time and hadn't served many goblins, and in fact couldn't remember any of them drinking anything much heartier than fern beer, but why would everyone say that if it weren't true? Maybe they had goblin pubs they went to—hadn't she heard something like that once?

"Yes, I'm . . . this is my tavern."

His finger-length nose twitched. "A happy meeting for me. *Hem.*" After the odd little throat-clearing noise, he leaned forward as though to impart a secret. "I am for the moment without gold of any coinage, fair lady, kind mistress. Not a fly-fleck."

She bit back a smile, unwilling to be charmed. It was too hot to encourage this kind of nonsense. "If you're after a free drink, you'd better try somewhere else . . ."

"No, no! That is a mistake you make of me. I ask for no favors and I want no drink." He rubbed at his nose, scratching it until it bent at least a couple of inches sideways. He was younger than she'd first thought, not even middle-aged, and fairly clean for a goblin, but he did have the infamous musky smell. "I wish only to know if there is a small task of some kind that needs attention—something that might earn me the price of a meal? At the moment, as I have said, *hem,* I have no coins."

She squinted at his tattered clothes and his long, bare feet. Her first impulse, to send him away, remained strong. He did have that slightly acrid goblin reek, and there was a still-nervous part of her that suggested tonight was not the night to do anything out of the ordinary. On the other hand, he was extremely polite for a goblin or anyone else, and he did have the look of someone down on his luck.

What if my dear old Semellus hadn't taken me in that night? Where would I be now? Rolling drunks down by the waterfront? Would I even be that lucky?

She decided she owed something, if not particularly to this strange little fellow, then to the memory of Semellus weft-Beebalm, who had taken in a young runaway and eventually made her the lady of the house, a wife in all but name.

"Right," she said. "You can do a bit of sweeping, I suppose. And then clear away and wash some glasses in the back. An hour or so should earn you some supper."

He made a courtly bow, his knee joints popping like wood knots in a fire. "Very kind this is, Madam Alewife. A blessing on your establishment. I call it down."

Now she did smile. "I see. And what would be your name?"

He raised a bristly eyebrow. "Ah. My name. Ah." He nodded slowly, as if asked to explain the secrets of the Elder Trees. "Button is my clan name. Mud is what they call me in the streets of this bright city. What I call myself, *hem,* that is too mysterious." He shook his head sadly, then looked up at her, his yellow eyes bright. "I wish you only well, you see."

It was too hot for goblin-riddles. Mary pointed to the broom.

The little fellow seemed to be a decent worker, and although he attracted some unfriendly attention from the young bloods sitting near the billiard table—a youth in Thornapple black and gold seemed to be the leader, and had already sent one of Mary's serving girls running to the back room in tears—the goblin applied the broom steadily and stolidly. As the evening wore on a party of older gentry came in, three prosperous-looking men and a woman, all a little cheerful with drink already, and their presence seemed to keep the noise down at the Thornapple table. Mary found herself relaxing.

When Button had finished sweeping, Mary caught him by his bony, furred elbow. "You've done well. Why don't you take a moment to have something to eat? Juniper has made up a nice rabbit stew tonight—I'd definitely take that over the shellfish if I were you. And I'll pour you a glass of ale to go with it."

The yellow eyes glinted and the long nose twitched; now he seemed to be the one holding back the smile. "Most and very kind, Mistress. If you would please put that meal in a sack for me, then I will take it with me when I have finished my work. I mean to share it with someone, you see. As for ale, so sad but your kindness is misplaced, as I do not drink. *Hem,* but now I have thought that perhaps my friend would like some. Is it possible to put ale in a sack?"

"Ah, not really, but I'll see what I can come up with. Come on, sit down and eat. You can take the rest with you."

He drew his arm away gently, but with enough force for

Mary to realize that although he was less than three-quarters of her size, he had a surprising, wiry strength. "No, with thanks. Not allowed to eat here in public. *Hem.* It is a strangeness of my own." He made a funny little bow. "Just clearing away the glasses, that is what I will do now."

She shrugged and let him go. After she had leaned into the service hatch to the kitchen to ask Juniper to find a spill-proof container for the stew, then handed the old greencoat a bottle of Orchid Lightning Pale to put into the sack with it, she found herself still shaking her head as she mopped down the bar. She hadn't ever really talked to a goblin before. Were they all this odd . . . ?

Juniper appeared from the kitchen, wings drooping in the heat, and set the sack down on the bar, but he didn't go away again. Absorbed in cleaning the taps, Mary found herself wondering with a measure of irritation what the old fellow wanted. Did he disapprove about giving bottles of ale to goblins? But that didn't explain why the whole room had suddenly become a great deal quieter, or why her neck hairs were all standing on end.

Juniper muttered, "Think this might be trouble, Mary."

She looked up to see a bit of jostling by the young bloods' table. The goblin was struggling to balance a tray of glasses while the young Thornapple blocked his way with an outflung leg. The young noble's companions were chortling in anticipation of a little fun.

"These glasses, they belong to the alewife," Button said with a certain nervous dignity. "It would be shameful, yes, if I were to drop them."

"Shameful for you or for me?" The Thornapple youth laughed—and he *was* a Thornapple, she could see him clearly now; there was no mistaking those white eyebrows—then flicked a calculating glance toward Mary. "Put them down if you're worried. I just want you to answer my question."

The goblin did not want to look him in the eye. "Yes. I answer you, yes. I am a goblin."

"We know that!" said Thornapple.

"We can smell it!" one of his companions brayed.

"I asked you if you were a *real* goblin."

Button again tried to get away, but Thornapple folded a long-fingered hand around the creature's skinny forearm. "Please, I do not know what you mean . . ."

"That's enough." Mary stepped around the edge of the bar. "Let him go."

The young Thornapple looked up at her with lazy satisfaction. She felt a shock of recognition when she saw that the eyes in his handsome face were two different colors, green and black. This wasn't just one of the young Thornapple cousins, this was Orian himself, the heir apparent, eldest son of one of the most powerful men in the City. Used to being recognized, he grinned at her expression. "I'm not harming anyone, Mistress." His use of the title was adroitly contemptuous. "Are you really going to call the constables over a conversation?"

Mary Mosspink hated bullying, hated it worse than almost anything. As a child growing up in the Merrowtown waterfront slums she had seen enough of it to last a lifetime, but the bullies of her childhood had possessed no other attributes beside brute strength. This kind was more insidious, less forgivable, bullying by those who had no need, who already owned the City and everything in it.

"Go back to your bar," said Orian Thornapple. "The little fellow is going to tell us a story, that's all. No harm to him. That's what a real goblin does, isn't that right?" He squeezed Button's arm companionably. "Tells true stories?"

The goblin turned his yellow eyes up to her. There was something in his look that went deeper than his words, but it was a far more complicated emotion than simple fear. "Do not worry for me, Madam Alewife."

Mary stood, tangled by indecision. She ought to throw them all out, the whole smirking table. But who would do it, with Shortspan out sick? And even if she managed, then what? The thing of it was, if the youth wanted, he could probably get her license taken away. Then she would find out how accurate her earlier musings about a life without The Forcing Shed had actually been.

She hated her own cowardice, but she was at least brave enough to recognize it for what it was. "You let go of his arm," she said at last. "Just let him go. Then if he wants to talk to you, he can." She stood in place until the handsome young man released his grip, then did her best to make her retreat to the bar look like the walk of someone who'd just defused a problem. When she got there, she half thought about pulling out the gun, but knew that would only make the situation worse—she certainly wasn't willing to shoot Orian Thornapple or one of his friends. That wouldn't just lose her a license, it would cost Mary Mosspink her precious freedom as well. At the least. Still, she stayed close to the register and the hidden package, certain now that her intuition had been right, that if there had been a wind on this sticky-hot night, it would carry disaster.

Some of the other patrons seemed to think that the disagreement was over and resumed their conversations, but the room was still tense. Mary watched as a couple of Thornapple's companions got up and went to the six-hazard table behind the goblin. They picked up cues and began to stroke the balls across the baize in a desultory fashion, but they were really just preventing a quick retreat by their leader's chosen victim.

"Now," said Orian Thornapple, "you did say you were going to tell us a story, didn't you? A real old goblin-type story? A true one?" He leaned forward unsteadily; for the first time Mary saw how drunk he was and felt a cold wash of terror. She should never have walked away. She looked for Juniper to ask him to call the constables, but couldn't see him.

"Tell me a story about fathers," said young Thornapple.

"But, young master, why do you want a goblin story?" Button seemed less frightened than Mary would have expected, or else he was hiding it well. "The tales that goblins make, they are well-known, and not very satisfying to folk like yourself. All goblin stories have a hole in the middle of them."

"Don't talk rubbish. Tell me a true story. About fathers who live too long."

By the Trees! Mary thought. *He is drunk—either that or he's mad. He's asking the little fellow to tell his fortune . . . or his father's fortune, which is a lot worse.* It was an article of folk wisdom, much-believed but never definitively proved, that goblins could sometimes foretell the future. But whether it could truly be done or not, it was certainly not allowed to try to spy into the fortunes of one of the High Council, and Thornapple's father was one of the Council's leaders.

Even some of young Thornapple's companions were looking a bit nervous now, but whatever expansive strangeness was upon the Flower lordling seemed to make him oblivious. Mary Mosspink wondered how much he had drunk. Or maybe it was something else—ghostweed, or even dust. "Talk, goblin," he said. "I don't give a rap about any hole in the middle. Tell me a tale."

Button bowed his head toward Orian Thornapple. "Be it so, then." He took a breath, held it for a moment in silence. The patrons sitting nearby, who had been pretending not to listen, now gave up all pretense.

"Once," the goblin said, "in a time when things that went around still went around, there was a very old fellow—a pinchpenny was he, who had little love for, *hem,* anything except gold. In his youth he had briefly taken a consort, and from this union a child had been born, a son. After she had left him the boy's mother had died in hunger and want, unhelped by the child's father.

"As he grew older he grew less capable of the working of his own land and keeping of his own house, but remained reluctant to spend any of his money, so the old fellow decided that he would bring his son back to live with him. He did this not out of love, but in the desire to have a servant he need not pay. Many people of the village saw this, and many whispered that the sooner the old man went to feed the Trees, the better it would be for all whose lives he touched."

Orian Thornapple seemed to like the goblin's story so far: he was smiling broadly, sitting back in his chair. He was alone at the table, now. His friends had moved to the six-hazard table, where they were talking quietly and a bit worriedly among themselves. "Better indeed," Thornapple said, and chuckled.

"Now the young one had a son of his own—yes, a very little boy—and they both came to live at the house, and the little one's father made him do many of the harder tasks his own father gave him to do, so that the small boy had scarcely any rest from sunrise to sunset. So there were three living together then in that house, the old fellow, his son, and the child who was the old man's grandson.

"One day the child discovered that there was, *hem,* a goblin living in a hole near the house, and because he had not yet grown cold to the world as had his father and grandfather, he shared what little he had to eat with the goblin, often leaving a crust of bread or a boiled root at the mouth of the hole. One day, he came back and discovered that the goblin had left him something in return—a toy of sorts, a bird made all of gold.

"When he showed this bird to his father and grandfather, both were consumed with greed. The grandfather insisted the bird should be his, since it was his house and grounds where the goblin lived. The younger man insisted just as strongly that since it was his own son who had tricked the goblin—as he saw it—into giving gold in return for crusts of bread, the bird belonged to him. They argued and argued until the younger fellow, in a rage, killed his own aged father. He then told the little boy that his grandfather had gone away, that they would have to work even harder now, and sent the child to bed.

"He had decided to make the goblin produce more gold, so he crept out beneath the moon's light to the goblin hole with a sack of flax seeds in his hands, then scattered a handful of the seeds all around it and laid a trail of them back to the house, where he flung the rest of the sack of seeds over the floor, knowing that the goblin was properly bound by the Laws of Things and so would have to, *hem,* count them all, and that since he would not be able to do so before the sun came up, the goblin would then be bound to the house and forced to do his bidding.

"He hid and watched the goblin walk past, nose close to the ground, eyes squinted as he counted the flax seeds. He waited outside the house until dawn's light began to shine in the belly of the sky, then he went in.

"He found the boy and the goblin sitting on the hearth rug together, drinking betony tea.

"Later, the little boy sold the house. With what it earned him, he was able to become a rich merchant, and never needed to sell either of his two golden birds."

The goblin, whose voice had become very singsong, suddenly stopped talking. He blinked slowly, once, twice, as if awakening from a dream. "That is the end of my story," he said.

A few of the patrons at other tables began to whisper. A woman laughed. Mary realized that despite her nervousness, even she had drifted into in a sort of half-sleep.

"What kind of nonsense is that?" Orian Thornapple struggled up out of his chair, stumbling a little. He loomed over the goblin. "What kind of story was that . . . that rubbish? It made no sense!"

Startlingly, a wide, sharp-toothed grin appeared in the goblin's face. "For the price, it seemed a very sensible story to me, Master."

"Why were they just sitting there drinking tea? What about the flax seeds the goblin was supposed to count?"

"The boy had come down in the night and found the seeds scattered on the floor. Fearing that his father and grandfather would be angry over the clutter, he had swept them all up."

"But . . ." Young Thornapple scowled. It made his face

much less handsome, and much less mature. "What was that babble at the end—the child sold the house? Where was his father? And you said two gold birds, but there was only one!" He grabbed the goblin's shoulder.

"Such are goblin tales," said Button, even as he swayed in the other's grip. "Can you really not guess what it was that happened to the child's father, who had tried to trick the goblin and failed? Can you not imagine where it was the second gold bird came from?"

The woman who had laughed earlier did it again, and this time she was joined by a few others, including the table of older Flower-folk. Orian Thornapple turned and glared at them, then seized both the goblin's shoulders and shook him. "You think you have made a fool of me, do you?" The little creature did not make a noise, but Mary could feel the storm-precursors of violence crackling in the air. She turned to pull the package out from beneath the register, shook off the covering cloth, and dropped the Cuckoo automatic into the pocket of her smock. "That's enough . . . !" she called, turning back to Thornapple and the goblin.

"So!" The Flower lordling's cry was triumphant. Even as his friends came forward, perhaps trying to prevent what was about to happen, the youth bent and snatched up something that had fallen loose and clattered to the floor near the goblin's feet. Thornapple held it up; it gleamed a smoldering yellow-green, making his fist glow. "What is this? What is this?"

"It is nothing," said the goblin, tugging at the youth's wrist in an ineffectual struggle to get it back. "It is only something to light my way home through the dark—a witchlight."

"Leave him alone," Mary said, but so quietly she barely heard herself.

"Hmmm, I'd say it looks like a weapon." Thornapple turned to his friends and the other patrons. "Wouldn't you all agree? Hasn't the Council spoken very firmly about the penalties for goblins and other noncitizens owning weapons?" He turned, holding the struggling Button at arm's length, and called to one of his companions, "Go fetch the constables. I think they'll be interested . . ." Suddenly he shrieked and began to shake the arm, trying to dislodge the very creature he had held captive a moment earlier. "Cursed thing! The little skin-eater *bit* me! He bit *me! I'll kill him!*" Thornapple flashed something out into his other hand—a blade, thin but wickedly long.

Mary yanked the pistol out of her smock. She was only planning to wave it around in a manner purposeful enough to stop everyone in their tracks, maybe fire it into the ceiling if necessary, but as she turned around a tall, scrawny stranger in tattered clothes came lurching up the aisle of the tavern, his eyes and mouth stretched wide with terror or pain. She lowered the pistol, confused. The newcomer staggered moaning toward the goblin and Orian Thornapple, his hands pressed against his ears as though someone had laid the grandfather of headache-curses upon him. The Flower lordling let go of the goblin, sizing up this bizarre new threat with a smirk that suggested he didn't think it amounted to much.

"Some kind of goblin-lover, eh?" Thornapple asked, lifting his long knife.

"Stop!" the apparition shouted at him. "Leave him alone! Stop all your voices! *Get out of my head!*" His voice rose to a shriek and something exploded with a *krrrooom!* like indoor thunder, turning all world into pure white brilliance followed by utter blackness.

For a single mad instant Mary thought she had pulled the trigger of her gun by mistake, but even a Cuckoo automatic didn't make a bang like that, and after the echo died down to a painful ringing in her ears she was still sightless, down on her knees and scrabbling absently with her hands for something she couldn't even imagine. People were screaming. A lot of people were screaming.

"Who turned out the bloody lights?" Someone grabbed her leg. "Who's that?"

"Juniper? The lights are off? You mean I'm not blind?"

"The bloody power blew out."

"Thank the Grove for that. I thought I lost my eyes."

The power came back on a few minutes later. Surprisingly, almost no one had left. Orian Thornapple certainly hadn't. He was lying on his back beside his table with his throat ripped out, surrounded by an extremely wide puddle of blood and beer. The hand that had held the goblin's witchlight no longer existed: the arm now ended at the wrist, a scorched stump.

The corpse looked quite surprised.

"Bad," Mary told Juniper. "This is very, very bad."

The goblin and the scrawny fellow were gone, of course.

The bad stuff started slowly, although Mary Mosspink had no doubt it would pick up speed soon enough. The leading Councillor's son had been murdered on her premises, even if no one quite understood all that had happened. The mere fact that she was completely innocent and that the young idiot had brought it on himself would be of little account when the wheels of officialdom began to turn. But the detective constable who interviewed her did not seem unduly vengeful and she allowed herself a little hope. When Mary told him what she remembered about the goblin, he quirked his mouth in a sour smile.

"But you know his name, if he didn't lie," she said. "People always say goblins never lie."

"Everyone lies," the constable said. "I don't care what they say about goblins. But it doesn't matter." He explained to her that there were some twenty or thirty thousand members of the Button clan in the city, and that at least half of them had been called "Mud" at some point in their lives. It was a bit like saying someone was named "Hey, you."

The constables extracted statements from all the employees and customers before leaving Mary and old Juniper to clean up the mess. It wasn't until hours after young Thornapple's body had been taken away that she realized that despite what must have been a fairly pressing need to escape in the darkness, the goblin had not only taken the time to finish off Orian Thornapple, he had also remembered to take the stew and the bottle of ale he had earned with him.

12

THE HOLLYHOCK CHEST

As consciousness sluggishly returned, all Theo could remember at first was what seemed an odd dream in which he had been a sack of potatoes. No, a sack of wet potatoes, and a sack being handled rather roughly, at that.

He kept his eyes closed and tried to figure out where he was. The bed was big and soft, so it wasn't the cabin. But he didn't live with Cat and her quilts-on-top-of-quilts fetish any more, unless the breakup had also only been a dream, like the potato-sack nightmare . . .

Wait a second. He had been a wet potato sack carried by a two-legged elephant. And there had been a bumblebee flying around his head, talking to him in a funny little buzzy voice. All of which meant . . .

. . . Absolutely nothing. Except that it had obviously been a really weird dream . . .

Hold on. Buzzing. Flying. Fairy. Fairyland. Applecore!

The whole grotesque adventure came flooding back as Theo's eyes popped open. A huge white comforter was draped over his legs, and beyond that was the footboard of a large wooden bed. Good so far. But beyond the footboard sat a gray, lumpy person the size of an industrial refrigerator.

Theo gasped and yanked the comforter over his head. A voice like someone dragging a manhole cover down a cobblestone street bellowed, "Hoy, Ted! Tell the boss he's awake."

It was comforting not being able to see, because the large gray person he had been looking at just before he had made the swift decision to pull the covers over his head and pray it would go away had not been a comforting thing to observe.

"You can come out, Pinkie." The voice was so deep and rough that just being in the same room with it made his kidneys hurt. "I'm a vegetarian."

"No, you're impossible," said Theo, but without much conviction.

The thing laughed. "Funny Pinkie. Come on out. The boss'll be seeing you in a moment. You might want to leak out some fluids or whatever you lot do after you wake up."

Just because I look at it doesn't mean I have to believe in it, Theo reassured himself. He slowly inched down the covers until the top halves of both his eyes were exposed. The commitment made, he did his best not to squeak with fear: the thing next to the bed gave the old playground expression "butt-ugly" a whole new meaning.

Is this what my life's going to be like from now on? Just one horrible, weird thing after another? That sucks for days.

The predominant color of the thing's bumpy, wrinkled skin was indeed gray, but not a simple gray: it held a complicated array of hues with strange undertones, like the exterior of an anciently decrepit concrete building left to weather and collapse, a gray that suggested the kind of walls where graffiti had been painted over and then re-graffito'd in a continuous cycle for about a thousand years. The thing's face, however, made the rest of its gnarled hide look positively kissable. Its eyes were just tiny little points of red light deep under brows so heavy someone could have tended bar from behind one of them. Between them was a formless gob of lumpy, crusty gray stuff that could only be called a nose because it had nostrils, and because it was more or less in the center of the thing's face. The mouth was open, displaying a grin so jagged and horrifying that Theo's fingers involuntarily tightened on the quilt again. The bald, gray, gruesomely massive thing was sitting cross-legged on the floor beside the bed, but even so its head was at least five feet above the ground. It must, he guessed frantically, weigh as much as a medium-sized car.

"Hello," it grated, and leaned toward him, batting eyelids like folk-art saucers. Its breath was what might more properly have been expected out of the southern end of a triceratops. "My name's Dolly. You know, you're kind of cute for a pink boy."

H e was fanned awake the second time by the wind from tiny wings. Whoever was standing on his chin was saying angrily, "It's not funny, you bloody ogre. If I'd been here, I'd have flown up your nose and gone on a three-month search for your brain, just so I could kick it back out your nostril."

"Oh, mulch," the deep voice said grumpily. "It was just a joke. They're such frail things."

"He's been through a lot." The fanning stopped. "Come on, boyo. Wake up."

Theo opened his eyes.

"And don't look up my skirt, you rude shite." With a flick she flew up from his chin and back a yard, forcing him to sit up, groaning, so he could see her. The massive gray thing was still sitting on the floor but it looked a little chastened. It was no wonder he'd mistaken it for an upright elephant in his first dream . . .

"Hold on," he said. "How did I get here? Did . . . you carry me?" He paused. "And is your name really Dolly?"

"Close as you'll get to saying . . ." and she belched out a gnashing, grinding noise that made Theo's kidneys ache again. "So it might as well be 'Dolly,' yeah. I carried you. My brother Teddybear took a turn, too."

"Teddybear . . . ?"

"That's how ogres name themselves," Applecore told

him. "They get their names as kids, called after their favorite toys. But before you get all sentimental, her brother's teddy bear was a full-grown live bear that he eventually squeezed to death by accident. And Dolly . . . well, boyo, you don't even want to know what she used for a doll."

"No. No, I don't." He looked around, as much as anything else to avoid looking at gigantic gray Dolly, who was grinning again. Except for his leather jacket, reassuringly draped over one bedpost, everything around him was a bit odd and unfamiliar. It was a good-sized room, full of tasteful little details of the kind that might be found in an upscale bed-and-breakfast. (Theo and Cat had stayed in one in Monterey once, and Theo had been amazed how much money you could charge to let someone sleep in your spare room if you had a vase of cheese straws on the mantelpiece and a needlepoint of an otter on the wall.) This room had soft, shimmering cloth hangings on the wall and very little ornamentation except for an upright wood-and-glass-object on the bedside table. He guessed it was a clock radio even though its face was triangular and there seemed to be more unreadable symbols on it than the numbers on a standard clock. But unlike the Monterey bed-and-breakfast, or in fact most rooms that fell into the category of "guest room" as opposed to "cell," this room had one door and no windows or vents of any kind, although something that looked a bit like an air conditioner with a covering screen made of silk was sunk into the stones of one wall. Air conditioners in Fairyland. He couldn't wrap his head around it at all. "Where am I, exactly?" he asked. "What happened?"

"You jumped into the river," she said. "And you didn't even ask first."

"Ask? What do you mean, ask? You told me to do it! There were people chasing after me!" But they hadn't been people, of course, he remembered, they had been angry fairies. That was part of the problem.

"Not ask me. You don't go jumping into someone's river

without getting permission," Applecore said sternly. "Ignorance is no excuse. Look at your arm. No, the other one."

He stared. Tied around the base of his left wrist was a single strand of wet green grass. He tried to slide it off but it wouldn't move. He couldn't unpick the knot, either, and the grass was as unbreakable as some kind of space-age carbon fiber.

"It's not going to come off. You should be grateful you got away so lightly, boyo. That's a nymph-binding, and it means you owe a powerful favor. I had to work hard to bargain that, so they didn't just drown you, or worse."

"Worse . . . ?"

"No more questions. I'll explain later. Just be glad that the Delphinion and Daisy commune people got together a while back and chased all the Jenny Greenteeths out of that river, or you'd be . . . well, best not dwelt on. Your Jenny doesn't haggle like the nymphs do, she just starts chewing. Now get up."

He looked from the band of preternaturally strong river-grass to the hovering fairy. It was plain that as long as he was in this damned Fairyland, he'd never, ever get the kind of answers he wanted to anything. He'd just have to try to catch up on the run.

"I still don't know where we are."

Applecore snorted. "The only place you could be without being dead, right about now," she said. "This is Tansy's house in the Daisy family compound—the Sun's Gaze Commune. I told you we were coming here."

"Bit mad is our boss," Dolly said. "Tansy likes lost causes and whatnot. Oddities and so on. Mortals."

"I wouldn't go so far as to say he likes 'em," said Applecore. "But he wanted this one, so we're off now."

Dolly shrugged. "You can take him. I made sure he wasn't carrying anything he shouldn't before I put him to bed." She gifted Theo with another leeringly jagged smile, and for the first time he realized he wasn't wearing his jeans and shirt any more, but instead something halfway between pajamas and a martial-arts costume made of slithery grayish silk. "You're smooth all over, aren't you?" said Dolly. "I like that. Novelty, I call it."

Theo was still shuddering as he followed Applecore out into a broad, carpeted corridor. He pulled on his leather jacket, which he had snatched off the bedpost on the way out. It looked strange with the silk ninja pajamas, but at least it was something familiar. In truth, though, not everything seemed as strange as he had expected: the soft, fur-lined boots that had been thoughtfully placed by his bed felt quite pleasantly ordinary, the walls on either side of him seemed nothing more exotic than pale, sandy stucco and although the light fixtures set at intervals along the passage were intricately ornamented, the lights themselves seemed to be . . . "Electric bulbs?" he asked Applecore. "Is there really electricity here in Fairyland?"

"I can't say I ever could make sense out of electricity when anyone tried to explain it. But, no, these lights are scientific. They work by magic."

Theo still felt like his brain wasn't entirely connected, but he couldn't help wondering why his uncle's book had described a kind of gaslight or even oil-lantern version of Fairyland—something like Victorian London: instead, from what he could see of the quite modern decor and appliances, Eamonn Dowd seemed to have gotten the similarities wrong by a good hundred years or more.

I'm tired of weird stuff, he realized. *I just want to go home. I'll go along and meet this old Tansy fellow, the one who likes mortals, and I'll answer some questions. Maybe he wants Uncle Eamonn's book?* In a sudden panic that it might be lost he groped at his jacket pocket, but however intrusive the rest of Dolly's search might have been, she had at least left him his great-uncle's journal.

So I'll meet this Tansy guy, give him the book if he wants it—it's not worth staying here to keep it, that's for sure—and then I'll get him to send me home. For a moment he could even imagine that things would be different for him now, after such experiences. *I'll change. I'll get my life together. Maybe I'll even write a novel and get famous—use Great-Uncle Eamonn's ideas, and what I've seen myself . . . how hard can it be to write one of those fantasy books, anyway . . . ?*

Theo was interrupted in these creative musings when another large, heart-attack-inducing figure stepped out of the shadows at the end of the hall. The floor gave a little under its weight. "Hello, Gnat," it rumbled.

"Don't get cute, you massive shower of gray shite," said Applecore, but almost fondly. "We're here to see your boss."

Teddybear, who was even less attractive than his sister (if such a thing were possible), nodded his huge head. "He's expecting you. Go right in." He looked at Theo. "And don't do anything stupid, Pink Boy. I took you out of the river and I can put you back in. From here."

Theo hastened after Applecore into a sparsely furnished antechamber, something that looked like it might have been designed by an unusually artistic Trappist monk. He looked over his shoulder to make sure they were alone before asking, "Are all ogres like those two?"

"No, not really." Applecore settled onto his shoulder. "The big ones you don't even want to have in the house. Really dreadful, they are." She reached over and pinched his earlobe. "You know, I think Dolly's a bit fond of you."

"Shut up. Just . . . shut up."

A stranger walked into the room, a tall, slender man apparently in his thirties with a long white lab coat and a long white ponytail. He looked Theo up and down coolly, then turned away. "Come along," he called over his shoulder.

"Who the hell is that?" Theo whispered to Applecore, who still rode his shoulder.

"Count Tansy, 'course. You'd best get on with it."

"But . . . but he's not . . . !" What had he been expecting? Old? Kindly looking? Just because Applecore had once referred to him as some kind of doctor . . . ?

Tansy led them out of the formality of the antechamber

and into something much more chaotic. To Theo's first, startled glance it looked like the early days of computing, of that time which he knew only from photos and magazine articles when people had mounted their first generation PCs in handmade wooden boxes, before such things had been replaced by mass-produced plastic cases. On second glance, the technology seemed more sophisticated than that, with unrecognizable machines stacked on every surface in the room, although there *did* seem to be rather an emphasis on attractive wooden cases, not to mention controls of fluted glass instead of workaday buttons and switches.

Tansy stopped at one of the tables and picked up a pair of spectacles which he donned before turning around to inspect Theo again. The lenses made the fairy's violet eyes seem larger, but did not make him seem any more like a kindly old inventor; rather they gave him the look of some kind of trendy European conceptual artist, which was in keeping with the techno-minimalist decor. The clothes he wore under the white lab coat—and now that Theo looked at it, it seemed a bit stylish for a lab coat—were also white. In his hawkfaced way, he was quite handsome—even beautiful.

He looks like the angel that tells you you're not getting into heaven because you didn't make a reservation, Theo decided. He extended his hand, feeling awkward. "Hi, I'm Theo Vilmos . . ."

"Yes, you are." Tansy nodded once and ignored the hand until Theo curled it away again. He turned to Applecore, who had sprung from Theo's shoulder and settled on one of the polished wooden surfaces, legs dangling. "You are a week late, sprite. What happened?"

A week late? Theo looked down at his grass-bound wrist. *Jesus, was I unconscious that long? No, couldn't have been. Did it take Applecore an extra long time to reach me in the first place?*

As she launched into a highly technical explanation of their encounter with the corpse-thing and their arrival in Larkspur territory, using words like "outflow" and "trajectory" and "proximate entry shift" that didn't seem like they belonged in a "magical-trip-to-Fairyland" kind of situation, Theo could not help noticing that his tiny guide's demeanor had changed. She was all business now—perhaps even trying a little too hard, flinging technical terms around like a roadwork foreman explaining to a company VP why his crew had accidentally put a jackhammer through a power cable.

"Yes, well." Tansy dismissed the rest of the explanation with a flick of his long fingers. He looked at Theo again, not angrily, but certainly not with a great deal of human warmth either, as if Theo was a guest's dog rather than an actual guest. In fact, after all the trouble of getting him here, Tansy hadn't really spoken to him yet.

Human warmth—that's the key, isn't it? Theo decided. *He's not human. And I don't even think he likes humans very much.* And if this purple-eyed fellow was one of the sympathetic ones, Theo had a sudden, chilling premonition of what it might be like to encounter some of the more unsympathetic of Tansy's folk.

Well, so I'll never be Fairyland's Mr. Popular. "Why did you bring me here?" he asked.

Tansy raised an eyebrow thin and white as a line of high-test cocaine. "Because I was the only one who could find you."

Theo puzzled over this for a moment. "That doesn't really answer my question."

"Wait until I finish with the sprite." The lord of the manor turned back to Applecore. "Is there anything else important you need to tell me?"

"Bunches, I'm afraid." She lifted off the tabletop and hovered, looking a bit frayed. "First, that dead-bodies thing'll still be following him. If it found him there, it'll find him here."

Tansy looked over the top of his spectacles. "I hope you're not suggesting I couldn't puzzle that out for myself."

"'Course not, Count Tansy. Right. Well, also, when we were leaving Larkspur's land, the lad here went into the creek. That's why I had to fly straight here and get Dolly and Teddy to bring him home."

"The creek? You mean the Graywindle? It's strange that the nymph gave permission . . ."

"She didn't, not exactly. Not at first." Applecore flew over and tugged Theo's left hand up so Tansy could see his wrist. "I had to let him be bound."

The fairy lord shrugged. "The mortal's affair, not mine."

"But it will affect how he travels, sir."

Tansy shrugged again. "He may not. Finish your recitation."

"Well, and when we bumped into Larkspur and his hunting party, I had to use my own charm because I used up all yours earlier, scuffling with that ugly thing. It wasn't much, just a small-and-secret thing, a Once-in-Thrice Misdirection I got through a friend's discount, but it was my last bit of protection. So I'm without defenses, sir, if you see what I mean."

"I'll see you compensated, of course . . ." Tansy began.

"Hang on a moment," Applecore said, then flushed—Theo could see it even from a few feet away. "Sorry for interrupting, sir. Sorry. I just realized, a moment ago you said, 'He may not.' What does that mean, if you don't mind my asking. May not what?"

Tansy looked like he did mind her asking, at least a little, but couldn't be bothered to make a point of it. "May not travel. You see, things have changed."

"How so?" Applecore moved a little closer to Theo, hovering almost protectively, he thought.

"As I may or may not have explained to you, I did not want this mortal for myself, but because certain others wished me to summon him." Tansy turned and moved to a low chair, settling himself into it with remarkable grace. For the first time, Theo noticed that this important fairy had no wings—nor had any of Larkspur's hunting party had them, now that he thought of it. Hadn't Eamonn Dowd written something about the upper-crust fairies and their wings?

"He was wanted at a conclave in the City," Tansy continued, "—a meeting of some of the most important leaders of both the Symbiotes and the Coextensives . . ."

Applecore flew close to Theo's ear. "Those are the Creepers and the in-betweeners—the groups who are against the Chokeweeds," she whispered.

Tansy frowned. He obviously had sharp hearing. "I must say I deplore those oversimplified names. It is the worst kind of common goblin-talk." He shook his snowy head in irritation. "Besides, we Coextensives are not "in-betweeners," a poor choice between two more dynamic parties. Rather, it is the other two parties who tend toward extremist positions, and we are the moderate and sensible majority on which society depends." In his strange way he seemed the most human Theo had yet seen him: a bit of color had even crept into the skin stretched over his pale cheekbones. "In any case, some of my fellow Coextensives felt it was important that this mortal be brought here . . ."

"Theo Vilmos. I have a name. I'm not just 'this mortal.' "

Another wave of the hand. ". . . That *Master Vilmos* be brought here, and although I am a busy person with many important projects, they convinced me to help. I was to bring him . . . you . . . here, and one of the young fellows of the Hollyhock household—a prominent Symbiote family, and good folk despite a certain political naïveté—was to come here and escort you to the conclave."

"But what happened?" Applecore asked. "Have they canceled this meeting or some such?"

Tansy shook his head. He sat silently for the space of a dozen or so heartbeats, then rose from the chair and walked over to a surface covered with wooden boxes whose shimmering screens were unlike those on any electronic device Theo had ever seen, as though they were not solid at all, but some kind of vertical liquid. Tansy moved his fingers slowly over one of the boxes and the screen rippled and glowed, then he closed the lid. Although he didn't much like Tansy, Theo had to admit these fairies were fascinating to watch. As with the folk in the hunting party, every gesture Tansy made, even the most apparently spontaneous, seemed like something choreographed and practiced. *It's like they've been in some kind of Applied Gracefulness crash course since the second they were born.*

Finished with his first task, the tall fairy pulled open a drawer, then lifted out a silver box the size of a hardbound book and put it on the tabletop. Applecore buzzed over to examine it; after a moment's hesitation, Theo walked over to join her.

"This was delivered yesterday," said Tansy. "The tommy-knocker who carried it was one of the workers from the mine on the far side of our estate. He did not recognize the fairy who gave it to him and bade him bring it here to me. In fact, the knocker said no one had ever seen this stranger within the bounds of the commune."

The box was an ornate thing, the silver chased with designs of birds and tree branches. In the center of the lid was an emblem of a round flower with overlapping petals.

"That's the Hollyhock crest, isn't it?" Applecore asked.

Tansy nodded. "It is. But I don't think it was sent by the family of the young man who was coming for Master Vilmos. Look." Tansy lifted the box's lid, unleashing a waft of spicy smells that held a faint acridity underneath. Inside, nestling on white petals, was a small object the size of a child's fist, wrapped in red paper.

"It's a heart," Tansy said. "Dried and stuffed with rue." He gave a short, sour laugh, but his face was turned away and Theo could not see his expression. "I rather think that means we shouldn't expect your escort, don't you? At least, not any more of him than this."

"Good God, the way he said it—like he didn't care!" Theo sat on the edge of the bed. His legs were still trembling. "Like it meant nothing."

Applecore was perched on top of the screen that looked like part of an air conditioner, vibrating gently. "They're not like us normal folk, those Flowers," she said, then looked up. "What am I saying? You're not like us normal folk, either."

It was almost as hard for Theo to accept the casual way Tansy had dismissed him as it was to have found out that one of the few people in this whole mad world who seemed to have a vested interest in his safety was dead before Theo had even had a chance to meet him. "This all just sucks. What am I supposed to do now?"

"Don't know. He'll talk to you again this evening, he said. Don't push him, Theo, that's my advice. They're a mad shower, the Flower-folk. You can't hurry them after anything."

"But what about me? I didn't want to come here. What am I supposed to do now?" He stood up and began to pace. "What about sending me back? Can you do that?"

She shook her head. "Can't."

"Can't? Or won't?" His voice was rising, even though a part of him was ashamed to realize he was shouting at a woman the size of a salt-shaker. "Doesn't anyone here care that I've just been . . . snatched out of my normal life, without anyone asking me? Just kidnapped, for Christ's sake!"

Dolly stuck her huge, blunt head in through the door. "You're hurting my ears, Pinkie. Sit down and talk nice."

He sat down, clenching his teeth. He might be angry, but he was not stupid enough to argue with a couple of thousand pounds of bone and gristle that, according to Applecore, could run faster uphill than most mortals could sprint downhill.

The little fairy came over and lit on the blanket beside him. "I'm sorry for how things have turned out, but don't go confusing the facts. I didn't kidnap you, I opened a door without explaining it because Tall-Dark-and-Crumbly was going to suck the marrow out of your bones, probably without even taking off the meat first. I didn't fetch that thing down on you, either—it was coming on its own. And when you went through that door, fella, I didn't drag you."

He stared at her for a moment then let his face sink into

his hands. "You're right. I'm sorry. It's just . . ." He sat up. "Look, just . . . talk to me. Maybe we can figure something out. Why can't you send me back to my home? If I stay here, won't that thing find me? That . . . zombie?"

"You're better off here, to tell you the truth. Tansy's got defenses. Besides, it's not that easy, just sending you back—it takes a lot of power, especially when you don't want anyone to notice. Even without the Clover Effect, getting someone through to the other world, it's like . . . like building some big, complicated ship. Takes a long time, a lot of work."

"But you did it once already."

"Because he arranged it. I don't think I could do it by my-self, even if I had a trip left—I'm not a scientist like Count Tansy."

"If he's a scientist, it must be the Dr. Mengele kind. The kind that thinks of people as lab rats." He thought for a mo-ment. "You said before that he couldn't go, and that's why he sent you. Why?"

"That's the Clover Effect, named after some experiment-ing Flower-fella. It's been so ever since we lost the king and queen of Faerie. We used to be able to go back and forth whenever we wanted, although there were some places that were easier for it than others. Now we can only go through to your world and come back here once apiece." She sat down on the comforter and combed her reddish hair out of her eyes with her tiny fingers. "That's our exemption, we call it, that one trip. Works coming from your side, too. Un-less you're pure spirit like that thing that tried to kill you, that is—they can go pretty much wherever they want and then get their meat from wherever they end up, but the rest of us can't. So you need someone like Tansy or his friends to get you back home."

"So I just have to sit around here and hope that your boss has enough magical oomph to keep that monstrosity away from me until he decides what to do with me."

"More or less. Sorry."

Theo slumped back against the headboard of the bed. "So what are you doing working for someone like this Tansy guy?"

"I grew up here on the commune."

"Why is it a commune, anyway? A commune's where everybody's equal or something. Seems to me like the whatever you call 'em, the Flowers are in charge here like everywhere else."

"It's just a name from something back in the old days. The Daisy family used to be radicals, back during the First Unusual Era. They like tradition no matter what, so they kept the name."

"So you live here?"

"Not really. I live in the City now, but my family mostly are still here. We Apples have the freeholding of an orchard and everyone who's at home works in it—even Pip and Seed, my two closest brothers, and they always said they were going to run away because they hated it."

"Your family owns an orchard?"

"Not the land, but like I said, we've got the freehold on the trees. Ten acres' worth," she said proudly. "A thousand trees and more."

"Oh." He nodded. "What kind of trees?"

She rolled her eyes. "My name's Applecore. My da's name is Applewood. Ma's called Applebough. I got brothers and sisters named 'Pip, 'Seed, 'Skin, 'Blossom, to mention a few. One of 'em's even called Applebutter. So what kind of trees do you think they are?"

"Oh. Yeah, I get it."

"Quick as a hummingbird's hind end, aren't you?"

He scowled. "I thought I told you to give me a break. How did someone so little get to be so damn snippy? Is it some fairy-thing? Did your mama dip you in the Nasty River when you were a baby or something?"

She laughed. "One to you, boyo."

"You didn't finish explaining why you're working for Tansy."

"Ah. Well, his cousin Zenion Daisy is the lord of the

manor here on the commune, at least as far as being the one
with the seat in Parliament—he's the one who grants our
freehold. But they're a tricksy lot, these Daisies, still sort of
freethinkers by Flower standards, and they all share in running the place or doing whatever else interests them—
Zenion's sister Dyspurnia actually makes most of the
decisions. Tansy's had me help him out before, mostly gathering herbs or other things—he's mad keen on science but
he's no herbwife. And I've run a few errands for him in the
City, found books he was looking for, obscure charms, like
that. I've had trouble finding much other work in the City,
though, so when he asked me if I'd do this—well, the pay
was good."

"But . . . but why didn't he send someone . . .
someone . . ."

"Bigger?" She scowled. "Don't pretend, you, I know
what you were going to say. Goes to show what you know—
that's why he sent me. The smaller the person going through,
the less disruption, so the less power it takes to send 'em. I'll
bet it still turned all the lights off here when I went, but."

Theo sighed. "So on top of everything else, sending me
back is going to take some huge amount of power or
something?"

"It's not easy," she said. "That's why they call it 'science.'"

"Then I'm just totally screwed." A wave of misery
washed through him. They said you never appreciated your
hometown until you moved away. How about your entire
world?

Applecore looked at him for a long moment. "Tell you
what," she said. "I'll go talk with him—with Tansy. He's
really not a bad fella by Flower standards."

Theo gave her a bleak look. "Yeah, probably hardly ever
beats the servants to death or anything."

"Just quit feelin' so sorry for yourself. Stay here and I'll
be back in a bit." She rose from the bed and hung in the air
for a moment, looking as though she wanted to say some-

thing more, but instead she turned and shot out the door in a fizz of swift-beating wings.

Bored and depressed, Theo got up and began pacing the narrow confines of the room, letting his hand trail along the hangings on the wall, which caressed his skin more like a liquid than like fabric. He stopped in front of the object that looked something like a clock and examined the strange glyphs arranged around the edges of its triangular face. *It sure looks like a clock radio,* he thought. *I could listen to some music while I'm waiting. That would be interesting, wouldn't it? Listening to music invented on an entirely different world?*

He touched one of the small silvered bumps on the surface of the wood, but if it was a button, it didn't do anything obvious. He pressed another, then dropped the object onto the bed in surprise when a voice whispered out of it, asking what sounded like a question in a language he did not understand. The thing bounced a couple of times until it reached the end of its cylindrical cord. The whispering voice said nothing else.

He waited a couple of minutes just to be sure, then picked up the clock radio or whatever it was in his hands and tried another button. At first he thought that this hadn't done anything either, until he realized that the wood was growing smolderingly hot beneath his fingers. He yelped and dropped it onto the bed again. A wisp of smoke rose from where it lay, so he jerked it up off the bed and held it by the cord.

"Shit! What do I do?" he said to himself, out loud—always a bad sign. *Old Tansy'll love me if I burn down the family manor.*

The thing was growing hotter—he could feel it on his exposed skin even with it dangling a foot away. In a growing panic, he shoved the bed a little bit away from the wall with his legs so he could try to reach the outlet while keeping the clock safely away from anything flammable. It was a tight fit, and the clock thing swung toward him as he bent, rummaging awkwardly behind the bed, and bumped against his head. It felt like the time he'd picked up one of Cat's curling irons without noticing it was plugged in and he let out a shriek of pain.

He finally got a grip on the cord down near what looked like an outlet, a rectangle of pale wood set directly into the stone of the wall. He yanked, but the cord did not come loose. The clock swung near his head again and frizzed a lock of his hair into a crisp curl. He braced his hip against the bed and yanked again, as hard as he could. The cord came away with a loud *pop!* and a flash of greeny-blue flame. For a moment he could see a round circle of teal fire still flickering on the outlet plate, then even the hole was gone, leaving nothing behind but smooth wood.

He looked at the cord dangling in his hand. The ivory-smooth knob at the end where it had connected to the outlet was as featureless as if it had just been sawn off the tip of an elephant's tusk.

The clock, or whatever hellish device it might be, was already cool.

Theo stuck his head out into the corridor. Applecore had been gone at least an hour and he was getting crazy with restlessness. Tansy's lab or whatever they'd call it here was down that way, but Theo had no intention of dropping in on him and reinforcing the fairy's dislike of mortals by blundering in at an inopportune moment. He'd just go for a stroll in the other direction. It wasn't like he was a prisoner or anything, was it?

Was it?

He stood in the corridor, wondering why it seemed longer than it had when he had looked down it before. How big could this place be, anyway? Was it the main manor house for the Sunny Days Commune or whatever Applecore had called it—Theo could only remember it had sounded like some kind of organic dairy—or was it a separate building?

Well, finding a window could tell him something, and getting outside into the air would tell him even more.

He glanced up at a bit of sky peeping in through the skylight. It felt like it should be late afternoon, and certainly the oblong of blue overhead looked like that was about right.

Maybe I should leave a trail of crumbs or something, he thought. Which reminded him that he hadn't eaten anything since he'd been in Faerie, nor had he drunk anything except river water, and most of that by accident. *There's a destination, then,* he decided. *I'll hunt for the kitchen.*

Of course, it wound up being a lot more difficult than it looked. The house, most of which seemed to carry on the spare white-stucco-and-color-accents look of the parts he'd seen so far, seemed not just large but oddly unintuitive in the way it was laid out. Every time he thought he'd figured out how it worked and expected to turn a corner and find himself back in a main corridor like the one outside his room, he found himself standing instead at the edge of some kind of sunken living room with a pond and live trees growing through carefully laid-out gaps in the floorboards, or at the door of a walk-in pantry whose shelves were lined with sacks and canisters. Some or even all of these might very well have contained food, but enough of them were jiggling by themselves on the shelf or even making little squeaking noises that he had no interest in closer investigation.

What was even more odd was how some of the rooms disappeared right in front of him, or seemed to, especially those that had windows to the outside world. He would spot a wash of sky peeping through at the far end of a series of linked, open rooms, but when he got to the last room he would find himself looking into another corridor with no window or in fact anything remotely sky-colored in sight. Once he found a sort of parlor room with big, low couches that had a picture window covering one entire wall—he could see an expanse of forested green hill, its crest just touched by the last slanting rays of sunlight, the clouds beginning to turn salmon-pink above it. But when he stepped into the room, the entire window was gone, replaced by a slab of polished black stone. Thinking it might be some kind of polarization trick, he stepped back to the entranceway of the room again, but although the light now gleamed very attractively off the polished surface, it was still opaque black.

Are they trying to keep me from seeing out? Or someone else from seeing me?

He could often hear people talking but could never find any of them. Once he even thought he heard Applecore's clear, high-pitched voice behind a cloth hanging, as though she were in a room just on the other side, but when he swept it back he found nothing but a wall of pale tiles. He heard voices that sounded like the slow, harsh cadences of the ogres, and others stranger still, but they all seemed to float to him from no discernible direction. A few times he wondered if there might be some air-conditioning ducts hidden in the wide wooden roof beams, piping not just air but sound from one part of the house to the other, but if such things did exist, they were hidden beyond his capacity to spot them.

When the lights suddenly dimmed and then went out, Theo had a moment of pure terror. He stopped, as rigid as a mouse when the cat door pops open. The darkness surrounded him like something tangible, something thick, but the abrupt, total silence was even thicker—no whispers, no dull, barely audible humming, just the silence of premature burial. He was suddenly all too aware that he was a stranger in a completely alien place.

Do they have regular blackouts here? He didn't dare move. *Or does it mean something worse?* A picture from one of his childhood books came to him, Theseus in the dark labyrinth, unaware of the brute Minotaur looming behind him.

He had no idea how long it took until the lights in the hallway came up again, but it was longer than he would have liked: the renewal of the phantom voices was as comforting as hearing the kindly neighbors in the next apartment come home.

The return of light and noise did not solve his other problems. He wandered on through rooms that would thrill the editors of *Architectural Digest* while confounding any actual architects, found singing shower-fountains in bathrooms made of what seemed like living but unbarked wood, discovered carpets so thick that they seemed to cling to his feet as if unwilling to let him leave and chattered to him in soft voices he could not quite make out, but still could not find a kitchen, or his own room again, or in fact any other living souls that he could recognize as such.

Panicked into a desperation beyond any fear of embarrassment, he stopped and began to shout: "Applecore? Applecore!" If that truly had been the sprite's voice he had heard earlier through a solid the wall, why shouldn't his own travel the same way? "Applecore? Where are you? Hello! Anyone?"

"What do you want?" asked a feminine voice, cool and collected as a stewardess reciting safety information to a planeload of bored commuters. Theo looked around, but except for a table with an ornamental tree in a rectangular vase, he was alone in the hallway.

"Where are you?" he asked the tree, just in case.

"In the house." As far as he could tell, the calm voice came out of thin air. *"Do you need help?"*

"Yes, yes I think I do. Who are you?"

"I am the hob," the voice said. *"I live in the house. You are one of Count Tansy's guests. How can I help you?"*

Jesus, was that all it took? I wish I'd thought of this earlier. "Can you help me find my way? Like, back to my room, if I wanted?"

"Certainly." It seemed unimpressed, as though it were not quite worth its disembodied time to handle such simple requests.

"How about outside?"

"Outside the house?" Now the dainty voice sounded a bit irritated. *"I'm sorry, you can't leave the house without Count Tansy."*

"Oh." Well, that told him something, anyway. Maybe a bit more than he wanted to know. "How about the kitchen? Can you give me directions to the kitchen?"

"You wish to walk there?"

Theo frowned. "What are my alternatives—rocket skates? Light rail? Yeah, if it's close, I'll walk."

"I could bring it to you if you prefer."

That just plain sounded weird. "No, that's okay, I'll walk."

"Very well. Go forward until you reach the end of this hallway. Turn right, then turn right again immediately."

"Cool. Thanks."

"Enjoy your visit."

He hadn't sensed her arriving, if that was what she'd done, but he did sense her going. It was an odd departure, something barely perceived, like a light going out in a building he'd been watching while thinking of something else.

It's all magic, he thought. *This whole world works on magic. And I don't understand any of it. Man, I'm in trouble here.*

Even with the directions, he had to retrace his steps three times before he found the kitchen, because he did not at first realize that *turn right at the end of the corridor, then turn right again immediately* meant just that. After he had gone up and down the close-ended corridor several times looking for a place to make the second right when there clearly was no such place, he tried to be a bit more literal. He went back to the ornamental tree, then walked to the end of the hall again. As soon as he had made the right turn into the corridor he immediately turned right once more, bracing against the smack in the nose he expected when he hit the wall. But suddenly there was no wall there.

The kitchen was a high room of pale stone and dark floor tiles, huge and warm, agleam with hanging brass pots and pans. At the far end a small bristly figure on a stool was leaning over a huge shiny stovetop, alternating between

shouting up into the rafters and doing something that looked
like conducting opera. Nearer stood a long refectory table.
There were only a few people sitting at it, less than a dozen,
but it looked like a lot more because two of them were ogres.

"Hoy! Pinkie!" shouted Dolly. Her voice made the crock-
ery vibrate in the hutches.

"There goes the neighborhood," rumbled Teddybear.

As Theo stood warily in the doorway the ogres' companions turned and examined him with interest. They were the
size of small children, round-faced and more or less human,
dressed in matching gray uniforms that gave the scene the
air of break time at some Munchkinland fast food restaurant.
The little people had long, curling eyebrows and the
males—Theo thought he was on fairly solid ground here—
sported wide, fluffy beards.

"Can . . . can I come in?" he asked.

"Course you can," said Dolly cheerfully. "We were just
telling the others about you."

"*You* were." Teddybear belched, a drawn-out noise like a
garbage truck hefting a Dumpster. "I was eatin'."

"The lights went out." It was strange to be relieved to see
anything as ugly as the ogre siblings. "Or did that happen
only where I was?"

"Happens all the time these days," said Teddybear.
"Power plant workers having a little holiday or something.
Somebody needs to grind a few of those lazy bastards into
jelly."

"You hungry?" Dolly asked Theo.

"Not for jelly," he said. "Not now."

"Come join us." She gestured for him to sit next to her
and pulled a basket full of bread closer to the edge of the
table. She elbowed her brother to move over, leaving a tiny
sliver of bench between the massive gray bodies. The little
people watched avidly as Theo wiggled into the space.

It's like taking my bike in between two semis, he thought.
If either one of 'em twitches, I'll be nothing but a smear. He
settled in gingerly. "Yeah, actually I am sort of hungry."

"Are you allowed to eat?" the ogress asked as the little people whispered among themselves.

"Allowed?"

"Isn't there something about mortals eating our food and then their heads blow up or something?"

"What?"

Teddybear shook his head. "Gah, Doll, you talk a load of old few mets sometimes. Their heads don't blow up—that's silly. They turn purple all over and die. And it's not just from eating—it happens even if they just put some stone in their mouth or even just jump over some branches. Mortals can die from doing just about anything here."

Theo, who had been reaching for a piece of bread, pulled back his hand. "What are you talking about? Is this a joke?"

One of the little people on the far side of the table stood up on the bench so his head was on the same level as Theo's. "They're giving you a bad time, Stepstool." He sounded like he'd just won the helium breathing finals. "Mortals don't die from eating our food, they just can't go back to Mortalia again."

"Mortalia?" one of the others asked.

"Where mortals come from," the first little man explained smugly.

"What the hell does a brownie know?" demanded Teddybear. He sounded angry, but considering that he could have stuffed half a dozen of the little people into his mouth at one time, they didn't seem very alarmed. "You're all idiots. Our mum told us the story. All about this mortal boy named Percy Faun, and how he covered himself with grease so he could slip through the door to here from . . . from the mortal place. He ate some pommy granite and died."

"Mortals don't eat rocks, sodskull." Dolly rolled her eyes. "Do they, Pinkie? You don't eat rocks, do you?"

Theo's hands were now in his lap. Despite the cramping of his empty stomach, he didn't want to touch anything that might be food. His head blowing up might be a fitting end to a very difficult day, but although he doubted that would really happen, he didn't feel like taking any chances—especially with the possibility of not being able to go home. "No," he said. "No, we don't eat rocks."

"All right, it wasn't granite then," said Teddybear. "Miss Clever. But it was something like that. He ate it, then he tried to go home but he fell over some sticks and died."

"You said they turned purple," Dolly pointed out. "Mortals, I mean."

"Fell over some sticks, turned purple, then died."

Theo could only sit and listen to his stomach rumble while they argued over the top of him. The brownies seemed to think it was all very funny.

13

A CHANGE
IN THE WEATHER

"Of course you can bloody well eat," Applecore informed him as she led him down the hall from the kitchen toward Tansy's lab. "What else are you going to do, ya thick, live on air?"

"But . . . but the ogres said . . ."

"Ogres!" She buzzed across the antechamber so briskly he almost had to run to keep up. "There's a reason Tansy didn't send one of them after you, you know. Even Dolly, and she's a bleedin' genius by ogre standards, couldn't find her arse with both hands and a treasure map. And our Teddy can't count to eleven without unbuttoning his trousers." She gave him a tiny shove toward the door into the lab. Inside his host stood waiting, arms crossed on his chest. "He hasn't eaten anything since he's been here, sir," Applecore announced, "because the ogres have been giving him some old shite about how it will keep him from getting home again."

"What?" Tansy appeared startled, as if he had been miles away. "Oh, he hasn't eaten?" He spoke to the air. "Fetch in some food for Master Vilmos."

"*Certainly, Count Tansy,*" said the sweetly reasonable hob-voice.

"I'm very sorry," Tansy told Theo. "When you first arrived,

I was quite . . . absorbed. I should have asked you if you had eaten. Terrible way to treat a guest. My apologies."

Theo could not help staring. A few hours earlier the fairy had looked at him like he was a bug. Now he was treating him like a real guest. What the hell was that about? "I . . . I just . . ." It took a moment to shake off his surprise. "Dolly and her brother, they told me that if I eat here, I can't go back. It's some old story, apparently."

Tansy nodded. "It's just that, I'm afraid—an old story. I have no doubt it has some basis in truth, mind you. I would guess that in the old days, when there was little to inhibit travel between your lands and ours, it was easier for a mortal to dally here and forget to cross back, so that by the time he returned the slippage would have meant a terrible dislocation on his return."

"Slippage?"

"Yes, the differences between our two worlds. The passage of time is perhaps the most obvious symptom, but not the only one. But eating or not eating has nothing to do with whether or not a traveler may return, then or now. I suspect it was a sort of ploy devised by wise mortals to keep your kind from staying here too long. If they left without eating, and hence only stayed as long as they could last on an empty stomach, the disruption would not be too great."

"Disruption?"

A female brownie had walked silently into the room wheeling a cart with a tray on it—at least, Theo assumed she'd walked, although he hadn't actually seen her enter. She was plump and rosy-cheeked and quite ordinary in her proportions, as though someone had simply shrunk a slightly short-legged young woman to about three and a half feet high. "Where, sir?" she asked.

Tansy nodded toward a low table.

The brownie put the tray of fruit and bread on a table, dropped a curtsy, then pushed her cart back out of the room. The fairy-lord gestured for Theo to take the leather-cushioned chair next to the table, which had a casual elegance that suggested it was Tansy's own. Theo seated himself a little apprehensively. Applecore squatted down beside the plate, sniffing. "Ooh, eglantine honey," she said. "That's nice, but."

"Help yourself." He turned back to Tansy. "So it's really all right if I eat?" He didn't want to be stubborn, but it was hard to believe the cool-eyed creature of a few hours earlier was suddenly itching to be his buddy-old-pal. "I'll still be able to go back home?"

"Eating this or any other wholesome food will have no effect on whether or not you can go back," Tansy said. "I swear by the Oldest Trees."

Theo looked to Applecore for a clue as to what was going on, but she didn't seem worried for him. In fact, she was scooping huge dollops of butter and honey off his bread with her hands and licking them off, so the food certainly wasn't poisoned or anything that crude.

"What did he call you, a sprite?" Theo asked her. "Is the definition by any chance, 'Mouth like a sailor, manners like a tiny flying pig'?"

She grinned behind a smear of honey. "Shut up and eat, you great big waster."

He broke off a corner of bread and picked a fruit that looked like a salmon-colored cherry. The bread tasted like bread (only much better) but the fruit was like nothing else he'd ever had, the bold sweetness undercut by a certain perfumed tang—a wonderful, exotic flavor. He was reminded again that he was starvingly hungry and he scooped up a whole handful.

"As I said, I'm very sorry for my earlier . . . abruptness," Tansy proclaimed. "I was preoccupied. But I have given the matter more thought and realized that it is still important for my principals to meet you, and also that you should not be left to fend for yourself in what must be a very disconcerting new world."

Theo still didn't trust the situation. Tansy was fairly convincing as a nice guy but it was hard to ignore the earlier behavior; Theo couldn't help wondering what might have happened during the course of the day to change things. Or was that just what these Flowers were like, these high-powered fairy-folk—able to shut off or turn on simulated emotions at will, like real-world sociopaths? It wasn't the most comfortable thought.

Either I'm paranoid or they're totally freaky. Two great choices.

"Could you just send me back instead?" he asked. "I mean, no offense, but I didn't want to come here in the first place. I really don't need to meet anyone . . ."

"Ah, but you do." Tansy smiled brightly. Theo thought for a disturbing moment that the ascetic, white-haired creature was going to walk over and chummily thump him on the back. "Surely you haven't forgotten about the spirit who found you in your home and attacked you."

"Not much chance of that."

"That sort of entity will not be long thrown off your scent, and could not be avoided forever even if you could cross back and forth between your world and ours every day. As it is, once you have settled back down into your normal life again it will easily find you. And next time you will not have Mistress Applecore to help you, or a door through which to escape."

Theo remembered the thing's raw face and oozing eyes; he suddenly felt clammy under the arms. "So what are you saying? That it's just going . . . going to *get* me someday? No matter what?"

"We hope not. But it will take a more cunning mind than mine, or a better equipped laboratory, to find exactly what the thing is and remove it or placate it. That is another reason why you should go to my friends in the City. They are better connected than I am, closer to the seats of power . . . and that means all sorts of power. I have chosen the life of a poor country philosopher and scientist, you see."

"You said, 'Another reason.' What's the first reason?" Theo suddenly wondered if Tansy or his allies might have set the corpse-thing on him themselves, just to make sure he did what they wanted. "Why me? You said there were these, I don't know, groups. Political parties. And one of them wanted to talk to me or something. Why?"

"I am not at liberty to disclose too much, in case you . . ." Tansy hesitated, then began again. "You see, you will have to travel a long way, and . . ." Apparently deciding this was just as unproductive a tangent, he pulled a stool out from behind one of the equipment-covered tables and sat down on it, his long legs bent at the knees. He wore what looked like very expensive fawn suede slippers, with no socks. "Let me explain a little." He pulled out his glasses and put them on, then leaned over to look at a display on one of his desktop instruments. He waved his hand over it and the screen changed from silvery to a sparkling blue-green; a cloud of mist drifted up from the screen but quickly evaporated as he turned back to Theo and Applecore.

"Your race, Master Vilmos, and my race have lived in each other's shadows a long, long time. Not always in harmony, it has to be said. When we first noted the rise of your kind, there were some of our folk who thought we should . . ." He paused.

"Thought you should what?" Theo demanded. "Wipe us out like bugs?"

Tansy waved a negligent hand. "Let's not get sidetracked."

"Sidetracked? Like, that's a small matter?"

"The fact is, despite early doubts, our two races have managed to share the world a long time—not the world as you know it, I should make clear, but the world as we *both* know it. It is not really one world, you see. They overlap. Or, rather, they coexist, your world and our world, although not always in the physical plane."

"Physical plane? Overlapping worlds?" Theo was irritated by Tansy skipping over what was clearly an important part of the story, namely the actual desire of some fairies to bump off all the humans. He was being treated like a child, which made him want to act like one on purpose. "This is beginning to sound like astrology or something," he said, slouching back in the chair. "I hate that stuff. I had a girl-friend once who was always telling me that I was retrograde or something when what she really meant was that I was being an asshole."

Tansy's smile regained a little of its earlier wintry chill. "Yes. Well. Without going into too much detail, in deference to your undoubted fatigue, suffice it to say that while our two races used to share the physical and metaphysical bounty of the world very closely, we have grown apart over the years and our needs have changed. I suppose the easiest way to say it is that your people now take much more from the earth than we do—and I am not talking about the spin-ning globe, the actual planet with its topsoil and air, but about something a bit more intangible. In a way, it is like two towns built on the same lake. Your town has begun to pump away a far larger share of the clean water, and to re-turn those waters to the lake fouled."

"This is about pollution?" He bit down on a pit and gri-maced. None of the other fairy-fruits had contained pits. He spat it out carefully into his hand and put it on the corner of the plate. Applecore, who had eaten quite a bit of honey and a few berries, rose unsteadily into the air and lit on Theo's shoulder.

"Nothing so simplistic or so . . . physical . . ." said Tansy, "but the analogy may stand. Let us say simply that you mor-tals are overutilizing and befouling our shared environ-ment." He leaned back in his chair and looked over the tops of his glasses. "It has a great deal to do with changing beliefs."

"Huh?"

"Changing beliefs, or more specifically, the diminishing of belief in what you call magic in your world, and which we think of as the true science. There have been several nexus points when things have changed in both worlds, some of them you would undoubtedly recognize as important mile-stones in your own world, when things have grown rapidly and significantly worse here. Most of these nexus points have had to do with voyages of discovery or moments of human innovation, but some simply with the brutalization of imagination there and the atrophy of childhood. Each point significantly changed your world and simultaneously reduced the power available to us here, and thus made our lives harder and emptier. Your last hundred years have been the worst of all for us.

"When it was realized what was happening, several changes came to our society. One was that we began to try new methods to use our resources more effectively, forcing us in a way to ape your race's path—what you call 'progress.' Another was that debating how to respond to these changes became the dominant political issue of our society, at least among those of us farsighted enough to recognize the problem."

"Or those with time on their hands because they don't have to work for a living," Applecore whispered loudly in Theo's ear. Oddly, she sounded a little tipsy, although he hadn't seen her drink even water.

"Thus," Tansy continued, "we have our major parties in this disagreement. First there are the Symbiotes, who believe that the continued rise of humanity is inevitable and that we must therefore find a way to live in the shadow of your race and subsist on your leavings—much like certain birds and fish who clean the hides or teeth of larger and more dangerous animals. The Symbiotes themselves put a braver face on it, but it is really nothing more than parasitism."

"He's talking about those Creepers I told you about," whispered Applecore.

"Then there are the extremists on the opposite side, those who believe there can be no accommodation with a race like yours—with a species that does not even recognize what it is on the verge of destroying. These are the Excisors." He frowned at Applecore. "The 'Chokeweeds,' as commoners call them."

"Yep." She giggled. "Chokeweeds!"

"The Excisors believe the only solution is to remove ourselves from the influence of your kind entirely. To be fair, there are some few in this group—scientists and philosophers for whom I have respect—who would like to find a way simply to separate your race and ours so that we could each live unaffected by the other, but they are the minority. Most of the rest would like to destroy, disrupt, or subjugate your civilization. Lately they seem to be losing patience with the normal and legitimate workings of the Parliament of Blooms. It is feared that they may even seek a more direct confrontation with those of us who disagree."

Theo was doing his best to make sense of this—it was similar to what Applecore had told him, but had more long words in it. "And you're part of which group . . . ?"

"As I said before, I think, I am one of the Coextensives—believers in a middle path. We feel we must find a way to live with your kind, but not necessarily simply by giving in. We have been active in various small ways even in your world, influencing events where we can. We have some surprisingly well-connected friends."

"Rich mortal loonies," Applecore whispered loudly, then laughed so hard that she slipped off Theo's shoulder and had to beat her wings hard to keep from falling to the floor. She hovered near his elbow, still chortling. "Humans who want . . . to believe . . . in *fairies!*" She did a midair loop. "Eejits!"

Theo looked at her, worried.

"Oh, by the name of . . ." Tansy stared at Applecore's oscillating flight. "Hob? Hob? When were those berries picked?"

"Last autumn, sir," the bodiless voice responded. *"When they were ripe."*

"Curses. The fermentation pixies must have gotten into them, at least enough to make the sprite here drunk as a selkie on shore leave." He got up and walked over to one of the standing cabinets, then pulled open the drawer. "There, you wayward dot, there is a pile of towels. Lie down and sleep it off."

Applecore bumbled around near Theo's face for a moment. "Not much weight, see," she said. "Me, I mean. Don't take much . . . that's what all the boys say . . ." She hiccuped. "Don't let him give you any of those berries," she told Theo in a stage whisper. "They're mad!" The sprite flew unsteadily toward the drawer and disappeared into it. Within moments Theo could hear a soft but incredibly high-pitched snore, like someone drawing a bow back and forth above the bridge of a violin.

"Well, after that interruption, I've forgotten what I was saying." Tansy shook his head.

"Something about the party you support . . . ?"

"Ah, the Coextensives. Well, we have our own agenda, but we definitely eschew the extremes. Desperate, violent measures are not needed. Not yet, anyway, and not for the foreseeable future. But neither can we simply let our destinies be written by other hands."

Theo heard the unmistakable beginnings of a party political commercial. "But what about me? Where do I fit into all this?"

Tansy swiveled toward him, clearly annoyed, then carefully made his face neutral again. "Ah, yes. You, Master Vilmos."

So he's not that good at hiding his feelings, after all, Theo decided. *Or else he's playing an even weirder game than I thought.*

"I can't tell you what my contacts want of you—and that is not by my choice," the fairy added hurriedly. "It is because I do not know. Some of the most important members of Parliament are involved, both Coextensives and Symbiotes, and they have not made me privy to the substance of their interest. But they want to see you."

"It's probably about my great-uncle's book," Theo said. "Why don't you just give that to them? If they're happy with it, then they can let me go home."

Tansy shook his head. "Sadly, it does not work that way. My orders were explicit—to send you to the City where they could meet with you in person. They were . . . most forceful about that."

Theo suddenly realized that Tansy's change of attitude might have come about because he had talked with these superior, powerful folk and they had let him know that they very much still wanted to see Theo, late or not. *Which means what? That I have a little power in this situation?* But if so, he didn't want to waste it with Tansy, who (whether or not he was faking this newfound courtesy) was beginning to seem like a mere functionary.

"So I have to go?"

Tansy nodded, almost a small bow. "I regret it, but yes, you must."

"But they killed the first person who was coming to escort me, you said. Someone definitely killed him. How am I going to find this place I'm supposed to go to, and how am I going to get past whatever killed that Hollyhock guy? And what if that dead thing comes after me again?"

"Yes, those are all problems. I have been thinking on the matter carefully. To show you how seriously I take this situation, and how I regret my earlier behavior—I really was very distracted, as I believe I told you—I will send a member of my own family with you."

"Thanks, but I think I'd rather have one of the ogres. They may not be the best company, but I bet nobody would f . . ." He paused to rephrase. "I bet nobody would mess with me if I had an ogre along."

Tansy shook his head. "Oh, no, most unsuitable. For one thing, they are needed here. They are personal bodyguards on loan to me from my brother—not to mention that they are of great help moving equipment here in the lab. For another, you betray your ignorance of our society. To travel with ogres in attendance is to signal yourself part of the highest Flower nobility and thus to attract attention. Someone would very quickly wonder why an unknown like you could afford two such large and dangerous servants."

"Oh, and they won't notice me without them?"

"Not if you wear the proper clothes and we make some other adjustments to disguise your appearance as well. Mostly it is your color, that brash, brownish tone to your skin. It makes you look like a laborer."

"Well, that describes my general position in society pretty well. If you add 'boneheaded' and 'ungrateful' to it."

Tansy gave him a sour look. "I will have all the details seen to, so there is no need for worry. I will send someone to help you with disguising yourself."

"Okay, we hide my tan so people think I'm an ordinary middle-class fairy." Theo shook his head. "This all makes me feel like this trip is going to be a little more dangerous than you've been letting on. Who's this relative you're going to send with me?"

"Do not worry, Master Vilmos—it will be easier than you fear. Come to me in the morning when you are up and dressed and we will finish the preparations." Tansy turned his back on Theo and then seemed to remember himself. "Can you find your way back to your room by yourself, Master Vilmos? Hob can take you straight there or give you directions."

"That would help. Otherwise you might never see me again."

"Yes, that's true." He said it quite seriously. "By the way, would you take this inebriated sprite with you? I have work to do."

Theo picked Applecore out of the drawer and cradled her in his hand. Her little eyes opened blearily for a moment, then she let out a minuscule belch, smiled, and went back to sleep.

"They are like starlings," said Tansy, frowning. "Never silent, and rude as can be."

Theo felt an urge to defend his only friend in this other-

worldly place, but from his own experience he had to admit
the fairy lord was speaking the truth.

"Ow!" "Hold still—you wouldn't want me to pull your
face off by accident, would you?"

When an ogre said something like that to you, even a
comparatively friendly one like Dolly, you paid attention.
Theo held still. "So you're the expert Tansy said he'd send
to make me up, huh? Ow! Careful, you're smashing my
nose!"

"By the Oldest Trees!" groaned Applecore, slumped on
the bedside table. "Can you two not talk without shouting at
the top of your bleeding lungs!"

"Someone's hungover," said Dolly, grinning. "It's funny
when the wee ones drink."

"Ha ha," agreed Applecore. "You great gray shower of
shite."

Theo didn't say anything at all because Dolly was rubbing white cream onto his face—and right through his skin
onto the bones, it felt like—with a gray thumb the size and
texture of an unpeeled avocado. For a moment he thought
she'd pushed his lips all the way around to the side of his
head, then he realized they'd just gone numb from the pressure. "What the hell is that stuff?" he asked when she let up
for a moment.

"White lead," Dolly told him. "It's what I always use
when I want to look like I don't have to work for a living."

"Lead! That's poisonous, isn't it? Do you want to kill
me?" Theo tried to struggle away.

"No, not after all the work I've done on you," Dolly told
him. "But I'd be happy to pinch your face up until everyone
thinks you're a Stroke Boy, then it won't matter what color
you are."

"It's too high up here," Applecore announced and flew

unsteadily down from the bedside table to the floor, where she began walking in eccentric circles like a smoke-stunned yellow jacket. "I feel like death, don't I," she moaned. "How could you let me do that?"

"Let you? I didn't even know it was happening." Theo turned his head to peer at the clock, then remembered he couldn't read it. "What time is it?"

"What are you looking at that for?" the ogre asked.

"Isn't it a clock?" They both looked blank. "You know, a thing to tell time?"

"A thing to tell time what?" Dolly looked at Applecore, who shrugged, uninterested in anything but the pain in her head. "My, you pink folk do have strange ideas. No, it's a charm-casket."

Theo tried to rub some blood back into his temples, where he felt certain he now had ogre-prints the size of beer coasters. "What the hell is a charm-casket?"

"Just something that will give you any little charms or cantrips you might need—direction-finders or hair-straighteners or love-stiffeners." She poked his side until he squeaked. "That what you were looking for, Pinkie?"

"Jeez. No wonder I almost burned the place down trying to get the radio to play. So how do you tell what time it is?"

"Those big round things in the sky." Dolly smirked. "Sun? Moon? You may have seen them."

"Okay, so I'm ignorant. We do it differently back home. Just tell me what time it is, will you?"

"Sunwise it's midmorning," Applecore declared. "You can tell because the light is pure poison and it stabs into your eyes like knives." She found a spot back against the wall. "Also because it's the time of day when ogres and mortals talk the most shite. Oog. Even my hair hurts."

"There," said Dolly. "I think he's done. Not top quality, but what can you expect?"

"I'm sure you did the best you could," Theo said generously, looking for a mirror.

"I'm talking about you, not the paint-up." Dolly smacked

him with a powder puff until he was choking, then brushed
off the excess with astonishing gentleness. "All done. Here."
She reached into a pocket of the voluminous something-or-
other she wore and produced a surprisingly small hand mirror; it seemed no bigger than a poker chip in her huge gray
paw. For a moment Theo wondered why she would carry
such a small thing, then realized that mirrors for ogres must
not be very commonly made—for obvious reasons. She'd
taken a fairy-sized mirror and made it her own. As he took
it from her he was suddenly and uncomfortably full of what
felt like pity.

He definitely looked . . . different. Dolly had curled his
longish brown hair and put something in it that made it look
more golden. The white grease had been applied with more
care than it had felt like from his end, rubbed in until it made
his skin seem palely translucent. That and a subtle brushing
of rouge brought out his cheekbones and narrow nose—his
"Vulcan features" as Cat used to call them.

"I look . . . okay," he said. "Not perfect, but . . . surprisingly realistic."

"You're very welcome," said Dolly.

"Sorry. Thanks, yeah."

"Oog," said Applecore. "Does that mean I have to drag
myself up now? Or can I take another few minutes and get
on with dying?"

As Theo pulled on the clothes that Tansy had sent for
him, a pair of boots and some loose and serviceable earth-
toned garments that he doubted came from the lord's own
closets, but more likely had been commandeered from one
of the more human-shaped servants, Dolly continued to
admire her handiwork. "You do look rather sweet, if I say
so myself." She grinned hugely, revealing teeth like
crooked shower tiles. "How about a kiss for good luck
then, Theo-lad?"

Theo was seized with panic, but it was a strangely familiar panic, the fear of someone who wanted things to be easy
when they never, never were. "You know," he said after a

long moment, "I'm really grateful that you did this and all, but . . . but you're not really my type, Dolly. Sorry."

She looked at him and her smile tightened. "You don't have much of a sense of humor, do you, Pinkie?" She stood up; her head almost touched the low ceiling. For a terrifying moment Theo thought she was going to wad him up like a candy bar wrapper. "In fact, I think you're a bit shallow, you know that?" She turned to Applecore. "See you when you get back from the station." She left the room with elephantine dignity.

"She's right, but," said the sprite, rising up from the floor like a helicopter with a bent rotor. "She didn't mean nothing by it—she was only messing. You must be a deft hand with the ladies back home."

"Yeah, whatever. I'm sorry. Aren't we supposed to be meeting Tansy?" It was bad enough having everyone back in the real world look at him like he was a complete loser— now it was starting to happen to him in Fairyland as well.

"Oh, 'course, wouldn't want to hold you up." She sounded angry.

As they walked down the hall—a different hall, Theo felt sure, but it had taken the place of the one that had been outside his door the previous night—he suddenly caught up to Dolly's parting comment. "What did she mean, 'see you when you get back from the station'?"

"Just because you act like an utter mean eejit sometimes doesn't mean I wouldn't see you off," Applecore said quietly. "I'm not spiteful, meself."

"You mean . . . you're not going with me?"

"Go with you? Back to the City? That's why Tansy's sending one of his relatives with you. What good would I be? Besides, this is where my family lives, I'm just back, and I owe my ma and da a good long visit."

"Oh." He was a bit stunned—no, worse than that: he was devastated. He had taken it for granted that Applecore would go with him.

By the time they reached Tansy's lab Theo was feeling

very depressed and could barely muster the strength to respond to the count's greeting. Another fairy was with him, one who seemed somehow a bit younger (as far as could be told with such ageless faces) and was certainly a bit plumper, which meant he was built like a slender mortal. And he actually smiled, although he did not go so far as to extend his hand to Theo.

"This is my cousin, Rufinus weft-Daisy," Tansy explained as he led them across the house. The day was dark outside the long windows, the sky streaked with charcoal-colored clouds. "He's going to accompany you to the city."

"Rather exciting it will be, too," said Rufinus. "Quite secretive. Like the old days of the last Flower War."

Tansy gave him an irritated look. "Something which you were not yet alive to see. In any case, let's not have any talk like that where outsiders can hear. It won't do to set people thinking."

"Yes, yes, certainly." Rufinus gave a vigorous nod. "Quite right, Cousin Quillius."

Oh, my God, Theo thought miserably. *I'm going off into horrible danger with an Upper-Class Twit for a bodyguard.*

"Now, in just a moment Heath will bring the coach around to take you to the station . . ."

"Coach?"

". . . And thus," Tansy told Theo sternly, "we do not have much time for chat. Cousin Rufinus will have ways of getting in touch with me, but on the very small chance that you two should become separated, I suppose you should be able to reach me, too. Using public communications may not be feasible, so . . ."—he reached into the breast pocket of his white coat—". . . I want you to have this."

Theo stared dumbly at the tiny leather case for a moment. At last, since it seemed expected of him, he flicked it open. A piece of golden filigree lay cushioned in the velvet interior, a slightly abstract sculpture of a bird about the width and length of two extended fingers. "What . . . what is it?" he asked at last.

"It is what we call a shell. It will give your words wings," said Tansy complacently. "Open the case and speak to it when you are in dire need and I will speak back to you."

"Oh. It's kind of like . . . a cellular phone?"

Tansy frowned ever so slightly. "It is a scientific instrument. Treat it with respect." He regained his bonhomie as they reached the large, sand-colored entry hall whose main feature was a sweeping minimalist staircase. Theo hadn't realized the house had an upper story. If in fact it did. "Hob," Tansy said, "has Heath come with the coach?"

"He is waiting in the courtyard."

"Then your adventure is just about to begin, Master Vilmos." Tansy smiled. He was pretty good at it, but still not quite convincing. "Come—I will show you the way to the front doors."

My adventure? Theo could not help remembering other great euphemisms of the past, such as a high-school girlfriend telling him that breaking up would be "a learning experience."

The dark clouds had rolled in overhead, turning morning's glow to a midday twilight and filling the air with the wet smell of an approaching storm. It seemed to match the change for the worse in Theo's mood. If he had half-hoped that Dolly and Teddybear and some of the other household folk would come out to bid him farewell, he was disappointed. In fact, even Tansy did not seem to want to linger too long in the outside air. As they piled into the back of the coach, which turned out to be something that looked just like a slightly old-fashioned beige Town Car, indistinguishable (except for some extravagant bits of silver and gold ornament) from a vehicle that Theo might have seen idling in a pickup lane at San Francisco Airport during his boyhood, Tansy spoke quickly.

"You'll do fine. Rufinus knows just where to go—don't you, Rufinus?"

"Most certainly, Cousin." Young weft-Daisy laughed in a confident sort of way.

Theo shook his head in a mixture of confusion and resignation. He had many more questions to ask, but Applecore was crawling across his shoulder trying to get onto one of the backseat headrests and Rufinus was bashing him painfully in the shins with a huge suitcase he had dragged into the car. By the time Theo had figured out what was going on, Tansy had already slammed the door and retreated into the house, which looked much more normally shaped on the outside than he would ever have dreamed, a long modernist manor of pale stone, pagoda roofs, and not-quite-transparent glass.

Theo flinched as a nightmarish face peered in on Rufinus' side of the car. It had a long, horselike muzzle and was a sort of pearly gray-green, a skin color that went nicely with its crisp navy blue suit and cap. It had huge nostrils but no eyes. "Can I take that bag for you, governor?" it asked Rufinus. The arms that came through the car window ended in gloved hands rather than hooves, although the fingers were thick and spatulate. "I'll put it in the back."

"Most kind, Heath," said the young fairy with lordly condescension. "Just that one—I'll keep the smaller one with me."

When the strange greenish creature had disappeared around toward the trunk of the car, Theo let out his breath. "What . . . what is he?"

"Too loud by half," growled Applecore from her perch on top of the headrest as Heath thumped the suitcase into the trunk. The sprite was apparently still feeling the effects of her overindulgence.

Rufinus leaned toward Theo. "Of course, you're a stranger here. Heath is a doonie. They are terrible ones for the drink, doonies—fermented mare's milk is their tipple, don't you know—but extremely loyal. And they're excellent drivers, of course."

"Excellent . . . ? But he doesn't have any eyeballs!"

"Ah, but he smells extremely well."

"I've smelled better." Applecore was lying back with her eyes closed. "Ooh, the bleeding Trees, me head still throbs."

"Oh . . . my . . . God," Theo said quietly to himself as the chauffeur with no eyes climbed into the front seat and pulled out of the courtyard and its circular road, tires spitting gravel.

Oddly enough, Heath did indeed prove to be a very good driver; after a few minutes, even Theo had to admit that perhaps vision was an overrated commodity in the chauffeur business. Whether it was his excellent sense of smell that allowed him to do it, or some other strange trick beyond Theo's understanding, he kept squarely to the middle of the country lanes, made the turns without anyone shouting, "Hey, you, go right!" and stopped in plenty of time for processions of small strange animals Theo largely didn't recognize to cross the road in front of them.

Applecore had slid down from the headrest and crawled across the seat to find a more stable spot to sleep off her headache, curled on top of Rufinus' coat. The young fairy lord had opened his valise, which seemed to be a sort of laptop computer or the equivalent, though what it looked like was a shallow box full of mercury that eddied and rippled but somehow never spilled over the edges. Tansy's cousin watched its sparkling movements avidly and closely, talking and even laughing to himself, waving his fingers above it.

"Reading my mail," he explained when he saw Theo staring.

The skies stopped merely threatening and began more active intimidation. The first drops of rain splattered against the windshield like fat rotten berries and within moments Heath had set the windshield wipers ticking back and forth. Outside whatever beauty made this Fairyland as opposed to just Any-Old-Land was obscured by gray light and swirling rains.

In other circumstances Theo might have wondered why a

blind driver needed windshield wipers, but at the moment he was using all his energy just being miserable.

It was nothing so simple as homesickness, although he was feeling that in spades, or even simple terror, which was in excellent supply as well. Dolly's remark about his shallowness was working away in the pit of his stomach. Was it true? Even Applecore was so disenchanted with him that she wasn't going to cut short a visit with her folks to spend time with him.

So I'm supposed to be a hero, a diplomat, what? I didn't ask to come here. I didn't ask to have any of this happen. Just because I've got the brains to say, "This sucks" instead of pretending it's some kind of wonderful fairy-tale trip, does that make me a bad guy?

Cat's pale face hovered in his thoughts, her dogged determination to add to the legend of Theo the Useless even from her hospital bed: *"It's always the same. You're thirty years old but you act like a teenager. The shit you start and never finish. Your going-nowhere job . . ."*

He had to concede a few points, but he wasn't ready to give in completely. Besides, when people said you were acting like a teenager, didn't that usually mean they were jealous because you had more freedom than they did? Was having an all-consuming job you didn't like very much, like Cat's, somehow proof of being a grown-up, or proof of having given up on the possibility of better things?

Well, nobody has to worry about my own going-nowhere job, because I don't have it anymore. And as for going nowhere in general, I've certainly gone somewhere now, haven't I? He sighed.

The horselike face of Heath the driver surveyed him in the rearview mirror—or seemed to: it was hard to tell with no eyes there to meet his. "You're the mortal, aren't you?"

"Isn't it obvious?"

"Not really. You smell a little foreign, but that's true with a lot of people who've been traveling, if you get what I mean."

"Yeah, I guess." Desperate for something to alleviate his gloom, Theo seized on the age-old diversion of Talking to the Driver. *Suicidally bored mandarins probably did this with the rickshaw guys back in ancient China,* he thought. "So how does someone get a job like yours?"

"Ah, you know, it's kind of in the family. My dad and granddad were both hackies. That's what we do, a lot of us."

"Doonies, you mean? Have I got that right?"

"Yeah, exactly. We all used to be road-guardians—each family would have their own patch and they'd take care of it, live off small offerings, reward good or kind travelers and punish bad ones, like that. Then the Flowers up in the City decided to begin building the Interdomain Highway System and . . . well, we doonies fought it. Organized ourselves, pleaded our case in front of the Parliament, you name it. I suppose a few roads might have got torn up as well." He shrugged, a gesture that looked strange until Theo realized he didn't have the same kind of shoulders as a human. "Anyway, we lost. Now the roads belong to all of Faerie, they say. Whatever that means. It don't mean doonies, I'll tell you that for free. So we made the best of it—it was a while ago. A lot of us started driving, like my granddad. We do like being near the roads, still."

There was a note of loss in his voice that Theo recognized very clearly. "And how long have you been driving for Count Tansy?"

"Well, not for him as such, y'see, but for the Daisy clan. Pretty much all my life. My dad hooked up with them in the old lord's day, would have been . . . six hundred years ago? Give or take a few decades."

Theo had to swallow before he could say anything else. "And how . . . how are they to work for?"

Heath darted a quick if eyeless glance at the other side of the mirror. Rufinus was still chortling to himself over his valise. "Oh, fine, fine. Better than most. Treat you pretty good, almost like one of the family."

"Urgh," said Applecore. She levered herself upright and

peered blearily from the folds of Rufinus' coat, then clambered slowly onto Theo's leg and up his sleeve, her wings waggling slowly. "I feel like a bugbear just shat inside me skull." From her new perch on Theo's shoulder she squinted out the rainy window at the wet country lane. "Where are we? We've gone way past Oxeye Station."

"We're not going there," said Rufinus without looking up from his shimmering valise. "Cousin Quillius thought it would be a bad idea—that if someone should be looking for us, they'd certainly be looking for any trains coming into the terminal from Oxeye—it is the Daisy station, after all. So Heath is driving us all the way to Penumbra Station. It should be usefully crowded because of the holiday. It's Mabon the day after tomorrow," he said to Theo by way of explanation. "The trains will be very full."

"Fairy trains," said Theo, still not quite used to the idea, even while riding in a fairy limousine. "And what the hell is a Mabon?"

"Stop the coach," said Applecore suddenly. "Quick!"

"What?" Rufinus frowned. "You heard what I said—Cousin Quillius wants us to go all the way to . . ."

"Stop the coach!"

"Why?" asked Theo, beginning to panic. "What's wrong?"

"I'm going to be bloody sick, that's why!" groaned Applecore, then immediately proved it.

As Rufinus hurriedly opened the window and began flapping his hand to get some air into the backseat and counteract the slight but acrid smell, Applecore wiped her mouth with her arm and looked at the small mess she had made down the shoulder of Theo's jacket.

"Sorry," she said sullenly. "It was those be-damned berries."

Theo sighed and tried not to look at it. He was in a car being driven by a green pony-man with no eyes, he was spattered with cold rain and pixie barf, and was about to be deserted by his only friend so he could continue on to an unfamiliar city with a companion right out of a Monty Python sketch. He tried to imagine a way the words "fairy tale" could be stretched to this meaning without destroying it entirely. He failed.

"Yeah, well," he told Applecore. "One of those days, I guess."

14

PENUMBRA STATION

"**Y**ou should be grateful you weren't wearing anything nice," Rufinus said solemnly as Theo used the rainwater-dampened handkerchief to remove the last of the spot Applecore had made. The fairy frowned. "If something like that happened to one of my Acanthus suits, I'd be perfectly murderous." The handkerchief was Heath's—even the thought of his own being used that way had sent Tansy's young cousin into shudders.

"Grateful. Yeah." Theo felt like he was hanging by his fingernails over a bottomless pit of bleakness.

"I didn't mean it to happen," Applecore said a touch defensively. "I told you to stop the coach, didn't I?"

Rufinus practically had his mouth pressed against the opening between window and doorframe where he sucked clean air as though he were trapped in a coal mine filling with deadly gas. "Yes, I suppose you did," he snapped. "But you could have been a bit clearer."

Theo was tired of their bickering and so depressed he felt like he might start screaming. Instead, he asked, "Where are we now?"

They were passing through something that looked almost like a suburban town, although it was a little different from the kind of places where Theo had grown up and spent most of his life. There were no sidewalks, and not only weren't the roads straight, they had clearly been made crooked on purpose, as though right angles brought out the same kind of reaction in the town's designers as too many fermented berries had in Applecore. The houses were small, or seemed to be—most were hidden in copses of leafy trees—but Theo had learned from Tansy's manor that you couldn't trust first impressions. The dwellings he could see were painted a riot of different colors and patterns, and came in a much wider variety of basic forms than Theo was used to—not just boxes, but cylinders, spheres, and more complicated shapes he couldn't define—and even, in the case of one upside-down pyramid balanced on its point, seemed actually to defy gravity.

"This is Penumbra Fields," said Heath. "It sort of grew up around the railway station. Commuter town, I think they call it. Lots of people with a house here work in the City, even though it's a long trip. Only come back on weekends, most of them."

The idea of fairies living in commuter towns didn't sit right, but Theo couldn't think of any specific reason why it shouldn't be so. It was definitely a suburb: they passed a park where a group of fairy children were chasing a small golden object that didn't look like either a ball or an animal, but was inarguably hopping; near them, other kids were fly-ing colorful kites that didn't seem to have strings. He watched a line of smaller kids in many different sizes and shapes, winged and wingless, singing as they were led along the road by a floating, shimmering rainbow bubble the size of a cantaloupe; he guessed they were being escorted to or from school. He wanted very much to hear their song, but before he could figure out how to get his window down the car had passed the small parade.

More confusing was that he could see shiny automobiles in many of the houses' driveways, smaller and less ornate than the car in which he rode, but otherwise not much dif-ferent: it was obvious that "coaches" weren't just for the rich. In fact, it seemed that the mechanized, early-Victorian nature of fairy civilization his great-uncle had written about as though it were the product of his own fancy, was not only true, that fairy civilization had advanced a great deal since Eamonn Dowd had filled his notebook.

But it's less than thirty years since he wrote that, Theo thought, *and they were still deep in the gaslight era then.* He stared at a very modern stoplight, similar to what you might find at an Earth intersection except for the colors of the lights, orange and lavender-blue instead of red and green—that and the fact that it hovered in midair, unsupported. *Has everything here really changed so fast? Or has the time passed differently from our world?* He remembered Tansy's talk of "slippage" and "distortion." What did that mean, exactly?

His thoughts were interrupted as Heath pulled the car through a wide turn, out of the tree-lined back avenue they had been following and into a wider road that dumped them into a busy town square. Theo stared at the row of tall, slender buildings surrounding the square like candles around the rim of a birthday cake. Some of them were over a hundred feet high, weird combinations of heavily decorated, almost Gothic architecture with unusual overall shapes and modern building materials. The large, low building just ahead that he guessed was the railroad station looked a bit like a pointless jumble of spiky objects, but it had a stately, dome atop it that wouldn't have looked out of place on a small state capitol, although the hemisphere of this dome seemed more spider-web than solid thing and was clearly open to the elements.

Must be miserable inside on a day like today, he thought, fighting a surge of homesickness so intense it verged on panic. *Just my luck.*

What he found most surprising was that they had passed out of a quiet country lane and in only moments were in a busy town center, even if the town itself wasn't very big. It was the first time he'd seen a lot of the so-called "coaches" in one place. Almost all of them were smaller than the town car in which he was riding, and came in a charming array of shapes and hues, from things that looked almost like Volkswagen Beetles to oddly asymmetrical creations whose front end and back end could only be ascertained for certain once Theo could see which way the drivers were facing. People were also traveling on things that looked like bicycles and motorcycles, and children rode on skimming boards and scooters, although calling them by those names substantially broadened the original concept—he saw at least one "scooter" that had weird coppery lizard legs instead of wheels. But if the road that went around the outside of the town square was full of odd conveyances, it was even more full of pedestrians, hundreds and hundreds of them.

"So many people here!" he said out loud.

"Ah, yes." Rufinus chuckled. "It must seem very large and loud to you, I suppose."

Theo scowled. "I didn't mean that. We have cities where I come from that are a thousand times bigger than this. I just . . . this is the first time I've seen more than a few of you people in one place." Although he had to admit to himself, "people" was another term that didn't quite fit. At a rough estimate, at least half of the folk in the square seemed much smaller than humans, although a few were much, much larger. Besides the knee-high gangs of young brownie toughs, the flocks of even more diminutive winged schoolchildren in uniforms, and the slender, wet, and sad-looking blue women pushing baby carriages or shopping carts, he also saw three or four hulking ogres and at least one weird scarecrow shape nearly ten feet tall that looked a bit like a man on stilts but clearly wasn't.

"Polevik," Applecore explained when she saw him staring at the tall fellow. "They can be shorter if they want to be. Probably got a job washing windows or something."

"Most of the other people in the square seem pretty small—um, no offense," he added quickly. "But a lot smaller than me, anyway. Why's that?"

"Ah, yes," said Rufinus. "I suppose that could be because they do not get the bracing country air we enjoy in the commune."

Applecore rolled her eyes. "Probably it's because lots of the big folks ride in coaches and the rest of us walk or fly, and that's why so many of the folk you see on the street are on the wee side."

"Ah." Rufinus nodded his head sagely. "I suppose you could be right about that, Kettledrum. Heath, be a good fellow and just turn here at the entrance." He scowled. "By the Trees, the holiday traffic is dreadful! I can understand the people needing to travel, but all these others hanging about—why are they not home spending Mabon with their families?"

"Because they can't get home," Applecore said a little sharply. "They can't afford it and their families live too far away."

"Hold on," Theo said to Rufinus. "You said somebody might be looking for us."

"Yes?"

"Well, shouldn't we find somewhere else to get out of a big car . . . big coach, I mean . . . like this? I mean, if there's anyone watching the station, wouldn't they be more likely to notice the coach than they would be to notice us by ourselves?"

Rufinus weft-Daisy nodded again. "Hmmm. That is an idea. Yes, you might very well be right." He turned to the doonie, who was already signaling for a left turn. "I've changed my mind. See if you can find us a place around the back to get out, won't you, Heath? Where we won't be so . . . so . . ."

"Conspicuous," Theo supplied, but he was thinking, *Oh, God, I'm so doomed. From reading part of a Tom Clancy novel in a doctor's waiting room, I'm already better equipped for danger than this guy is.*

It was quite a different scene around the back of the station; Theo had his first look at a less savory side of Fairie. Some of the shopfronts were boarded up, the walls were graffittoed—crosses and Stars of David were among the symbols used, he noticed in a bemused way, perhaps for shock value—and the streets were littered with what looked like drifting bits of paper. Fairy-folk in an interesting assortment of shapes stood in the doorways or thronged on corners. Theo had to keep reminding himself that none of them were wearing masks. He was in Fairyland and this was just how people looked, this bizarre aggregation of what he thought of as purely human characteristics along with horns and hooves and fur and bat ears. Some of the locals seemed to be having fun, laughing and talking or even playing musical instruments, which briefly made him want to get out of the car and spend some time listening, but many of the others looked lost—abandoned. A large portion of these street-fairies were of one particular type. They were all thin and almost all barefoot, with toes and fingers that stretched like tree roots, and the parts of their bodies he could see were covered in an uneven pelt of hair that might be greenish-gray or brown or several shades in between. They stood anywhere from half to three-quarters human size, and their skinny noses were as long as human fingers.

Theo pointed to a group of these creatures as they turned to watch the car roll past; he could not help noticing that they all had disturbingly bright yellow eyes. "What are those?"

"Goblins," said Rufinus. "There are so many here now! I can't imagine where they all came from."

"They came to work in the fields," Applecore said. "And they did, until the crops were in and the jobs ended."

"Then they should go back to . . . wherever it is they go," pronounced Rufinus. "Goblin Land. There is really no point to them standing around, cluttering the streets."

"I'm sure they feel the same way," Theo said, but quietly. At first it had just been his own situation that dragged on him, but now he had discovered that Faerie itself could be depressing, too.

As if worried that the troop of indigent goblins might follow them, Heath drove carefully over a sidewalk and down a narrow alley before stopping behind the station. Theo realized, with a jolt of sorrowful panic, that it was time to say good-bye to Applecore, but before he could think of anything to say—and while he was still worrying he might start blubbering like a child and completely humiliate himself— she buzzed up into the air.

"I think I'd like to go in and have a bit of a wash," she said. "It's a long ride back and I don't want to sit with meself that long just stinkin' like a day-old mackerel. Plus I need to go for a slash in the worst way."

"We have plenty of time," declared Rufinus airily, although Theo could tell he thought the sprite vulgar. "You can use the facilities, then we can all have a cup of tea together before you go. Heath will wait. And I will carry my own luggage!"

Heath, who was already unloading the bags, nodded his equine head. "If you're sure, your lordship. Yeah, I'll be here waiting, so take your time, missy." The doonie straightened up and turned to Theo. "Hey, I bet you were wondering about the window wipers, weren't you? My first-time passengers usually do."

"I think I guessed," Theo said. "It's for the rest of us, right? Because we'd get nervous if we couldn't see out the front, even though it doesn't make any difference to you."

If he'd had eyes, Heath might have had a twinkle in them. "Pretty good. That's part of it, yeah. But there's also the flying muryans."

"What are those?"

"They're little guys that look a bit like bugs. They hover over the roads and go splat on the windshield, which they deserve, because it's pretty stupid to hover over the Interdomain Highway even if it does cut through your ancestral land. It doesn't kill 'em most of the time, but it can't feel very good. Anyway, the wipers sweep them off before they have time to put a curse on you." He set Rufinus weft-Daisy's suitcase down on a relatively dry spot on the sidewalk, then raised a blunt-fingered hand and saluted before he swung himself back into the driver's seat. "Have a good trip, your lordship. You too, buddy," he told Theo. "Stay lucky."

"Now, let me think," said Rufinus as they ducked out of the rain and pushed their way in through the back entrance. "Where was that tea shop?" An old fairy with draggled wings and skin like an orange peel, bent over and coughing vigorously, shuffled a bit to the side to let them pass out of the vestibule and into the high-ceilinged station concourse.

Theo followed weft-Daisy, but slowly because he was staring around the station. There was something odd about the place, something that nagged at him. It wasn't the hundreds of fairy-folk of all shapes and sizes—he was growing used to that—or even the signs in a completely unfamiliar language and alphabet that he could nevertheless read, against all logic. (The one in front of him, written in what appeared to be some long-defunct Middle Eastern script, clearly had too many consonants, not to mention a few vowels that he'd never seen before, yet just as clearly said, *"Citizens who appear to be Luggage must be prepared to Present their Tickets for Inspection at Any Time."*) Neither was it the bronze statue they passed, although it was also fairly odd: what seemed to be a wingless sprite standing on the head of a sleeping, normal-sized figure, its arms raised in muted triumph. The plaque on the bottom said *"We Will Never Forget Our Dead."* It was only a moment later, when he saw the smaller words *"Penumbra Veterans, Second Gigantine War"* and puzzled out what "Gigantine" meant that he realized the two figures might just as well represent a normal-sized person standing on a dead giant. Someone had set a small pyramid of ripe apples in front of the monument, perhaps an offering of sorts.

Giants? he thought uneasily, and could not help looking up, as though even now some vast hand might be reaching down toward him. As he stared into the vaulted spaces of the ceiling, into the gray light streaming through the latticework

of the dome and glinting across the silhouettes of tiny, flying humanoid creatures, all as strangely super-real in its own
way as the scenery in Larkspur's forest, Theo suddenly realized what had been nagging at him. As he had seen from
outside, there was no glass or anything else in the open fret-
work of the dome, but although light was leaking in plenti-
fully, the rain that had been splashing down all across the
town was not.

All the rules are different here, he realized. *Even the
physics or whatever. Just . . . different.*

Some things, though, seemed to be the same in both
worlds. Women and their bladders, for instance.

"I'm burstin', Vilmos," Applecore confessed suddenly.
"Oh, you walk slow, but. Can you just tell me where you're
going and I'll meet you?"

"There's a cozy little tea shop in the corner near Track
One, I believe," said Rufinus with the air of a veteran boule-
vardier. "Nothing much, but a bit better than average. We'll
be there. What would you like?"

"The shortest possible distance to the jacks," she said; an
instant later she was off like a wasp fired from a slingshot.

Theo, meanwhile, could not help his slow progress. For
the first time he was getting a chance to see faces up close—
fairy faces of all types. There were the little people, of
course, brownies and gnomes (he guessed they were
gnomes; they certainly had the boot-tickling beards for it)
and many other types who did not even reach his waist, most
of them with faces as wrinkly and knobby as dried-apple
dolls. Even smaller were the sprites like Applecore, little
more than swift shimmers in the air until they stopped to
hover. There were plenty of goblins as well, some working
menial jobs in the station, some waiting for trains, others apparently just hanging around, doing a bit of panhandling.
The goblins seemed of all ages and many economic stations,
but all of them seemed actively to avoid eye contact with
Theo and Rufinus.

Are they supposed to do that or something? he wondered.

Do they get in trouble for looking at the upper-class fairies? Or do they just hate our guts?

Our? He was amused despite himself. *And what makes you think that if you lived here in Fairyland, you wouldn't be a goblin or something even farther down the totem pole? It's like reincarnation, those people who believe in previous lives always think they were dukes or queens or something, ignoring the fact that most people back then spent their whole lives up to their knees in shit before dying of toothless old age at thirty.*

But it was the faces of the upper-class fairy men and fairy women that were most intriguing—the women in particular, of course. Not just because the "nobles" were by far the most human, or because by human standards they were all good-looking (although they certainly were) but because of *how* they were good-looking.

They weren't perfect. In fact, although by and large they had a greater regularity of feature than the average set of human train station visitors, they weren't more attractive in aggregate than your average Hollywood party full of wanna-be actors and actresses. But what kept them from being per-fect—and thus perfectly dull—were features Theo couldn't quite define, features which pulled them away from the human norm and which were fascinating precisely because he didn't recognize where they came from.

When he had first met Count Tansy he had thought him something like a Celtic-Asian or Scandinavian-Asian mix-ture, but with skin tones lighter than either. Now, seeing all this fairy nobility at once, he began to see a fuller example of the types that he had only been able to classify with human approximates before. The "Asian" eyes were by and large set wider in the face than in most humans. What he had thought an extreme Northern European lightness of skin in Tansy actually seemed to be near the middle of the fairy scale, and there were subtle colors in that skin type, green and purple overtones so faint as to be almost invisible, that made even the most linen-pale of Irish maidens look like a ruddy Sicilian dock roustabout by comparison.

That was what made them so interesting, and the women so alluring: these average fairies were not much more beautiful than humans, but they were compounded of so many different—and to Theo unfamiliar—types that each face seemed almost a new world in itself.

Not that it was always easy to get a good look at the faces, especially those of the women. At least one aspect of the fashions which Eamonn Dowd had described appeared to have survived into this more modern era—all-enveloping clothing for women: gloves and long soft skirts and calf-length coats of crisp, pale fabrics. Dozens of upper-class fairy women waited on benches or took tea with friends in the small station restaurants, but there was scarcely an ankle to be seen among them. Big hats and head scarves seemed to be in fashion, too. The whole scene was bizarrely Edwardian: if it hadn't been for things like swooping sprites and little men with heads like pug dogs working the shoeshine booths, Theo could have been watching a costume drama on public television. He wondered for a moment if the rainy weather was making them cover up, but if so, the working fairies, big and small, seemed to pay it little mind, dressing for comfort and blithely displaying bare arms, bare legs, bare wings . . .

"Hey, why don't any of *you* have wings?" Theo asked suddenly.

Rufinus turned in obvious irritation. "What are you talking about?"

"Wings. You don't have 'em. Your . . . cousin, whatever, Tansy—he didn't have 'em either. I thought maybe it was only the little ones that grew them, but there goes somebody your size," he pointed to a young fairy woman in a funny white hat that looked like a flattened seagull, "and *she's* got 'em."

"She's a nurse," said Rufinus, as if this explained something.

"But why don't you and your cousin have wings?"

Rufinus shook his head slowly. "The better people . . . don't. Now, here is the tea shop. I hope they haven't changed proprietors—I've not been here in months."

Theo shrugged and followed him in.

As Rufinus ordered three teas, two large and one extra-small, from a red-faced woman with stubby wings who had to stand on a stool to see over the countertop, Theo found himself staring at the various delicacies behind the glass. The pastries were lovely, each one a piece of staggeringly careful craftsmanship. He was just about to ask Rufinus to order one for him when he noticed that the dainty little torte whose shimmering colors had caught his eye appeared to be made from real butterflies. Real, living butterflies, since the wings were still gently moving. Another had a pile of what seemed to be sugar-dusted fish eyes mounded on its center.

His appetite in retreat, he followed Rufinus and the tray toward a table in front of the tea shop which afforded them a grand view of the concourse—and the concourse a grand view of them. "Ummm, I hate to be a nag," Theo said, "but shouldn't we sit farther back? Just to keep a low profile?"

This time Rufinus could not hide his annoyance at Theo's suggestion, but he shrugged with what was probably a fairy lord's equivalent of good grace and let Theo lead him back to a more shadowy spot along the shop's inside back wall. As Rufinus poured the tea, Theo watched Applecore appear in the shop's open frontage, a small shadow zigzagging in place as she hunted for them. "Over here!" he called.

She saw them and buzzed across the room so quickly that one of the patrons was just beginning to swat absently at a spot above his head as Applecore landed on the table next to Theo's saucer.

"Nice of you to join us," said Rufinus.

"Yeah, cheers." She turned to Theo. "Don't turn around too sudden-like, but there's some fellas I don't much like the look of across the station. In front of that Wingworks shop. They're watching you."

He looked. "I don't see anybody there."

She rose up off the table for a quick survey. "They've gone, now." She turned to Rufinus. "Three fellas, your size but a bit strange. No, a lot strange. Cool and collected, though—not street hooligans. Wearing dark coats."

Now Rufinus was squinting too, but with the absent air of someone examining a cloud that a child has claimed looks like a duckie or a horsie. "Maybe you were mistaken, Kettledrum. Of course, there are lots of people in long coats. On account of the rain, you know."

"It's Applecore," she said, but without the heat Theo felt sure he'd have received in Rufinus' place.

It's a class thing, he realized. *She treats me like an equal and expects the same back. But she doesn't think she's going to yet it from him—and she won't either, from what I've seen.*

"Still, it's good of you to be concerned," allowed weft-Daisy. "And I am not altogether unprepared. Fear not, Master Vilmos, should something happen, I will protect you. Cousin Quillius gave me some quite fine little counter-charms against attack, for one thing. And I also have more than a bit of experience with other forms of defense. Did you know I captained the fencing team at Evermore my last year up at school?"

"His intramural team," Applecore whispered loudly. "From his residence hall."

"But you don't have a sword," Theo pointed out.

Rufinus smiled so happily that for a moment Theo almost liked him. "Ah—so you believe, my mortal friend. But look here." And he lifted his valise and tugged something out of the bottom. As it slid out, Theo saw that it was either a short sword or an extremely long knife—the blade seemed a good half a foot longer than the width of the valise.

God help us, he's one of those guys who thinks he'd be good in a fight. Now Theo was beginning to feel really, really nervous. He had been in just enough serious combat himself, mostly because of playing music in nasty little dives, to know that not only wasn't he any good in fights, but that being good just made it more likely someone would bust a pool cue across the back of your head when you weren't looking.

"So let's finish our refreshments, shall we?" said Rufinus. "We have the best part of an hour until the train leaves."

Theo forced himself to sit still and drink his tea. There was nothing he could do to get home any faster or any more safely. It was like being in trouble up on top of a Himalayan mountain: you could moan and scream about it all you wanted, but ultimately you still had to find your way down.

"Goodness, two cups of Gossamer Hills has gone right through me," weft-Daisy declared, pushing back his chair. "But there should be plenty of time for me to take a little walk and find the first-class lounge—so much nicer than using the facilities on the train."

Theo had still not entirely got used to the idea of fairies urinating, but it was growing clear to him that within their own world, or universe, or dimension—whatever the hell this place was—they were just as physical as humans on Earth. "So should I just wait for you here?"

"No, I think you should go to the train, Theo," Applecore said firmly before Rufinus could speak. "Don't want to cut it too close. I'll help him find the track," she told the fairy lord. "Then you can just meet him there."

"Ah, very kind of you. Well, if you'll excuse me." He started away across the restaurant, then came back for his valise. "Wouldn't do to leave this behind, would it?"

Tansy's cousin had only just disappeared from sight when something yanked hard on Theo's earlobe.

"Hey! What the hell are you doing? That hurt!"

"Come on. You're not going to sit here, and you're not going to sit on the platform, either."

"What are you talking about?"

"I saw those three fellas who were watching you and they weren't nice. Do you trust me?"

"More than anyone else I've met here, yeah."

She wrinkled her tiny nose for a moment, weighing the remark. "Well, that's as much as I can expect, I s'pose. Anyway, I think Tansy's lad is a bit of a dobber, and I think you need to be watching out for yourself."

"That makes sense to me."

"Good. Then we're going out of here through the back door and see if we can't find a bit less obvious way to get you on the train. That's one of the reasons I didn't try to hurry you lot out of here. Just as well to wait 'til just before the train goes out to board. Follow me." She rose into the air and led him down the aisle toward the employees-only section of the tea shop.

"What are we doing?"

"Nipping out the back, like I said. It'll be easier to get across the station without attracting attention if we just go round that way, where they dump the rubbish and all."

She led him through the kitchen, where two fat little manlike creatures, both smoking clay pipes—he guessed they were what Applecore called "bogles"—stood on stools that raised them to the necessary height to do their work. One of them was tending the fry basket, the other lifting and inspecting pastries in the open oven with a long-handled paddle.

"Whither goest, tinyfry?" the bogle by the oven asked Applecore lazily. He sounded like a Shakespearean comic rustic, with a broad accent that sounded vaguely northern England to Theo, who didn't know much about English regional accents beyond the Beatles. He still couldn't figure out why fairies should sound like British and Irish folk, anyway.

"Out the back, you great ball of guts," Applecore said. "It's lucky you're good-looking, because you'll never be a cook—your *millefois* tastes like shoe leather."

As the fry cook laughed, the oven-bogle grinned. "And it's lucky for you that you're such a sweet-talker," he said, "because you're going to need to be able to make new chums—your boyfriend just stepped into the walk-in refrigerator."

Theo heard this last just as the door swung shut behind him with a resounding *ka-chunk*. He was suddenly very, very cold.

But I didn't touch the damn thing, he told himself. *It just closed, like . . . magic.*

Shit.

He had to stand, shivering, as Applecore argued with the cooks about opening the door. He heard her call the bogles lots of names, which made him feel a little better, but unlikely as it seemed, there were moments when she seemed to be laughing as she did it.

His teeth were chattering pretty hard when the door finally popped open again.

"What use dating a petalhead such as yon when he can't even muster a cantrip for latchlifting?" the fry cook chuckled as he beckoned Theo out. "Come out, our frosty master. Else we might mistake you for something edible and put you in a stew, then go up before the Assizes for floricide."

"Sass," said Applecore, but Theo didn't think she looked very indignant on his behalf.

"If thou shouldst grow bored and pissed off with petalheads, small nifty, and return to dating your own social equals," grinned the fat oven-bogle as he waved good-bye, "you'll know where I might be found."

"Yeah and some verily" said the other. "Up to his overworked mouth in flour, as always. Door to the service corridor's that way."

"Nice enough fellas," said Applecore as they made their way down the narrow hallway that ran behind the row of shops.

Theo had a feeling that if Rufinus had made that comment, he would have automatically added, *"for bogles."* "They liked you," he told Applecore.

"Get away with you."

"Oh, they didn't? So why are you blushing?"

"Am not. Shut your gob."

As they reached the last door in the corridor, Applecore

flew up close to his face. "Now, when we step out, don't
look around—that's the kind of thing people notice. Remember, you've just been doing something you're supposed
to do and now you're on your way to do something else
you're supposed to do. *Don't look around.* That's what
guilty people do."

"Wow. You're pretty impressive. Like a miniature John
LeCarré out of a box of Cracker Jacks."

"I don't even know what that means, but I'm sure it won't
keep me from kicking you in your earhole. Now shut up and
push the door open."

He wondered briefly how people Applecore's size
opened doors like this when there weren't people Theo's
size around, then they were out and walking past the ladies'
room for another station restaurant. At least, he assumed it
was the ladies' room, since one of the several silhouettes on
it looked humanoid and female, although most of the other
silhouettes looked more like vacuum cleaner attachments.
Theo decided it didn't bear too much thinking about.

The business was a book and magazine store full of
browsing travelers. The place was festooned with harvest-
holiday decorations, sprays of leaves and piles of produce on
almost every surface and stylized moons hanging from the
rafters. At least he assumed they were decorations—it was
hard to tell, here in Faerie, what might be just the normal
weirdness. As he followed Applecore down the rows of
glossy magazines, he experienced the strange cognitive dis-
sonance again: he could understand everything written on
them without understanding a word of the language or
script. "Making Oak Blight Work for You!" trumpeted
something on the cover of one that his brain translated as
Roots—the Dryad Magazine. There were dozens of others,
all equally unlikely—it was like walking through the set of
some expensive Hollywood comedy: *Wingspan—for Working Mothers* with articles like "Forget Your Frost-Charms—
A Fresh Mabon Feast in Minutes!" and newspapers called
The Trooping News and *The Arden Intelligencer* with head-

lines proclaiming "Coextensives Fighing to Hold Coalition Power" and "Holly's Generator Outages Blamed on Worker Morale."

The browsers were just as unlikely a collection as the periodicals, everything from be-hatted and veiled fairy women who looked like they'd been flown in from a remake of *A Passage to India* to a group of talking hedgehogs all wearing what appeared to be matching rugby shirts and carrying pennants and coolers, shoving and arguing good-naturedly while one of their number bought a bag of salted grubs.

"You're looking around too much," Applecore hissed in his ear. "Walk faster. You're on your way somewhere."

He had hesitated in front of a magazine rack, staring at something called *Aodh's Harp*—he figured that of the two kinds of periodicals he generally liked, in a land of women who always wore head-to-toe clothing he was probably going to have better luck with music magazines—but he realized she was right. Thinking about how little he knew here made him feel hopeless and twisted that skewer of homesickness in his guts again. It was one thing to make him up to look a bit more like a fairy, another thing entirely to expect him to pull it off. It was like dumping an ice cream vendor into a particle physics conference and telling him to fake it. If all he had to do was sit and look like he knew what was happening—well, maybe. But ask him to get up and discuss quarks? Disaster.

"Track Twelve," Applecore said as she led him out of the magazine store and onto the concourse. They were half a dozen storefronts down from the tea shop, which reduced the chance of someone spotting them coming out. Applecore quickly found a group of people moving generally toward the tracks and Theo wrapped the crowd around him like a cloak.

I guess I should be grateful everyone else here isn't Applecore's size. Then I'd really have trouble blending in. He saw no sign of the sprite's trio of rough-lookin' fellas, and for a moment wondered if Rufinus might not be the

more sensible after all. Why would anyone send some kind
of professional fairy detectives after a know-nothing mortal?
Maybe the whole thing with that poor Hollyhock guy's heart
had been some kind of mistake, nothing to do with Theo at
all. He basked for a moment in the warmth of the idea, although he didn't really believe it. After all, *somebody* had
sent that dead thing after him.

Applecore hissed at him. "Over here! I've just seen 'em!"

His heart now bumping along quite quickly, he let his
winged companion lead him to a sheltered space just across
from Track Eleven, between a pillar and a little windowed
kiosk with the name *Ariel's,* a spot where he would be out of
obvious sight while she went to investigate. Theo tried to
look as though he were reading the advertising in the windows carefully. The kiosk sold what he at first thought were
waffles, but after a while spent watching the hair-netted
brownies handing out the little bundles wrapped in waxed
paper, Theo decided their product was some kind of pre-
processed frozen honeycomb dessert.

Something touched his ear. He jumped.

"Don't do that!" Applecore said in a strained whisper.
"Just stand still! Look through the window and out the door
on the far side. See?"

He did. Twenty steps on the other side of the kiosk, three
dark, lanky figures stood by a bench watching people go by
without being obvious about it. Even though their faces were
mostly shaded by their hats, he could see the suggestion of
something pale and shiny-wet between brim and collar, a
sandcrab gleam.

"Oh, my God."

"Just stay here. The train won't board for another few
minutes, but we may be all right. They're looking down the
other way so they don't know we're already past 'em." She
settled on his shoulder. Her presence was oddly but unquestionably comforting. "Hollow-men."

"Hollow-men? What does that mean?"

"They're a sort of troll. Underground folk. Man-stealers,

they used to be, when their caves still opened in your world. They're good at what they do and they keep their mouths shut. Someone's paying a pretty penny for you, boyo."

"Jesus! What does everyone want with me? I'm just a guy!"

"Ssshhh." Her tone was more urgent now. "There's Tansy's cousin. Bloody eejit certainly took his time."

Theo started to say something, but the hollow-men abruptly slid away from the bench and moved toward Rufinus, smooth as wheeling sharks. They vanished for a moment into the crowd at the edge of the railheads, then closed in behind him and on either side as the young fairy reached Track Ten. He looked at one of them without seeming to notice, but then his head swung to the other side and he stopped. The hollow-men quickly surrounded him at arm's length. For a moment no one seemed to do much of anything: the foursome could have been chance acquaintances chatting about the dodginess of railway schedules. The creatures' chins were close to their chests and their faces were mostly hidden by collars and hats, but Theo felt sure they were talking to weft-Daisy, because the alarmed and cautious look on his face was becoming something else, an expression almost of contempt.

"Call for help, you daft fool!" Applecore said urgently but quietly. For a confusing second, Theo thought she was speaking to him.

Instead, Rufinus weft-Daisy turned abruptly and began to walk along the concourse. The trio of trolls walked with him, surrounding him. One leaned close and whispered in Rufinus' ear; the fairy stopped and lifted his valise in both hands.

He's pulling that blade, Theo realized, but in the instant it took for the thought to form the black figures had already folded around weft-Daisy like a gloved fist. Rufinus slumped a little, as though he had suddenly grown dizzy. The hollow-men helped him walk a few steps toward the bench where they had originally been waiting and let him sit down there.

They leaned together briefly, then turned and glided toward the tea shop in loose formation.

"What . . . what happened?"

"Stay here, Theo. Don't make a sound!" Applecore dove from his shoulder to floor level and shot away. He had one brief glimpse of her slaloming around the legs of other station patrons, then he thought he could see her hovering beside weft-Daisy, who still sat on the bench with his mouth open as though he were the recipient of stunning news.

Which, in a way, he had been.

Moments later Applecore dropped back onto Theo's shoulder from nowhere, making him jump again so that he bumped his nose against the *Ariel's* kiosk window. A pair of young goblins sharing a honeycomb looked up at him in amusement.

"He's dead," she whispered.

"What?"

"When you're not alive anymore! Dead!"

"I know what it means!" Panic rose higher now, threatening to choke him. What kind of world was this? "How can he be dead? He had charms or something! What happened?"

"Cathedral knife, I think—no charm can stop one of those. They opened up his belly—he's got a lapful of his own guts. Terrible." Her crisp words hid her own shock and fear, but not completely. "And they took his case, too. He's just sitting there. Someone will notice any moment."

"I should damn well hope so!"

"Well, you'd better hope it doesn't happen before you get on that train or the constables will hold everyone here and start checking identification." Her voice was tight with desperation. "You'll wind up in the Penumbra Fieldshire jail and sometime before Tansy's solicitor gets here you'll decide to hang yourself in your cell."

"I'll what . . . ? But I wouldn't . . ." He suddenly realized what she was saying. His heart was thumping away like a methedrined woodpecker. "How could that happen?"

"Whoever hired these fellas isn't joking around, Theo.

There aren't but a dozen or so Cathedral knives in the whole of the land—they're made of spell-hallowed glass from the ruins on the Old Mound itself. They don't get handed out to every Tom, Dick, and Hobthrush, y'know—those fellas are working for someone important."

"What do I do now? Oh, shit, poor Rufinus—he was an idiot, but I can't believe he's dead!" Theo wiped sweat off his face. The only idea he could come up with was to run screaming across the station, but it didn't seem like a good one. "How will I get to the city without him? I don't even know what it's called!"

To his amazement, Applecore burst into shrill, near-hysterical laughter. "By the Trees, fella, you really do take it all. What's it called? The City, man, the City! There's only one! It's like saying you don't know which 'up' someone's talking about." The sprite fell silent. She seemed to be oscillating between terror and a kind of fast-thinking omnicompetence. After a long moment of close-eyed concentration, she said, "I suppose I'm going with you, then, amn't I?"

"Oh, Jesus, can you really? Will you?"

"Stop saying that blasted name—you made that lady over there shiver and she didn't even hear you. No more talking." She shot off for a moment, then returned. "Those three fellas are still poking around down by the tea shop. Step out from behind here and just start walking toward Track Twelve. See if you can find some other people going that direction. Whatever you do, don't look around!"

Rufinus' body had begun to sag and now stared down at the floor with glassy eyes, as though it had lost something and was looking for it there. A little fairy woman with a rolling basket full of parcels had seated herself at the other end of the bench from the corpse. At the moment she was oblivious to her companion's condition, but how long could that last?

"Let's go, then," Theo said. "I might as well have my heart attack walking as standing."

The sea of unfamiliar fairy faces which at first had seemed fascinating, and for the last half hour had mostly gone unnoticed, now swirled past him like a nightmare. At any moment he expected someone to point at him and shout, *"Impostor!"*

Most difficult of all was the feeling—no, the certainty—that something with a clammy white face was moving up behind him, reaching out a hand for the back of his neck . . .

"Don't you dare turn around," said Applecore.

As he fell in with a group of people his own size moving down the platform of Track Twelve, heading for the first-class section, something came to him like a splash of cold water.

"Oh, my God, Tansy's cousin must have the tickets!"

"No, he doesn't. I took 'em off him an hour ago and stuck 'em in your coat because I didn't trust the poor daft lad not to lose 'em."

"And I didn't notice?"

She snorted. "I could have shoved the Parliament building into your pocket and you wouldn't have noticed. You were lookin' at girls. Now turn here—get on!"

He stepped up into the third-class compartment. Inside it was a zoo, almost literally, as creatures of all shapes and sizes struggled for a place to sit down. Applecore whispered that it would be just as well not to get wedged in, so they moved to the far end of the car and stood near the door, among a group of other human-sized but apparently lower-class fairies who eyed Theo's clothes and quickly turned away. He wondered what that meant.

"Why won't this stupid train leave?" he whispered to Applecore. He could feel the trio of hollow-men out there as though they were fins circling his leaking boat. He wanted to run down to the engine and take the driver by the neck and bang his head until he throttled up and pulled out of the station.

As if the distant engineer could feel this potential threat to his well-being, the steam whistle let out a great pteranodon shriek.

"Thank God," Theo gasped. An instant later two corpse-faced, black-clad shapes hustled past the windows of their railway carriage. For a moment he thought the hollow-men would come into his car and his stuttering heart would stop completely, but instead they shoved onward through the crowd on the platform, heading toward the first-class cars. A few moments later the train began to ease its way out of the station.

"Did they get on?" Theo asked Applecore. "Or did we leave without them?"

She shrugged, but she did not look either happy or confident.

It rode the planar winds like an invisible kite, a shapeless presence stretched wide, wide, every bit of it alive and alert to the thing it sought. It was close now—even in the midst of all the similar creatures surrounding its quarry, the irrha *sensed its target as easily as an owl might spot a single small motion of warm life in the midst of a forest of undergrowth.*

Following that target had not been easy this time: the journey between the two planes was more difficult than the irrha *had, in its unthinking way, anticipated—rougher and more strenuous. Things had changed during the slow millennia it had sleepwalked in the dark between-places. If a tireless thing could be weary, it was. If a thing without emotions could be frustrated, it was that, too. To be so close to its goal—to touch the quarry, nearly—but not to close and seize and complete its burning directive, had filled the* irrha *with a sensation it had not experienced in so long that it did not remember what it was. But one thing the hunter did know: it did not like the sensation at all.*

Closer, closer . . . there. It had located its target precisely. All that remained was to cross that last fragile membrane and become embodied, to take form by joining with something that could move through this plane before the quarry slipped away again. It had chosen badly in the last place, first wearying itself dispelling the body's living

*inhabitant, then finding that the fleshy envelope was so dam-
aged that it had been forced to spend valuable time supple-
menting the damaged parts with bits of other bleating, warm
meat-things. The quarry was so close here, actually within
reach—the hunter could not afford to be slowed again by
such resistance or such incompleteness.*

*It swooped, spun, fell closer. So much life here, so con-
fusing for senses honed in the chasms of the deepest, most
lightless and warmthless dimensional oceans! But the* irrha
*was determination itself. It found what it was looking for
and moved to take possession, bursting out into a jittering,
exploding worldsphere of light and color and sound.*

Cornelia Yarrow surveyed her purchases—a flying toy
powered by a simple but long-lasting charm, a goblin
doll in traditional dress of feathers, beads, and dragonwing
cloak, not to mention a selection of sports pennants with the
insignia of leading houses and butterfly-patterned scarves
that friends had assured her were being worn by all the fashionable ladies and gentlemen in the City, as well as dozens
of other trinkets. She thought she had spent a little more than
she should have on a few of them, but the main thing was
that she still had half an hour until her train back home to
Willow and she had finished buying gifts for everyone on
her list, her niece and all the many grandnieces and grand-
nephews. Out in their little forest village, her relatives considered Penumbra Fields to be almost as big as the City
itself: they would have been terribly disappointed if Aunt
Cornelia had not brought back gifts from her trip to the Honeysuckle Academy for Girls' tricentennial reunion.

Thinking of her grandnieces, one of whom was going up
to Honeysuckle next year, she suddenly felt old. Could it
really be three hundred years since she had walked those
echoing halls as a student? Sometimes it seemed only a few
seasons in the past.

As she put her parcels back in her wheeled basket she could not help noticing that the unpleasant odor around the bench had grown worse. She looked at the sleeping man down at the far end. He was well-dressed, but you never knew what these upper-class folk might get up to, especially the young ones. Out on some kind of sustained rag, no doubt. Still, he didn't smell drunk, he smelled . . . unclean.

The stranger's head turned toward her and the eyes popped open. Cornelia Yarrow could not suppress a gasp of surprise. There was something wrong with the Flower lord's eyes—they seemed blank and dull, almost blind.

The mouth worked. When he finally spoke, the young noble sounded as if he had never used any language before, let alone the proper diction his social station demanded.

"Where . . . ?"

"I beg your pardon?"

"Where . . . is . . . ?" The blank-eyed man shook his head as if the effort to speak was too much, then stood up. A messy something slid off his lap and onto the station's tiled floor with a wet slurp.

That's extremely inconsiderate, Miss Yarrow thought, *he's just dropped his lunch on the ground, what kind of manners do they teach these young people today . . . ?* But as she looked at the red, slippery mass of tubing lying beside the bench and the bits that still hung out of the young man's tattered shirt, Cornelia Yarrow came very close to screaming. Instead, she fainted dead away onto the bench.

The *irrha,* apparently satisfied with Rufinus weft-Daisy's body, which although most decidedly dead was still flexible and not too badly disabled, turned away from the bench and began walking slowly across Penumbra Station, stuffing its dangling innards back into its clothing.

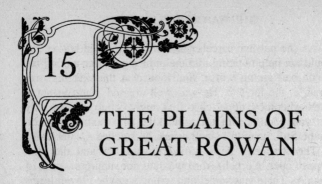

15

THE PLAINS OF GREAT ROWAN

The shape of Faerie itself is even stranger than the nautilus plan of the city I call New Erewhon—for it is no shape at all. To accurately reflect the experience of traveling there, a map of that land would have to revolve like a child's top or go through some other metamorphosis I cannot quite conceive, for Faerie simply will not lie flat and behave itself . . .

"Reading something?"

Depressed by what was for Fairyland a rather brooding landscape smearing past the rainy windows, mostly hilly meadows empty of trees, and by the crush of weird creatures and their strange smells in the third-class compartment, Theo had been trying to reexamine a little of his greatuncle's book. He looked up to see the owner of the voice, something vaguely sheeplike, leaning in from the seat beside him, its belligerent little red eyes squinting beneath knotted gray fleece.

"Uh . . . yes. I'm reading something."

"Can't read, me. Never learned." It showed long, flat yellow teeth in what might have been a smile, but might just as easily have been a smirk of menace.

"I'm sorry. To hear that."

"Oh, I admire you clever folk who can." It didn't sound very admiring. It leaned a little closer, giving him a whiff of breath like souring milk. "You must think them like me are stupid."

"No, I don't . . ."

"Just a stupid padfoot, you'll be thinking. And who could blame you? You with your education and advantages and all."

Theo was beginning to wish quite desperately that Applecore would come back from her inspection of the rest of the train. He had hoped that just keeping his mouth shut and avoiding eye contact would keep him out of trouble.

"Hey, yarnback," said a more human-looking fairy, one of the few Theo had seen that actually looked middle-aged. This one was dressed in worn but clean clothing and had a few lines on his face and the closest thing to a tan Theo had yet glimpsed. But he was also wiry and strong, and he was not looking at the padfoot kindly. "Why are you pestering the lad?"

"Is it your affair, old-timer?" the sheeplike thing asked. "Or are you just certain that anyone with manshape is in the right?"

"Manshape's got nothing to do with it," said another creature that certainly did not fall into that category, with an armadillo-like hide and a tiny, plated head that barely poked out of the top of the bony armor. "You're just looking for trouble. Before we even got into Penumbra you were bumping and swearing at some poor boggart because you said he spilled your lunch."

"He did! Clumsy little needlenose knocked over a whole box of hayslaw!"

While the argument continued, Theo slowly sank back into the corner. He lifted his book up to block out these impossible train companions and struggled to focus on his great-uncle's handwriting.

Faerie is divided into regions called "fields," and these regions are not always the same. That is, they re-

*main the same within themselves, but they are not al-
ways in the same relationship to each other—at least
that is the closest I can come to explaining it, or even
grasping it myself. It sometimes seems as though the
lands of Faerie are in rings which move, so that one
week two lands seem to be beside each other, then the
next week it is not so. But it is even more complicated
than that, because there are no clear rules to this either in amount of movement or regularity. One day
you cannot get to the field of Gateway Oak from Ivy
Round or from Great Rowan to Hawthorn Scathe.
Then the next day the paths from Oak to Ivy are again
clear, but Rowan and Hawthorn may remain divided.*

*I traveled little outside the City so I did not see
many of these effects myself, although I did once, as I
will describe. But I often heard it spoken of in precisely the same way that people in my world might talk
of the weather without bothering to explain why you
should take an umbrella on a rainy day—assuming
that any sane adult listener would know. Thus,
acquaintances of mine would say, "Alder is far this
year, but so beautiful at this season. I think we should
gather a traveling party and go—we could be there in
a few days." At some other point I might hear that
same person say, "I was in Alder Head yesterday
evening . . ."*

Something tickled Theo's neck and he stiffened, imagining it was the woolly muzzle of the sheep-man again.

"There's no sign of the hollow-fella," Applecore said into
his ear.

Theo tried to keep his voice low. "He's not on the train?"
To Theo's immense relief, as the train had pulled out of
Penumbra Station they had seen two of the slug-faced
hollow-men standing in a crowd on the station, but since one
was still unaccounted for, Applecore had been searching the
other compartments.

"There's no sign of him, which isn't quite the same thing. The train's pretty full and he could be in the jacks or somethin'. I hope you didn't expect me to force my way into every lavatory on the bleeding train."

"No. So what do we do now?"

"Talk a little quieter, for one thing. I'm standing right next to your jawbone, remember? I can hear you even if you barely whisper, but most other folk can't. What do we do now? Keep on to the City, I guess. I'll get you to these people who want to see you, then I'll head back to my old ones and my brothers and sisters."

"Should you . . . call someone in your family? Let them know where you are?"

"Nah, I'm a big girl. But that reminds me—we have to tell Tansy what happened."

"How?"

"He gave you that speaking-shell."

"Oh, yeah, we'd call it a phone."

"Whatever. He needs to know. At the very least, the Daisy-clan folk should know that someone's killed one of their family."

"Call from here?" Theo looked around. The padfoot had lapsed back into sullen silence, and was winding a lock of fleece around its dirty gray hoof-hand while glaring at the fairy who had intervened. There were perhaps two hundred other living creatures in the compartment and very few of them looked remotely human. Some of them had ears like bats, and for all he knew were listening to his and Applecore's every word.

"You're right, for once. When's the next stop?" She looked up. "It's a good long way to Starlightshire still, so you probably won't lose your seat if you get up and go to the jacks."

"That's the toilet, right? Let's go."

The restroom was at one end of the car. Theo lost his balance several times, once having to steady himself on what he thought was the back of a seat and found out only when its

owner grunted in irritation was actually the raised neckplate
of something strange and lizardlike.

"Maybe we should have snuck into Second Class instead
of settling for Third," Applecore whispered as Theo backed
away with fulsome apologies. "Seems they'll let anyone on
a train these days."

He opened the restroom door, which other than a very
low, very wide toilet and a sink with a tiny ladder running up
the wall beside it, did not contain anything too frightening in
the way of facilities. "Do you want to come in?"

"I should keep an eye open for trouble."

"Looks like there's a latch on the door. Come in. What if
Tansy asks me something I can't answer?"

She frowned. "I've never gone into a public toilet with a
fella. Not since my da took me when I was a little one."

"We seem to be experiencing a lot of firsts this week,"
Theo said. "Come on."

With the door closed, it would have been a tightly uncomfortable fit with any second person except Applecore.
She dragged a paper towel out of the dispenser and spread it
on the edge of the tiny sink like a picnic blanket, then sat
down. "At least the place isn't too horrid," she said. "I hate
the mess some people leave in places like this."

"I know what you mean," said Theo.

"No, you don't," she said. "Not until you're my size and
the mess is twenty times bigger."

"You win." He stared at himself in the mirror. "I'm going
to scrub off this make-up Dolly put on me. It's starting to rub
off on my clothes, and anyway, there are lots of people on
the train who are as tan as I am."

"Yeah, but they're workin' folk."

"I don't care. There are so many different kinds of people
on this train, no one'll notice. I just want to get it off." He
washed his face with warm water, then used a dispenser-
towel—it felt more like silk than paper—to scrub away the
small creamy traces left around his ears and jaw. Feeling a
bit more comfortable, he lifted the case out of his pocket and

opened it. "Now we get down to business." He looked at the
filigree bird-shape nestled on the velvet. "Do I lift it out?"

"Just talk. Call Tansy."

"Call him how?"

"By name. His first name's Quillius."

Theo leaned in until his breath misted on the golden object as he said Tansy's name. Nothing happened. He tried
again; after a moment the statuette began to gleam as though
it had been lifted and turned toward the sunlight.

"What is it?" Although the ornament was in the case, the
voice was in Theo's ear and it was unmistakably Tansy's.
"I've just sat down to eat."

"Things have gone very wrong," Theo said.

"Who is this?"

"Jesus!" Applecore glared at him. Theo tried to speak
more calmly. "Can't you even guess? How many other people have you tossed to the wolves lately?"

"Vilmos?" Suddenly the fairy lord's voice was sharp in a
very different way. "What do you mean?"

"Your cousin, nephew—whatever he was—he's . . ." He
paused. He might not like Tansy, but that didn't mean he
should deliver bad news this way. "I'm afraid something bad
has happened. Rufinus has been attacked and killed."

"What? Where are you? What's going on?"

Theo tried to explain as succinctly as he could. Tansy
seemed very surprised, but if he was brokenhearted it did not
show—he might be hearing from the gardener about what
looked to be an expensive case of lawn-blight.

Maybe I'm not being fair, he thought. *They're not like me.*

"Is the sprite there?"

"She is, yeah."

"I wish to speak to her, too. Applecore?" There was a
sudden *pop* in Theo's head. When the little fairy answered,
her voice was suddenly in his ear as well, as though she were
perched on his shoulder instead of sitting fastidiously on a
disposable towel.

"I'm here, Count Tansy."

"Thank you for staying to help our guest. What Master Vilmos has said . . ." He hesitated—he clearly wanted to ask, "Is it all true?" but felt that would be an insult to Theo. ". . . Is there anything you want to add?"

Maybe he's a little bit human after all, Theo decided.

"Not much, sir. We're in a great steaming pile of trouble, though, that's sure."

"When you get to the City, you must go straight to Hollyhock House. No, wait. Someone also killed the young Hollyhock lad who was sent here. That could mean a number of things, not least that there are spies in their household—or in mine, which seems more likely considering that there were people lying in wait for you and poor Rufinus as well." Tansy was silent for a long moment; when he finally spoke, he seemed strangely hesitant. "The most trustworthy and sensible Coextensive outside of our Daisy clan is Lord Foxglove. He's a clever man and as well-acquainted with the City's eddies and undertows as a nymph is with her river."

Reminded, Theo looked down at the knot of rivergrass on his wrist. What the hell was a nymph-binding, anyway? He would have to ask Applecore to explain properly.

"Lord Foxglove is certainly clever, sir—too clever, some say," the sprite was telling Tansy.

"Eh? What do you mean?"

"It's just that some people say he's friends with Lord Thornapple."

"As are many others, from many houses."

"You would know better than me, sir. It's just that Thornapple is . . . he's . . ."

"An Excisor—a Chokeweed, as you'd put it? Yes, Thornapple is of that party, although he is also one of the more intelligent and flexible of their number. In fact, most of his positions are not that far different from those of us in the Daisy clan—except for his dislike of mortals, of course, which is excessive. But whatever Thornapple may be, Lord Viorel Foxglove is *not* a Chokeweed, but one of the more sensible moderates, a member of my own faction in Parliament. And there is nothing wrong with having friends who differ in their politics—we are not at war, after all, Applecore."

She frowned. "Begging your pardon, sir, but what happened to your cousin looked like war to me. And what with that young fella's heart showing up in a box, the Hollyhock folk might disagree with you, too, and all."

Theo could almost hear Tansy's mouth pursing in disapproval. "The ties between the great families and their Houses, especially between the masters of those Houses, are long and deep, Applecore. They do not cease simply because of political friction. And Foxglove and Thornapple have been friends since their days at Dowsing."

Theo watched Applecore squirm in frustration on the sinktop, but she said nothing more.

"Now," Tansy went on, "when you two get to the City, you must proceed immediately to Foxglove House. Applecore knows where it is, but if for some reason . . ." his hesitation this time had a grim shadow even Tansy could not hide, ". . . well, if the two of you happen to become separated, Master Vilmos, then you must go to Springwater Square by yourself. You cannot miss Foxglove House—it is the tallest tower on the square. Simply tell the guards that you bear a message from me to Lord Foxglove. Show them the device through which we are speaking now. That alone should be enough to ensure they take you seriously. If not, ask them to send a message to their master saying, 'Tansy bids you remember the River's Edge.' "

"The river's edge?" Applecore asked. "Did you save him from drowning?"

"What? No, it is the name of a tavern. One of the lower sort, I am ashamed to admit. But when we were both students at Dowsing Academy I helped Vivi Foxglove, as we called him then, out of a scrape there. He will remember."

Theo was having trouble wrapping his head around this. Here they were, making a secret phone call from the restroom of a train after having just watched their companion stabbed to death, and Tansy was acting like it was some Jeeves-the-Butler story. "You're taking what happened to your cousin pretty well."

"Does that mean you find me insufficiently upset about my loss, Vilmos?" Tansy's voice suddenly grew cold. "If so, we will have to agree to disagree. I will not lower myself to quibbling with your ill-informed interpretations."

"Sure. Whatever." Theo realized he had just insulted a guy who could help keep him alive, and he certainly needed help with that just at the moment. *Chased by living corpses and slug-men,* he thought. *Hey, why not some of those—what are those bastards from* The Hobbit *called, black riders? Just to make things complete.* "Sorry. I didn't mean to offend you."

"Don't be ridiculous—I am not so easily offended," said Tansy, although his every tight-jawed word suggested otherwise. "Call me when you reach the City and I will instruct you what to tell Foxglove. I may contact him myself eventually, but until I find out where this terrible flaw in our security lies, I prefer to use only private devices like this."

An instant later, like a soap bubble popping in Theo's inner ear, the connection ended.

"Well," said Applecore as Theo put the phone-case away. "Well, well. Isn't *this* a shower of shite, and aren't we standing in it? I guess we might as well go back and sit down. No, I've got a better idea. Follow me."

Theo fell in behind her as she flew slowly toward the front of the train. Within moments they had moved into the next third-class coach, as full of odd shapes and faces as the one they had left. Still, it was interesting how quickly he was beginning to get used to it—if he half-shut his eyes, he could almost believe he was back home. Most of the passengers seemed to be drowsing as the train rushed and rattled on through the rainswept meadows.

"Where are we going?" Theo whispered.

She fell back to fly beside his ear. "Those hollow-fellas may not have got on the train, but they'll have been in touch with whoever hired 'em. That means if they were watching you, they'll have given out a description and someone may be looking for us when we get off."

"Shit, I should have thought of that. But why are we going up toward first class? I thought you said we'd be too obvious up there—that's why we're in the back."

"We're not going to first class—at least not to stand around. Now just walk and shut up talking."

Theo did as he was told.

"Here's where we should have put ourselves at the start," Applecore whispered as they passed through the nearest of the second-class coaches. There were a few of the more un-usual fairy types here, but most of the travelers seemed to be office workers and laborers of more human shape. One or two of them glanced up as the pair made their way up the aisle, but they seemed more interested in the sprite than in Theo himself. "Would have blended in a bit. Wouldn't be getting into barneys with padfeet and your other trouble-making riffraff."

"I know I keep asking this, but where are we going?"

"Private compartments. Just this side of the dining car."

"But aren't those the really expensive ones?"

"Yes. But they're also the ones people won't be sitting in if they're having a meal or a scoop in the club car."

"I don't understand . . ."

"By the Trees, Vilmos, but you ask a lot of bloody ques-tions! Just shut your gob for a bit and you'll see!" Her hiss-ing voice was loud enough to make a few of the second-class passengers look up from their magazines or their own con-versations. Theo's heart sped. *This isn't just about making a scene,* he reminded himself. *This is about getting noticed and maybe getting killed. I have to trust her.* He stared straight ahead and kept walking.

They stepped through into the rattling space between coaches. He could smell something in the agitated air here, something like electrical ozone, but also a bit like burning sugar—the magic that made the train run, he guessed. "Now

I'll explain!" Applecore said, almost shouting to be heard above the noise of the wheels. "We're looking for somebody's luggage. We need to steal you some new clothes, in case anybody's looking for what you're wearing when we get off in Starlightshire."

"We're getting off?"

"We're sure as hell not going all the way to the City on this train—we might as well show up waving a flag with your name on it. Like Tansy said, they must have their hands on someone in his house. Those pale-faced fellas knew exactly what train you were supposed to be on—that's why they were waiting down by the platform, and why they rushed right to this train when they couldn't find you after they killed Tansy's cousin."

Theo flushed with embarrassment. "I hadn't thought of that."

"I noticed. So we're getting off, then we're going to find some other way into the City, or at least a way onto another train."

"And meantime?"

"We're thieving. So look for anyone's luggage left in their compartment. We'll hope they're in the bar instead of just the toilet, but we should be quick about searching anyway. You need some plain men's clothes, nothing too fancy." She tugged his ear again. "Stop—one more thing. Get out the shell Tansy gave you and look like you're talking on it. That'll give us an excuse to be walking up and down the passageway."

He again did as he was told, marveling at the difference between traveling with Applecore and with that idiot Rufinus—a dead idiot now, but that was no reason to sugarcoat his failings. Theo tried to look like all the self-absorbed businessmen he'd ever seen on his trips through office highrises, so involved in their private conversations that Theo would have to dodge out of their way even though he was carrying a huge potted plant and they were carrying only a phone the size of a cigarette pack. As he walked he tried to cast surreptitious glances into the compartments. Most of them had at least one passenger; in general they seemed a prosperous and almost entirely wingless bunch who might all have been human for as much as a quick inspection would have told him.

"Quick—over against this wall," Applecore ordered as they reached the end of the coach. She tugged him over toward a small space between the end of the private compartments and the wall with the door leading to the dining car. Theo leaned against a fire hose and pretended to be deep in conversation as a conductor with tiny wings, a bluish cast to his skin, and a worried and distracted look on his face banged through the doors and walked briskly toward the back of the train, hardly sparing a glance for Theo.

When he had gone, Theo turned and started back down the length of the coach, still miming an urgent and absorbing conversation. Applecore, who had buzzed ahead of him down the passage, abruptly pulled up and began to wave her arms at him. Fairy-folk were observing him from inside their compartments so he tried not to run, but he felt terribly exposed and wished very much that he could find a seat somewhere and just hide behind his great-uncle's book.

"What is it?" he whispered.

She pointed. The compartment beside him was empty. A good-sized suitcase in shimmering midnight-blue fabric sat on one of the two overhead luggage racks. "And the one across the way has got its curtains pulled, so no one will see what we're doing," she said in his ear. "Let's get in and pull the ones on this side, too."

He took one brief look at the closed compartment across the passage, then slipped into the empty compartment and closed the black curtains.

"Take your time!" Applecore hissed. "Act as if you belong here, ya great eejit."

"Easy for you to say." He reached up, heart thudding, and fumbled down the surprisingly heavy case. "It's hard to

imagine anyone in the universe who belongs here less than
I do."

"You're a bit of a whiner, Theo, do ya know that?"

"And you're a bit of a . . . shit." He stared at the suitcase.
"It's locked."

"Bugger. Let me have a look." Applecore put her eye
against the bag's latch, then turned to Theo. "You wouldn't
happen to have a hairpin, would you?"

"You know, I usually carry one . . ." It was a poor joke,
covering rising fear. Any moment now the bag's owner
would come back, there would be shouting and conductors
called and then he'd be thrown in some weird Brothers-
Grimm jail, just like Applecore had said. And then at night,
when no one was paying attention . . . "Jesus. *Jesus!* Isn't
there anything else we can use to open it?"

"I told you before, that name won't do anything but make
people itch. Hold on till I think a bit."

Theo stood and stared at the suitcase with nervous intensity. "What else could we use besides a key?"

"Well, I've got a hatpin," said a new voice behind him.
Theo jumped and dropped the suitcase onto the floor. It
popped open, scattering clothes and small parcels of toi-
letries all over the compartment. "Oh! I suppose you won't
need it now."

It was a girl, standing in the open doorway, dressed all in
black with a long coat and close-fitting hat. No, maybe not
a girl—how could you tell anything with these folks, anyway, especially age?—but certainly with every appearance
of young womanhood. She had a heart-shaped white face
and wide, startlingly violet eyes; all he could see of her hair
beneath the hat was a tar-black curl on her forehead. "Oh,
God," Theo said miserably. "Is this your suitcase?"

She looked at him curiously for a moment, almost startled, then a mischievous smile curled the corner of her
mouth. "No. But now I'm rather certain it isn't yours, either.
Are you thieves?"

"It's all a mistake," said Applecore decisively. "Just a

mistake. Let's put this back and find our own compartment. Sorry if we disturbed you, my lady."

"Oh, a mistake. Well, that's all right, too. It's a long, dull trip." She smiled, showing Theo her small, perfectly white teeth. "If you're bored and want some company, my compartment's just across the corridor."

Applecore, who had flown to Theo's shoulder, gave him a little kick. "Oh!" he said. "That's very kind . . . my lady. But . . . but my . . . associate and I, we . . . we have a lot of work to discuss."

"Do you want any help picking up those clothes?" She seemed to be enjoying the whole terrifying, embarrassing mess more than she should have.

Good Christ, Theo thought, *this is the first time I can ever remember in my whole life wanting a tornado to come down and suck an attractive woman out the window.* "No! No, ma'am, we'll be fine. Thank you."

"See you in the dining car, perhaps? Are you going all the way to the City?"

"No." Another kick from Applecore. "I mean, yes! Perhaps we'll see you."

When the girl had slipped back into her own compartment and discreetly drawn her own curtains again, Theo clawed through the clothes, which did at least appear to be a man's (as far as he could tell with his weak knowledge of fairy-fashion). He found a pair of shimmery gray trousers and a white shirt with long, wide sleeves. "Should I look for anything else? Shoes?"

"Don't make it too obvious—besides, you're not trying to look rich, just different than you looked before. You can roll up the arms on the shirt and we'll get back to Third Class. You'll look like a mill worker who had a job review today or something."

Theo stuffed the rest of the clothes back into the suitcase and heaved it onto the rack, then rolled up the purloined shirt and pants and tucked them under his arm. He opened the compartment door and let Applecore check to see if the passage was empty, then followed her out. Except for what might have been a twitch at the drawn curtains of the young woman's compartment, nobody seemed to notice. His pounding heart finally began to slow a little—but not much.

They stopped at the first lavatory once they had reached second class. "Go change," Applecore told him. "Then we'll head on back to one of the compartments where they won't be so likely to notice you weren't there at the beginning of the trip."

"You mean we're not going back to the same seats?"

"And sit down wearing different clothes that just got stolen from first class? It's asking for it, isn't it?"

He stepped out of the restroom a few moments later, as exhausted from all the anxiety as if he had run several miles. The clothes were a decent enough fit, although the pants were a little on the short side. "Good thing I lost weight after my mom died," he said.

"Sorry to hear about your ma, Theo," said Applecore gently. "Now shut it and walk."

Applecore chose a seat on the aisle in a cluster of sleeping house-boggarts—or that was how she described them; to Theo they just looked like more midgets, with bristly beards and bristly eyebrows at least as thick as the beards. The land outside hadn't changed much during their sojourn among the upper classes; the skies were still murky gray above the rain-soaked meadows, so that Theo couldn't even guess what lay beyond the mist that topped the first line of low hills, although he imagined it was more of the same.

"Do you think she's going to tell anyone about us?"

Applecore, who was nodding on his shoulder, gave a sleepy grunt. "That girl? P'raps. Not much we can do about it, 'less you were planning to murder her."

"No! But . . ." Of course, what else was there for them to do? This might be quaint and picturesque Fairyland, but the train was still moving fast enough to kill anyone who jumped off. "I just . . . why didn't she get upset? She knew what we were doing."

"She's a Flower—who knows what that lot thinks? Probably thought it was some kind of prank."

Theo sat back and pulled out his great-uncle's book but he couldn't focus on the words. *Come on, Vilmos. If you ever needed to study, this is the time. Just because you screwed up college doesn't mean you can't learn something important now . . .* But his brain felt like an animal in a too-small cage. "Where are we?" he asked suddenly.

"Root and Stem! Can't you let a body get some rest? It's bad enough I have to chase around without you murder me sleep, too." She rearranged herself. "We're still in Great Rowan, but we started out close to the border. Be glad—you could be traveling for days, otherwise."

"Which border?"

She groaned again. "And now he's going to make me think." She did so for the space of several heartbeats. "It's two days 'til the moon changes, right? So we'll be crossing into Hazel Wand. That's where Starlightshire will be this time."

"This time?" He had been reading something about this when the padfoot had started making trouble, but it hadn't made any sense. "You mean your towns and cities aren't always in the same place?"

"No, ya thick. The towns are always in the same place, it's the railroad stations that aren't. Well, they're always in the same place on the railroad, I guess, so you're half-right."

"What the hell are you talking about? You're telling me somewhere like that big town we were just in—that it moves? What, just gets up on its legs and walks to somewhere new?"

Applecore fluttered over to the seat in front of him, balancing carefully just behind the furry head of something large enough to take up two seats by itself, and whose snores Theo had mistaken when they first sat down for something caught in the train's wheels.

"Look, you." She leaned forward and lowered her voice. "Penumbra Fields—that's a commuter town, I told you. Grew up around Penumbra Station. So it's always, what is it, eleven stops from the City, no matter what province it's in. Starlightshire will be the same way 'cause it's a station-town. Oxeye Station, though, that's the Daisy station, see, and it's always in Great Rowan Field because the Daisy commune is always in Great Rowan. The train that goes through Oxeye Station is a local line—that's how you can *tell* it's local, see, because it's always in Great Rowan."

Theo shook his head, which was beginning to hurt. "But you said we could have left from Oxeye Station, we just thought it would be more dangerous," he said quietly. "How would that have worked if the stations that connect to the City are always moving around? I don't think I'm getting this."

"All local lines connect to a main station—it's just not always the same main station."

"Oh." He let his head fall back against the seat. "Well, that's crystal clear."

"I'm glad." Applecore was either missing the sarcasm or just wanted to get back to her nap.

He picked up Eamonn Dowd's book again, hoping for some mortal's-eye clarification of Fairyland's insane transportation system, which was beginning to seem like some high-school roleplaying game full of arbitrary, nonsensical rules, but Theo still couldn't concentrate well enough to read. He gave up and stared out the rain-spotted window, exhausted by his terrifying day but trying not to doze, waiting for a heavy (and probably anything but human) hand to fall on his shoulder, a voice to announce that the jig was up. It took him a moment to realize that he was staring at moving shapes in the distant hills.

Dark figures, perhaps a dozen in all, were riding down into one of the meadows. They dropped out of sight behind the train so quickly that he thought for a moment he had indeed been drowsing and dreaming, but a few moments later the train passed another cluster of riders reined up in the deep meadow, watching the train with a yellow-eyed intensity that made Theo extremely nervous. This group was much closer: even in the brief moments while the train swept past he could see that their clothes were dark but fantastical even by fairy standards, voluminous head scarves and billowing robes tied with strips of ribbon. The downpour did not seem to bother them. Each of the riders had a spear or goad in his hand and what looked like a rifle strapped on his back. What he could see of their narrow, long-nosed faces looked oddly familiar, but even that was not what made Theo reach up a hand to poke the little fairy on his shoulder awake.

Each of the horselike animals on which the riders were mounted had a single glossy horn in the middle of its forehead.

"Applecore? Applecore? There are people . . . or whatever . . . outside the train. Watching us. They're . . . they're riding unicorns."

He felt her wings buzz into motion beside his ear, tickling him. She hung before the window watching as they passed another group of the riders, these a bit farther away and riding parallel to the tracks, their every sure-seated movement suggesting that they could go as fast as the train if it were worth the bother. Looking at their lightning-legged mounts, Theo wondered if that might not be true.

When they had passed this last group, the stormswept plains were deserted again.

"Shite and onions!" Applecore said, but it sounded more like wonder than apprehension. "You don't see that very often."

"Who are they?"

"Grims. Wild goblins, I guess you'd call 'em. They live out in the wastelands and the mountains with their herds of sheep and cows, but they almost never come near the railroad or the cities. I've heard of some towns out in Ash and Alder where they show up to trade hides and some herbs and

things, but that's the first time I've seen them in Great
Rowan."

"Are they going to attack us?"

She gave him a look of puzzled amusement. "No, why?
Is that something that happens where you come from?"

"No." He thought of all the Western movies he had seen
with vengeful Indians riding down on a train, whooping and
blazing away at the helpless passengers. "Well, not lately.
Not where I live."

"Well, there used to be bandits here, too. But it's been a
deadly long time, and I've never heard of it happening since
the last Goblin War, and certainly not since the Winter Dynasties." She shook her head. "Grims on the plains of Great
Rowan. I wonder where they're going? Strange days."

She was just settling herself back on his shoulder, and he
was trying to decide whether he dared fall asleep himself,
when the pitch of the train's engines began to change. At
first Theo wasn't even certain what he was hearing—the locomotive already sounded quite different from its earthly
counterpart, the engine sounds more a low rushing and humming than a puffing *choo-choo*—but he found himself leaning forward. He could feel the motion changing even before
the first screech of the brakes.

"The train's stopping." Whatever was happening, he was
pretty sure that he wasn't going to like it. "Are we there yet?"

"We bloody well are not," Applecore said. "We're an
hour out of Starlightshire, at least."

"Maybe those goblins are angry and they've blown up the
tracks. Maybe your Great Fairy Chief spoke to them with a
forked tongue or something." The train had definitely stopped.
Many of his fellow passengers had woken up and were talking
among themselves, clearly less worried by this than he was. He
tried to calm himself.

"You do talk a load of old shite sometimes, Theo. But it
won't hurt to find out." She buzzed up off his shoulder and
started down the aisle at ankle level, but passengers were beginning to get out of their seats and she quickly rerouted to

an airspace just below the ceiling. Theo sank down and did his best to look like a half-asleep fairy on the way home from visiting perfectly normal fairy-friends or something. He couldn't see where Applecore had gone—some of the other passengers had stopped on their way back from the restrooms and were standing in the aisles, looking out the windows and speculating.

He spotted her coming back to him about a second before she arrived; she was going so fast that she had to beat her wings hard to stop.

"This is very bad, Theo," she said. "They've stopped the train."

"I know they've stopped the train! Who are 'they'?"

"Constables have just got on. But that's not the bad part. One of those hollow-men is with 'em. He's leadin' 'em down the aisles, looking for someone. What do you want to bet it's us?"

"Oh . . . fuck."

"Hold on till I get into your shirt."

"What?"

"If it's one of those fellas that was in the station and he's just been up with the driver till now, then he'll probably be looking for a big one like you with a little one like me. So I'm going to get out of sight. Meanwhile, you're dressed different. He may not recognize you—we don't know how close they saw you. And that sort of troll doesn't see that well, anyway."

"Are you suggesting I just sit here? What do you mean, don't see that well?"

"With their eyes. They're cave trolls. But their hearing and smell are sharp, so don't you say a damn word no matter what—it would only get you in trouble anyway. Just show your ticket and pretend you're deaf or somethin'."

"No, bad idea." He shook his head frantically. "Stay here—bad idea. Run away—much better idea."

"What, you think they won't have someone at the back of the train? I saw the uniforms—these aren't village plodders or even shireblades, these are Field Special Constables and that lot aren't stupid. Just sit tight." And with those words she clambered down his shoulder, over his collar, and into his shirt. A moment later he could feel her feet and hands as she braced herself against the inside of the stolen garment and belayed herself a little farther down, her torso pressing against him as she flattened herself against his chest. It was a bizarrely intimate sensation, like having a living Barbie doll squirming against his bare skin.

Thank God I'm probably going to die right now, he thought in a surge of near-delirium. *Because otherwise this would put me in therapy for years.*

"Don't you dare bump into anything," she hissed from a spot just to the side of his left nipple. "You'll smash me like a bug."

"Should I call Tansy? Maybe he could vouch for me or something."

"He'll do no such thing. He's not a fool. If they've stopped the train and put the Specials on to find you, it's probably because they've found Rufinus and someone's blamed it on you. Tansy on the phone won't make them change their minds and it will make him look very bad."

"Shit! So there's nothing we can do?" For a moment he thought he might throw up, then his stomach and everything else inside him seemed to turn to a single block of ice as the door at the front end of the compartment opened and a pair of armed fairies with padded vests stepped through. Behind them came a horribly familiar shape dressed all in dark clothes, slouch hat pulled low, face gleaming beneath the brim like the belly of a fish.

Theo watched helplessly as the two officers, prompted by whispered comments from the hollow-man, moved slowly down the aisle. The constables both had wings, or seemed to: their padded, dark-gray body armor certainly bulged behind their shoulders. They wore wraparound mirrored sunglasses, the kind Theo had seen on every highway patrol officer who had ever pulled him over and listened with blank-faced contempt to his stammered excuses, although these seemed to shine with a light of their own, like luminous mother-of-pearl. In fact, their heavy gloves had a faint glow to them, too—not so much a radiating light as a weird visual intensity. But most disturbingly, both constables carried what looked like heavy machine pistols, menacing slate-colored things whose magazines were not rectangular but shaped instead like . . . hand grenades? No, something more organic . . . pineapples?

No, bees' nests, he realized—they looked like some kind of modern-art beehives.

Something wriggled on his breastbone, then Applecore poked her head up above his collar to sneak a look. "Shite!" she hissed, "they must think you're the one who burned down the Cathedral or somethin'. They've got Hornets." With a little grunt of despair, she slid back down under his shirt again.

The police weren't actually asking many people for tickets or documents. As they got closer, Theo was fractionally relieved to see that the constables themselves looked a little bored, as though they had already decided that their superiors had sent them on a wild goose chase. But the hollowman was not bored in the least: like a dog reluctant to be led away, he leaned in between the policemen to sniff as the group moved slowly down the aisle.

Theo sank lower in his seat. He thought about lifting the book, but such a show of nonchalance seemed no different than screaming out his guilt. Every other passenger was watching the threesome coming down the aisle with sick fascination and many of them looked only a little less full of guilty panic than Theo himself.

This isn't a happy place, he realized. *It wasn't before I got here. Fairyland is in bad times.*

To his astonishment, the police moved right past him, the dull glow of their sunglasses sliding over him as though he were nothing, a bug.

Yes! he wanted to shout. *I'm a bug! I don't matter!*

The hollow-man's shadowed face swept across him and for an instant Theo thought he saw a glimmer as the tiny, piggy eyes beneath the hat touched his, paused for a split-instant, considered. Theo's heart seemed to swell until it was too large to beat. The hollow-man peered at him, flicked a glance at the trembling boggart next to him, then stepped past and began surveying people in the next row.

Theo's gaze rolled up to the ceiling and he sagged. For a moment, he thought he might faint from sheer, hysterical relief. Then, just as he was about to let out the breath he'd been holding for so long that sparkly lights were dancing along the edge of his vision, the pale, half-hidden face swiveled back in his direction. The head went down and Theo heard a loud, whuffling noise, then the hollow-man reached out a hand, flashing an inch of clammy white between black glove and black sleeve, and touched the elbow of one of the police constables.

"Back here," the hollow-man rasped. The voice was awkward, aphasic, as if the creature spoke with organs forced to adapt to speech but meant for some other task. "There is . . . something . . . someone . . ."

The police turned around and came back in Theo's direction, following the damp-faced thing as it sniffed the air like a hunting hound. From beneath the hat's brim, the tiny eyes sought Theo out and found him again and this time they did not slide away.

"Yes," the troll said. "Ah, yes. There you are."

16

POPPY

"*There you are!*"

Theo knew the voice, but he was too stunned with terror to figure out whose it was or why he recognized it. The armed constables had turned around and the hollow-man was leading them right back to him, but they all stopped at the sudden cry.

"What are you doing back here, you wicked thing?" The violet-eyed girl in black swept down the aisle from first class, her long coat flaring like the wings of a bat. The police stared at her openmouthed, and Theo was no less boggled: she seemed to be talking to him. "Did you think I would nap all day?" She turned and announced to the entire carriage, "It's true I'm a liberal employer, but really! I ask you!" She stopped beside Theo and gave him a little slap on the back of the head. "Get up, you great oaf. I am very angry with you. I rang my bell for simply *minutes* and there was no sign of you. Back here gambling and trading filthy stories with the rest of the no-accounts, I'm sure." As Theo stared at her in stunned surprise and Applecore squirmed in blind confusion beneath his shirt, the young woman turned a brightly amused smile on the two police constables. "Has my servant stolen something? If so, you have my permission to take him out and shoot him on the spot!" The smile bent into a mock-frown. "But Daddy and Mummy are so very fond of him. Perhaps I shouldn't have him shot after all."

"It is . . . some kind of trick," the hollow-man said, lurching forward. He turned toward the Field Special Constables. "He is the one—I am sure of it . . ."

"Get up, Quaeus, and tell me what you have done to offend this . . . moist person." The young woman got her hand under Theo's elbow and pulled until he struggled onto his feet. Everybody in the entire car was watching, every slotted eye and triangular bat ear aimed straight at them. Theo was so nonplussed that it took him long moments to realize the girl was trying to push something hard and thin into his hand. For an insane moment he thought it was a knife, thought she was trying to encourage him to attack the well-armed police.

"I . . . I don't know." He could barely form the words.

"He is a murderer," the hollow-man grated. "He has killed a young Flower lord in Penumbra Station only a few hours ago." Many of the onlookers gasped at this assertion and stared at Theo with bright, fascinated eyes. Whispers ran through the carriage like wind through wheat.

"Rubbish," said the young woman. "He has not left my side all day until I lay down to take a nap a few minutes ago. We never even got out at Penumbra Station. Show them your ticket, Quaeus."

Theo looked down at the thing in his hand, a wafer-thin rectangle that seemed to have been sliced off a gemstone like a piece of pastrami, then looked up at the woman. She smiled encouragingly. "He is a bit stupid as you can see," she told the officers, "and he's a trial to me sometimes, but he would never harm anyone."

Theo held out the special ticket in a shaking hand. The constables looked at it with something like awe, but the hollow-man ignored it, staring at Theo and the young woman with a hatred that even his hat and shrouding garments did not conceal.

After he had held the ticket for a moment in his radiant

glove, one of the constables passed the crystalline wafer back to Theo. The expression on the fairy-policeman's high-boned face, bored a few minutes earlier, was now electrified. "All in order."

"Now come back to the compartment, Quaeus," the young woman said. "When we get home, I'm afraid you will have to be punished for causing such trouble."

"Sorry to have bothered you, milady," said the other policeman.

"Yes, sorry to have bothered you, Lady Thornapple," said the one who had examined the ticket, who still looked as though he had briefly been allowed to tread on the steps of heaven.

The young woman laughed. "Lady Thornapple is my mother. You need only call me 'Mistress Thornapple.' "

"Yes, La . . . Yes, Mistress Thornapple."

The hollow-man let out a hiss that turned into a sputtering whisper. He shook his head in fury, writhing eel-like, as though he had no bones in his neck. "Are you fools going to let him walk away? Are you going to be taken in by this crude trick?"

"Shut up, you," one of the constables said. "First off, I told you, nobody's found a body in Penumbra Station. We checked."

"Then it's been hidden by this man or his associates," the hollow-man declared. "I witnessed the murder!"

The constable looked at him with obvious distaste. "Fine. Then how do you like this? This woman's father is First Councillor of the realm—what are you but a jumped-up private op? Now, do you want to finish this search, or are you going to waste more of our time here?"

The hollow-man seemed about to let out a shriek or leap at the constable's throat. Instead he turned toward Theo's rescuer and made a rubbery bow, but there was a nasty glint from the eyes beneath the hat brim. "I do not know what game you are playing, milady, but for now you have the advantage."

The woman in black's only reply was to laugh as she tugged Theo away up the aisle.

"I think we'll go to the club car," she said cheerfully as they passed through the loud connector between coaches. "That horrid person seemed extremely angry. He'd be a fool to try anything after all that, with so many witnesses, but we won't tempt him by isolating ourselves."

"What in the name of the Trees is going *on* out there?" shouted Applecore, struggling to fight her way loose from inside Theo's shirt.

"Ah, it's your little friend," said the young woman. "Well, I suppose she can come too. What do you drink, dear?"

Applecore fell back into the shirt as they bumped through the sliding door into the club car; her reply was lost against Theo's midsection.

"I'm so pleased." The young woman collapsed into a booth. "This looked like being such a dull trip." Theo sat down carefully, not only to protect Applecore, who was still squirming around inside his clothing, but because he felt that if he moved too quickly his head might come off and roll under the table.

"Uh . . . thank you," he said. "For everything."

"Not at all," she replied. "What would you like to drink? You really must have at least one drink before we begin our torrid affair."

A head the size of a grape poked out of Theo's collar. It scowled. "Begging your pardon, ma'am, but what the hell are you playing at?"

"Why—is he yours?"

"Not as such, no—but I'm the one looking after him. Did I hear that you're a Thornapple?"

The young woman rolled her eyes. "By birth, not by choice. The Trees know I'd just as soon have been born into an ordinary family like the Stocks or the Loosestrifes."

"An ordinary family with pots of money, then," said Applecore quietly, but the woman did not seem to hear. Theo could only stare in dazed astonishment at the exotic black-haired creature who had saved him. Just five minutes earlier he had been certain he was going to die; now his personal Tinker Bell was apparently arguing with this glamorous Goth princess about whether the newcomer would get to make love to him or not.

"So who are you?" he asked suddenly. "How did you get them to leave us alone, exactly? And who's . . . Kways?"

"Quaeus. He's one of our servants. He often travels with me—that's why I carry an open ticket for him—but he's back helping the family get ready for the funeral."

"Funeral?"

She went on as though he hadn't spoken. "They sent my old governess and a bodyguard to come back with me instead, but I wasn't going to put up with that so I left before they arrived."

Confused, Theo looked to Applecore, who had clambered out and was sitting on a saltshaker, her feet dangling above the tabletop, but the sprite only shook her head. Theo decided she didn't look very happy about what was going on, which was odd considering the alternatives.

"You don't know about the funeral?" the young woman said. "It's been on all the mirror streams. I'll tell you, but be a hero first and get me a drink . . . oh, I don't know your name!"

"Theo." As soon as he said it, he looked guiltily at Applecore, who was indeed scowling. *Ah, well, too late to come up with a pseudonym now.*

"What an odd name! Sounds like it could be something out of Ash or Alder—or one of the Willow farming families." She smiled dazzlingly. "My name is Poppaea, but everyone calls me Poppy. Now do be an absolute Rose and get me a drink, will you?"

"Ummm, what should I get?" *And how should I pay,* he also wanted to ask.

"Don't be silly—the barman knows what I want. Just tell him to put it on my tab."

That problem solved, Theo wandered off across the dark compartment. He was grateful to see that most of the tables were unoccupied, perhaps only a dozen drinkers in the entire long coach, mostly solitary or in quiet-talking pairs. The whole club car had a hush about it that he had experienced only on his trips bearing floral tributes to high-powered executive offices—the stillness of lives heavily insulated by money. Almost everyone in the car was on the handsomely human end of the Fairy spectrum. *They must have another bar for riffraff like me and the guys with wings and hooves,* Theo thought.

If the bartender had wings, he kept them well-hidden. He had the long, saturnine look of an actor who might have been asked to play Iago a few times. "For Mistress Thornapple, yes?" He already had a cocktail shaker in his hands. "Anything for you, sir?"

"Yeah." Theo realized he had no idea what constituted a social drink in Fairyland. Did they have vodka? Or would it be something more like eye of newt, toe of frog? "I'll have the same as she's having."

He brought the two frosted glasses and the two shakers back on a tray. As he slid into the booth, Applecore gave him a hard look from atop the salt-shaker. "Did you get anything for me?" she asked. "Or was the simple pleasure of having been inside your shirt supposed to last me all day?"

Oh, my God, what's this about? Theo wasn't always the quickest guy around the block, but there was something going on here that sounded a lot like jealousy. This from a tiny person who had already said she thought he was shallow and selfish? He took the shot glass—the smallest he had been able to find—out of his pocket and put it down beside her. "I thought you and I could share."

She was a little mollified, but not much. "Share that? What is it?"

He shrugged and turned to Poppy Thornapple, who was sipping her drink with obvious and even somewhat theatrical relish. "I got myself the same thing as you, but I don't know what it is."

"It's called a Wingbender—it's dreadfully lower class. I love it." She took in Applecore's flinch but didn't quite seem to understand. "Hawthorn berry liqueur and pomegranate juice, mostly, plus just the tiniest pinch of mandrake and something else I've forgotten, now. And a little honey-sugar on the rim of the glass, of course." She took a long, savoring swallow.

Applecore shook her head. "I don't think I want any more fermented berries," she said quietly to Theo. "Thanks, but."

"Father hates it when I drink in public," the young woman said suddenly. A tiny spot of color came to each impressive cheekbone. "Father hates it when I do *anything* in public."

"You said you were going to a funeral, didn't you?" Theo shook his head—already he was losing track of what they were talking about. He lifted his drink and sampled it cautiously. It was strange, quite bitter around the edges, which played surprisingly against the honey flavor, but not out of the range of the odder cocktails ordered by some of his dates in the pre-Catherine days. It did set up a tiny humming somewhere at the back of his head, and now he seemed to remember that mandrake could poison you. He set the glass back down.

"Oh, yes, the funeral." Poppy rolled her eyes again. "Dreadful, the whole thing. It's my brother, Orian. He got himself killed in some waterfront dive. They say it was a goblin. I suppose it could have been." She gave a strangely cheerful little shudder, like someone recalling a particularly good horror movie. "It's all a ghastly waste of time. I hate traveling during holidays."

Applecore almost slipped off her salt-shaker. "Your *brother?* Your brother was killed and you think the funeral's a waste of time?"

The look she got back was half-annoyance, half-amusement. "You didn't know him, dear. A horrible, mean boy even when we were all little." She looked at Applecore. "Oops. Didn't mean to be rude. When we were young, I should have said. Anyway, he tormented my sisters and me. He killed my little dog. On purpose, in front of me." Her voice had grown very flat. "And he got worse when he left school. But he was the apple of Father's eye, so everyone in the family is acting terribly, terribly bereaved." She waved her hand. "Call me heartless if you want to. Father insisted I come back for the funeral, so here I am." She stared at her drink for a long moment, then suddenly looked up at Theo. "Why don't you come to the funeral with me? We wouldn't have to stay long. It's going to be at the family vault in Midnight, just outside the Trees. I know a very nice private club less than an hour away from there, in Eventide. We could slip off." She emptied her glass and clicked it down on the table, staring at Theo with feverish interest; he suddenly realized this wasn't anywhere near the girl's first drink of the day. "I'm sure your small friend has other things to do in the City. Wouldn't you like to spend a little time with me?"

He sat blinking in startled silence for so long that he decided she would think he was trying to communicate in semaphore. There was a painful brittleness to her. She was beautiful, but just as obviously a bit unstable—not to mention the fact that several different kinds of unpleasant things were busily trying to kill him. Embarrassed, he glanced at Applecore, but she only stared stonily at their rescuer. "I . . . I . . . that's very . . . generous . . ."

"Ooh," Poppy said suddenly. "That's gone right through me. You will excuse me while I make a quick trip to the necessity, won't you . . . Theo, wasn't it? Funny name."

"Uh, sure. Certainly."

She slid out of the booth and made her way with a kind of unbalanced grace down the aisle and out the far end of the compartment.

"Rich hussy," said Applecore. "That's the way they get, some of them. No one ever to teach them right from wrong, and nothing to do with their lives but spend the family's gold."

Theo almost smiled. His companion, for all her stated disdain for politics, was a bit of a pocket Marxist. "She's all right. She saved our lives."

"It's a game to her, Theo!"

"Well, maybe we can get her to play the game a bit more. I don't really want to stay on this train. That . . . troll-thing . . . it wasn't happy."

Applecore nodded. "True. He won't do anything while those Specials are still on the train, but since they won't find any murderer, they'll get off again in Starlightshire. Of course, even if he lets us alone 'til then, he might have more of his friends waiting when we reach the City."

"So maybe the girl can help us somehow. She saved us once. And who else is going to help us? Who?"

"You can't trust her just because she says she likes you! She's a Thornapple!"

"So?"

She buzzed so close that trying to watch her angry face made him cross-eyed. "Do you pay no attention at all, ya thick? She's a Thornapple. Her da's the First Councillor—one of the biggest fellas in all of Faerie. *And* he's a Choke-weed—he's Lord Hellebore's number one ally, which means he wants to see all your kind dead. Some girlfriend you've chosen!"

"Girlfriend?" He pulled his head back so he could focus. "What are you talking about? We need help. Badly. Now sit down where I can see you and talk to me. Please."

Applecore lit on the table, scowling. "You're a babe in the wilderness, Theo. Do you have that expression where you come from?"

"Yes. And maybe I am, but . . ."

He was interrupted by Poppaea Thornapple, making her way down the aisle with an absorbed expression on her face—a face that was looking less and less alien to Theo: he was beginning to see her just as attractive. Very attractive. And he hadn't been with a woman in quite some time . . .

"Just back me up," he whispered to Applecore. "You know, make sure I don't say anything too stupid." The sprite looked as though she'd rather push him off the train, but she didn't argue.

Young Mistress Thornapple was moving with exaggerated care because she had a Wingbender in each hand. "I brought you another," she said as she slid into the booth. Theo couldn't help wondering if she was as slender under all those clothes as she looked.

"I'm still drinking the first one."

"Ah, well. Wouldn't do to be caught short. They close the bar when they pull into Starlightshire." She turned to look out the window. The landscape was less wild here: an occasional house could be seen half hidden in the forested hills, and some of the open meadow actually looked as though it had been mowed. "We'll be there soon."

"The thing is, Poppy . . ." He took a breath. He had spoken confidently to Applecore, but the little fairy was right—he didn't know much of anything, and he was about to cross a line. This young woman was part of a powerful family that wanted him dead. He was nervous all over again. "The thing is, what that troll, that . . . hollow-man . . . said was partway true."

"That you're a criminal? Darling, I know that. I found you and your little friend opening peoples' suitcases, didn't I?" Her long, uptilted eyes suddenly widened. "Oh, did you truly kill someone? That's . . . that's quite impressive!"

"*No!* No, we didn't kill anyone. But we know the fellow who was killed. We were traveling with him. It was that white-faced troll and his friends who killed him."

"By the Inner Ring!" Poppy Thornapple seemed almost more pleased than upset. *She thinks it's exciting,* Theo realized. *She's treating this all as some huge diversion.* "And now they want to kill you, too! And I'm the one who saved you."

"Yes, yes, you did. But that's not going to make any difference if we stay on the train all the way to the City. They'll just be waiting for us there."

"Then you must come home with me!" She leaned forward. "We have a huge place. Daddy never minds if I bring anyone home. Daddy never even notices—he's always working."

Great, thought Theo, *I didn't think of that. Sure, we'll just drop over to the Fuhrerbunker for the weekend.* He looked helplessly at Applecore.

"Yes, well, that's very kind, your ladyship," said the little fairy. You could hardly tell her teeth were clenched. "But when we get to the City, we have important business. The safety of the realm, like. And . . . and . . ." her inspiration dried up for a moment, but then came flooding back, "And we wouldn't want to put you in that sort of danger."

"No," said Theo gratefully. "Don't want to put you in danger. But we do need your help. Is there some way you can help us get into the City without taking the train all the way in?"

Poppy Thornapple was looking at him now with an interest that went beyond the merely carnal and had instead become something like real fascination. "Oh, yes," she said. "Of course. We can hire a coach. I don't carry much cash but I have oodles of tallies." She hadn't touched her most recent Wingbender at all. Now she pushed it to the side so she could set her small black purse on the table and begin sorting through it. "I even have a schedule—here!" She lifted out a small translucent oblong very much like the ticket she had earlier produced on Theo's behalf. "Oh, we're in luck—Starlightshire's in Hazel now. Otherwise we would have had to stay on until Trumpet Windhome."

"You'd do that for us?"

"Of course." She smiled hugely. "Oh, but look at me! Here I am, acting like a silly schoolgirl, when your friend's been killed." She tried, not entirely successfully, to look sad. "What was his name?"

Theo hesitated and Applecore jumped in. "Rufinus weft-Daisy, ma'am. I expect it will be in the news. He was Theo's . . . cousin."

"Such a strange name—Theo, I mean! Is it short for Theodorus or Theolian, or something else?"

"Theodorus, ma'am," said Applecore solemnly. "Theodorus weft-Daisy." She leaned toward her after casting a brief look of pity toward Theo. "Poor as ditchwater, ma'am," she whispered confidentially, "his whole branch of the family."

"Oh," said Poppy. Her violet eyes didn't leave Theo. "Brave, resourceful, and poor. *How wonderful.*"

As the train passed through what was obviously the outskirts of a fair-sized town, they went back to Poppy's compartment and made sure to draw the curtains. When the train stopped, they waited for a couple of minutes that seemed much longer to Theo. Just as the conductor was calling the last boarding, they sent Applecore ahead to scout, then hurried down the corridor to the end of the compartment—or at least hurried as fast as they could with all Poppy Thornapple's luggage in tow.

"I can't believe you didn't call a porter," she said to Theo.

"No sign of Mister Tall-Dark-and-Damp anywhere," Applecore announced.

They joined the milling throng on the platform just as the doors closed and the train pulled out again. Theo looked up and saw a flash of white, masklike face pressed against the window in a darkened compartment like a greasy thumb on the glass, watching them with helpless rage.

"That's him," Applecore said. "We've done it, for a bit, anyway."

"Look, there are those charming little constables," said Poppy cheerfully. The commuters heading down the platform toward the station were eddying around the armored bulk of the Specials as though they were two large stones in a stream.

"I don't think we want them to see us," Theo said. "Since

your tickets must have said you were going all the way back to the City."

"I suppose you're right . . ."

Theo took her hand—it was as cool as marble—and led her back up the platform. He didn't hold on very long, although she clearly didn't mind. They stopped by what he took for a phone booth (it was unlabeled and could have been some altogether stranger contraption for all he knew) and waited. When the constables had finally vanished into the station concourse, Theo picked up Poppy's two largest bags and began trudging down the platform.

"What have you got in here?" he asked breathlessly. "Homework from sculpture class or something?"

She laughed. "Shoes, in that one." She pointed at the smaller bag, which was still large enough that Theo felt like he was dragging a St. Bernard dog with a handle on its back. "A girl can't go home for two weeks and not have any shoes. The other one's mostly clothes."

Theo heard Applecore snort just behind his shoulder. He couldn't really argue with her assessment. "Haven't you people invented wheels on luggage here?"

"But all the porters have lovely little wheeled carts. Why would you want wheels on the cases, too? Is that some kind of fad out in Rowan this season?"

Theo shook his head.

Starlightshire Station was about the same size as Penumbra but without a dome, a long, low, barnlike structure with an open scaffolding roof trussed by metal bars. The space between the bars was not apparently empty as with Penumbra; instead there was a shimmer in the open spaces, a moving swirl of faint color like a soap bubble film waiting for breath. Theo didn't bother to ask about it. He had experienced enough inexplicable strangeness for one day.

As he watched the swirl of fairy nobles and rougher, stranger creatures moving across the concourse, Poppy pulled something that looked like a smooth silver wand out of her purse and spoke quietly into it. "They'll be here very shortly," she told Theo when she'd finished.

"Who?"

"The coach-hire people, silly. In fact, we should probably go wait out front."

"Then I'll have to hit the jacks again," Applecore announced. "Sorry to be crude, but facts are facts and my bladder feels like a frightened blowfish." She rose into the air and flew above the crowds toward the nearest wall. To Theo's surprise, instead of dropping down to door level she skimmed along about ten feet off the ground, then ducked into a hole in the front of a small cubicle about the size of a shipping box, mounted high on the wall like a birdhouse. After spending a great deal of time in the restroom on the train, Theo had been wondering what kind of facilities there were for people Applecore's size; now he had a better idea.

"Is the sprite a . . . special friend of yours?" Poppy asked suddenly. "A sweetheart?"

"Applecore?" He was startled. Didn't the fact that he was about a hundred times bigger make the answer pretty obvious? "No. She's just a friend." He felt disloyal. "A very good friend. She's done a lot for me."

"Ah." She nodded and seemed satisfied. "Of course. Anyone else?"

"What?"

"Is there anyone else, back home or wherever? For you?"

He thought of Cat, so far away and undoubtedly so very happy not to be with him. "No. Not anymore."

She brightened, then suddenly grew morose. "You must think I'm a little fool."

"No, of course I don't. You've been wonderful to us."

"I have . . ." She wouldn't meet his eye. "Well, I have a confession to make. Because I like you, Theo, and I wouldn't want you to go on thinking that . . . that . . ." She trailed off.

Oh, my God, he thought. *She's called her family and they're on their way right now to arrest me and torture me*

in some weird fairy-dungeon. "Confession?" His voice was
not as steady as he would have wished.

"I'm one hundred and five."

"What . . . ?"

"I'm one hundred and five years old." She still couldn't
look at him. "I just wanted you to know. Because I do like
you. Now you probably hate me."

He could only stare.

"I know I seem older. Well, sometimes. My parents think
I'm a child, but I'm not—I've had lots of lovers already. But
I didn't want you to find out and think I was trying to trick
you. I'm not at university like you probably thought—I'm in
my last year of Swansdown Academy. But I'm old enough
to marry, you know, so I'm not *that* young!" Now she finally
looked up, but seemed puzzled by the stunned expression on
his face. "I don't mean you have to marry me!" She narrowed her extraordinary eyes a little. "So how old are you?"

Theo's stammering was interrupted by the return of
Applecore. "Right," she said. "Me kidneys have sighted
land again. Should we get going?"

O utside the station it was early evening and the lights
were coming on all over Starlightshire, streetlamps
and advertising signs, but they all seemed fainter than the
electric lights Theo knew, even the simplest more silvery
than ordinary white light and also more . . . *witchy*, was the
only word he could summon. Thus, when the huge fog-
colored car rolled up to the sidewalk in front of the station,
silent as Charon's barge, he jumped a little. The driver
stepped out and Theo was startled by what at first seemed
like a familiar horselike face.

No, he realized, *it's not Heath, just another doonie. He
said a lot of them were drivers.*

"Are you the parties wanting a ride to the City?" the
driver asked. His greenish skin was heavily mottled with
white—Theo wondered if he might be from something like
the pinto branch of the family—and he wore a gray uniform

whose sheen was only a little less pearlescent under the station's flood lamps than the car itself. "I need someone to signify, please."

Poppy bristled. "I told them who I was!"

"No offense, Mistress Thornapple. It's just the way things are these days. It's a shame, but there you go." He wagged his eyeless head apologetically and produced a small leather-bound book from the pocket of his coat. "A formality." He opened it to what seemed to Theo a pair of blank pages and held it out. Poppy held her small hand over it for a moment; the driver nodded and put it away again. The whole thing was so much like ceremonial magic and yet so similar to using a bar code reader that Theo was suddenly struck not by the strangeness of the Fairie world but by the previously unremarked strangeness of his own.

When they were seated in the deep and spacious passenger compartment with all Poppy's luggage stowed in the trunk, the car slid out of the station parking lot. Theo looked anxiously out the tinted windows for signs of someone watching them, but the crowd hurrying in and out of Starlightshire Station's lunar light seemed oblivious to them.

"It's about three hours to the City from here," said the driver. "Would you like to hear some music?"

"Oh, yes, please," said Poppy. From out of nowhere—or more likely from hidden speakers, but Theo couldn't simply dismiss the "from nowhere" theory after what he'd seen lately—a mournful air filled the car. The music seemed to occupy the center of a previously unimagined triangle whose three sides were Arab flutes, quiet polka changes played backward on the glockenspiel with a lot of reverb, and the noise of running water. Theo listened with fascinated attention. It was enchanting, almost literally so, like being hypnotized in the nicest possible fashion. At last the tune ended and a new one began, an even more improbable combination that was something like "Danny Boy" played at one-tenth normal speed and arranged for gong and sitar. This one had a vocal, a helium whisper like something sending back its last transmission as it drifted away into the void of space. The only words Theo could make out were *". . . far far far the mirror we are, the nearer star . . ."*

"I love this tune," Poppy said happily. "Whatever happened to these people?"

"One-hit wonders?" Theo guessed.

Despite the fact that the third passenger was no larger than a parakeet, Poppy had squeezed herself against Theo and showed no signs of moving away. He was having a hard time not reacting to her; the feeling of a woman's firm leg pressed against his own was exactly as distracting in Fairyland as it would have been back in good old Mortalia.

But she's a hundred and five years old! Old enough to be a great-great grandmother—no, old enough to be dead! The mere thought of her in a romantic light should have felt like that film *Harold and Maude,* but it didn't, quite. *Or what was that other one with Ursula Andress, where she's really like a million years old and turns into a mummy at the end . . . ?* But that was bullshit, he told himself—she wasn't some really old woman who looked young by magic. She *was* young. Just not by the standards of his own world.

The real, seriously bad problem is that she's some important rich guy's daughter, and as far as they're concerned, she's just a schoolgirl. Like they don't have enough reasons to want to kill me already.

He looked over to Applecore, feeling guilty about the fact that he had somehow come to be holding one of Poppy Thornapple's hands again, and equally guilty that after realizing it he still hadn't disengaged, but the sprite had made herself a sort of nest in the corner of the seat, curled on Poppy's cloche hat, and was apparently sound asleep.

Thanks, he thought bitterly. *Leave me here to figure out this weird-ass stuff by myself. Thanks a lot.*

Poppy stirred beside him. "Can you open the roof?"

He only realized she wasn't talking to him but to the invisible driver when a panel opened in the ceiling of the car.

Above them hung a sky full of huge stars like jellied fire, like Van Gogh's maddest visions made real.

"It's always nice in this part of the world," she said. "I can't wait until we're outside of town."

Theo was still catching his breath, staring at the stellar fireworks. "Why?" he croaked.

"Because it's so built-up around here these days and so bright, all the streetlights and everything make it hard to see the sky properly." She snuggled in close against him. "Do you like me just a little, Theo? Tell the truth."

"Yes. Yes, of course. You're a very nice ... young woman."

He could hear the pout in her tone of voice. "That's the kind of thing people say about girls in the Young Blossoms—the girls that put together cobweb drives and bake sales to relieve starving goblins in Alder Head."

"All right, you're beautiful, too. But you know that."

"Really?" She rubbed her face against his upper arm, slow and comfortable as a fire-warmed cat. "That's better. Will you make love to me, then?"

He took a breath. "I don't think it's a good idea, Poppy. I'm ..." He couldn't think of a way to say it that didn't sound like the worst kind of letting-someone-down-easy cliché. But it was true! It was actually true! "I'm not a very good person to be involved with right now. But you're lovely. I'm really glad I met you."

She raised her head a bit and regarded him with those huge eyes, the purple so dark that they seemed pools of total shadow even underneath the fierce starlight. "Truly? You wouldn't be lying to me just because I'm a hundred and five, would you?"

He nodded. "Truly."

"All right." She nestled into him once more. "Perhaps we shouldn't rush things, anyway. I don't want you just to go away like the others always do. Well, the ones I didn't *want* to go away. Some of the rest I couldn't chase away with black iron." Her eyes remained closed, but she smiled and covered her mouth with her fingers; she was still a little tipsy. "Sorry. Everyone says I have a shocking vocabulary." She yawned. "I think I'm going to sleep for a little while. It's been such a busy day . . ."

There was no sense of transition, but after a while he could tell by the limp heaviness of her body against him that she was asleep. The music played on, a long tapestry of soft flute-noises and droning chords that made him think of the wind moaning around mountaintops, but with a strange little backbeat that kept surfacing and then fading down into the mix again. Theo was reluctant to move or in any way break the spell. He felt as though he had stepped out of the tumultuous events of the past days into some dreamlike pocket of his own past, an eddy of time from his teenage days—a girl, a quiet car, the countryside sliding past the windows. *But this girl's a century old and the countryside is full of unicorns and monsters.*

For a moment the music dwindled. *"Everyone all right back there?"* asked the driver.

"Just fine," Theo replied. The music came back up, throbbing mysteriously, sugared now with the faint chirping of some stringed instrument. If there were crickets in Heaven, Theo thought, then listening to them must be something like this.

Music really did mean something to him, he realized, and it always had. It called to him, although there were no words to describe what it promised. It was like a secret language he never forgot how to speak, a hometown he could always return to when he tired of what life was throwing at him. From the moment he had first heard himself imitating the sounds that came from his mother's radio, before he even knew that what he was doing was called "singing," music had seemed like a place only Theo knew about and in which he was always welcome. Now he listened with joy to this strange, new music—the first hint of an entire world full of music he had never heard or even imagined, an idea as inviting as a kiss—and as he did so he stared at the sky. As Poppy Thornapple had suggested, the stars, already insanely bright, seemed to be growing even brighter as the car rolled deeper into the countryside darkness. At the same time, their gleam did not turn the sky around them blue, but made it seem even more unashamedly black.

The dark sky got darker. The stars got brighter. The music surrounded him, lifted him, even seemed to teach him things about this world he hadn't understood before he'd heard it. After a time he could not compute, Theo found himself carefully disengaging himself from Poppy Thornapple, moving her head from his shoulder and propping it with his own folded jacket. He lifted himself from the seat, putting first his head and then his shoulders out through the moon roof until he could spread his elbows on the roof of the car. The air that lashed his face was warm and just a little damp; he found himself wondering absently if rain clouds here moved like they did in the real world, or had patterns as confusing as the inconstant towns of Faerie.

But sweet as it was, the fertile-smelling air was barely on his mind or in his senses: with the lights of the town now far behind them and only the silvery beams of the car's headlights smearing the road ahead, the stars seemed to grow even grander and more dramatic, to flame like novas. He could see both their living, burning, gaseous immensity and their diamond hardness, as though they were cosmic and magical objects simultaneously. They filled the sky in all directions, and even the smallest shone so clearly that for the first time in his life he truly felt the world beneath him to be something adrift in a spherical sea of lights. At the same time, as the strange fairy melodies rose up around him and the moist wind tugged at his hair, he could see that beyond doubt they were also gems scattered across the fabric of the sky, or even the eyes of gods.

It was only when he slumped back down in his seat half an hour later that Theo realized that his cheeks were wet, and that he had been crying for a long time.

*   *   *

He woke to find something brushing against his nostril and a sneeze building.

"Don't you dare!" Applecore said sharply.

"Then get off my face." He scratched his itching nose and tried to sit up, but discovered that the Thornapple girl was draped over him, lying on his arm. Outside the car it was quite dark; the stars framed in the moon roof, while spectacularly beautiful by any earthly measure, were vastly reduced from what he had seen before.

"We're not in what's-it-called anymore," he said groggily.

"Starlightshire. Not for hours. We're just cutting across the edge of Ivy. We'll be in the City soon." The sprite's wings buzzed briefly as she lit on his knee. From what he could see of her by the dimly illuminated panels over the doors, she looked strained and edgy.

But why wouldn't she? he thought. *This hasn't been any easier on her than me.* Still, he did not want to be conscious right now—it felt like he hadn't slept in days. "Why did you wake me up?" he complained.

"Because we're going to be there soon and I need to talk to you before *she* wakes up."

"She's not so bad, you know."

"You would think that, wouldn't you?" Applecore crossed her arms over her chest. "But that's neither here nor there. We have to decide where to get out."

"Aren't we going to that, what was it . . . ?" He ransacked his fuzzy memory. "Springwater Square? To see that Foxglove guy?"

"No. Not unless you want to find out what happens to bad mortal boys who don't listen to their elders."

"Elders? Oh, my God, how old are *you?*"

"Old enough to think with my head and not other parts of me, thank you very much. I don't care what Tansy says, we're not going to put ourselves in that Foxglove's hands. Those Flowers think they know everything, but I've been in the City lately and I've heard what people there are saying. That Foxglove and . . ." she lowered her voice, making Theo

lean as far toward her as he could with Poppy's head in his
armpit, ". . . and this girl's father are thick as thieves. And
they're both chummy with Lord Hellebore, and *that's* about
as bad as news can get."

"Who's Hellebore? I think I've heard the name before."

"We've time to talk about it later. Right now, you let me
do the talking to your girlfriend here."

"She's not . . ."

Poppy was stirring. She lifted her head and brushed a
strand of ink-black hair out of her eyes. She wore it cut
short, shorter even than Applecore's hacked red bob, but
without the hat her bangs seemed continually in her eyes.
"Theo . . . ? Are we there?"

"Not yet," Applecore said shortly. "Go back to sleep."

She sat up, yawning and stretching. "Shade and stream, I
must be a terrible sight! I'll have to ask the driver to stop
somewhere so I can freshen up before we reach town."

"That's just what I wanted to talk to you about, Mistress,"
Applecore began, but the girl sat up straight on the seat and
took Theo's hand.

"Look, we *are* here. I told you it wouldn't take long."

They were coming around a hillside bend and for a moment Theo, looking a bit stupidly at the smoked glass that
separated them from the driver's seat, couldn't understand
what she was talking about. Then he saw the first of the
lights framed in the window beside him.

It was immense, so wide that it seemed to fill the entire
horizon. At this distance he couldn't make out individual
buildings but only the lights that filled the wide, flat valley
between the hills, a monstrous wash of lights as though
someone had spilled a wheelbarrow full of diamonds, emer-
alds, and sapphires across the ground, as though the stars
through which he had flown earlier had drifted down from
the sky and piled up like snowflakes.

"It's . . . it's big." He wasn't certain he'd ever seen any
earthly city so large—it had to be in the range of New York
or Tokyo or Mexico City, at least—but he also found he

didn't care much about comparisons just now. It was majestic and stunningly beautiful and, because the lights were just a few tones off from what he was used to, more than a little alien. His heart was beating very quickly, and not simply from wonder: there was fear, too, at something both so monumental and so utterly indifferent to him.

He swallowed, staring in silence for what might have been half a minute, then at last began to sing in a quiet voice, *"They say the neon lights are bright, on Broadway . . ."* He gave the old tune a long, slow bluesy read, then, when no one objected, sang "I Left My Heart in San Francisco," and an old Journey song from his childhood about city lights, and finished off his impromptu urban medley with "New York, New York."

"If I can make . . . it . . . there, I'll make it anywhere . . ." Yeah, they call this whistling past the graveyard, he thought as he neared the end. *But what the hell.*

"You have such a pretty voice, Theo," Poppy said, squeezing his hand. "I've never heard any of those songs— I haven't even heard music like that. Where is it from?"

"Another world," he told her, then fell silent again before the awesome spread of light.

17

THE HOTHOUSE

The Remover of Inconvenient Obstacles admired the way in which he had been kept waiting. Even in the midst of world-changing events, Nidrus, Lord Hellebore, had taken the opportunity for a small assertion of power and status. An hour sitting in a deceptively uncomfortable chair in his lordship's outer office, with only Hellebore's pale and silent secretary for company, had made the point handily.

The Remover wondered if the secretary was always so pale and silent, and whether it was her habit so scrupulously to avoid looking at those her master kept waiting. He did, after all, have a certain effect on people, even when he was spruced up to go visiting. Even very strong charms could not make him look entirely . . . acceptable.

"His lordship will see you now," she announced with her back still toward him. A door opened in the wall, silent as a petal falling to the ground; reddish light spilled onto the carpet. The Remover stood and made his deliberate way into the office of the master of Hellebore House.

Lord Hellebore sat half in shadow, a ghostly presence. The Remover recognized his own habit when receiving his rather infrequent visitors; that part of the Remover's face which could still smile twitched a little as he sat down. The

white flower in its spotlit vase glowed like phosphorus between them.

"Dramatic lighting, my lord."

Hellebore flicked his fingers and the light grew more
even. "You will forgive me. I was thinking."

"A worthy occupation for a nobleman."

"And the worthier for being unfashionable, eh? So, do
you bring me news?"

"Nothing you do not already know, my lord."

"Yes. Well."

A long time passed in silence.

"Explain to me," Hellebore said at last, "why you have
failed."

The Remover's tone was mild. "I have not failed, my
lord. I simply have not succeeded yet. Remember, you
wished me to begin this while the person in question was
still in the other world. When he escaped the initial attempt
and crossed over, he gained days. But the pursuer has
crossed over now, too. I think your quarry's hours of freedom are numbered." The Remover allowed himself another
little smilelike tightening of the mouth. "I gather you have
made an attempt of your own, my lord. I am surprised that
after you spent so much to purchase my services you are
willing to spend still more on what I must honestly suggest
are less likely methods. Really, my lord—hollow-men?"

"The cave trolls are not such bunglers as you make out.
And what is the purpose of being rich if you cannot employ
multiple weapons against that which stands in your way? I
would rather be paying a second assassin to stab the corpse
than have an enemy slip away."

"But the task here is more delicate than a murder, my
lord. That is why you hired me in the first place. Do you
know the expression about cooks and broth? Would you
choose to have several chirurgeons wrestling each other for
pride of place while you lay ill on an operating table, or
would you rather have only one, the best man at the craft,
standing over you?"

Hellebore made a quiet noise of irritation. "When you have brought me this mortal, then you can gloat. If you succeed, I will make you official tame monstrosity to the Parliament of Blooms."

After an almost invisible flinch, the Remover said quietly, "But I am not tame, my lord."

"Enough of this." Hellebore stood, unfolding gracefully from behind the desk like an exquisitely crafted machine. "I have another with whom I would consult—I think you know who I mean. I would like you to come, too. You have not actually met him, have you?"

"Just the once, my lord."

"Ah, of course. I had forgotten." Hellebore waved his hand and a door opened in the side of the office. "You don't object to meeting him again, then?"

"On the contrary, my lord, I will find it most interesting."

They had been walking for only a few minutes, but already the temperature was noticeably warmer. "He likes his rooms heated," said Hellebore. "That won't cause any problems for your . . . condition, will it?"

"Only minor inconvenience."

"Lady Hellebore calls this part of the tower 'the Hothouse.' "

"And how is your wife?"

Hellebore gave him a strange look. The Remover of Inconvenient Obstacles was not generally known for making polite small talk. "She is well. She spends little time in the City these days, though. She has taken the younger children out to Festival Hill, our place in Birch. She is afraid there will be a war."

"But of course there will be a war. You are seeing to that."

"That is why I have not talked her out of staying at Festival Hill."

They reached another waiting room. Seated at the desk in this one was not a secretary but a man in a white cloak with a single band of white silk knotted about his dark hair. He

looked up at their approach, then rose. "Ah, Lord Hellebore." His eyes slid to Hellebore's guest, stopped for a moment, then rapidly returned to his patron. "Have you come
to see him?"

"Yes, but I'd like to hear any news, first."

"He is well—quite healthy. His appetite is uneven, but
that is common in a child his age—some days nothing,
other days we are calling down to the comb over and over."
He looked worriedly for a moment at the Remover, clearly
hesitating.

"Go on," said Hellebore.

"He had another seizure a few weeks ago, but otherwise has
responded well to the medicaments. Interestingly, though, he is
a bit allergic to both moly and the most quotidian sleep-
charms . . ."

"Yes," said Hellebore. "Thank you, Doctor . . . Doctor . . ."

"Iris. Well, weft-Iris. But how could you be expected to
remember, my lord? You have so many important things on
your mind."

"Open the door, please."

"Of course!" Doctor weft-Iris sprang back to the desk and
waved his hand above it, murmured something. A door appeared in the wall where there had been no sign of it before.
Lord Hellebore stepped toward it, then paused and gestured
for his guest to go in first.

As he did, he heard the doctor quietly ask Hellebore, "Is
that . . . ?"

"Yes, it is." Then the door closed and Hellebore and the
Remover were alone in a short, steam-dampened hallway.
"You are a celebrity of sorts," Hellebore said with a cold
smile.

"To the medical craft. And to a few other crafts as well."

When the door to the larger chamber opened, it was at
first very hard to see anything through the swirl of warm
fog. When the air currents caused by the door had abated a
little, the huddle of white-clad bodies on the far side of the
white room became clearer.

The two nurses stepped to the side as Hellebore approached, so quickly it almost seemed they must be guilty of something, clutching the towels they had been employing to the bosoms of their uniforms, their faces heavy with the look of foreboding common to the staff of that household. But their master apparently was in no mood to find a reason to punish anyone today. He simply waved them off, and, gratefully, they went.

"Hello, Stepfather," said the small figure in the thick white bathrobe. The boy's voice had a strange throatiness, as though it came from a full-grown woman imitating a child's way of speaking. The skin visible on his bare feet, hands, and slightly round face was quite pink, perhaps with the heat of the bath he had just left. His curly light brown hair fell in loose, wet ringlets to just above his eyes. "You can come forward—I'm really quite clean."

"So I see," said Hellebore, but did not move. "I came to talk to you. I've brought someone. This is . . ."

"I know who it is," the boy said with a grin. Even the Remover of Inconvenient Obstacles, no stranger to disturbing sights, could not help noticing that the child's smile went his stepfather's grimaces one better: it did not touch his eyes or warm the rest of his face in any way, a grin like someone pulling up the corners of a corpse's mouth. "We're old friends, he and I."

"Ah. Yes. In any case, I wanted to ask you a few questions. Get your advice about something."

"About Theo Vilmos."

It was surprising in itself to see Hellebore surprised. "Yes."

"He's still free."

"How did you know?"

"Oh, come, Stepfather, that doesn't require any great art. What else would bring the two of you here? Your esteemed guest scarcely ever leaves his house in the waterfront district. And if you had managed to get your hands on this Vilmos, this . . . *mortal,*" he gave the word an unusual, even poisonous emphasis, "then why would you be asking me for advice?" The boy stretched, then beckoned to one of the nurses. She came, shamefacedly sneaking glances at Lord Hellebore to see if he objected. The boy shrugged off his robe and stood, rosily and plumply naked. "Dry me. I wish to be dressed now."

As the nurse began to rub him with a towel, Lord Hellebore sent one of the other nurses for chairs. He sat, stretching out his long legs. "Well, then. Tell me why we have not succeeded."

"Because this is not a runaway servant or a spy from one of the other Houses you seek. Success will not come so easily."

"Are you suggesting that somehow this creature is outwitting us?"

Where another child might have rolled his eyes or snorted, the boy only became more still. Even as his outside was being briskly rubbed, he seemed to retreat into some quiet place within himself, barely within shouting distance. "No," he said at last. "I am saying that things like this— things of which this Vilmos person is a part—are never simple. He is an attractant of sorts, especially now that he is in our world, and so he will draw unexpected forces, cause unforeseen accidents, spawn unlikely coincidences. Look at the things that have happened around him already, consider the momentous events of which he has unwittingly been a part. Is a fish powerful? But throw one into a quiet pool where cranes and crocodiles are sleeping and things begin to change." The boy turned his exotic, brown-eyed stare on the Remover of Inconvenient Obstacles. "You should know that."

"I do. But you put it nicely."

"Thank you. My stepfather has sacrificed much so that I might have a good education."

The Remover nodded. "Let's hope he has not sacrificed too much." Silence fell. Hellebore did not break it, but rose and gestured. The other nurse came forward, her arms full of soft pale clothing, and the two servants began to dress the boy. "Come," the lord said to the Remover. "I have kept the car waiting for you."

"Give my love to Stepmother," said the boy, smiling again.

Hellebore grunted as if he were too distracted to reply. He did not look back, and did not speak again until he and his guest were out of the steamy room and moving down the corridor, the air cooling with every step.

"Everything that was ever written about creating a Terrible Child is true," said Hellebore thoughtfully. "He is an abomination."

The Remover nodded. "Then you got what you wanted, my lord, didn't you?"

18

SIDEWALKS OF
NEW EREWHON

"Y ou have to tell her, Theo. You know you have to."
He didn't want to do anything of the sort. He much
preferred looking out the window at the nighttime streets. It
was a place strange beyond all imagining, this city of muted
bronze and jade and shiny black glass, even here on its outskirts with most of the skyclawing towers still miles away.

Johnny Battistini had gone to Japan once as a replacement
drummer for a metal band past its prime—"They made me
wear a wig, Theo, no shit. I looked like Phyllis Diller!"—a
one-shot gig that he had talked about for years afterward. At
the time Theo had been frustrated by Johnny's inability to describe Tokyo and why it had made such an impression on
him. Although he spoke about it frequently, summoning up
the memory without warning from a haze of post-practice
weed smoke, he could never explain his fascination more
clearly than: "It was just . . . weird. It's like a regular city, but
then it's all different and shit. But to them, it's not different.
And that's the really weird part!"

I finally get where you were coming from, John-boy.

Theo felt a sharp, sharp pang of homesickness, as though
a less substantial version of the knife that had killed Tansy's
nephew had sliced him open and left him helpless against

the strangeness of this new place. For the first time in his life, he truly missed Johnny B. The drummer would have reduced the whole of the experience to, "Wow, this place is crazy!" and by doing so made it palatable.

Other than the bizarre variety of creatures going about their lives just as though they were normal people in Theo's normal world, it was hard to say what about the City was so alien. The buildings, although a bit strange in shape and decoration compared to those back home, were still within the bounds of comprehension—no matter how gossamer-thin the walkways between buildings or shimmeringly translucent the stone facades, general engineering seemed at least similar to the mortal world: sprites and other fairies might fly, but the buildings largely resisted such notions. The nature of the City's artificial lights was different, of course, but he had seen that from a distance—he was just seeing it more closely now. The limousine had come out of a long stretch of darkened industrial warehouses on the outer rim of the City and was rolling through a lively network of streets lined with stores and theaters and clubs and restaurants, many decorated with stylized moons and apples, apparently for the harvest holiday, all with signs ablaze, but these arrangements of glowing tubes and bulbs had a spectral, twilight quality, as though even the fiercest, hottest spotlights were draped with shrouds of pale green and silver and gray. They weren't, of course: it was the light itself that was unusual, the otherworldly radiance of Faerie, a spectral glow beneath which mortals first lost their way and then lost their souls . . .

"Theo!" Applecore's whisper was so loud it hardly qualified as a whisper anymore; it felt like she'd stuck her head all the way into the hole of his ear. "You have to tell her."

"Why can't she just let us off somewhere near where this Foxglove guy lives . . . ?"

She shushed him with surprising force. It felt like she'd stuck a bicycle pump in his eustachian tube. *Jesus, she sure has a loud voice for a tiny person,* he thought, wincing. *A friggin' six-inch-tall drill sergeant.*

"We're not goin' anywhere near that shower!" she hissed. "I told you, I don't trust Foxglove. And don't mention any names, anyway!"

Theo shot a glance toward Poppy, who was sitting with her head tilted back against the seat, listening to the music with her eyes closed and a little smile on her face. She was holding Theo's hand quite tightly. "Okay, but why can't she drop us off near wherever it is we really are going?"

"Because the more she knows, the more dangerous it is for us—and for her, if for some reason you're suicidal and my life doesn't mean much to you. We don't want her able to tell anyone anything except she dropped us in the Deepshade District."

He started to raise an argument, but he knew Applecore was right. "So when do we get out?"

"Now. We can get a bus anywhere around here."

"A bus? My God, trains are weird enough. There are buses in Fairyland, too?"

"Shut it, you! Do you want to give yourself away completely? Now tell her. And don't go looking to me to fix it, or to make you look like a nice fella." She lifted off his shoulder and flew over to sit on the door handle at the far side of the car, fitting her back into the curve of the padded handle with her wings on either side. "Go on," she said loudly.

Poppy opened her eyes. "Sorry," she said. "This is just so much nicer than that old train. Father's factor will have a fit, of course—he's one of those old-school hobbanies who acts like every penny you spend is a hair plucked out of his own backside." She giggled. "My, Theo, you must think I'm a foul-mouthed creature."

"Poppy . . ." Theo hated being a bad guy. He tried to think of a half-truth, but could not ignore the fierce attention of Applecore, watching him from the door handle with her arms folded across her chest. "Poppy, we can't go all the way into the middle of the City with you. You have to let us out here."

"What do you mean?" She looked from him to Applecore; the sprite shrugged. "Where are you going?"

"We . . . we have lots of places to go. You're in danger now just for knowing us, for helping us. We don't want to make it any worse."

"But . . . but I thought . . ." Her expression hardened. "You used me."

"No! No, Poppy, I swear . . ."

"You don't really care about me at all. You just acted that way so you could get a ride into the City. I should have let the constables take you away." In the dim light of the back-seat, she seemed to have gone chalky white except for her staring eyes and the dark line of her mouth, which quivered. "You probably *are* murderers. No, that would at least mean you were really desperate. You're probably just thieves, just petty, nasty little thieves." She pounded on the partition that separated them from the driver. "Stop the coach!"

"Pardon, Mistress?" asked the doonie's disembodied voice.

"Stop the coach. These people are getting out."

The car pulled smoothly out of the slow traffic and over to the curb. The door swung open without a sound, Applecore still clinging to the handle. Outside, a sign advertising some kind of gambling parlor splashed shuddering blue-gray light all over the pavement.

"Look, Poppy, we're very grateful—*I'm* very grateful," Theo began, "and I really do like you. I think you're . . ."

"You think I'm stupid. You think I'm a stupid child. Get out. Go to the Well, for all I care."

Applecore, ever the pragmatist, was already out and hovering above the sidewalk. A trio of husky young ogres slowed down to peer inside the limousine.

"Hello, seedling!" one of them said to Poppy, bending his immense form almost double to get his huge head into the open car door. He had fists like Virginia hams and he smelled like something sluiced out of factories in big pipes. "Looking for fun? Come down from the pollen palaces for a little of the gray stuff?"

"If you touch my coach," Poppy snarled at him, "—if you even breathe on the windows, I won't bother to have you killed, I'll have your family killed instead. Every one of them." The young ogre blinked at her. "Then you can explain to the neighbors that Mumsy and Daddy and your brothers and sisters are all dead because you were thinking with your knob when you should have been minding your own business. Now, consider the whole thing carefully before you decide, Gray Stuff—do you really want to fuck around with Thornapple House?"

The ogre had time only for one more dumbfounded blink, then his two companions grabbed him by the arms and pulled him away with a force that would have easily yanked a normal-sized person into pieces.

"Wow," Theo said as he watched them hurry away. "You're tough . . ."

"Get out of my coach!"

He turned. There were tears in her eyes, which made him feel like one of the lowest life-forms imaginable, but there was also something in her face that made him shut his mouth again without the protest of regret and innocence that was halfway up his throat and rising. Instead he turned and scrambled out onto the sidewalk. The door scraped his ankle as it slammed closed. A second later the limousine pulled back into traffic, which parted for it as though it were a dynamite wagon.

"You certainly can pick 'em," Applecore observed.

"Shut up." He didn't really want to alienate the sprite as well, his only friend, but he was too full of boiling misery to keep his mouth shut. It didn't matter, though: he couldn't think of anything else to say.

He followed Applecore down the sidewalk in a daze, trying to sort out his feelings, all but oblivious now to

even the strangest surroundings and most unusual life-
forms, glad only that the night skies were clear so he didn't
have to add wading through puddles in a driving rain to his
list of miseries.

The thing was, he felt bad because he hated being misunderstood, but there was more to it than that: he had genuinely liked Poppy Thornapple. In the midst of all that had
happened, it had been lovely to have a few hours of nearly
innocent flirtation, the cheerful companionship of an attractive young woman who also liked him. And there had been
something about her, a what-the-hell quality, that he had
found fascinating. "What did I do wrong?"

Applecore, who was doing her best to find the right sort
of bus stop, ignored him until he asked again. "What do you
mean, wrong?" she said.

"I didn't lie to her. I didn't promise her anything!"

Applecore shook her head. "We don't really have time to
talk about this now, Vilmos. And you probably don't want to
hear what I have to say anyway."

"But I don't get it. I was really careful . . ."

The sprite dropped onto his shoulder, grabbed his earlobe, and leaned out in front of his face. "By the Trees, fella,
have you ever actually had a girlfriend?"

"What the hell does that mean? Lots."

"Then you must have worked really hard not to learn anything about women. Is that why you had so many? Easier
just to dump 'em when they started making sense?" She
snorted and sat down on his shoulder.

Theo groaned. "My life sucked already and now I'm getting lectured about my relationships by a fairy the size of a
dog's chew toy. Perfect."

She didn't say anything for a long moment, didn't even
move. When she spoke, even with her head so close to his
ear, he could barely hear her over the noise of the traffic.
"I'm going to give you one chance to apologize."

"What?"

"You heard me."

"What did I say? I'm sorry!" He was turning his head so sharply trying to make eye contact that he had to stop in the middle of the sidewalk. A two-way procession out of an illustrated children's book eddied around him. "Applecore, please don't leave me. I said something stupid—okay, I'm sorry. But I don't even know what it was."

"Theo," she said after a pause, "almost everything you say is stupid."

"Probably," he said, relieved. Her voice had sounded almost normal again. "And you shouldn't pass up an opportunity to kick me when I'm down, anyway—you might not get another one for at least ten minutes. But I really don't know what I said."

"Do you think my size makes me stupid?"

"No!"

"And do you think I'm a woman?"

"Of course I do . . ." He swallowed down the "I guess," reasoning that it might muddy the situation.

"And the problem you're snivelin' about—would that be a problem with a woman?"

"Yeah, but . . ."

"So why would I not be qualified to give you the benefit of my experience, being as I'm a member of that particular sex?"

"Jeez, that wasn't what I meant. I just . . . Shit. Forget it. I'm wrong and so what else is new?"

"Quit whinging and start walking, ya thick. And listen a little bit."

"Okay, okay."

"What did you do wrong—isn't that what you asked? You said, 'But I didn't promise her anything!' as if how someone feels about you was some kind of court case or a contract, like you can solve it just by taking out the agreement and waving it around—'See, I never said it!' But how people feel isn't like that, Theo, especially women. And the thing is, you know it, too."

He groaned again. "I don't know *anything.*"

"Oh, yes, you do. I used to have a gentleman friend just like you. Sweet-tempered most of the time—he could be lovely, he could—but he just took everything that was given him and never wondered what was expected back."

"So what the hell *is* expected back, will you tell me that? Or are we men just supposed to read your minds?"

"By the Trees," she said, "it's like talking to a faun in the springtime. Look, fella, so you didn't tell her you loved her or that you were going to live with her in a cottage by the sea. Did you hold her hand? Did you listen while she talked about how happy she was? Did you or did you not tell her she was lovely and that you were glad you met her?"

"I thought you were sleeping! You were listening!"

"Fair play to you. This is my life, too, remember. Can you blame me for being curious about what stupid things you might tell the daughter of one of the people who are trying to kill us?"

He was walking again, all but oblivious to the grotesque and beautiful faces watching him through the windows of restaurants and bars, to the shouts and the foreign musical tones of the coach horns, even to the snatches of intriguingly exotic melody wafting out of stores. "Okay," he said at last. "You were listening. What was I supposed to say? She was nice."

"You're just like that other fella I went with. Theo, what do you lads expect? You make us work for every word out of you. Half the time if we let you have what you want, we never hear from you again, or if we do, you've gone all strange on us. We have to try to read you like a book in some language we don't know, then when we make a mistake, you tell us, 'Ha! I never said that! You can't prove it!' Look, you, you can't hold a girl's hand, cuddle up with her, tell her she's beautiful, then pretend that because you didn't ask for her hand in marriage it's all a mystery why she's upset when you piss off at the first opportunity."

Theo shook his head. "But you didn't even like her! You wanted me to stay away from her!"

"I like her better for not sitting around listening to your excuses. But you're right, I didn't want us mixed up with her at all. Which, you may have noticed, is why you didn't see me playing finger-tickle with her, or rubbing me leg on hers when I thought me companion was asleep. Turn right here."

"What?"

"Turn right here. There's a stop down this street for the bus through to the Morning Sky District."

The stop, an ornate bench beneath a small but equally ornate, leaf-shaped roof, stood in front of a boarded-up storefront. The sign over the store's front entrance had been pulled down, but in the silvery streetlights Theo could still see the bolts that had held the letters in place, spelling "Lily Pad Sundries" in that strange gibberish-but-he-could-read-it way that Fairyland writing usually appeared to him. There was only one other person waiting at the stop, a goblin sitting with a very straight back at the end of the bench. He did not look over when Theo sat down, but there was a change in the quality of his attention to the street that suggested he was not entirely oblivious.

"Okay, you win," Theo told Applecore. "You're the zen master of relationships and I'm the whatever, the uncarved block. Teach me."

She laughed sourly. "As if I need to add to my list of impossible jobs. Just use your brains, fella. I think you've got some."

"Is that a compliment?"

"Of a sort." She frowned. "If this is the right bus, we can stop at my place first before we go on to . . ." She stopped and shot a quick look over to the goblin, who was still solemnly watching the traffic slide past, his long nose pointed at the street like a finger. "To the other place."

Theo couldn't even remember where they were going— to see Foxglove? No, Applecore had vetoed that. "We're not going to go . . . wherever it is tonight, are we?"

"I don't know," she said. "It's getting a bit late. But I don't know where else you can stay."

"You said we were going to stop at your place. I'm not picky—I'd be happy to sleep on the floor or something."

She cocked her head, looking puzzled, but before she could answer the bus came around the corner, the engines humming with a sound like drowsy wasps, the brakes screeching a little as it pulled up at the stop. It was shaped a bit like a caterpillar, with accordion folds and a humped back, but still recognizably a bus.

I'm getting used to things here already, Theo thought as he went up the steps, then stopped when he got to the top. It wasn't the driver who gave him pause, a squat, donkey-eared woman half Theo's size on a special booster seat, with modified pedals in reach of her dangling feet. "Damn! I don't have any money," he whispered to Applecore.

"Doesn't cost anything," she said. "But that's a good thought. We need to get our hands on a bit of the yellow stuff pretty soon—I've pretty much emptied my tallybank."

The little goblin had got on ahead of them and had already made his way back to the rear of the bus. Since all the seats at the front were full, Theo followed, with Applecore on his shoulder. The passengers hardly looked up as he went past.

They wound up in a seat in the second-to-last row, beside a sleeping fairy woman with a faint lavender tint to her skin, who seemed a bit the worse for drink or something: she had an odd smell to her, almost like camphor. Her cheek was mottled with an old bruise and her wings were bedraggled, one of them even tattered along the edge. The goblin had taken a seat behind them in the last row, and was still staring ahead as though afraid to do anything else.

The bus had gone a few blocks when Theo realized he had been drifting, thinking of the look on Poppy Thornapple's face as she threw him out of the car and wondering why it hurt him so much to remember it. "About money," he said. "Why don't we just have Tan . . ." He paused: Theo was learning the trick of discretion, too. "Why don't we just ask your boss to wire us some. You can do that here, can't you?"

She frowned. "Not as simple as you think, but for reasons I don't want to talk about now. And I still have to puzzle out where we can put you up for the night."

"But . . ." He hesitated. "Listen, I don't want to cause trouble. I mean, if there's some religious reason or something that an unmarried sprite can't bring home a member of the opposite sex a hundred times her size . . ." He suddenly thought of something. "Wait, is this your parents' place? Is that why you don't want to bring me home? But I thought they lived back in . . ."

She stood up and touched his lip, silencing him before he could say more. "No, you great eejit. It's just that when I'm staying here in the City, I live in a comb."

He didn't get it. "And, so, what, do you have a hairbrush you keep as a weekend place? If you don't want me in your house, just say so."

Applecore rolled her eyes. "A comb! It's a place where people like me live. You don't think I rent something the size of what you'd live in, do you? What a waste! It's a special place just for sprites and us other wee folk, ya thick."

"Oh. Is that . . . comb like 'honeycomb'?"

"You get the prize, boyo."

"And I take it that it's not big enough for me to sleep on the floor."

"Theo, if you took the roof off you could just about wedge your head into the parlor, but you wouldn't have space left to wink. As for my room, well, I've got the biggest in our part of the place, and you couldn't probably spread your fingers on the floor without touching the walls."

"Our?"

"Me roommates. We're all in and out, but there's near a dozen of us altogether. That's just in our bit—the whole comb's got thousands." She looked out at the street. "We're almost there."

The thought of thousands of winged fairies in one place

was faintly disturbing—like termite-hatching season. "Okay, I see why that wouldn't work. So what am I going to do? I sure don't have any money myself. Can I sleep in the park, or will the constables or whatever they're called come roust me out?"

"More likely you'd get eaten by werewolves." She didn't look like she was kidding. "Truly, you don't want to be in the park at night if you can help it. This is our stop."

As the bus shuddered to a halt and a few of the other passengers, gnomes and spriggans and various bogles squeezed their astonishingly disparate and in some cases quite awkward shapes out of the seats and into the aisle, a furred hand suddenly appeared beside Theo's head holding something small and vaguely white. He turned to see the goblin who had shared the bus stop with them leaning forward.

"Please forgive my too-sharp ears." The goblin smiled, showing sharp little teeth, and cleared his throat. "I had no intentions to destroy your privacy, but I could not help hearing something of your dilemma. If you should find yourself without a roof in this the very large and not excessively friendly city, come to this place. My friends and I share it. Not much, it is not much, but it is safe." He nodded emphatically. "Safe."

"Time to go," Applecore said, hovering noisily by Theo's ear.

"Thank you." Theo took the paper and stared at it for a moment, then closed his fingers around it. "That's very kind."

"We all wait on the hilltop." The goblin nodded his head again, just once this time—it almost looked like a benediction. "And we all wait for the wind to change."

Still trying to make sense of the last two remarks, Theo followed Applecore down the stairs and onto the sidewalk. "What was *that* about?"

"Who knows? Some kind of cult—goblins go for all that shower."

Theo stared at the slip of paper. The goblin had written on

it in a surprisingly neat hand, "Beneath the old Fayfort Bridge." He showed it to Applecore.

"Not your high-rent cult, then," was all she said.

He was about to crumple it and throw it away when he remembered where and what he was: in a strange city in an unfamiliar land, penniless and homeless. *Can't afford to throw anything away,* he thought. *I might need to leave a note for someone and not have any paper. A suicide note, maybe* . . . He folded it instead and put it into the inner pocket of his shirt.

"Here we are," she said as they turned another corner. "Orchard Flower Comb."

His first impression was not what he had earlier thought it might be, a termite nest, but of a vertical meadow full of fireflies: the air in the small side street was absolutely ablaze with flickering, swooping lights—gray-green, pink, yellow, and pale blue, like a blizzard of radioactive snow. Some of the glowing shapes stood on the banks of tiny balconies that stretched the length of the street, but most of the gleaming spots were actually flying in or out of the hundreds of doors.

"What are all those lights?"

"Sprites," Applecore said. "A few pixies and kinky-punks and hob-lanterns, too, but all the flying ones are sprites. Why, what did you think?"

"But . . . *you* don't glow in the dark."

"Can't be bothered. Come along, you." She tugged at his ear, then flew on ahead of him.

Theo took a breath and followed. Bright shapes shot past him with every step, and although many of them were indeed tiny little people as human-looking as Applecore, the phenomenon felt more like walking through tracer-fire: for every self-illuminated winged figure, at least a half dozen that were unlit whizzed past him in the evening darkness, making themselves known only by the wind of their passing, an occasional wing brush through his hair, or in a few cases, a small voice shouting something that he could not make out. In fact, now that the rumble of traffic from the

larger streets was behind him, he could hear high-pitched
chatter all around—laughing, shouting, gossiping from balcony to balcony as the residents hung clothes or just enjoyed
the evening. The firefly-colony metaphor was beginning to
fail; with its rush of wings and the background of barely audible voices, the alley that contained Orchard Flower Comb
was beginning to seem more like a cavern inhabited by talking bats.

The housing complex extended all the way along a wall
that Theo only realized after some moments was the back of
another, full-size building. The comb started at about the
level of his knees and extended several yards up above his
head, something between a high-rise tenement and a dove-
cote, row after row of box-shaped buildings joined side to
side so that it looked almost like someone had mounted an
immense set of wooden post office boxes on the wall and
cut little birdhouse doors in each one. Most of the dwellings
had balconies added onto them, although some of these
seemed little more than fruit baskets fastened just below the
doorway.

Theo's first impression of something as swarming and
impersonal as an insect nest did not last long: the residents
had clearly worked hard to put their individual stamp on
their homes. Many of the fruit basket terraces had potted
flowers, hanging tinsel or streamers of cloth and other decorations, and most of the tiny houses had windows cut into
the front walls as well, with curtains or blinds which colored
the light that shone inside so that the pastel flickerings generated by many of the residents were matched by the more
static colors of the windows. Some of the dwellings had
been modified even farther, perhaps by a single family
which had bought anywhere from two to a half dozen of the
boxy apartments and then connected them in a number of
clever ways, with exterior stairways and sliding poles. A
few, to the secret delight of Theo's inner child, were scaf-
folded by a complex arrangements of chutes and ladders.

Not all the ladders led from one dwelling to another.

Long accordions of steps hung down to the ground from most of the buildings, and looked as though they might be meant to be pulled up in an emergency.

"What are those long ladders for?" Theo asked.

"Pixies don't fly," Applecore said. "Now, you, wait here. I'll be back in just a wee while." She rose a yard or so above his head and then flew into a lighted door he could just barely see. A few small shapes poked their heads over adjacent balconies to look at him but didn't appear overwhelmingly interested.

The sprite didn't hurry back out. As he loitered in front of Orchard Flower Comb, Theo found himself wondering for the first time what it was like to be Applecore—how he would feel if he had grown up in a world of giants who were, proportionately, as tall as ancient redwoods. He couldn't quite wrap his head around it.

Somebody from my world who knows something, a college professor or somebody, ought to come here and study this place. No, researchers, a whole bunch of them. Because you could live here for years, I'll bet, and only just start to get a handle on how different it is . . .

"Ooh, he is a big one," someone said above him. For a moment, the pseudo-Hibernian dialect made him think it was Applecore poking fun at him, but the voice wasn't quite right.

"Well, of course he is," said someone else. "She told us he was a big one."

"I meant he's a big one *for a big one,*" protested the first. "He's got shoulders!"

"Will the two of you quit it, you silly starlings?" said a third unfamiliar voice. "I'm getting me headache back."

Theo squinted upward. On a balcony just above his head a trio of Applecore-sized figures stared down at him. All three were young women, as far as he could tell, two with dark hair, one cut short, the other long, and the last with an immense fluffy mane of gold half-rolled in curlers. All three had wings poking out of the back of their housedresses.

"Are you Theo?" asked the blonde. "You're a big one, aren't you?"

"Can you think of nothing else to say, Ginnie?" snapped the one with short dark hair. "You're doing my head in." She looked down. "Pay no attention to this lot. They've only been in from the country about two hours."

"Ooh, Pit, it's terrible you are!" said the other brunette. "She's been here about a month longer than us and she puts on such airs!"

"Ummm . . ." He tried to let his brain catch up. "Are you . . . are you some of Applecore's roommates?"

"Yes," said the long-haired brunette, "although for as much as Core comes around these days, you'd think we were sharing the place with a will-o'-the-wisp." She made a little mock-curtsey. "I'm Fuzz. The one with the sour face is my sister, Pit."

"Fuzz . . . Pit . . ." Theo nodded, still struggling.

"We're Peaches. And that one with her hair all sticking out like Peg Powler is Ginnie."

"Don't tell him that! That's just a nickname," the blonde said, and sniffed at her roommate. "It's really Auberginnie. I'm an actress and that's my stage name."

"Yeah, back home in Hawthorn she was just another Eggplant," said Pit.

"Oh!" said Ginnie. "You're so stroppy tonight!"

"Well, me head hurts, doesn't it?"

Theo cautiously raised his hand. So far he had not been endearing himself to the female population of Faerie, and at the moment he was outnumbered three to one. He had a feeling that the size differential wouldn't make any more difference than it had with the power balance between Applecore and himself. "Hello. Nice to . . . nice to meet you. Yeah, I'm Theo. Is she . . . um . . . almost ready? She didn't tell me how long she'd be."

"She's faster to get ready than most." Fuzz leaned over the balcony, squinting, her hair dangling. It looked to be almost as long as she was tall. "So, are you really a Daisy? You don't look much like a Daisy."

"What would you know?" demanded Pit. "When have you ever seen a Daisy?"

"I saw one on the news talking about some parliamentary thing. Don't be such a gull."

"Saw one on the news." Pit shook her head. "Just ignore them both. They only came out to ogle you."

"What?" said Fuzz. "Are you saying it wasn't your idea? What a liar you are!"

"He'll think we're terrible," Ginnie wailed.

"See what I mean?" said Pit with grim satisfaction. "Farm girls. Fresh out of the branches. Still have pollen in their ears."

"Take that back!" Fuzz demanded.

Fortunately, just as Theo was seriously contemplating making a run for it, Applecore appeared beside them with a small suitcase in her hand. She lifted off the balcony and began to descend toward Theo, then flew back up and hugged her roommates.

"Where are you going?" asked Ginnie. "We've hardly even seen you!"

"Not certain," said Applecore. "I'll let you know. We just have some business to take care of . . . some Daisy business . . . and it's better we don't advertise ourselves."

"Does this have something to do with those fellas who were asking about you?" Fuzz wanted to know.

"What?" Applecore was clearly startled. "What fellas, when?"

"You mean you didn't tell her when she first came in?" said Pit. "What's wrong with you two?"

"You were in the next room, just watching the mirror-stream. You could have come in and told her . . ."

"Shut up, the lot of you!" shouted Applecore, and the heat of her response was so unexpected that her three roommates all fell silent. "Tell me what you're talking about. Now."

"A couple of pixies we haven't seen before came to the

door," Pit explained briskly. "They said they were friends of yours from back in Great Rowan, but they seemed nervous."

"Shite and onions." Applecore shook her head. "I don't know any pixies from back there. What did you tell them?"

"That you were gone and we didn't know when you'd be back, what do you think?" Pit scowled. "I didn't like the look of 'em at all. Just as well I came home—these two probably would have had them in for tea and cakes and let them go through your room."

"That's not fair," said Ginnie, almost crying now. "And if you chased them away so well, then why did I see them just this morning? Sitting out on the front sidewalk, watching the comb?"

Pit glared at her. "You *what?*"

"Oh, Ginnie, why didn't you say anything?" demanded Fuzz.

"Because before I had a chance to remember, Core came back . . ."

"You had time to eat an entire sesame cookie by yourself before she got here . . ."

"Enough!" Applecore quickly gave her roommates another hug. "Don't fight, you three. And if those fellas come back, don't let them in. In fact, call the superintendent and tell him the pixies are harassing you. Talk about it on the terrace, get some other folk paying attention to them. Chances are they'll get tired of watching for me, but for all your sakes I want you to make it uncomfortable for them to hang about here." Her wings hummed and she rose off the balcony.

"But where are you going?" asked Fuzz. "This doesn't sound good at all."

"It's not, so it's better you don't know. Don't worry, dear ones, I'll be fine. I've got my big, strong friend Theo, after all." She settled on his shoulder, leaned into his ear. "Let's get going. The Trees alone know who's watchin' us right this moment."

Theo gave Applecore's roommates a distracted wave as

he stepped out into the alley. "Go where?" he asked. "You never really told me."

"I've been thinking. Walk that way, back toward the bus stop, and try to look normal, will ya?" When she had him facing the right direction, she settled on his shoulder again. "Is that your best normal? Then I'm sorry for you, fella."

"What are we worrying about—pixies? Aren't they little like you? But wingless? How the hell are they going to follow me, anyway?"

"They can ride, y'know. Ratback. Birdback. And pixies may not have wings, but not all sprites are sweet and helpful like me, either, so let's keep moving and keep our eyes open. I think we're going to be okay if we stay out in the lighted areas. Even if they have poison arrows, they'd need a lot of 'em to knock you down and keep you from getting away."

"Poison arrows? What the hell are you talking about?"

"But that doesn't mean they won't do their best to follow us, find out where we're goin'. So we've got to scramble around on the buses a bit, then get to a safe spot."

"But not Foxglove's place, right?"

"No, definitely not. Hang on here a moment till I have a look." The bus stop was in sight. She lifted off his shoulder and buzzed away into the darkness. She was back hovering in front of him before he reached the empty bench. "Don't see any sign of anyone watching, but that doesn't mean much. A pair of pixies with the right charms . . ." She let it hang as though Theo would know about this sort of thing already. "As to where we're going . . . see, I'm not a Flower. Tansy and those other gentry types, they think they've got more in common with each other than with anyone else, so when times are bad he'd rather send you to someone in his own party. But Tansy's party, they're deal-makers, and like I said, I've already heard a few things I don't like about Foxglove. I'd rather take you to someone who's got something to lose—someone who can't make a deal because they're mortal enemies with the folks who are trying to kill you."

"You want to take me to the . . . the Creepers, right? The ones who wanted me in the first place."

"But not the Hollyhock clan. Tansy's right about that—who knows how Hellebore and Thornapple and that lot found out about that young fella coming to the commune to escort you—the one who wound up with his heart in a box? But they did, and in times like this it's usually an inside job."

He couldn't help smiling at the phrase. "You're pretty hard-boiled, Tinker Bell."

She scowled. "Call me that name again and you'll be wondering how your bollocks wound up lodged in your windpipe—from below. Just because we don't get to your side of things much anymore doesn't mean we don't know anything. 'If you believe in fairies, clap your hands!' If you believe in fairies, kiss my rosy pink arse is more like it. Now are you going to shut your gob or not?"

He shut his mouth.

"That's good, then. So we're not going to talk about this on the bus—if a goblin can hear us talking, so can a lot of other folk. We're going to get on and off the buses a couple of times, but in the long run," she moved in close and lowered her voice to a whisper, "we're heading for Daffodil House. There's someone there who'll want to meet you, and luckily it's someone who doesn't like Hellebore and his Chokeweeds very much."

If it had been something past ten at night by Theo's reckoning when they visited the comb, it was approaching midnight when they got off the last bus. Theo stood shivering on the sidewalk beside a wide thoroughfare—the night air had turned sharply cold—while Applecore sniffed the breeze. "I don't think we're being followed."

"Followed?" He looked around at the silent walls and dark windows. Actually, he realized, there weren't that many windows, at least at ground level. "There isn't anyone here at all."

"This part of Gloaming District's like that. No restaurants, no night life, just government buildings and some of the bigger house-towers. Once everyone's in for the night it's pretty quiet. Let's go."

She led him down a street full of tall buildings that, like everything else in this city of alien shapes and colors, were both like and unlike what he knew. Many of the Faerie office complexes were squat structures like old castles, with walls around the outside that hid all but the tops of the buildings within, and although they were covered with bright spotlights and had quite modern looking guard stations in the massive gates, they did not look much different from the medieval districts of his world that were still inhabited. Theo remembered seeing plenty of similar arrangements during his one trip to Europe with Cat: museum-quality stonework with spanking new technology bolted right onto ancient structures.

The family compounds—the "house-towers," as Applecore named them, were a bit different. For one thing, while the office buildings averaged five or six stories, the house-towers ranged anywhere from twice to ten times that amount. One of the first they passed, a huge structure lit by upward-slanting footlights which Applecore told him was Snapdragon House, was a good example of the type: it was not cylindrical but polyhedronal, and although it had regular rows of windows on the upper floors, there were none at all within fifty feet of the ground, probably for security: the only entrance to the building seemed to be through a gate-house set well back from the street, its massive doorway set deep in a thick wall. But although there were few windows in the first hundred feet, the tower was not without decoration: the windows were a number of different sizes and shapes, and most of the available wall space was covered with ornamentation as complex as the gargoyles and carved saints of a Gothic cathedral. Even in the glare of the spotlights

Theo couldn't quite make out the nature of the carvings, but they seemed to run across the side of the tower he could see in slanted bands, as though the whole thing created a single picture spiraling around the structure.

He asked Applecore about the decorations.

"Goblins gettin' killed, mostly," she explained. "Snapdragons made their names and their fortune in the last Goblin War. You should see Phlox House. They were big in the wars with the giants. They've got carved giant heads and shoulders built into the foundations—them big fellas look like they're not having a real good time holding up the building, either." Her voice took on a thoughtful tone. "At least I *think* they're carved."

She led him across a wide expanse of trimmed lawns and meandering paths, all quite empty in the pale, bluish light of the streetlamps. "Hoarfrost Park," she told him.

"Do we have to watch out for werewolves?" he asked nervously.

"I think they've just planted the new wolfbane—you see those hedges? They take better care of downtown then they do the parts where us working folk live."

Keeping his ears open for the sounds of something lupine in the shrubbery—because who knew what you could expect from disgruntled gardeners? Theo could just imagine them planting ivy instead of wolfbane by mistake—Theo slowed to look at a statue. It was the first he'd been close enough to see. It was of some strange, silvery metal, and seemed to represent a fairy lord in full armor, holding his swan-winged helmet in the crook of his elbow. He looked out across the park in a heroic pose that Theo had seen on dozens of statues back in his own world.

"Who's this?"

"How should I know?" Applecore flew in impatient circles. "The first Lord Rose, or maybe Speedwell, one of that shower. Come on." Theo stared a moment longer at the sharp-featured face. If the subject of the statue was not one of the most arrogant creatures that ever breathed, the artist had done him a disservice.

"... *Cold,*" said a weary, infinitely mournful voice. Theo jumped. *"So ... cold ..."*

He looked around, heart pounding. "My God! That statue just talked to me!" The voice had seemed miles away and yet right inside his head.

"No, it didn't." Applecore was beside him now. "Come along."

"It did! It talked to me! It said 'Cold!' "

"That wasn't the statue. See, when they cut down what was left of the forest that was here to make the park, the tree-nymphs ... well, their trees were all destroyed. Some of them got into the statues as sort of a protest, but it didn't do any good. They're still in there." She shook her head. "Can't be nice for them."

"When did all this happen?" He was still shivering—the voice had sounded so lost, so miserable.

"Least fifty years, must have been, maybe a hundred. Nobody cared. It's sad, I suppose, but what can you do? Now hurry up."

He could not help looking back over his shoulder at the gleaming, silvery figure. Fifty years or more! He might only have fancied it, but he thought he could still hear a faint, miserable echo as he caught up to Applecore. "How can anyone put up with that? It's ... it's horrible!"

"Nobody who lives around here stands next to 'em long enough to hear. You just learn. Anyway, here we are."

They looked down from the top of the grassy hill onto the edge of the park and a huge complex, the biggest he'd seen yet, perhaps four city blocks square, so wide that the whole of Hoarfrost Park was its front garden. The main tower was large, perhaps as much as thirty or forty stories high, but it was not the tallest he'd seen—the Snapdragon house-tower and a couple of others had been higher. However, three of the four corners of the complex also held towers that were each about half the main tower's height, so that the landscaped lot looked something like the gathering of Giza pyramids.

Like a cemetery full of monuments. The encounter with the dryad had upset Theo deeply—he could still hear its voice, the exhausted disbelief of an abandoned child.

"Daffodil House," Applecore announced. "Although really that's only the center tower-house. The other towers are Iris, Jonquil, Narcissus, and that low one's the conference center." The fourth corner, the only one without a tower, was filled by a sprawling complex of low buildings.

"Jeez," he said. "This is all one family's place? It's huge!"

"They're a big, powerful family," she said. "In fact, they've practically been bankrolling the Creepers all by themselves, so if it weren't for them . . ." She fell silent; Theo realized she had decided against finishing her sentence.

"If it weren't for them, what? Your kind might be busily wiping out my kind?"

"I'm tired, Theo. Let's just try to get off the street before someone catches up to us. Wouldn't you rather be inside those walls than outside just now?"

That was true. He had been out of Tansy's house less than twenty-four hours and felt like he had been on the run for weeks. He was exhausted, frightened, and had no doubt that he smelled pretty rank as well. One of those hollow-men could probably spot him from a mile away. "Okay, yeah. Let's go."

She led him to a tunnel barely higher than he was. It went all the way through a stone outer wall at least twenty feet thick. "The guard station's through here."

"Isn't this a bit of a weak spot in the defenses?"

"Have you ever seen a pastry bag?" Applecore asked. "You know, how you squeeze on it and this little stream of goo comes out the end?"

"Yeah?"

"Somebody in Daffodil House or in the guard tower says

a word and these walls slide together." She made a squelching noise. "Whatever's in here—goo."

He thought very carefully about turning around and running back out again. "Is it a word someone might say by accident?"

"Hardly ever happens."

"Oh, I feel much better. How do you know so much?"

"Been here before."

The guard station, which was only the bottom floor of a large guard tower in the front wall, was an odd combination of medieval and modern: the interview room was mostly behind walls that seemed to be transparent glass or plastic. At this time of the night Theo and the sprite were the only people on the visitor side of the barrier, but that did not hasten the approach of the guards, a group of uniformed ogres who were playing some kind of card game on the far side of the room. At last one of them sauntered over and spoke to Applecore through a slot too small for even a sprite to get through, while Theo tried to look interested in the *Daffodil— the Dynamic House!* and *Explore Historic Hawthorn Scathe* brochures in a rack by the chairs. After a drearily long time the guard sauntered off, stopping on his way toward what looked like the communication center to kibitz on the card game.

"Aren't they going to figure out pretty quickly that I don't have the right identification—that I'm not really a Daisy?" Theo asked quietly when Applecore came back to him. He was almost too tired to be afraid. Almost, but not quite.

Applecore looked surprised. "Didn't Tansy give you anything?"

"No."

She shook her head, troubled. "Well, no matter. While we were at the comb I called the person we're going to see. Those Jimmy Squarefoots are just double-checking. If she's coming, it won't matter if you're wearing your pants on your head and dancing a jig."

They were kept waiting long enough that Applecore buzzed to the slotted window after a while for another exchange of ideas with the guards. The sprite's main idea seemed to be, "Get off your fat gray arse and call again." Theo did not really want to hear what the object of her disgust—a seven-and-a-half-footer almost as wide as he was tall, wearing something that looked very, very much like a wooden submachine gun on a shoulder strap (and with a dozen or more similarly sized and similarly armed friends ranged around the guardroom behind him)—might think about some of Applecore's more critical opinions, so he huddled on his chair by the brochure rack and tried to look as though he were just innocently waiting to get his work visa for Mother Goose Land stamped or something.

Even this tension couldn't last forever, and at last Theo found himself nodding. He was startled awake by Applecore hovering very close in front of his face, tugging cruelly on his eyebrow.

"Get up," she said.

"Stop it," he mumbled.

She leaned in close. "You don't know how lucky you are, boyo. Her ladyship came *herself.*"

Theo opened his eyes wider and staggered to his feet. Standing just inside the barrier was a slender, handsome fairy woman, indistinguishable at first from any number he had seen in the train stations and on the streets. This one had light brown hair with an actual streak of gray in it, and although there was little else in her features or posture to suggest she was anything but in the bloom of young adulthood, he suspected he might be meeting one of his first older fairies.

"Marvelous," she said, looking Theo up and down. "Just marvelous. We are so lucky to have you." Her voice was deep and fell into the category he would have labeled "no-nonsense" back home—she sounded like the kind of aristocratic woman who would stick her arm up a pregnant horse without a moment's hesitation. "Just think," she said to Applecore. "An actual mortal!"

"She knows?" Theo was a little surprised.

"Of course I know. And I am really thrilled." She extended her hand. "Please forgive me—I am being a terrible hostess, but that's what happens when the thirst of inquiry is on me, I'm afraid. Welcome to our house. I am Lady Aemilia Jonquil. Lord Daffodil is my brother."

It took Theo a moment to realize that the hand he was shaking wore some kind of latex glove. Maybe she really had been helping a horse give birth, he thought. Or, more likely, a unicorn. "Nice to . . . meet you."

"Oh, and you, too, Master Vilmos. Now, I know this should really wait until tomorrow when we can get the testing under way properly, but before we put you to bed I'd like to perform just one or two small—and, I'm afraid, a *bit* more than moderately painful—experiments on you."

With Applecore hovering just out of range and ignoring Theo's increasingly nervous questions, Lady Jonquil took him by the hand and led him through the guard tower into the stony fastness of Daffodil House.

19

A HOLIDAY VISIT

The wind had changed and that morning had shifted into the northeast, a stiff breeze from Ys that moaned through the bending treetops of True Arden, a wind with a bite to it, first messenger of still-distant winter. It was the day before Mabon, and many of the staff would be traveling home for the holiday to visit family out in the countryside whom they had not seen in months. The younger employees, including some who could not afford the trip back home, were making the great house festive with corn dolls and acorn mazes and piles of apples on the tabletops. One of the caretakers had made a wine moon out of wicker and birch bark and hung it above the front door where it jiggled in the freshening wind.

It was an exciting day at Zinnia Manor, and not just because of the holiday, or the weather change, or any of the more usual reasons—sympathetic madness among the clinic-hobs nearing retirement, or an escape by one of the Feverfew twins (each time they immediately went to ground in the hilly countryside that surrounded the manor; sometimes the director had to hire a Black Dog and handler to track down the shapeshifting escapee). Instead, what was causing excitement among the nurses as they passed each other in the old halls or huddled over tea and lavender-oil muffins in the break room was the knowledge that the patient they called the Silent Primrose Maiden was going to have one of her rare visitors. The fact that it was almost always the same visitor, and that he came most holidays, did not make him any the less interesting to the manor staff. Not only was Erephine Primrose's visitor handsome even by the high standards of his folk, and also the heir-apparent to one of the most powerful family houses, he was known to be unattached. Dynastic pressures were strong, and he was said to have fathered a child or two on the weft side, but that did not mean he would never marry. And, as one of the youngest nurses pointed out, there was no law in Faerie that said he could not marry a commoner if he fell in love with one.

The older nurses laughed at this—the youngster who had spoken of the Primrose lordling as though he lived in the same world she did was a farm girl still damp behind the ears with the dews of Ivy Round, one who followed the romance fables available through Zinnia Manor's mirror-stream with the same deeply absorbed belief that other fairy-folk reserved for news about the latest debate in the Parliament of Blooms or announcements about interfield trade statistics or distant border skirmishes between the giants and the smaller but more ambitious mountain trolls. Still, all but the most hardened of her coworkers found something naively charming in the young nurse's insistence that even her large and pretty wings were no barrier to an alliance with a scion of one of the Flower houses.

"It's not as if I couldn't do something about that," she protested. "People are having their wings off all the time."

"Even more than once, some of them," another nurse pointed out. "Like Mr. Lungwort. His just keep growing back no matter how many times he has 'em pruned." The others laughed. The sanitarium's administrator was not particularly popular and his ambitions were the subject of frequent discussion.

"If you're lonely, what you really want is a mortal," said

one of the older nurses. "Smelly and hairy and savage. Ooh, that'd do me right. I've not had any of that for centuries."

"Getting one of them's no more likely than getting a fellow out of one of the Six Houses—not these days," said another.

"'Sides, if that Primrose lad even looked at you too long, I imagine there would be more than a few ladies from the High Houses who'd be happy to set a Stroke Boy on you," the older nurse said cheerfully. "That happened to a girl I know who was in service. They don't like to share with our sort."

"Look," the farm lass said, blushing. "I know it's not going to happen, but a girl can dream, can't she?"

At least they could all agree on that. And the Silent Primrose Maiden's brother, most of them also agreed, was someone worth daydreaming about.

"Erephine?" he said, as though he might be interrupting her at something. She sat in her chair, still and warmthless as a statue. "Good Mabon Eve, dear one. It's me, Caradenus. I came to see you."

He closed the door behind him and checked to make sure it latched. There had seemed to be an unusual number of nurses in the corridor as he had made his way to his sister's room, all doing their best not to watch him too obviously but not entirely succeeding. It was difficult to believe they all had business in the same part of the manor at the same time. Lately he found himself swimming in strange political currents; he wondered if the staff might be spying on him. But who would go to such an extreme? The Excisors? They must have larger matters to worry about than the duty that brought him to Zinnia Manor. His own father? Surely the two of them hadn't moved so far apart, for all their differences. No, he could make no sense of it. Perhaps it was only his imagination. Still, the staff had all seemed so . . . interested.

"I've come to see you for a reason." He reached out and took his sister's cold hand. "I'm involved in some things that might make it hard for me to come see you for a while." He moved a little closer, lowered his voice, for all the world as though he were sharing a secret with someone who could understand it. "Things are . . . difficult all over just now, especially in the City. There's talk of another Flower War." He closed his eyes, suddenly feeling very weary. "I fear it may be true. What a horror that would be, after all these years of peace."

He let go of her hand and sat back, examining her face. She continued looking at nothing. He made himself smile, but it was difficult. "Do you remember when we were both young and we went to go see our cousins at Pimpernel Rise in Alder Head, that big house in the hills? You were afraid because someone told you there were manticores in that wood, and I said I would protect you, that I wasn't afraid of anything." He shook his head. "I was only a boy, with my first sword and a few charms I'd learned. I promised you I wouldn't let anything happen to you. Ever. I promised."

For a long moment he could not speak.

"The old goblin," he said at last. "It's just come back to me. Do you remember him? We met him on the Bonfire Road. He was riding to market with some rabbit skins and he let you pet his unicorn." He summoned back the smile. "You were so brave! It had bells around its neck and it shied at the smell of me, or perhaps at one of the charms I was wearing. The bells all jingled. But it lowered its head so you could stroke it. How big your eyes were!"

He took her hand again and they sat in silence for a long time.

"I will come back to see you as soon as I can," he said as he stood up. "I do not forget. I will not forget." He bent and kissed a cheek like clay. "And if the day ever comes, I will see you avenged for this. I have sworn it by the Well." He hesitated, then bent and kissed her again, his eyes blinking. "I love you, my Erephine, my sister." She still had not moved except for the small expansions and contractions of her chest. "Farewell."

*   *   *

"He is fine to look at, isn't he? But he seemed sad when he went out," the young nurse from the farm country said. "Didn't you think so?"

"You can't tell with those Flower-folk," one of the others said. "Stiff as statues, they are."

"But maybe he's unhappy about his sister . . ."

Her coworker shook her head and went on measuring out the bite-me-not elixir into small cups: it was medicine time in the Active wing. "They don't waste their strength on feelings, those Flower lords, and especially not about the girl children of the families. They do what's right so that everyone can see it, of course. Very big on making the right show."

"Besides," said one of the older women, "She's been in here for years, so they must all be used to it by now. No, you're just being a romantic, my girl. It's easy to do with these rich, fair-faced chaps—they can seem however they want."

"Do you really think so?"

"Mark my words, girl, and don't let yourself be fooled. They rule the world, that lot. All of Faerie bends the knee to them. What would one of them have to be sad about?"

20

AMONG THE CREEPERS

"What the hell is that?" Theo squinted at the jar Lady Aemilia was holding, which glowed a pale yellowish green like something out of a low-budget movie.

"Don't be such a big girl's blouse," said Applecore, kicking her legs on the edge of the dispensary table.

"And what's *that* bizarre expression supposed to mean?"

"It shouldn't hurt at all," said the fairy noblewoman, but Theo felt she could have put a bit more feeling into the assurance.

"You said the last thing would only smart a bit and then it felt like someone stuck a dental drill in my spinal column. So 'shouldn't hurt at all' means what? No worse than a severe beating?"

"Certainly no worse than that," Lady Aemilia agreed. "Just lie on your stomach. Aren't we glad we didn't put our shirt back on?"

"Oh, yeah, we're thrilled." Theo clambered back onto the medical table and its white linen cover. He couldn't escape the feeling that this sparsely decorated room was actually a veterinary surgery, but he supposed he should be grateful that at least it was clean. Still, this was not the bargain he would have preferred to make—painful experimentation in return for sanctuary. "You still haven't told me what's in that jar."

"A leech, of course. We need some of your blood."

Theo was halfway off the table before Lady Aemilia grabbed his arm, but he got no farther. She was surprisingly strong for someone who looked like a willowy hundred and ten pounds at the most. "Don't make such a scene, young fellow." She turned to Applecore. "Does he really know so little about science?"

"Science—you're calling leeches 'science'? What do you call thumbscrews and the rack—'probation'?"

"We simply need some of your blood so we can determine how . . . so we can do some other important testing. We so rarely get the chance to study someone like you."

"I thought this city used to be full of visiting mortals."

"Oh. Well, not . . . full, exactly. In any case, it has been a long while since we have had anyone of your type here, and our science has moved forward rapidly since then. This is a priceless opportunity to increase knowledge. Now would you please stop being such a soppy boy and lie down."

"Her ladyship knows what she's doin', Theo," said Applecore.

Theo didn't want to embarrass the sprite, but then again, it wasn't like she'd consulted him before getting him into this, either. He stretched himself facedown on the table and stared at the wall, which except for a stylized daffodil in bas-relief was as tastefully blank as the rest of the room's walls. He tried to relax, but when Lady Aemilia's cool hand suddenly touched his back muscles he barely stifled a shriek of alarm.

"Silly. Tensing up will only make it worse. Don't worry, these leeches are specially bred in the most scientific surroundings." Something was set gently on his back below one shoulder blade and settled there with a small wet shrug; he tried not to think about it too much. It nipped him sharply, then he could feel numbness spreading. "It should be better now," his hostess explained. "They have anaesthetic saliva. 'Anaesthetic' means that it suppresses . . . ."

"I know what it means." It was probably bad form to interrupt fairy women of high social standing, but right this moment he didn't give a shit. He was tired of being treated like Charlton Heston on the ape planet. "It's Greek for 'We just added another five hundred bucks to your hospital bill.' " The puzzled silence lasted several seconds. "That was a joke."

"Ah, of course," said Lady Aemilia. "Oops, I think this little fellow is full. Cumber! Could you bring in another leech, please."

"Another one? Why don't you just poke a hole in me and fill a bucket?"

"What a good idea!" She tightened her grip to keep him on the table. "That was also a joke, Master Vilmos."

After Lady Aemilia had disappeared—off to instruct little fairy children on the evils of chewing gum or something similar, Theo suspected—he pulled his shirt and pants back on. The noblewoman's assistant, a small male fairy with skin the color of butterscotch pudding and hair only a shade lighter had remained to straighten up the examining room.

"How long have I been in here? It feels like it's been all day."

"It's late afternoon," Applecore told him. "Are you hungry?"

"Oh, yeah. Nothing like having a huge glowing leech on your back to put a man in the mood for chow."

"Would you like to wash your hands before I clean the sink?" asked the assistant. Theo shook his head and the slender fellow went to work scrubbing the shiny bronze.

"You're a grump, Vilmos," observed Applecore.

"Why are they so interested? I mean, there must have been half a dozen people in here today, staring at me. Not that any of them bothered to talk to me. I felt like the Elephant Man or something."

"I can tell you," said the assistant. When Theo turned to

look at him, he blushed a little, or seemed to—it was hard to tell with his skin color.

Applecore fluttered up from the table and buzzed over to Theo's shoulder, balancing on it carefully as he buttoned his shirt. "Yeah, why don't you? He never listens to me."

The fairy bobbed his head and smiled. He seemed shy, but not in the servile way Theo had encountered so often during his single day at Daffodil House: the goblin house-maids who would not meet his gaze, the wingless but still obviously lower-class functionaries who hurried to one side to let him pass. In fact, there was a gleam in this fairy's eyes as he spoke that Theo could not at first understand. "It's just . . . oh, I'm certain that coming from a magical world like yours, we must all seem very drab to you, Master Vil-mos. But it's an honor to be part of these examinations. You cannot imagine how exciting it is." His cheeks grew a little more brown; he was definitely flushed, now. "Speaking for myself. I mean, I'm certain Lady Aemilia is quite interested too, of course she is. But for me, it's . . ." He took a breath. "I earned my graduate degree in Mortal Studies. So this is . . . I never even hoped . . ."

Theo could not help liking this fellow. There was some-thing pleasingly childlike about him, and not just his ageless features, or the fact that the top of his head only reached Theo's shoulder. "Well, I can't say I'm happy to be of serv-ice—not quite—but I suppose I'm glad someone's getting something out of this. What's your name?"

The fairy seemed caught entirely by surprise. "My name?"

"Shit, did I say something wrong again? Do you come from some fairy-place where you're not allowed to have a name until you've turned at least one pumpkin into a coach or something?" Theo regretted his sarcasm—the fellow looked confused and almost on the verge of panic. "Never mind. Is it all right to ask your name?"

Applecore snorted. "You see what it's like, running

around with mortals? Put that in your next lab report, fella.
I could tell you stories . . ."

"No, I just . . ." The assistant shook his head. "My name
is Cumber. Cumber Sedge."

"Pleased to meet you." Theo began tying his shoes. "Now
where am I supposed to eat? They brought some little seed-
cakes this morning, but I haven't had a bite since." He
turned to Applecore. "They put you in some other part of the
complex. Have you got a cafeteria over there or something?"

"I'm staying in Daffodil Comb under the main tower,"
she said. "I think you'd find the portions a bit small. But we
should be able to get you set up in the refectory, or maybe
they'd even bring something to your room, although it's usually only the high muckety-mucks that get that kind of treatment. Speaking of your room, did they do right by you? I
didn't get much of a chance to look it over this morning."

"It's fine—kind of like the Wonderland Holiday Inn, but
no complaints. I'm afraid to touch any of the appliances,
though—I almost set Tansy's place on fire when I was
there."

Cumber Sedge straightened, the gleam back in his eyes.
"You know Count Tansy?"

Theo hesitated and looked to Applecore, but she seemed
unconcerned. "Yeah, sort of. I stayed with him for a couple
of days."

"He has some fascinating ideas about etheric vapors,
quite original. One of the few Flower lords who is more than
simply a gentleman scientist." He looked around guiltily
after uttering this bit of *lesé majesté*. "Have you read his
work on Circular and Triangular Utterances?"

"Uh, I'm afraid I've been a bit busy lately, but I'll be getting to it any time now." He winced as Applecore tweaked
his ear. "Stop that. So, where can I get something to eat?
Dinner, supper, whatever you call your evening meal?"

"Would . . ." That one word seemed to have bankrupted
Sedge's courage; he plunged his hands deep into the pockets
of his white tunic and swayed a little, then had to take a deep

breath before trying again. "Would you like to go have a
proper meal? After all, it's Mabon Eve. I could take you—
both of you. It would be an honor. There is a small restaurant here in Daffodil House, near the park, that's very nice."
He flushed again. "Or so I'm told."

Theo shrugged. "Sounds good. Applecore? Or have you
got something hot and heavy going on back at the comb—a
date with Tom Thumb, maybe?"

"You're vulgar even for a mortal, you are." She dropped
from his shoulder and buzzed over closer to Sedge. "Do I
have time to smarten meself up a little?"

"Cer . . . certainly. I have to finish cleaning up here,
anyway."

"Am I just allowed to go off like this?" Theo asked. "I
mean, don't these Daffodil people want to know where I am
at all times or something?"

Applecore snorted. "These aren't the folks who asked for
you in the first place, Vilmos—those were the Hollyhocks. I
had to beg to bring you here to Daffodil House, but now
you're safe. It's a good thing for you that Lady Aemilia is so
interested in mortals."

"Yeah? Any interest that centers around the application of
leeches I can do without." Still, he found himself vaguely
disturbed that his hostess and the rest of the Daffodil nobles
seemed so little concerned with his whereabouts. "Did you
tell her ladyship that people were trying to kill me?"

"Oh, yes. It was one of the things that interested her."
Applecore rose and hovered. "I'll go make meself beautiful,
boys. Shouldn't take more than a few hours." She laughed as
she turned and flew out.

Cumber Sedge watched the fast-disappearing glint of her
wings. "She's . . . really nice. Are you . . . if you don't mind
my asking . . . have you . . ." A hectic patch on each cheek
darkened all the way to milk-chocolate. "Is she your girlfriend?"

*   *   *

It was better than a cafeteria, Theo had to admit. The Gatehouse was a small, pleasant restaurant at the base of the Daffodil House tower on the edge of what was more or less a moat, halfway across the complex from the real gatehouse in the outer wall. Bathed by the silvery gleams of concealed spotlights, the moat might have been the remains of something that once had been practical, but now instead of guardsmen or walls it surrounded thick banks of rushes, a few artfully pruned willows, and a good half-mile of paths with ornamental bridges and benches set out at intervals so that the most picturesque spots could be viewed in comfort. The food in this newer gatehouse was good, although Theo was not entirely in love with Fairyland cuisine, which relied a bit too much on honey, clotted cream, and flower petals for his tastes.

"So were these places here before there was a city?" Theo asked.

"Many of them, I suppose." Cumber Sedge was on his second glass of wine and was beginning to loosen up. He already had a splotch of mint jelly on his gray shirt. "I'm afraid I'm not very good with ancient history. The City is built out from the site of the first mound, you know—some even claim it began before there was a king and queen, but I don't believe them—so it's very, very old. Anyway, I'm pretty certain that the Daffodil family castle has been in the same place a long time, like the Helebores and the Primroses. Apparently the established families like to build on the site of older buildings, or incorporate them."

"You say it like you've only heard about it. Aren't you one of them? A Daffodil?"

Applecore, sitting on a tiny chair and eating at a tiny table set on the tablecloth between Theo and Cumber, gave a little snort, then picked up her tiny bowl of dandelion wine and had another drink.

Cumber smiled apologetically. "She's laughing because I'm not a Daffodil—I'm not from one of the Flower Houses at all."

"That's not why I laughed," she said. "Some great eejit just fell in the moat outside." A few of the restaurant's other patrons were also staring out the picture windows at the commotion down by the water.

"Ah. That looks like Zirus and his friends. Zirus Jonquil—Lady Aemilia's son. He and his friends can be rather . . . sporty. We were at school together. Not that they ever took much notice of me."

"So you're from a different family?" Theo asked. His venison had been quite good, simple but well-cooked; now he was enjoying the wine and beginning to wonder if people in Faerie smoked cigarettes or even cigars, and how he might get hold of such a thing. "I was wondering why your name wasn't Titus or Taurus or Doofius or something like that."

"A different family?" Cumber let out a sort of shamed giggle. "A different species, almost. I'm a ferisher."

"A what?" Theo was distracted by a thump and jingle from the front door as several youthful-looking fairies pushed into the restaurant and up to the bar, talking and laughing loudly.

"Ferisher. You haven't heard of us? We're domestic fairies, mostly. My mother was one of Lady Aemilia's nurses." He looked sideways at Applecore. "She's been very kind to me, Lady Aemilia. When she found out how much I liked to read, she always gave me books. And she even sent me to school with her own boys. I was the first ferisher they ever had at Great Ring Academy . . ."

"Look who's here! It's old Cumberbumber!" A figure lurched up to their table, his appearance so loud and sudden that Theo flinched. "Well, Good Mabon Eve to you, Sedge. I can't believe my mother actually let you out of that dungeon of stinks where she keeps you locked up!"

"Hello, Zirus." Sedge's smile was a little nervous. "Good Mabon Eve to you, too. I like it in the lab. I like the work."

"Work—bloody Bark and Root, who wants to work? Had enough of that back in school." The tall young fairy yanked an empty chair away from another table, startling the table's occupants, and sat on it splay-legged and backward, tipping back and forth between Theo and Cumber. He was dark-haired, very handsome—the resemblance to his mother's chiseled features was easy to see—and seemed by the standards of his kind to be quite, quite drunk. "Who's your chum, Cumberbumber? Old family friend?"

"Yes, he's a friend," said Cumber, and gave Theo what looked very much like a warning look.

The young fairy lord offered Theo his hand and Theo took it, not quite sure of what he was supposed to do. He gave it a shake that turned into sort of a squeeze, then let go. If he had done anything wrong, the scion of Jonquil House appeared not to have noticed. "Pleasure to meet you, all that. Zirus Jonquil, me. Don't mind what those others over there tell you—they're all potted." He gestured at the bar, where several of his friends were standing a little unsteadily, although their natural grace was such that Theo was only now getting to the point where he could tell the difference between sober and unsober fairies. "You are?"

"Theodorus," he said. Applecore flitted up to his shoulder and whispered a suggestion in his ear. "Theodorus weft-Daisy."

"A country cousin!" said Zirus. "Welcome to the big, bad City. What do you think? Your first visit?" He turned to his friends. "There's a lad here fresh in from Rowan." He turned back to Theo and Cumber Sedge as his friends at the bar shouted what sounded like genial insults at the out-of-towner. "Say, what are you fellows doing tonight?"

"We're just having dinner . . ." Cumber began.

"No, you're coming with us—it's a holiday, isn't it? Bring your friend." Zirus squinted blearily just a bit to the side of Theo's face, and for a moment Theo thought the fairy lord was going to be sick. "Hoy, who's that? There's someone on your shoulder, Daisy."

"Her name is Applecore."

"I'm a friend of your mother's," the sprite said, a bit sternly.

"Ooh." Zirus grinned. "Then you'd better come along too, so she doesn't find out where we're going until it's all over."

"Go where?"

"The most wonderful club. Very new. Everyone's talking. And they will be until it closes in a week or so and they're talking about something else." Zirus chortled. "Come 'long. I insist. Haven't seen old Cumberbumber here for a shuck-dog's age." He grabbed Theo by the arm. He had his mother's grip, and Theo found himself pulled up onto his feet. "I insist. We'll go in my coach. The rest of this lot can find their own way." He tugged Theo toward the front of the restaurant with Applecore buzzing along beside their heads and Cumber Sedge hurrying along after.

"Don't we have to pay for our dinners . . . ?" Theo asked as they reached the door.

"Pay? Rubbish. Hoy, Needle! Put it on my bill!" The bent old fairy behind the counter didn't look pleased, but didn't say anything as they banged out the door and into the cold evening air. "He's probably a bit miffed because I haven't settled my tab in a few months," Zirus confided to Theo as he hurried them down a winding path toward the compound's front gate. "Mother is being dreadfully stingy about advances on my allowance. Hoy! I'll go wake up that lazy driver of mine. I can see him sleeping from here!"

As Zirus skipped off toward a long limousine that was idling in a little parking lot just beside the gate, Theo slowed down until Cumber Sedge caught up with him. "Do we have to do this?"

Cumber shrugged, embarrassed. "It's not a good idea to say no to Zirus. He's like his mother—curious about things. He'll just get even more interested in you and start asking questions, and not necessarily only around Daffodil House. I'm lucky—most of the time, he forgets I exist."

"Come on, you lot!" Zirus shouted.

"I don't like it," said Applecore quietly in Theo's ear.

"But at least we're not likely to get picked up by the constables while we're out with him—nobody arrests a Flower."

"It's not being arrested I'm worrying about," whispered Theo, remembering Rufinus weft-Daisy slumped on the train station bench. But Zirus Jonquil was trotting back toward them in a not entirely straight line, waving his arms and urging them to hurry.

"Sorry, sorry, this is all my fault," said Cumber Sedge.

"By the way" Theo asked Applecore, "I understand the 'Daisy' part, but why do you keep telling people my name is 'weft-Daisy'? What does 'weft' mean?"

"Bastard," she said. "Don't look at me like that, ya thick—I'm just telling you what the word means."

Zirus Jonquil kept talking as they rode across town, a drunken but also highly entertaining recitation about silly people and unusual events that Theo felt sure he would find even more amusing if he knew any of the subjects or even a bit more about the world in which they all lived. A lot of the stories seemed to be about people getting into trouble in places they shouldn't be, off their own turf. To hear Zirus tell it, these shenanigans sounded a bit like the early parts of *West Side Story,* funny and more exciting than dangerous, but as Theo looked out the car window at some of the bleak, run-down neighborhoods they were now crossing, he thought the area itself looked like some of the less charming parts of Los Angeles, more like Bloods and Crips than Sharks and Jets.

"Where are we going, exactly?" he asked Cumber. "This club?"

"I'm not certain," said the researcher. "But it does seem a bit far—I think we're already at the far end of the Eventide District. Zirus, where are we going?"

"Just into Moonlight." Their host's tone was light, but Theo could tell by the uneasy look on Cumber's face that it was not such a minor thing.

"This isn't good, Theo," Applecore whispered in his ear. "Ask him what the name of the club is."

When Theo did, Zirus smiled and drained another glass of something he had poured himself from the bar built into the car door. "Oh, you probably haven't heard of it—it's only been open a couple of weeks. It's called Christmas and it's quite good." He laughed as Cumber Sedge flinched. "You really have to get out more, Cumberbumber. If the name of the place bothers you, wait until you see the decor!"

"Where exactly is this place, Zirus?" Cumber asked. "I didn't think there were any clubs in Moonlight, just house-towers and government buildings and places like that."

"Ah, but that's what makes this club so good," the young Jonquil lord said. "It's in the basement of Hellebore House."

A six-inch tall sprite had to gulp loudly to be heard so clearly. Theo's uneasy feeling suddenly grew a great deal more intense.

"Not good?" he whispered.

"*Very* not good," she whispered back.

"Oh, stop it, you two," said Zirus. "Everybody makes such a massive fuss about the Hellebores, just because the father's awful and political and the heir is a bit of a strange weed. But some of the younger ones are quite fun in a wild sort of way. Besides, how else would any of us from Daffodil ever get to see the inside of Hellebore House?"

"But I don't want to see the inside of Hellebore House." Cumber had clearly had more to drink than he usually did, and had become ever more silent and morose during the journey. "They're our enemies."

"Enemies!" Zirus shook his head in amused astonishment. "Do you believe all that nonsense about a Flower war? It will never happen. Bark and Root, they're always squabbling in Parliament. The goblins will rise up and execute us all before the houses go to war with each other. Speaking of, this part of Eventide really has gone to seed, hasn't it?" He frowned. Outside the window the streets were crowded again, but it did not seem like a happy scene. Most of the folk on the sidewalk were goblins and what looked to Theo's untutored eye like various kinds of doonies and squat boggarts and other not-quite-human-looking folk. They seemed listless and unfocused, standing or even sitting on the sidewalk in the harsh silvery light of the streetlamps, collected in little knots. Many of them looked sullenly at the car as it slid past them.

Theo remembered something from his great-uncle's book about the shape of the City being a sort of spiral. "So, Daffodil House is in Gloaming, right?" he asked Applecore. "And this is, what, Eventide? And we're going to Moonlight. So does it just keep going? I mean, does it get darker and darker? Is there a Middle-of-the-Night or something?"

"Let's not talk about it," she said.

"Why?"

"Because."

"No whispering, you two," said Zirus. "Blast, we're out of brandy." He settled back in the seat and crossed his legs. "What brings you to the City, Daisy?"

"He came with me," Applecore said quickly. "He'd never been and he wanted to do some sight-seeing."

"Sight-seeing?" Zirus groaned. "Don't let her drag you around to all that nonsense—Winter Dynasty Bridge, Knocker's Walk, all that. Stick with me, I'll show you the real City."

"That's very kind of you." Theo was wondering how quickly they would be able to shed this young Jonquil lord and get back to Daffodil House. He did not like the idea of being introduced around—what if they ran into someone who really was from Daisytown or whatever the damn place had been called? He could only pray that this would be one of those clubs where the music was so loud you couldn't do anything but nod and smile while people yelled unintelligible questions.

"Speaking of the real City," said Zirus, "we're just coming into Seven Blooms Square. You know all the old stories from the last war with the giants, I'm sure—Sweetpea's

Charge, the Battle of the Twilight Bell, all that." Theo knew
nothing of the sort, but nodded and tried to look intelligent.
"Well, it's all rubbish, at least about the Seven Blooms, and
I should know because we Daffodils were one of them. Well,
it's not *all* rubbish, but the bit about the people all cheering
when the Seven families announced they were going to create a new parliament, that certainly is. It was all done in secret, and only because they were all tired out from trying to
kill each other after the giants were defeated. Nobody was
cheering because the king and queen were dead and everyone was terrified. My great-uncle swears on all the Trees
that old Otho Primrose was so frightened and shaking so
badly that he couldn't have signed the treaty except Lord
Violet was helping to hold up his arm."

Theo had no idea what any of it meant, although there
were a few faint resonances with things he had read in his
own great-uncle's book. He was having trouble thinking
clearly and wished he hadn't had the wine. A light spatter of
rain on the coach windows broke the strange, witchy lights
of the city-center up into a smear of silver and green and
blue spots, but it seemed to be getting darker outside rather
than brighter, as though they were leaving the well-lit areas
behind. In the middle of a long patch of blackness broken
only by an occasional streetlamp, the coach slowed and
stopped.

"What's going on?" Cumber Sedge didn't seem nervous,
just confused, but then he probably didn't have as much to
worry about as Theo did.

"Checkpoint," explained Zirus. Theo could vaguely make
out a dark shape blocking the way, some kind of wall. Low
voices spoke for a moment, their own driver no more intelli-
gible than the guards or whatever they were, then the coach
again moved forward, but more slowly this time.

"There it is," said Zirus. "Hellebore House. Mad bastards, the lot of 'em, but you have to admit the old place has
style."

Theo couldn't make out much of anything until the young

Daffodil lord flicked his fingers at the door and the window slid silently down, letting in a spatter of misty rain. After Theo blinked the water out of his eyes he saw the huge pale spike.

It was so strange an object that it took him a moment to get the perspective. If it had looked more like an office building or a castle tower it would have happened immediately, but it looked like nothing so much as a kind of ivory chess piece out of some abstract set—a very slender rook or a predatory queen. It was not cylindrical like the Daffodil towers, but four-sided, as far as Theo could tell, although neither of its visible sides were rectangles—not quite, although they looked like they might have started that way. The whole structure seemed to have been stretched out of true, as though a great hand had reached down, grabbed the tower by its spiky, many-gabled roof—an odd contrast with the simplicity of the rest of the building's lines—and yanked on it, pulling it up into the dark sky like a piece of bone-colored taffy. It was lit by carefully arranged spotlights, some with a reddish tint, and all its windows were black. It looked like the shell of an alien animal or a skull with hundreds of eye sockets.

"I . . . I don't like that place." There was more to Theo's aversion than he could express, an alien coldness that came down on him suddenly and with great weight. It reminded him queasily of something—a nightmare?—but he could not remember what it was. He only knew that he was having trouble getting his breath, and that he wished he were somewhere else.

"Why should you like it?" Applecore asked. "They're not nice people in there." Cumber Sedge only mumbled as he stared out the window—the ferisher, Theo realized, was pretty seriously drunk.

"Wait until you see the club," said Zirus, pouring himself another drink. "It's *really* interesting."

Theo had now heard the word "interesting" several times from Lady Aemilia and her son. He was beginning to suspect that it had two meanings for them, and neither of those matched the definition of the word as he had previously known it. One was *"horrible."* The other was *"especially horrible for mortals."*

"I don't think I want to see any more interesting things," he announced, but it was far, far too late. They were already in the driveway that led to the main gate. He felt as though something was waiting for him, something dreadful. He hoped it was only that he wasn't used to fairy liquor.

At first it seemed like it was going to be even worse than he had thought—the hulking ogres at the massive gate shining lights into the car, the long wait which Theo was convinced would end with them all being dragged out and handcuffed, or put into stocks, or whatever restraints they used on wanted criminals in Fairyland. Applecore had moved to his shoulder; he could feel her sitting there, a tensed, hard little object that seemed made of springs and knobs. He realized he'd never seen their driver, and had a sudden suspicion that the creature behind the wheel was one of the corpselike hollow-men, that this whole episode had been an elaborate trap. But instead the ogres stepped back and the limousine suddenly rolled forward again through a renewed flurry of rain that slapped against the windshield, then down a dark and disturbingly long tunnel that dumped them into an underground parking lot about five seconds before Theo's paranoia hit the critical point. In a daze, he followed Cumber Sedge, who didn't seem any more eager to go than he was: Zirus Jonquil almost had to push them both out of the car. As they walked across the echoing, silverlit garage, Theo looked back at the limousine but could not make out the driver's face through the darkened windows.

They could already feel the music as they waited for the elevator, a thumping, jarring sensation as though something extremely large was trying to escape from the floor below them. A few more fairy lordlings joined them, laughing and talking so fast and in such emphatic slang that Theo couldn't understand a word. He let himself be moved into the elevator like a puppet.

When the door opened the sound hit him like an explosion, a walloping bass and strange polyrhythms he couldn't quite wrap his head around, topped with a soaring wind instrument like a clarinet. Two huge gray hands patted him down in a rough but cursory fashion, then shoved him through into the noise and the flashing lights and the crowds of extravagantly dressed (although some were nearly naked) and almost uniformly gorgeous young fairies. Transparent shapes gyrated in midair among the dancers, shapes that looked like nothing so much as ghosts and which popped like soap bubbles when the dancers touched them. But nothing stunned him as much as realizing what the club actually was.

A church . . . ! He had been expecting something more in keeping with the name, some kind of mock-horror decadence with a Yuletide theme—serial-killer Santa maybe, mutilated elves, black tinsel, and scorched trees. Instead he could have been in the chapel—albeit a large one—of an Episcopalian church. There were stained glass windows, lit from behind, and a simple altar near the far wall beneath a large crucifix, from which even the most frenetic of the dancing fairies in their extravagant finery seemed to keep a respectful distance. The Jesus on the cross was not even one of the more tormented, bloody sorts he had marveled at in Mexican churches during his traveling days. He was about to say something about it to Cumber Sedge—bellow something, since that was all that could be done—but the ferisher stumbled against him and almost fell.

"This . . . is . . . horrible," Cumber groaned.

"We have to get him out of here," Applecore shouted in Theo's ear.

"Is he drunk?"

"It's that." She pointed a tiny hand at the crucifix. "These people . . . they're all crazy. Sick."

And suddenly he remembered what she had told him

about swearing, and realized that it was the Christian symbols themselves which gave this place its nasty cachet. They didn't need to have pictures of mangled children or evil toys: it wasn't the Christmas bit that was the draw here for Faerie's jaded gentry, it was the Christ bit—not modern Christmas, but Christ Mass.

"Where are you going?" Zirus shouted. He had already found a drink, somewhere. "This is fabulous, isn't it? They've actually hired Bishop Silver to do the music. All those great old music charms—everyone wants to get him. He's absolutely the most vaporous tune-smith in the city. Makes his own phantasms, too, you know."

Theo waved his hand in a distracted way. He guessed that the phantasms must be the transparent, faintly glowing figures flying around the dance floor. The music certainly was interesting—he could hear all kinds of strange fragmentary resonances, and could sense noises in it that he couldn't quite catch with his ears. He would have loved to learn more about it, but not here, not now. "Yeah, it's great," Theo roared back above the din.

"Can I get you something?"

"Cumber's not feeling very well." Theo struggled to keep the ferisher upright. He'd been in this position before, but it was the first time he'd ever had to carry someone out of a club because of too much Jesus. "Is there another room?"

Zirus laughed. "You're doing okay, though, country boy. A bit more than you seem, eh? Right, I think there's a quiet room just up the stairs. I'll catch up with you—I've just seen some friends."

The room was open to the dance floor, and the noise boiling up from below didn't make it a whole lot easier to talk, but at least they couldn't see the crucifix from the table in the dark room. Theo got Cumber sitting upright and Applecore fanned his face with her wings until he seemed a bit more himself.

"Sorry" he mumbled. "Just . . . not my sort of thing."

"That's okay" Theo said. "Do you want some water?"

"No, another drink."

"Are you sure?"

The ferisher nodded his head grimly. "It'll make it easier. We'll be here a while."

"Well, why don't we just go home by ourselves? Catch a cab or something?"

"And how are we going to pay for it, boyo?" asked Applecore. "Do you have any tallies? No, I didn't think so. Cumber?"

The ferisher shook his head. "I paid for the meal in the restaurant. I left it on the table. It's one thing for Zirus to walk out on a bill, but I'm not the Jonquil heir." He sighed. "But that was all I had, so we'll have to wait for him to take us home. Could I have that drink? I'll be perfectly happy to put it on Zirus' tab."

"I'll go find a waitress," said Applecore, and hummed straight over the railing into the seething mass of creatures below.

Another group of fairies, apparently upper crust and dressed in a weird mixture of what looked to Theo like High Victorian and slashed and smeared punky Goth fashions, piled into the quiet room and settled around a table in the opposite corner, making it much less quiet. Theo frowned and moved a bit closer to Cumber Sedge. "I don't know how much you know about me," Theo said, "but I really don't want anyone to . . . well, notice me. There were people trying to kill us on our way to Daffodil House. I shouldn't even be here."

"Nor should I," said Cumber mournfully. "Don't belong."

"I'm just saying that I don't know enough to pass myself off as anything, really. So please, help me out. We can't afford to draw any attention. We just need to stay sort of quiet and unnoticed until your Jonquil friend takes us home again."

"Understood." Cumber tried to lay his finger alongside his nose in a gesture of secret solidarity and managed to poke himself in the eye. Applecore buzzed back in, followed a few moments later by a waitress, who took one look at Theo and Cumber Sedge and went to take orders at the other table first.

"How are you boys?" Applecore asked. "Enjoying this charming place?"

"I was just telling Cumber that we need to be . . . inconspicuous."

"No worries about that," the ferisher said. "Nobody here wants to see you. These Flower folk, they could care less. One of the lesser classes—even worse, one of the other *races* . . . !" He shook his head. "Wouldn't help you if you were lying dead in the street."

The waitress appeared, an attractive fairy woman with surprisingly prominent wings. She was wearing an odd costume that Theo only figured out after she had left—bearing their drinks order and instructed to charge it to the young laud of Jonquil House—was a nun's habit shortened and slit into a minidress.

"But Zirus seems like an okay guy," Theo said.

"Oh, as far as they go, he's a good one." Cumber had recovered from his initial shock, but had become morose and distant. "But most of them wouldn't piss on you if you were on fire."

"Unless you were lying on an expensive carpet," said Applecore.

"So are you telling me that no matter what language I spoke back in my world, I'd be speaking Fairy here?"

"You'd be speaking the Common Breath," Cumber said, working very hard to enunciate his consonants above the musical din. He'd had three drinks on Zirus' tab, and what he had gained in cheerfulness he had lost in articulation. "That's the language all the races of Shaerie fare. Bugger. Faerie share."

Applecore, who had downed a few thimblefuls herself,

giggled. She had left Theo's shoulder and was sitting in the middle of the table.

"Okay, I guess I get that. But what if my normal language was, I don't know, Arabic? No, Chinese. Isn't it kind of weird that I'd arrive here and I'd see all you fairy folk from, like, old Irish stories and whatnot?"

"That *is* an interesting question," said Cumber, downing the last of his drink. "You see, Seed, we don't thee . . . we don't *see* . . . ourselves the way you do. And we don't see you the way you see you. Right?"

"You've lost me."

"See, there have always been people of Faerie visiting the mortal world. Well, until recently—the Clover Effect has cut back on that." He frowned. "And until just lately, there have always been mortals who have crossed over into Faerie. So most of the difference between what some mortals call us and what some others call us is just the difference in mortal languages. You call us fairies, other mortals call us peris or whatever the Chinese word or the Balinese word is. See? But there is another difference, too. It was a ferisher who did the important work on it, actually." He nodded slowly. "Holdfast Buckram. A few centuries back. Wrote a marvelous book called *The Mortal Lens*. About how mortals tend to see what they want to see. No 'fense." He belched. "'Scuse me."

Theo was trying to pay attention—this was something he hadn't read about in his great-uncle's story—but a fairy lordling at one of the other tables in the quiet room was smoking what looked very much like a cigarette in a long cigarette holder, and Theo found himself wishing he had the courage to go bum one. But that would be asking for trouble, wouldn't it? He tried to refocus on Cumber Sedge. "So I see most of these fairies as looking like . . . like the kind of fairies I expect to see?"

"More or less." Sedge got the attention of their waitress and ordered another round of drinks. Theo shook his head. He had been drinking only a sweet wine, and was only on his second glass since reaching the club, but he was already feeling more fuzzy than he wanted to. "So if you had grown up in some quite different datrition . . . bugger . . . tradition, you'd bc seeing and hearing things a bit differently."

Theo had now stopped listening entirely. The young, pale-haired fairy with the cigarette holder had leaned back to laugh at something. Sitting on his far side was Poppy Thornapple. "Oh, my sweet Jesus," said Theo.

"That only hurt a little!" Cumber announced cheerfully.

"Vilmos, I told you, don't do that," said Applecore.

"There . . . over at that table, it's the girl we were on the train with." Poppy was dressed quite differently now, no longer wearing what he realized had been her meeting-her-family clothes. In a sort of elaborate mourning-outfit with a surprisingly low bodice, and makeup that looked like it belonged in a Japanese play, she blended in well with her companions, but he knew without doubt it was her. He was surprised by the flipflop in his stomach. Remorse? Or just jealousy? She was leaning her head against the young lord with the cigarette.

"Well, I'm not surprised," Applecore said. "This is just her sort of place, isn't it?"

Before Theo could reply, Poppy looked up and saw him. She had been speaking, and for a moment she simply froze, mouth open, eyes suddenly wide and startled. Then she looked away and finished what she had been saying, forcing a laugh. When her companions responded and the conversation eddied away, she looked at him again. This time it was as though a gate had been slammed down behind her eyes: she stared as though she had never seen him before and never wished to see him again. After a moment, she whispered something to the pale-haired fairy and got up and left the room, her stiff, wide skirt swinging.

"Just a minute," Theo told Applecore. "I'll be right back."

"Don't you dare, Vilmos . . . !" the sprite began, but he was already up from the table and heading for the door.

She wasn't on the stairs. He went down into the full blare of the music and pushed alongside the pulsing swarm of dancers, looking for her on the floor or in one of the alcoves that lined the wall, dark places where people were kissing and groping, inhaling things out of odd little crystalline tubes, or engaging in other activities he couldn't quite make out, but about which he felt he could make a good guess or two.

He found her at the bar, waiting for a drink. "Hello," was the only thing he could think of to say.

"Do I know you?"

For a moment he wondered if he had mistaken a mere resemblance under thick makeup. But then he remembered the way she had looked at him across the tables, the anger and hurt. "You know me, Poppy. From the train."

"I don't think so. I certainly never talk to country riffraff on trains, so you must be mistaken. Very badly mistaken." She would not meet his eye.

"Look, I'm sorry it turned out that way. I didn't want to leave, but we had to."

Still looking toward the bartender mixing her drink, she said, "I'd hate to have to call for security—they are extremely rough here in Hellebore House, as you might guess. They would probably break your legs at the very least. And the wings that you are no doubt hiding under that ill-fitting jacket—well, they would probably rip them right off."

"All right. I'll leave you alone." It had been stupid coming after her—what had changed? And he could only hope she was exaggerating for effect and that she wouldn't really call security. The last thing he needed was for that to happen. "I just wanted you to know that I was sorry, and that I didn't lie to you about anything. It was just . . . bad timing." He turned and walked away.

"Stop. Come here."

He turned and looked at her, wondering if she had changed her mind and wanted to keep him in sight until she could call for the bouncers. She had an odd look in her eyes, a staring, red-rimmed intensity.

"I just want you to know," she said quietly, making him lean forward to hear until his face almost touched hers, "that I hate you, Theodorus weft-Daisy, or . . . or whoever you really are. Do you understand? I'll be staying at Thornapple House for another week before I go back to school, and you are not under any circumstances to call me there on my private line. Because I hate you, you wretched, horrible, heartless monster."

She abruptly reached up and pulled his head down toward hers, then kissed him so hard that her teeth banged against his. When he let go he tasted blood from his own lip. She was crying.

"Now go away," she said. "You've spoiled my evening." She wiped her eyes with her sleeve, smearing her makeup, then turned to shout at the bartender, "Running water and black iron—where is my drink?"

Theo stumbled back across the club, a bit overwhelmed. Someone grabbed his arm near the bottom of the stairs. It took him a moment to recognize Zirus Jonquil: the young fairy lord was even more happily drunk than before, his hair disarranged and his shirt unbuttoned to reveal ivory skin almost to the navel. He looked quite wild and beautiful—there was something deeply, weirdly attractive about him that had nothing to do with sex. At least Theo hoped it had nothing to do with sex.

"Daisy! There you are. Where have old Cumberbumber and the fingerling girl got to?"

"Upstairs."

"Well, you're missing the most tremendous fun—one of the Campion lads was teasing the Hellebore security, who didn't take it well. They just took Campion out on a stretcher, but he was still ragging them even as they put him in the hospital coach . . . !' "

"Hysterical." Theo was distracted by the sound of someone shouting at the top of the stairs—shouting very loud, he realized, if he could hear it over the thump and whine of the music. As he reached the door, something flew into his face like a confused bird, battering him for a moment in a flurry of wings and tiny limbs.

"There you are!" Applecore said as she fluttered backward. "Oh, and you, too, your lordship. I was just coming to look for you. It's your friend, Sedge."

But Theo for one did not have to be told that. Cumber Sedge, who had apparently had a bit more to drink than was absolutely optimum, was standing on the tabletop shouting at the gathering of fairy lordlings of which Poppy had been part. Theo was grateful to see there was no sign of her now—it was bad enough trying to figure out what was going on between the two of them without adding a shitfaced ferisher into the mix.

". . . And just because you were born to the right families you think you're better . . . better than ev'ryone . . . !" Cumber swayed and pointed a wavering finger at the fairies. "You think ev'ry one wans . . . wants . . . wants to be like you!"

Poppy's companion, the young fairy with the cigarette holder, saw Zirus and called out, "Ah, there you are, Jonquil. Is this one of yours? If he is, you'd better silence him before someone takes offense and has his head."

"Point taken, Foxy," said Zirus. "Maybe we'll just trundle him home . . ." But Cumber Sedge would not be so easily muzzled.

"I don't belong to anyone!" he screamed. "You wingless bastards run everything, but you don't own me!"

Everyone in the room was watching now, and Theo saw someone on the stairs below him turn and head back down toward the ground floor, perhaps looking for the massive security guards. If Cumber went to jail, Theo had a feeling he might wind up there as well. For a moment he considered making a run for it—what did he really owe the little ferisher, anyway?—but the thought of wandering the alien streets showed that for the foolishness it was. He was relieved when Applecore settled on his shoulder again. "We have to get him out of here," he said. "Now."

"You have a gift for the obvious, boyo."

Poppy Thornapple's former companion was actually debating with Cumber—debating, or playing with him as a cat with a mouse. "Wingless?" the young fairy said with a lazy grin. "And did you not choose to be the same? If you are so fond of wings, little class-warrior, where are yours?"

Cumber Sedge gave out a drunken shriek of frustration. He crouched down, and for a horrifying moment Theo was positive he was about to leap onto his tormentor. Theo and Zirus both sprang toward the ferisher, but he was only setting his drink down on the table; an instant later he straightened up and yanked his shirt over his head. Somehow he managed to keep upright long enough for Theo and Zirus to reach his side and take his arms, but Cumber fought with surprising strength, and though Jonquil hung on, Theo could not; Cumber Sedge turned halfway around toward the table of young fairy nobility to show them the pair of jagged pink scars on his back.

"Where are my wings?" he shrieked. "Gone! Cut off! Because my mother wanted me to be like you! But I wish I had them still! Do you hear me? Because a fairy without wings is . . . is nothing! A flightless abomination!"

Zirus tugged the ferisher roughly off the table and wrapped his shirt back around him before shoving him toward the door. Theo followed closely, Applecore hunched down and riding his shoulder like a jockey. The Jonquil heir stopped in the doorway and bowed to the crowd, most of whom seemed more amused than anything else.

"Well," Zirus shouted above the music, "another exciting evening at Christmas, hey? But I think we'll get this fellow home now."

"Someday all their houses will burn down," Cumber Sedge murmured, "and I'll be one of the ones cheering." Only Theo heard him.

In the elevator down, Zirus was still cheerful. "Hidden depths, eh, Sedge?"

"None of you ever liked me," Cumber said quietly. "The whole time we were in school together, you ignored me. You didn't even bother to pretend."

For a moment Zirus Jonquil's face revealed something startlingly cool and hard. "Oh, stop blubbering, Sedge. What did you expect? You're only a ferisher, after all."

21

IN THORNAPPLE HOUSE

The big coach slid past the gates and down the long driveway lined with poplars. The lower part of the tower stood mostly dark, as was to be expected—it was halfway between midnight and dawn, after all, and even the most powerful families had to be seen conserving energy—but there was a cluster of lit windows on one of the top floors.

Father, up working late, she thought.

As she stepped from the car she could just hear the quiet moaning of the tree-nymphs in their restless sleep. The spells on them were powerful, but even so they could not be entirely silenced. "They're mourning all the other trees gone here in the middle of the City, all their kin killed or dispossessed," one of her childhood nurses had told her. "A terrible thing that was done here, terrible." That nurse had not lasted long, but her words had stayed with Poppy. In the small hours there was no traffic to hide the nymphs' lament and it left her shivering.

Malander Foxglove slid out behind her, pulled her back toward him. He twined his long arms around her and searched for her lips. His mouth smelled of myrtle pastilles, which he sucked to cover the faintly corrupt scent of pixie dust. "Shall I come in, fair Poppaea? Shall we have a little Mabon Eve drink?"

"I'm tired, Lander."

He raised an eyebrow, then leaned back against the side of the huge coach. "You've been strange all night, Pops. Not your normal entertaining self at all." He rubbed up a bit of elemental fire between his fingertips and lit his cigarette in its long holder, then blew a twining snake of smoke. "I hope this won't be an all-the-time thing, little one. That would get boring."

She hated it when he called her "little one." It was the kind of name her father used on those long-ago and extremely rare occasions when he had tried to be affectionate—the kind of nonspecific endearment that Poppy suspected allowed Lord Thornapple not to have to remember which of his seven daughters he was talking to. And it also reminded her of something else she would rather have forgotten, namely that she was half a head shorter than any of her friends. She stiffened in his arms. "I'm sorry to offend you, Master Foxglove."

His eyebrow lifted again at her tone. "Black iron, what crawled into *you* and died?" He let go of her and stretched lazily. "That's my ancient father's bodyguard Gummy waiting there at the door, so the old fellow must be here discussing affairs of the realm with your daddums. Surely you don't mind if I come in and see whether he wants to catch a ride home with me?"

"Your father must have his own coach."

"Not if he came with Lord Hellebore, which he probably did—the three of them are close as the Unseelie Host these days." He sniffed. "They seem to think that if they stopped interfering with everything, the whole place would turn back into the Wildwood again."

"I told you, Malander—I'm tired."

"No one wants to get under your petticoats that badly, Pops, least of all me. There are a million fish in Ys, so don't be so full of yourself. All I'm doing is coming in to see if my father wants a ride home."

"You hate your father."

"Yes, but only to keep things interesting."

She shrugged, too tired to argue, but the idea of having to talk to anyone, let alone having to fight that person off, made her feel almost ill. She was growing weary of Malander Foxglove. In fact, the entire night had been a mistake. After the terrible funeral for her brother, the oppressive stillness of the Grove, the weight of tradition around her like a thick fog, then the relatives and friends at the wake talking about Orian Thornapple as though he had been some kind of young Rose instead of what he was—a rotten little shit—she had thought it would do her good to go out with her friends somewhere loud and dark. But the fact was, she had to admit she didn't really like most of her friends.

And seeing Theo hadn't helped. She had all but begged him to call her. What kind of way was that for a young woman of her class and connections to behave? He was probably laughing at her right now with his lowlife friends, especially that snippy little sprite.

Malander gave the large gray person a mock-salute. "What's the good word, Gummy?"

"Overtime," grunted the bodyguard.

Poppy dropped her black spiderweb cloak behind the front door. It was worth thousands, but she half-hoped someone would steal it, or at least step on it so she'd have an excuse to go out shopping to get another. She didn't want to be home. She hated this place. Then again, she didn't particularly want to be back at school either.

"By the way, who was that fellow you were talking with downstairs at the bar?" young Foxglove asked suddenly. "A bit heavyset, strange haircut? I didn't recognize him."

"What were you doing—spying on me?"

He blew a smoke ring. "I was on my way to the gents, as it happens. My, we *are* self-absorbed tonight, aren't we? And a little tense. Why, is he some new flame of yours . . . ?"

The question, and the hopelessness she felt even trying to answer that question in her own mind, still hung over her like the smoke ring when the lights in the hallway suddenly flickered once, then went out.

"Another cursed blackout." Malander Foxglove's sharp features flicked up like a red ghost as he drew on his cigarette. "You can't get those bloody-minded power plant workers to do a decent day's work. They need culling. There hasn't been a real crackdown in years." He curled an arm around Poppy. "Don't worry—I'll make a little light."

As fire sputtered silently between his fingers, she ducked out of his grasp. "I don't need your help, thank you."

"You're being very strange tonight, Pops. Come on, give me a kiss and let's make up."

For a moment she hesitated. She didn't know what she wanted, not really, and it would be nice to be held. Lander wasn't the worst boy in the world, even though he was irritating her a bit just now. But as he moved toward her, finger and thumb curled, elemental fire dancing between them, she saw something repellently acquisitive in his face, as though the foxfire revealed something that had been hidden. He was his father, or would be very soon. In fact, he was her own father, or as near as made no difference—just another in the legion of privileged lordlings who passed the world back and forth between them as though it were an object of little interest, and handled the lives of their women and servants with the same blithe unconcern.

The queen wouldn't put up with it. It was a startling thought because it was so unexpected. All those lessons learned in childhood that she thought she'd long since forgotten, all those famous old stories that she and the other girls used to ridicule after Young Blossoms meetings—they hadn't gone away at all. And whether they were true stories or not, what did it matter, really? The ideas were right. When the king made the queen angry, she didn't just bow her head and take it. She left him whenever the mood struck her. She took lovers, showed him up for a fool. *She was Titania the Glorious, and if they irritated her, she would have burned up my father and Foxglove and all this lot like sawdust.*

"Leave me alone, Malander," she said, and turned and walked across the dark entry hall.

But he would not leave her alone—she heard his footsteps behind her. "Ah. So we want to be chased, do we?"

She could call the guards. One word, even one strong thought, and the hob would have half a dozen brawny creatures down on him in seconds. She wasn't some servant girl to be trifled with, even if he was the son of one of the leading families. She was a Thornapple—her father was First Councillor. But if he didn't go quietly, if there was a ruckus and a public scene, Daddy would be so tiresome about it . . .

She reached deep into her memory for a charm. It was something she hadn't used in years, since the days of sneaking out of the residence hall with Calpurnia and Julia, the Woodbine sisters, and coming back late to find Miss Stonecrop waiting for them, Old Stony so angry her spectacles were heat-fogged. Poppy whispered the words under her breath, felt for the thought in the way her tutors had showed her—it was a wriggling thing, small, shiny, and hard to grasp as a fish in muddy water—and caught it.

"Poppy? Iron and blood, where did you go? Poppy?"

Suppressing a giggle, which would give her away to Malander Foxglove's sharp senses no matter what the charm did, she turned and went right past his outstretched hand, retaining the memory of his stunned, irritated face in the glow of the elemental light to enjoy later. He was sharp, though—he felt the faint breeze of her passage and lunged at her, but missed. She hurried toward the stairwell. She would take an elevator from the next floor up.

The irritating thing about elevators, she told herself as she trudged onto what by her count must be the twenty-fifth floor landing, was that they didn't *work* in power blackouts. These more and more frequent outages were becoming very annoying, and this one was certainly inconvenient. She could muster enough force on her own to run one or two small appliances—she might not have applied herself much during her tutoring, but she had natural ability—however the elevators were all slaved onto one main circuit. To make one work, she'd have to be able to make them all work, and even her father with all his years and experience didn't have the power to do that on his own.

We've made ourselves prisoners in our own houses, she thought, although she had to admit that might be a touch overdramatic.

"I am attempting to engage auxiliary energies," the hob said into her ear—and into the ear of everyone else in the building. *"I will return the house to normal as soon as possible."*

Poppy had passed a few servants and family functionaries on the stairs, some of them groping blindly, some of them carrying their own little lights they had made; if she had not been used to the deference of underlings she might have thought it strange that they did not look at her, and even more so that many of them almost bumped into her and did not stop even to sketch a bow or a quick curtsy. But climbing more than two dozen floors at the end of a long, confusing, and ultimately rather dreadful night made her less observant than she might have been, and she had also underestimated the strength of her own conjuring: it did not occur to her that they could not see her or sense her at all—that the charm was still in place.

Even without the inarguable darkness, she would have known the power in the building was off by the effortless way the door swung open at the lightest push. The entrances to the family's private section of the Thornapple tower were all so crisscrossed with charms that ordinarily a large coach would have bounced off it, should such a thing be found in the twenty-fifth floor lobby in the first place. But now, and without her even having to breathe her own secret housename, it opened for her like a lover's arms. In the green flicker of the emergency witchlights she could see the corridor stretch before her but little else. Something was strange, but of course everything was strange in a blackout, and she was still thinking about the door.

No, we're not just prisoners, we're slaves to our own assumptions. Because with the power off, anyone could just walk in here and do anything. The arrogance of our strength! she thought. *Not even a bolt on the door.*

It was only when she was halfway down the corridor and the startlingly tall figure of Lord Hellebore stepped out in front of her, glowing with witchlight of his own manufacturing, that she understood her mistake. She was on the office floor, not the residence. She swallowed a squeak of surprise at seeing him, dark-haired and glowering, his skin corpselike in the nimbus of sickly fire, and then had to suppress another gasp when he walked past her.

I'm still wearing the charm!

He stopped and hesitated, thin face lifted as though he scented something, and she knew she should speak up—it was rude to be invisible, even in your own house—but something in his hard face choked off the admission as thoroughly as a hand around her throat. Nidrus Hellebore shook his head once, not so much a movement of confusion as a refocusing of feral attentions, then strode to the window at the end of the passageway. As he turned and came back, Poppy shrank against the wall and held her breath, although she still couldn't have quite said why. Even if he caught her, the worst that could happen was a scolding, certainly. She was in her own house. She hadn't done it on purpose.

"What is it?" Now Lord Foxglove, Lander's father, had come out into the corridor. "Are we attacked?"

The contempt in Hellebore's voice was quite impressive. "If so, then someone has attacked a third of the city. No, you bloody fool, it's another power breakdown."

Foxglove's own halo of witchlight shrank a little, as though he had been slapped. "It's just . . . the matter we're talking about . . . it makes me . . ."

"If you're going to say it makes you act like a coward, don't bother. I noticed." Hellebore stopped again, turning his head from side to side. "But it does feel like there's been someone here. And not too long ago."

Foxglove did not appear to be listening. "It's just . . . I don't think . . . there must be another way . . ."

"What are you two doing out there?" called another voice—Poppy's father. "Come in here and close the door. The hob will sort it out."

"On our way, Aulus." Hellebore said it in a loud, cheerful voice; an instant later he turned back to Lord Foxglove like a viper. "You *are* a bloody fool," he said, just loud enough for Poppy to hear a few feet away. "I should have brought in Monkshood instead of you. He may be mad, but at least he has some grit. Who needs your ridiculous Coextensive faction, anyway? It will all be meaningless soon. Look out there! Miles of black. No power. It's all coming apart and you know very well it's not going to get better. The question is, are you with us or not? This is the time for great decisions and, yes, taking risks. Even more important, we've risked everything, Thornapple and I. If you think you can just back out now . . . well, I'm sure you remember what happened to Violet."

"But I just . . . is there no other way . . . ?"

"If you think that, you're living in a magical world, Foxglove. You might as well be a mortal and go fly to the moon. I asked, do you remember what happened to Violet?"

"Of course, but . . . !"

"And think about Violet House. Think about the empty lot in the middle of Eventide where it used to be. Black, burnt trees. The ground sown with salt."

"But . . . !"

"Just think about it from time to time. Now come—our host is waiting." Hellebore took Foxglove's arm—for a moment their halos of light blended, shimmered. Then they went through the door into her father's office and the corridor was dark again.

"*I am attempting to engage auxiliary energies,*" said the hob, and this time, with her nerves pulled tight as lute strings, Poppy did indeed let out a little squeak of surprise. *"I will return the house to normal as soon as possible."*

She hurried back toward the stairwell, hoping now that the charm would last long enough to get her onto the right floor, past the servants, and into her bed. She didn't care if it was in the dark. She just wanted to be able to pull up the covers and make the world go away for a while.

It's none of my business, she told herself. *Whatever they're doing, it's none of my business.*

I hate this house.

22

STATUS QUO ANTE

It was not easy to fall asleep after an evening like that, but he managed at last. He probably would have been better off staying awake.

The old, familiar bad dream came back for the first time since he left his own world, although in truth he had felt its presence all evening, from his first view of the bony, angular heights of Hellebore House.

In many ways the dream seemed the same as before, Theo imprisoned in his own body, sharing it with an alien presence. As with the other nightmares, he stared out through a surrounding murk, but in this version it wasn't mist that encircled him but smoke: he was looking down from the top of a tall building, the stars hugely bright and close, the air sour with the smell of burning. The City below him looked like a lava field, with dozens of patches of bright red glow, each signifying an entire neighborhood in flames, providing the only light in the dark city. Screams drifted up to his high perch, as thin with distance as the mewing of kittens, but what was worse than the suffering going on below him was that he could feel himself enjoying it, savoring the terror that ran wild in the shadowy streets. The alien presence was completely in control. Every shriek gave him a jolt of pleasure. It was like sex. It was *better* than sex, because he, or rather the thing that wore his body like a suit of clothing, was having his way with an entire world.

Theo woke up sweating and whimpering, and was helplessly grateful to find himself in his room in Daffodil House. He asked for the time and the hob-voice told him in a desultory way that it was after midnight. Fairies didn't seem very specific about time, he had learned, and their houses followed that pattern.

He knew he was not going to be falling asleep again any time soon, not while his heart was still rattling in his chest. He asked to have the lights on, then went into the bathroom and got himself a glass of water, marveling anew at how bizarrely ordinary a place this could seem, as though he were spending the night in a decent but not overwhelming hotel instead of in the heart of magical Fairyland. The tap turned, the water came out. Experimentally, he flushed the toilet. The water went around and around—not even backward, the way some people claimed it did in Australia. He could only be thankful it didn't have a little paper strip across it reading "Sanitized for your Protection."

Mints on the pillow would be okay, though.

It was no use trying to jolly himself. No matter how apparently ordinary the setting, he was stuck in a very strange place. People, no not even people, *things* were trying to kill him. He didn't know the rules. His only friend was the size of a ballpoint pen.

He pulled Uncle Eamonn's book out of his jacket pocket. Both leather jacket and notebook were looking a little the worse for wear, wrinkled from being sat on, a bit water-stained in places. He had felt sure that the book was the reason he had been dragged out of his own world, but so far no one had asked to see it or even asked him about it, even though he had mentioned it to Lady Aemilia and Cumber Sedge, just to name two people here in Daffodil House.

Theo still had no real idea of how things worked here, and he was wondering if a rereading of the notebook might help. There were things in it that he'd barely paid attention to at the time because he'd thought it was fiction—because who could ever have imagined it wasn't?

It's like someone gave me a manual on lion-taming to read, but didn't warn me I was about to be smeared with gravy and parachuted into the African veldt.

But the frustrating thing was that it wasn't an instruction book. There was no handy dictionary, no index of facts or explanation of local etiquette. It was a story written by a visitor, the areas of detail apparently arbitrary and maddeningly inconsistent.

Theo began browsing through the notebook, skipping the early autobiographical sections entirely. He wasn't even certain what he was looking for, but in the few short days since he'd crossed over or passed through or whatever the hell you called it, he'd become steadily less certain he knew what was going on. Strange as it had been, the Larkspur family forest where he had first arrived had at least felt something like what he would have expected Fairyland to be. Now it was clear that it had been no more than a private game preserve, the grounds of a rich clan's stately home. The real Fairyland was here, in this vast city—or at least it seemed to contain most of Faerie's residents. At the same time, the weird modernity seemed to carry over into other areas as well, class struggle, the power of wealth, the importance of technology . . .

A word dimly remembered from high school social studies caught his eye and he stopped to read.

Although present-day Faerie is an oligarchy, and there have always been powerful families, as far as I can tell some kind of shift happened about two hundred years ago, their time—I cannot be exact, because time in Faerie is a slippery thing, and comparing it to our own world makes it even more so.

Faerie was once a true monarchy, ruled (as mortals themselves have described in poetry and folktale) by a king and queen. Shakespeare called them Oberon and Titania, but they have many other names, like Gwynn ap Nudd and Maeve (or Mab). In fact, they seem to have many names and no names because they were the only king and queen, and had been so for most of the memory of the fairy race, just as what I named New Erewhon was called simply "the City" by all in Faerie, since there were no other cities, only towns and villages.

In any case, during the time of the last Gigantine War—a war between the fairy folk of New Erewhon and the race of giants (whose origins and habitat no one can explain better than that they come from "the Giant Country") something happened to the king and queen. They are commonly held to have been literally killed by the giants, but I have heard other explanations that suggest the king and queen died exerting some great and final force that saved the City and defeated those terrible enemies; there is a song of armored giants approaching the heart of Faerie, burning and smashing all before them, that makes them sound more fearsome than even the most modern war machines of my own world. Whatever the case, the monarchs of Fairyland fell during the last struggle in the ruins of their stronghold (which for some reason seems to have been called by a name that translates as "the Cathedral," instead of "the Palace" or anything else you might expect) and the reins of power were afterward taken up by what are commonly called the Seven Families—seven of the most powerful clans who (either heroically or opportunistically, depending on how much cynicism is applied to history) created a power structure to hold Faerie together in the vacuum that followed the death of the king and queen.

All of the famous Seven—the Daffodils, Hollyhocks, Primroses, Hellebores, Thornapples, Violets, and Lilies—were already among the land's most powerful families. Each had the normal clannish proclivi-

*ties found among the high houses—the Hellebores and
Daffodils fascinated by science, although in very different ways, the Violets and Lilies skilled in the creative arts, Thornapples drawn to business, and the
Hollyhocks and Primroses engaged by politics. One
trait they all shared, though, was a desire to rule over
Faerie. After the initial panic was over and order restored they were forced by popular will to reinstate the
Parliament of Blooms, but real power remained—and
still remains—with these clans and their closest allies.*

Then the lights went out.

For a moment Theo felt certain something really bad had
happened—that someone had discovered he was reading
something he shouldn't and now they were coming to get
him—but then he remembered the blackout in Tansy's house
and various comments he'd heard about Faerie's untrust-
worthy power situation. When the hob-voice proclaimed
that alternative power operations would begin soon and that
the proper authorities had all been contacted, he could not
entirely forget he was trapped in pitch-blackness in a very
strange house in a place full of ogres and worse things, but
he felt at least a bit reassured. Thus, when someone suddenly
knocked at the door he let out only a very small scream of
surprise.

"Who . . . who is it?"

"Cumber Sedge to see you," explained the hob, persist-
ing in its duties even in the middle of a blackout.

"Me, Cumber," said the person in question.

The ferisher had brought his own light, a sphere the size
of a large marble which gave off enough radiance to illuminate the young fairy's mournful face but not much more.
"Sorry to bother you, Master Vilmos. The hob said your
light was on. Well, until all the lights went out."

"Call me Theo, please. Come on in. How are you feeling?"

"You mean from the drinking? Not bad. It'll be worse
when I wake up tomorrow—good thing it's Mabon and

Lady Aemilia isn't expecting me to work. But about how I behaved? Pretty wretched, to tell you the truth." He followed Theo into the room and, perhaps in some kind of penance, declined a chair and sat cross-legged on the carpet.

"Ah, it happens. Everybody has to let loose sometimes." Theo hesitated. "Unless they're going to execute you for it or something."

"Nobody goes to the Well for saying things like that," Cumber said. "At least, not unless they're a goblin."

"Well, that's good. Not for goblins, I guess, but I'm glad they're not going to have you shot for insulting a Flower or something."

The ferisher nodded. Even in the thin glow of the magic marble or whatever it was, he looked profoundly unhappy. Theo had thought of the long-faced Cumber Sedge as about grad-student age, but he realized now the butterscotch-colored fairy was probably at least five times that—ten times, for all Theo knew. He sipped his water and waited for the other to say something. It was a long wait

"So, does this happen all the time?" Theo asked at last. "This blackout thing?"

Cumber shrugged. "It's been getting worse. All the power plants are strained—Lord Daffodil has three of them in Ivy and I hear they're all having problems. That's one of the reasons for the big meeting they're having."

"Oh, yeah?" Theo wondered what had brought the young fairy to his room. Cumber seemed to have something on his mind, but perhaps he just wanted the company of someone who didn't think he was a disgrace and embarrassment. "Interesting. What big meeting is that?"

Cumber looked stricken. "You haven't heard? Why hasn't anyone told you?"

"Told me what? Why should they bother to tell me?"

"Because you're one of the other reasons for the meeting."

"I'm . . . Hang on, what?"

"Lady Aemilia was talking about it yesterday. Lord Daffodil knows that some of the other Houses were trying to get hold of you, and since you're staying here, he figures he has a bit of a bargaining chip."

"Bargaining chip?" Theo felt a sudden chill. "You mean they're going to make some deal, hand me over to those people who were after me?"

"No, no!" Cumber said hurriedly. "No, I can't imagine that—Lady Aemilia's way too interested in you, for one thing. But Lord Daffodil knows the Hellebores and Thornapples and that lot want you, so apparently he's decided he's going to make them worry a little, wondering what secrets you're telling him. Which reminds me, I've been kicking myself for letting Zirus drag us out tonight, especially onto Hellebore family turf—it was madness. Your friend Applecore's wrong, though—the people in charge here do care what happens to you, at least as long as you're valuable to them. And if something had gone wrong while we were outside the compound, they would probably have blamed me." He had the look of someone who'd eaten something that was not agreeing with him.

Hold on, Theo thought. *Thornapples? Poppy's family? They're after me, too? Could she have known that?* "I don't get this—any of it. These bad guys think I'm telling secrets to Daffodil or something? What secrets? I don't know anything. Why are they all so interested in me? These people don't even *like* mortals."

"This is why I wanted to come talk to you, Mast . . . Theo. I feel terrible that no one's telling you anything. Not that I know much. But I do know one important thing—something that you need to know, too." Cumber took a deep breath. "Can I get myself a glass of water? I feel like one of the Great Beasts is nesting in my mouth."

"Of course. Be my guest." The bathroom and the tap were only a few steps away, but Theo didn't relax until the ferisher had returned with his water and sat down on the floor again. In movies, someone who was about to explain something important always got shot in the back or stabbed or something just before they could tell you the Astonishing Truth.

"Well," Cumber said, "first off, you're not a mortal. You're one of us."

"What?" Theo had to think for a moment to make sure he'd actually heard what he thought he'd heard. He was suddenly finding it hard to breathe. "You're joking. You must be joking, right?"

Cumber Sedge shook his head. "I don't know why they haven't told you, but I know it's true. I've seen the test results. The readings on your Index of Humors—well, you're on the low end of normal, but you're certainly not mortal. No, it couldn't be anything else. And I heard Lady Aemilia talking to her brother about it."

"Her brother . . ." He was dazed.

"Lord Daffodil. She called him when the results first came in."

"But . . . but . . ." He tried to find something he could use as a weapon against the enormity of the attack. "I'm not human? That's bullshit! I . . . I had *parents,* for Christ's sake!"

Cumber flinched as if struck, but kept his eyes fixed on Theo even through obvious discomfort. "You had people who raised you," he said quietly. "Mortal people. I'm sure they were very good to you, but that doesn't mean you're related to them. Changelings seldom recognize the truth on their own. And after a certain point in their lives, they are human. You probably wouldn't have passed our tests after you'd been there a few more years, not to mention all the other things that could have accelerated or even finished off the mortalization process—having a family, undergoing a religious conversion, a serious illness . . ." For a moment the ferisher's guilty gloom was brightened by discussing his subject of expertise. "There have been cases where changelings in the mortal world have even denounced other changelings without for a moment reflecting on why they were so certain . . ."

This was like one of those topsy-turvy dreams, where

someone could tell you things that you knew were wrong yet you couldn't summon a useful argument against it. "Hold on, hold on!" Theo waved his hands. His own voice sounded distant, as if someone else was speaking. "If I'm one of these . . . these fairies . . . then why are they so interested in me? Why all the tests? They couldn't have needed all that just to tell whether I was one of them or not—those reflex tests, the color recognizing stuff . . ."

"As Lady Aemilia said—she was telling you the truth about this, anyway, Theo—they haven't seen anyone like you for a long time. There isn't much travel between your world and ours anymore. There aren't many changeling babies, and I haven't heard of any that have crossed back over to our side for ages."

"But . . . I *feel* like a mortal, damn it!"

"You probably do—that's how you were raised. But more importantly, you feel like you. When have you ever been anyone else to compare it to?"

He tried to think of a reply but couldn't. This new dream, this nightmare, was defeating him. "Did Applecore know about this?"

"Not as far as I know. It only came up after Lady Aemilia saw the test results. Anyway, your friend doesn't seem like the type who'd keep her mouth shut about something important."

Theo had dozens more questions, but Cumber Sedge had very few answers. Tests could not show who his real parents were. The ferisher knew of no famously missing children, nor as far as he could tell did Lady Aemilia—Theo's original identity was a mystery. Switching babies with mortals had been very common in the past but was almost unheard of these days, largely because of the Clover Effect.

Theo felt like he wanted to cry, but at the same time he felt like he was drifting in a vacuum, unable to touch or even to remember the normal life he had been leading until moments earlier. Even in the midst of such abnormal events as he had experienced lately, he had still felt himself to be a very ordinary person. That was gone now: he literally had no idea of who or what he was. He sat for a while in silence, full of anger and confusion.

At last, he let out a deep, shuddering breath. "Listen, I appreciate you telling me this and everything, and someday I'll probably thank you—but for now could you get the hell out? I'd like to be on my own."

"Certainly. I understand." Cumber got to his feet, not entirely steady. "I'm sorry, but I thought you should know."

"Right." He showed him to the door, tried to find something else to say as the ferisher stood awkwardly in the hallway outside, but couldn't. It was only after he slammed the door that he realized he'd sent away the only light.

He groped back to the bed and lay there in the dark, his mind a flurry of fragmentary images that did not ever quite coalesce into sense—his childhood, his mother's dying, the crazy things he had seen here, even Cat's angry, pale face. It went on for hours, or seemed to, a helpless roller-coaster ride through seemingly unending confusion.

What am I? Where did I come from? Is my whole life just a stupid, made-up story?

A sudden, ugly thought, alone in a lightless room in a strange land: *Is that what the dream's about? That thing inside me, looking out through my eyes? Maybe I've got some kind of evil fairy side and now it's starting to come out.*

Mom said she couldn't love me the way she should have, he suddenly remembered. *Because I didn't seem right. Wasn't that what she said? She knew.*

She knew.

The power was still off when he finally fell asleep, a transition from one helpless darkness to another.

Daffodil Comb was in a barnlike structure underneath the main tower, a vast room that resembled a high school gymnasium. The power had come back but the overhead lights in the huge room were dim and there were enough small flying people in the air to make details hard to discern, so Theo could only guess at its original purpose.

Do these people even play sports? he wondered. *Normal ones?* It was depressing how little he knew about the world in which he was presently forced to live—and worse, how little he knew about these creatures who were apparently his own kind. He couldn't think about that just now, though—it was like his whole mind was an aching bruise. Easier to concentrate on things that didn't matter.

Poor, snobby Rufinus had said something about being on a fencing team—that was the reason he had thought himself capable of handling the hollow-men. He had been horribly wrong, of course. So this world had fencing, but what else? It was hard to imagine fairies playing field hockey or football. In fact, the ruling class seemed more like an entire nation of country club tennis players—much easier to picture them sipping drinks on the patio after a match, expensive sweaters draped across their shoulders, than getting into a sweaty half-court basketball game . . .

"Hey, giant feet, you want tae watch where you're going," shrilled a thickly accented voice. "Or is that how you spend your days off, stravaigin' aboot and crushing innocent people?"

Theo froze and looked down. The floor was as alive with traffic as the air above him, tiny pixies and other small creatures filing in and out of the comb, scurrying across the floor to the propped outer doors of the room in long lines, like mice leaving Hamelin.

"Oh, sweet Jee . . ." He caught himself. "Sorry! Sorry. I didn't . . . step on anyone, did I?"

"No, but not because you're bluidy graceful or anythin'."

Theo carefully got down on his knees. The creature standing in front of him was a little larger than Applecore, but a uniform gray-green and covered with bristling spikes; Theo couldn't help thinking he looked like some kind of mascot for the Artichoke Council. He was carrying a toolbox. *Oh, my God,* Theo suddenly thought. *If Cumber's right, this guy's kind of a relative of mine—all these little bugs are. Closer to me than Mom, at least biologically.* The thought was yet another in the category of too-big-and-too-strange; he simply couldn't do anything with it. "Hey, I really am sorry, man. I was . . . I'm new here."

The spiky little person stared at him for a moment, then shrugged. "Aye, it happens."

"Could you help me, maybe? I just need to find someone named Applecore. A sprite. Do you know her?"

"No. Don't like 'em, either. Bluidy wingers think they rule the roost. Hang on." He put two fingers small as the points of sharpened pencils to his mouth and whistled, surprisingly loud—*preet, preet, preet!* Theo didn't know what he was supposed to say, so he didn't say anything.

An instant later another little person dropped out of the air from somewhere just above Theo's head—a male sprite, as far as he could tell, a handsome, graceful little fellow wearing a sort of toga. The winged man hovered, looking at Theo with only limited curiosity, then shouted down to the creature on the floor, "What do you want, thistlehead?"

"I'm late tae work. This big lummox is luiking for one of yours and he almost stepped on me—some flappy bint, hight Applecore. Ring any chimes?"

The flying man ascended a couple of feet and examined Theo's face with some interest. "I think she's staying in the guest quarters," he called down.

"Fine. You take care of him, then. I have tae go clean the silvertangs for the muckle stoorage battery and I don't have time tae waste on flutterby business." The spiky little man turned and stalked away, joining one of the lines of small creatures snaking toward the outer door.

"Friendly guy," Theo said.

"Those thorns aren't just for show," said the sprite, laughing. "Hogboons are a grumbly lot. But he's all right, as they go. I'll see if I can turn her up. You just stay here. Step on one of those little needlenoses, you probably won't hurt them—they're tough as old leather—but you'll get a nasty prickle in your foot and no mistake." His wings blurred into invisibility and he was off.

Daffodil Comb had its own open-plan cafeteria, as Applecore had told him, in another large room just off what he now thought of as the gym. The smallest tables were the size of a silver dollar, but some were large enough to accommodate half a dozen diners the size of a G.I. Joe doll. This was still a bit small for Theo, however, so he made his way carefully to one edge of the eating area so he could sit down on the floor with his back against the wall. Applecore perched on his knee with her tea and scone. At midmorning there weren't many other people in the cafeteria, but those who were seemed to find the spectacle of the sprite and her monstrous friend quite amusing; they giggled and whispered behind their hands. He felt like he was back in high school, except that even during the worst adolescent traumas of high school he'd never had to worry about whether he was actually human.

"I don't know what to say, Theo, truly."

"You didn't know?"

"By the Trees, I didn't! I swear!"

"Could Cumber be lying? Or wrong?"

She took a sip, thinking. "Anything's possible. But it doesn't seem likely. He's a good sort, that young fella, and he strikes me as a smart one, too."

"But . . . but I don't *feel* like one of these people! Besides, it doesn't explain any of this other crap, even if it's true. Do you think that's why those other people were after me, the ones who hired those cave trolls? Because they wanted to do experiments on me, like Lady Aemilia did?"

"Doesn't seem likely." Her little forehead furrowed. "Fact is, boyo, this still doesn't make any sense."

"Just tell me one thing. What are *you* doing here?"

She frowned. "What's that supposed to mean?"

"Just what it sounds like. I've been wanting to ask you,

but I was too scared. You're the only friend I've got here."
He thought for a moment, tried to smile. "To tell the truth,
even back home I've only got one other friend to speak of,
so you're in some pretty select company." What would
Johnny think of the news that Theo had fairy blood? He
wouldn't believe it, of course, but he'd enjoy the chance to
comment on the possibilities, that was for sure. "Back at
Tansy's house, you were going to let me go to the station and
that would have been that. Instead you've come all the way
here, risked your life, you can't even stay in your own home
with your friends—all for someone you don't know that
well, and who's probably going to get his ass killed anyway . . . !" She glared as one of his self-pitying hand ges-
tures almost knocked her off his knee. "Sorry. But I don't get
it. Even if it's not my fault, I'm into something deep. Why
are you risking your life hanging around with me?"

She finished eating and brushed the crumbs off on his
pants leg. "It's not for the fancy accommodations, that's for
sure. That scone was baked in a goblin sweatshop or I'm not
an Apple." She stared at him for a moment. "Why am I still
here? I'm not entirely certain, and that's the truth. Part of it
was . . . well, because when I first met you, I was surprised.
See, I've never met a human before . . ."

"But I'm *not* a human, apparently!"

"You might as well be, the way you interrupt. Root and
Bough, Theo, you're a pig sometimes and no mistake." She
brought back the glare for a moment; he put his hand over
his mouth. "Better. See, I'd never met a human before. And
I expected you to be, I don't know, big and mean and stupid,
I guess. Like a giant. But whatever else you are, you're not
mean."

Now it was his turn to glare.

"That's more like it," she said, grinning. "It's true, but.
You may be a pain in the arse, but you're basically a good
sort. Anyway, when I brought you through, you were so . . .
helpless . . ."

"It just gets better and better."

"Be glad you have at least a few appealing qualities, boyo, however pathetic. Now pay attention. I didn't feel good about what was going on from the first, the whole thing about bringing you here. See, it was my job to get you through that gateway no matter what. That ugly dead thing showing up just meant I didn't have to argue with you or trick you. So it was a hard decision to let you go off to the City on your own, but to tell the truth you were a rude little shite with Dolly and that made it easier. Then everything went to buggery at the station."

"So that's why you're here? Because I'm a loser and you felt sorry for me?"

"If you want to think of it that way, Theo, then I suppose so." Her face had become surprisingly serious. "Good friendships have started with less."

He remembered what he'd said to Dolly and found he didn't like that Theo very much, either. "Yeah, okay. You're right—friendship is friendship, I guess."

"That wasn't all." She finished her tea, rolled off his knee and buzzed over to put the little tray on the counter; a few moments later she had settled again. "See, I didn't entirely trust Count Tansy. Not saying he meant you any harm, just that I doubted he had your best interests at heart. One of my brothers used to be his errand-runner and wound up in trouble because of it—Skin, the oldest. It's ancient history now, but because of it my brother's only got one working wing and he's pretty much housebound. He does the family accounts and helped look after us little ones while we were growing. Tansy was playing some complicated political game and using Skin to send messages. My brother got jumped by a gang of hard pixies and got a terrible beating. You probably think that sounds funny."

"No, I don't. I'm learning. And I've been through something like that myself once upon a time, but I was lucky enough to get away without being permanently damaged." That bad night out in the parking lot of that bar called the

Stop Sign—it seemed like centuries ago now. "But was what happened to your brother Tansy's fault?"

"Not because he arranged it, but because he put Skinny in a bad situation without giving him the proper information, then didn't seem too sad when it all went wrong and my brother got hurt bad. Sure, the Daisy clan arranged a nice little pension for him, but which do you think he'd rather have, money or both his wings?"

Theo sighed. "I'm trying to understand it all, but I keep coming back to this one huge thing I can't get past. Someone's telling me that I'm not human. I've been human all my life! How am I supposed to take that?"

"You didn't know there was anything else *but* human to be all your life," Applecore said. "Try to think of it like you've just been told you weren't—where was it you're from? America? That you weren't American, like you thought, but Frankish or something."

"French," he said absently. It was a good suggestion, but he wasn't quite ready for that kind of mental calisthenics yet. "But I still don't get it. How could something like that happen? I wasn't adopted. My mother told me about when she went to the hospital to have me. She was upset because I arrived at a bad time and she didn't get solid food for twenty-eight hours or something."

"Changelings aren't adopted, they're—what's the word? Substituted. Usually before the wee one is old enough to talk. At least, that's how it used to be when it happened more often. Someone took your parents' real baby away, or it died. Either way, there was an . . . opening, and they were given you instead."

Theo shook his head. "So . . . so somewhere I must have . . . fairy parents?"

"Stands to reason."

"Can I find them?" Although the idea was not entirely pleasant. He suddenly remembered a song he had written years earlier, a bluesy little piece of braggadocio about having a lightning storm for a father. Man, this is even weirder.

I thought it was boring, coming out of the middle-class sub-urbs. If I only knew!

"You can try, I s'pose. But people here in Fairie—at least among your kind, if you'll excuse the expression, the larger folk—aren't all that interested in their families at the best of times. It's the way they are—you saw it with that Thorn-apple girl."

"Poppy."

"Whatever her name was. And, let's be honest here, boyo, leaving your child with mortals, probably never to see him again, that isn't exactly the act of a loving parent, now is it?"

"You're saying they wouldn't be interested in meeting me."

"What's the kindest way to put it? No, I'm thinking, they would not. Especially if powerful people want to kill you. You're a bit of a mixed blessing even for those of us who like you . . ."

"Theo Vilmos," a soft but steely voice said in his ear, *"Lord Daffodil commands your presence in the Audience Chamber."*

"What's wrong?" Applecore looked concerned.

"You didn't hear that? A voice just told me I'm supposed to go to the Audience Chamber and see Lord Daffodil."

She pursed her lips and let out a near-inaudible whistle. "You're moving up in the world, fella. Do you know where it is?" When he only shook his head, she said, "Then I'll take you. Maybe see if I can stick around for the audience. Lord Daff doesn't show himself all that often."

"I'm glad that my miserable life is at least providing you with a few interesting moments."

She chortled. "Yeah, something new every minute with you, boyo."

The Daffodil House Audience Chamber seemed to take up a large part of the main tower's twenty-sixth floor. It certainly had its own very large lobby. After a brief inspection, Theo was waved toward the door by the creature sitting behind the desk—which, Theo decided, since it was almost seven feet tall and had a tusked, wrinkled face a bit like a warthog's, was probably more security than secretary—but it took one look at Applecore and shook its misshapen head. "Not on the list."

"She's with me," Theo said with what he hoped was an admirable determination.

The Appointment Beast looked at him with something that might have been amusement in its tiny, red-rimmed eyes, except amusement seldom looked so much like the urge to chew off someone's face. "Oooh," it said. "Very chivalrous. The sprite stays out here anyway. Now, how many pieces of you am I sending in to see the boss? One? Or more?"

"It's not worth arguing, Theo," she said. "He's just a pig with a little too much authority."

"You cut me right to the tenderloin, girlie." The beast turned his malevolent eyes back on Theo. "You going in?"

"I'll meet you here," Applecore said. "You'll find me just far enough away from the desk that the air-conditioning starts to take the edge off this fella's breath."

The warthog-thing chuckled in appreciation as Theo stepped past him. He wished he could feel so cheerful. The fact that the door was whispering like an idiot beggar didn't help.

"Clean as a bean," it fluted as he walked through, its childlike voice suddenly quite loud, *"Clean as a bean. One nymph-binding. Strange clothes. No weapons. Clean as a bean."*

The Audience Chamber, which had sounded as though it should be all tapestries and stained glass windows, was instead a large and extremely modern room, one entire wall a floor-to-ceiling window with a magnificent view of the corner of the Daffodil compound that contained the conference center building, and also of the City beyond. The window glass—if it was glass—seemed to bend the light in an odd way. Three figures were waiting for him, still as statues: Lady Aemilia sat between two male fairies, one light, one dark. He wondered how long they'd all been sitting in silence. Did they talk with their minds or something? He seemed to remember Applecore saying something like that about the Flower families. Creepy.

Hold on, if I'm one, could I do that too? Or is it too late for me? That would be typical Theo Vilmos luck, of course—to have all the disadvantages of being nonhuman, with none of the benefits.

Lady Aemilia stood up, smiling graciously if a bit perfunctorily. She was wearing a sort of suit made out of a rough, pale fabric—something that, like a complimentary bathrobe from a five-star hotel, managed to look both simple and extremely expensive. "Good Mabon to you, Theo Vilmos. It is kind of you to join us. I hope the power outage didn't inconvenience you too much. They're such a problem for us these days." She indicated the dark-haired man. "This is our honored guest, Lord Hollyhock."

Theo was a little startled. The Hollyhocks were the family who had commissioned Tansy to get Theo to the City in the first place, so this must be some blood relative of the guy who'd ended up a mummified heart in Tansy's silver box, but in all the excitement since then he had almost forgotten about them. The fairy lord didn't look much like he'd suffered any major losses lately. He wore a beautiful, slightly shimmery suit and was handsome in a long-boned way, as so many here were, but seemed small by Flower-fairy standards. Hollyhock wore rimless spectacles, but otherwise had a face that Theo thought belonged in a Renaissance painting, as if he should be standing beside the throne smirking at Columbus while the poor fellow tried to talk Isabella and Ferdinand into loaning him some ships. He surprised Theo by smiling at him in a way that was almost nice. "Master Vilmos. We meet at last."

"And this is your host," said Lady Aemilia, "Lord Daffodil."

Theo's first thought was that the fellow's name should be Lord Dandelion instead. He was tall by anyone's standards, with a great mane of hair that stood out in all directions, a handsome, heavy-jawed face, and a closely trimmed beard that was little more than pale stubble. His sand-colored, unstructured suit was impeccably casual. His whitestreaked hair was sand-colored, too. Of all the Flower-folk Theo had seen, he was the only one who actually looked like he was past the prime of adulthood. Theo suspected that meant he was very, very old indeed. To look at, he might have been a vigorous sixty, the kind of man who'd buy your business, fire you, and then steal your girlfriend as well and take her away on his yacht.

"You have been treated well, I trust?" Lord Daffodil's tone suggested he could think of a thousand things that were more important.

It was hard not to get on his knees to this impressive personage and genuflect, harder still not to say something that was at least politely reassuring, since it was obviously no more than a courtesy inquiry, but Theo was beginning to think that whatever his own actual heritage might turn out to be, his mortal-world approach to things was of some use here. "Well, the roof didn't leak in my room or anything, but I haven't exactly been showered with information."

Lord Daffodil allowed one brow to climb just the exact distance to connote slightly amused disdain, a piece of precision engineering that Theo could not help admiring. He wondered if the master of Daffodil House had some goblin woman pluck and shape those impressive eyebrows. "You feel you have been tricked in some way? That we have taken advantage?"

"I feel that there are things going on here that concern me, but I'm the last to know about them. Lady Aemilia," he said abruptly, "I've just been told that your tests prove I'm not really mortal—that I have fairy blood. Is that true?"

She smiled. It was a sympathetic one, ever so slightly sad. *Damn*, Theo thought, *can't you ever catch these people off-balance?* "You must have talked to young Cumber. I was told he had a bit too much to drink last night. I am fond of the lad—I've known him since he was born, and his mother is very dear to me—but despite the advantage of his schooling, he has failed to learn much discretion."

"Begging your ladyship's pardon," Theo said, "but fuck discretion. Is it true? Do I have fairy blood?"

Lord Daffodil stirred, but Lady Aemilia only offered another regretful smile and nodded. "Yes. You are . . . one of us."

"One of you? Does that mean . . . I'm a Daffodil?"

The master of the house let out a snort. "By the shattered Cathedral, you certainly are not! There are no missing children in our house!"

"Please," said Lady Aemilia. "Forgive my brother. He does not mean to be rude, but we do take good care of our offspring, unlike some of the other houses. You have met my son Zirus, I'm told—does he seem like the child of a house that could lose a baby and not care?"

He seems like the child of a house that gives him too much money and too little responsibility, Theo thought but didn't say—he knew that kind of parenting wasn't confined to Fairyland. "Fine. So then where do I come from?"

"We don't know, Master Vilmos," said Lord Hollyhock. "What we do know is that certain of the other leading houses have been watching you for a long time. That something recently happened or is happening that has made their interest more personal and more intrusive. A . . . well, let us say a source of ours with access to those houses made it clear that they were about to change the arrangement—to do something more than simply observe you." He was watching Theo carefully, perhaps to see how closely he was following what was being said. "At that point, we decided to step in. Do you know much about what is going on here? About our factions?"

"Enough to know that it's confusing. But, yeah, Creepers,

Chokeweeds, that stuff. Everybody fighting over whether to kick the mortals in the ass or not. It's been explained to me."

Hollyhock allowed himself a small grin. "I would have enjoyed hearing that explanation. So, if you know something of that, you will understand perhaps why we didn't feel we could allow our adversaries simply to do whatever they wanted. And why we became a bit curious about you."

"I still don't understand—why me? These are, what, the Hellebores and Thornapples we're talking about, right? What could they possibly need me for?"

"We don't know," Hollyhock admitted. "But no doubt they will be very upset to learn that you are with us."

"You're going to tell them?"

"He is cursedly full of questions," said Lord Daffodil. "Whatever his true nature, his mortal upbringing quickly comes to the fore." He didn't sound like he thought that was a good thing.

"Hang on, I thought you were one of the families that *liked* mortals."

Daffodil stared at him as if from a great height, which was actually more or less the case. "We Symbiotes don't feel that the mortals should be destroyed, but that the two races must find a way to coexist. That is hardly the same thing as *liking* them."

Theo sat back in his chair, weary and depressed. He might not be a human being but he felt like one and thought like one. It wasn't much fun constantly being told how much everyone hated his kind around here. "So, excuse the mortal rudeness, but I still want to know why you're going to tell these people who want to kill me that I'm here?"

"They don't actually seem to want to kill you," said Hollyhock, who at least seemed to be able to talk to Theo as though they were both of the same species. "That's part of the puzzle. We want to know why they've been chasing you just as much as you do. We're hoping that when they find you're here, they'll think we *do* know, and they'll either give up their plan or give it away."

"So, mine shaft parakeet or whatever that bird is—that's me. Be honest, that's what you mean, right? Let's find out if I'm really important by seeing if they try to kill me again."

"Even if they wanted to kill you," Lord Daffodil said, "they would not dare. Not as long as you are under my protection. That could bring about another Flower War, and nobody wants that, not even the most hotheaded of the Excisors like Hellebore."

Theo looked out of the window. Beyond the walls of Daffodil House the city stretched out as far as he could see, except for the great dark expanse of Ys, the lake or ocean or whatever it was, full of boats that looked like silver clipper ships. The worst of the clouds had rolled through and the skies had turned a clear if muted blue. Theo realized for the first time that although he'd seen modern trains and automobiles here, he'd seen no sign of airplanes. Was that because some of these people could fly by themselves? But the wealthiest, most powerful group had no wings, so that theory didn't hold. Could it have something to do with the way the topography changed, the thing with the train stations and all that? He was about to ask about it when Lord Hollyhock suddenly said, "This has been very difficult for you, Master Vilmos, hasn't it?"

He turned in surprise, assuming he was being mocked, but if the fairy lord was insincere he hid it well. "Yes," Theo said. "Yes, to tell the truth, it has. Dragged right out of my life into a world I didn't know existed, chased by monsters and a bunch of other imaginary creatures—imaginary to me, anyway. No offense. And now I'm told that I'm not actually a human at all, that my parents weren't my parents? Yeah, it's been a bit tough."

"Please believe that we were not to blame for most of those things," said Hollyhock. "That we have indeed tried to help you."

"Yeah. Yeah, I know. I may be pissed off, but I'm also grateful, especially for Applecore. She saved my life." A memory suddenly returned. "That thing that first came after me in my world—do you know about that?"

"The undead thing?" asked Daffodil. "Doesn't make any sense, that. Why would Helleborne and that lot send something like that after him?"

"Perhaps because it could go after him in his own world, where they thought we wouldn't discover what was going on," said Lady Aemilia. "Yes, Master Vilmos, we know about it."

"Well, Count Tansy said that the thing was going to keep coming after me. I don't know when it's going to show up again, but I know that next time I may not have a convenient magic door to jump through. Tansy said you guys might be able to, I don't know, get that thing off my scent. Did he mention that?"

"I have not spoken to Tansy in days," said Hollyhock. "But I was furious that he sent you to the City without a proper escort. My nephew Dalian was supposed to accompany you, but he was murdered on Mistletoe Green the day before you were to be brought from your world to ours. I suspect Helleborne's people—it has the smell of something of theirs, the careful cruelty."

"They cut out his heart," said Theo.

Hollyhock looked at him sharply. "How do you know that? Only the family saw the body and knew what was done to him."

"I saw the heart. They sent it to Tansy in a silver box. I think it had, like, your house crest on it or something."

The dark-haired fairy lord shook his head. "It was sent to Tansy? Tansy has the heart? Why? It makes no sense."

Theo could only shrug.

"Enough of this," said Daffodil. "These are small matters. The crime against you was terrible, Malvus, but I do not believe Lord Helleborne himself had anything to do with it. There are factions in his household and allied houses, some of them quite wild . . ."

Lady Aemilia deftly cut in. "Whatever the case, it is time

to move on to other matters—think of the summit conference. It begins this afternoon."

"Summit conference . . . ?" Theo had almost entirely forgotten what Cumber had told him the night before, but it was coming back.

"Yes, a meeting of the Six Families," said Lady Aemilia. "Where we will find out what the Hellebores and Thornapples think about you being our guest. They will be here, along with Lords Foxglove and Lily and their retinues, in a very short time."

"Hang on a second." Theo suddenly had extremely damp palms. "You're telling me that the people who tried to kill me or capture me or whatever . . . are coming *here,* to Daffodil House? Today?"

"We have asked for an Exigent Gathering, yes. There wasn't time to arrange use of another site because of the holiday," said Lady Aemilia. "Parliament is out of session and Lord Monkshood said he couldn't possibly provide sufficient security there on such short notice . . ."

"What is he asking?" demanded Lord Daffodil. "You, Vilmos, do you think you should have some say about when the Six Families, the masters of the realm, should meet with each other?"

"I think I should have some say about when I get trotted out for a bunch of people who seem to want me dead, and certainly want to see my friends and family back home wiped out, yes. Yes, I goddamn well do."

"Perhaps it need not be that way, Master Vilmos," said Hollyhock. "Lady Jonquil, do we need to involve him in a face-to-face confrontation?"

"No, probably not." She turned to Theo. "I will make an arrangement so you can watch the proceedings without having to be physically present. Would that satisfy you?" She said it nicely, but still managed to sound like she was soothing a child's tantrum. Theo, however, was not going to be drawn into the fairy nobility's stilted manners and old-world behavior.

"Yeah, maybe. If it's safe."

"Does the fool creature think someone is going to assault him in my house?" growled Lord Daffodil. For a fairy, he had turned a rather choleric shade of beige-pink. "Nonsense!"

Lord Hollyhock turned to Theo. "I would like a little conversation with you before the meeting, Master Vilmos. Have you had lunch? No? Then perhaps you will join me for a meal in the chambers Lord Daffodil and Lady Jonquil have been kind enough to provide me. Let my hosts and I just finish discussing a few things here. Would you wait for me outside?"

Theo nodded and stood. He still had a lot of unanswered questions, and so far the Hollyhock fellow was the only person who'd shown any signs of being willing to talk. As he walked out they fell silent behind him. He caught a reflection of them in the floor-to-ceiling window and saw that they were all staring at each other. Talking, it looked like, maybe even arguing, but without moving their mouths or making a sound.

The outer room seemed to be empty except for the warthog-thing sitting behind the desk. "Applecore?" Theo called.

"She went out," said the tusked creature. "She saw something on my security eyes." He gestured to the row of framed mirrors on the desktop. Theo leaned over to look. Each one appeared to contain a view of some part of the compound or the surrounding streets. "She's quite a sweet little nutcracker, that one," the warthog said. "Not exactly the sugarplum variety, but I like a little spice myself." His overfilled mouth pursed for a moment and his brow furrowed. "Listen, can I ask you a question? Don't want to cause no offense. Are the two of you . . . you know, are you two an item?"

"What is this?" Theo growled. "Why do people keep asking me that? Doesn't the fact that she's the size of a candy bar and I'm about a hundred times bigger than her tell you anything?"

The warthog's tiny eyes opened wide. "Say, where are you from? Must be the farthest island in Ys or something—the hogboon-docks, for sure. Haven't you ever heard of cosmetic surgery?"

"Cosmetic . . . ? You mean . . . ?" It was too bizarre. He didn't want to waste any more brainpower on the ins and outs of this cartoon world. "Look, did she say when she was coming back?"

"No. She just said to tell you she thought she'd seen someone you knew and she was checking it out."

"Someone *she* knew, it must have been."

The secretary shook his bristly head. "Hey, I know my job, pal. She said someone *you* knew. She even said the name—Rufus or Findus or something."

Theo thought for a moment. "Rufinus? But it couldn't have been him—he's dead."

"Then she was probably wrong." The creature settled back and crossed one broad, pants-stretching thigh over the other. "But she's still pretty cute. Sassy, too—the way I like 'em."

Theo was still trying to figure out what Applecore might have been talking about when Lord Hollyhock appeared and led him away to lunch.

23

THE SHADOW
ON THE TOWER

The well-dressed brownie who brought lunch was so swiftly efficient that every time Theo saw him the brownie was in another part of the room, arranging the rolling tray, setting out drinks, adjusting the lighting and the blinds on the window with such nimbleness that it was hard to believe Hollyhock had sent his secretary and the rest of his staff away: the room seemed to be filled with other people. The last time Theo looked up, the dapper little fellow had vanished. Theo hadn't even heard the door open or close.

"I'm glad you joined me," said Hollyhock, leaning forward to peruse the tray. Outside the Audience Chamber he was almost informal. "Have some of the melon—it's only in season for another week or so." He speared a piece with a long two-tined fork. With the fruit in his mouth, he waved the fork in a strange little pattern; immediately the air in the room felt closer, tighter. Theo's ears popped as if he had just changed altitudes. "Just a small discretion-charm," Hollyhock explained. "I'm certain our hosts respect my privacy, but too much trust of even one's allies is not a healthy idea in these sad times." He smiled, but his eyes were intent. "I said I was displeased with Tansy for having sent you unescorted. I am also unhappy that the Daffodil clan have been so slapdash in their care of you."

"They took me in off the street," Theo said.

"They have given you no guidance, no warnings, nothing. It's regrettable, but the City is not a safe place these days for almost any one, and certainly not for you. I heard that Lady Aemilia's son took you to a club right inside Hellebore House. Is that true?" When Theo nodded, he scowled. "Criminal. Like putting your purse down on the sidewalks of Goblintown and expecting it to be there when you return. You seem to have been incredibly lucky. Perhaps a little *too* lucky." He lifted his fork again, held it up as though it were a baton and he were about to conduct Theo in an aria from *Madame Butterfly.* "Do you mind?"

"Mind what?"

"If I give you a brief inspection." He saw the puzzled way Theo was looking at the fruit fork. "Ah. It's silver, you see—a good conductor. Not a perfect item, but good enough to save me going through my belongings to find my wand." When Theo did not object, Lord Hollyhock closed his eyes and began to move the fork in lazy circles. Three different times he stopped and extended his free hand to snap up something invisible as though he were catching mosquitoes.

"Just as I suspected," Hollyhock said when he had finished. "You were covered with them. But, to our fortune, they are all of the minor variety. I doubt it's anything deeper at work than the usual run of security policy at Hellebore House—they sprinkle them on everyone. You have a few on you from the Daisy commune as well, but they are days old and inert."

Theo suddenly felt itchy all over. "Some what? Covered with what?"

"Charms, I suppose you'd call them, although they're a bit more . . . manufactured than what that word generally connotes. Since you haven't any background in our sciences, as far as I know, it's a bit difficult to explain. Tiny surveillance devices."

"Bugs!"

Hollyhock smiled. "No, not living creatures at all. As I said, it's hard to explain . . ."

"Oh, for God's sake, I know what a surveillance device is." Theo took a breath—he didn't want to offend this man. "That's what we call things like that back on . . . back in my world. Bugs." A chill tightened his skin. "Hang on—you mean I've been wearing those things? That the people at Hellebore House not only know exactly where I am, they've been listening to me?"

Hollyhock shook his head like a kind father—*No, son, you can never go down the drain in the bath.* "I very much doubt it. These are minor charms, manufactured to attach themselves indiscriminately to anyone from outside Hellebore House who steps into their compound. Most of them weren't even working—disabled by Daffodil House's own counter-charms when you returned, no doubt. The three I've just destroyed have been sending something back, but it couldn't have been much, since they were badly damaged by Daffodil defenses. These are common practices in the City." He set the fork down. "But it *is* evidence that this is all not being taken seriously enough. Tansy, Daffodil, even Lady Aemilia, although she's sharper than most of them, are all treating this like it's a bit of interfamily espionage over who will win the Trooping Banner at the Old Hill Day Games."

Theo had been picking his way without much appetite through the fruit, bread, and cheese, although the melon was as good as advertised, with a curious minty, perfumed taste. In fact, everything on the tray was exotic and wonderful, but any urge to eat had now left him for good. "What exactly *is* 'this'?" he asked. "I keep hearing about a Flower War. Everybody says there's not going to be one, no one would dare start one, blah, blah, blah. That sounds to me like a divorce or somebody dying—whenever people talk that much about how something's *not* going to happen, it's usually because they're scared to death it *will* happen."

"Your mortal background does you credit," Hollyhock

said. "You see more than many in this city. Yes, I agree—I think they're all being foolishly optimistic, but I think that secretly they know it. It is a common cliché to say that no one wants a Flower War, but the fact is that there have been three of them just in recent history, one of them a very short time ago, and for much the same reasons as far as I can tell—major disagreements among the ruling families."

"But what does it have to do with *me?*" Theo rubbed his face. He was beginning to feel the lack of sleep: it was getting harder to ignore the dull throb in his head from too much to drink the night before. "It's crazy."

"I suspect it has something to do with the rumors I've heard, the truly chilling rumors. They say that the Hellebores have raised a Terrible Child."

Theo shook his head. "I don't get it. They've got a bad kid?"

"No, no. A Terrible Child is not an ordinary child, not by any stretch. It is a . . . thing, in a sense. The product of a very old and now shunned science from an earlier era. A child who is not born of woman in the normal way, although I do not know much more about the process than that—it is a thing you only hear about in old stories, so if Hellebore has managed it, he has managed something significant, however evil."

"Evil?"

"A Terrible Child is a sort of living invocation, if what I understand about it is true. A gateway to the Old Night."

"Old Night. I have a feeling that's another one that means something really unpleasant."

"It is the primordial crawling chaos out of which all order arose. It can only be restrained, not destroyed." The fact that the fairy lord could say such a thing as though he were talking about the weather was what frightened Theo most. *I'm stuck in a world where things like that are the plain truth. Magic is real here, even black magic. And I don't know shit about anything.* "It has retreated now and touches the world only in a few shadowy spots," Hollyhock explained, "but out of those few places dreadful things erupt, madness and murder. To unleash Old Night in all its power would mean an entire era of blood and savagery and delusion, the twisting of everything known into its worst possible configurations."

Theo wished he hadn't eaten. He had a sour, nauseating taste in his mouth. He lifted the crystal goblet of water that the fairy lord had poured for him and drank like a man in the desert. "It sounds horrible," he said at last. "But I still don't know what it has to do with me. Besides, why would these Hellebores want to do something like that, anyway? I saw their place—they're rich and powerful. If they ruin Faerie they'll be ruining themselves, too, won't they?" He took another drink.

Hollyhock showed a grim smile. "I have no idea what any of it might have to do with you except that the coincidence seems too great to be ignored. But as to why the Hellebores would do such a thing, you have misunderstood me. They do not mean to unleash Old Night here. It is your world that they would plunge into an epoch of torment—or at least what was your world. The world of mortals."

It took Theo a while to finish coughing and wheezing. As he dabbed at his wet shirtfront with the napkins Hollyhock handed to him, he tried to make sense of it. "You're saying that . . . that these crazy bastards, the Hellebores and Thornapples . . . that they're planning to destroy my entire world?" He had absorbed the idea that Applecore's Chokeweeds—Excisors, as they seemed to like to call themselves—bore a grudge against humans and even might want them wiped out, but he had put it in the category of some kind of terrorist cell—the source of occasional acts of violence, perhaps, but not of an actual plan for total genocide.

"Unleashing Old Night would not destroy it so much as transform it out of all recognition," said Hollyhock. "But the results would still be horrible."

"But why do they want to do something like that?"

"I suspect it has something to do with power. You experienced the outage we had last night, I assume, or did you sleep through it?"

"Power? Not political power, but you mean like ... electricity?"

Hollyhock looked puzzled for a moment, then nodded. "Of course, that is the science of your world, isn't it? Here that word describes a discredited superstition of half a millennium past. Yes, the power that runs our society, lights our buildings, warms our rooms, and moves our vehicles. These outages—blackouts as some call them—have been getting more frequent and more serious. It is no coincidence, Master Vilmos, that the fiercest Excisor families are those that own the machineries of power production. For some reason, perhaps due to our rapid expansion and the growing demand, perhaps because of something more peculiar and less obvious, our science—and particularly those families—are having trouble meeting the power needs of our civilization.

"What *is* known about the problem is that there is a connection between the growth of what your world calls technology *there* and the shortages *here*—that advances in scientific progress in the mortal world somehow cause setbacks here that are growing increasingly painful. Many people feel that your world and ours make a closed system—that we need your ignorance to keep ourselves strong. If so, this is a bad time for Faerie in more than one way. Humanity is slowly abandoning its old beliefs, the beliefs that give power to our world, at the very same time that our civilization is exponentially expanding its need for that power."

The reference to the ignorance of mortals, even from this unusually well-disposed fairy, rankled a little, but it also reminded Theo of the deeper paradox that had been gnawing at him all day. *They keep saying "you," and "your people," he thought, but that's the point, isn't it? I'm not a mortal at all, unless everyone here's lying to me ... and that must have something to do with why I'm in the middle of this.* But he had been raised to think of himself that way, and a life-

time's worth of self-image could not change in an instant—
might not ever change. *So how can I understand why these
Excisors might want me when I can't think like they do?*

"I'm trying to follow all this," he said. "Really trying.
You think that somehow they want to bring on this Dark
Night thing, and then people—mortal people—will be,
like, plunged back into the Middle Ages and get supersti-
tious all over again? Make it easy for you fairies to draw
power from us?"

"Old Night. Perhaps that is what they want, yes. I confess
I cannot see all the sides of the figure—it is a strange, complex plan, whatever it is, and one that has been years in the
making—but it is the only thing that makes sense of what
has happened."

"And that somehow they need this Terrible Child—and
me, too?"

"Again, perhaps." Hollyhock sighed. "I am certain of
only one thing—our opponents will not be contented merely
to argue about it in the Parliament of Blooms in the ordinary
way, or even at today's summit conference, as Daffodil and
the other old guard seem to think. Neither will they be
bluffed into giving up. Hellebore is a man of action. He relies on others to waste their time talking while he plunges
ahead."

Theo had momentarily forgotten the conference. Now the
idea that the masters of the Hellebore and Thornapple families were going to be right here, in this place, made him feel
nakedly vulnerable. He stared at the rain-spotted window of
Hollyhock's suite. A series of drops joined together, formed
a vertical stream. When they reached a small leaf stuck to
the pane they did not push it out of the way but flowed
around it. *What was it Dolly Ogre called me? Shallow. Like
that rainwater. Just going with the flow, sliding away,
changing direction—whatever's easiest. Is that what Cat
meant, too?*

Now here he sat, the World's Shallowest Man, in an utterly strange place with his very life at stake among these

coldly selfish fairy-folk. He resolved to do better than he had done in the past. He also resolved for once to keep a resolution.

"What about you?" Theo asked suddenly. "Why are you so different? How do I know you don't have your own agenda?"

"Good question." Lord Hollyhock toyed with a piece of bread. "The answer is, I *do* have my own agenda, of course. But I'm one of the few whose agenda coincides with yours, Master Vilmos."

"Why is that? And why should I take your word for it?"

"I can only answer the second question by saying you shouldn't, but I'm afraid I can't offer you any proof. As to what we have in common, other than our basic essence, well, I am not really one of the old guard, although my family is a powerful one. My mother and father died during the last Flower War, so I have that reason to fear and distrust conflict between the families. Also, I am a radical of sorts, at least by comparison to most of the other house-lords. I do not believe we can trust the old patterns to hold things together, or that tradition is still the most important force in our society. We are a long-lived people and thus slow to change, but we *do* change. We must. And our society has not really been stable since the king and queen died—I suppose that will mean little to you, but it's true. Hellebore is another radical, but his ideas only benefit Nidrus Hellebore and people like him—a very small part of our folk. Not to mention what he would do to countless innocent mortals, against whom I have no grudge."

Theo's concentration had snagged on the idea of the death of the king and queen, which he had read about in his great-uncle's book—that it had been their passing which had forced (or was it *allowed?*) the seven ruling families to take power in the first place. Whichever the case, it was all becoming a bit much, too many facts, too many confusing new ideas, and no matter what his blood might say, his mind still told him that he was a mortal: he was far more concerned with protecting his own skin, whatever its genetic heritage, than continuing a crash course on the Royalty of Faerie.

"One more question," he said to Hollyock. "Were you the one who wanted me here? In . . . Facrie? And if that's true, why did you have Tansy do it instead of just doing it yourself?"

Hollyhock made a graceful gesture of surrender. "I drive the others mad because when I believe something is important, I treat it that way. So, yes, if pushing and pushing until Daffodil and Lily and the others gave in and agreed to have you brought here from your world means I am responsible, then the blame is mine." He smiled a little. "I hope in the long run you will have cause to thank me rather than hate me, but the future is still churning in the Well. We could have brought you directly here—to this very house, if we had chosen—but such an expenditure of power, and of such a singular and unusual focus, would have drawn attention, especially when we knew you were already being observed by Hellebore and his allies. Tansy is one of the few men outside the city who has the skill to effect a thing such as this. His experiments are well-known, but even the most suspicious of the ruling families consider him a largely harmless eccentric—he does not dabble much in real politics, although he talks about it a great deal—and so I thought if he were the one to contact you and attempt to bring you through, it might go unnoticed." He frowned. "Apparently I was wrong. In any case, I put a little pressure on him through his cousin, Lord Daisy, and he finally agreed."

"But not with everything you wanted."

"Certainly he did not fulfill his charge with the care I would have desired. Imagine, sending only a sprite after you!"

"She did pretty well," Theo said. "No, she did damn well."

"In any case, Tansy began to be fearful when he heard about my nephew Dalian's death." Hollyhock's frown returned. "I still don't understand why they sent his heart to the Daisy clan. But whatever the case, he was in a panic and wanted to back out of the whole thing. It required Daffodil and Lily and some of the others exerting the full weight of their authority to get him to agree to keep his bargain with us."

Theo sat back. He finally understood the change in Tansy's demeanor from irritation and what seemed like disinterest at first to an almost fawning kindness. It didn't explain everything, though. "So," he said after long silent seconds, "what's going to happen today? How do I really know Lord Dandelion and his pals won't sell me out to Hellebore? They sure don't think much of me."

"Lord Dandelion." He grinned. "That is amusingly apt—I will remember that for the Parliamentary Follies, if such a happy, ordinary thing should occur this year. As far as them somehow betraying you, don't worry too much, Master Vilmos. I may be a young troublemaker as far as they're concerned, but I head one of the ruling families and am not easily ignored, even by an old warhorse like Daffodil. Also, they are finally beginning to feel nervous about Hellebore's machinations, whatever they say. They have heard the rumors of the Terrible Child. They know that such a thing only comes about by the application of a hideous science, by the study and practice of many forbidden things. You are a pawn, but until we know more, an important one. They will not give you up as easily as you fear."

"Somehow that doesn't make me feel a whole lot better."

Now Hollyhock laughed. He was quite likable for the master of a Flower house. Theo didn't know if that should make him suspicious or not. In any case, his suspicion-sensors were beginning to fatigue from overuse. "I've arranged for you to watch the whole thing from a safe part of the conference center," the fairy lord said. "You will not even be on the same floor of the building as Hellebore and his contingent. Come along, it's almost time for the show—I'll lead you to your seat."

Theo stood. "Is there a way I can find someone who's staying here? It's Applecore—the sprite who got me here.

She went off a while ago and I'm beginning to get a bit worried about her."

"I will pass a message to the hob," said Hollyhock, leading him toward the door. "I am sure your friend will be found quickly. You are an important guest, after all, however it must sometimes seem."

It was at least a ten minute walk from the lobby of the Daffodil house-tower to the conference center, around the moat and along the edge of a memorial garden that seemed to be dedicated to the Daffodil clan's war dead, although which war was not specified; Theo was more than a little weary of fairy history and did not ask. He concentrated instead on enjoying the breeze and the muted afternoon sunshine, indulging his senses with what he would have thought of back in California as a typical autumn day. The air smelled of apples and something earthier, wet loam and leaves. The Daffodil House compound was huge and its grounds were carefully landscaped so as to look almost like wild forest and meadow: with his back to the four towers, the much lower conference center still hidden by hedges and old stone walls, Theo could almost forget where he was.

There were not many people on the paths for some reason. A work gang of wrinkly little men digging away in a drained ornamental lake stood up to watch them pass, then touched their foreheads and turned back quickly to their jobs when they recognized Lord Hollyhock. Farther on, a group of male sprites were painting the detail-work on top of one of the ornamental lampposts beside the path, three on a brush, buzzing and chattering. They swept down and made a couple of circuits around Theo and Hollyhock, swift as a storm of midges. Their greetings sounded more mocking than respectful, but his lordship paid no more attention to them than he had to the diggers.

The conference center was low compared to all the other

buildings in the Daffodil complex, only four or five stories at its highest point, but that didn't make it small. It stretched over a large area inside the wall and had its own manicured gardens, less wild than the rest of the Daffodil grounds. It also seemed built in a more modern style, at least as far as Theo could tell: the outside walls were mostly glass or some Faerie equivalent, and the different buildings were connected by exterior catwalks and bridges, so that it looked a bit like a giant model of some unusually flat molecule.

Even with the fairy lord accompanying him, Theo spent a rather long time being pressed and poked by unsmiling ogre security guards before being allowed to pass through the wide front doors. Hollyhock led him across a lobby full of busy functionaries in a variety of exotic shapes and into an executive elevator.

"We could have walked up—it's only one floor—but you don't want all the folks gossiping on the stairs to see you," Hollyhock explained.

The "seat" Theo had been promised for the proceedings proved to be in a corner office suite, two floors beneath the main meeting hall. This room was probably only thirty or forty feet off the ground, but the view outside its windowed outer wall was so dense with the tops of trees it was impossible to say for certain. The suite was empty but for a long table, a few chairs and other pieces of furniture, and a large greenish personage wedged firmly into a desk just inside the door.

"I'll just leave you then, shall I?" said Hollyhock. "I've got a few things to attend to before the meeting begins."

"And I just stay here, right?"

"Oh, I should think so. If you need anything, Walter can help you." Hollyhock pointed to the thing behind the desk, then nodded and went out.

Walter was another large Appointment Beast, at least as ugly as the one Theo had met earlier. He was pudgier than the musclebound warthog, with skin like a crocodile and a round, scaly face. He silently directed Theo to the table in the center of the room, then flicked his fingers over the surface of his own desk as if trying to shake water off them; a large mirror rose from a previously invisible slot in the center of the table. Its reflecting surface appeared to steam over, then the mist vanished and was replaced by the Daffodil family crest which remained in the center of the mirror.

"The Test Patterns of Fairyland," Theo murmured.

"Beg pardon?" said reptilian Walter.

"Nothing."

The Appointment Beast nodded, slowly extricated itself from behind the desk, and brought Theo a pitcher of water and a glass.

"Do you mind if I eat my lunch?" Walter asked. "Seeing as I'm working today when I'm supposed to be on holiday?"

"Not at all."

The scaly head nodded. "Very kind." Walter took a white cardboard carton that might have contained Chinese takeout out from beneath the desk, opened it, and looked in. *Flarp!* A long gray tongue shot out and plunged into the box like a piston, then withdrew almost as quickly, bringing back something with tiny wriggling legs. Theo turned away, unsettled.

The mirror in the center of the table grew misty again and the Daffodil crest faded, replaced a moment later by a view of what Theo guessed must be the conference center's meeting hall a couple of floors above him. It was at least as large as the vast basement room that held the comb, and like the much smaller suite Theo was presently occupying, seemed to have one wall entirely made of glass. A long table bisected the hall, running perpendicular to the floor-to-ceiling window; Theo's viewpoint looked down its polished length. Banks of seats surrounded the table on either side—diplomacy as spectator sport. Outside, the towers of the city's greatest houses spiked the skyline like the unfolded components of a Swiss army knife, a group of silhouettes much quirkier than anything he would have seen back in the world of his birth.

Lord Daffodil and Lady Jonquil were already sitting on

the side of the table visible to Theo's left, surrounded by various underlings. Lord Hollyhock had just taken his place, too, although he had a much smaller contingent which included some young fairy women in smart suits. Beyond them, nearest the floor-to-ceiling window, and clearly constituting another household, was a group centered around an extremely tall and slender fairy lord with long silvery tresses and sad but self-absorbed eyes; he looked even older than Lord Daffodil. This mournful presence was surrounded by a group of what might have been acolytes, young fairy men with identical haircuts wearing simple, loose garments that resembled religious robes.

"Who's that?" Theo asked, pointing at the silver-haired fairy.

The Appointment Beast looked up, cheeks bulging. He chewed a few times, delicately spat a shell into his napkin, then set the box down and leaned forward, squinting. "Ah. His Radiant Honor, Garvan, Lord Lily," he said. "Mad as a mudfly that one."

Theo tried to remember what he had been told about the Lily household. Allies of the Daffodils and Hollyhocks was all he could remember.

So everyone here so far is on the same side, he thought, and it was literally true, because the side of the table to Theo's right was still entirely empty. *No Hellebores yet, no Thornapples.* That should have made him feel better, but it didn't. Waiting was worse than knowing, really. He surveyed the crowd of fairies filling the seats behind Hollyhock, Daffodil, and the rest. "Who are all the folk at the back?" he asked. "Some of them look pretty rich and important."

The lizard man leaned forward again. "The usual lot. The Primrose clan over there, they're another of the Six Families. A lot of the others are Lord Daffodil's allies. Those are Peonies, and Bluebells, and . . . I can't quite make those out in the back, but I saw the guest list so I'm fairly sure they're Snowdrops. Beyond them are . . . Stocks, yes, no question. Hard to tell which Stocks just by looking at them—huge family and they all look much the same—but you can't mistake the look. Weak chins, the lot of them."

"And the other side, the empty chairs, those are for the Hellebores and the Thornapples?"

The functionary briefly consulted a list on his clipboard. "Yes, and some others who asked to be seated with them. The Foxgloves, Larkspurs, and . . . let me check . . . Monkshoods, Buttercups . . ."

Foxglove. It tugged at Theo's memory, but his head was spinning with horticultural names, an overgrown garden of half-understood fairy civics and history.

"That lot will arrive late, no doubt," the scaly fellow continued. "With Hellebore and some others it will be a purposeful gesture of contempt. With Lord Larkspur, it will be because he has caught the wrong train from the country. He will spend ten minutes blaming the rail system."

Despite his nervousness, Theo was amused. "You seem to know a lot. What's your name?"

"Spunkie Walter, sir."

"Nice to meet you, Spunkie."

"No, my name is Walter. A Spunkie is what I am. You met my cousin Spunkie Tim earlier."

"The warthog guy? Oh, sorry, is that rude?"

"People can think what they like." Walter shrugged at the ways of the world. "Some people think I look like a lizard."

"Imagine that."

The Spunkie nodded. "Would you mind if I finished my lunch, sir? They said they might want me to bring you up later, so I'd just as soon eat now. I hardly get a chance to sit down around here, let alone eat."

"Of course." Now Theo was nervous again—very nervous. He didn't much like the idea of being brought up later, or at all. He did his best to calm himself, watching the fairy lords preparing for the conference. Well, one side was preparing. The other still hadn't made an appearance. Spunkie Walter had called it a gesture of contempt. *Or,* Theo couldn't help thinking, *maybe it's something much worse. Maybe they're*

going to attack Daffodil House and try to kidnap me or some-
thing. But it was hard to believe that, hard to attach that much
significance to himself, no matter what Hollyhock had said,
let alone believe that any of the other fairy houses were desperate enough to attack the Daffodil clan here in the heart of
their power, behind their mighty fortifications. Still . . .

"Hey, Walter? Does Lord Daffodil have . . . I don't know
what you call it here. A standing army? A personal security
force?"

Walter slurped down another wiggling something. "Yes,
sir," he said glumly. "Over a thousand of them. They have
their barracks in the outwall. And there are always a hundred
stationed in the main tower. After the last Flower War, nobody gets too trusting around here."

"Thanks." Theo suddenly felt much better. And there must
be magic too—lots of magic, all the charms and things Hollyhock had mentioned. These rival houses must be like the US
and USSR during the Cold War—opposing forces too well
balanced to start anything for fear that even the aggressor
might not survive. No, it was leaving this armed fortress that
he needed to avoid. His stupidity in letting Zirus Jonquil take
him right to his enemy's doorstop was really beginning to
rankle. *Come on, Theo. You can't be shallow anymore. You
can't just go along. That will get you killed . . . !*

Lord Daffodil was standing now, talking down the table
to some of the others on his side, but Theo couldn't hear a
sound. "Is there a way that I can hear what they're saying?"

"Say, 'To my ears,'" Walter instructed him.

Theo did; a moment later Daffodil's voice was in Theo's
head, full of well-bred irritation that his counterparts from
the other families had not yet arrived. It was not an external
sound like the sort you got from speakers, however good:
the fairy lord's voice was right in his head. It was such a
strange and fascinating effect that Theo almost didn't look
around when the door to the office opened.

The ruling class were still similar enough to Theo's eyes
that it took him a few seconds to recognize the fairy stand-

ing in the doorway. The handsome, bespectacled figure nodded to Theo, then turned to the lizard-secretary and said, "Do you recognize me?"

"Of course, Count Tansy."

"Good. I have a message for you from Lord Daffodil." He passed the spunkie a piece of paper. Walter looked at it; a frown crossed his scaly face.

"It should come through the hob."

"It was not given to the hob, it was given to me. I was just with your lord a few moments ago."

"Then I must go at once," Walter said, rising. "There is a drinks cabinet on the far wall, Count Tansy. Please forgive me if I leave you to serve yourself. This appears to be urgent."

Theo had been staring. "Tansy. I didn't expect to see you here."

The other smiled a little. "I cannot say the same—I have heard a great deal about you lately. I gather you have had many near misses and close escapes, but it seems you have been lucky. Still, I am very displeased that Applecore brought you here, against my orders."

"Yeah, that's right, you wanted me to go to . . . to . . ." The recalcitrant memory escaped for good, replaced by another thought. The din from the conference room had diminished when he gave his attention to Count Tansy, but it had not gone away, and it added to the confusion in Theo's head. "Hang on, it must have been you!"

Tansy, who had been approaching the table, stopped suddenly. "What does that mean?"

"Applecore left me a message—said she saw someone I knew outside Daffodil House. I thought from what the secretary said that she meant she'd seen Rufinus—but he's dead."

"Yes, he most certainly is, the poor fool." Tansy slid into the seat beside Theo.

"Nice relative you are," Theo said. "But she must have

meant you. I haven't been able to track her down—did you see her?"

Tansy shook his head. "I have not, and I doubt it was me she saw, since I came not in my regular coach but a jitney from the station. My presence here is not generally known, you see." He looked at the view of the main meeting room. "I see that Hellebore and the others have not arrived."

"Yeah, Walter the spunkie said they'll come late, all of them, the Thornapples and the Larkspurs and the . . . Foxgloves, too . . ." He was suddenly as cold as if fever-chilled. "Oh, my God. That's who you tried to send me to, wasn't it? Foxglove?"

"Foxglove? I might have." Tansy spoke in a distracted way. He was watching the mirror intently. "What of it? It has only been widely reported in the last few days that he has thrown in his lot with Hellebore's people."

Theo's heart was hammering. "Hollyhock couldn't figure out why you sent me to the City with so little protection. But that wasn't a mistake, was it? You . . . you sold me out."

"Sold you out? What nonsense is that? I have done my best to help you, you rude, ungrateful creature . . ." Tansy paused. "Look, Hellebore has arrived."

Theo's eyes flicked to the mirror, but everything looked much the same—one side of the vast conference table crowded, the other side empty. Lady Aemilia was suggesting that there was much to be discussed even without all the six leading families represented, and her words distracted Theo for what was almost a fatal second. He saw movement from the corner of his eye and turned just as Tansy tried to clamp a piece of cloth across his mouth. One smell of it, an acrid, moldy scent like something that had been growing a long time under dark wet ground, was enough to make him fling himself backward. Tansy had not had a chance to get his other arm around Theo's neck. He managed to break free and tumble off the chair and onto the floor, but it felt like some of the fumes were inside his body now, turning his muscles to rubber.

Idiot! He scrabbled away from the table, trying to get control of his limbs so he could stand. *I'm an idiot for not seeing it coming! He sent Walter away! He sold me out and now he's here to finish the job!*

Tansy was on him in a moment, grabbing him with slender but still astonishingly strong arms. As if in alliance with his attacker, the voices from the conference room grew louder in Theo's head as he struggled to keep Tansy's cloth away from his face.

"We are being treated outrageously. You know I do not like leaving my mountain for anything except the most important business, especially on a sacred day that should be spent with my family and folk . . ."

"Please, be patient, Garvan."

"I have been patient, Lady Aemilia. My meditations have been disrupted, I have been forced to travel out of season through all the field of Holly Crown trying to find a station, and now this!"

"You have every right to be upset, my good Lily . . ."

"And that is enough from you, Hollyhock. You are only a pup, and if you think I will stay here and be insulted by that Hellebore and his jumped-up set simply to further your political ambitions . . ."

"Wait! I am being given a message . . . "

"What is it, Brother?"

"Just a moment, Aemilia, the hob is saying . . . it makes no sense . . ."

Theo's battle, in terrible counterpoint, was almost completely silent. He rolled toward the table with his enemy straddling him, hoping to knock the fairy's head against the furniture and dislodge him, but Tansy saw his plan and managed to get one foot against the table leg as he again forced the cloth into Theo's face. Theo held his breath, but he was already exhausted and needed air: he knew he could not last much longer. He tried to remember the fights he'd been in, but the only things he could recall were either getting hurt or making a run for it at the first distraction.

The slender, pale hand was pushing the cloth down on him despite his strongest efforts to keep it away. In another moment he wouldn't be able to get any air at all and the struggle would be over. Theo hesitated, knowing he would only get one chance, then forced himself to stop resisting and go limp. He had managed to take only a small breath before surrendering and prayed that the cloth wasn't something magical, that it only worked if you inhaled the fumes. He made himself lie still and hold that tiny, insufficient breath against the screaming of his instincts as the reeking fabric closed over his mouth and nose.

"I have him," Tansy announced, apparently to the air. "I will be out of this place in moments. You may proceed."

Under the cloth, Theo's eyes were stinging so badly he thought he might be blinded, but that was the least of his worries. He had to wait, lungs burning until his every fiber shrieked at him to fight for breath no matter what, and then wait seconds longer, until he felt Tansy's hand loosen the pressure and the fairy's weight shift a little on Theo's chest. As soon as the rag came off he twisted his head and got his teeth into the side of Tansy's hand, then bit down as hard as he could. The fairy shrieked in startled pain and the cloth dropped from his fingers. Theo yanked back his head, gasped in air, and heaved himself upward with what felt like his dying strength, lifting Tansy off the ground with him before throwing himself backward into an explosion of blackness.

The blackness did not go away swiftly. For a long time, minutes and minutes, Theo could only lie helplessly on the floor of the office, wondering whether he had hit his own head while smashing Tansy against the table, or if the poison on Tansy's cloth really had made him blind. At least he couldn't hear anything else moving, either: Tansy had not scrambled up to finish him, although Theo could feel the weight of the count's arm across his chest. When vision and control over his limbs finally returned, Theo shook the fairy off, turned over, and stared blearily down at him.

Tansy was not dead, but he had hit his head very hard and his eyes were rolled back under their lids. He quivered like a rabbit Theo had once seen, shot by a friend's pellet gun. Theo crawled across the floor and picked up the cloth, then brought it back and shoved it against Tansy's bloody face. The fairy's trembling became less, then stopped.

I hope he's fucking dead, Theo thought, but he doubted the drugged cloth was meant to work that way. It was a lot of trouble for everyone to go through just to kill him, like on the train. Kidnapping seemed a more likely intent.

He got the upper half of his body onto a chair, then managed to pull himself up until he was standing, swaying beside the table. The voices in his head had grown quieter again, but he could still see the people in the huge meeting room. He wondered who he could call. He had to tell someone—Hollyhock needed to know what was going on.

"Hob?" he called up toward the ceiling. Nobody answered.

"I am afraid I must stand with Lord Lily," Daffodil was saying angrily. *"This is more than irregular—sending this mandragorum is a calculated slap."*

The Hellebore side of the conference table was no longer empty. A single figure dressed in a black robe now stood there, facing Daffodil and the others. What Theo could see of the face was so pale that at first he thought it was one of the hollow-men. When it pulled back its hood, he saw that the features were bizarrely unformed, two completely dead eyes, a lump of nose, a slit of a mouth, the whole thing as lifeless as an uncooked gingerbread man. It reached into its robe and guards leaped forward from all around the room; in an instant the barrels of several dozen weapons were pointed at the unfinished thing, but it continued in its slow, clumsily deliberate way.

Theo could only stare at the mirror and watch it all unfold, brainsick, exhausted, and confused.

"Don't fire," Lord Daffodil said loudly. *"No weapons known to science could have gotten past our detection*

charms. The mandragorum went through five checkpoints before it was allowed in here."

The pulpy white hands emerged, each holding a golden rod. Despite Lord Daffodil's words there was a flurry of humming and clicking noises as those guards who had not already cocked their weapons did so, but the pale thing only spread its two arms, holding the rods out vertically at the extent of its reach. A flicker of light passed between them, then the space between the rods was filled with the image of a coldly handsome, dark-bearded face.

"Hellebore!" said Daffodil in outrage. *"What are these mummer's tricks? Why are you not here? Why do you send this poor manufactured creature in your place, this . . . walking root? Are you afraid to meet with your equals?"*

A smile spread across the face in the shining image. *"My equals are here with me."* The image stayed the same size, but the field of view widened until the men sitting on either side of him could be seen, one dark as Hellebore, but with white eyebrows, the other with fair hair and beard. *"You know Thornapple and Foxglove, I think."* Thornapple only smiled—and except for the eyebrows and that unpleasant smile, Theo realized, he was disturbingly like his daughter Poppy—but the other fairy lord's mouth was a tight line. Even through the ache in his head, Theo thought Lord Foxglove looked ashamed and maybe a little frightened.

What the hell am I doing watching this? It's not a damn TV show—they just tried to kill me! I have to get out of here, tell someone . . . But it was all he could do at the moment to stand upright and stare. Hellebore was dominating the picture again, his pale, amused face so handsome as to verge on pretty were it not for something horrifying about his eyes: even through the medium of the screen and the mirror through which he was watching from a distance, the man's coal-black stare held Theo like a candle flame in a dark room.

"So is this it?" Hollyhock was asking. He alone seemed to have grasped what was going on. Daffodil and Lily and

many others were still bellowing outrage at this breach of protocol. *"Do you no longer feel yourself safe in our houses, despite all our ages-old traditions of questing? Does that mean it is to be war?"*

Hellebore laughed. *"Let us say that I would not feel safe in that house, no. As to war, yes, my young lord, it is. And more than that. The game has not merely begun, it is over."*

Despite Hellebore's face on its magic screen in the middle of the mirror, Theo felt his attention drawn upward, to the transparent wall that ran all across the side of the conference center meeting room. Others in the great room had seen it too: a small shape coming through the sky toward Daffodil House, moving very fast, a black, wide-winged silhouette swooping down out of the sun.

Lord Daffodil was up on his feet, shaking his fist, but his face was as bloodless as the inhuman thing that held out Hellebore's screen—the face of a man who sees his own death on the wind. *"But it cannot be! You could not have made such a flying device! All our laws forbid it! We would have known if you had worked the science to build such a thing . . . !"*

The thing was coming straight toward them like a kite being reeled in. Now Theo could see its shape, the scalloped wings, the thread of whiplike tail. People in the meeting room were shrieking, fighting with each other, stumbling over chairs, falling.

"You're right, my lord," said Hellebore. *"So we have returned to an earlier science, one our people had almost forgotten. Why build something that flies and flames and kills . . . when we had only to wake one up?"*

It was over the center of the city. Theo gaped. It was huge—he had not realized how fast it was moving because he had not dreamed how big it was, long as a football field from snarling mouth to the tip of its snakelike tail.

Lord Lily was staggering, held up by two of his acolytes. *"You have wakened a dragon? Then you are cursed! Cursed!"*

A high-pitched hob-voice began to shriek, both in the

Audience Chamber and in Theo's head: *"Danger! Attack! Danger! Attack! Danger!"*

"Cursed? Perhaps," said Hellebore evenly. *"But you are dead. Which fate would you prefer?"*

The black shadow covered the window, plunging the room for a timeless second into something deeper than twilight. Light smoldered in every crevice of the vast shape, the black scales surrounded by glowing red like stones floating in molten lava. Then the mouth gaped open in a hellish flare of incandescence and a six hundred foot span of wings spread wide to slow the thing as the great serpentine neck snapped forward, vomiting fire.

The huge window of the meeting room blew inward, an explosion of burning liquid glass—for an instant Theo could see the inhabitants flung before the spray, withering to black bone and ash—then the mirror went dark. The entire building spasmed beneath his feet and a blast of thunder like God's own hammerblow threw him to the floor and smashed the ceiling in above his head, raining pieces down on him like the stones of shattered Jericho.

Part Three

FLOWER WAR

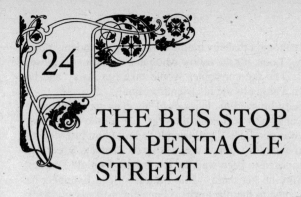

24

THE BUS STOP ON PENTACLE STREET

Streedy Nettle looked very carefully at the street sign to make sure it still said the same thing. He didn't think that streets usually changed names from one block to another, but he wasn't absolutely certain. In fact, he wasn't absolutely certain about very much, except that he was quite certain he wanted to get on the right bus and get home. He could only take shallow breaths because he was so nervous his chest hurt. This was the first time he had been out on his own since his new friends had found him, and although a part of him was proud to be doing something to help instead of just eating their food and taking up space, he didn't like standing in the middle of the sidewalk by himself under these gray afternoon skies. Still, it was an important errand. They had told him so. They had also told him that only he could do it—no one else! That had really made him wonder. But that didn't make being on the streets alone any easier. He wondered why . . . why . . . he struggled to remember the quiet, serious fairy's name . . . why Caradenus hadn't met him like he was supposed to do.

Sometimes he had to stop walking just to think, to make himself remember what he was supposed to do next, but when he did people often looked at him with anger on their faces as they stepped or flew around him. That frightened him. He thought that any moment they might suddenly point and say, "Look, it's the fellow who ran away from the power plant!" Then the constables would take him away and he would never get to see his friends again.

Streedy brushed his hair out of his eyes and squinted at the street sign. It said Pentacle Street like all the others had, which was good. His small friends had told him just what to do, and one of the things was to stay on Pentacle Street. He was supposed to keep walking toward the Twilight District, but before he got there, while he was still in Eventide, he would come to the place where Pentacle crossed Sour Milk Way and find the bus stop there. He didn't know this because he had got off the bus this morning at the exact same stop on his way into the middle of the City (although that's just what he had done with Caradenus) but because his friends had talked with him about how to get home over and over if he was ever left on his own. They had tried to draw a map for him, but it was too hard to read and understand. Easier to learn things like they were the words to a song, the way he learned that song he liked so much, "Broceliande Blue," just say them again and again and again until he knew them as well as his own name.

And he really did know the way home that well, and perhaps even better, because there were moments when he didn't remember his name at all—when the only thing that Streedy Nettle could think of to call himself was not a name at all but an idea, a memory of that horrifying golden instant in which the power of the entire plant had moved through him, had lived inside him as though he weren't a person at all but a beast of freezing fire as big as the sky. In those moments he was not the Widow Nettle's gangly son anymore, not the country boy from Hazel or even the new Streedy who found it hard to think but who wanted so badly to help his new friends: in those moments he simply *was,* a glorious, terrifying memory of being so full of light that he thought he might explode into glowing white fragments . . .

People bumped against him and cursed as they hurried

past. Someone tried to brush by and must have felt the crippled wings hidden beneath his loose coat, because she—it was a woman, a young girl in a servant's cap, with wings of her own that glittered even in the dull autumn light—gave him a very odd look.

"All right for some," she said, then walked on quickly.

Streedy realized that he had stopped in the middle of the sidewalk again. He was in the way. People were noticing him. His friends had been very firm about that, as firm as they had been about him learning the route: he was not supposed to do things that would make people pay attention to him.

It was so *difficult* to think while he was walking, not just because thinking was hard work, but also because he was afraid that he would go past the place he was looking for while he was still trying to remember. And there had been so much to remember today! Not just how to get to where he had been, and how to get back to his friends again, but also not to stop in the street or say anything that would make anyone wonder about him. And then all the hard work to remember the things his friends wanted done in the middle of the city without Caradenus to help him! That had been the hardest part in some ways, but he was finished now, which was a relief.

But was he really finished? He stopped again, just for a moment, because suddenly he wasn't sure. He thought and thought, panic making his chest feel tight again. What if he had gone to the place but had forgotten to do the thing he had gone there for in the first place? "Go with me," he had begged his friends, "it's too hard to remember all these things!" but they wouldn't do it. "We can't go where you're going, Streedy," one of them had told him—he thought it was Doorlatch. "They'd follow us. They'd be watching us the entire time. It has to be you."

Suddenly, he remembered the bag he was clutching in his hands. The bag! Of course! If he hadn't done what he was supposed to do, the bag would be empty. He opened the top just a little, just enough to peer in. It was full of Truename cards, just like it was supposed to be. He sighed, relieved. He had done what he was supposed to—he could remember it now that he wasn't so nervous. Yes, now he could remember walking right in and doing all the things they had told him to do, in just the right order.

He was bumped again. Stopped in the middle of the sidewalk. That was bad. Time to walk again. Walk along Pentacle Street. Look for Sour Milk Way. That was how it was supposed to go. But was this really still Pentacle Street? What if he'd turned down the wrong street somehow?

He found a sign at last. Pentacle Street. So that was good. He resumed his march toward the bus stop.

"Get out of the street, strawhead!" someone shouted. Streedy Nettle at last pulled his attention away from the blinking blue light on the pole. It felt like it was blinking behind his eyes as well—such a strange sensation. And there were little smeary bits of light around everything, even the big black coach which had stopped in the center of the intersection, and whose driver was now shaking a fist at him, yelling out the rolled-down window. "Go back to Alder!"

"But I'm not from . . ." Streedy shook his head. The traffic light still seemed to be in his eyes, even when he looked down. A horn honked again. He hurried across the intersection and up onto the sidewalk on the far side. What street was he on? Pentacle Street? Good.

It hadn't always been like this. He couldn't exactly remember how it *had* been, but he knew it had been different before the accident. He didn't used to forget things so quickly, hadn't had to be reminded by his friends that he was going somewhere when they found him standing and staring. Blinking lights hadn't sort of put him to sleep like they did now, hadn't whispered in his ear, *on off on off on off,* ticking like midnight footsteps in a tiled room. In fact, he had hardly ever noticed lights at all before the accident. Now he could see them for what they were, a certain kind of cold heat flowing back and forth from brilliance to blackness like water sloshing in a bowl, but so fast that most other people couldn't see the changes. Streedy could, though, or could at least feel them. He was glad he didn't have to go out in the nighttime. Even from a distance the lights of the city center at night made his head ache.

He looked up at the next intersection and saw a sign that said Sour Milk Way. This time he remembered to move over close to the window of a store while he considered it. Yes, that was the name he had been looking for. Where Sour Milk Way crossed Pentacle. He was supposed to look for something. He frowned, but the frown didn't last long. *The bus stop.*

Pleased and more than a little proud, Streedy looked all around the intersection. There was a big store on one corner, a very high building with brightly glowing letters over the wide glass doors that said "Loosestrife, Licensed," and people coming out with bags and boxes. That wasn't it—no, that was some kind of store. He remembered stores. He remembered his mother taking him all the way into the town of Twelvetrees to get a winter coat, and the department store— much smaller than this one—called "Zinnia Brothers," which had been so full of unattainable objects like an entire small mezzanine floor of toys that to young Streedy it had seemed like a dream.

He blinked. Was he supposed to go to a store? No, the bus stop. *Remember, Streedy!* He was angry with himself.

He spotted it at last, just a few yards back up Pentacle Street. He had walked right past it. His friends were so smart, telling him to look for Sour Milk Way! It was just like the one a block away where the bus had dropped him off this morning, with glass walls and a gray-green copper roof in the shape of a giant elder leaf.

The Warstones and Dockyards bus, he told himself. *That's what they said. Don't get on the wrong bus. Warstones and Dockyards.*

There were already a half dozen people on the bench,

three of them old women dressed in black or gray. There were also two younger women in domestic service uniforms, one of whom was small enough that she might be half-brownie, and a man whose expensive coat fit so snugly it was clear that he had no wings at all, not even crumpled and melted ones like Streedy Nettle's. He had a mirrorcase open on his lap and didn't even look up when Streedy almost bumped him. A few of the others did glance at him, but only for a moment. Streedy decided to stand, even though his feet hurt. He was afraid he might fall asleep sitting up as he sometimes did. It was harder to fall asleep when you were standing.

He was just wondering if the man in the suit had gone to a doctor to have his wings off, like people back at the power plant said that the supervisor Mr. Dogwood had done, when the little serving-woman tugged at the other woman's sleeve and pointed at the sky, saying, "What's that?" She didn't sound scared, just surprised.

Streedy looked south down Pentacle Street and was dazed by the succession of orange and blue traffic lights stretching away into the distance. It took him a moment to see what she was pointing at, a strange, angular shadow coming across the sky like a fallen leaf caught up by the wind.

"It's so big . . . !" said her friend.

Streedy wanted to laugh because it wasn't big at all, it was small, he could have reached out his hand and covered it like a spot on the wall. But then he saw that it was getting bigger and bigger very fast and he realized he was wrong, that it had only been so small because it was far away—he'd forgotten how that happened—and then he saw what it was and he couldn't think about anything else at all because he was freezing cold all up and down his body. He felt like he'd swallowed a block of ice as big as his own head.

"Bloody black iron . . . !" someone shouted—it must have been the man with the mirrorcase, but Streedy didn't look at him. He couldn't look at anything except the thing that was growing bigger and bigger in the sky.

"But there isn't any such thing!" one of the old women shrieked. "Not any more! There isn't!"

The thing blocked the light as it plunged down. The bus shelter fell into shadow, the air perfectly still for just half an instant. Then wind filled the street like a living thing, sending papers, leaves, dust spiraling up to cloud the sky. Coaches skidded, crunched into each other. A horn blared and would not stop.

As it leveled at the base of its dive, only a few feet above the top of the street's tallest buildings, the huge black dragon spread its wings—Streedy could hear the wind roaring and thrumming in the membranes. Signs tore loose from the walls and tumbled clattering into the street. Lights popped and fizzed with the gassy green light of escaping power, something that normally made Streedy want to run away as fast as he could, but his feet seemed stuck to the sidewalk. Glass spattered down the length of the sidewalk in a sudden downpour as windows broke all along the block, some of it clattering on the bus shelter roof. The people around him had been knocked to the ground, battered or terrified into silence. Streedy clung to the shuddering wall of the shelter as the huge black wormshape twisted in midair, its wings snapping up then down as it writhed back into the high sky. A moment later it was hurtling away north, no longer on the same line as the street. It did not vanish, though: Streedy saw it rise, wings spreading even wider, like the petals of some exotic hothouse flower, then a line of bright fire leaped down from its mouth toward the ground, toward some target Streedy could not see. The dragon flame was so searingly bright, as though someone had scratched a burning stick across his eyes, that for the first time Streedy Nettle shrieked and lost his grip and fell to the sidewalk like a half-empty sack.

Even through his closed, dazzled eyes he could see a great white flash, then something roared like a long peal of thunder. The ground jumped beneath him as though struck by a giant's hammer, bouncing Streedy over onto his belly. The cold pavement against his face was the only real thing for a moment—

that and the stinging sight of dragonfire still painted on the inside of his eyelids like a razorslash of burning light.

"The dragons are going to kill us all!" someone shrieked. The voices crowded together—people were shouting up and down the street. More coaches crunched into things.

"That was Hollyhock House—that thing just burned down Hollyhock House!" screamed someone else.

"They'll kill us all!"

"It's war!"

"It's the end, the end, the end . . . !"

Streedy pressed his cheek against the cold concrete and listened to the winds rise. He didn't want to remember anything more. He didn't want to.

He was walking, although he didn't remember why. It was snowing, just like back in Hazel, which seemed wrong, somehow, but there it was, a constant flutter of gray and white flakes everywhere, in the air, sifting and swirling around his feet, getting into his nose and mouth so that he could hardly breathe or see for crying. Strange snow. The street was winter-dark, too, but nighttime had come only in certain places, great inky clouds of blackness in front of the sun but with bits of blue-gray sky peeping through. He didn't understand any of it.

No bus had come. He couldn't remember exactly why, but everyone else had stopped waiting before he had. In fact, they had all run away, except for one of the women, who had spread her wings to fly, but she was clumsy like she hadn't done it much, and also crying hard. She had fluttered awkwardly through the snowy wind until she ran into a wall and fell and then didn't get up again.

Streedy hadn't seen a big fairy like her fly in a long time. Something really bad must have upset her. He felt he should remember what that something had been—it seemed like it was important—but he couldn't. So now he was walking, his special bag still clutched in his hand. He didn't want his friends to be upset. He hoped he was walking in the right direction. Pentacle Street? He was pretty certain that was the right name, but he had no idea if he was still on that street. He tried to ask people where he should go, but most of the folk he saw hurrying through the gray snow, some holding things over their heads to keep the stuff off, some with scarves or shirts clutched over their mouths, didn't want to stop and talk. He finally found someone, a little ferisher in a suit who was standing on a streetcorner talking into a shell. Streedy asked him whether he was going the right way to get the Warstones and Dockyards bus.

"Warstones . . . ?" The little ocher-colored man put his shell in his pocket. He laughed, but he looked like he wanted to cry. His face and suit were very dirty. He looked like the kind of person who should know Warstones, Streedy thought, but the ferisher disappointed him. "Cracks in the Floorboard, how should I know?" He wiped sweat and gray snow off his forehead, giggling. "Three of the great houses—Lily, Daffodil, Hollyhock, all gone in an hour! Somebody said Parliament is shut down. It's war!" He stopped laughing and burst into tears, just as Streedy had thought he might. He seemed to be a very emotional fellow. "I can't help you. I can't help you. They say everyone's to be off the streets by sunset. It was that Thornapple fellow who was saying it, Lord Thornapple. Seemed very calm . . ."

The Thornapple name frightened Streedy, although at the moment he couldn't remember exactly why, but he also was confused by something else the man had said. "Sunset? But it's already night!"

The ferisher shook his head, wiping at his eyes with the sleeve of his suit coat, smearing the dirty snow on his face even more until he looked like he was wearing a mask. "Go home! Go to your children!" He turned and began trotting down the street. In a few moments he was lost in the swirl of gray and white.

"I don't have any children," said Streedy, but there was no one to hear him.

He walked on for what seemed like hours. He forgot what

street he was supposed to be on and stopped looking at the signs, stopped trying to remind himself. It was hard to see, anyway—his eyes burned and burned and for some reason his lungs did, too, just as they had in the days after his accident. He kept stumbling and falling down, and each time it was harder to get up. But his friends were waiting for him back home. He clutched at his bag. His friends were waiting.

In a dark street where the snow was not so thick, a small, narrow street crisscrossed overhead not with streaks of fire but with washing lines, he crawled up onto a porch and fell against a door that had a smaller round door in the middle of it, set about the height of his stomach. He didn't know where he was anymore and he didn't know whose apartment or business this might be, but he remembered this kind of door—his friends had told him about doors like this with a hole in the middle. He slapped at it until he remembered to close his fingers into a fist, then went on knocking on the door, trying to remember what his friends had taught him about the right way to knock—*three fast, two slow, two fast, then do it again and again and again . . .*

The goblin that finally opened the inset round door and peered out did not say a word, but he did not close it again, either. Instead he watched Streedy with wide, fearful eyes. Voices washed out from behind him, buzzing goblin voices raised in argument, as well as the familiar tones of the mirrortalkers that had greeted Streedy every night back home when he came in from the fields, before he went away to work in the plant. His mother had loved her mirror. "My company," she called it. "My friends."

Friends. "Help me," said Streedy, and suddenly he was looking up at the goblin's face instead of down. He had fallen, somehow, and it was very hard to breathe, as though the snow was filling up his lungs, hot snow that smoldered inside him and pushed out all the good air. "Help me . . . find my friends. They live . . . under . . . a bridge."

25

A MILLION SPARKS

For long moments he waited to burn.

There was noise all around him, distant shrieks and the disembodied voice of a hob reporting danger and destruction, listless as a feverish child, but at the moment it seemed to Theo he was surrounded by, and sunken in, a deep and stunning silence.

I'm going to die, was the only coherent thought, and so it seemed his only thought: *I'm going to die.* But after a while he became aware that the silence was a kind of pall of shock, and that just as the world around him was actually filled with frantic noises, so his own mind was full of disconnected thoughts flitting, squeaking, and colliding like startled bats in a sealed chamber.

I'm going to die here. In Fairyland. Why had he sat waiting for this? Why hadn't he seen through Tansy before? Why had all the fairies he'd met been so certain that there wouldn't be a war? *Well, they're all dead now so they're probably feeling pretty stupid.* Through all the disconnected fluttering in his head, he knew he was stuck in the middle of a moment of great change, a point from which everything else could be seen as strands leading backward. He could only hope—but not quite believe—there might be strands leading forward as well.

If I don't die.

Gradually, through the dust and the sound of crippled beams creaking like the timbers of a storm-strained ship, he realized that if he *was* going to die it might not be for many minutes, or even longer. It was not his own floor that had been incinerated by that terrible winged shadow but one farther up in the building. He was half-flattened by bits of ceiling but not crushed; he could feel his feet moving, his toes flexing when he tried them. But he could not expect things to stay this way very long. Smoke was already beginning to creep down from whatever hell had been created above his head—he could smell it, the weird odor of things burning that he could not identify, combustion without familiarity. Already he was having trouble taking deep breaths. If he stayed here he wouldn't survive, but all else was vague and difficult.

Theo reached out in his dust-blindness and scrabbled at what was restraining him, but could make no sense of it by touch alone. He mopped at his eyes, turned the loose grit into a more general, stinging slime of sweat and dust. There was dust everywhere, clouds of the stuff mixed in with the smoke. Something crawled across his hand and he snatched it back with a shout, knowing even as he did so that it was ludicrous—as if any living thing could come close to the horror he'd just witnessed, a thousand square feet of glass turned to liquid in an instant, flame like glowing acid. His shout turned into a helpless, heaving cough. Little dusty bugs were crawling all over him, or at least they looked like bugs, though they were almost perfectly round. Their legs stuck out in all directions; none was bigger than a silver dollar, but some were small as confetti circles. One scrabbled across another a few inches from his hand and he saw gold gleam where the dust was scraped away.

Sitting on the floor, as helpless as an infant, Theo suddenly realized that Hellebore's pale, calm face had been talking soundlessly in the back of his mind all this time, a sort of horror tape-loop that didn't end, featuring the fairy lord's smile of infinite cruelty in the moments before the world caught fire. Hellebore was as empty as a ghost—was that what a ghost was, something that looked like a person but had lost all its kindness?—but he was also powerful, more powerful than even poor dead Hollyhock had dreamed. Lord Hellebore and his allies had sent a reptilian monster to deliberately and cold-bloodedly kill everyone in that conference room, along with God knew how many other hundreds or even thousands in Daffodil House as well. And the destruction might not be finished. If he was to have a chance of living, Theo had to get out.

What was pinning his lower body, he finally realized, was not part of the roof but the dust-caked length of the conference table on which the mirror had sat, its legs gone, one end propped by debris. It was far too heavy for him to push it off, but by shoving at it until he was breathing in ragged gasps, Theo managed to get one of his legs loose. The whole limb throbbed and he had to wait some time in the increasingly smoky dimness until he could use it to help shift the conference table a bit off the other leg, make enough space that he could turn his foot sideways where it was hooked under the table's far edge. He rolled completely onto his side and wriggled until that foot was also free, then he lay panting for a moment until a coughing fit got him up onto his knees, retching and spitting bits of gray-white mud. He shrugged off his leather jacket and his thin fairy-shirt and tied the shirt across his mouth and nose like an outlaw's bandanna. It seemed to keep out a little of the smoke. He was going to leave the heavy jacket behind and let sentiment be damned, but a piece of flaming debris dropping down from above made him think again. Despite his exhaustion, he pulled the jacket back on.

Where's the door? The room was getting extremely hot now, like an oven just starting to work. He had a brief vision of himself baked as dry and powdery as the ash that covered him. *You can't catch me, I'm the Gingerbread Man . . .* Finding the door seemed an impossible task.

Debris lay everywhere, mountains of the stuff piled
jaggedly to the collapsed roof. He couldn't make out
where the walls were and which one was closest.

Groaning, coughing, Theo started to crawl. Within moments he put his hand down on someone else's hand.

Numbly, he scraped away at the dust and fragments of
ceiling, working his way up the arm to the face. He had
enough time for a dull shock of recognition before Tansy
opened his eyes behind his shattered spectacles. "Help
me . . ." the fairy whispered.

Theo looked at him for a moment. *Hellebore didn't want
me dead,* he realized. *He sent Tansy to get me out first, but
it went wrong.* Knowing that he was to have been spared was
no comfort. The Excisors wanted him alive, but probably
only so they could torture him for some information they
thought he had.

"Who is . . . ?" Tansy blinked away blood. "Help . . . !"

"Danger," murmured the hob from everywhere and
nowhere. *"Attack."*

Theo just shook his head and crawled on.

The idiot voice of the hob grew fainter and fainter and
then stopped at last as he made a painfully slow
progress across the room. Collapsed structural elements
were what made it difficult, the fallen beams and large
pieces of wall and ceiling which hung down or were piled in
front of him like abstract sculpture, but Theo dimly recognized that it could all have been much worse—although that
wasn't much solace. The interior of a modern fairy building
seemed mostly built of very light materials, which meant he
was digging his way through piles of shaped, very strong
glass, strips of wood, and metal hammered almost as thin as
gold leaf, all covered with a sifting snow of dust, instead of
through concrete and cast iron. Still, by the time he had
reached the door he felt as though he'd moved several hundred cubic feet of rubbish. He was sweating from the heat
beating down from the burning floors above, but periodic

showers of smoldering fragments from the dark spaces above made him glad he'd put the jacket back on.

Once or twice he thought he heard Tansy moaning in the rubble behind him, but it wasn't as hard to ignore as he had thought it might be: even with the hob silent, Theo's head was still full of yammering voices.

It took him a few minutes to get the office door open when he finally reached it—the whole floor seemed to have gone slightly out of true. The corridor ceiling had also collapsed. As he made his way out on his hands and knees into the wreckage and smoke he found bodies, all motionless and pretty clearly dead—half a dozen fairies, all full-size, who had been caught in the corridor when the ceiling had come down. He paused to peer through the floating dust, trying to decide which end of the hall was closer, but it was useless. He could only pick a direction and start crawling over and around the obstacles and past the silent victims, some of which were no more than feet or hands sticking out from under heavy wooden beams.

The smoke was getting thicker and the voices inside him were growing strong again, too, nattering away without much regard to what was really going on, like a bus full of querulous old people stopped by the roadside. He heard Cat talking about his many failures, Applecore calling him shallow. He heard Tansy's contempt and Lord Daffodil's scorn.

They all want me to die. A waste of space. He felt sorry for himself, because they were probably going to get their wish. But it hadn't always been that way. Everyone had always known he could make something out of his music. He had sung, and people had sat and listened, or stood and cheered. Even when he was back in elementary school the teachers had sent home notes, put it on report cards, *"Theo sings like an angel . . ."*

Or like a fairy. So was even that to be taken away from him? It turned out he wasn't special, he was just from another species. *But Poppy liked my voice . . . She said so, and she's never heard anyone else but fairies . . .*

The smoke was getting so thick that he kept forgetting where he was, kept thinking it was fog, that he was on one of the hills back home in San Francisco watching it roll down out of the west. Or back in his cabin with the trees turning misty and ghostlike outside . . .

Simply to make some homely noise, he coughed dust out of his mouth and throat and began to sing the first thing that came into his mind:

> *". . . But . . . I'll sing no more now . . . 'til I get a drink.*
> *For I'm drunk today . . . and I'm rarely sober . . ."*

He barely made a sound at first, just a hiss of air with words, muffled by the shirt tied across his face. He found a bit of strength, coughed, and went on a little louder.

> *". . . A handsome rover from town to town.*
> *Ah, but I'm sick now, and my days are numbered.*
> *So come all ye young men and lay me down."*

It was the old tune he'd sung to his mother as she lay dying. It didn't make a very brave sound—his voice was an unintelligible muddy croak and every syllable scraped his throat like steel wool—but it was a sound, something other than the internal drone of horror. He dug away at the wreckage and sang in a voice not much above a whisper.

> *"I wish I was in Carrickfergus,*
> *Only for nights in Ballygrand.*
> *I would swim over the deepest ocean,*
> *The deepest ocean, my love to find . . ."*

An ocean. It would definitely be worth drowning if he could do it in blessed, cool water, just open his mouth and swallow it down . . .

He looked up, blearily aware something had changed. He was having so much trouble clearing the four-foot section of collapsed ceiling in front of him that he had failed to realize that what it was snagged on was a door handle.

Door handle.

Like Saul's revelation on the road to Damascus, it seemed blinding. Door handle. Which meant . . . door. A door. He had reached the end of the corridor.

He managed to slide the sheet of ceiling material to one side before lifting it again and this time he was able to get it upright then push it away so that it toppled onto some of the other rubbish that had accumulated at the end of the hall. Now he could see the actual handle, covered with dust like a tomb-artifact. His fingers curled around it. *Opens in, that's what I need. Please, God, make it open in. If it opens in toward me, that means . . . what does it mean, again?* He fought to keep his mind from wandering away and leaving him alone. *Right. That will mean it's an exit—the stairwell, probably. But if it opens away from me, it's another office.*

He couldn't bear to think about that much. He twisted the handle and pulled. It didn't open.

For long moments he sat in the dust, completely devastated, his eyes blurring with gritty tears. He turned and pushed but when that didn't work either he succumbed to a twinge of hope.

Maybe it's an out door and it just jammed.

He set his legs, grabbed the handle in both hands, and pulled hard. It didn't open, but he thought he felt the smallest little tremor, something wanting to budge that couldn't quite. Delusion—a dying man's self-delusion, that was what it had to be. But he squatted again, got a grip on the handle, and then set one foot against the doorframe. He pulled, straining for breath, almost screaming with the effort. The door popped open with one swift crunch like a bone breaking and in that moment he felt he could hear a sudden choir of angels drowning out all other voices in his head.

The stairway was nearly as full of rubble, dust, and smoke as the hallway, but he could see a way down through the leaning timbers. Hundreds or even thousands of the little golden beetles were on the stairs already, pouring out of broken pipes and then forming themselves into semi-orderly lines that went nowhere, pooling against obstacles, driven by some instinct he could not understand. In fact, their headless determination reminded Theo of himself. He would have laughed but his throat and lungs felt like they were full of singed wool.

Only a couple of floors to the ground, he told himself. *Don't lose it yet, man.*

He was halfway down the first set of stairs when something above him collapsed with a sound like a bomb going off, an impact that knocked him to the floor. The dust clouds billowed with the pressure change and his ears buzzed, a high foul tone that didn't go away again and made him feel sick to his stomach. He sucked air through his improvised mask and waited to be crushed into jelly, but again, Death seemed to be holding back—a giant skeletal fist trembling over his head. He clambered to his feet and began staggering down the stairs again.

What am I doing in the middle of all this? I'm a singer— a goddamn singer! I'm not even one of the guys that plays the guitar . . .

As the ringing in his skull finally began to die down new voices surrounded him, disembodied like the hob but not utilitarian, humming, chanting, even singing, a hundred different keys, a cacophony. He couldn't help wondering if something had fallen on his head and this was a symptom of brain damage or just some broken magic of Daffodil House spewing like a plumbing leak.

At the bottom of four flights of stairs that each seemed a mile long, he found himself in front of another door. Now, to his slow astonishment, he realized he was hearing voices that originated outside his head—real voices, loud and rough and fearful. He slipped and fell on the landing, then got up and pulled the door open, only to be nearly trampled by three dust-covered figures in the gray body-armor of police constables, their hooded silhouettes so bulky and distorted beneath their dusty cloaks that for a moment he took them for ogres.

One of them grabbed him, a hard clutch on his upper arm that made Theo cry out even as he marveled at the existence of other living people. Beneath the hood and the dust the constable was wearing prismed goggles like the compound eyes of a fly. A small shape holding a tiny glowing sphere hovered just above the constable's shoulder, dressed in a bubble-mask and blast suit like a toy space alien. Theo guessed it was some kind of rescue-sprite. One of Applecore's kin.

"Is there anyone else up there?" the constable shouted. "Anyone alive?"

"I don't know." The shirt over his face muffled his words and he had to say it again, louder. *Applecore,* he thought suddenly. *My God, where is she?*

"Right. Get out." His interrogator steered Theo roughly through the doorway. "Go on! Straight down that hall and then up into the lobby!" The constables pushed past him and started up the stairs.

Tingling, almost hyperventilating with relief, Theo hurried along the hallway. He would live. Much of the rubble had been pushed against the walls, leaving the way clear. He would escape out into the air. He would escape the dust and smoke and the moaning phantom voices and the horror, run away from this ruined place and keep running, didn't matter where, until he could breathe. Until he could sleep . . .

The hallway branched. There was a sign in the illegible fairy-script that he somehow could always read: *Lobby,* it proclaimed, with an arrow pointing the way to life and freedom like the kindly hand of a guardian angel. The cross-corridor sign read: *Daffodil House Tower.* It also had an arrow.

He paused without at first knowing why. Where had Applecore been when that . . . that horror had happened? Outside—or at least that was what he wanted to believe. She must have gone outside, she must have—that was the

message she had left for him before he went to the conference center. The sprite was no idiot, either: if she had been
anywhere out of the building she would have seen that thing
coming through the air, that terrible winged shadow, and she
would have gotten the hell out of Dodge City. Of course she
would have.

But as Theo started into the corridor leading to the lobby,
another thought struck him. *Even if she did spot Tansy, she
didn't follow him into the conference center where I was.
What if she went upstairs to the big meeting, instead?*

He stood at the place where the corridors crossed. *If she
went up there, she's dead and there's nothing I can do. If
she's outside, she may have lived, but there's nothing I can
do until I get out there. Where else could she be?*

The comb. He didn't want to think about it, but he
couldn't push it away. *The comb underneath Daffodil
House.* He had no idea what had happened to the main
tower, but he found it hard to believe that Hellebore and his
allies would leave that proud, tall symbol alone. What if she
had gone back to the comb? What if she needed help?

No, it was foolish even to think about it. Go into another
damaged building to look for a person who probably wasn't
even there, and would be almost impossible to find if she
was? But even with his head buzzing and all his limbs
achingly exhausted, Theo could not forget how she had
flown against that undead thing like the world's bravest
hummingbird, trying to save his miserable life with nothing
but a corkscrew. And he could not forget her on the train,
staying with him to the bitter end, huddled under his shirt
even as the constables and the horrid, sluglike hollow-men
approached. What had she owed him? Nothing. What did he
owe her? Everything.

Just head up that corridor to the lobby, you idiot, the sensible part of his brain told him. *She's probably outside, and
if she isn't, what could you do anyway?*

Shallow. The word jumped up like the blackest curse.

Shallow. He could feel himself, all surface, empty as a plaster statue. *Heartless. Gutless.*

Better to be shallow than dead.

What else do I have, though? What am I holding onto? I'm not even human, I'm some kind of unwanted, rummage-sale fairy. She's my friend.

He turned around again and stepped into the corridor with the *Daffodil House Tower* sign. Maybe the main tower had escaped the worst damage, he told himself without quite believing it. It would have been the conference center Hellebore and those other sons of bitches really wanted, wouldn't it? All their enemies gathered in one place. Theo was shaken to dizziness by a sudden flashback of the meeting room collapsing in a gush of molten glass and billowing flames, of what must have happened to Lady Aemilia Jonquil and Hollyhock and even Spunkie Walter, working on a holiday. . . .

Because it was mostly empty of rubble, anyone who had been in the offices along the corridor between the conference center and the main tower had not lingered: the doors gaped open on either side and the long hall was empty except for a fine haze of dust. After he had gone perhaps a hundred paces he reached a wider place where four other corridors radiated out, making a five-pointed star of hallways, not counting the smooth-sided vertical shaft that led upward from the crossing-point to some kind of skylight window at the surface a dozen yards away. Theo could see that it was dark outside now, a deep gloom pierced by beams of greenish-gold light filtering through the dusty murk. He didn't know whether the sun had actually set or the air outside was simply black with smoke. Either way it was depressing and disorienting: he had no idea what time or even day it was, could not guess how long he had been struggling to escape.

Only a few dozen paces beyond the star-crossing the corridor began to get hot and Theo began to have a pretty bad feeling about what might have happened to the main tower above his head. Within twenty more steps he was sweating

profusely. Then the corridor dead-ended in a wall of gently
smoking rubbish where the ceiling had collapsed.

Oh, my God. Here, too.

He stood, swaying. It seemed clear that the destruction
above must be general, and that it extended all the way down
to this place, a floor beneath ground level. Which meant that
he had just forced his way into the most dangerous parts of
another crippled building.

But it's not as bad down here as where I was before. He
clung to that thought. *She might be trapped in there and the
doors are just stuck closed.* No more time to stand around: it
was painfully hot and seemed to be getting worse. He pulled
his jacket sleeve over his fingers and gingerly touched the
vertical rubble, looking for a safe place to apply pressure,
but it did not move when he shoved it. He turned and retreated back up the corridor.

Theo tightened the shirt over his mouth and wiped at his
streaming eyes as he reached the five-way crossing. He
chose one of the two closest corridors and followed it until
he again reached another spot where deadfall from the ceiling sent him back.

Golden beetles with charred shells dropped from the
crevices above, pattering on his shoulders and head, crunching underfoot when he walked. At least the humming,
buzzing voice-leak had finally gone silent, dying as the hob-
voice had died. He chose another corridor and followed a
succession of twisting passageways, struggling to keep himself focused on which direction was the one he wanted, but
he hadn't had time to learn much about the main house
tower's geography and it was even more baffling from underneath. He stopped at another ragged wall of collapsed
ceiling, heartsick and exhausted, but just as he was about to
turn back once more he saw that one of the open doorways
on the edge of the destruction led to a short passageway and
another door.

Theo fought through the debris, protecting himself with
the jacket as he pushed heavy pieces of beam out of the way,

their charred edges still glowing in places. When he reached
the other door he found it was blocked by an obstacle on the
far side, but at last he managed to shove it open. An arm fell
across the gap as he stepped through; he almost tripped over
it and fell down another set of stairs. The fairy-corpse at his
feet had been crushed by a large chunk of metal from above,
which after doing its murderous work had tumbled on down
the open stairway. The air duct or whatever it was had finally
lodged about halfway down the steps, a black-smudged clot
of silver.

Neither corpse nor fallen duct held his attention very long:
beyond and below, spread across the massive chamber and visible only because much of the smoke was being drawn up into
the ruined ceiling, lay a bewildering panorama of devastation.

Theo's first thought was that somehow, through some incomprehensible fairy-magic, he had stepped right out of
Daffodil House and was viewing the great complex's destruction from some perch high above. It took a moment to
realize that what he was seeing instead was an accidental reflection in miniature.

The ceiling of the huge, vaulted room that contained Daffodil Comb had come down in a tumult of flaming beams
and shattered ducts and material, smashing the center of the
comb flat and setting the remnants on fire: tongues of flame
still leaped toward the ruined ceiling, filling the air with a
swirl of ash and sparks, a storm of white flecks and orange
glitter, so that the wide space seemed like nothing so much
as a souvenir snowglobe out of Hell's giftshop. Bodies were
scattered everywhere, on the floor and in the rubble. A dozen
or so were Theo's size, ordinary fairies who had been visiting the comb for work or social reasons, but the ghastly majority were pixies and sprites and other small creatures,
uncountable hundreds or even thousands of tiny bodies
burned black, translucent wings curled and crisped, so that
what had been an entire city of speaking, singing people
now looked like drifts of dead flies. But not all had died in
the first destruction: small cries of shock and pain filled the

air, and Theo finally realized that what swirled through the
chamber was more than bits of fiery ash, that the upper
reaches were full of tiny, awkwardly fluttering shapes, some
of them actually aflame, others just beginning to smolder—
flying sparks hunting madly for escape but instead being
sucked upward by the hot drafts. Others that had managed to
stay below the updrafts were battering themselves against
doors and walls as they died, blind and brainless. It began to
seem like half of the million sparks that filled the air were
dying fairies.

Theo stumbled down the stairs, batting out the flecks of
burning ash that settled in his hair and threatened his eyes,
but he already knew it was hopeless: the heat was too intense. He could not stay in the burning room long enough to
reach the worst of the destruction, let alone search in that
horrid, charred pile for one little body. He felt as though his
eyes were coming out of his head, raw and so dry he could
not even blink. The smell was terrible.

He stopped when he reached the floor. A great piece of
burning beam fell from the hole in the roof and clattered into
the rubble of the comb, sending up a massive plume of
sparks and flame. In the momentary glare he saw that someone was kneeling on the ground not far away—someone his
own size. Although debris had fallen very near and floating
embers were settling on the figure's back, the fairy did not
look badly burned. He was even moving, although very
slowly, trying to pull himself across the ground.

"Stay there!" Theo shouted, but it came out as a garbled
yelp. He pulled the shirt away from his mouth so he could
make himself understood. "I'll help you!" The figure's head
came up and glanced around, half-blinded by the smoke. To
Theo's astonishment, he recognized him. *"Cumber?"*

He crossed the floor as quickly as he could, leaping over
piles of burning debris, edging around those that were too
large to vault, struggling to stay upright, blocking any
thought about what was crunching and smearing underneath
his feet. He reached the ferisher's side and dragged him up-

right, ignoring the protests of his own agonized muscles. Cumber Sedge looked at Theo for a long, stunned moment without seeming to recognize him.

"Come on, it's me—Theo! I'll help you. Can you walk?"

"My leg—something fell on it." Cumber took another step and almost fell. Theo got under his shoulder.

"Yeah, me too. You forget about it after a while. Hold on."

They went staggering back through the smoke like some sickly two-headed, three-and-a-half-legged monster. It was incredibly difficult for Theo to pull the fairy up the stairs— Cumber was nowhere near his size, but he was no thing of swansdown and dandelion fluff, either. Something buzzed past Theo's face whimpering and trailing sparks. The ceiling groaned and another large piece shifted and then smashed down, throwing gobbets of fire past them as they struggled to mount to the landing.

"They killed everyone," Cumber said sadly. "Everyone."

"Not you and me," Theo said through clenched teeth. He was beginning to think he'd have to put the ferisher over his shoulders. "Not yet."

The most difficult part was getting past the lump of metal that had killed the fairy at the top of the stairs. It had over-balanced since Theo had passed and rolled down another length of stairway and was now wedged crossways across the steps. Theo's only option was to climb past it himself, then lean back and try to help Cumber Sedge over the obstruction.

As the ferisher was struggling to climb over the hot metal, the duct began to shift again. Cumber more or less leaped off the chunk of metal, gasping with pain, just as it shifted, slid, and then tumbled on down the stairs to the fiery floor of the Daffodil Comb chamber.

Theo just stepped over the corpse at the top of the landing, but Cumber Sedge balked, although he had been surrounded by charred bodies only moments earlier.

"The rest of the roof is going to come down any second," Theo told him. "Step through this door or I'll slug you and

drag you." He had actually raised his hand—he was coughing and his eyes were so teary he could hardly see, but he
was definitely going to do it—when Cumber swallowed and
stepped over the ruined body.

"That was Drift Burdock," he said as Theo pulled him
through the doorway. "I've known him since I was small. He
worked with my mother."

"We're heading for the stairs." There was nothing else to
say, really. Theo got under Cumber's arm again, hobbling
with him toward the star-shaped crossing. Behind them
something began growling in such a deep voice that for a
terrified instant Theo thought that the winged shadow, the
dragon, had returned, had come down to the ground and
forced its way into the vast room behind them. Then the
walls of the corridor shook hard, the floor bounced, and the
growl became a crackling groan. "The ceiling!" Theo
shouted. He bent and got hold of Cumber Sedge as best he
could, draping him awkwardly over his shoulder, then ran,
his heart swelling in his chest until he thought his ribs would
explode outward. He made only a dozen steps before there
was a loud scraping, squealing sound followed by a titanic
slam and a blast of hot air from behind them. The floor convulsed beneath their feet and Theo pitched over, Cumber
falling awkwardly beneath him.

After a few dazed seconds, when the rest of the roof and
walls had not come down on top of them, Theo dragged
Cumber up and hurried him toward the only place that he
knew for certain led up and out to safety.

By the time they reached the stairs leading to the conference center lobby, smoke was roiling around their feet like
swamp-mist. Cumber, dazed and in great pain, wanted to
stop to get his breath, but Theo would not allow it.

The last moments went like a falling dream, like the instant between realizing you were about to be in a car accident and the first smash of metal on metal. As they staggered
up out of the stairwell Theo saw that the lobby was full of
people, mostly hooded constables helping victims out to-

ward the open doors, but all those other living creatures might as well have been in some kind of parallel dimension, a place that although visible had nothing to do with Theo Vilmos. His only thought, the one thing that kept his legs driving, was to get out of the building, to reach air and light and to have nothing above his head but sky.

A huge daffodil made of wood and gold leaf had fallen from the wall and shattered, flinging pieces everywhere; it seemed an exhausting insult at this late point to have to lift his weary legs over the fragments, but he did. They stumbled out of the doors to stand stunned beneath black sky and the burning hulk of the main tower, the flames reflected a thousand times in the windows of Daffodil House's other buildings. The shorter, slenderer tower of Narcissus House was standing almost untouched just a few hundred feet away, although many of the windows were broken and some leaked smoke. The grotesque scene should have looked like something out of Dante—it *did* look like something out of Dante—but to Theo it was beautiful beyond description. It was the world again, the open sky, things he had been certain many times in the last hours were now lost to him forever.

They let hoarse-voiced constables shove them away from the door. Cumber disengaged himself and limped along unsupported. Theo smelled air that didn't have smoke in it, or at least that had more air than smoke.

Escape, he thought, blurry and tired, struggling to make something of his rattling thoughts. *I'm out. I'm alive. Now what?*

He couldn't think of much of anything that mattered, except taking a long, cool shower and then sleeping for a hundred years.

26

LOSING A FRIEND

The air outside was almost as smoky as what had been choking him inside the buildings, but when Theo could stop coughing for a moment it seemed almost deliciously pure, the breath of angels. He unknotted the sooty shirt around his face and threw it to the ground, then stood sucking in the wonderful stuff. He resolved to celebrate every single breath he ever took for the rest of his life.

Rivulets of golden beetles scuttled over the walls that still stood and across the ground, crackling under his feet as he trudged away from the conference center doors. Giant emergency lanterns had been set up all through the grounds of the Daffodil House gardens, out of reach of most of the falling debris, their lamps roofed over with lenses that beamed their mustard-colored light upward through the dark, swirling pall. Shouting constables and singed and dust-smeared victims were everywhere, as purposeless as the golden bugs except for one group of about a dozen fairies in long gray robes who stood in a circle at the farthest edge of the open space around the building, waving their arms in the air and singing. Some kind of religious group, he assumed, the fairy equivalent of the Salvation Army praying at a disaster scene, but then he heard a rumble of true thunder from high overhead and felt a spattering of rain on his face, and just at that moment the singing jumped up a key. Not holy-rollers, then, but a fairy version of the volunteer fire department, perhaps, their true mission meteorological rather than missionary. Theo shook his head. Time after time Faerie had almost killed him, yet he still understood so little about this place! But he could not afford to stand, dazedly watching them—he was still too close to the two most badly damaged buildings, the conference center and the main tower which seemed to be barely holding together. Bits of roof and façade came whirling down at intervals from the spotlight-painted heights to shatter against the ground, deadly as grenades.

With Cumber still in tow Theo staggered out toward the Daffodil House gardens and at last fell to his knees to retch up what felt like pounds of soot, coughing so hard that he could only lie on the ground when he had finished, too dizzy and weak to get up. For a long time he lay gasping, watching sparks drift past as he slid in and out of a fractured near-sleep while Cumber sat beside him, mumbling to himself and moaning. At last a female fairy appeared out of the murk, her eyes wide but her ash-smeared face wearily blank. She handed each of them what looked like an expensive goblet before she wandered off again into the near-darkness and the new rain. Theo sat up and drank a little of the water, coughed most of it up, then drank again. For a brief moment his entire life was in that silvery thread of water running down his throat, a thing of indescribable sweetness and wonder.

As he sat, feeling for the first time in hours that there might be some point to being alive, another shape came staggering toward them like a broken toy. *That poor bastard's in worse shape than we are,* was all Theo had time to think, then the wind pushed the smoke away and he could see a familiar face. For a moment he thought he must be wrong, fooled by the dim light, but as the figure came closer, ten paces away, nine, eight, he grew certain. Stunned and exhausted, he could not think of the name or remember why this sudden visitation should seem so unlikely, but he did know that filmy-eyed face, he did.

"Iron and blood," Cumber groaned, watching the approach. "Look at that poor bastard. He's been blinded."

"It's him," Theo said, almost too quiet to hear himself. "It's Tansy's cousin." A moment later the name came back too, but so did the memory of Rufinus weft-Daisy being stabbed to death in Penumbra Station. Before Theo could speak again, Rufinus' long coat flapped open to reveal the wrinkled, black-rimmed gape where the slit belly had collapsed inward and Theo felt an electrifying terror run through him. This was not Rufinus but something that wore his body, and Theo knew exactly what it was.

The dead thing came straight toward him. Air hissed through its gaping mouth as the hands came up, shriveled fingers flexing. Theo scrambled to his feet and tripped over Cumber Sedge. A moment later the corpse was on him, clutching at him with idiot strength. So frightened he could not shout for help, Theo smashed at the familiar but empty face that loomed over him, slamming his hand against it until he felt bones crack, but although he forced a belch of carrion air out if it, the thing did not lose its grip. The hands on his neck were icy cold. He grabbed at its body, trying desperately to push it away, and gobbets of flesh came loose in his hands like boiled chicken. The clutch on his throat grew colder, seemed to bury his thoughts in frost, turn his muscles into silt bleeding from the bank of an icy river. He could see nothing, think of nothing but the slack-skinned face . . .

Abruptly the fingers came off his neck and the living corpse tumbled from on top of him. He could hear Cumber's frightened grunting as the ferisher beat at the thing's head with his water goblet. Theo rolled over, gasping for breath but strangely dreamy and slow-minded as he watched the thing fight back in near-silence. It clutched doggedly at Cumber Sedge's scorched pants legs, crawling up him even as the whimpering fairy beat its head—the head that had once been Rufinus weft-Daisy's, and which still had the look of a grisly caricature—into a shapeless knob.

Shaking off the frost on his thoughts, Theo crawled across the ground and tackled the dead thing, which pulled Cumber down as well. For a moment they both thrashed in panic, tangled in each other as well as their clawing, relentless adversary. Theo got away first and kicked the thing as hard as he could, felt ribs break underneath the mummified flesh. He kicked it again and again until it had to let go of Cumber to protect itself, curling like a silent, stinking spider, but even after the ferisher was free Theo kept kicking it in a screaming fury of horror and disgust, kicking the torso into broken meat and fragmented bone, until Cumber Sedge yanked him away.

"It's dead now!" the ferisher told him. "It's dead!"

"It . . . was . . . already . . . dead," Theo gasped. He pulled free and kicked it again. The thing's eyes seemed completely dimmed now, the body finally motionless. "Hurry up," he said. "We have to get out of here." He grabbed at Cumber and began to pull him away from the body.

"Wait," Cumber said, "you need help. You're bleeding . . . !"

Another shape appeared out of the murk and stopped beside the huddled thing on the ground. "Here, what's going on—what have you done?" the newcomer growled at them. "Come back!"

"It's a constable," Cumber said, relieved. "Hold on, he'll help us . . . !"

Theo had no strength to spare on such nonsense. He sped to a staggering trot, tugging Cumber Sedge after him.

"That man attacked us!" Cumber shouted back at the constable; he was dragging at Theo's arm, trying to slow him down. "We didn't want to . . ."

"Shut up. Where do we go?" Theo demanded. Cumber was still staring. Theo looked back and wished he hadn't. The constable was kneeling over the body on the ground, and for a moment it appeared that he was giving the victim the kiss of life, but the thing's ragged arm was around his neck, holding him in place, and it was the constable who was twitching and struggling. "Oh, sweet Jesus," Theo murmured.

Cumber ran on half-heartedly, still staring back at the bizarre scene. "But what's . . . ?"

"It's taking a new body!"

"New body . . . ?"

Theo slowed down until Cumber Sedge was in front of him, then gave the ferisher a rough push that made him stumble and almost fall. "Damn you—run! That wasn't a person! It's that corpse-thing that already tried to kill me once!"

They had only gone half a hundred yards when the dark, bulky shape of the constable stood up and let Rufinus' limp body slump to the ground like a sack of rubbish. The constable swiveled his head in a very unnatural way until he located Theo and Cumber; then, like a mechanical toy or an insect, he turned the rest of his body to face the same direction before starting after them at a heavy, awkward trot.

Theo put his hand on Cumber's backbone and shoved him forward, propelling the ferisher back toward the smoking, spotlit hulk of the Daffodil House conference center and the greater safety of other people.

But would the frightened constables trying to save lives at a disaster site intervene to save him from what looked like one of their own? Even in his exhaustion and confusion Theo could see that it was much more likely they would hold him up long enough for the thing to catch him. As he suddenly veered from the glaring lights and confusion near the front door, Cumber slammed against him and they almost fell down. He looked back and saw the constable-shaped thing had narrowed the distance to only a few dozen yards.

"Where do we go?"

"There!" Cumber pointed to a door in what looked like a small hut or a public restroom just to the side of the looming outer wall of Daffodil House.

"Are you crazy? We'll be . . . trapped in there . . . !"

"Do what I say!" Cumber bumped him toward the door. Theo scrabbled it open and they plunged through onto a small landing, then almost fell down the stairs when the door closed behind them, sealing them in darkness.

"What the hell is this?"

"Down. Hold onto the railing."

They had reached the bottom of the fourth short flight when Theo heard the door groan open above them and the first sounds of booted feet on the stairs. He and Cumber spilled off the bottom landing and out into a flat space. Suddenly a greenish light leaped out all around them: Cumber had produced one of the small glowing spheres from his pocket. They were in a vast room, low but wide, and they were entirely surrounded by . . . parked cars.

"A garage? We're going to die in a garage?" A sudden spark of hope flickered through him. "A car—you have a car here!"

"No," said Cumber. "But there's a way out of here that leads to the other side of the grounds. This way!"

They stumbled to the far side of the garage, but when they pulled open Cumber's escape door it was to find the corridor full of smoking wreckage from above, the way blocked. Their pursuer had just come down off the stairs at the far side and started across the garage floor toward them, boots knocking echoes, a stone-faced, stiff-legged shadow.

Theo turned to the smoldering wrack, hoping that at least he could find a piece of burning wood to use as a weapon. Comic books and fairy tales and movie images flickered through his head—*a torch, they're scared of fire, monsters are scared of fire, aren't they?*—then Cumber began to pull in a different direction.

"Over there! The main stairs!"

"Are you crazy? We'll just get trapped inside the building and it'll fall down on our fucking heads! At least here we might be able to get past that thing, get out into the air . . ." Theo didn't want to die in some hole like this and he certainly didn't want to die gasping for breath inside the smoking husk of Daffodil House after he'd fought so long to get out.

"No," Cumber shrieked, "the stairs go down! There's a stop for the train!"

Theo stared. The constable-thing was moving swiftly but not hurriedly. Its arms were spread wide, and for a hallucinatory moment Theo imagined them stretching to fill the garage from wall to wall. Cumber yanked his elbow so hard he almost fell over. Hopeless, helpless, he allowed himself to be pulled back across the open floor toward the blockhouse structure at its center. The door would be locked, Theo knew it as surely as he knew his own name. He would have to play hide-and-go-seek around the structure like the smart pig locked out of his brick house, the wolf getting closer and closer until exhaustion ground him down and the hungry thing grabbed him at last.

But the door was unlocked.

When they had slammed it behind them, Cumber wasted a few critical seconds searching for a latch that wasn't there. They gave up and headed down.

More stairs, tripping, stumbling, sometimes falling in the shaking, near-useless light of Cumber's torch. *Stairs. This is hell. Hell is stairs,* was all Theo could think. *I'd sell my soul for a goddamn elevator.*

But I don't have a soul, do I? I'm some kind of fairy.

Okay, settle for an escalator, then.

"Do you actually think there are going to be any trains?" he gasped. Above them, they heard the stairwell door rasp open.

"Of course there aren't going to be any trains with the complex on fire! But there are tracks . . . and tunnels and . . ." Cumber tripped and caught himself, moaned with pain.

"Your leg—I forgot." Theo got under his arm. "Do you want me to carry you?"

"You can't do it. Just help me. I'll manage."

Two more flights, both of them gasping now, then they skidded out onto a platform, slipped and got tangled and fell to their hands and knees. The dimming light of Cumber's globe showed a tunnel mouth at either end of the tiny station, dark holes that the swampy light could not pierce.

"Look, that thing doesn't want you," Theo whispered as he helped the ferisher up. They could hear the steady slap of footsteps coming down the stairs, still distant but magnified by the echo. "Just me. It probably won't even notice you. Just wait until it comes after me, then go back up the stairs."

"Shut up," said Cumber wearily. "You make a wretched hero. Let's get down onto the tracks."

"Which way?"

"Away from where half of Daffodil House has probably collapsed onto them, don't you think?" Cumber Sedge crawled to the edge of the platform and began trying to let himself down onto the siding a couple of yards below. Theo, who despite his countless bruises and aches and his raw-scraped lungs was in much better shape than his companion and at least a foot taller, hurried to climb down first so he could help him. Here was another one who hardly knew him, he could not help thinking, but was risking his life on Theo's behalf.

"Thanks," he whispered as he lowered the ferisher down to the tracks.

"Let's not die. That would be thanks enough."

Gravel crunched underneath their feet as they limped toward the tunnel, the greenish light wavering on the walls, making everything seem misshapen.

"Back home you have to worry about stepping on the electrified rail. Is there something like that here?"

Cumber snorted. "Nothing so easy to avoid."

"And you're really sure there won't be any trains running?"

"You'll hear them if I'm wrong."

Theo sneaked a look back. The little station platform was still empty.

The darkness began to grow thicker and thicker around them. Theo worried that the tunnel was filling with smoke, that he had breathed so much now he could not smell it or taste it anymore, could only guess the air was thinning by the dimming of his sight. "Shit," he said when he finally understood what was happening. "Your little flashlight thing. It's dying."

"It's not meant to be used this long. It's for taking notes in lecture hall." Cumber narrowed it from a glowing orb to something more like a flashlight beam, but it did not seem to grow any brighter.

And when it finally goes out? Theo could not help thinking. *When it's just us in this pitch-black tunnel . . . with that thing behind us . . . ?* He strained for the sound of boots crunching behind them, but their own dragging feet were making too much noise. He stopped so he could hear better.

"Blood and iron, have you lost your wits?" Cumber turned and staggered back, grabbed Theo's jacket, and pulled him hard. "It's either behind us or it isn't—what good is standing there listening going to do?"

Theo let himself be led forward again.

The light from Cumber's little globe had grown so faint that it took him a moment to notice that the roof of the tunnel was gone and that they were in the open again—or at least as open as anything could be this far underground. It was too dark to see much of anything, but he had the impression of vast spaces and thought he could smell something more primal than the tunnel smells, a yeasty funk primarily made up of mud and growing things and . . . water?

"It's a canal, a bit of Ys," Cumber confirmed. "Or rather, it's some tributaries that flow into Ys—it's all practically a sewer down here now."

"And think I see little lights out there, too." Theo squinted into the middle distance. The pinpoints of glow mounted up on either side of the track as though he and the ferisher were walking into some amphitheater built expressly for fireflies.

"It's Deeping Hollow, the kobold city," said Cumber.

"Well, not just kobolds—all kinds of folk who've lost their places in the city up top. Goblins, tommy-knockers, undocumented bogles . . ."

"Would they help us?"

"Are you joking? The only reason we haven't been robbed and murdered so far is probably because they're all terrified by what's been happening aboveground so they're lying low."

"Then where are we going?" Theo suddenly did not like the look of the clusters of small lights, and he liked even less the series of distant whistling cries that began a few moments later along the upper reaches of the invisible valley, like coyotes howling to each other from the tops of desert buttes.

"I don't know. But wherever it is, it has to be better than standing around and waiting for that dead thing to get you, doesn't it?"

Theo could only grunt. It had already been the murderous mother of all bad days to begin with, and now he had to drag his bone-weary body through the depths. He was tired of pain, tired of endlessly walking, tired of being pursued. He was tired of darkness. *I guess the only thing I'm not tired of is living,* he thought. *Which is why I'm doing all this other bullshit.*

The cries from the sparkling darkness in the upper reaches of the kobold city were getting louder and more insistent. Theo bent to pick up a few good throwing-stones from the bed of the railroad track and the blood that rushed to his head almost tumbled him over. Then, abruptly, the whistling noises changed pitch, became more frantic, more confused. A moment later, the invisible observers all fell quiet—a blanket of silence that started behind Theo and Cumber Sedge and rolled over them. Theo looked around in surprise as the countless tiny lights began to wink out.

"I think they just spotted our friend," whispered Cumber. "And they don't like him any more than we do."

Theo supposed he was grateful that at least the ambush

seemed to be on hold. He squinted back down the tracks,
trying to figure out where the sudden darkening of the lights
had begun. "It couldn't be more than a quarter of a mile,
maybe less," he whispered. "That thing's slow, but it never
stops—I don't think it even gets tired. Good God, it must
have walked halfway across Fairyland with its guts fallen
out just to get to Daffodil House . . . !" He turned back to the
track ahead of them and looked up, startled. By the fading
light of Cumber's globe he saw what seemed vertical towers
looming up only a short distance ahead of them. "What the
hell is *that?*" he hissed.

"Railroad bridge."

Theo didn't like walking on trestle bridges. He had almost been caught on one by a train while larking around
stoned in the Marin hills with Johnny and a couple of the
guys from one of their earlier bands, and although he had
laughed about it in later years, he had never shaken off the
memory of the few moments when he had not been certain
he would get off in time, when he had been forced to think
about jumping down forty or fifty feet into a rocky gorge.
Now another such bridge loomed right above them, the tres-
tles no more than a ghostly filigree, stretching away over an
expanse of dark water that the failing light could not even
touch, so black it might have been starless space.

"Do we have to go over it?"

"Unless you want to turn back and try to outwrestle that
thing that's following us, yes, I'd say we have to." Cumber's
voice was brittle with pain, but Theo was not going to be so
easily silenced.

"How long is it?"

"How long? I've only ever been over it on the train. Not
that long—a few hundred steps, I should think."

"Good." Theo clambered out from between the tracks
and started down the embankment at the side. "Then we
can swim across instead." He cocked his head to listen.
The waters below were almost silent—there couldn't be
much current.

"You are mad, you really are." Cumber staggered after him, clutched at his arm. "Look at this, Theo. Look!"

Theo couldn't understand what he was talking about. "Look at what? The bridge? I damn well see it!"

"No, look at what's on your wrist, fool." Cumber pushed up the sleeve of Theo's jacket, exposing the bracelet of grass. "That's a nymph-binding. Have you forgotten?"

Theo was nervous at how loud Cumber was getting. "Sort of, yeah. So what?"

"So what? You belong to the nymphs. The next time you get into any body of water bigger than a bathtub, you're theirs. No arguing. You won't be able to bargain your way out of it, either, unless you've been picking up some pretty fancy talismans on our little trip today and I just missed it."

"What are you saying? That . . . that I owe them my life or something? But I didn't agree to anything like that!"

"No, but Applecore did, to save you. A nymph-binding's an old loophole that gives you a chance to go find treasure to exchange for your servitude." He shook his head. "You may have fairy blood, Theo Vilmos, but you don't know anything, you really don't. Faerie works on bargains and agreements. Our science is all about agreements, not like that silly randomness they believe in your world. You ask, you get, you pay for it."

"So if I just dove in there . . . ?"

"Then whoever lived there would get to claim you. And I promise you, it wouldn't be a pretty little river-nymph like the ones Applecore saved you from, oh no. It would be something that lives deep in that black water and drinks and eats whatever the City spews out."

Now Theo was beginning to panic, and not just from the unpleasant picture Cumber was painting: they had been standing and talking far too long. "All right," he whispered, "you win! We can't swim. We'll have to cross the bridge. But let's hurry—that thing is going catch up with us any moment!"

They scrambled back up to the train tracks and onto the

trestle bridge, forcing their endlessly aching muscles into
yet another effort, stumbling every few steps. Theo did his
best not to think of the distance down to the water that
lapped at the pilings and what might swim beneath its
opaque surface. They had only gone a few dozen yards when
the tracks beneath their feet began to vibrate, a soft but distinct bumping that slowly grew louder.

"Footsteps?" Theo gasped. They looked back, but there
was no sign of their pursuer. Cumber then swung the light
around; nothing was visible ahead of them, either. Theo
turned and took a few steps back, peering into the distance.
The little globe still gave off enough light that he felt he
should be able to see anything that made so much racket.

"Theo . . ." Cumber sounded very strange.

He whirled to see a nightmare shape climbing up over the
side of the bridge in front of them, surprisingly nimble for
its huge bulk. It was vaguely humanoid, with pale, warty
skin that glowed like the underside of a luminous mush-
room. It looked only a little taller than a man but about five
times heavier: as it slouched confidently toward them it almost seemed to fill the bridge. It blinked a few times—its
eyes were small and black as raisins—but did not seem otherwise put off by their light. The creature's rubbery mouth
looked big enough to swallow Theo up to the shoulders. It
stopped in front of them, but its body continued moving for
a long moment afterward, like gelatin—it was hard to tell if
the bulbous creature was sagging with fat or whether its skin
merely bunched and accordioned like the folds of a rhinoc-
eros' hide. The only thing certain was that it was mon-
strously big and incredibly ugly, and that it stank like a tidal
flat.

"Yum," it said in a deep, bubbling voice. "Strangers on
my bridge. What have you brought me?"

"I've crossed this bridge on the train a hundred times and
never had to give you anything!" Cumber's righteous indig-
nation was undercut a bit by the quiver of terror in his
words.

"Ah, got a deal with the railroad, I have," the thing said cheerfully. "Family rights—we've had this bridge for centuries and I get my little slice, regular. But folk traveling on foot—that's a different matter. Tell you what, though," it said to Cumber, "you give me your chum's head, I'll let you have a free pass for three whole years." It leaned forward to examine Theo, who was rigid with fear and did not move a muscle even as the thing's dreadful breath washed across his face. "Well, two years," it said.

"We just need to go across this once," Cumber said. "We're being followed by something very, very bad."

"Worse than me?" The thing smiled, showing jagged teeth of many different lengths. "Come, now. You'll hurt an old troll's feelings."

"It might be," said Cumber, struggling to keep his voice even. "And it doesn't bargain."

"We'll see." The troll looked intrigued. "But first things first, if you're in a hurry." It scratched its chin—or the great shapeless pouch of leathery flesh where a chin should be—with a huge, cracked fingernail. "All right, then, I'm thinking . . ."

"Maybe you'd accept my rail pass?" Cumber asked hopefully.

The troll laughed, a sulfurous hiss. "Rail pass. That's a good one." It brought talon to chin again. "Tell you what. I can afford to be generous, since times have been good—not only my stipend from the railroad, but now that all these folk have moved down from aboveground there are always little ones playing on the tracks, so it's been a jubilee year for me. And if they're blowing each other apart up there, it will only get better. So I'll give you a bargain. A finger."

"A finger . . . ?" Theo had thought things were already at rockbottom. "You want to have a finger from one of us before you'll let us cross?" He darted a look back and was half-certain he could see something coming down the tracks toward them out of the dark distance.

"No, no. A finger from *each* of you. That's a very generous offer, you know. In the old days, I'd have just eaten one of you. At least one."

Theo stared at the nightmare beast crouched in its armor of pale folds like some kind of giant sumo toad. He had a moment's fantasy of simply running past it, but somehow knew without being told that it wouldn't be so easy. He also thought that the bargain might not be so agreeable after it caught him.

This is crazy! This is a bad dream . . . ! He looked back. Something *was* coming toward them out of the shadow, a moving bit of darkness; it was only a distant speck, but getting bigger every moment.

"All right," he said out loud. He felt suddenly cold all over, sick to his stomach. No good delaying. "You can take them from me." He stuck out his left hand, tried to make a joke despite his spiking terror. "At least I'm a singer, not a guitar player."

"He can take one from each of us," argued Cumber.

"Now *you* shut up. You wouldn't even be in this if it weren't for me."

A huge, bumpy hand with skin like damp rubber folded around his own so that only his fingers stuck out, his hand and wrist gripped as though by an industrial vise. "Oh, you sing, do you? If you're ever back this way, you should drop in again—I love music." The immense mouth yawned open and Theo stared in horrified fascination at the tangle of rotting teeth. How would he be able to wash himself down here, clean and bandage the wounds? What kind of horrible diseases would infect him? He couldn't look. He curled his middle finger and index finger to keep them away from that filthy maw, shut his eyes tight and concentrated on not throwing up as he waited, waited . . . waited . . .

He opened his eyes again. The massive face was close to his hand, but the horror-movie mouth was closed, as were the eyes. The thing was sniffing, or at least its two pinhole nostrils were twitching.

"What is that smell?" the troll rumbled. "Like cow, but . . . but different."

It took Theo a moment. "My leather jacket?"

"I've never smelled anything like it." It flared its nostrils and inhaled deeply. "Cowskin! But not like any I know."

"It's from the mortal world," said Cumber. "That skin comes off a cow from the mortal world. Very rare."

"It's . . . lovely. Makes my mouth water something fierce." The troll turned to stare at Theo over his prisoned hand. The little eyes narrowed again in a cunning squint. "Tell you what, not that your fingers aren't nice in their way . . . but I'd be willing to make do with only one in exchange for this piece of skin."

"No fingers," said Cumber. "You get the cowskin, but that's all."

For an absurd moment, Theo almost argued—his beloved jacket! He'd had it for years. Then he thought about how long he'd had his fingers.

"Well . . ." The troll frowned a doughy frown then released Theo's hand. "Right, then. A bargain."

Theo hastily shrugged off the jacket, but pulled out his great-uncle's notebook before he handed it over. "It's yours."

"Nice," the thing said in its deep, suety voice. "I'm not even going to eat it all at once. I'm going to savor it. Thanks. Say, if you ever pick up anything else like this, remember— I love to bargain . . . !"

But Theo and Cumber were already hurrying across the bridge as fast as their weary legs would carry them. It was only after they had left the bridge and its guardian far behind that Theo realized he had left Tansy's telephone-brooch in the pocket of his jacket. He had no plans to go back for it, of course: as far as Theo was concerned, that piece of two-legged ugliness was welcome to blow out Tansy's long-distance bill or download a ton of troll-porn and charge it to the Daisy commune.

Betray me, huh? Taste the Revenge of Vilmos!

They collapsed at last and lay gasping for a long time until they regained the energy even to sit up.

"Come on," Theo said at last, climbing slowly to his feet despite every muscle in his body shrieking at him not to do it. Cumber's globe was only a flicker of green now, no stronger than a nightlight in a child's bedroom. "We can't stay here. That thing was right behind us."

"But it has to cross the bridge to catch us."

"You don't understand how bad that thing is, how hard to stop." A sudden and unwanted memory of it coming through the screened bathroom window of his cabin like cheese through a grater weakened his legs so much he almost fell down again. "You have no idea."

"Perhaps," said Cumber, "but you're probably underestimating how difficult it is to get past a troll guarding its own bridge."

"What if it takes the troll's body, like it took that constable's?"

Cumber considered for a moment. "I don't know if that's even possible. If it is, it will be slower but a great deal stronger. But it would have real trouble following us above-ground, I think. A troll like that probably hasn't seen full daylight for centuries. It would be like making it walk through an oven of red-hot coals."

"That zombie-thing won't care—it probably doesn't even feel pain. It kept Rufinus' body even with all the insides fallen out."

"Yes, but it would also be very conspicuous—people would certainly notice a cave-troll stumbling around like that. Make it a lot harder for the thing to sneak up on us." He frowned as Theo helped him stand, then they began to walk rapidly along the tracks again. "Yes, I think we need to think about going back aboveground once more."

"But where do we go? Do you have some friends that . . . that could hide me?" He felt ashamed for asking—he had already brought this young fairy nothing but trouble and terrible danger.

"Not in the City—not anymore. I've never lived anywhere here but Daffodil House. Let me think. We certainly do need to find someplace safe—I can't believe that Hellebore and his cronies would stage a monstrous attack like that and then let everything else go on as normal. It must be an all-out Flower War. They'll have troops out rounding up their enemies, most of whom won't be seen again."

Not only am I the strangest stranger I could ever be, Theo thought as they limped along the tracks, listening always for the sound of pursuit. *Now I'm a fugitive, too. Everybody's trying to kill me. And at this very moment my favorite jacket that I've had since I was a teenager is being eaten like steak tartare.* A laugh came out that was half sob, or perhaps it was the other way around.

This has to be the worst fairy tale there ever goddamn was.

Cumber's globe of light had shrunk to the strength of a dying, green-glowing match by the time they found a worker's ladder leading up from a switching station to the surface. Wearier than he had ever been in his life, it took Theo half an hour to climb the one hundred or so rungs, pushing Cumber up ahead of him step by cautious, exhausted step. They emerged at last out of a service hut on an empty railroad siding beneath a muted dawn sky full of dark, sooty clouds. Surrounded by trees and hedges, they could see little of the city, but at least half a dozen vast pillars of smoke still rose to the heavens around them.

"They've burned all their enemies' houses down," Cumber whispered.

Too tired to speak more, they climbed down off the railroad embankment and found themselves in an industrial district, but one in which there were few signs of life; the only movement came from swirls of snowy ash picked up and dropped by the circling winds. They found a bus stop and waited with dumb hopefulness, but after a quarter of an hour it seemed obvious that no buses were coming.

"We have to put some room between ourselves and that

thing," Theo said. "We probably can't lose it completely—
it's already followed me all the way from my world, and it
certainly tracked me from the train station where it got Rufinus' body—but we can buy ourselves some time."

"Let's head for a main road," Cumber suggested.

It almost seemed a cruelty beyond any of the horrors
Theo had survived to have to walk again when he was so
tired and sore, to have to put one foot in front of the other.
The streets were so empty that he could not help wondering
if Hellebore and his army of Excisors hadn't done more than
simply attack their enemies, if they hadn't found some way
to destroy the entire populace of Faerie as well. But as
they moved into what seemed more of a commercial district
they saw a few signs of other living beings—a car passing at
the end of a street, faces peering out through upper windows, and finally a line of people waiting to get into a small
corner store—stocking up on necessities, Theo imagined.

Cumber abruptly hobbled out into the street, leaving
Theo to gape after him. A moment later a tiny little truck appeared out of a side street and began to head away, but Cumber caught up to it at a limping run and stood talking with
the driver for long moments, then waved Theo over.

"It's the end of the world," the little bearded fellow was
saying as Theo approached. His skin had a distinctly azure
cast and he had ears like a kangaroo rat. "Stone's honor. I'm
heading out toward Birch where my people are. You'd be
wise to get out, too."

The truck was of an appropriate size for its gnomish
owner: since Theo and Cumber could not fit in the tiny cab,
they stretched out on the bed of the truck, making themselves as comfortable as possible in the middle of a collection of weird tools and artifacts that seemed as though
they'd only be useful for sitting on top of other things to
keep those things from blowing away. The little truck moved
agonizingly slowly, but it was bliss not to walk and they
made fairly good time with so few other vehicles on the
road. The knotted black pillars of smoke seemed to stare

down at Theo like monstrous cobra gods, but even that could not keep him from sliding in and out of sleep as the little vehicle jounced its way across town.

He woke up, his head aching horribly, to find that the truck had stopped and Cumber was trying to get him to climb out of the back. The driver did not wait for thanks: as soon as they were both on the sidewalk he put it in gear and puttered away.

It seemed to be a public park. Theo did not care. He let Cumber lead him down a dirt path and then off the trail and into a grove of trees. They clambered into a tangle of ivy that blanketed a hillside and stopped. Within moments Theo had dropped into sleep like a stone falling down a well.

27

BUTTON'S
BRIDGE

His first dream was a surreal horror, chewing and chewing on something that fought against him, something that actually struggled in his mouth. He was full of dark rejoicing but also horrified by his own casual cruelty, simultaneously exalted and revolted. He passed on into other dreams that were more ordinary but no less dreadful, full of images of tiny bodies falling to dust in his clumsy hands, of a mulch of crisp black wings whispering beneath his feet like drifts of charred onionskin.

He woke up shivering beneath a sliver of moon. The world was cold and dark and he hurt all over. He was alone on a hillside, tangled up in ivy. He was alone.

"Cumber!" Theo's voice was a raw croak and the effort made him cough until the stars that should have been in the sky but weren't frolicked right in front of his eyes.

"Ssshhh." A shadow came toward him. "Don't make so much noise!"

"I thought you were gone."

"I've been looking for firewood. Well, and I've been out getting the news. Here, put this on." He tossed him a tattered, dirty thing that might have been a bedsheet; after a few puzzled moments of examination, Theo decided it was supposed to be a shirt. "I found it in a rubbish bin," Cumber explained.

Theo realized he was naked from the waist up. *Of course, my jacket . . .*

He pulled the shirt over his head. It was so big on him that he wondered if it had belonged to an ogre. "Getting the news? How?"

"You don't think you and I are the only folks hiding out in this park, do you? In fact, there are a lot more folk here than usual—not just the homeless ones, but all kinds of people who suddenly don't want to be in buildings anymore, who want to be under trees and sky like the old days. Everyone's terrified." Cumber sat and produced a small collection of twigs from his pockets. "I thought I'd never want to see anything else burning," he said. "But right now, I need a fire."

Theo sat in silence while the ferisher arranged the sticks, then took a piece of what looked like newspaper out of his pocket and rubbed it between his finger and thumb until the edges curled and began to burn. As he held it to the bits of bark he'd piled around the sticks, Theo asked, "Was that the paper? Or did you do that?"

"Make the spark?" Cumber shrugged. "I did. Quite an easy charm, really—you could probably do it yourself with only a little practice. But I couldn't have done it yesterday. Too sore, too tired to think."

"How are your legs?"

"Nothing broken, but they hurt and the burned parts itch like a gnome's knickers. How are you?"

"Miserable. Scared. Alive, though, and that's something." He stared at the small flames beginning to climb the pile of kindling. "What do we do now?"

Cumber Sedge shook his head. He had managed to clean some of the worst of the dust and soot from his yellow-brown face and looked almost like the young lab attendant he had been when Theo had first met him. "I don't know. It's chaos out there."

"What do you mean, 'out there'? Where are we?"

"Rade Park, in the Gloaming district. One of the biggest parks in the City—kind of a reminder of how things used to be, before Hellebore and the others—yes, good old Lord Daffodil too—tore down all of True Arden so the City could grow." He blinked. "It's hard to believe Daffodil is really dead, the old tyrant. Actually, he wasn't all bad. And Lady Jonquil was always kind to me, when she remembered I was there—I wonder if there's any chance . . . ?"

"No." It sounded harsher than Theo meant it to be. He reached out and gave the ferisher an awkward pat on the arm. "I'm sorry, but I don't think so. I saw what happened. Nobody got out of that meeting room alive."

"And Applecore . . . ?" Cumber Sedge seemed to be trying to keep hope out of his voice—out of his heart, too?

"She might have got out. Or not even been there when it went down. She left a message that she was going to go outside." A thought struck him. "Oh my sweet . . . of course! Applecore left me a message—said she saw someone I knew hanging around outside Daffodil House. I've been thinking she meant Tansy, but he said he didn't know anything about it . . ."

"I have no idea what you're talking about."

Theo explained his brief, brutal encounter with the treacherous Count Tansy. "So he was the one who set me up in the first place, it seems pretty clear. But that doesn't matter. What I was saying was that I thought Applecore meant *him*—that Tansy was who she'd seen. But it wasn't, it was his relative Rufinus she'd spotted, or anyway it was his body walking around. And of course she found that a bit surprising because the last time we'd seen him, well, he'd been pretty much dead as a doornail. So she went off to find out why someone we thought was on the ex-citizens list was hanging around out in front of Daffodil House." He nodded. "Makes sense."

"So you're saying she went to go have a better look at . . . that *thing?* The thing that tried to murder you? The thing that followed us?"

"Yeah, exactly." He sobered as he realized what the fer- isher was worrying about. They sat for a while in silence, staring at the flames. It was no good talking any more. They had little reason for hope, and nothing more practical to rely on. "So what did you hear while you were out getting wood?" Theo finally asked.

"It's war—the real thing." Cumber sighed and poked the fire. "The mirror-streams are full of it. Hellebore and Thorn- apple and their allies are claiming they only did it because they were going to be attacked, that it was self-defense. No- body believes them, of course, but no one's in a position to argue with them, either. They have Parliamentary troops out all over the city, looking for what they're calling 'conspira- tors,' which basically means anyone they consider an enemy."

"Like you and me."

Cumber smiled. "Well, like you. I could probably still plead ignorance and be allowed to go back to the country- side—find a job herding goats or something." His smile faded. "Unless the mere fact of knowing you makes me an enemy, too."

"I don't think you want to find out," Theo said. "I think the questioning would be very bad for you."

Cumber let out a long breath. "Well, then I guess I'm a fugitive too."

"So is that it? It's all over—Hellebore burned down his enemies' houses and now he's the winner?"

"Not quite that simple. For one thing, he's made a lot of the other houses rethink things, even if they're not going to say or do anything about it right now. After all, how could you trust someone who'd do that to three of his oldest allies? Hellebore and the other Excisors are on top right now, no question about that, but they're going to be like the old kings of the giants who murdered to get their thrones, then always had to sleep with one eye open, watching for the one who was coming to murder them in turn." Cumber spoke with grim satisfaction. "And that's not all. The rumors—the least

mad and unbelievable ones I've heard this evening, anyway—say that a lot of people got out of the houses or
weren't around when the attacks came, including Lady Jonquil's son, Zirus. The rumor is that he's found refuge with
another family, and even that he's planning to raise an army
and fight back. A study of history suggests that the first reports are nearly always wrong, but it could be that Hellebore
and the others haven't done as thorough a job as they'd
hoped."

"Well, it's not as if that's going to do *us* any good," Theo
said. "We don't have any influential friends. Of course,
Zirus seemed to have a fond spot for you. Would he take
us in?"

"Maybe. If we could find him. But of course, no one's
going to admit just now that Lord Daffodil's nephew is their
guest—not with Hellebore and Thornapple running the Parliament of Blooms like it was their own corner nectar-shop."

"So what do we do? Stay here?"

"Maybe for a day, but we're too vulnerable out here in the
woods. We don't know how long it will take that dead thing
to track you down, and this park has also got a bit of a werewolf problem at night during the best of times . . ."

"Say no more." Theo moved closer to the fire. The darkness of Fairyland, he had come to realize, not only might
harbor nearly anything you could imagine, it almost certainly did. "So what do they want, Hellebore and Thornapple and those people? We still don't know why they're
interested in me, either. Why go to all that trouble to try to
kidnap me out of Daffodil House?"

"Power. That's usually the reason for everything." Cumber sighed. "As to where you fit in, I can't even guess. I'm
used to reading about these things in histories or hearing
about them from survivors. I never wanted to *be* a survivor."

"Maybe not, but it beats the hell out of the alternatives."

"True." The ferisher held his slender hands up to the
warmth. "Well, whatever's going on, we can't stay. And
we can't wander the streets, either. Most people don't like

the Excisors, but they've got a firm grip on the City right now and there will be lots of folk interested in getting on their good side by turning in a couple of wanted fugitives."

Theo was thinking about werewolves now. He had already been thinking about walking corpses and wished he could have left it at just that, ghastly as it was. "God, it's cold. I can't believe you made me give away my jacket, Sedge. At least having fewer fingers wouldn't have made me any colder."

"That's gratitude for you." Cumber squinted at the lump in Theo's pants pocket. "What is that—if you don't mind my asking? I saw you take it out of the jacket."

"You already know what it is—my great-uncle's diary, notebook, whatever. I told you about it. I thought it was the reason that Hellebore's people wanted me, but now I know that's not true."

"You saved it?" Cumber brightened; he looked like a young boy holding his first Fourth of July sparkler. "That's wonderful news. Is there . . . do you think . . . would it be too much for me to ask to look at it?"

"Go ahead, knock yourself out." As Theo handed it to him, something small fell out and into his lap, a curl of white not much bigger than a receipt.

The ferisher stared at the book cradled in his lap with a sort of happy greed. "An actual record of a mortal's impressions of Faerie in the recent past! Mortal Studies is my specialty, you know—I've waited my whole life for something like this."

Theo lifted the piece of paper that had fluttered out of the book. He squinted, struggling to read it by the fire's flickering light. *"Beneath the old Fayfort Bridge.* What the hell *is* this?" Then it came back to him—the little bright-eyed creature on the bus. "Oh, right. A goblin gave it to me. I think it's some kind of mission or homeless shelter. Told me if I ever needed a place to stay . . ." He turned to Cumber. "Hey!"

The ferisher seemed more alarmed than pleased. *"Who* gave it to you? A goblin? Let me see that." He stared at the slip of paper as though he hoped to turn it into something else by force of will. "Fayfort Bridge—that's down by the Fenland, past Warstones, even—all the way on the other side of the City. And it's a terrible place, dangerous, full of poor people, criminals . . ."

"Are there werewolfs?"

"Were*wolves.*" Cumber pursed his lips. "No, of course not. It's down in the wetlands near the city docks."

"Well, that's enough to recommend it to me—no werewhatevers."

"But . . . goblins!"

"You know, you fairies have some real problems with prejudice." Theo even smiled, pleased to have some direction again, a destination. "No goblin has ever done anything bad to me. Why are you all so set against them?"

"I can't speak for anyone else," Cumber said primly, "but a group of them ate my great-grandmother. Surely that's reason for a bit of prejudice."

Theo woke to dawn and skies that were still black with smoke, fouled like a mountain pool trampled to muddiness. Cumber Sedge was building another small fire. "About time you woke up, considering you slept the day away yesterday," he said. "I've already been up and visiting some of our fellow nature lovers." He held up something that looked like a coffee can with the words "Wing-Kleer" on it in big white letters. "I brought back some water from the stream." He produced a wrinkled bag from his pocket. "Oh, and got us some bread, too—here, break your fast."

Theo hadn't realized how hungry he was until he put the heel of crusty bread into his mouth. He barely chewed before swallowing it down, then took his time with the second piece. "How did you get this? You said you didn't have any money." He looked at Cumber more carefully. "Hey, where are your shoes?"

"I don't really need them. In fact, a lot of people in Daffodil House thought it was pretty funny I even wore them.

Among the Flower-folk, there's an old expression for taming things up in a vulgar way—'You might as well put shoes on a ferisher.' Eat up. It's better than walking across the City on an empty stomach."

When Theo had emptied his bladder and they had put out the fire, fastidious Cumber insisted these be two separate activities, which Theo thought was a waste of water—he discovered that he actually could walk fairly well if he ignored the fact that he felt as though he had been run through some kind of industrial laundry-folding machine. "If I hurt this much, your leg must be killing you," he said to Cumber, wincing as he tried to get circulation into various suffering muscles.

"I'm not doing too badly. We ferishers heal quickly and we work hard without much complaint—that's why the nobility regard it as such a waste when one of us wants to use his mind instead. Come, let's get going. Luckily we can go some miles through the park without having to go near a public street." Cumber seemed to have shed some of his civilized pessimism along with his footwear—he seemed almost cheerful as they set off through the trees. The ground was still wet, steaming with mist; it was hard to tell where the hilltops left off and gray sky began.

"Explain to me again how your grandma got eaten by goblins. I kept nodding off."

Cumber sighed. "I wish you'd quit going on about that—it's not a particularly pleasant story. I told you, she was mostly unlucky. And it was my great-grandmother. She and her husband were . . . what would you call them? They wanted their own land, so they made a farm in a very wild area."

"Homesteaders, that's what we'd call them back home. Pioneers."

"I suppose. Anyway it wasn't all the goblins' fault. They were wild and it was their land, I suppose. This was just before the last goblin war. The local clan got into a dispute with my great-grandfather and he shot a few of them."

"With a gun? One of those . . . beehive things?"

"This was centuries and centuries ago, Theo. They didn't have modern weapons. It was an old-fashioned crossbow. Anyway, the goblins came back and attacked them. My great-grandfather got away but my great-grandmother was killed. So they ate her."

"Yeesh." Theo made a face. "I can see why you don't approve of them, I guess."

"Well, to be fair, they ate their own as well, if they were killed in a battle. Sort of an honor, I suppose. Perhaps they were even trying to show respect for old Great-Grandmother, by their lights. But my great-grandfather didn't take it that way."

"Wow. That's like one of those Old West movies or something. So why are there all these goblins in the City now? Do they still eat people?"

"Only as a mark of high honor, I'm told. And only their own kind." Cumber led Theo over a ridgetop where they had a fleeting glimpse of some of the City's highest towers, gold and rose in the smoky morning light, before they made their way down into cover again.

The highest towers that are still standing, he thought. His lighthearted mood evaporated.

"After the last goblin war," Cumber resumed, "when we had well and truly defeated them and the City began expanding out onto what had been goblin lands, there was a lot of argument about what to do with the goblin tribes. Some of the Flower families just wanted to do away with them, kill them all, but some of the more farsighted suggested that there would be a growing need for cheap labor. So the goblins were put to work. A lot were brought into the City itself in the last couple of centuries as the expansion began in earnest." He made an awkward gesture. "Now that things have slowed down, what with the energy shortages and all, there's not enough work for all of them, but they don't really have anywhere to go back to. It's a problem."

"But there are still some living wild, right? I saw some on the train, in Great Rowan."

"Grims?" Cumber looked surprised. "You saw grims in Great Rowan? Are you sure?"

"Yeah. Applecore saw them too." He pushed on past the moment's sad silence. "They looked like, I don't know, Genghis Khan's Mongols or something. Wild. Fierce."

"I don't know what Gengus Konsmongles are, but I've seen the grims too, out in Ash where most of those who didn't come into the City and into the towns still live." For a moment his eyes lost focus and he slowed his brisk pace. "Stirring, in a way."

"So your family were settlers, then? Country folk?"

Cumber laughed, a touch bitterly. "Oh, yes. Still are. Rustic as dirt."

"But you're, like, a college graduate or something."

This time he didn't even laugh. "You saw my back, Theo. Do you think the trade was worth it?"

"Good God, is that really the entrance requirement for fairy universities? And the kids back home think *they've* got it tough."

"It's not that straightforward, of course." Cumber shook his head, watching his own bare feet crunch through the undergrowth. This shoeless stuff didn't seem to bother him at all. "My mother came to the City from the Jonquils' country place—she was a favorite of Lady Aemilia's, kind of a pet. When she had me, well, of course she raised me here around her mistress' children, and Lady Aemilia indulged her. But I wasn't the same as the Flower children, and one of the most obvious ways to tell was that I had wings. They haven't had wings in the Daffodil Clan for several generations now, not even rudimentary throwbacks. So Mum saved up her money—she wouldn't even let Lady Aemilia help out! There's pride for you, won't even take charity to help mutilate your son. And I had the operation. But you know something, Theo? Even the ones who didn't see my back, even the first day I was at the Academy with Zirus and the rest, the other students knew. I was a ferisher, wasn't I, and ferishers are supposed to have little wings. They thought it was funny. Well, the nice ones did. Some of the others thought I was getting above my place and let me know it, regularly and forcefully."

Theo couldn't think of much to say. Except for occasional run-ins with the jock crowd, his cheerfully stoned high school days back at Hillsdale High didn't really compare.

"It's just the way things are," Cumber said. "Not much use complaining. They'll be worse, now, with Hellbore and his lot in charge."

"So I guess even before this, some folks weren't too happy with the way things are around here." Theo had barely ever considered Fairyland before winding up as an unwilling guest, let alone the real possibility of class warfare.

"All too true. But it hasn't always been like this. In the old days, things were a lot simpler. Everyone had his or her patch, and everything just sort of went on. Boring, maybe, but you didn't see gnome children begging on street corners. Things began to go bad when the king and queen died. That was really the start of the whole thing. The seven most powerful families—six now—got into power and began changing things right away." The sudden realization was painful to see. "*Three* families now. And probably before long it will be down to one. The Hellebore Empire."

Theo supposed that some things weren't that different from his own world. The people in power were always trying to get more of it. It wasn't enough to be eating the best meat while the rest of the population chewed old bones. The big dogs all seemed to have the same secret goal, each one dreaming of the day when he alone would be the one biggest dog, eating sweet bloody flesh until he was full to vomiting while others starved.

"Did it hurt? Having your wings cut off?"

"Hurt? No, no, of course not. This is the modern age.

They can cut away your entire life and you'll never feel a thing."

It took them most of the morning to make their way across Rade Park. The intervening day had made his emotional wounds a little less raw, and Theo was at last able to talk about Applecore, although neither he nor the ferisher could bear to speculate over what might have happened to her. Theo found himself telling Cumber at great length about her bravery and the deep well of kindness guarded by her exceedingly sharp tongue, and was surprised to discover how much Cumber already knew about her—the ferisher and the sprite seemed to have had a few long talks during the time in Daffodil House. The conversation began to feel like a wake—Cumber seemed at least as miserable as Theo about the fact that they had lost her, and that it was probably forever. At last, in frustration and sorrow, they fell into silence.

They stopped to rest about an hour past noon and Cumber produced the rest of the bread he had acquired that morning. Theo was astonishingly hungry and happy to have it, but he was beginning to want more. Real food. A real bed. Safety.

But you're not going to get it, are you? Not anytime in the foreseeable future. So live with what you've got. Complaining was more than useless, it was a display of foolish ingratitude. He had survived what should have been certain death several times with nothing worse than a bruised, aching body and miserably crusty lungs. He had a companion—a friend, perhaps—who was risking his own life to help him. Theo was fairly certain that even though the City might not be a safe place for Cumber Sedge right now, there were spots in the countryside where even a wingless ferisher could find shelter and aid, yet here he was, patiently answering questions so basic that he must have felt like a kindergarten teacher at the end of a long, long field trip.

Speaking of questions, Theo was still having trouble

getting the hang of the local chronology. "So you said the seven families took over, what, a few centuries ago?"

Cumber gave him an amused look. "Are you planning on taking a test? I don't think it will be your uncertain grasp of history that will be the biggest strike against you for citizenship at the moment."

"No, I'm just trying to figure things out—mostly where I fit into all this. Hellebore and his cronies want me, so the reason I'm here has something to do with him. But he certainly didn't need anything I could give him or tell him to launch his little Flower War." Theo frowned, struggling to think and keep up with Cumber at the same time: the barefooted and apparently revitalized ferisher was proving an exhausting hiking companion. "I know I keep saying this, but I'm not anybody. I'm just an out-of-work musician. It doesn't make sense."

"No, it doesn't."

"Right. Well, there must be something I don't know yet. So help me out. I'm supposed to be a fairy, okay. My only other connection with this place is that someone I thought was my great-uncle was here about thirty or forty years ago. That's in my-world time. How much is that here? How long ago?"

Cumber shook his head. "It's not that simple, I'm afraid. The time flows differently in our world and your world, and often it seems to flow faster here—but not always. You're combining two unstable systems. And there are geographical effects to factor in as well, which won't make much sense to you. I've studied your world enough to know that places that are proximate in your world stay proximate."

Theo considered that for a moment. "Yeah," he admitted. "Generally, if a train goes from San Francisco to LA, you don't wake up one day and find out that suddenly it stops at New York between the two."

Cumber smiled. "What amazing names. I never get over them. The pictures they make in my head! San Francisco! Like a name from a dream."

"Yeah, you should see the fair folk dancing down in the Castro on Hallowe'en." Theo snorted. "It's something out of an old folktale, all right."

"Time to be walking again. We're moving along the edge of the Twilight District now, but we still have a very long way to go and I'd like to get there before nightfall."

Their path began a long descent. The hills were more and more sparsely covered with trees and now Theo could see glimpses of a great expanse of silvery water to their right.

"Ys," said Cumber. "The islands of Hy Breasil are just out of sight beyond the horizon to the east there. I've often thought I'd like to go there. Get away from this terrible city . . ."

"So is it an ocean? Or a lake?"

"It's just the water," Cumber said, and shrugged. "If you go out far enough, it's the ocean. But here it's a lake—well, kind of a bay in places. I don't think I can explain."

Theo could also see vast stretches of urban housing and industrial blocks between the park and the water, but the district below them had little in the way of the high towers that dotted the city center. "Is that where we're going?"

"No, that's Eastwater. We'll go through one end of it on our way. Mostly warehouses and very, very cheap flats for very poor people. Farther north—see out there, where there aren't so many buildings? That's the edge of the Fenland. It's a sort of swamp between the City proper and the dockyards. The Moonflood River lets out there, and the old Fayfort Bridge is one of the last bridges across the river. Hardly ever used now, I think, because the railroad and the main highway bypass it and come in through Eastwater."

"I still can't get used to hearing the word 'railroad' used to describe something in Fairyland, let alone 'power plants.' When did all this happen?"

"When the City expanded, after the Seven Families took over. Lord Hellebore may hate mortals, although I can't think of any reason he should, particularly—they say he used to visit the mortal world regularly, before the Clover

Effect was in place—but he and his kind certainly love all
the things that mortals have come up with. It's one of the
reasons we have so many power problems—the Flower families have built so much, so fast. It used to be that the power
for all the charms and cantrips and spells of Faerie could be
provided by the king and queen—well, by what the king and
queen did."

"What exactly did they do?"

"I don't know, really. Provided the power, or perhaps
channeled it—they simply *were,* and somehow that was
enough. But with them gone and the City growing so fast,
the Seven Families and the Parliament had to find other
ways to provide power to make everything work. So they
developed the plants."

For a moment, Theo was confused, imagining some
utopian scheme of deriving energy from soybeans. "What
kind of plants?"

"Power plants, of course. Where they make the scientific
energy that runs the lights and the coaches and the trains
and . . . and everything. And so Parliament passed the Power
Generation Laws and they began the conscription."

"Hang on, you've lost me again. A conscription—that's
like a draft, right? Like when they pick you to go into the
army, whether you want to or not?"

"Is that what it means in your world?" Cumber nodded.
"I knew you used the term, but since your science is so different—we don't even think of it as science, to be honest—
I couldn't imagine what it meant, and it's so hard to find
reliable texts even in the university libraries."

"I'm still confused. Why do people get . . . conscripted
here? Not to go in the army, I take it."

Cumber shook his head. "No. You really didn't know?
Sorry, but it's the kind of thing every schoolboy learns even
if he's only going to spend his life grazing sheep. The conscription determines who goes to the power plants."

"That doesn't seem so bad—it's a job, anyway. Why do
they have to force people?"

Cumber Sedge stopped. "Theo, when I say that people are conscripted to go to the power plants, I don't mean to go work there, supervise, take care of the machinery, do the bookkeeping. They have ordinary employees who make decent wages who do that, people who go home to their families every night and live in houses or flats. No, the people who are conscripted are the ones who generate the power. Or rather, after they lose the lottery, they're taken off to the plants and the power is drained out of them. A few years—ten at the most—and then they're retired, but there's not much left after the plants are done with them, no matter what the government propaganda claims. *'I did my bit, and now I've a long, golden retirement in front of me, thanks to Thornapple Generation, LPB!'* or whatever they call it. I've seen a few of the real survivors, people from my own village, before the operators wised up and started shutting them away in Power Worker Retirement Hostels so their potential replacements didn't have to walk past them every day on the village high street and see them shuffling and drooling."

"You mean these power plants somehow . . . suck the power . . . out of people? Out of live fairy people?"

"Where else would it come from?" Cumber's sour laugh returned. "And why do you think my mother was so anxious for me to go to school and get my name taken out of the lottery? Modern power generation is the wonder of science, Theo. *'So few giving so much for so many.'* That old darling, Lord Daffodil, who was just burned to crackling yesterday, invented that phrase—he used to get a tear of pride in his eye when someone quoted it back to him. He used to talk a lot about the good old days when the farm boys would come spilling off the wagons, anxious to take their place in the generators and do their bit for the good of Faerie."

Theo had to walk without speaking for a while. Bile was swimming in his throat and he was afraid if he opened his mouth he might throw up.

*   *   *

By the time they left the park and the trees behind them for good and descended by a series of winding, cobblestoned roads back into the City, an industrial area full of boxy warehouses and equally boxy flatblocks, with washing rippling on the line on every balcony like flags of surrender, it was midafternoon and Theo was losing the surprising energy that had kept him going through the morning. The pall of smoky gray clouds overhead mirrored his mood.

As he stared at the long blocks stretching before him, the buildings featureless except for the surreal silver rooftop sculptures called mirrormasts (which Cumber's confusing explanation seemed to suggest were a bit like television antennas) and the occasional flowering of graffiti on a wall, the symbols even more cryptic and abstract than what he was used to back home, he found himself thinking of Anna, a girl he had dated for a while in the mid-Eighties. She had been a self-proclaimed Wiccan, although her version seemed largely self-invented as far as Theo could tell. She never cursed or thanked in the name of "God" but always "the Goddess," and had a deep and reverent love for dragons, unicorns, and fairies. Theo had thought she was a bit dippy, in fact, but their off-and-on relationship, built mostly around long days spent under her hand-made quilt in her tiny apartment, had lasted for the better part of a year and had been a bit of a refuge for him during a fallow period of his life. He had not thought about Anna in a long time, but now he found himself remembering her solemn explanations of what the fairy-folk got up to with both cynical amusement and a kind of regret.

It's just as well old Anna never made it here, he thought, watching a tiny housewife out on her balcony, pulling so many different children's outfits off the line that he was almost certain she was only renting the until she had the deposit together for a shoe. *This is the actual place she used to talk about so much—"Where all the magic comes from," she used to say. "They live off our dreams." And you know what? She was right. But not in a very nice way.* He remembered what the now very dead Lord Hollyhock had said about Hellebore's plan, about something called the Terrible Child. *And it's going to be even less pleasant soon. They're going to be living off our dreams the way leeches live off blood, except leeches don't have to destroy their victims' whole society.*

"You look dreadful, fellow," said Cumber. "Don't worry, we'll be out of the City and into the Fenlands soon."

"It's not that, not really. I just . . . I was just thinking about how people—my people, or at least the kind of people I thought I was . . ." He paused, having confused himself a bit. "About how so many human stories are about Fairyland. Poetry, songs. And whether they think the place is wonderful or scary, they always imagine of this place as . . . beautiful. Magical. Terrible but glamorous. And there is some of that. But a lot of it's . . . . like *this.*"

Cumber nodded slowly. "If you find that depressing, imagine how someone like me feels about it. This is where I live."

Gently but effectively silenced, Theo kept walking.

They ate the last of the bread as they passed through a district even less prepossessing than the one they had just traversed, a sprawling shantytown that looked like it was constructed of white plywood. It was a bad neighborhood by any standards, but the locals who came to watch them from the doors of their hovels or peered down at them from low rooftops, a rabble of dirty and distracted full-sized fairies along with brownies, gnomes, and squint-eyed pookas, seemed far too beaten-down to pose much of a threat. Still, as they walked through the narrow, twisting alleys, Theo kept an eye out for Fairyland muggers.

They were just about to cross the local equivalent of a main road, where the shanties stood some half-dozen paces apart and tire-treads rutted the muddy street, when Cumber suddenly grabbed Theo and pushed him back into the shadow of a doorway. They watched as a strange, open car rolled past, more like a jeep than anything else, but with differences in shape and line that would have irritated or even panicked most mortal designers. Half a dozen constables in heavy cloaks and helmets were perched on it, all armed with the beehive guns, their outfits decorated with the abstract flower-glyph that Cumber had told him was the parliamentary insignia. A rabble of children from what looked like a dozen species followed in their wake, little goblins among them, begging for food and money. The grim-faced fairies on the jeep paid no attention to the children but Theo was grateful for the noise and distraction: the vehicle did not even slow as it drove past their hiding spot.

"How far do those guns shoot?" he asked in a whisper when the constables were well past them.

"As far as they need to," said Cumber. "Well, the hornets get tired after flying awhile, especially if they've been in the clip for too long without being fed."

Theo shook his head. "You mean there are real live bugs in there?"

Cumber nodded. "Sort of. They're made out of metal. It's a scientific thing."

"Metal, but they still eat? What do they get fed?"

"Bronze shavings, mostly."

Theo sighed. He sometimes thought he could live here for years and still not understand a thing.

Soon after the brush with the constables, they left the last of the Eastwater shantytown behind them. The whole of Ys now seemed to be spread before them, but it was strangely uninspiring. The land between them and the water was a descending set of rolling hills studded with rock outcroppings, patchily covered with low trees bent into bizarre shapes by the constant wind—a wind that was already making Theo's clothes snap and flutter.

"It's pretty gloomy out here."

"Didn't use to be. Do you see that silvery line, there? That's the Moonflood River. It used to be the lifeblood of the place—went right past the Great Hill where the first fairies lived. But when they began building the City up they dammed it and re-routed it, and cut channels so it could be used to irrigate the lands west of the City, until it wasn't much more than a trickle." He swept his hand across the flat, dismal prospect. "This was all True Arden, covered with trees. The queen used to have her dances in the forest meadows past Warstones, below what's now Battle Hill—you can see the hill if you squint, over there. Yes, that ugly piece of rock. But they blocked the river and cut down the forest and this all became mudflats, rocky hills . . . well, you can see for yourself."

The view wasn't particularly inspiring, but the walking was a little easier across the sparsely forested hills and Theo was grateful for that. Still, he couldn't help contrasting the emptiness with the almost hallucinatory beauty of the woods on Larkspur's land and said so.

"Oh, that." Cumber shrugged. "That's not a real forest, that's a rich man's preserve. It used to be part of the Silverwood—in fact, all of Larkspur's lands used to be a tiny section of the Silverwood. It's the same old story, Theo. You must be tired of hearing it by now—I'm certainly tired of telling it. It's gone. They just saved a little piece for Larkspur and his friends to hunt in."

"You people really *do* like to imitate my world."

Cumber only smiled sadly.

An hour later they had reached the Moonflood, more a sluggish canal than a river, hemmed by stone embankments on either side which were the highest features for miles other than a few lumpish hills. The sun had fallen low in the west, the beginnings of a spectacular red glow illuminating the smoky skies behind the peak Cumber had named Battle Hill. The temperature was dropping and mist was rising from the flat, muddy lands around the river. Theo shivered. It had been bad enough sleeping out of doors in the park, with its sheltering ivy and trees. The idea of spending a night exposed in this glum wrack, listening to the distant shriek of seabirds, was miserable indeed. Even Cumber seemed doubtful.

"There it is—the old Fayfort Bridge." He pointed to what looked like nothing more than a pile of wreckage, visible now as they crested a long shallow slope. It squatted over the river like a discarded parade float, a fantasy castle that had been sat on by a giant.

Good God, Theo thought, *around here that could have really happened.*

The bridge towers had mostly collapsed: great round shards of wall lay half-submerged in the moving water, causing the only curls of white Theo had seen the whole sluggish length of the river. A few sections still stood atop the bridge, but only one tower had kept most of its stones. It stood at one end of the wide span like a single tooth in the mouth of a cartoon witch. On either side, where the bridge met the muddy riverbanks, lay more tumbles of fallen stone, half-vanished into the muck and looking so much like the turds of some immense animal that Theo found himself wishing he had never thought about giants at all.

"This bridge used to guard the river, when that was the City's most vulnerable and important artery," Cumber said. "When the river mattered."

"I don't see anyone around."

"Maybe they've been chased away." Cumber didn't sound anywhere near as sad about it as Theo was.

"No, wait—there's someone moving up on top of it." Theo shielded his eyes. "Not very many of them. I think they see us, too." Whether they did or didn't, a moment later the distant figures had vanished from the bridge's crumbling fortifications and the landscape seemed entirely lifeless again.

It took them another quarter of an hour to follow the river's course down to the foot of the bridge. The space under it was choked with refuse, pieces of wood, piles of stone—Theo could barely see water and was amazed that the river could find places to flow through it toward the Ys. Up close, he was even more surprised by how big the ancient structure was, hundreds of feet from one bank to the other. Its single remaining tower was almost half the height of Daffodil House. He was still staring up in amazement, wondering how many carefully chiseled stone blocks had gone into such an immense thing, when someone shouted at them to stop.

"Do not move." They could barely hear the invisible sentry over the wind sawing through the bridge's broken stones. *"There are guns looking upon you."*

Theo and Cumber kept very still as a wiry little shape clambered down from one of the broken towers near them. It was a goblin, dressed only in a loincloth and vest despite the wind. At first Theo thought it might be the one who had given him the slip of paper, but after a moment he saw that this one was smaller and older, with grizzled white whiskers surrounding his wide mouth. Still, his movements were sure: he leaped down from stone to stone until he reached the lower fortifications, then clambered down the outer wall on a rope that Theo had not even noticed and came toward them.

"What do you seek?" The goblin looked more put out than nervous, despite the fact that even Cumber was almost a head taller than he was. *Maybe there really are guns pointed at us,* Theo thought. It was a depressing idea. He felt too tired to outrun a banana slug, let alone magical metallic bees. He started to reach into his pocket, then remembered all the television shows he'd seen about police standoffs and hostage situations.

"I have a piece of paper," he said slowly and clearly. "A goblin gave it to me, invited me to come here. I'm going to take it out of my pocket now."

The white-whiskered goblin looked distinctly unimpressed. "Produce this paper, then, or a mighty stinging is what you will receive."

"Friendly folk around here," Theo said under his breath. He reached into his floppy fairy-shirt and experienced a moment of real panic before he finally found the paper crammed down into the bottom of the pocket.

The goblin squinted at it, then held it up to the western sky as if looking for a watermark. His eyes grew round and his finger-length nose quivered. He looked at Theo and Cumber with something like astonishment, and for a few bad seconds Theo thought they were both going to be shot.

"Follow me, kind fellows," the goblin said. He actually bowed before turning around to lead them to the foot of the bridge.

"By the Trees, look at this!" Cumber had stopped to lean over the side of the bridge. Theo, who had been surreptitiously scouting around for the hidden marksmen with whom they had been threatened, checked with their goblin guide to see if it was all right to look. The goblin didn't seem to care, so he went to stand by the ferisher.

The shanties had been invisible from the direction Theo and Cumber had come, but they were packed up against the other side of the dilapidated bridge along both banks as though a great flood had left them behind. The little town extended far down the riverside toward Ys; Theo thought he could see the end of the shanties about a mile away, but it was hard to tell through the growing shadows. The camp was full of many kinds of fairy-folk, although the slender brown and gray goblins seemed to be in the majority.

"There must be hundreds of people here," Theo murmured. "No, thousands."

"And another thousand or so right under your feet, a-living in the fortifications of the bridge and beneath the pilings and even on rafts in the river underneath." The whiskered goblin sounded quite pleased with these arrangements. "But you young masters probably have heard these truths already, if intimates you be of our great Button."

"Button?" Theo shook his head. "Who's Button?"

"Ah, yes." The goblin shook his head approvingly and laid a finger beside his long, long nose. "The more quiet now, the less shouting later."

Theo could only wonder what that was supposed to mean, or what weird misunderstanding he had started with his slip of paper. He noted with some surprise that instead of taking them down toward the shantytown along the river-banks their goblin guide was leading them over the length of the bridge toward the one remaining tower. As they neared it, two large creatures stepped out of the shadowed doorway. They were ogres, Theo was surprised to see, and at least as large and ugly as Tansy's bodyguards, Teddy and Dolly. They glared suspiciously at Theo and Cumber, but at a cheerful gesture from the old goblin they stepped back, their misshapen gray faces suddenly more respectful.

The two new arrivals were led up a narrow flight of stone stairs into the tower. Theo was already exhausted, and after they had climbed what he guessed was about five floors' worth he was hoping that if for some reason this was all an elaborate trick to capture them, the capture would quickly be followed by an execution, just to stop his legs from aching. Instead, they reached a heavy wooden door at the top of the stairs. The goblin pushed it open and stepped aside, waving for them to walk through.

"He speaks to some perry dancers who've come all the way from Gateway Oak," their guide whispered as they went past. "So it is possible that you may have need to wait a while before you can be in audience with him."

At the far end of the room sat another, slightly larger goblin, wearing a brown robe so basic that it might have been something a Franciscan monk would put on while his good clothes were out being cleaned. Behind him sat a half circle of goblins and other fairyland creatures, perhaps a dozen in all, of which only one was the kind that looked mostly human, a handsome, golden-haired man in the ageless middle years of his sort. He and the others looked up as Theo and Cumber came cautiously forward, but the goblin did not take his eyes off the trio of almost impossibly slender beings who sat before him, dressed in diaphanous silks and looking more like dream-creatures than things of flesh and blood.

The goblin at last held his hand up and spread his fingers, bowed his head briefly toward the fey trio, and then for the

first time looked to the newcomers. Theo recognized him as
the one who had given him the paper in the bus station. A
smile curved gently across the goblin's thin face.

"You have come. I hoped that it would be so. I am honored by your trust." He shut his eyes for a moment as if
dropping off to sleep. "Sad, I am sad, but at the moment I
have these other honored guests who have need of, *hem*, my
poor thoughts and meager assistance." He made a graceful
gesture toward the sylphlike creatures that Theo guessed
must be the perry dancers the other goblin had mentioned.

"Do you need me longer, Button?" the white-whiskered
goblin asked.

"Doorlatch, thanks to you. Go if you wish. Oh, but would
you be so kind as to bring my friend Nettle up to see me before you return to your post?"

The old goblin called Doorlatch gave an oddly casual
wave and headed back down the stairs.

"Now," the one called Button said to Theo and Cumber,
"until I can give you of my time and offer you to drink as is
proper, I think perhaps you will have the most comfort with
one of your own kind." He turned to the yellow-haired fairy.
"Caradenus, perhaps you could see that these guests are well
hosted?"

"Certainly." The fairy rose. He was quite tall, and wore a
kind of loose, unconstructed suit that looked like it belonged
on the veranda of a sugarcane plantation. "Come with me,"
he told Theo and Cumber. "Very many thanks to you for
your patience," called Button as they were led back to the
stairs, Theo groaning inwardly at the thought of having to go
all that way back down. "Soon we will speak together."

"Excuse me for asking," said Theo as they started down,
"but who the hell was that?"

The golden-haired fairy turned to look at him in surprise.
"If you do not know, what are you doing here? And why
should you receive such kind treatment?" His eyes narrowed, more puzzled than hostile. "You speak strangely,
friend. Where are you from?"

"A long way away. Are we safe here?" He didn't know how much he dared to give away just yet. "I mean, can we spend the night here? We're very tired."

"Of course," the one called Caradenus said. "By the falling light through the leaves, of course you can. Button has said so—nobody here would dare say otherwise."

"So he's . . . in charge? That goblin?"

Again Caradenus looked at him. He turned away for a moment as they stepped down off the stairs and nodded to the ogres by the door, then turned back to stare at Theo again as they walked out of the tower and onto the bridge. The sky was already much darker; fires had been kindled all through the shantytown. "Forgive me, but there is something terribly familiar about the way you speak—like something I've heard in a dream. Where are you from?"

"Rowan," said Cumber flatly, "he's from Rowan," but it was clear by the yellow-haired fairy's face that he did not believe it. He continued to stare at Theo, then his frown suddenly turned to something else—a wide-eyed look of surprise.

"I have it. You speak like a mortal I once knew. You speak like someone from the mortal world. It is faint as the scent of a flower beneath the snow, but it is there. How can that be?"

Theo was tired. He didn't like subterfuge, and he didn't want to stand here in the middle of the bridge with everyone down in the shantytown staring at him.

"Because I *am* a mortal," he said wearily. "Or at least, I come from the mortal world and thought I belonged there until a couple of days ago. I'm not quite sure what I am. Does that explain it?"

Caradenus was still staring, even more intently if possible. "And do you know a mortal man named Eamonn, of the house of Dowd?"

"Eamonn Dowd? You knew Eamonn Dowd?" Theo was so shocked that he lost his grip on any kind of discretion. "He was my great-uncle!"

The fairy took a step backward as though he had been struck across the face. His astonishment turned into something more complicated, an expression of puzzlement and perhaps even sadness. "Then I am in a terrible situation," he told Theo.

"Why?"

"That's enough," said Cumber, a worried edge to his voice. "Let's not say any more until we've had a chance to talk to this Button fellow again."

"Because I fear I must kill you." With a gesture as economical as it was graceful, Caradenus reached into his loose jacket and drew out a knife as long as Theo's forearm. He lowered it until the blade pointed unwaveringly at Theo's heart. "And yet, you are the guest of one I hold dear. But the honor of my entire house rests on me." He shook his head, his narrow face now miserable but very determined. "I see only one solution. After I kill you I will have to end my own life. It will not expunge all the dishonor, but there is nothing else I can do."

Theo looked at the tall fairy and his terrifyingly sharp blade. "Oh, shit," was all he could think of to say.

28

GOBLIN JAZZ
BANDWAGON

"If you have a weapon," said the fairy who seemed quite sincerely intent on murdering him, "this would be a good time to produce it. The obligations of honor do not extend so far as to prevent me killing you if you are unarmed, but I will feel better about things if you defend yourself."

Theo kept backing away. His weariness had burned away in the rush of fear, but he knew he was too exhausted even to run, let alone fight back against a taller man with a long, sharp blade. "You don't need to do this," he said, but the one named Caradenus was still walking toward him. Theo tried to think of something else that might save him but his brain seemed to be short-circuiting. "Jesus Christ, Buddha, and Mohammed! Saint Francis of Assisi! Hooray for the Pope!"

Cumber winced and lifted his hands to his ears, but the fairy with the knife only blinked.

These people are hanging out in clubs named "Christmas" now, Theo thought miserably. *I guess they're getting over the whole God's-name thing.* "Why are you doing this? I've never met you—I've never met my Uncle Eamonn, either, for Christ's sake!"

Not even a blink this time. "You have my pity but nothing more. I am sure you are innocent, in your way, but your blood is not. Just as punishment is a dynastic responsibility, so is the original crime." The blade began to move in small circles, mesmerizing as the sway of a cobra's head. "Your great-uncle defiled my sister and disgraced the Primrose clan. Be glad my father is dead." For a moment the fairy's face twisted with something like grief. "Be glad the traitor Hellebore has murdered him, because my father would not have offered you the kindness of a quick death."

"But Hellebore is my enemy, too!"

The face had again settled into an expressionless mask. "It does not matter. This is not political. This is a matter of a blood oath on the waters of the Well." The fairy lunged.

Theo stumbled as he dodged backward, which probably saved his life, but the tip of the blade still pierced his shirt at the shoulder; a moment later he felt a cold sting that told him the skin beneath had also been cut. The fairy did not stop, but continued toward him, the blade hunting his heart again.

"Stop!" said Cumber Sedge. "He is not who you think he is!"

"Trickery will do him no good. He has confessed from his own mouth."

Theo flung himself backward again as the blade snapped out and suffered no more than another, longer rip in his shirt, but there was stone behind him now and he could go no farther. He had backed across the width of the bridge.

"But that's just it!" Cumber started to step between Theo and the fairy; the slender blade almost took him in the eye. The ferisher's dark golden skin lightened a full shade. "He calls him his great-uncle, but he's not! Theo, tell him what you've learned!"

"Huh?" His heart was thumping so hard he felt like someone had hooked an industrial compressor to his arteries. It was like the worst speed rush ever. The blade was wavering only inches away from his chest. It rose until it danced a slow weave in front of his throat. "What? Tell . . . ?"

"What you learned! At Daffodil House! About what you are!"

"Oh! I'm . . . I'm not a mortal. That's what they told me."

He couldn't take his eyes off the silver blade decorated with twining symbols of deer and flowers.

"What is this nonsense?" the fairy demanded. "What has that to do with the honor of Primrose House?"

"Because if he's not a mortal—if he's really one of our kind—how can he carry the blood guilt for something that Eamonn Dowd did to your family? He only *thought* he was related to Dowd, but he's not—he can't be!"

It was almost as surprising to Theo as it was to Caradenus Primrose. He had only begun to think about what it all meant—his mother not really his mother, his life a kind of lie. But Cumber Sedge was right. If he wasn't mortal, then Eamonn Dowd wasn't really his great-uncle.

There was some kind of coincidence there, something big and strange and significant, but at the moment all Theo could think about was the tall, yellow-haired person who wanted to kill him.

The fairy stared, first at Cumber, then at Theo. The blade stopped moving, but stayed very close to Theo's neck. At last he turned back to Cumber. "Do you swear this is true? That you are not merely trying to save your friend? Do you swear on the timeless Trees?"

"I do."

The blade wavered for a moment, then dropped until it pointed at the stones of the bridge beneath their feet. "I . . . I do not know what to say." Primrose looked so confused that Theo almost felt sorry for him, until he remembered how close the fairy had come to pushing that shish kebab skewer into his heart. "If I have accused you wrongly, I beg your pardon. Someone else must be your guide. I have shamed Button and myself." He turned abruptly and walked a few steps up the bridge, then vaulted onto the wall and leaped down out of sight.

"What did he do?" asked Theo, stunned. "Kill himself?"

"It's only a few yards down," Cumber reminded him. "And unless he landed on a sharp tent pole, I think he's probably doing just fine." The ferisher made a disgusted face. "These bloody Flower-folk and their debts of honor."

"He wanted to kill me. I never even met him before and he wanted to kill me!" Theo leaned against the side of the bridge trying to catch his breath again, waiting for his heart to slow down. "He said Hellebore murdered his father. There were Primrose people in that conference room when . . . when the dragon came. That must mean . . ." Theo already felt sick to his stomach with fear; he did not want to think about what he had seen in Daffodil House. It was still hard to muster sympathy for the golden-haired fairy, but if his father had been in there with Hollyhock and Lady Jonquil and the rest . . .

"Since what we told him is true, I don't think you'll have to worry about him any more. That honor thing cuts both ways and he seemed pretty upset he might have killed you for a bad reason." Cumber's smile was not a cheerful one. "Anyway, nothing's really changed. We still need to decide what to do next."

Discussion was put off by the sudden appearance of two figures, one familiar, one not. "What am I hearing?" asked the goblin Doorlatch, his wizened face full of concern. "A fight between guests? Between the friends of Button? But this is a terrible thing!"

"All is well now," said Cumber. "A misunderstanding."

"But you have no one to be your guide . . ." the old goblin began, then suddenly the second figure lurched forward. The man's movements were so awkward that for a long, heart-stopping instant Theo thought his undead nemesis had found him again.

The tall young fairy was dressed in little more than rags. He had an unruly thatch of hair like a comedy wig and was so thin that he made an ordinarily slender fairy like Cumber look like the first Rotarian in line at the all-you-can-eat pancake breakfast. He also had eyes that did not quite focus, or rather focused a little bit past the apparent subject of their attention. Despite the incomplete eye contact, though, he seemed fascinated by Theo, or at least by something in Theo's vicinity.

Whatever it is that's caught this weirdo's interest, Theo decided, *he certainly is standing uncomfortably close . . .*

"Ah, well." The goblin darted a nervous glance at the skinny fairy, as though he were a dog that might suddenly decide to run out onto the freeway. "Once I have brought our friend Nettle to esteemed Button, I will come back and help you myself. Did I share my name? I am called Doorlatch."

"Yes, I'm Cumber Sedge. And this is my friend, Theo."

"You . . . !" The tall thin fairy leaned even closer to Theo, who had a sudden nightmare vision of the rest of his time in Faerie consisting of a series of vengeance-duels, but Nettle only squinted and raised his long-fingered hands as though he wanted to feel Theo's face. "She . . . she knows you," he said. "She . . . talked about you." He spoke as though he had some kind of problem thinking and expressing himself, as though he had suffered brain damage or some kind of birth defect.

"Who?" Theo was beginning to feel more than a little overwhelmed by the way everybody in this damned camp seemed to know him. "Who are you talking about?"

"Poppy. Her name is Poppy. I like her."

"Poppy Thornapple?" Of *course* it was Poppy Thornapple—Theo only knew about three women in all of Fairyland. "Wait a minute, you know her?"

The thin fairy shook his head. "I hear her." He tapped his long skull. "In here."

"I don't understand."

"Do not alarm yourself, master," said Doorlatch. "Our friend Nettle, he is not like others. He is full of strange ideas." He curled dark fingers around the fairy's wrist and began to lead him away toward the bridge tower. "Come. Button wishes to see you."

"Button is good to me," Nettle told Theo. "He brought me food. He helps me think."

Theo was rapidly losing his grip on what was normal.

"But I *do* know the woman he's talking about!" he shouted after them.

"We will speak when I return!" Doorlatch called back. "Wait for me!"

"I think I've reached my saturation point," Theo said as they disappeared into the tower. "Fairies who want to kill me for family honor, telepathic fairies—I can't take any more strange stuff."

"I must say, you certainly seem to attract it," Cumber observed. "Back home, my luck was just bad. Here, it's bad and weird." He slumped down on the bridge, his back against the wall that only a few minutes earlier had blocked his retreat and almost killed him. "And all the people who could send me back are dead now, aren't they? Killed in Daffodil House?"

Cumber frowned sympathetically. "Well, it's not sending you back that's the problem so much as getting rid of that dead thing that's chasing you. It's probably safe to say that most of the people who *could* get that thing off you and send you home—and who also don't want to kill you—well, they're dead, yes. I suppose there might be some other possibilities . . ." He sighed. "But believe me, Theo, some of them could turn out worse than just staying here. Actually, some of them could turn out worse than being stabbed by that Primrose fellow."

Theo squinted into the orange-streaked distance. The long sunset of Faerie was over and twilight was rushing on. "That's a lot of help, Cumber. Thanks. I'm grateful that you kept that guy from killing me and everything, but if any other encouraging thoughts like these occur to you, could you just keep your mouth shut?"

"There we are, cozy as toast, eh?" Doorlatch carried a slim torch; behind him, the sky was velvety black and the frozen-firework stars of Faerie had sprung into view. Theo realized he had dozed off sitting against the bridge wall. A little panicked, he looked around for Cumber and was relieved to discover the ferisher sitting beside him.

Theo climbed onto unsteady feet. He'd had just enough of a nap to feel even more exhausted and groggy. "Who was that tall guy, that . . . what was his name? Nettle?"

"He is a very kindly young fellow, like yourself," said Doorlatch. "And a great favorite of our Button, oh yes."

"What did he mean when he said he heard Poppy Thornapple in his head?"

The little goblin shrugged. "It is all too deep for this old fellow. He often says things I do not understand. He is . . . damaged." The goblin didn't seem to want to talk about it much. "You must ask Button. He is the one who found young Nettle. He thinks very highly of him, so of course the rest of us also do, oh yes."

Cumber had fallen in alongside them as they made their way down to the end of the bridge and off, then clambered down the crude wooden stairs to the riverbank below and the shantytown. Theo looked at the ferisher's alert face with no little irritation. *If we're both fairies,* Theo thought, *how come he looks rested again and I feel like shit?* "Are all these people homeless? Is that why they're here? Is the goblin named Button in charge of all of them?"

"You have many questions, young master. Too many for old Doorlatch. You must save them for those who can give proper answers." He led them through a jumble of tents and cook fires as crowded and active as a Moroccan marketplace, but with a variety of inhabitants a hundred times stranger. There were many of what Theo thought of as "ordinary fairies"—the ones who looked mostly human, either with or without wings—and even more goblins, but there was also an impressive sprinkling of other types.

A group of small, sullen looking fellows who were covered with short fur just like a Weimaraner dog's glared at the passersby as though the intruders might be intending to steal the flames out of their campfire. "Capelthwaites," Cumber explained quietly. "They're shape-shifters, or at least they used to be. They formed a union and now nobody can afford to pay them to do it, so they just stay like that. Rather an unfortunate, liverish color to be all the time, it has to be said. And those nice-looking ladies over there are Green Women. They might ask you to dance. Don't do it. They used to keep young men like you up all night dancing, then eat them. They don't do that anymore—at least they're not supposed to—but they'll still happily take your purse and your clothes and leave you to wake up naked and bruised in a meadow somewhere."

"Charming," said Theo. They made their way through the crowd, ducking the ubiquitous sea birds and marsh birds and crows that seemed to swoop down and take up any space left momentarily free of people.

"Don't get me wrong. I'm not a bigot. Most ferishers are just thrilled about doing household tasks—they hate disorder—but I'm not one of those kind of ferishers, so I suppose there are also Green Women who are vegetarians or who don't like to dance, and tommy-knockers who are uncomfortable in enclosed places. But by and large, one of the differences between mortals and fairies is that humans are all pretty much the same and fairies have . . . well, we have roles, I suppose. We're most comfortable when we're doing what we're expected to do."

"Like doonies becoming drivers when the roads were taken over by the government."

"Yes, perhaps, although I'm not sure . . ." Cumber suddenly grabbed Theo's arm and swerved to the right. "Careful! Don't step on the klippies."

Theo looked down to see a group of tiny people with dark faces staring up at him. A moment later they scattered, running under the wall of a tent.

"Almost there, almost there," said Doorlatch. "I was going to put you with young Master Primrose—ah, how very sad, I have just realized he must be Lord Primrose now! But since you aren't getting on together, hmmm, I'll have to make another arrangement."

Cumber was still thinking about what Theo had said. "Yes, I suppose you're right. The doonies would rather come down in the world—they used to be quite a powerful clan, you know—than give up their beloved roads. And look at me! I think I'm so different, the first ferisher ever to take an advanced degree, but what do I wind up doing with it? Working as a helper in a great house instead of in a small one, that's all. Tidying up. I'm still a servant. I might as well be hauling firewood for some provincial farmer for a bowl of milk and a place to sleep in the barn. I couldn't stand to see the way Lady Aemilia left that laboratory, you know, and so long after she'd gone down to supper I'd still be there, putting everything back to rights . . ." He shook his head. "She wasn't all bad, though, Lady Aemilia."

Theo was watching a group of what looked like gamblers, mostly brownies and goblins. Someone had drawn a ring in the dirt near one of the fires, and two beetles were walking around in the circle—walking very eccentrically, Theo thought, as though someone were prodding them with an invisible stick to make them go in one direction or another. Finally one of the staggering beetles crossed the perimeter and immediately rolled over on its back as though the effort had nearly killed it, kicking its legs feebly as a cheer went up from the winners and the losers cursed.

"But you don't work for Lady Aemilia any more," Theo said as the collapsed beetle was snatched up and a new one was tossed into the ring next to the champion of the last bout. The shouting began again. "You don't have to be . . . whatever you were. Daffodil House is gone. If there was ever a time to change . . ." *And me, what do I need—a boulder to land on my head? I've been yanked out of my own world. I'm a stranger. This is my chance, too—my chance to be something I can be . . . what? Proud of? Is that what I want? That elementary school civics stuff?*

"You're right, Theo," Cumber said. "And you have helped give me my life back, give me this chance to do something different. I thank you for that."

"Me?"

"I would never have made it out of Daffodil House. I had given up. I would have died there."

"Well, you've saved me a few times. I think we're even."

"Here we are!" said Doorlatch. "It is small, but it will be chummy and so friendly, I think."

Theo stared at the rectangular yellow tent. It leaned to one side, but it was a good eight feet from end to end and more than half that wide—quite reasonable for two people who had been sleeping rough in a park. "That looks like it should be fine."

"Splendid. I will just come in with you and introduce you to your new . . . what is the word? Tent-sharers? Room-companions?"

"Huh?" But before he could ask any questions, Doorlatch had pulled back the flap and stepped in. It was a very low door, and Theo had to concentrate on getting under it without getting tangled in the flap. By the time he was all the way in, Doorlatch was already talking.

"Here are two fellows I have brought, and very fine fellows they are. Button himself has asked that you show them every courtesy and share your home with them."

The cramped interior of the tent was lit only by a foxfire lantern whose light had a faintly green-gray tinge, but it was enough to see that neither of the two people already in residence seemed exactly delighted to see their new roommates.

"Two more of Button's special friends?" asked a small, round-faced creature dressed in nothing but red overalls with silver buttons. The pugnacious face and fringe of orange hair made the stranger look a little like a tiny ginger lion; it took Theo a moment to realize that at least one of their new roommates was female. "That was the excuse you used to inflict Streedy on us, and the Well take me if we don't spend every night listening to him thrash and talk to himself. And when he farts, the whole room lights up like the signs in Strawflower Square! Makes it cursed hard to sleep."

"None of your joking, Mistress Twinge. You know you're fond of that lad." Doorlatch shook his grizzled head. "And he relies on you!"

"Well, he does make a ghastly lot of noise," she said, but Theo could see now that she was smiling. "Right, bring 'em in. We might as well get crammed in together—probably won't have much less room than this in the cells under Hellebore's place after we all get arrested for harboring anti-Flower ideas. What do you think, Coathook? Guests okay with you?"

The tent's other inhabitant was a goblin, but a different sort from Button and Doorlatch, smaller and even more wiry, and with more black than brown or gray in his bristly hair. His yellow eyes blinked slowly as he considered Mistress Twinge's question. "Don't care," he said at last.

"Splendid!" said Doorlatch to this less-than-ringing endorsement. "It's all settled. You two newcomers get some sleep. I'll come back for you near midnight. Button's going to tell a story."

"A story? At midnight?"

"Of course. Everyone will be there. Mistress Twinge, Coathook, help these two find their way around while I'm gone, will you?" Doorlatch backed out through the flap.

Something came flying across the tent and almost hit Theo in the head, but he got his hands up and managed to catch it. It was a battered metal flask, the kind that fit closely in a hip pocket. "It's wine. Have a swig," said Mistress Twinge. "Welcome to our humble home. We call it Poison Ivy House." Her eyes narrowed as she looked at Cumber Sedge, who seemed a little stunned. "Is that a problem for you? Are you one of those Flower-folk like young Primrose whose sense of humor died of starvation years ago? Or is it just you don't like the idea of living with emancipated women?"

"N-no!" Cumber shook his head for emphasis. "No, neither of those things. I'm certainly no Flower." But he looked almost pleased to have been misidentified. "It's just . . . I've never met a wild goblin before."

"Coathook? He was born wild, but brought up here in the filthy bad City like the rest of us, right, Hooky?" The goblin didn't reply. "He's not the strangest here at the bridge," she said with a laugh. "He's not even the strangest living in this tent."

"I gather there are going to be five of us," Cumber said.

"Ah, yes." Mistress Twinge gestured for Theo to hand the flask to Cumber, who took a careful sip, then a larger and more enthusiastic one.

"The stories are true!" Cumber Sedge was smiling now. "You pookas do have the best wine. What is it, dandelion?"

"And burdock. With a few bumblebee behinds to give it some sting." She laughed loudly but briefly. "Sting. Shite, but I'm funny."

"Is that what you are?" Theo asked. "A pooka?"

"Isn't it obvious? But I don't know your name, lad. I'm Piper Twinge of Blind Pig Street. You've met Coathook."

"Theo. Theo Vilmos." His own name sounded odd to him now. It had been a little weird growing up with a Hungarian last name in the suburbs, where most of the other kids had been named Johnson and Roberts and Smith, but once he had moved to cosmopolitan San Francisco where he was surrounded by Nguyens and Battistinis, Chavezes and Khasigians he had never thought about it much. Now for the first time in decades he again felt awkward—it almost seemed he should be named Honeysuckle or Cauliflower or something, just out of courtesy. "And this is my friend, Cumber Sedge."

Why did Mom and Dad move up from San Mateo, anyway? he wondered. He had never really thought about it before. *Dad was retiring and didn't have to commute to the city anymore, so it didn't really make any difference for him. Could it have been that . . . that Mom, or even both of them, wanted to be closer to me?* It was a strange and novel thought, made even more strange by the still almost incomprehensible idea that they had not been his true parents.

"We are all well-met, then," said Mistress Twinge, breaking his reverie. "Although not everyone feels that way."

"What?"

"Our friend, the young laird of Primrose, came mumbling and hissing past here a little while ago." She produced a cigar and lit it with a raspy flick of her fingers. Within moments the tent began to fill with foul-smelling smoke. "I tried to get him to tell me what was on his mind that had set him so palely loitering and he said something about a young mortal lad, or a not-quite-mortal lad, another stray puppy that Button had brought back. Seems he'd had a falling out with him, matter of honor, so on, woof woof woof—it wasn't very clear. Primrose is a good lad, but he talks rubbish at the best of times. Anyway, he was in a dither about it. You've got a mortal name. You've just arrived. You're a friend of Button's, apparently. So I'm jumping to conclusions. Am I landing on anything?"

Theo blinked tears out of his eyes. Mistress Twinge's cigar in the small tent was almost as bad as being back in Daffodil House. Still, he couldn't help being amused by the little pooka-woman's easy manner—she was a bit like Johnny Battistini with a sex-change and a leprechaun makeover. "Yeah, we had sort of a run-in. A misunderstanding." But inside himself it was not so easy to dismiss. Primrose had clearly intended to kill him—had been only moments away from it—and you didn't just forgive and forget something like that as though it were a schoolyard argument. Theo took the proffered flask and drank. It burned a little on his still-raw throat, but it set something warm glowing in his stomach. His muscles relaxed and the smoky confines of the tent suddenly seemed comfortable.

Good God, he realized, *I'm drunk on one long swallow. This shit is potent.* It didn't help that he was exhausted. "Where can I lie down around here?" he asked, and suddenly realized that, uncomfortable as it might be for him to be crammed into such a small space, it must be more so for the ones who had already been living here and had become used to having that much room. "Just a corner. I'm dead on my feet."

"Can he fit in over by you, Coathook?" asked Mistress Twinge.

The goblin scrabbled up a few carefully folded bags that looked as though they might have contained fast food about a century or so in the past—Theo could read the faded words "Willow Farms Fresh!" on one of them—and produced a bundle of dark cloth that looked too small even to be a prison blanket. "Have a bedroll?" the goblin asked. His voice was flat and his face didn't show much emotion, but he had very intense, bright eyes. "No? Use my cloak."

"That's really nice. Thanks." Theo spread it and stretched himself out on what felt like scratchy black wool. Beside the natural lanolin of untreated fleece, he could smell another scent, something strong, almost musky, but not altogether unpleasant. It was a bit like sniffing the interior of the big cat house at the zoo, he thought, growing groggier by the second. Or something else. *The fox house? The wolf house? Do they have wolf houses at the zoo . . . ?*

The last thing he heard was Cumber Sedge saying in a grim but almost proud way, "We were there. We were in Daffodil House when it happened . . ."

Theo woke up with a heavy, fuzzy head and a mass of aches where he should have had a body. The tent was dark, but some light leaked through from a fire outside. A shadow moving on the fabric of the tent told him he wasn't alone.

Theo poked his head out cautiously and saw the goblin Coathook sitting cross-legged before the fire cooking something, or perhaps just burning the end of a stick. The yellow stare swiveled toward him.

"Where is everybody? Is it midnight? Did I miss this storytelling thing?"

Coathook pulled his stick out of the fire and examined it, then rubbed the point on a flat stone for a moment before putting it back into the flames. "Not midnight yet. The pooka took your friend over to the beetle game."

"Cumber doesn't have any money, so I guess that's safe." Theo wasn't sure what to say. "Thanks again for loaning me your cloak."

The goblin shrugged. "Won't need it much until winter comes. You use it. Friend of Button's, so."

Theo sat down across the fire from him. The goblin moved very slowly, but gave the impression he could move much faster if he wanted to—and those eyes! Theo remembered his brief semi-dream about the zoo's wolf-house. He looked at the dark, silent Coathook. Could a goblin be a werewolf? It seemed a bit much—over-egging the pudding. Mistress Twinge the pooka had said he was half-wild. What would wild mean in a goblin—was he one of those grims Theo had seen from the trains? They had been, as he remembered, distinctly impressive.

"Can you tell me a little bit about this place?" he asked. "I mean, I only came here because Button gave me a card that had the name of the bridge written on it. Everybody seems to think we're friends of his, but we don't really know him at all."

"He knows you." Coathook examined his stick again, tested the end with a finger. "He invites only people he knows are right. He lets the rest of us bring in other new folk." At the end of this, the longest thing Theo had heard him say, the goblin put the stick back in the fire.

"So he's . . . what, the leader?"

Coathook shrugged. "He's the smart one. The one with the ideas. He . . . knows things."

Theo shook his head. "I don't really get it. I mean, is Button sort of the mayor of this . . . tent city? Was he also the one who started it?"

Coathook grinned. His teeth were yellow too, and quite sharp. "There have always been people here since the river

changed. Poor people. Hungry people. Button helped them.
But the . . . mayor?" He laughed, a noise like a wheezy
cough.

"Maybe I'm using the wrong word . . ."

"No, I know that word. Fairies who are chiefs of towns,
of cities. Fat ones who make important-sounding speeches.
No, Button is not that. He is not a mayor. I think he is a
general."

It took Theo a moment to catch on. "You mean, this is . . .
an army?"

"Not yet. Soon, maybe." Coathook withdrew the stick to
test the point again.

Unsure of what to think, Theo stared at the blackened
piece of wood, scraped against stone until it had a needle-
sharp point. "What are you going to do with that? Anything?"

The goblin nodded his head. "Oh, yes. If we do not soon
get a chance to kill some of those Flower bastards, then I am
going to go across the camp and stick this into the ear of a
brownie I met named Wicker—all the way into his thinking
organs." Again he let out the wheezing laugh but there was
an unpleasant glimmer in his eyes. "Which will teach him
not to cheat me at cut-stones."

"It will certainly make sure he doesn't do it again," Theo
said earnestly. "Did I tell you how grateful I was for the use
of that cloak?"

He left the goblin behind, not without a certain relief,
and went to find some food. He hadn't eaten since he
had shared bread with Sedge in the late afternoon and the
day's walk had been a long one. Coathook had told him that
there would be a meal after Button's speech or story or
whatever it was, but Theo didn't want to wait that long—he
wasn't actually certain he wanted to stay up all night just to
hear some goblin-mullah toss parables or rabble-rouse or
whatever it was the guy did.

The camp was an even stranger place by night with the
birds gone and fires burning everywhere. Weird shapes

loomed up before him, each more alarming and startling than the last. Theo still had to remind himself that the people around him weren't wearing Hallowe'en masks or hanging around backstage at some children's theater: they really looked like that. In fact, many of them probably felt that an arrangement like he had, with two eyes, two nostrils, and a mouth all laid out in a symmetrical fashion on the face (and *only* on the face) was downright disturbing. But since they were almost all polite enough to hide this sentiment, he decided he could be too. He nodded and smiled at two old women with storks' legs who were dangling their clawed feet in the river, and then smiled as he patted a small child with the head and tail of a fox. He did his best to keep smiling even after the child almost bit his finger off and the mother—or perhaps it was the father—came running after him, pointing and barking and calling him names.

By the time Theo was a few yards away the yappingly anxious parent could barely be heard above the general din of the camp, of fairyfolk laughing, shouting, and arguing. The place was so full of noisy life that he had wandered quite far from the tent by the time he noticed he had been hearing an interesting sound for some time now without ever quite being conscious that he was listening to it. It was music, at first only a distant drone and snap of drums with the occasional wail of what sounded like singing voices, but getting louder and more complex to his ear with every step.

Since he had been unlucky about getting himself fed (he had quickly realized that since he had no money he would have to beg food off people who clearly had little to spare) he now let himself be tugged across the camp by his ears instead of his stomach, following the exotic strains through several wrong turns that either nearly dumped him into the sluggish Moonflood or dead-ended him at its muddy upper bank, or landed him right in the middle of someone's private space—particularly embarrassing and even traumatic when one such private space proved to be occupied by two ogres making love. He did not stay long—in fact, he turned and

ran—but the sight of all those acres of wrinkly gray flesh in
spirited congress was something he felt sure would come
back to him in nightmares for years.

The music drew him, although he couldn't say why, except that it was music, however strange. It was not the sort
of thing he liked even at his most eclectic, altogether too
alien, a kind of endless, whining drone that did not yield
very much information to his untutored ear, but he had no
other destination. Fairy children watched him pass, some
with sharp interest, others with eyes dulled by hunger or illness. *Can I catch the diseases they have here?* he wondered.
*I sure as hell wasn't vaccinated for any of them before I
came.* The sudden worry only underscored how lost he felt,
how strange. All these folk, some with wings, some with
donkey ears, some so small he could barely see them by the
light of the campfires, were part of a different world. He
might as well have been the first man on Mars in some old
science fiction book.

No wonder Eamonn Dowd wanted to write about it, he
thought as he watched a group of children with dirty faces
and wings playing an elaborate game with a stick and a
wheel off what looked like a baby carriage. *It's so different.
It's not even like the fairy tales. You could live here your
whole life and not understand how everything works, the assumptions, the rules.* An abrupt realization that he might indeed have to live here his whole life brought an intense pang
of homesickness. *It's not missing cheeseburgers and television and things like that, it's missing a place where I know
the rules. Where I know what someone means when they say
something, where I'm not always having to guess.*

Now, to add to his vast fund of ignorance, he had another
pressing mystery to deal with: *What did Eamonn Dowd do
to get that Primrose guy so crazy? Or what does Primrose
think he did, anyway?*

The music was quite loud now. Theo turned down a long
narrow space between two clusters of tents and found himself at the end of a cul-de-sac where the camp backed up

against the river's old stone walled banks. A crowd had gathered around the musicians; Theo felt a little touch of unease when he saw that they were all goblins, and not the friendly, civilized sort like Doorlatch, either. The musicians and most of the crowd were small, lean, and hard, most dressed in tattered, earth-colored clothes. A few were wearing brighter fabrics, robes of what even in the dim light were clearly bright reds and yellows, and many of the goblins dressed this way were dancing. It took him longer than it should have to realize these must be goblin women. Their long-nosed faces, or what he could see of them, since many of them wore hoods, were a little different than the men's, but what made him sure at last was what he could see of their bodies, slender above the waist but with wider hips than Coathook or the other goblins he'd met.

A few paused to look at him—some a bit suspiciously, he thought—but did not stare long before turning their attention back to the music. There were at least half a dozen goblins playing, long fingers moving like spider's legs, one goblin blowing on an instrument with long twinned pipes like a forked recorder, another couple playing more ordinary fifes or whistles. A tall, long-whiskered goblin held something that looked like a boat's paddle with strings on it across his lap, and the rest seemed to be playing different kinds of drums and shakers. It was hard to tell for certain, because the dancing women, and some dancing male goblins, kept swaying back and forth in front of the musicians.

The strangeness of the scene and the almost painfully unfamiliar music sent another wave of melancholy over him. He closed his eyes, half-listening to the wind instruments skirling around the drone of the musical paddle and the complicated, nearly arrhythmic scatter of drumbeats. *What the hell am I doing here? Besides the obvious, trying to stay alive? The greatest adventure anyone could ever have, and I can't even appreciate it—I just want to go home. If I were Great-Uncle Eamonn, I'd try to write about it, but I couldn't even hack those essay exams for junior college. What am I, really? A bum.* A fairy, maybe—he still couldn't quite believe it—but definitely a bum, no matter what. *An out-of-work singer. A delivery guy for a florist, with no girlfriend and no family. That's the funniest part of the whole thing— the idea that someone thinks I'm worth trying to kidnap or kill. Give me a break! I can finish myself off. Just give me another thirty or forty years . . .*

He was beginning to hear patterns now in the poly-rhythms, odd percussive ellipses, things left out that emphasized the things that were left in. He found himself swaying. *Look at me—like a stockbroker at a jazz festival,* he thought derisively. *Too dumb to know he's uncool.* But that wasn't really fair, was it? He'd believed most of his life that you didn't have to be cool to appreciate music, that it didn't even matter if someone liked uncool music. That was one of the things that had driven him crazy about Kris Rolle and his bandmates, that youthful certainty that there was good music and bad music and that they knew which was which. "Bullshit," he'd told them once. "A teenage girl creaming while she listens to some boy-band, a monk digging on the God he hears in Gregorian chants, or John fucking Coltrane himself climbing up into the sky on a staircase made of sixteenth notes, it's all the same. If it takes you there, it's good." That was when he cared enough to argue with idiots like Kris. That was when he cared.

Theo was beginning to hear some of the sounds in the music, to get a tiny glimmering of what it was, and also, perhaps more importantly, to get an idea of what it wasn't. When people heard something or saw something unfamiliar, they had to compare it to something they knew. That was fine. But breaking away from that first identification was important or you'd spend the rest of your life thinking of it as a subset of the familiar thing. Theo was listening closely now, feeling the beat but also realizing that the goblin music wasn't any number of things it had sounded a little like at first hearing: it wasn't Middle Eastern music, wasn't Indian, wasn't Asian. It had too many strange unplayed bits in it to be any of those. If there was anything he knew that came close, it might have been the Qawwali stuff, the Sufi devotional music he had listened to for a while as a matter of rebellion when all his musical friends had suddenly discovered African music and were raving to him about King Sunny Ade and Ladysmith Black Mambazo. Not that they weren't fine, but he simply hadn't wanted to be the last guy onto the bandwagon, any bandwagon.

Hey, now I'm definitely the last guy on the goblin jazz bandwagon, at least on this world. But if I ever get home, I'll be the first goblin jazz guy on my block—on anybody's block.

He smiled, his eyes still closed, head nodding to the beats he was beginning to hear, even the ones that weren't being played. *That's what I am, when you come down to it, he realized. I may not be making any money off it, but I'm a musician. I'm a singer.*

Time passed—five minutes, half an hour, he couldn't tell. The dancers, male and especially female, had shied away from him at first, but now it was as though they no longer noticed him: he had sunk into the music with them until he was invisible. He was hearing things he couldn't have heard when he first arrived in the dead-end street, his brain making some sense out of the larger patterns of the music, some of which seemed to last for minutes before repeating. The musicians gave out occasional bursts of vocalization, swooping cries that scurried up the minor scale before holding for a moment, but they never lasted for more than a few seconds. Occasionally someone in the crowd would join in, singing a quick babble of unfamiliar words or even letting out a wordless cry, but otherwise the music had no singer's part.

What was odd, though, was that there seemed to *be* such a part, or at least a place for another instrumental voice of some kind, implied in the shape of the music as he now understood it, commented on by the instruments and percussion as though it were actually being heard. Sometimes this gap disappeared, filled by the frantic, almost colliding sounds of the musicians; other times, especially when the drone softened and the drumming dropped to a faint purr of fingers on taut skin, the gap seemed so obvious that Theo yearned to fill it. He found he was humming, half-singing to himself as he swayed, trying not simply to fill the perceived emptiness with something of his own creation, a blues vamp or jazz scat, but to create what *should* be there.

The music wound around him, compelling as a drug, endless as a necklace of bright beads running continuously through his fingers. Someone was filling the space in the music now, cresting the drone then dropping back into the sinewy muddle of instruments, moving in delicately wordless, staccato sounds through the quiet stretches.

When he realized that he was the singer, and that he was as loud as any of the instruments, he stopped singing and opened his eyes in shock. The dancers nearest him were watching him, but they were still dancing. He looked up to the musicians but the only one looking at him was the long-whiskered goblin with the string instrument, who met his eye and nodded. He was not smiling, but he was not frowning, either. The string player nodded again, then moved his head in a way that looked very much like *"Go on."* Tentatively, Theo began to vocalize again. The goblin still did not smile, but he nodded once more and closed his eyes as he lowered himself back into the river of music.

Theo kept his own eyes open as he sang, at least at first, but although many of the goblin crowd looked at him with interest and even a little surprise, he saw nothing else—no resentment, no bitterness. He began to breathe more easily. He didn't want to be some American tourist crashing into someone else's ceremony, but unless goblin body language was completely upside down from his own, they didn't seem to mind, even seemed to accept and enjoy it. He let himself bask in the music once more, let the worried thoughts drop away until he found again the place he had been. The hole in the music led him on like a firefly over evening hills, like a will-o'-the-wisp through midnight swamps. He did his best to follow, to fill the space without filling it up entirely, to let the music breathe around him. When he worked hard, when he tried to think too much, he lost his way, but when he simply felt for it the bright thing was there before him, leading him through a world that was completely foreign and yet somehow at least a little familiar.

This is who I am, he thought as the musicians crashed in with a loud, discordant break and he caught his breath. He was high, light-headed, happy. The more he forgot himself and sang, the more he felt like he truly was himself. *Whatever else I might be, human or not, I'm a singer. No one can take that away from me.*

The frenzied blare died away. For a moment just the drums went on, an expectant, slithering patter as quiet as a small rock bouncing down a steep slope. Then the paddle-shaped instrument began to caw like a blackbird in a bare tree and Theo talked back to it in a high keening wail like the wind and his words and thoughts went away and he disappeared into the music again.

29

THE HOLE
IN THE STORY

Theo was just taking another long hit from the ivory pipe and marveling at stars stuck on the celestial firmament like lumps of burning napalm—whatever else about Fairyland might be disappointing or terrifying, he had to admit that the stars were almost worth the price of admission—when Cumber found him.

"Theo, I've been looking all over for . . . *what are you doing?*"

He held it in for a few more seconds before replying. "Hanging out with some new friends. Smoking some ghostweed." He turned to the goblin musicians. "That's what it called, isn't it? Ghostweed?" The musicians had not been particularly chatty before, but with Cumber's appearance they had all gone silent. "Whatever," Theo said. "It's pretty cool. You want some?"

"No!" Cumber waved his hands. "No. You'd better give that . . . thing back. We're late. We're going to miss Button's story."

Theo shrugged. "These guys said that he never starts until everyone who's supposed to be there is there. Right, Bottlecap?"

The stringed-instrument player nodded slowly. "He always knows the right time."

"Well . . . well, I think we should go anyway, Theo. There are things to talk about."

Theo handed the long-stemmed pipe to Bottlecap, who tapped out the ashes against his bare heel and slipped it into his baggy coat. "Okay. Well, thanks, guys. Thanks for letting me sing with you, too."

"You *sang* with them?" Cumber seemed unusually agitated. "Theo, you didn't let anyone give you anything called philtre, did you?" His voice dropped. "Or . . . pixie dust?"

The goblin musicians glanced at each other and began to disperse. One of them began to hum a plaintively droning little air. Bottlecap looked back at Theo and smiled deep in his furry face. Apparently some things were universal, and one of them was how musicians reacted to straight people.

Cumber had his elbow and was practically dragging him away. "Man, what's the problem?" Theo asked. "Those people were nice to me." He couldn't get very upset, though. The ghostweed had crept into some of the draftier cracks in his mind and sealed them up. He felt warm and connected to everything from the smoldering stars on down. "What's with this pixie dust you're in such a panic about? Is it addictive or something?"

"Yes, it is, but the main objection is that it's made from real pixies."

"Say *what?*"

"Mummified. In any case, just stay away from it if someone offers it to you. I was worried because everyone says that the goblins come into the city and sell it—mostly to the rich Flower kids."

"Those guys were just players. Good, too—you should have heard them! And I joined in after a while. We had fun."

Cumber shook his head. "You never cease to amaze me." He had let go of Theo's elbow but was moving purposefully and Theo had to move faster than he wanted to keep up. "What's it like?"

"What? Singing?"

"No, ghostweed. I've . . . I've never tried it."

"Not even when you were at the university? Man, what were you doing?"

"Studying." There was a stiff edge in his voice. "Some of us couldn't afford to ease our way through. Some of us couldn't have Daddy and Mummy send special tutors down to help us cram for our Transmutation finals."

Theo had been about to tease the ferisher a bit, but there was too much pain in Cumber's answer to ignore. "Well, you didn't miss that much. It's . . . I don't know, it's just copping a buzz. Sort of like marijuana back home, or a few beers. At least I think so, but this is my first time—maybe an hour from now I'm going to be screaming and seeing green tigers."

"Once a term, after finals, Zirus and the others used to drag me out and make me drink with them. The first time I was a bit proud and excited—these were the children of very important families, you know, famous families. But I drank too much and made a fool of myself, started crying about how much I missed my home. Do you know what Zirus did the next day?"

Theo shook his head.

"Invited me out again. You see, they loved it. They thought it was hilarious. The little ferisher who couldn't hold his liquor."

"Well, based on what I saw at that Christmas club, maybe you're the kind of guy who shouldn't drink—weird things start to happen when you loosen up. That's just how it is sometimes with people who are a little too tightly wrapped. Don't take offense—you know what I mean."

Cumber nodded sadly. "I do."

"Hey, what's going on up there?" Theo had just noticed that they were not the only people moving toward the bridge, and that most of the camp seemed to have arrived ahead of them. A row of torches had been set along the wall of the bridge with an empty spot in the middle where a small knot of people were standing, looking down at the crowd. "It looks like Elfapalooza or something. Is there going to be more music?"

"Button's going to tell a story. Everybody's been saying that for hours. Don't you listen, Theo?"

"Yeah, I listen." He was not going to let Cumber take the sheen off his mood, or harsh his ghostweed buzz, or whatever it was. "I just didn't think it would be like this."

It was strangely quiet as they worked their way into the densest part of the crowd, nearest the bridge. Most conversations around them were being carried on in low tones; only the cries of birds and the occasional happy or angry shrieks of children lifted above the abnormal stillness, which gave everything a tense, expectant air.

They had reached a point in the gathering where if they were going to get any closer they would have to squeeze between a group of ogres who were passing a hogshead of something around, and even in his cheerfully stoned state Theo could see it might not be a good idea to try to shove past drunken ogres. They moved back a little bit so they could see over the large gray folks, who were even taller than they were wide.

"All this for Button?" Theo marveled. "The little guy who gave me the card? What is he, some kind of rock star? A magician? Does he do tricks?"

Cumber, who had fallen into a morose silence, did not reply.

As if Cumber and Theo were indeed the two he had been waiting for—although they were surely too far back in the crowd for him to have seen them—the knot of people at the center of the bridge split apart and a small, slender shape stepped forward to the edge. Theo couldn't be certain, but he thought that beside a couple of ogre bodyguards, one of Button's companions was Caradenus Primrose, the fairy who had tried to kill him. At least Primrose didn't look proud of himself: from what Theo could see of his long face at this distance, the fairy seemed as depressed as Cumber Sedge.

"By the Taproot, there are many of you here today!" said
Button cheerfully, surveying the crowd. Somehow, either by
particularly fortuitous acoustics or magic of the more ordinary Fairyland sort, his voice seemed to fly to Theo's ears as
though the little goblin stood only a few feet away. "So
many have come since the terrible day when the dragons
flew. But you all are welcome! My clan name is Button. In
the nest I was called Mud. My other name—well, *hem,* we
shall talk about that. Goblin names, like goblin stories, always have a hole in the middle."

"We're hungry!" someone shouted in a rasping voice. A
few others echoed the cry, but on balance the crowd seemed
patient and interested in what Button had to say.

"And we shall feed you. Many kind people have brought
food to this place and it will all be shared. First, though, because there are so many new ones here, I ask you to listen to
my story.

"But this is not truly *my* story, no—it is not the story of
Mud of the Button tribe, although I am in it, as you are in it,
and you, and you. In fact, we are all in it. Rather it is the
story of a very beautiful land of forests and fields and rivers.
The goats and cows and sheep grazed the hills that the sun
warmed, roaming as far as they wished—or at least as far,
hem, as their herders would let them. In the evening the
white stag came stilting out of the forest to watch the moon
rise. There was room for all, food and shelter for all, fire and
water and earth and sky for all. Do you know this place, this
wonderful place? Faerie, it was called."

A few people laughed as though it was the punchline of a
joke, but Theo was feeling the effects of the ghostweed quite
strongly and had been slipping into a pleasant reverie, seeing the pictures Button made in his mind's eye; he didn't like
people laughing at them.

"Yes, it seems strange now, when most of the trees stand
behind the walls of the great houses or are fenced in as part
of those households' country estates to shelter the animals
our lords hunt for pleasure, to know that once the forest cov-

ered much of Faerie. Most of you remember, but those of you who are too young—imagine! Only imagine! A black squirrel, leaping from branch to branch, tree to tree, could spend her entire life crossing Faerie without ever touching the ground. Trees like an ocean! Trees more ancient than Flower lords or gnomes or even goblins. Trees which saw the first sun, which were old when the first mountains thrust up from the ground, trees so broad that an entire town such as you find at any railroad station could have sheltered under the branches of one, trees so tall that their leaves touched the clouds and their roots were set in the very scales of the world-worm. *Hem.* Is it any wonder that the fairy-folk, when they arose in the long grass of that first evening, looked on those ancient trees with awe? That in the long days that followed, those among them who distinguished themselves in power and beauty took the names of trees for their own? Where have they gone, those ancient Tree lords and Tree ladies? We know their names, for we live in their old fiefdoms, the fields of Lord Rowan of the fair hair, of Lady Birch tall and slim, of Oak and Alder and stately Willow, all of them lovely and wise beyond our understanding. Where did they go? Why is there nothing left of them but their names?"

The crowd was silent now. Theo had begun to forget that Cumber was standing next to him, let alone that he was himself only one in a crowd of hundreds—no, it must be thousands. It seemed like the little figure standing on the bridge was talking to him alone.

"But, *hem,* I hear you ask, what does a goblin know of such things? What does a goblin know of the beautiful masters of Faerie who tamed the world but wisely left its heart wild? Well, I will tell you an astonishing thing—there were goblins there too! Ah, yes, it is hard to believe! But there were in those long-lost days the ancestors of my own people, and they too were handsome and bold. They walked the plains and the deep forests, they spoke to birds, they swam in icy rivers and feared no water-spirit, they ran beneath the stars and sang to those stars as they ran—and the stars sang back. Stranger still, they served no one but themselves. When one of the great Tree-lords wished to cross goblin lands, he brought gifts and gave them to the goblins and they feasted together. And when he had crossed the goblin land or hunted in the goblin forest, he gave them more gifts and thanked them. And when a goblin chieftain wished to cross the lands of a Tree lord to follow the birds, or to find new grazing for his horses or sheep, he brought gifts to the Tree folk and they feasted together.

"Yes, I know, to our civilized ears it sounds strange indeed, but those were the most ancient of days, when no one knew any better.

"And watching over all were the king and queen. Lean closer and I will tell the youngest among you a very, very surprising thing. All those who have grown to maturity must surely know this, but the children will find it most astonishing."

Theo found himself bending forward, one stalk of wind-blown wheat among thousands of others, all leaning in the same direction.

"Here is the secret. The king and queen—they were king and queen of the goblins, too! King Goldenstare and Queen Silverclaw, we called them. Yes! And they were also monarchs of the dwarves and the pixies, sprites, gnomes, hobbanies—all the creatures of Faerie! One king! One queen! Deep in the Old Hill at the center of Faerie they sat on their thrones, robed in darkness and crowned in air and light, and had the ordering of everything in their hands. If they loved the tall Tree lords of the shining hair, no less did they love the clever, nimble-handed gnomes, the arrow-swift sprites, or the laughing, freedom-loving goblins. There were some creatures who did not venerate them, like the giants, but even the wind that bears them up is not, *hem,* loved by every bird.

"This is a goblin story, of course, and as all but the very youngest of you know, goblin stories always have a hole in the middle. The Tree lords are gone now, gone to their graves in the Cathedral Grove that circles the Old Hill in Midnight. Their grandchildren and great-grandchildren and great-great-grandchildren rule Faerie in these days, and where the tall trees once covered the land and drank from the sun and moon, yet still made shelter for all who stood beneath them or harbored in their branches, the Flower lords of this day are too busy covering themselves with bright colors and climbing toward the light to make shelter for others.

"The king and queen are dead now too, and with them has gone the order that gave to each goblin and fairy and troll and woodwight an equal share. Yes, it is astonishing, especially to those of you who are children—the rest are old and wise and knew these things already—but there was a time once when there was no City, when there was no servitude, and when the power to make a fire or to call the rain or to cure an illness came not from the factories of Flower lords but directly from the king and queen themselves, flowing like the waters of a great river, so that each and every man and woman and child could go down to its banks and take what they needed. So old-fashioned! So impractical! Because, of course, as any goblin or fairy child who has ever played on a sandy shore knows, you cannot spread your sand widely if you wish to make something stand high. You must push the sand together, pile it up and up, and that is how you make something tall and impressive like the house of a Flower lord, or even like our great City. If that means that you must take from elsewhere to have enough for a proper pile—well, then! The magic of Faerie is not sand on the riverbank for all children to share together, goblin and pooka and fairy lordling alike, especially since there is not as much of it to go around as there once was, it seems—perhaps because we no longer have our king and queen. In any case, only the mad or the selfish would suggest that the beauties of our City and the power of its lords and ladies might have been put to better use if shared with all. Those days are over! Who could wish such old-fashioned ways to return?"

The crowd was beginning to murmur now. It was a noise of unrest, and even through what had been a general haze of well-being, Theo could not help worrying that the things Button was saying were angering them, that any moment they might storm the bridge, ogres or no ogres, and pull the little goblin down. Theo's mood took a sudden downward turn. The crowd around him seemed strange and menacing. *I don't belong here. What am I doing? What does all this talk mean?*

Button went on as though he did not hear the growls and the growing chorus of angry shouts. "Some would say that we goblins should feel particularly aggrieved, oh yes. For although all the races of Faerie now serve the Flower lords, only the goblins were brought in chains to help build the City, were stolen from their forests and plains and loaded onto railroad cars—women separated from their men, parents from their children. When the jobs were done, we found the lands where we had lived now belonged to Flower lords and Flower ladies, that the forests were fenced and the plains had been plowed and covered with towns and railroad tracks."

"You're not the only ones they stole from! The dwarves did not give in without a fight!" someone shouted in a deep voice from a few yards in front of Theo. "They broke our guild. They starved our families. Eight hundred and twelve of us died just in the battle at Golden Mountain, cut down like rats in a grain house—the goblins are not the only ones who've suffered!" A few other voices echoed him. Someone else shouted something about wood-nymphs and the rape of True Arden, and Theo suddenly realized that the crowd's growing anger was not directed at the little goblin.

"Ah," said Button. "Well, there you see, I am only a foolish goblin, a young one myself and thus ignorant of history, *hem*. Perhaps it has not been my people alone who have suffered for this mighty flower of truesilver and crystal we call the City." He was swaying a little; his voice moved again into its singsong cadence. "But listen. It is late and I have not finished my story. It is late and the children should be asleep.

"I told you that all goblin stories have a hole in the middle—like all goblin names. It is not for me to tell you what fits in that open place, that well of mystery at the center of Faerie. On one side were the Tree lords and all other fairy-folk living together. Today we stand on the other side of that hole, with the Tree lords gone and the Flower lords now masters of all, with the goblins and the dwarves and others forced to serve at their tables and hope for a crust they may take home to their families. On one side was Faerie in the days of the king and queen, when the land was rich and belonged to all. Today we stand on the other side of that hole, with the masters of the Flower houses fighting among themselves for power, unleashing great dragons, burning not just their enemies but any who must live where they are fighting their war. What is in that empty space? It is not for me to say. The stories of my people do not work that way."

"The Flower houses must fall!" someone shouted.

"They've robbed us!" screamed someone else. The crowd began to make noises like an animal waking up, a huge and unhappy animal.

"Careful, my friends!" said Button. "In these days, when all power rests with the feuding Flower lords, it is foolish to offend them. Who would speak ill of Lord Hellebore or Lord Thornapple when it is their charity that keeps the poor of the City alive without jobs, and their forebearance which keeps armed soldiers from coming to this camp and arresting all of you who left your homes without permission during a time when the Parliament of Blooms has set the City under military law? Why, at any moment, it would be within the mandate of Parliament to send in troops and haul every citizen of this wrongful enclave away to a work camp, or even to execution."

"Let them try!" screeched a tall, celery-colored woman. A dozen other voices echoed her.

"Calm, calm," said Button. "We must have calm. For the

lords of the Flower houses surely have your best interests in mind, and the power to keep the City under their just governance, and the rest of Faerie under governance of the City." He paused as if listening to the discontented murmuring, gazing slowly across the sea of torchlit faces. Theo wondered what it must look like from the bridge. Carnival. Hallowe'en squared.

Above the cries of discontent, a lone wolf-voice howled out its misery.

"Did I think that the Flower lords were corrupt and their rule criminal," cried Button suddenly, "then I would have to tell you a very different kind of story." The crowd fell silent. "I would feel honor-bound to say that the day is coming when the Flower houses must give up their power. *Hem.* I would feel compelled to say that for once there will be no hole in a goblin tale, to point out that the death of the king and queen was observed by no one but the masters of the famous Seven Families, and that those families are now down to three, as a troop of bandits may slit each others' throats in the night over the swag from a rich robbery they have just committed. That the king and queen who ruled all with an even hand have been taken from us, and perhaps that was no accident. Now their successors set each others' houses on fire and drive our children through the streets with whips.

"In fact, if I thought that the rule of the Flower houses needed to be resisted, I would not only fill the hole in my story, I would tell you that until the day comes when all is made right or I breathe my last, I would no longer hide behind the hole in my own name."

A hoarse goblin-voice shouted, *"No!"*—whoever it was sounded quite shocked, even frightened. A small chorus of other voices joined him, trying to stop Button from doing something Theo didn't quite understand, but Button only smiled.

"Oh, my friends, if I thought resistance to the Flower houses was important," he went on, "I would have to say that secrecy, even when it is an old tradition, is for cowards—that sometimes even mystery must go naked." He raised his slender arms in the air. "I would stand here before you as though a child at my Naming Song, and say to anyone who can hear that my clan name is Button, the name I was given in my nest is Mudlark . . . and that the name I call myself, my name-of-secret-despair, is Bug." Another shocked cry rose from the goblins in attendance. "I would tell it to everyone, because the day is coming soon when even the smallest, crawling things must stand up and be counted.

"That is what I would do. 'My name is Mud Bug Button,' I would say, 'and I shall not rest until I have back my home-soul—my honor!' And on such a day as that, I would ask you all to join me."

Many of the goblins in the crowd were still reeling with obvious horror at the revelation of Button's other name—apparently it was a big deal, although Theo found it only another confusing detail buried in the mass of myth and rabble-rousing and strange conditional declarations. But even among those goblins there were a few who recovered quickly, who seemed fired with excitement, and they began to chant the full name. To look at their faces made clear that something was happening beyond even the powerful anti-Flower rhetoric, whether Theo could grasp it or not.

"Mud-Bug-Button. Mud-Bug-Button." The chant grew, but it was celebratory not threatening, and others beside the goblins were now chiming in. The initial moment of frenzy was past—Theo had felt it like dry tinder all around him, that if the little goblin had given them a target to attack, the crowd would have thrown its bodies against that target, no matter the consequences—but the madness had not altogether cooled. The gathered fairy-folk were elevated and strangely bonded. They shouted at each other, even argued loudly, but there was also laughter and cheerful boasting, embraces between different types of fairies and curses against the effete Flower clans, even some music and dancing starting up underneath the fiery stars. As Theo slowly

came out of his dreamy state he saw that goblins and other folk were moving through the crowd with baskets of hard bread and river fish, passing out food.

A tall shape appeared in front of him. "Button was right. He said you were here. He has sharp eyes." It was Primrose, the young fairy lord who only hours before had held a knife to his throat. Theo's first response should have been to flinch away from him, but the ghostweed he had shared with the musicians had left him feeling strangely detached, as though nothing quite mattered.

"What do you want?" It was Cumber, oddly enough, who sounded angry and defensive.

"First and most importantly, to tell you that Button has asked for you. He and some others are taking a meal and he would like you to come and share bread with him." Primrose hesitated. "The other thing is that I would like to make an apology to you. I . . . I have not left behind as much of the world I came from as I thought, and when I heard two days ago that my father had died, it . . . it reminded me of loyalties to him I once felt strongly, loyalties to the family name, even though I had turned against them, to his sorrow and my unhappiness." He lowered his head as though waiting for the executioner.

My God, Theo realized after several long seconds had passed, *he really wants me to forgive him. He's waiting for it.*

"You tried to kill him," Cumber said.

"Any of my kind would have done the same," Primrose replied with a hint of angry pride. "I am one of the few who would stop to learn why I might be wrong. I am perhaps the only one who would come to you and apologize."

And it was true, or seemed that way: Theo could see that the fairy's whole demeanor suggested someone doing something incredibly difficult, that Primrose was stretched tight as piano wire. If he rebuffed him, Theo did not fear that the fairy lord would attack him—the time for that had passed—

but he suspected that Primrose himself would suffer some deep wounding.

It's hard to learn to be flexible, Theo thought. *It's hard to trust.* He had been there himself, fighting with Cat about things, afraid to give an inch.

"If you promise to tell me what you know about my . . . about the man I used to think of as my great-uncle," Theo said, "I'll be happy to forgive you. No, I'll forgive you anyway, no conditions. But I would like to hear what brings you here—and also what you know about Eamonn Dowd."

Something like a grateful smile flickered on Primrose's androgynously handsome face, but it did not last long. "It is shameful, what happened. Shameful to my family."

"Okay, I won't force you. But if you're going to trust me with an apology you can probably trust me with some family shame as well. And even though Dowd wasn't *really* my uncle, I've thought of him that way for some time, so I think I'll have to share this shame you're talking about."

"I'm . . . I'm rather hungry," Cumber ventured. "I was out with our tent-mate Mistress Twinge this evening while Theo was . . . singing. She took me out to see some sights, meet some people. Most of it had more to do with drinking than eating and my stomach aches. Could we go?"

Primrose nodded. He suddenly seemed much more relaxed, less stilted. "Come. Button's table will be good, simple food. Just the thing for someone who has been keeping company with a pooka."

Even with all the people now in it, the top room of the bridge tower seemed bigger than it had the first time Theo had seen it. At least two dozen fairy-folk of all different shapes and sizes were sitting on the floor around a carpet covered with bowls and cups, eating and talking. The old goblin Doorlatch sprang up at their entrance and almost skipped over to greet them.

"Ah, Master Vilmos and Master Sedge, very good, very good. And we have made up our quarrel with Lord Primrose,

I see. Splendid!" He took Cumber by the arm and steered him to an open space next to an attractive young fairy woman who had tattered clothes but magnificent, shimmering wings furled tightly against her back. He politely directed Primrose to sit next to Cumber, then took Theo by the arm. "An honor for you, young master. Button has asked you to sit beside him."

It required convincing a bodyguard ogre the size of a midsize sedan to move over and make room, but Doorlatch got Theo shoehorned in next to Button before vanishing off to pursue some other errand.

"Please," said Button, who was again wearing what Theo thought of as his Franciscan habit, "make yourself welcome at our table. The field mice in honey are very good."

Theo tried to keep his smile. "Thanks. I think I'll just have some fruit and bread and . . . is that cheese?"

Button nodded. Up close, he was much the same small, unassuming figure who Theo had seen on the bus. It was hard to reconcile that with the demagogue who only half an hour earlier had been so deftly playing the crowd. "May I serve you?"

"That's really kind, but I can do it myself." He busied himself trying to get a small object with a shiny rind like a melon out of a stack of fruit without tipping the whole thing over. "I'm . . . I'm confused. When I first met you, I . . ." He took a piece of bread from a woven basket. "What were you doing riding the bus?"

The goblin smiled. His teeth were yellow like an old dog's, and sharp. "It is, *hem,* faster than walking."

"Yeah, but you seem a little too important around here just to be sitting on the cross-town bus handing out cards to people like me."

The smile broadened. "From what I understand, Master Vilmos, there are not very many people like you to be found here in Faerie."

"Fair enough." The little guy was hard work. Theo looked down to see Cumber trying to listen to something earnest Primrose was saying while still keeping a conversation going with the attractive sorrel-haired fairy woman on the other side of him. *Poor Applecore,* he thought. *We're neither of us being very faithful to your memory.* It made him feel guilty and it hardened his resolve. "Look, I guess I'm trying to figure out what you're doing here, for one thing, and why you invited me—why you care about me at all. You're obviously an important guy."

Button turned to whisper something to the ogre on the other side of him, who looked at Theo with something like amusement on his elephantine face before going back to his energetic chewing. "I told him you were the one who was singing with the goblins this evening. There is much talk about you already. You wonder why I invited you? As I said on the bridge tonight, perhaps it will soon be time to fill empty places in some important stories. You have been here less than a day and yet you already found a very powerful empty space to fill. Your kind and my kind do not make music together."

"Really?" He was flattered and a little nervous. Apparently he hadn't just been jamming, he had been performing some kind of weightily significant cultural exchange. Theo was suddenly very grateful he hadn't known. "Okay, it worked. I'm distracted again. And I'd love to talk music sometime . . ."

"Then you must speak to Doorlatch. He was a sacred hill-top singer, once."

". . . But that's not really what I want to know now." He took a breath. "Please, if it's not rude to keep asking, what's going on here? Who *are* you?"

Button's laugh was easy, unforced. "I am just what you see—Mud Button." He made his face solemn. "No, I forgot, I have abandoned mystery. I am Mud Bug Button. I am a storyteller."

"And the stories you tell sound like you're trying to start a revolution. That makes you pretty important."

"What goes on here *is* important. I simply happen to have come here at a particular time. It is the others who are also here, and the reasons that brought them to this place, that are important."

Halfway between a blood-and-thunder preacher and a politician, Theo thought. *He seems like the best kind of each, but how the hell would I know for sure, especially here where all the rules are different?* "Are people going to fight back against Hellebore and his friends? Because if they are, maybe I am in the right place after all. I owe those bastards something."

"More than you guess, I suspect." Button again made his strange throat-clearing noise as he returned his attention to the bread and the sopping, glazed field mouse on his plate, making it all into a sort of sandwich.

Theo didn't really want to see the mouse go down, so he concentrated on filling his own stomach with some less avant-garde delicacies. He poured himself a cup of wine that smelled of oranges and cinnamon, then offered the jug to Button, who shook his head. Theo drank off the whole cup before venturing another question. "I met someone who was coming to see you today . . . a pretty strange guy named Nettle . . ."

Button looked up, smiled, nodded. "My good friend, yes. You will get to see more of him since you are sharing a tent."

"Hold on, *he's* the other roommate? They said it was someone named Streedy."

"Streedy Nettle, yes. That is his name."

Theo recalled the unfocused gaze with more than a little dismay. "We're sharing a tent with *that* guy? The tall one? The . . . strange one?"

Button was about to laugh, but he managed to keep it off his face. His eyes betrayed him, though; they glittered with amusement. "So you have met him. Good."

Theo shook his head. "All the more reason for what I was going to ask you. So what's with him? I mean, he said he knew someone that I know—that he heard her voice in his head."

"Is that someone in the, *hem*, Thornapple family, by any chance?"

"Yes!"

Button nodded. "Let me tell you a little bit about Streedy Nettle."

"Is this another story with holes in it?"

"You must judge for yourself. But since there is no such thing as a story with a true beginning or a true ending, then they must all be circular, and if they are circular, it stands to reason that they will all have a certain . . . open space in their center."

Theo waved his hand in surrender. "Streedy Nettle. The Thornapples."

"Yes. He worked for the Thornapples, did my friend Streedy, if you can dignify it with such a name. Do you know anything about how power is generated in Faerie, Master Vilmos?"

"I've heard a little," Theo said grimly. "Slave labor until they burn out, basically, right?"

"A fair summation. And Streedy was one such producer of power, working in a Thornapple power plant as a capacitor, which suggests he had some native abilities beyond what is normal. In any case, long before he had reached his natural age of diminishment, Streedy was involved in a very bad accident. It is hard to say what happened, exactly, but there was a terrible overload of power for some reason and he was right in the center of it."

"When you say power here, you're talking about what I call magic, right?"

"Ah, yes, you are of the mortal world originally. I suppose that is right. But whatever you call it, it was a terrible event. Streedy was almost killed—he should have died, in fact, but for some reason he did not. When he felt well enough, he ran away. Delirious and slowly starving, he found his way to the outskirts of the City and wandered the streets of Eastwater. I found him. I fed him. I brought him here."

"Well, that explains about what he's doing here at the bridge, I guess, but not about . . ."

"The Thornapples?" Button took another bite of bread, then wiped his mouth daintily with the sleeve of his garment. If it weren't for the finger-shaped nose and the yellow fangs, Theo would have felt himself to be in the company of some Bedouin chieftain. "That is a mystery even to me. Something about his accident, the way he was changed. He hears voices. At first I thought it was only madness from a damaged mind, but it is more than that. I have heard enough to know that somehow he has made, *hem,* a connection of sorts with the power systems of Thornapple House—a fleeting and irregular connection, but it is there—and that he hears things, learns things, because of it. He cannot explain them all, and even though he now seems to understand what has happened, it is still very troubling to him to hear those voices in his head."

Theo sat back. He was full and almost happy: the despair of the past days was, for the moment, at an acceptable distance. *Ghostweed and music,* he thought. *And a good dinner. It may not be the best way to get through something, it may not rebuild your life or bring back your friends, but it's better than a sharp stick in the eye.* "Well, *that's* all pretty weird, for sure," he said to the goblin, "but at least it makes some sense. I have to stop thinking that the rules I know apply here. It makes me stick out like a sore thumb. It gets me in trouble."

"Oh, but that's just what you should not stop doing, my friend." Button pushed his own plate away. "It is important that you keep thinking like what you are, or what you long believed yourself to be—a mortal."

"What are you talking about? And how do you know I'm not a mortal, anyway?"

The goblin did not smile this time. "You have few secrets left in this camp, Theo Vilmos. But do not fear. We are your friends, or we would like to be. And we need you."

"Need me? For what?"

"I am not sure yet. But the bad days are coming, the days of fire. No, they are already here. And I sense that we will need you, and need you very badly. Even so, it may not be enough. We live in the days of a Terrible Child, Theo Vilmos. Days when bad dreams walk living under the sun."

It was too much to absorb. Theo closed his eyes, let the babble of the table flow over him. "Can I ask you one more question?"

"Of course."

"You telling your other name tonight. Was that as big a deal as it seemed?"

"I do not think any other goblin has ever admitted it to any outside his nest, and certainly not to any who were not of his own tribe. But these are times of change. It seemed the right thing to do."

"The other goblins seemed to take it okay."

"Most here are almost mad with anger—yes, and with hatred of the Flower clans. They are willing to go through nearly anything to find their home-souls again, although some will feel uneasy tomorrow to have heard such a private thing spoken in a public place, and said in front of Uneaten as well—those who are not goblins." He showed a small, yellow smile. "And I daresay there will be more than a few of my kind who will want to kill me when they hear, the tradition-lumbered folk of the Ash Plains Covenant, others who fear the new more than they fear death. And of course there were spies from the Flower families among those gathered tonight. But Choo-Choo and Topsy will protect me." He reached out to pat one of the ogres, who grunted with a mouth full of food. "Long enough, anyway, for me to accomplish my work." Button straightened up. "Come, we have talked enough of such things. Tell me of your world. We goblins seldom see those lands in these painful days. Do mothers still frighten children with our name?"

Theo considered. "Not really. I suppose there are monster movies, things like that . . ."

"Monsters moving?" Button looked at him with a shrewd

eye. "I am sure your world would be stranger to me than mine is to you. Tell me a little, then I will let you go and sleep, for I know you are tired."

And so as the lamps burned down and the fairy-folk talked and laughed and whispered all around him, Theo did his best to stay awake and tell the goblin stories of a strange, magical world in which everyone grew old, the trees had no spirits, and none of the people, not even the lowliest folk, had wings.

30

FAMILY MATTERS

The limousine full of bodyguards was already loaded and waiting, a cloud of tiny powersparks drifting up from the coach's exhaust vent. The air in the underground garage was thick with the stuff—Poppy could feel it prickling on her skin. They had been waiting for her a long time.

Good. She couldn't care less.

She saw glimpses of thick gray faces as her father's guards looked out at her through the smoked windows. Even behind darkened glass, their expressions were respectful. Everybody knew what had happened to an ogre named Blocks who had been caught leering at the daughter of his employer, Lord Periwinkle. What was left of the body had been sent back to Blocks' family in twelve attractive ceremonial cases, each bearing the Perwinkle crest. None of the boxes had been very large, although Blocks in life had been a massive fellow. Lord Periwinkle had been voted an official Bestowal of Praise by the parliament for his gesture—more for its deterrent effect on bodyguards and servants everywhere than for the courtesy shown to the bereaved family.

Wayside, the driver, stood by the door of her father's coach. He nodded his blind, equine head at her as she approached. He was bigger than the average doonie, tall and broad across the shoulders, effectively giving the Thornapples an extra bodyguard: if other doonies were slender thorough-breds, he was a plowhorse.

"Afternoon, Mistress."

"Good afternoon, Wayside. I suppose my father's in a horrid mood because I've kept him waiting?"

"I've seen him more cheerful, Mistress." He opened the door for her, then closed it behind her with a silent thump that always made her ears pop.

As she sat down, her father gave her the withering look that used to send a spasm of panic right through her when she was a child, from the nape of her neck to her groin. She was impervious now, or as close to it as you could get when the person in question could still have you killed with a snap of his fingers.

Would he do that? she wondered. *If I made him angry enough?* Her stepbrother's murder had left Aulus, Lord Thornapple, with no heir, so presumably he had some use for his daughters, although she felt sure that was the only reason he cared about them. After Orian's birth had killed his first wife, her father had married three more times, but to his secret shame and public irritation the succeeding wives had produced only five girl children. The other four daughters were all married to scions of important client houses . . .

Client, as in rhymes with "pliant," thought Poppy.

. . . But none of them seemed the type to which her father would entrust what was now, with the destruction of the Daffodils, one of the two most powerful houses in the city.

Fine, she thought. *Better than fine. Let Lavinia's husband Saxifrage have it all. The faster he runs it into the ground, the happier I'll be. Murderers.* She stared at her father, mirroring the emotionless mask he habitually made of his features. *You and that monster Lord Hellebore. You all deserve to die.*

As that dreadful, cold thought grew in her like ice crystals, the luxury coach bumped up out of the garage and slowed to be waved through the gate and out into Henbane Square. The usual rabble of beggars, protesters, and supplicants was gone; instead, the square was full of well-armed parliamentary constables, a mark that the ruling families were still not entirely certain of their victory. Wayside slowed to let the coach full of bodyguards clear the gate-house and catch up.

Her father finally broke the glacial silence. "You have made me wait." With his pale skin, snowy eyebrows, and thick, tar-black locks, he looked like a marble statue that someone had painted hair on for a prank. "By making me wait, you have made our host Lord Hellebore wait, too. Two of the most important people in all Faerie, on whose words and thoughts thousands of people depend, have lost half an hour of their precious time because of a slip of a girl who cannot be punctual."

"I didn't want to go in the first place." She hated the sound of her voice—dealing with her father seemed to leave her only two choices, frightened or spoiled and whiny. "What do you need me for?" *You can think up new ways to murder people on your own,* she wanted to say but did not. Poppy's rebellious streak had always stopped well short of suicidal candor, but she was finding it harder than ever these days to keep her mouth shut. The news of the destruction of the great houses and the deaths of her father's and Hellebore's rivals in the Six Families, along with hundreds of others—not to mention the incessant discussion of it among even her most unpolitical friends—had shocked her profoundly when she thought her brief life had made her a complete cynic. The magnitude of the destruction still gave her nightmares.

And all because my father and Foxglove and that evil, evil man Hellebore wanted more power. I heard them planning it! That was in some ways the hardest part of all, though even now she recognized there was nothing she could have done, not without knowing exactly what was about to happen.

"What do I need you for?" Her father had been silent so long she had forgotten they had been having what passed in Lord Thornapple's chill, reptilian way for a conversation.

"Is that all you can think of to say to the one who has given you every advantage? To one who has raised you in a luxury which even the children of the other high houses would envy?" He shook his head. "It is not as though I ask much of you, Poppaea. To make an occasional appearance at family functions. Not to disgrace us with bad behavior in public. It is not much to ask in return for the life you have been given."

No, she thought. *It's not much. You could ask me to care about you and the family, and that would be a price I couldn't pay.*

"Well, then, Father," she said. "How may I pay you back for all the kindness and generosity you've shown me?"

He flashed a tiny smile, sudden and cold as a patch of ice on the road. "You have your mother's tongue. It's too bad she was . . . that she could not learn to control her impulses more carefully. I hope you will not follow her in that way."

Follow her to what? A philtre overdose that might or might not have been an accident, and might not even have been self-inflicted? *At least she knew how to love. She even loved me.* "No, sir. I wouldn't want to do that."

His smile flickered out like a weak flame. It was a miracle it had lasted so long. "I hear your friend, young Foxglove, has announced his engagement to Monkshood's eldest daughter. What do you think of that? Were you two not . . . close?"

She shrugged. She didn't really know what she felt about Malander and his new totsy, but it wasn't much. It was abundantly clear to Poppy that the city was full of Flower boys who wanted to get into her pants. What did she care who their daddies were? What did she care about any of it? And, more importantly, why should her father care about it?

He settled back against the seat. "Enough of this. You will mind your manners today. It would not hurt for you to apologize for making us late. Nidrus Hellebore is tolerant and understanding of the foibles of children, but a little courtesy goes a long way."

Silence returned, the familiar waters in which her father swam like a shark. The great window-speckled ivory tusk of Hellebore House was in view now; looming above the smaller buildings. People on the sidewalks peered at the passing luxury coach; Poppy thought their faces miserable, even haunted. She ached to make some noise, to disperse the oppressive quiet, but there was something in her father's manner that she couldn't quite understand.

Guilt? she wondered. After murdering all those innocent people, after he and Hellebore had filled the streets with soldiers and turned the Parliament of Blooms into nothing more than a dog house for their tail-wagging sycophants, could it be something as ordinary as guilt?

No. She felt quite certain it wasn't that.

A phalanx of ogre bodyguards cleared the ordinary workers of the house-tower lobby out of the way like they were trash, shoving them back to the walls as Lord Hellebore himself came down to meet the guests. It was an honor that her father appreciated immensely, she could tell, although the handclasp he shared with the master of Hellebore House was a mere brush of the palms—the respectful salute of two predators.

But Father is still the smaller animal. He wouldn't have thought up something like that attack on his own, or had the courage to do it. In another time, another place she might almost have admired Hellebore for his boldness—there was something quite attractive about ruthlessness—but she could not get past the death of innocents. And all for what? More power, more *political* power, for the man who already more or less ruled Faerie.

He looked it, too. He wore a suit of hand stitched cream-colored spidersilk that a dozen indentured ferisher women had probably gone blind making, and his hair was cut at the youthful and slightly trendy shoulder length. "Poppaea," he said and took her hand, looking her over. His skin was

cool and extremely dry. "You are more lovely each time I
see you."

"Thank you, Lord Hellebore," she said at last. "I'm sorry
we're late. It . . . it was my fault."

"It is Beauty's privilege to keep others waiting," he said,
so smoothly and kindly that for a moment it almost seemed
like there might be a heart beating inside his chest. His black
eyes flicked over her again, slowly but not unduly so, an expression of power so great that it did not need to insult others to prove itself. It was like being examined for preferred
cuts by a goblin who had every expectation of eating you
one day. "Yes, very lovely."

Her father was nodding ever so slightly. Her breath
caught in her throat. Was this the plan, why she had been
brought here? Was she simply going to be given to the master of Hellebore House as a kind of tribute?

With only the most gently proprietary air, Hellebore took
her arm and led her and her father toward the largest elevator—the "ogre box" as it was sometimes called in the great
houses. It had to be large and strong: two pairs of bodyguards got in with them, shoving their huge bodies back
against the walls to maximize the protection and also to
leave as much room as possible in the middle of the elevator for their smaller employers. All four guards had set their
lumpy faces in expressions of blank seriousness. She was
sure her own expression wasn't any more cheerful, and her
father nearly always looked like the funerary portrait of
some famous general. Only Hellebore, murderer of thousands, appeared to be enjoying himself. He caught Poppy's
eye and winked. She managed through sheer strength of will
to keep her knees locked and her body upright.

It had been years since she had been on the upper floors
of Hellebore House—some kind of parliamentary holiday
party decades back was the last time she could remember—
and she was a little surprised now to see how relentlessly ordinary it was. The décor was fashionably sparse, the paint
fashionably luminous, but other than a certain drained and

nervous look on the faces of the employees scuttling past (who all stopped to bow and tug their forelocks before passing their master, though he never acknowledged the tributes) things did not seem much different than in Thornapple House or any other of the most powerful family housetowers. It was only in backwater operations like Loosestrife House or the Bluebell-Mallow Cooperative that you heard someone whistling or singing, or saw people stopping to converse within sight of one of the ruling clan. Only in those families where they had given up on attaining power did things ever get lax.

How she longed to live in such a family!

"I hope you'll forgive us, Poppaea," said Lord Hellebore suddenly as they stepped out of an elevator on the fifty-second floor into a wide lobby with a midair fountain at one end, an endless curl of running water hovering in the air. "I have some important business with your father—it will not take us long. If you'll wait here for just a moment, I'll find someone to show you around."

"Oh, no, please." The idea of being left on her own for a while was the most hopeful thing she had heard all day. "Don't bother anyone just for me."

Hellebore smiled and winked again. Her father was smiling too, which made her skin crawl. "No trouble at all. And then we'll see you for lunch. They do a rather nice white venison here in the house restaurant."

The pale woman behind the desk—very pretty, with the ropy hair and drowned, woeful look that suggested she might have nymph blood, nodded respectfully at Poppy as she rose from behind the desk. "Can I get you anything, Mistress? Betony tea? Some spring water?"

"No, I'm fine, thanks." Poppy took a seat. A magazine rack suddenly glimmered into view beside her where a moment before there had been only bare wall. *Impressive touch,* she thought. She plucked out a copy of *Tower Life* and opened to a fawning article on Lord Lily and the massive re-decoration of Lily House. A chill ran along her spine as though someone had slipped an ice cube down the back of her blouse. Lily House was gone now, rubble and ashes. She looked at the date on the magazine and saw that it was only a few weeks old. She supposed it had come out just before the attack. The real question was why the Hellebores still had it in their waiting room.

But they'd think it was amusing, she realized, and went cold and prickly all over again.

"Mistress Thornapple? Poppy Thornapple?"

She looked up, startled. The figure looming over her was so tall that for a moment she took him for a polevik. When he stepped back she saw that although he was extremely long and lean, several handspans taller than she was, he was still only an ordinary fairy like herself. Then she got a good look at his face, emotionless as a mandragorum's, and started wondering again.

"Yes, I'm . . . that's me."

"My father wants me to show you around."

"Father? You're . . ."

"Antoninus Hellebore." He nodded slowly, as though someone was whispering the instructions on how to do it in his ear. "They called me Anton at school. You can call me Anton."

Poppy was startled again. She knew the name—Lord Hellebore's eldest had been at school with Orian—but had never met him before. Among the Flower houses he had always been said to be a bit unusual. Once, as a very young girl, she had even convinced herself that "unusual" could mean "kind," and had developed a short-lived fantasy of Anton Hellebore being someone who might take her away to live in a beautiful castle full of singing birds. She was glad her younger self had grown into a woman who could look at this slack-jawed scarecrow without feeling disappointed. "Hello, Anton. You knew my brother Orian back at Dowsing Academy, I think."

"Oh, yes." He nodded again. "Orian died recently, didn't he? I remember someone telling me that he was killed." She expected him to say something about how sorry he was, but instead his next words were, "Follow me."

As he led her on a rather perfunctory tour of the family-compound portion of Hellebore House, Poppy had a chance to observe him. She couldn't quite put her finger on what made him so strange, other than his polevikian physique. He was a little dull, especially in the social niceties, and your average stone had more of a sense of humor, but she could also see streaks of intelligence, and sometimes more than streaks: his explanation of the family tower's complex mirror-system was dizzyingly technical and far too offhand to be mere show. But there was something damaged about him, as though at some point his brain had been removed and then restored and the connections hadn't grown back just right. It was more than faintly creepy. He talked with something approaching genuine pleasure about inanimate objects, especially things that were dangerous, but he not only didn't acknowledge any of the employees, servants, and distaff family members who saluted him, like his father he didn't even seem to notice them, as though they were vibrating at a frequency that Poppy could see but he could not.

Finally, though, a family member arrived that he *did* see—that he couldn't avoid seeing.

"You have a friend!" The woman was sharp and shiny and beautiful as the blade of a saber, her hair a brilliant gold that belonged on the head of a dairymaid, and perhaps once had been. She wore a youthful pants and shirt combination—perhaps a little too youthful, but that was Poppy's opinion, the harsh judgment of actual youth. Poppy could smell expensive anti-aging charms. So far, they seemed to be working. "Anton," the woman said, "you must introduce me."

His face churned with emotions she could not read, but he only said, "Yes, Mother. This is Poppy Thornapple."

"Oh, of course, we met at your family's Midwinter's Day party a few years ago, didn't we?" She took Poppy's shoulders in her hands and placed kisses like the nudge of a parrot's beak on each cheekbone. "So nice to see you here. How are your . . . how is your father?" She seemed to have remembered at the last moment that Poppy's mother was dead.

"Fine. He's with Lord Hellebore right now."

Aurelia Hellebore showed an impressive amount of teeth. "And so Anton is keeping you company. Charming! I tell you, you must come for tea some day and we can get properly acquainted. And shame on your father for not bringing you here sooner, although these hostilities have been hard on us all. How old are you now, dear? At least a hundred, yes? Well, you've grown into a most delightful young woman." She waved her hand. "Now you must excuse me—I have ever so much to do today. I'm only in town until tomorrow then it's back to the country. You young people have fun!"

Lady Hellebore vanished, followed by a small retinue of servants.

Poppy was still trying to figure out why the meeting had felt so unspontaneous—it was Lady Hellebore's house, after all, so why shouldn't they run into her?—when Anton Hellebore made a strange growling noise in his throat. His face had grown even more childishly sullen, as though the presence of his mother had momentarily sucked away half his age.

"I don't want to get married," he said.

For a long moment Poppy had no idea what he was talking about. Then, just as she made sense out of the whole day and abruptly found herself fighting a wave of nausea, Anton turned to her. "Do you want to see my stepbrother?"

"What?"

"My stepbrother. Well, my adopted brother. Everybody always asks me about him—they all want to know what he's really like. Mother and Father won't let anyone meet him."

So this is your little thwarted bit of revenge, she decided. *A rule you can break. Because they're thinking about pairing you up with me, and you're probably not even interested in girls. Or boys, either.* "I've heard about him. People call him . . ."

"A Terrible Child." Anton smirked, then turned and walked toward the elevator, this time without even a *Follow me.* "It's a stupid name," he said over his shoulder. "He doesn't do anything." He waited until the elevator door had closed behind them, then leaned close to her. His breath smelled like copper. "I've killed *lots* of people," he told her in a conspiratorial whisper.

She didn't know any way to respond to that except to keep her mouth tightly shut and to breathe shallowly.

"I have!" he said, a little defensively. "In my experiments. You don't find anything out if you don't. I'll show you my laboratory later if you want." The elevator opened and she had to move out because he was behind her. "Just this way," he said.

The air on this floor was noticeably warmer, as though the household hob had forgotten to keep it circulating. It was damp, too—Poppy was suddenly conscious of her blouse sticking to her back. She was not conscious of much else except a distinct queasiness. She felt like she was floating, as though her head were a bit of dandelion fluff being carried on a breeze down the hot, moist corridor.

The window began halfway along the passage and continued for a dozen paces. The room on the other side of the glass was so cloudy with steam that it was impossible to make out anything except a few vague shapes—furniture, as far as she could tell, low white chairs and a white table. Even the walls seemed to be white. The whole scene reminded her uncomfortably of an underground mirror-show one of the girls at school had gotten hold of, and had shared at a late-night party. Supposedly copied from a scientific research project, it purported to show the ghost-world—the place where all the mirrors connected—and at the time, surrounded by giggling housemates, Poppy had thought it mostly boring, but the roiling emptiness of it, the suggestions of faces and contorted shapes, had come back to her in several nightmares.

As if summoned up by those unsettling memorics, something emerged from the back of the steamy room and came toward her, only stopping when it reached the long, water-beaded window. It was a child, a boy, quite ordinary looking at first except for the curly sparrow-brown hair and slightly plump face, but there was some other subtle oddness about him that she could not immediately name. He was a little shorter of limb than most children his age, and his eyes were a most unusual color—not violet or emerald green or robin's egg blue as she was used to among the Flower families, but brown. It was only after a moment that she realized his features and proportions were not simply outside the usual norms. He was a mortal.

"There he is." Anton was striving to sound jocular, but was not altogether succeeding. "Wave to him."

The little boy watched her, expressionless, separated from them by a pane of glass and less than an arm's length of distance. It was his eyes that held her, and not just their strange, earthy color, like a mud-stirred puddle: they had a quality of intelligence that did not match the rest of his childish features, a regard as deep and cold as a cloudless winter sky. Then the boy smiled at her, a slow exposure of teeth that made his adoptive father's predatory grins seem warm and benevolent. She turned away, gagging.

"Wait!" Anton Hellebore called after her as she hurried back toward the elevator. "Don't you want to see my experiments . . . ?"

She found her way back through the maze of corridors to the waiting room. The nymph-secretary looked a bit startled to see her, but offered tea again.

"Nothing." She could barely make herself speak. It felt like something was screaming in her ear, telling her to run as fast as she could. She sat, tapping her fingers, a magazine unread on her lap. What was she doing here? Being led around like a prize heifer while the Hellebores sized her up, that was what. But even though they might want to marry her to that gangly freak, she had no illusions as to which bull she would be expected to service. There was no misreading the cool, satisfied look that Hellebore Senior had given her.

And that thing in the foggy room . . . !

She stood up, thinking for a moment that if she did not get to a bathroom to splash cold water on her face she would faint. But once she was on her feet she kept moving toward the door.

"Mistress Thornapple?" called the secretary. "Are you leaving? You really shouldn't walk through the house by yourself."

She opened the door to the corridor and the elevators. "Is there a message for your father . . . ?"

She pulled the door shut hard behind her.

31

IN THE BLOOM YEARS

Cardenus Primrose came into the tent with the rigid face of a man submitting to judgment. *No, not just an ordinary man,* Theo thought, *but some king forced to answer to commoners.*

"You have been here several days now," the fairy lord told him, "and my debt is still undischarged." His voice sounded much more troubled and sorrowful than his expression would have suggested, and Theo immediately softened.

I guess he can't help it—it's like he went to some stick-up-the-ass private school. Well, he probably did, but even for a Flower fairy he's pretty puckered. "I think I said that I wouldn't force you."

Primrose shook his head. "You did say that. But to be candid with you, Master Vilmos, it is my own knowledge that I did wrong to you that causes me pain, not any compulsion you have put on me."

"Did someone just fart?" asked Mistress Twinge. "I mean, either someone just squeezed off a real goblin-barker or someone's talking about principles of honor. Either way, it's getting pretty thick in here for folk like us pookas who don't have any honor to worry about. Believe I'll take a stroll. Coathook, you want to help me find Streedy? I haven't seen him since breakfast and I want to make sure

none of your goblin chums are cheating him out of his shoes
or something."

"Goblins do not cheat," said Coathook, brow furrowed.

"As in, 'Goblins don't cheat anyone who doesn't deserve
it'? Could be. Could be." Mistress Twinge jabbed a cigar
into the corner of her mouth, lit it with an ostentatious flick
of her fingers, then sashayed out of the tent leaving a trail of
smoke thick as molasses hanging in the air. Coathook followed her, grumbling.

"The pooka is always trying to shock me, but without
much luck," Primrose said when they had gone, and almost
smiled. "They are kind people, your friends."

"They've been nice to us. But I don't think I know them
well enough to call them friends yet. I'm not sure I know
any of you well enough for that. Sorry, Cumber, no offense.
But just . . . I don't really get how things work here." *How
about Applecore?* he asked himself. *She was a better friend
to you than most of the people you've called that over the
years.* But he didn't want to think about Applecore just now.
"Speaking of, should we offer you something? I don't think
we've got much but we might have a bottle of Twinge's dandelion wine under a blanket somewhere."

"No, thank you." Primrose sat down in a comparatively
uncluttered corner. The fairy was graceful in everything he
did, but he still couldn't make himself look comfortable with
the present cramped and—it had to be admitted—smelly circumstances. Theo wondered if getting the story about his
great-uncle was going to be worth the trouble.

"So you actually knew my Great-Uncle Eamonn?" he
asked. "Or the man I used to think was my great-uncle?"

"Would you like me to leave, Theo?" asked Cumber.

"No, please stay. You've already kept Lord Primrose and
I from having one . . . unfortunate misunderstanding. You're
kind of like my translator for the fairy world."

Primrose made an interesting hand gesture, bringing his
palms together until they almost touched. "I am grateful to
you too, Master Sedge. And perhaps, Master Vilmos, you

would be good enough to call me 'Primrose,' or even 'Caradenus.' "

Now Theo did laugh. "Sorry! It's just that if you want me to call you Caradenus, you'd better find something to call me besides 'Master Vilmos.' Agreed? It's Theo. Now go on. Tell me how you knew Eamonn Dowd."

"It was a goodly time ago—between the last two wars. I met him at a house-party."

"When you say 'between the last two wars,' remember I'm pretty shaky on the history of Faerie. Which two wars? How long ago?"

"Between the final Gigantine War and the most recent Flower War." Primrose's face hardened. "Most recent before this one, I should have said—and may that murderer Nidrus Hellebore go screaming into the Well for dragging us all into such suffering again!"

"About two centuries to a century and a half ago," Cumber volunteered. "Our time."

"Good God," Theo said. "So while thirty, forty years went by in my world—that makes it four or five times longer here?"

"It isn't always that direct a correlation," Cumber reminded him.

"In any case," said Primrose, "it was during what we call the Bloom Years. People look back on it now as a golden age, a time of high living and exciting changes, but even though I was much younger then, I still should have guessed things couldn't be that simple. And so should a lot of other people, but most believed what they wanted to believe. There was a sort of giddiness in the air. People were relieved because even though the king and queen had died in the war, the City hadn't fallen, Faerie hadn't disappeared, things seemed to be continuing—something nobody had been quite sure would happen. It's almost hard to believe that now, but you have to remember that back then no one could remember a time when Oberon and Titania hadn't ruled all the known lands—there weren't even any books in the libraries about such a time! And now they were really gone, but things hadn't collapsed, so of course we were relieved and thrilled. And the Parliament of Blooms seemed to be making changes everybody had wanted, as though the king and queen had been holding back the modern age simply by existing, so now things could move forward. It wasn't as clear then that the Parliament was pretty much controlled by the Seven Families—and for people like me it was even less clear. My family was one of the Seven, so I didn't really notice that not everyone was so very happy, that there were beggars on the streets everywhere, that the war with the giants had destroyed thousands of peoples' homes and livelihoods. There are probably folk out there in the ruling houses today who think what Hellebore and the others have done is just a bit of upset, and who are still going on about their lives, worrying about things like who'll take the Trooping Banner this year. A hundred years from now they won't remember the beggars and corpses, either."

Theo could not help but think of Poppy Thornapple, of her schoolgirl cynicism and ennui.

"I suppose it was at one of the parties at Stock House where I met him," Primrose continued. "The Stock clan had made a lot of money during the Gigantine War and wanted people to know it, so they used to throw the most tremendous parties almost every week's-end. The new horseless coaches would line up at the gates, trailing back for miles, and all the windows of the tower would be lit up. You could hear the music from blocks away." He smiled. "It may have been false in some ways, but it was certainly exciting.

"Anyway, at that time there were very few mortals left in Faerie. At the height of the Gigantine War the Parliament of Blooms had passed a number of laws to make it harder to get in and out of Faerie—not that the giants were likely to be sneaking in unnoticed. The Clover Effect dates back to that parliament. Powerful science was put to work to make sure no one cheated on the travel restrictions and it made a lot of hardships, especially for those with strong ties to the mortal world. But that was the mood of the time. You know, we almost lost that war. That's the thing you have to understand, why people ignored so much and let so much happen that should have been resisted. Because we almost lost. In the last battle alone the giants destroyed what seemed like half the City. Right near where we're sitting, most of the Longshadow district was smashed to dust by their catapults during the invasion—that's why we call it Warstones now. I don't know if you've seen it. It's never really been rebuilt properly. The fight was terrifying, even from a distance—if you've never seen a giant fully armored for battle . . ." He shook his head. "Forgive me. I'm losing the thread of my story.

"In any case, because there had been so few mortals around after the war, your uncle was a little bit of a celebrity—a very minor sort, but still well-known and welcome in many high houses. The Stocks were what are now called Symbiotes or even Creepers—sympathetic to mortals—and so Dowd was a regular at their weekend gatherings. Tertius Stock sort of made a younger brother of him. Tertius is dead now—killed in the Flower War that happened a few years later. He and his family sided with the Violets against the other six ruling families and lost the gamble, but that's another story . . ."

"So what was Eamonn Dowd like?" Theo asked. "Remember, I never knew him. He'd been dead a quarter of a century or so when I first learned of him."

Primrose sat silent for a long moment, considering. People were shouting outside the tent, children shrieking, laughing, enjoying the afternoon sun by the ancient river. "It's hard to describe him fairly, since my view of him has been so colored by what happened later, what he did to my sister . . ." He closed his eyes; Theo waited as patiently as he could. Cumber Sedge, he saw, was actually making notes in a small writing book. "He was amusing, that was one of the first things you noticed about him. He knew that to us he was very strange, that his appearance and habits seemed hopelessly odd, so he played them up. That was one of the reasons the Stocks liked him, I imagine—he was their trained mortal, as charming as a dog dressed up like a person and standing on its back legs. I beg your pardon if I offend, but that is how we felt about mortals, and that was why Eamonn Dowd proved so clever. It is hard to fear something that mocks itself."

"What did he look like?"

The fairy gave him an exasperated look. "What did he look like? A mortal. I find it hard to tell one of that kind from another, to be honest with you. I suppose by the standards of his race he was fairly ordinary—not too short, not too fat. He had skin like yours, dark hair, and dark whiskers on his upper lip."

"A mustache."

"Just so. We do not wear them here, although there are some kinds of gnomes that do, who in fact grow them extremely long. Your great-uncle used to make this part of the joke, often signing himself 'the Tall Gnome' in his letters."

"He wrote letters to people here?"

"We all did. It was considered rude in those days to use one of the swifter but more scientific means of, say, answering an invitation. I was too young then to be much concerned with such things myself, but I remember when one of our cooks, worried that she would be too late to buy the best something-or-other for that night's dinner party, actually flew to the market. Used her wings while on house business! Mother was horrified, of course—nothing like that had happened in our family since the Winter Dynasties. So, yes, we all sent letters and notes, usually hand-carried by servants."

"Did you like him?"

Primrose frowned. "Again, it's hard to say. I suppose I did, but not in the same way as the Stock clan did. I found it admirable that he worked so hard to fit in, that he took his rebuffs—and there were many rebuffs, of course—without rancor. Insulted in public by one of the mortal-hating families, he would make a joke of it and continue on. Balked in some business or social scheme by the same attitude, he would smile and try to find another way to manage. I wonder now if he was not all the time hating us for what we did to him, how we treated him . . ."

"Not from what I've read."

"Pardon?"

"I have a notebook of his. Cumber has it at the moment, actually. I've read it and most of what he has to say about New Erewhon—that was his name for this city—is pretty admiring. Of course, it doesn't cover his whole time here . . ."

Primrose leaned forward, alert now, his long body almost seeming to tremble as though he were a pointing hound. "What does he say about my family? About my sister?"

The sudden intensity of the fairy lord was unnerving. "Nothing, really. I went back and re-read after you . . . after you and I met. He doesn't say anything about your sister, not if she's also named Primrose, but he does mention you in passing—that he saw you coming back from a moon-brandy party or something with some kobos . . ."

"Kobolds," said Cumber.

"Ah. Sphene and . . . and Jasper." Primrose's eyes were focused near the tent ceiling.

"Huh?"

"The two kobolds. I cannot remember their family names. We were great friends during the Bloom Years." It was the first real smile Theo had seen from him. "They were lovers—not of mine, but of each other. They were artists. No one remembers them now, I imagine—even back then very few people wanted to see art that wasn't sanctioned by the Flower elite. They were a little bit fashionable for a while during the Bloom Years among the more adventuresome crowd, but I lost track of them when the Flower War came. I wonder where they are?" He came back from his reverie. "Please forgive me. What were we discussing?"

Theo shrugged. "I was telling you about Eamonn Dowd's notebook. It ends kind of suddenly. His last entry sounds despairing. Probably because of whatever happened with your sister."

"Might I see the book sometime? It is possible I might recognize things that even Master Sedge would miss, since I was there."

"Sure. You and Cumber can work it out. So, not to open the wound or anything, but what *did* happen with your sister?"

The fairy's thin face darkened, a pale golden flush that almost matched his hair. "It is not a surprising story, really. We Primroses pride ourselves on our open-mindedness, and my sister Erephine was always a rebel. Mother and Father liked to say tolerant things about mortals? Well, she would take a mortal for a lover and see what they thought about that! That was bad enough, of course—my father and mother did not really want their principles tested to that degree—but then Eamonn Dowd went too far. He dishonored my sister and the family, although the first dishonor was milder than the later, crowning blow."

"What did he do? Did he . . . did she get pregnant?"

For a moment Primrose's look of anger turned to confusion, then he laughed, a sharp bark. "Shade and Stream, no! We live long lives. Even a mortal lover is more a notoriety than a disgrace, and a halfling child—well, suffice it to say that in the old days, it's said, fully a tenth or more of the children of Faerie were half-mortal. Short-lived but fertile, your adoptive race. No, he convinced her to marry him."

"Marry . . . *That* was the dishonor?"

"It is one thing to make love to a mortal, even to bear a half-mortal child—a woman may have many children in her life by many men, after all—but quite another for that mortal to force himself into one of the oldest clans. By marrying a daughter of Primrose House your great-uncle was inserting himself into something almost as old and precious as Faerie itself. It was a disgrace my parents could not simply ignore."

Theo shook his head. "You'll have to bear with me, but

to me it doesn't . . . it doesn't seem like that big a deal. No offense."

"I suppose to one raised among mortals as you say you were, it might be hard to understand. But here it is a grave insult to the family. Worse, it is dangerous to a family like ours. Our bloodlines and the handing-down of family power are important to us in ways you may not understand . . ."

"Yeah, but even so, why is it only Dowd to blame? Wasn't it her fault at least as much as his?"

Caradenus Primrose scowled but his words were civil. "She would not have done it unless he pressed her. Something so shocking—it had happened here only one or two other times in recorded history, although there are many more instances of it happening in the mortal world. But with a daughter of one of the famous Seven Families? He might just as well have set Primrose House itself on fire. No, it was worse, because the house could have been rebuilt, but honor can never truly become spotless again." He was shaking. "I apologize for my anger. It is still close to my heart."

"I've gathered. And I'm sorry I don't get it," Theo said. "I'm not just sticking up for my . . . for Eamonn Dowd. Maybe he just didn't understand the rules as well as you think he should have."

Primrose was fighting hard to find his equanimity. "I might, with the greater knowledge and maturity I now have, be able to agree with you that part of his crime was due to misunderstanding our ways, despite all the time Dowd had lived among us. But you have not heard the second part.

"The marriage was brought before the Parliament of Blooms to be unmade. It was a terrible blow to family honor to have the union paraded in public, but it was the only way to separate them in accordance with the Old Law. My sister at first did not wish to part from Dowd, and had even gone so far as to move into his terrible little house out in Forenoon, doubling our family's shame. The parliament, to its credit, did not waste time and promptly ended the marriage. Dowd was banished from Faerie and my sister returned to the care of her family. She was angry, but I truly believe she was already regretting her headstrong decision to marry a mortal. She raged against my parents and their interference in her life, but I never heard her profess to be brokenhearted at losing Dowd.

"Dowd himself perhaps felt differently, but whatever the case, his banishment was mandated and carried out, although for some incomprehensible reason it apparently was not effective. These were unsettled times—the Violets were feuding with some of the other Seven Families and everyone could feel the growing likelihood of a Flower War. In any case, somewhere in the early days of open and violent hostilities between the ruling families, Dowd reappeared, to our complete surprise. In truth, we did not *know* he had reappeared at first, we only knew that my sister was stolen right out of Primrose House. In fact, at first it was suspected to be another move in the already deadly struggle between the great houses. It was only later that we caught the lawless gang of cave-trolls who had perpetrated the act and learned that Dowd had been their ringleader, that they had delivered Erephine to him. But by the time we discovered that, it was too late. Dowd was gone again and my sister was . . . ruined."

As the fairy fell silent, remembering, Theo wondered how much of this dramatic story was true and how much was Primrose family legend. The Eamonn Dowd who wrote Theo's book might have taken great risks for love, but it was a little hard to believe he would do anything quite as criminal as this sounded. Still, Theo did not want to voice any open doubts—his relationship with this fairy lord was far too fragile. Instead, he ventured another question.

"I'm sorry—I'm sure this must be painful—but why do you say he was banished and came back as though that was such a surprise? I mean, he got here in the first place, didn't he? It might have been illegal or dangerous or whatever for him to come back, but it wouldn't have been that hard, would it?"

Primrose was still brooding, so Cumber answered. "It's

the Clover Effect, Theo, remember? People—mortals and fairies—can cross from one world to another, but only once each way. Once your uncle was sent back, he couldn't return. Not wasn't supposed to—*couldn't*. Lord Clover and the people working with him invested a lot of powerful science to make sure that would be true. If there are loopholes, none of us has ever heard of them."

"So if I finally manage to get out of here, I can't come back." Not that at the moment that sounded like a bad thing, but this was the first time he'd even considered it. "Ever?"

"Not unless the law changes, and that would take a unanimous vote in the Parliament of Blooms," said Cumber. "Then they'd have to undo it, which would be terribly hard—just the thaumaturgic foundation for the Effect took months to install. But as Lord Primrose said about something else, that's another story."

There was still much of Primrose's tale Theo didn't understand. "Back to your sister, if it's not too hard to talk about it. Ruined, you said. How? What happened to her?"

"It's been many years," said Primrose. "It should not hurt so much. It happened in the middle of many larger and, yes, more terrible things, but it still causes me great pain. My parents never really recovered. We rescued her, you see— that's how we know it was definitely Eamonn Dowd who took her, why his guilt is proved by more than the word of the hired kidnappers who never actually saw his face. The place she was held in had been paid for by money out of Dowd's accounts here in Faerie, and the letter he had written to welcome her was found, too, and it was unquestionably in his handwriting. But he was gone by the time we found his lair. He left her behind like a cast-off shoe." The fairy took a deep breath. "We do not know what happened, what he did to her, but when we found her, she was mad— unalterably mad. No, worse than that. In those who are mad there is at least a trace of what they were, sometimes far more than that. In my sister there was—and still is—simply nothing of the woman we knew."

"What does that mean?"

"She is empty. What we found lives and breathes, nothing more. She is a husk. Dozens of the most esteemed doctors have examined her over the years but none of them could help her. She seems to have had her thoughts and . . . and her entire person . . . expelled from her like a yoke blown out of a hole in an eggshell." A tear glittered in the corner of his eye, shocking Theo: he had never seen one of these people cry, or even seem close to doing so. "It would be far better if she had died. Then we could have given her to the Well, mourned, and gone on. Instead she is a walking corpse in a sanctuary for the mad located outside the city. I go to see her a few times a year. It used to be more often than that—I would arrive with plans to read to her, to tell her family news and sing to her songs from our nursery days. *She must be inside that shell, somewhere,* I would tell myself, *the pretty, kind little Erephine you knew.* Now I visit her only on festival days and cannot wait to leave again. I do not read stories to her. I sing no songs."

After a long silence, Primrose abruptly stood. "But this is not your fault, and my attack on you was wrong and unfair. My tragedies are not yours. I hope we can be friends, Master Vilmos."

"It's Theo, remember? And . . . I'm really, really sorry about your sister."

"Thank you." He gave Theo and Cumber a kind of salute, one long finger touched to his jaw, and then went out of the tent, eyes still a little shiny in the corners.

"Wow," said Theo after a bit. "Just . . . wow."

"I will not deceive you," said Mud Bug Button. "It will be dangerous for you to go. But I fear it will be even more dangerous for you to stay here."

This is certainly our day for visitors, Theo thought. More surprisingly, the most important person in the entire refugee

camp at the Old Fayfort Bridge had come alone to see them
in their tent, without even his bodyguards. *He's got the common touch, no doubt about that.* "You want us to leave here
already?" he asked.

"No, you misunderstand me." The goblin looked far more
at home squatting on the dirt floor than had their previous
visitor. "Only for tomorrow. Certain voices have spoken to
me, told me that tomorrow will be a bad day for you to be
here."

"Voices?" Theo looked uncertainly to Cumber, who was
listening quietly. "Do you mean spirits or something?"

Button smiled. "No, Master Vilmos, no spirits. I speak of,
hem, certain employees in the Lord Constable's Chamber
who are sympathetic to our cause. They tell me there will be
many, many parliamentary constables here tomorrow. The
reason they will give is to protect those distributing food and
supplies to the many poor people who have fled their homes
and come to the bridge, but the real reason is to look for you
and Primrose and others wanted by the Parliament of
Blooms. Perhaps for me, too, but I do not think they know
my name yet, only my . . . shape."

"Shape?"

"Hellebore and the others know that someone is resisting
them. I have arranged certain . . . events that have probably
been noticed, although I flatter myself our enemies do not
understand my reasons or my plans. But they will have gathered that someone is playing an opposing game to theirs. In
fact, I hope you will assist me with one such small event tomorrow, thereby helping me and also keeping you out of the
hands of the constables."

Good lord, what are we into here? "What exactly do you
want?"

Since it was almost sunset, Mistress Twinge, Coathook,
and Streedy Nettle had gone off to stand in the food lines,
leaving Cumber and Theo the only people in the tent with
the little goblin, but still Button low-eyed his voice. "The
less you know the better, but I will tell you that Streedy's ac-

cident has made him . . . useful to me in many ways. I have
put him to those sorts of uses several times already, but he
must always be accompanied because he becomes confused.
Last time it was to be Primrose to help him and ensure he got
back to us again, but by misfortune it was the day of Hellebore's attacks on Daffodil and the other houses. Caradenus
Primrose left here as a member in good standing of the ruling elite—an extremely useful ear and eye for me among the
Flower clans. A few hours later he was a wanted criminal,
his family dead, their house-tower besieged and then in-
vaded by parliamentary forces. He had to flee the City center at risk of his life. Streedy was left to make his way back
alone through that chaos, and if not for the help of some of
our sympathizers in Goblintown . . ." Button shook his head.

"But we're probably wanted too," Theo said. "At least I
know I am. What good will it do sending us?"

"Because tomorrow I need Caradenus Primrose for
something else—something only he can do in a place only
he of all of us could go. You two will have to help Streedy
Nettle in a rather more public place. You are wanted by
Hellebore and his tame parliament, yes, but the mirror-
talkers have not spoken of you to the populace at large and
there are no pictures of you yet in circulation." The goblin
shrugged his small shoulders. "Still, it will be dangerous. I
will not lie to you. You might be caught. If you are, I am sure
you will be taken straight to your enemies."

"But we can't stay here, either. At least not tomorrow."
Theo looked to Cumber again. "What do you think?"

"I'll go if you go, Theo."

He turned back to Button. "And with whatever we're
doing . . . will it be something against Hellebore and those
bastards?"

The goblin smiled his yellow smile. "Oh, yes."

"And it won't hurt any innocent people? I'm not going to
plant any bombs or anything."

"I promise you, no one will be hurt by what you do tomorrow. But I must warn you that the day will come when

it, *hem,* may not be possible to fight Hellebore and Parliament and still keep your distance from things that might harm people. Nothing less than a war will defeat them." He showed his yellow teeth again, this time without humor. "War is suffering, after all."

"I'll deal with that when we get to it." Theo took a deep breath. "Okay, I'm in. Tell us what we need to do."

Streedy Nettle's odd appearance and even odder behavior—he twitched and mumbled even when he was at rest—had attracted the attention of some of the other passengers and Theo was beginning to feel nervous. He had never been a wanted criminal before, if you didn't count a bench warrant for unpaid speeding tickets, and he was beginning to think he wasn't cut out for it. All this, and somewhere out there an undead something was hunting for him, too. It didn't seem fair.

"Streedy's so conspicuous," he whispered to Cumber. "Wouldn't it have been better if we walked?"

"Yes, if you didn't mind arriving in the center of the City at sunset, after all the offices are closed. It's a long way, Theo."

"Ssshhh! Don't use my name." He tried to smile at a chubby brownie woman sitting in one of the half-size seats, who was watching Streedy Nettle with disapproval. She sniffed and looked away. In an effort to get the runaway capacitor's attention, Theo took his hand; Streedy immediately calmed. *That's just great,* Theo thought. *I'm going to have to literally hold his hand the whole time.* The fairy's skin was warm and seemed almost to tingle, so that Theo felt like his own hand had gone to sleep. The little hairs on the back of his arm stirred as though charged with static electricity. *Jesus, what if he electrocutes me or something? Can you get electrocuted by magic?* He looked at the fairy's dazed face, thought about the charred wing-stubs he had seen when the young fairy took off his shirt to bathe, and decided that whether it was like being electrocuted or not, he really didn't want it to happen to him.

Still, it was either hang onto Streedy's hand or have people stare at them. Theo hung on.

The bus climbed through the Sunset district. The houses were small and boxy, but near the crest of the hill they were neat and well-cared-for, most of them painted in vibrant colors and topped—as if to make up for the similarity of their shapes—with highly individualized roofs. Some looked almost like pagodas, others like folktale castles in miniature, sprouting tiny conical towers like crayons sticking out of a box. A few children were out early, probably on their way to school, the younger ones accompanied by parents or even occasionally by one of the rainbow nanny-bubbles he had seen back in Penumbra Fields. If it were not for the coaches full of armed parliamentary constables cruising slowly up and down the streets—Theo had seen half a dozen so far— it would seem to be a fairly ordinary day in an ordinary and fairly prosperous working class neighborhood.

The bus reached the top of the hill. Theo could see most of the City laid out before him like a patterned quilt, lumpy with hills where he was, sloping down toward the bright blue-green waters of Ys. Except for the strange shapes of the towers in the center of the City, gleaming in the morning sunlight, he could be looking down on any modern and attractive human city—Geneva, perhaps, or Sydney.

"That's Rade Park where we went the first night we escaped," Cumber said quietly, pointing to a band of dark green shadow that cut across the middle of the Gloaming district like a cummerbund. It suddenly made Theo aware of how little vegetation there was in New Erewhon, as Dowd had named the place, how just as in one of the human cities it resembled, the fairy metropolis had subordinated trees to houses and factories. *They really have done their best to imitate us,* he thought as the bus bumped down a

steep street and the city-vista disappeared again behind the
nearer buildings.

"Okay," he said, "I guess I understand why we're taking
the bus. But if Coathook is helping us, how come he's not
here too?"

"Button said that a goblin traveling with three of us might
attract attention. And apparently he also needs to arrive
alone for whatever part he's going to play to work properly.
He's taking another bus."

Theo sighed. "You sound like you believe everything
Button says already. Like you've joined Button's army for
real."

"Don't you believe him, Theo?"

"What he says about what he means to do, sure. But that
doesn't mean I believe my life is as important to him as it is
to me, just for instance."

"What do you mean?" Cumber looked around before
leaning closer. "He thinks you're incredibly important! He's
said so several times!"

"Yes, but that's a politician talking—no, a general. He's
important too, but he seems to be very casual about the possibility of some other goblins assassinating him for an-
nouncing his middle name in public or whatever that was he
did." Now Theo was leaning close too, his lips almost touching Cumber's ear. "Look, Button's fighting a war. He expects there will be casualties, maybe including him. I don't
care if I'm important to anyone else. I just don't want to be
a casualty, especially the 'oops, we underestimated' kind.
It's not even my war."

"But it was Hellebore and his allies who've been trying
to kill you."

"And if I get my fingers around somebody's throat who
deserves it, don't worry—I'll remember all that. But if I can
get home and avoid the war altogether . . ." He shrugged,
leaned back. "No offense, Cumber, but I don't feel like one
of you and I don't really understand most of what goes on

here, let alone care about it. I certainly don't want to die in a power struggle between rich fairy families."

"Most people don't risk their lives for power, Theo, even here. Most people do it to protect other people—people they care about."

Theo did not have a reply to that, but even if he had, he was suddenly finding it hard to concentrate. He had been trying to pull free from Streedy's grip for several seconds without much luck: the fairy was clutching his hand very tightly. Hair rose on Theo's head and a strange prickly feeling had begun to throb up and down his spine.

"Slow 'em down," Streedy's long face was full of panic but the calm voice coming from his mouth seemed to belong to someone else entirely. *"Wave 'em over here to the side. I'll take the front, you take the back."*

"It's the constables, Theo." Cumber was clearly frightened. "They're all over these days. They're stopping us."

As the bus slowed and pulled over to the side of the road, Theo realized that somehow Streedy had heard and repeated the communications between the two parliamentary constables who were about to board the bus. "What's my name supposed to be again? I can't remember!" he whispered to Cumber, but the ferisher was already sliding down the seat, putting a little distance between himself and his companions. Theo felt a burst of panicky resentment until he remembered Button's instructions. Cumber was a different kind of fairy: they would attract less attention if they didn't appear to be traveling together.

"Bloody iron!" Cumber Sedge squeaked as the first constable got on at the front of the bus. Theo's heart pattered— Cumber almost never swore. "They've got a Black Dog!"

Theo could only sit and watch as the constable worked his way down the bus, an ebony mastiff the size of a pony filling the aisle behind him. The dog was silent and made no overtly hostile moves, but the passengers on either side shrank away from it. Red eyes glowed like barbecue briquets as the huge animal padded silently after the constable.

Even with sunlight streaming through the windows the creature reflected no light: but for that terrible stare, it was only a dog-shaped shadow.

I have fairy blood, Theo told himself over and over. *There's no reason it should notice anything wrong about me. But what if it smells fear?* He stared at the shadowy head and decided that if it did smell fear, the dog must seldom smell anything else. He ransacked his mind for what he was supposed to say if they asked him questions, but it was horribly difficult to think with the mastiff slowly moving toward him, nose up and sniffing. *Oh, my God,* he thought, *what if Streedy starts babbling radio-speak again?*

A heavy hand fell on Cumber's shoulder and the ferisher jumped, which made Theo jump too. The other constable had come in through the back door of the bus and had reached them first.

"Identify yourself." His voice was muffled by his helmet. The mirrored visor gave him the look of a man-sized hood ornament. "Your Truename card."

Cumber fidgeted out the prismatic piece of shaved stone or whatever it was—Theo had never been able to figure it out—that Button had given him. The constable stared at it for a moment, flicked his eyes over Cumber, then handed it back. Theo had his in his hand already and passed it to the looming constable without being asked. "You're from out in Hazel Wand," the faceless man said to Theo. "What are you doing here?" He turned toward Streedy, who sat bobbing his head, eyes closed, locked in what Theo could only pray would remain a silent paroxysm of fear. "What's wrong with him? Where's his Truename?"

Theo reached into Streedy's pocket. The capacitor whimpered at Theo's touch but allowed him to take out the forged credential and pass it to the constable. "He's my cousin," Theo said, trying to stay calm, struggling to remember what he was supposed to say. "He's a bit . . . touched. Hurt his head in a farm accident. I'm taking him into Elysium House to help him with his worker benefits."

The other constable had arrived and blocked the aisle going forward. The dog was close enough now that Theo could almost have reached out and touched the matte-black muzzle—not that he planned to do any such thing. Other passengers on the bus were turning to watch, interested and also relieved that someone other than themselves had attracted the official attention.

"And your name is . . . ?" It was a trick; the constable had already looked at his forged Truename card.

"Stonecrop." Theo was so thrilled he'd remembered he almost let out a cheer. It was a country name, common as grass. "Jacky Stonecrop, that's me. And my cousin Paddy here's a Myrtle."

The constable stared at him a long time, then exchanged a visored glance with his companion, who had let the dog's leash go slack. The animal moved a step closer, until it was leaning across terrified Cumber Sedge to sniff at Theo and Streedy, pulling in so much air that Theo could feel the breeze. The light in its eyes flickered like a torch behind thick glass. It was quite hypnotic . . .

"I said, where are you staying in the City?"

Theo shook his head, trying to reassemble his thoughts. "Pigwidgeon Acres. My uncle lives at the hostel there, but he's too frail now to go out with Paddy. That's why I came up to the City." They weren't leaving. He hazarded a bit of extemporizing. "Is it always like this? I heard there were some people tried to overthrow Parliament. Is that what all the fuss is?"

The constables exchanged another mirrored glance, then the one who had been questioning Theo handed him back his card. "You're to be back in the hostel by sundown. And while you're at Elysium House, make sure you report your address. All non-residents have to go on the list. Otherwise you'll wind up visiting Lord Monkshood's cells, and that wouldn't make a very nice holiday for a country boy like you." He waited while his companion pulled back the Black Dog, then they all headed toward the front of the bus.

Theo could not even talk for several minutes after the bus was moving again. Streedy Nettle appeared to be crying.

They wound slowly into the heart of the City, through Twilight and across the edge of the Gloaming district and into Eventide. Perhaps because of Theo's mood after their brush with the constables, the downtown districts seemed gray and cold despite the clear, fairly sunny skies. The streets were emptier than he remembered—on his trip to Hellebore House with Cumber and Zirus and Applecore this district had seemed to throb with life, even at night. That journey seemed years away, now, and not just because of what had happened since. Eventide's sidewalks were nearly empty, the fairy-folk waiting for buses huddled deep in their coats as though to avoid attention. The people who were walking hurried, and did not even seem to see the others who shared the sidewalks. Only a few of the fairy-light signs glowed. Theo shivered. He wished he had his leather jacket back instead of the flimsy fairy-garb he was wearing. Then again, his old jacket would have probably just made him more conspicuous, and he definitely didn't want that.

As they rounded a corner into a canyon of tall buildings, Theo suddenly spotted the strange bulk of Hellebore House in the distance, its hundreds of windows like flyspecks on the curd-colored facade. He could not help staring at it, despite the disturbing sensation that the windows were shadowed eyes that watched him in turn. "They're all dark," he said. "It looks deserted."

Cumber Sedge looked up and knew without asking what Theo was talking about. "Some kind of special shutters," he guessed. "They're at war, Theo. The whole City's at war."

Streedy gave a little moan.

The bus stopped on the corner of Hedgerow and Springfair. Almost all the passengers who had watched their interrogation with such interest were gone; no one even looked up as they made their way down the stairs and onto the street.

"It's over there," Cumber said, pointing at a low, broad building at the far end of the block. "We've made pretty good time, all things considered, but we can't afford to dawdle."

With Streedy between them, swiveling his head like some kind of mechanical toy, they walked toward Elysium House. They stopped in front of a mirrorcase store a few yards away from the entrance to review Button's instructions. The storefront behind them was filled with rows of display shelves full of gleaming mirrorcases where dozens of identical scenes flickered: serious faces in the Parliament of Blooms, shots of armored constables in the streets, and once a view of the smoking ruins of Daffodil House. Theo turned away.

". . . So even when we see him, we don't go near him, understood?" Cumber was saying.

"Got it. We pretend we don't know him." Theo looked to Streedy who was staring up at the carved facade of Elysium House, his lips moving as though he prayed. "But I still don't understand what we're supposed to *do* in there."

"Nothing." Cumber shook his head. "Well, not after we make the first application, as Button said. We're mostly here for Streedy to help him get here, do what he needs to do, and then get home."

"You mean he's going to know what to do by himself? And manage it without attracting attention? Look at him!"

"Yes, but apparently he's done this before, or something like it. Now come on, Theo, before I lose my nerve."

The great hall of Elysium House was a bizarrely perfect representation of a forest grove created entirely in multi-colored stones and gems. The sky—in reality the interior of the dome—appeared to be a mosaic of pure lapis lazuli, big as a football field, with pearl clouds. The tree-columns had crusty bark in a variety of brown and silvery tones; one near the door rang like a chime when Theo rapped it with his knuckles. The fat-bellied redcap guard gave him a look of irritation and Theo quickly put his hands back in his pockets. Even the birds were picture-perfect creations with feathers of jade and alabaster and polished coral—but they did not move or sing. The dozens and dozens of fairy-folk who milled around the wide-open spaces were not singing either. They were filling out forms at the small carrels dotted about the massive chamber like flat mushrooms growing up out of the grass-patterned green tiles, or waiting in lines to speak to one of the row of Elysium House functionaries sealed behind glass like ambered flies. If he had seen this wide array of creatures a few weeks ago, when he was newly arrived, Theo would have been amazed by the woolly padfeet and tiny but dignified gnomes. Instead, he looked at them all with more familiar eyes now and saw just a group of sad and frightened people. For a moment, surrounded by petrified birds and diamond-hard flowers, Theo found himself nostalgic for places he had never seen, the original forests of Faerie that this stone grotto so carefully yet lifelessly imitated.

"There are some application machines down there," Cumber whispered, pointing to a spot along the wall between a pair of marble birch trees. "That's the shortest line I see."

"But aren't we supposed to wait for Coathook . . . ?"

"We're supposed to be ready when he gets here, and who knows how long it will take us to get to the front of the line?" Cumber indicated the huge sundial which, against all common sense, hung flat against the wall, out of any direct sunlight, and yet displayed a prominent wedge of shadow that had crept up the face until it was standing almost straight up. "He'll be here at noon. Come on."

They got into line behind some kind of possum-woman who had what looked like a couple of dozen children draped all over her, in her pockets and on her shoulders and one even sitting in her grocery bag, which she rested on the floor after each shuffling step forward. The possum-fairy child in the bag stared at Theo with round brown eyes as it licked the remains of something sticky off its pointed muzzle.

They reached the front at last. Streedy had his eyes closed

again and was talking to himself, fingers twitching as though he conducted an invisible orchestra. Cumber Sedge stepped up to the machine. Theo would never have known it was a machine if Cumber hadn't told him: it had the shape of a large, very realistic rock, tall as a Neolithic standing stone, with a large chunk broken out of it about chest high to reveal a crystalline interior like a geode.

Cumber put his hands on the stone and leaned in toward the glittering, faceted opening. "Entry permit application," he said.

"Purpose?" the rock asked him in a calm tenor voice.

"Visitor and livestock."

"Number of livestock?"

"One."

"Number of visitors?"

"One."

"Originating field of visitor . . . ?"

While Cumber answered questions, Theo looked around. The time must be drawing near when they would have to finish their business and let the next person in line use the machine, and the sundial on the wall was definitely reading noon, but he saw no sign of Coathook. He wished he knew what exactly it was that Button planned.

"By the Elder Trees," someone shrieked, *"what's wrong with him?"*

Terrified that Streedy had done something bizarre, Theo whirled around, but the tall, shaggy-haired fairy was still leaning against the wall beside the application machine. Everybody else had turned to look at something in the middle of the vast room. Theo turned too, and saw a group of different kinds of fairies beginning to crowd around a brown figure twitching on the floor. It took him only a moment to grasp what was going on.

While the other folk in line were facing away from the permit machine, watching the thrashing goblin and the excited throng around him, Cumber grabbed Streedy and pulled him forward to stand in front of the glittering geode-machine. The damaged fairy let himself be shoved closer, until his palms touched the stone, then the hair on Streedy's head began to stir as if in an unseen breeze—no, more slowly, Theo realized, as languorously as seaweed in the clutch of the tide. The fairy leaned forward until it seemed he might kiss the exposed crystalline interior. The geode glowed and Streedy's head became, for a moment, no more than a shock-haired silhouette.

Cumber leaned toward Theo. "This will take him a few moments at least," he whispered. "Go help keep people's attention over there."

Theo had a moment of pure panic as he ran toward the spot where Coathook was still snapping and moaning on the green tile floor. Several fairy-folk seemed to be considering helping him, but none of them appeared willing to get very close to his sharp yellow teeth.

"Someone help him!" Theo shouted. "Someone get a doctor!" A few bystanders turned to stare at him blankly. *Shit,* Theo remembered, *that's not the word for a regular doctor here. What did Applecore and the others call them again?* "A chirurgeon!"

He kneeled close to Coathook and put his hands on the apparent victim's shoulders to make sure he wouldn't get cut accidentally by the goblin's long nails. "Just a little longer," he whispered. "We're almost done, I think." He straightened up and announced, "I think he's starting to come out of it!"

The fat security guard had finally worked up the courage to approach. He kneeled, not without effort, keeping Theo between himself and the still-twitching Coathook. "What is it?" he asked breathlessly. "Is he dying?"

"No!" Coathook gasped. He really did look and sound dreadful. "Just . . . a goblin fit."

"Drunk, most likely," the guard said quietly to Theo. "They're like fish in Ys, always wet."

"I need water," Coathook panted. "No, not you, him. Bring water!" he rasped at Theo.

"I'll be right back," he told the guard reassuringly as he

got up. "See, he's getting better already." And indeed Coathook was beginning to twitch more slowly.

He pushed his way through the crowd gathered around the goblin and almost ran directly into Cumber and Streedy Nettle coming from the other direction. Streedy could barely stand and looked as though he'd been badly beaten. At any other time the tall, staggering fairy would have caught the attention of many of the people in Elysium House, but at the moment they were all far more absorbed watching Coathook trying to climb back onto his feet, using the fat security guard as his crutch before tumbling them both down onto the floor. People were laughing now and Theo could even imagine that Coathook would manage to walk out of the building again without being handed over to the constables.

"Did it all get done?" he asked. Cumber nodded his head in reply, but he was too busy keeping Streedy upright to talk.

They went out the massive front doors, down the stairs, and headed along Hedgerow Avenue toward the bus stop, but had only gone a few steps when Cumber abruptly stopped. "Theo, look!"

Theo's first response to Cumber's despairing tone was to glance back at the doors, expecting to see a crowd of angry fairies chasing them, but Cumber was pointing in another direction entirely. Theo turned to look at the shop window where they had stopped before entering Elysium House.

The rows of display mirrorcases all showed the same face. Theo's.

"Jesus! Shit, that's me!"

His face—a startled, candid image he'd never seen before, but which was still quite recognizably him—looked back at him for only a moment longer, then was replaced all across the window by the replicated faces of Lord Nidrus Hellebore—but Hellebore's image was not still. He was talking.

As Theo and Cumber dragged Streedy Nettle forward, half-hoping to block the display from the other people on the street, the viewpoint pulled back to show Hellebore sitting at a vast black desk that was empty but for two objects, a crystal vase with a single pallid flower, and a bell-shaped bottle, almost more like a specimen jar than anything else. It was hard to see what was inside, but it appeared to be moving.

"What's he saying? I wish I could hear the sound," Theo said.

"Do you really need to?" said Cumber miserably. "It's almost certainly something to the effect of, *'We want this fellow. Bring him to us and we'll make you rich. Help him and we'll have your skin off.'*" Cumber turned away from the shop window, eyes already roving up and down the street. "We have to get out of here fast, Theo! We have to get back to the bridge before someone recognizes you."

But despite the chill of terror that had raced through him at the sight of his own face being broadcast across the City, the knowledge that he was not only a fugitive now but a famous fugitive, Theo could not move from the spot. The camera, or whatever medium brought the picture to the ranked mirrorcases, had finally managed to bring the bottle on Lord Hellebore's desk into sharp enough focus that Theo could recognize what was huddled inside it, wings beating weakly on the inside of the glass.

"Oh, Cumber, that's . . . that's Applecore. He has Applecore."

32

TRENDY FUNGUS

All the way back he felt certain everyone on the Warstones-Dockyards bus was staring at him, a few only trying to decide why he looked familiar, but others no doubt whispering into their shell phones, alerting some parliamentary tactical squad that they had spotted a wanted criminal. Or maybe Hellebore and the others wouldn't bother with anything so subtle as a troop of constables. Maybe they'd just send another dragon swooping down out of the sky to roast the whole bus like a canned ham in a blast furnace, meat and bone and fairy-metals fused together into one grotesque mass . . . *No, Hellebore and Thornapple tried to capture me before,* he told himself, fighting panic. *They sent Tansy. So they probably won't just kill me.* He was shivering and almost sick to his stomach.

Of course, the idea that instead of being killed in a flaming second he might wind up in some soundproofed modern dungeon in Hellebore House did not provide much solace, especially since he still had not the slightest idea of what they wanted from him.

And they have Applecore. She's alive, but they have her. Knowing that was worse in some ways than being a fugitive himself. She was bait for a trap, of course. Theo had seen it in enough second-rate action movies: get the hero's sidekick

as a hostage, force him to enter the Evil Villain Lair. It
would have been ludicrous if it weren't so horrible when it
was really happening.

Besides, what makes anyone think I'm the hero?

*No, if I'm smart, I won't do anything. Because I'm not
some guy in a movie. I couldn't even buy groceries and make
change here, let alone pull some big* Die Hard *rescue.* But
that seemed too terrible to think about—how could he just
leave Applecore to be . . . what? Tortured? *Maybe with help
I could do something . . .* He looked over to Cumber, who
had not lost the shocked look on his face in the half hour or
so since they had seen Hellebore's broadcast. *Look at him—
he really cares about her and she didn't even save his bacon
twenty times like she did with me. I bet he'd risk his life for
her in a heartbeat.* But what could either of them do? Cumber was a lab assistant, not a master spy or an ex-soldier.
And Theo was . . . a musician, basically. *Look out, evil-
doers!* He felt weak and miserable. *Test-Tube Boy and
The Man Who Sometimes Plays the Tambourine are coming
for you!*

No, it was pretty clearly hopeless. But did that mean that
he should avoid trying? Even though he would probably
wind up being razored into pieces by Hellebore and some
crazy fairy-doctors because they thought he knew something
that would help them conquer the fairy universe? *And what
the hell is it they think I know, anyway? Something about
Eamonn Dowd? Or something he wrote about? But I have
his actual notebook and nobody's been interested in it so far
except people like Cumber. If the bad guys wanted it, they
could have had a maid steal it out of Daffodil House easily
enough.*

Still, it couldn't just be a coincidence that his great-uncle
had lived in Faerie and that now Theo had been dragged
here too, could it? But maybe it wasn't anything to do with
the book. It certainly hadn't led him here—he had still
thought it was a novel when all hell came shambling after
him. Maybe there was something about Theo himself . . .

Theo felt someone's eyes on him. A male brownie with a package on his lap was watching him suspiciously; for a moment he felt certain he was about to be denounced. Then he realized he had probably been squirming and mumbling to himself. He tried to give the brownie a reassuring smile. *Jesus,* he thought, *I'm turning into Streedy.*

The fairy into whom he was turning sprawled at the end of the seat as though someone had folded him up and then he had come violently unfolded again. Streedy Nettle was so exhausted by whatever effort he had put out at Elysium House that he wasn't even talking to himself: he stared out the window with the stunned look of a combat survivor. *So this is how it is,* Theo reflected. *I'm a fugitive but I don't know why. I'm working for a goblin, promoting a revolution I don't understand. My best friend here is stuck in a bottle on the desk of the most evil bastard in this world. What else can happen?*

Something made a loud popping noise and the bus swerved violently. Theo threw himself onto his belly in the aisle and lay there, waiting for whoever was shooting out the windows to get on with their job, but the bus rolled to a bumpy stop and the windows stayed where they were. Theo peered up from the middle of the aisle to discover most of the nearby passengers staring down at him in surprise. He hastily climbed back into the seat.

"What are you doing?" Cumber whispered. "Everyone's staring!"

"I thought someone was shooting at us. At me."

Cumber shook his head. "A ruptured tire, that's all. Try to look a little more normal, will you?"

"Oh, sure. No problem."

The bus driver, an old gray doonie with a receding mane and a straw cap perched between his ears, climbed back onto the bus after a few minutes, shaking his head and clicking his huge flat teeth in disgust. "We'll have to wait a bit," he announced. "They'll send another bus along for you while we get this fixed."

"How long until the new bus gets here?" asked a harried-looking gnome woman with two small but extremely active children.

As the driver began explaining some complicated formulation that seemed to add up to "I have no idea," Theo began to panic again. The idea of sitting by the roadside under the casual scrutiny of every jeep full of constables that passed was more than he could stand. "How far back to the bridge?" he asked Cumber.

"It would take us a couple of hours to walk."

"Do you think Streedy can make it without us carrying him?" Taking off on foot felt at least as dangerous as staying, especially when that undead thing was almost certainly still looking for him, but they'd be getting closer to sanctuary with every step instead of waiting to be recognized and arrested. "Yeah? Then let's go."

Theo's terror eased a little as they escaped the center of town, leaving only a dull ache in his stomach. Although several convoys of armed constables drove by them, he and his companions were part of an entire throng of goblins and short-legged dobbies and other poor fairies making their way back to the outskirts of the City ahead of the curfew. None of the troops seemed to give them more than a cursory glance. It was, however, a long, hard walk; by the time they left the crowds behind and had climbed to the highest of the hilly streets along the border between the Sunset and Twilight districts and were on their way down the other side toward the fenlands, Theo was so exhausted and footsore that even the prospect of being captured by Hellebore's minions didn't seem quite so dreadful. *At least they'd probably drive me somewhere before they started torturing me—I'd get to sit down far a while. Jesus, I'm in terrible shape. You never see one of those action-hero guys wheezing before he's even started climbing up elevator shafts and all that.*

As they trudged down a winding street into the glare of the late afternoon sun, seemingly alone in the neighborhood but for furtive movements at the round, curtained windows as the local gnomes and boggarts peered out at them, Cumber squinted toward the coppery line of the river stretching below them and particularly at the dark mass of people and tents sprawled along the banks beyond the Old Fayfort Bridge. "There are a lot of coaches and trucks parked beside the camp," he announced.

"Do you think it's Hellebore's soldiers?" Button had said something about an inspection, a spying mission by the Parliament of Blooms, but it had blown out of Theo's head in the confusion of the afternoon. Were they going to have to spend all night hiding in the weeds?

Cumber shaded his eyes. "I don't know—there are more trucks than coaches, but they don't really look like the kind of thing that constables would be driving. Still, we'd probably better go carefully."

At the bottom of the hill they picked a more indirect path across the hilly waste ground between the edge of the City and the fens, and were fortunate enough to meet up with a party of goblins who were passing around a bottle of something as they returned to the bridge after having spent the day looking for work in the City. At first the goblins looked at Theo and the two fairies with distrust, and they did not seem to recognize Coathook's name when Cumber tried to use him as a reference, but when Theo asked them if they knew the musician Bottlecap, and demonstrated a little snatch of the song he had sung with the goblin musicians his first night in camp, they began to smile. One of them even recognized him then, laughing and calling him "the petal-head throathonker" in an almost friendly way—which Theo assumed meant something like "the fairy who thinks he can sing"—then offered him the bottle full of brackish liquid. Courtesy dictated he try some. It tasted like it was made out of tree-moss and had a kick that made his eyes water. The goblins enjoyed his expression and noises very much.

They continued toward the bridge together, Theo and his friends now at least with the dubious camouflage of the returning laborers—dubious because Theo and even Cumber were obviously too big to be goblins themselves, let alone Streedy, who was nearly a yard taller than any of their new companions.

"I don't see any constables," Cumber said as they neared the bridge, "although I see quite a few civilian bodyguards around. In fact, it looks like other than the bodyguards, most of the ones I don't recognize are women—Flower-folk, by the look of them, or at least they're dressed too nicely to be people from the camps. I think they're giving away food. And clothing." He squinted again and shaded his eyes. "And stuffed toys."

"Oh, man, I keep forgetting we're living in a refugee camp. Button did say something about a charity thing." Theo shook his head. "I knew my life was screwed up, but I never thought I'd end up on the wrong end of a bunch of rich ladies doing good. Can we avoid this entirely?"

"Well, if we keep circling around to the riverbank instead of going straight in past the bridge, we can probably get down into the camp without attracting too much attention." Cumber frowned. "But there are a lot of people at this end of the camp. They *are* giving away free food, after all."

The goblins had also figured out what was going on and were heading toward the bridge to investigate. Theo didn't want to go near enough to risk being recognized by any of the outsiders. In fact, all he really wanted to do was get back to the tent as fast as possible, lie down, then pull whichever blanket was the least filthy over his face for a while and just be hopeless and pathetic.

They skirted the bridge and all the activity there but as they crossed the broad levee toward the river Theo's attention was arrested by one of the Flower women, part of a group of nearly a dozen standing on a flatbed truck as they handed down sacks of something or other. It took a moment to be certain it was her: she was dressed in something a great deal less fashionable than the dress she had been wearing when he last saw her.

"Oh, my G . . ." He grabbed Cumber's arm. "It's Poppy."

"Who?" Cumber had to let go of Streedy, whom he had been helping. The tall fairy wavered like a radio tower in a high wind, but stopped before tipping over.

"Poppy. This girl I met on my way to the City." She was a good twenty yards away and her raven-black hair was confined under a scarf, but he felt sure he wasn't mistaken. She had on a sort of shimmery, earth-colored jumpsuit which he guessed might be the Flower equivalent of worker's clothes; with her headscarf, she resembled some idealized Rosie the Riveter off a Second World War propaganda poster. Actually, even in his miserable mood he had to admit she looked quite fetching. "Poppy Thornapple."

"Poppy Thorn . . . Y-You mean the First Councillor's daughter?" Cumber sounded like he'd just tried to swallow a hedgehog.

Theo stared at her, full of revulsion for what she represented, but also a surprising longing. The Thornapple name had not meant much to him when they had first met—an intellectual rather than a visceral understanding that she was one of the enemy, if not herself personally guilty. Now it was hard to separate her from the smirk Hellebore had worn as the dragon swept down on Daffodil House with a belly full of murder.

Still, it was impossible to watch her and not feel a twinge of regret for what might have been. He remembered her pushing herself up against him, warm and soft and trusting . . .

And her father helped murder a thousand people in Daffodil House. An image of the scatter of charred bodies on the comb floor swam up to him. He was at war with himself, that's what it felt like. *Even if it wasn't her fault, she's part of that, right? Like one of those pretty little frauleins that went to Hitler's parties and never wanted to know what was really going on.* He turned his back on her and gestured to Cumber that he was ready to continue. *After all, that's what her daddy does so she can go to her private school and hang out in clubs snorting pixie dust with the other rich Flower kids. While her daddy's partner Hellebore keeps my friend in a jar on his desk . . .*

Oh sweet Jesus, of course—Applecore! Maybe she can help me get to Applecore! "Hang on," he said, and turned back again. Cumber sighed wearily but snagged the back of Streedy's shirt. The tall young fairy stopped again without comment or evident curiosity, like a toy whose battery had run down.

Theo examined the scene more carefully. Not only was Poppy in the middle of around a dozen other Flower women, but even if he wanted to dare it and could elbow his way through the crowd of refugees until he was close enough to make her hear him, the truck itself was surrounded by huge ogre guards and a few almost equally tough-looking doonie drivers. Even if they hadn't seen Hellebore's little version of *Fairyland's Most Wanted,* (or didn't just beat the bejesus out of him on principle) they might still remember his face when they eventually *did* see it on the local equivalent of the nightly news. He had no right to risk bringing parliamentary troops down on the camp. Even if he happened to be gone by then, it would probably land Button and Primrose and the rest in a dungeon somewhere and destroy the little goblin's plans.

So much for the sudden idea that Poppy might be some use to him getting to Applecore. He couldn't reach her without too much of a risk and in a little while she'd be gone. He obviously couldn't go to her house and ring the doorbell: *"Hi, Mr. Thornapple, I'm the guy you wanted to torture—can Poppy come out and play?"*

Unless . . .

It was a ridiculous idea, but so was being a fugitive in Fairyland, not to mention dragons and goblins and every other damn thing that had happened to him; he turned to the gangly figure beside him. "Streedy, you said you know Poppy, right? Poppy Thornapple?"

"Theo, what are you doing?" Cumber looked worried. But Cumber always looked worried.

"I'm asking him a question. Streedy? Did you hear me?"

It was like watching a piece of an iceberg crack, break loose, and tumble into the sea, a process so achingly slow that you could only sit back and wait. After what seemed half a minute, the tall fairy blinked and said, "Poppy. She's nice. I like her voice."

"Because you hear her talking sometimes, right? I want to talk to her now. Is there some way you can make that happen?" He looked at the long, puzzled face and his heart sank. It was ridiculous, of course. Most of Streedy's strange abilities seemed to be involuntary. Just because he seemed to be able to hear Thornapple House communications didn't mean . . .

"But Theo," Streedy Nettle said slowly. "You don't have a shell."

Shit. He'd just assumed something magical could be done—that Streedy could somehow connect him directly to Poppy. But Fairyland magic seemed to work in a much more mechanical way than that, or at least it did in this modern era. Of course he didn't have a shell.

"So I can talk to her, I guess," said Streedy. "But how can you talk to her?"

"I know, I know, it was a stupid idea." He scuffed his toe in the dirt. She was standing up now, wiping her forehead with the back of her hand, staring off across the fens. He wondered what she was thinking. "Whoa, hang on," he said as the fairy's words caught up with him. "*You* can talk to her?"

Streedy nodded. Cumber's worried look grew by a brow-furrow or two. "What in the name of the Trees are you trying to do?"

Theo ignored the ferisher. "Then will you talk to her? Will you tell her what I tell you to say?"

"I'll try, Theo. But my head . . . it hurts a bit."

"I know, and I'm sorry. I'll keep it short. Go ahead—see if you can reach her."

He was surprised to see Streedy lower his long chin to his chest and close his eyes instead of facing the truck where Poppy and the other women stood, then realized that unless he had been paying a lot more attention than he usually did, Streedy probably did not even know she was a few yards away. He thought about telling him, but across the camp Poppy was already reaching her hand into the pocket of her garment. She took out a slim object that Theo felt sure must be the same silvery wand she had used in Starlightshire Station and lifted it up, listening.

"Have you ever talked to her before, Streedy?" Theo asked suddenly.

Streedy started to repeat his words, then shook his head.

"Then don't bother to tell her who you are. Just tell her that Theo wants to see her—no, meet with her. That you're a friend of his and it's important Theo gets to meet with her."

Streedy spoke the words into midair, paraphrasing awkwardly. Theo watched Poppy. He could not quite make out her expression from such a distance, but she turned away from her companions and walked a few steps up the bed of the truck as though seeking privacy.

After a pause of some seconds Streedy Nettle opened his eyes and looked at Theo, face full of distress. "She says how does she know I'm a friend of yours. How does she know, Theo?" He was shivering a little; Theo felt a pang of guilt at putting him through what was clearly a difficult task after the heavy lifting he'd been doing at Elysium House.

"Ask her if she remembers the songs I sang to her." But she probably wouldn't recognize the words to *"New York, New York"* even if he could coach Streedy through singing it. "And tell her that I still remember how old she is, but I don't care."

Jesus, what are you thinking, Vilmos? he asked himself as Streedy haltingly relayed the message. *You had to pick two things that are all wrapped up with romance. What are you doing, messing with this girl's feelings?* He took a breath. *Saving Applecore, of course.* And it wasn't entirely false, either. He did like Poppy Thornapple. He had been confused, and he was even more confused now, after what had happened at Daffodil House, but there was still something there. *Yeah, but she's a schoolgirl,* he told himself. *A schoolgirl old enough to be your great-grandmother,* came the predictable rebuttal from somewhere deep in his hindbrain. He looked up and saw that Streedy was waiting for him patiently. "What does she say?"

"She says she has to finish doing something this afternoon, but she'll meet you this evening. Where?"

"Tell her to pick a place and a time." He was pleased with the success of using Streedy as a conduit, feeling a little of the ebullience he had felt that first night, rolling into the City despite all that had gone so disastrously wrong. "And tell her to make it close to where she is now. I know what she's doing today."

Streedy dutifully recited Theo's words, then listened to the reply.

"She wants to know how you know what she's doing."

"Tell her to look just east of the bridge."

"Theo!" Cumber's worried look had taken a turn into real fear but Theo ignored him. As Poppy turned from side to side, staring out from the back of the truck, Theo took a few steps away from Streedy and Cumber Sedge and waved. Again, he couldn't quite see the look on her face, but this time he could guess. "Tell her that's to show I trust her."

Streedy listened to her reply for a long time. Cumber was pacing. "She says she'll meet you at a place called The Chamber of Congregation, on Glaistig Haven Road between Twilight district and Eastwater. When the Queen's Ring rises."

Theo had no idea what that meant—a star, he guessed—but he figured someone could explain it to him. "Tell her that's great. I'll come alone. I hope she will too."

"Theo!"

"Shut up, Cumber. Tell her that, Streedy, then we're finished. You can hang up or whatever you do."

She was still staring in his direction. He waved again, a
little less broadly this time, then turned away. He had a feeling he couldn't quite explain, a certain faith that she
wouldn't immediately call in her father's bodyguards or the
constables, but there was no sense standing out in public in
case he was wrong—and no sense getting Streedy and Cumber into trouble too if he had let himself get overconfident.
"Come on, Cumber. I want to think. And someone has to tell
me what time it is when the Queen's Ring rises."

It rose at what would be about eight o'clock, mortal time,
a fat yellow star near the western horizon. Theo saw it
gleaming bright against the black sky as he found the restaurant and ducked in through the low door.

The Chamber of Congregation was a kobold place, a
small, windowless, self-consciously hip establishment in an
alley just off Glaistig Haven Road, which was at the center
of a sort of raffish shopping district near the Eastwater
docks. Kobolds were cavern-creatures and the lobby was
very dark, but Theo still felt unpleasantly conspicuous. He
wedged himself into a corner behind the maitre d's table,
next to a glass tank full of blind white cave salamanders, and
hoped Poppy would show up soon. It was the kind of place
where every customer who came through the door gave him
at least a quick inspection—not because they recognized
him, he realized after some panicky moments, but because
they were hoping he was someone worth recognizing. It was
just the kind of place where everybody checked out everybody else just as a matter of principle.

Trying to look natural, Theo turned away from the front
door and examined the slate walls that gave the restaurant
the look of having been carved directly into solid rock. All
around the lobby strange pictures of what he guessed were

kobolds and various underground animals had been incised
into the dark surface and then lightly brushed with some
phosphorescent chemical so that they seemed to float a few
inches out from the walls. Theo had no idea if they were
purely decorative or based on actual kobold folk-art. In fact,
he didn't even know if there was such a thing as kobold folk-
art, and even if there was, he couldn't guess whether it was
ultra-cool, just respectable—sort of "last year"—or tacky as
bullfight pictures and card-playing dogs. Of course, even a
black velvet bullfight picture, in the proper context, could be
cool again . . .

*I just don't know how any of it works here, from the most
important stuff to the least important. I should make a note
to myself: under no circumstances try to pretend you're
someone who actually grew up in Fairyland . . .*

"Theo?"

He turned and felt his insides lurch just a little. Even in
the dim light she didn't look like an enemy, but like a friend.
At the least. "Hi. Thanks for coming." He paused, uncertain
of what to do, then took her hand and held it for a moment
before letting go. *Oh, that's smooth,* he told himself. *Maybe
after you finish shaking her hand you could give her a free
sample of floor wax or something.*

"I didn't think you'd really be here." Poppy was still not
quite making eye contact. She was dressed up a little more
than when he had seen her at the bridge, black coat and long
skirt and a simple gray sweater, yet somehow there was a de-
terminedly bohemian air to the outfit. Perhaps it was the flat
sandals, or the gleaming strand around her neck of something that looked like silver but glinted in colors of firelight.
Theo knew enough about women and their clothes to recognize she was trying to strike an appropriate balance between . . . what? Between liking him and hating him?
Between wanting to look good and not wanting to look too
available? Just because he knew a mixed message when he
saw one didn't mean he knew exactly which messages were
being mixed.

After an awkward pause, he said, "Could we sit down? I'm feeling a bit . . . conspicuous today."

"Who called me?" she asked as a little kobold in a decorative hooded jacket led them to a table. "He was very strange."

"Stranger than you know. I'll explain later." The table was along one of the back walls, out of the direct line of the firelight. As he relaxed, he realized he was extremely hungry. "What do they serve here? Is the food good?"

"It's lovely, although I've only been here a couple of times." She looked around. "You know, my brother was killed in a tavern just down the street."

"Oh my . . . ! Poppy, that's terrible. Are you sure you want to eat here?"

She shrugged. "I know you think I'm ghastly, but we were never close. In fact, I didn't like him at all. He was a nasty, cruel boy." Clearly uncomfortable, she opened up her menu, which glowed with a thin ivory light of its own. "What are you going to have? It's almost all fungus but they do amazing things with it."

Mushrooms, he reminded himself after a slight flinch. *Mushrooms are fungus. Lots of fungus in Chinese food, too.* Still, it was hard to get too enthusiastic. "You order for me." The ethereal light from the menu bathed her face as though she were a portrait by Vermeer. It was seductive—all of it, not just the pretty young woman across the table from him. It was wonderful to be sitting in a restaurant again, just as though he had returned to normal life. If he squinted his eyes so he didn't notice the bird-headed woman in a booth nearby, if he pretended another customer's aggressive display of wings was a costuming affectation rather than living appendages, he could imagine he was back in his own world.

In fact, it was *too* seductive.

A kobold waiter stood by the table. Theo had not even noticed him approach. He was not the most attractive type Theo had seen in Fairyland—kobolds, although humanoid, had a bit of the look of hairless rodents, their noses large and prominent so that the rest of their faces seemed to lag behind, their almost translucent pale pink skin wrinkled like someone's toes who had been in the bath too long. But despite the underslung jaw, the waiter had a shy, sweet smile, and Theo suddenly wondered if he were like Cumber—a student working in a restaurant to pay his way through university, determined to make a life among those who thought themselves his superiors. Had he fought his way up from someplace like that midnight-dark kobold village under the railroad line . . . ?

Yeah, everybody's got a story, he thought, and looked at Poppy. *Do I know hers as well as I think I do?*

"Did the masters want anything to drink?" the waiter asked. Exhausted and overwhelmed, Theo asked for water. Poppy, perhaps being cautious for reasons of her own, ordered a glass of wine instead of a Wingbender.

"Look," he said when the little waiter had retreated, "there are some things I really need to talk to you about . . ."

"Oh, me too. I've run away from home."

"What?"

"I've had a terrible fight with my father. The real kind, not just the shouting-a-lot kind. He wants me to marry Lord Hellebore's son, Anton. It's impossible. He's completely mad—disgusting. And that stepbrother of his, or whatever he is . . ." She shuddered. It wasn't a theatrical gesture. "It would have happened anyway. I just can't live with those people anymore. And after what they did to Daffodil House and the Hollyhocks and the Lilies . . . Theo, I saw you with Zirus Jonquil, you must have heard what happened to his family's house—to his whole family."

He looked at her, stunned. She had run away. Good for her, of course, but for him . . .

"What's wrong, Theo? You must know about Daffodil House, even if you are from out of town."

"I . . . I was there. I was in it. When it happened."

"Bleeding black iron! Were you really?" She stared. "I

wondered why you didn't call when I practically . . . Oh, Theo, that's . . . I'm sorry." To his chagrin, she began to cry. "I'm so sorry."

"It wasn't your fault." What had happened to the careless schoolgirl who dismissed her own brother's death as an inconvenience? He tried to hand her his napkin but she had already found a handkerchief and was half-heartedly wiping her nose. "It wasn't your fault, Poppy."

"It was my family. My horrible family."

"Have you really run away? Could you go back?"

She shook her head and then blew her nose again. "My father has the household guards looking for me all over the City. That's why I couldn't meet you at one of the places I usually go. He doesn't like being defied, the old monster."

Theo took a deep breath. Not only wasn't he going to be able to use her to get to Hellebore as he had half-hoped, he now had the added danger that he might be picked up by her father's troops if they happened to find him with her. *Well, there it is—I'm fucked. That's it. Period. End of story.*

He supposed it didn't really matter, anyway: even if she could have got him into Hellebore House, he hadn't had even the ghost of an idea where to go from there. In a way, it was liberating. He still had to think of something to do about Applecore, but he didn't have to manipulate Poppy to do it. He hadn't felt very good about that.

He looked her over carefully. He wanted to open himself to her, but he couldn't quite shake the image of blithe, pretty Hitler-maidens going to lovely parties in Berlin while the SS dragged the undesirables off to camps. "Have you really left? Not just having a little moment, then you'll go back if Daddy says you don't have to marry the Hellebore kid, maybe raises your allowance?"

The tears were still rimming her eyes, but her face abruptly went cold. "Is that what you think? That I'd go back and live with those . . . murderers? For a bigger allowance?" She picked up her purse and began to stand. Theo reached out to take her arm but she shook him off. "I really am a fool," she said. "I tried to tell myself that what my father was doing was just politics. Wrong. And I tried to tell myself that I had misjudged you, that it was my fault for playing games, that you were really a nice guy. I was wrong about a lot of things, I guess."

Theo stood up as she started to turn away. His chair fell over. Other diners had begun to look at them. "Poppy, please, I just needed to know. To test you a little, I guess. Please, come back, I . . . I have some things to tell you." The fairy-folk on either side of them were whispering. *Shit,* he thought, *if they don't recognize me, they'll probably recognize her.* "Sit down, please!"

She let herself be drawn back down. He righted his chair and hunched over the table. "Tell me what?" she asked, dabbing at her face again.

"I have to confess something." *What the hell, right?*

Her face became still and her eyes mistrustful, as though a curtain had been drawn and she were peering out from behind it. "You have a wife back home in Daisyland, right? A little suburban place in Rowan? Children? Your own second-hand hob?"

He laughed despite himself, even though he felt like he was about to jump out of a window without knowing what was on the other side. "Oh, no. Nothing like that. No, I wanted to tell you . . ." He leaned forward. The other diners appeared to have lost interest again, but there was nothing wrong with taking precautions. "I'm thirty years old, Poppy."

"What? Do you think that's funny?" She started to get up again.

"Don't! It's the truth."

"Liar! How could that be . . . ?" She stopped, goggled. "Black iron, you're a mortal!"

"Ssshhh!" He took her hand to keep her close. She tensed, but did not pull away. "No. Well, sort of. It's a long story. Do you want to hear it?"

The little waiter picked this juncture to arrive with plates full of food that Theo could not even identify—ethnic cooking gone mad and then confined in a lightless cave for centuries—and began setting them out, ignoring with professional skill the abrupt silence that had fallen over the table. Theo couldn't tell what was garnish and what was dinner, and could only identify which things were plates because they were on the bottom. It didn't matter, though: he was far too nervous to eat.

When the waiter had slid off again, Theo told her everything, starting with a capsule summary of his life before crossing over to Faerie. It was tempting to glamorize things but he didn't do it, giving her instead the exact and accurate picture: thirty years old with a dead-end job, pretty fair musician, less-than-overwhelming people skills, especially when it came to relationships. He tried to gauge her mood but what he thought of as the austere Flower mask was still on her face: she sipped at her wine, picked at the food, and listened, but she kept her thoughts to herself. He told her of finding his great-uncle's book, about the sudden entrance of the sprite followed closely by the undead thing, about his startling arrival in a place he had never believed existed.

By the time he got to the part about Applecore leading him to Daffodil House, the first wash of adrenaline was gone and he was beginning to feel how hungry he was. He chose one of the least disturbing things in front of him, speared a piece on an odd, long-tined fork, and put it in his mouth. It was not too bad, although the combination of sweet and musky was a little hard to get used to at first, but the easing of terror made a very good sauce. As he told her the rest of what had happened to him, carefully avoiding any mention of Button or his plans and activities—he had no right to put the lives of the goblin and his comrades at risk, after all, no matter what he thought about the girl—he tried more and more of the kobold delicacies. The discovery of an arrangement of candied millipedes atop one of the dishes put him off for a moment, but he eventually made a mound of those things he liked best on his own plate. Eventually, almost every sentence of Theo-history was punctuated by forkfuls of food.

She was silent for a while after he finished. She drank off her wine, then picked up her purse and stood.

"Are you leaving?" The fear suddenly clamped him again. He had let himself relax too much. Was she angry enough to sell him out? "No, I'm going to the toilet. Is that all right?"

He nodded. He wanted her to assure him she wasn't going to call someone, that he wasn't going to be sitting here like an idiot when the special constables came crashing through the door, hornet-guns blazing or buzzing or whatever they did, but he knew that if he was going to keep her on his side he would have to trust her. *People have died for worse principles,* he thought. *But I'd rather not die.*

It was perhaps the longest ten minutes he'd spent since escaping from the burning wreck of Daffodil House. He sipped his water, pushed the remains of the kobold cuisine around on his plate, and did his best to appear to be someone not worth a second glance from any of the other diners. When he saw her coming back down the aisle, the mask of indifference still on her face, he had two simultaneous and completely different reactions.

So was I an idiot? Did she make a deal with her father— her freedom for mine?

She's really beautiful.

Poppy settled in, not making eye contact. "I just want to know one thing," she said at last. "I have to know. Did you come here because you wanted to use me to rescue your friend?"

He suddenly wished he'd ordered a real drink, too. "Yes. That wasn't the only reason, but I hoped you could help me, somehow. She's been more than a friend . . . I mean, she saved my life. More than once."

Poppy nodded slowly. "But that wasn't the only reason, you said."

"I like you, Poppy. I always did. When I saw you at the camp, I realized that I'd . . . missed seeing you."

She squinted at him. "If you're trying to weave a glamour over me, Theo Whatever-Your-Name-Really-Is, you'd better remember that you're a beginner. If you're lying to me I'll do worse to you than that lizard Hellebore could ever dream of." Her gaze dropped back down to the table again. "I can't help you, Theo. Even if I went back—and I'll never go back—they wouldn't let me onto the family floors at Hellebore House, not after the scene I made getting out of there. But I don't blame you for wanting to save your sprite friend, even if she is a snippy little bitch. So if you want to leave now, just tell me the truth and go. You don't have to worry about me—I won't betray you. But if you lie to me and pretend you care about me, thinking that you'll find a way to use me to help your friend after I've told you I can't, then I'll make you wish you hadn't ever met me. I truly will. Understood?"

He was so relieved that he almost laughed. "Did anyone ever tell you that you're pretty scary for a hundred-and-five year old? I'll bet that ogre kid still has nightmares."

She looked blank. "Ogre . . . ?"

"When you threw me out of the car, back when I first came to the City." His smile began to feel uncomfortable. He still didn't feel very good about that day. "You'll be happy to know that Applecore told me I was a jerk about the way I treated you."

"Jerk?"

"Sorry. A mortal expression that doesn't translate, I guess. An idiot. An inconsiderate fool."

Poppy nodded. "Then I hope you do save her. At least she's got some sense."

"What is it with women? You can hate each other's guts but you all still band together to agree that men are pigs."

"Because men *are* pigs." A little bit of a smile had crept onto her face now, but as if she too felt she wasn't quite ready to deploy that particular bit of her arsenal, she grew serious again. "So does this mean that you believe me when I say I can't help your friend?"

"Yeah. I'm trying not to think about that too much. It makes me feel like the lowest scum in the world. Here I am, sitting in a nice restaurant, and she's in a bottle."

"But if they want you, they won't do anything to her. She's just a sprite. She doesn't matter."

"Do you believe that?"

"I used to, I suppose. But I meant she doesn't mean anything to them. Hellebore is cruel but mostly he's about power. His son and . . . and that other creature, well, they might do anything, but he won't let them have her until he doesn't need her anymore. Which means when he has you. As long as you're free, she's probably more or less all right."

Theo sighed and sat back. "It all makes me feel sick. Let's talk about something else. What are you doing? Where are you staying? Are you going to go back to school?"

"Do you really want to know?" Her neediness scared him a little, but he remembered that there was steel in her, too, that he shouldn't underestimate her. That street-punk ogre probably did still have nightmares.

"Yes, really. And I think I'll have a glass of wine, too."

She was staying with a friend named Drusilla, it turned out, a girl she'd known from school who had dropped out to get married to a young fellow studying to be a chirurgeon. The two of them were living in a little house in the rundown Forenoon suburbs at the city's extreme southern end— "Practically on the moon, but it's a sweet house and Drusilla and Donnus are very happy," she explained. She didn't know what she was going to do about school. "It's my last year and I hate the place. They don't want you to ask real questions, they just want you to learn enough to make polite conversation at dances with the boys from Dowsing Academy." She shook her head. "That's not for me, Theo. I've been trying to help out with some of the organizations like the Daughters of the Grove that are doing things for people who've been hurt by the fighting—it's the least I can do, considering my monster of a father started it all—but I don't think I can stick with that either. Most of those women are more worried about getting seen doing these good things than just getting them done. Yesterday, when you saw me, we were half an hour late starting because they wouldn't unload the truck until the scribes and the other mirror-people were in place. It's like the Young Blossoms, except that everyone's surrounded by a cloud of youth-charms so thick you could choke. I hate that."

He had finished his wine and despite feeling more relaxed than he had for days he was beginning to worry about staying in one place too long. "Could we go for a walk? I'd like to get out of here."

She gave him an appraising look. "A walk? Like on our legs? Sure." She paid the bill by apparently, waving her fingers over it. He wondered how easy it would be for her father to track her down by her purchases. Rich girls, he suspected, didn't often think about things like that. He hadn't known many, but the few whose acquaintance he had made before Poppy hadn't led him to believe otherwise. There had been Sandra, for instance, a famous musician's daughter he had met at a club and briefly dated. She would simply walk out of restaurants and bars without paying, not intending to cheat anyone, but simply assuming—usually correctly—that everyone knew who she was and would bill her father. Or bill her father's manager, to be more accurate, since the eminent bass player and sybarite who had sired her didn't take care of his own accounts any more than did the Queen of England.

The Chamber of Congregation was less than a mile from the dockyards and the smell of Ys was very distinct outside, much more like an ocean than it had seemed to him in the muddy flatlands next to the Old Fayfort Bridge. She led him down some of the narrow lanes of Eastwater where the leaning buildings and dark alleys felt like something out of the mortal world's early 1800s—New Orleans, perhaps, or the backwater districts of Naples. Strange music, as strange as that of the goblins but undeniably different, drifted down from some of the upper stories.

"Kobolds?" he asked, thinking of the restaurant.

Poppy laughed. "You really are the ultimate out-of-towner, aren't you? You couldn't get a kobold to live on an upper story if you gave them the flat for free. No, most of the people around here are regular working fairies, but that sounds like pixie music. There are more than a few of them out here, but most of them live right down in the dockyard area or even on barges and houseboats."

Theo liked the music and he liked walking, feeling almost normal. He liked Poppy, too. He considered for a moment then took her hand, knowing that he was crossing a sort of Rubicon, no matter how small the gesture might seem. They continued for a while in silence, the two of them for this moment moving effortlessly through the warm, damp night like dolphins slipping side by side through tropical waves.

She pulled him to a halt against a shadowy wall, just outside the will-o'-the-wisp gleam of a streetlight. For a moment he thought she had seen someone she knew in the crowd of young men laughing and talking loudly as they spilled out of a tavern across the street, but when they had vanished into the night he realized that she had not stopped him out of fear at all. He put his arms around her, felt her fitting herself against him with the careful absorption of someone building something important. "I'm glad you called me," she said. "I thought about you a lot."

He didn't want to say anything stupid. He didn't want to say anything at all. He had got himself into trouble in the past by struggling with the question of what to say in these situations and he was even less certain now. But he hadn't told her a lie: being with her was enough, for now. So what else needed saying?

She was a very good kisser. She went at it with fierce determination—not in a hurry, but not playing games, either. There were only a few moments when he could concentrate enough to wonder why fairy kissing was so similar to human kissing, or to ask himself whether all fairy-folk kissed each other like it was the most important thing to do in the entire universe, or was it just Poppy Thornapple? The fact that she was technically a schoolgirl, which had worried him ever since she had first made her feelings clear, began to seem less important. However she might fit into her own society, by the chronology of his world she had been living her life since somewhere before Teddy Roosevelt was in office, and that meant if anybody was jailbait around here, it was him. By fairy standards Theo was probably in kindergarten or first grade.

Her work in assembling their connection had not been in vain: she was molded against him so closely that it almost felt as though they were growing together, and every small movement she made seemed to touch him in several places at the same time. He was beginning to wonder if he might not just be blasted out of his mind on that single glass of Faerie wine: his head felt quite floaty and the rest of him warm and pleasurably itchy. Was it love? Now there was a staggering thought. It was certainly lust, but there seemed to be more.

He pulled himself free, just a little, and laid his face against the side of her head. Her hair smelled like vanilla, like honeysuckle, like other things he couldn't even name but which he wanted to keep smelling for the rest of his life. Half an hour ago he had been arguing with himself about whether he was leading this girl on, but now he was beginning to feel that he was the one in danger of falling hopelessly and helplessly. Could she have used some charm on him? He didn't believe that—maybe when she had first met him, but after she had screwed up her courage to give him that ultimatum, leave or stay, but be honest about it?

God, I think it's real. I think it's . . . real.

Lost in the warm night, leaning against the wall and holding Poppy so close that he kept forgetting which way was up and other important things, it took him half a minute to notice the shape at the far end of the street. She was breathing in his ear and kissing and nibbling on it at the same time, and it was the most amazingly, distractingly nice thing that had happened to him in some while, but there was still something about the movement of the distant figure as it staggered from pool of light to shadow and then out into the light again that seized his attention. It lurched into another wash of light from a streetlamp, perhaps a hundred feet away from them, and he saw that it was wearing the armor of a police constable.

His heart suddenly froze into a lump in his chest. He stepped away from the wall, almost knocking Poppy over, grabbed her arm and began to walk away so quickly that she stumbled.

"What is it?"

"Behind us. That police . . . that constable. You can look, but for God's sake keep walking."

"But we'll make him suspicious, dashing away like this . . . !"

"Not unless it's a real constable—and I don't think it is. I told you about that thing that was after me. The last body it took was one of the constables at Daffodil House. Walk faster. When we get around the corner we're going to run."

"I'm not going to run from some . . . bugbear, Theo. I have a protection charm in my purse . . ."

"You don't understand, Poppy. This thing is bad, bad as it gets. Unless you have a charm that's the equivalent of a small-scale atomic bomb, we're better off just getting the hell out of here. Is it running?"

This time she sounded a bit more disturbed. "It's . . . it's walking fast. It moves really strangely."

"It probably has some pieces missing by now. How did you get here tonight? Please tell me you drove."

"I borrowed Drusilla's runabout. I hate trying to get a hired coach back from Eastwater at night."

"How far away is it? Never mind—we don't have any choice. I don't think even going into a place that's full of people is going to stop it. It just doesn't care. Here comes the corner." He squeezed her hand hard.

"You'll have to lead us. Wait until we're out of its sight . . . now . . . *run!"*

They did, pelting up the street, heading back across East-water toward the restaurant. A few older fairies coming out of another building had to jump out of their way and shouted genteel imprecations after them, but Theo had no time to waste on someone's hurt feelings.

Poppy had parked the small, sleek little car on a side street around the corner from the Chamber of Congregation. Theo could only bounce from foot to foot in nauseated panic as she fumbled through its unfamiliar door-charm. On the third unsuccessful try, a bulky silhouette lurched around the corner and into the dark street, pausing for a moment to swing its helmeted head from side to side, more like a radar array than like a person actually looking for something. If Theo had retained any doubt about the identity of their pursuer it was gone now. The thing did not move like any normal person, fairy or mortal. The arms hung slack at its sides and the head swiveled like something mechanical.

"Got it!" Poppy said as she yanked open the door. Theo ran around to the far side and climbed in, vaguely conscious that the seat seemed to wrap itself around him in a disturbingly lively way but in too much of a panic to think about it.

"Just drive," he said. "Distance." He turned to look. The thing was coming up fast now, stiff-legged but still horribly quick: He could see the face bouncing slackly under the helmet as it ran, its wearer uninterested in conveying mortal emotions, perhaps not even comprehending such things. "Now! Hurry!"

The car hummed to life and almost jumped away from the curb. Theo had only a moment to pray that they were not parked in a dead-end street. They weren't. He looked back again to see the thing watching them go. There was nothing in its posture that spoke of defeat or frustration. It would simply start all over again—already it was walking after them as it dwindled from view. Theo was suddenly extremely grateful the thing hadn't captured any bodies that had wings. It didn't really seem to plan, so its horrible single-mindedness had at least one useful side effect.

Still, given a choice; he would rather have not been chased by a relentless, deathless monstrosity, even if it did have a character flaw. But nobody was giving him a choice.

Half an hour later she pulled into the access road that led to the Old Fayfort Bridge, parked and turned off the runabout's lights. He reached across and took her hand. "Well, pretty interesting date, huh?" He tried to laugh but couldn't really manage. It was all a bit too awful for anything but the grimmest kind of humor.

"What are you going to do now?"

"About Applecore? Or about . . . you and me?"

She shrugged, smiled sadly. "Both, I guess. It's not a very good time for us, is it?"

"I don't know. I don't know much of anything. But I'm not going to just disappear or something, if that's what you're worrying about. Well, I suppose I might, but it won't be by choice."

"Don't say that, Theo. We'll think of something. I have friends—some of them know important people . . ."

"Yeah, but nobody, no matter how important they are, is going to make Hellebore stop what he's doing, and for some reason nobody can explain, I'm wrapped up in that." There were dozens of questions he should ask her, he realized, things that the daughter of Hellebore's partner might know that others wouldn't, but it was too late and he was too damn exhausted. "Can I see you again?"

"Of course." She took his hand, held it to her lips, then pressed it against her cheek. He stroked her black hair. "Of course."

"I need to think. I need to ask questions. I know some

people too. But I'll call you soon—if I can figure out a way,
I'll even do it myself this time."

Their kiss again threatened to turn into something much
more involved. It was extremely hard for his conscious mind
to raise a quorum for letting go of her—his feet and legs
wanted sleep after a day of walking and running, but the rest
of his body thought the feet and legs were idiots, and the bits
between his legs were on the verge of staging a full-scale
mutiny. He pulled himself free while he still could, kissed
her a few more times, then backed clumsily out of the small
car. It wasn't that it was too early in their relationship—it
was wartime, for God's sake!—but more that he didn't have
a place for her in his life yet, and feelings this surprisingly
serious and strong would just blow him apart, otherwise.

"Theo?" she asked as he came back around to the driver's
side window to kiss her good-bye again. "Do you really
share a tent with a goblin? And sing with them?"

"Yeah, pretty much." He hesitated, worried that she
would say some stupid upper-class thing about them being
dirty or criminal and, without meaning to, make him feel
wretched about liking her so much.

"That's so great. I always wanted to know a goblin. My
father never let me go near any of them."

He thought of Button's apparent plans for revolution.
"Everyone may get to know the goblins better one of these
days." He kissed her. "Goodnight, Poppy. Thanks for . . . for
everything."

"I shouldn't say this," she told him, "but I'll say it. You'd
better call me."

Theo waved as she made a laborious three-point turn and
then headed back toward the City. He felt more like a
teenager than he had in years. *Yeah, been here before—I live
in a world that makes no sense, the authority figures are all
out to get me, and my glands have taken over.*

He walked back to the refugee camp feeling a bit like he
should sneak in quietly so he wouldn't wake his parents.

33

THE LAST
BREATH
THEY TOOK

"I am pleased that you have come to see me, Theo Vilmos."

Theo took a seat on the woven mat across from Mud Bug Button. The goblin handed him a bowl and poured steaming water into it from something that looked pretty much like a teapot, but Theo was learning not to make assumptions. "Thank you. What is it?"

"Tea."

"Good." He sipped, blew, then sipped again. It tasted a little bit like root beer and a little bit like cilantro, but it wasn't too bad and there weren't any small animals floating in it so he decided he'd leave the inquiry at that. He sat for a moment just holding the bowl, letting his thoughts settle like the bits of leaf drifting down through the tea, although it was a bit hard to concentrate with all the grunting going on at the far end of the bridge's tower room. The two ogre bodyguards were taking turns doing two-handed lifts with a chunk of granite the size of a home entertainment system.

"Why are they always in pairs?" Theo asked. "Ogres, I mean. Nobody's ever got just one."

Button smiled his pointy smile. "Is that truly what you came up here to ask me? The reason is that they are usually brother and sister, at least among what the fairy lords call the

better houses—'better' meaning of course 'richer.' It is a superstition among the Flower-folk that siblings work together
better than any others, and since ogres often give birth to
male and female twins, and since the security trades draw
ogres in the same way that housecleaning draws ferishers
and home-management draws hobs, it is not, *hem,* impossible to find brother and sister pairs willing to work as guards,
especially since they can draw the highest salaries." He
looked over to Choo-Choo and Topsy, then lowered his
voice. "In fact, the belief runs so strong that when one sibling is killed, even when that death saves their master's life,
the other is almost always let go afterward. Can you imagine something so terrible? To lose your twin and then your
job as well? But it is only a belief, as so many things are, un-
questioned and even foolish. A surviving ogre twin, called a
'widow' or 'widower,' will often be a very fierce protector
for the next master, since they no longer have divided loyalties." He shook his head. "The Flower-folk never understand
that, or do not want to believe it, and they continue with their
fetish of sibling bodyguards. It is a common insult among
the fairy lords to say, 'So-and-so's guards had never even
met until they started working together,' meaning that, *hem,*
So-and-so was too poor to afford to hire twins."

Theo watched the gleam of sweat on leathery hides, the
bulge of muscles. "So are your bodyguards brother and
sister?"

Button laughed. "These two? They are indeed. But I am
no slave to Flower fashions, I hasten to say! They are the
bodyguards of Caradenus Primrose. They came with him,
but he has, *hem,* transferred them to me, I suppose. He fears
for my life. He is a kind fellow, Primrose."

"I wouldn't have agreed with you the first day, but I think
I do now. How did he come to be here? He's never said anything to me about it."

Button poured himself another bowl of tea. "I sense that
you are avoiding the true concern that brought you here,
Theo Vilmos. But I am in no hurry, and we may reach the

mountain by many roads." He sipped, contemplated. "Actually, how Primrose came to be here is very closely wrapped up with how I came to be here."

"I wondered about that, but I didn't know if it was rude to ask . . ."

"It is never rude to ask a goblin anything because we love to tell tales, but what you will get—as you must know by now—is a story with a hole in it, as we always say.

"Perhaps you have thought on this a bit, Theo Vilmos. Perhaps you have said to yourself, 'Button must have suffered some terrible loss at the hands of the Flower-folk, to bear them such a grudge.' Perhaps you imagined my family, *hem,* brutally slaughtered, or my mate ripped from my arms and dishonored by young fairy lords. But it is nothing so simple. In fact, I wonder how often it is that people who have suffered such losses can work usefully toward the sort of changes of which I dream. It seems to me that when the wheel on which a pot is made is crooked, the pot will be crooked also, however ambitious the potter. The bigger the pot, the more severe will be the flaws. Make it big enough and that original crookedness will cause it to shatter the first time you set it over the fire.

"That is how I feel. I believe a change is coming for the way we live. I look back and see I have been on a long journey, and some of it has been through evil times, but nothing so simple as, 'They killed my family, and thus they must be overthrown.' My mother and father are alive, living here in this City. My father is a gardener, now with a business of his own, taking care of the grounds of some of the greatest houses. He is happy—or, *hem,* he thinks he is. My mother, too, after many years washing windows and cleaning floors, now has the leisure to spend time with her grandchildren. You see, Theo, I have several brothers and sisters and they are not so concerned with the machineries of Faerie as I am. They have lived more . . . conventional lives. So my mother, too, believes herself happy. Perhaps she is.

"Ah, but you see, I had the evil luck to achieve some

education. I was the youngest and so by the time I grew my
parents could scrape together enough money to send me to
one of the goblin academies. You look surprised! There are
such things, truly."

"I didn't doubt it," Theo said. "I only . . . are they just for
goblins?"

"Of course. The Flower families and their admirers are
hard put to share schools and neighborhoods with lesser
fairies of their own type. I imagine your friend Cumber
Sedge could tell you some stories of what it means to be a
ferisher living in one of the high houses . . ."

"He has."

"Just so. No, the Flower gentry are not yet ready to see
their children studying alongside goblin children. For one
thing, it might make them question the differences between
us that they have always seen as beyond dispute. And now
you may hear a little bitterness in my voice, Master Vilmos.
Because of course, I did not conceive these ideas by chance.
There is no tale of some singular terror, but there is of course
a catalogue of petty insults and small denials, heaped one
upon the other, day after day, until taken together they weigh
more than any one event. I do not know much of the mortal
world but I imagine there are people there who experience
the same things I have . . ."

"There are. Of course."

"Then I wish I could have met such mortals—it would
have been instructive to consider the similarities and differences. What drives me is not what you would think, perhaps.
The worst was not when some rich idiot would curse me and
call me a 'skin-eater' or suggest I was dirty or a drunkard
without bothering to learn anything about me. Even the
knowledge that had we goblins proved useful for their
power-generation needs our entire race would have been
burned away like kindling by the Flower lords with scarcely
a second thought was not what galled me most—that is almost too big for one home-soul to encompass. No, the worst
was that even the kinder fairies I met, the decent sort, had to

keep reminding themselves that I was another living, thinking being. The surprise when I said something intelligent! The praising of almost any achievement by me as if I were a farm animal who had learned to solve cipher-charms! It was this more than the outright cruelties that ate at me, Theo Vilmos. And when I came out of the academy, afire with new ideas and puzzled that all my classmates were not blazing, too, it was to discover that, *hem,* my own family no longer understood me either, and that there was no occupation awaiting me where I could usefully employ my mind. Unless I were to strike it lucky and be taken up as a sort of curiosity by one of the more unconventional Flower families, as with your friend Cumber, I could look forward to nothing more challenging than clipping the hedges of the wealthy or, perhaps, owning a small store on the edge of Goblintown.

"Years went by and I could find no satisfying uses for my learning, for my ideas. You have seen the condition of our society, Theo Vilmos. It is not a happy place and the more I studied it, the more I learned of what had happened since the Gigantine War and the death of the king and queen, the more I became convinced that the edifice was rotting from within. Perhaps it is wishful thinking, because if the system survives I doubt I will see any change for my own people within my lifetime, however much longer it lasts." He smiled and looked over at Choo-Choo and Topsy, who were resting and drinking from a bucket of water. "Which will likely not be long, no matter how well-prepared Primrose's ogres might be."

He poured himself more tea. "There are no great surprises in this tale, Theo, as I mentioned. I met Caradenus Primrose while my father had the contract to maintain the endless north lawns of Primrose House. We are great ones for agreements and contracts, we goblins. We hold our honor dearer than our lives and we have always considered our given word the most sacred bond. Thus a contract, any contract, is to us a thing of powerful science. To my proud

father this compact with a Flower family seemed a sort of
acceptance by his betters, whereas to them he was only another sort of servant. But that is beside the point.

"Caradenus has always been an unconventional member
of a very conventional class and he went out of his way to
talk to us and the other laborers on the family estate. He had
even learned some words of Goblin, which, *hem,* he liked to
practice." He chuckled, then had to wipe tea off his lower
lip. "By the Taproot, he speaks it abominably! Like a man
with a cockatrice struggling to get out of his mouth. But
never tell him I said so!" He looked quickly over to the
bodyguards again in case they had heard. "It is admirable
Caradenus has tried to learn, but the first time he tried it on
myself and two of my comrades he actually came up to us
and said, in our tongue, *'Greetings, my head is Primrose the
smallest and you are commanded to eat your names with
me.'* The habit of subservience runs very deep—not surprisingly, when my people have been killed in the past for insufficient respect in nearly all the high houses, and every
work camp in Willow and Birch has a grave pit where the
bodies of those goblins who have been worked to death or
have resisted authority can be discarded—so we did not
laugh. I found out later he would not have minded, or rather
he would only have minded that he had the words so badly
wrong."

Theo didn't want to think too much about grave pits. "So
you became friends?"

Button looked surprised. "Oh, no. Not so easily—I still
am not sure whether we could call each other friends. He
and I are from different worlds, almost as much as you and
I. But we spoke often and learned from each other. He,
hem . . . hem—your pardon, I have an old injury to my
throat—he thought more about the problems of the world
than any Flower I have met, although we did not always
agree on the solutions and he was still bound very strongly
to some of the most conservative ideas of honor and tradition, even as he questioned things that were more funda-

mental, like the difference between types of fairies and the inequalities of our society."

The goblin took a long drink of his tea. "Primrose was a great help to me when I most needed him, although it troubled his principles, I think. But it is a mark of how different he is from his fellows that, just as he weighed his debt of honor against you in the light of what he learned, then decided he had been wrong, so he put even his own beliefs to the test when it mattered. In any case, he helped me to escape when no one else of his class would have even considered it.

"So I left my family and our little foothold in society behind. When Primrose found me again he too had begun to break with his own clan, although it was more in his heart than in his head. He loved his family, you see, and could not entirely separate who they were from *what* they were." Button poured himself a little more tea, then filled Theo's bowl as well. "He was not ready yet to break entirely with the way of life in which he had been raised and I think he still harbors some hopes that it can simply be . . . reshaped. I do not feel the same." He showed his long teeth; it was not a smile. "But we agree that change must come, and he is honorable. So, no, Theo Vilmos, Caradenus Primrose and I are not quite friends—I fear the gulf between our peoples is too great— but we have found something that is useful and perhaps even comforting to both of us."

Theo sipped the tea. Somewhere, he had lost the thread. "But you said he helped you to escape . . . Escape what? It sounded like you were just working for your father and . . ." He lowered the bowl. "Oh. I get it. That's the hole in the story, huh?"

Button took a little more tea.

"Do I have to guess? You had to escape because you did something—got in trouble. Right?"

Button swirled the dregs in the bowl and looked back at Theo.

"But you didn't do anything to his family, because then

he would have thought he had to kill you, like he did with me." He pondered. "And you didn't just run away, or put up some inflammatory posters or something, because you said 'escape' and you also said his principles were troubled. So you must have done something really bad." Theo suddenly found the yellow, slot-eyed stare difficult to meet. "Did you . . . kill someone? One of the big-deal fairies?"

Button's very sharp teeth appeared again. "You are practically a goblin yourself now, Theo Vilmos. You have filled the hole in the story. More tea?"

"Hang on. I've been helping you because . . . because you seem like you're trying to do the right thing. But I think I need to know about this." He looked over to the bodyguards, who had finished their workout and were regarding him with an offhand but nevertheless focused sort of interest, as though they could feel his tension from across the room. "What happened?"

"Nothing surprising when you consider how my ideas had been changing. I was in the street, waiting for the bus. A very simple thing! And just in front of me a fairy began to beat a goblin porter who had, *hem,* dropped one of his packages. I still do not know that poor goblin porter's name, and I fear he may have suffered badly—that the authorities must have afterward assumed that he knew me, but in truth I was a stranger to him. In fact, perhaps it happened because he *was* a stranger to me. In that moment, while the fellow I only found out later was a member of the Hydrangea clan bludgeoned him with a heavy walking stick until he could not get up, then continued to kick and beat him, that huddled, whimpering figure became every goblin I knew—myself, my father struggling through night courses at a shabby school to learn polite words to soothe his fairy masters, my brothers and sisters living in urban hovels, six to a bedroom, and still calling them 'nests' as if that would make them so, and all the nameless corpses in the lime pits of Willow—to me he was every one of us, and his self-promoted master was the dead hand of the Flower nobility, who had not been content to take our lands and our forests away, but now must crush us like insects.

"That is where my other name comes from, Theo, the one I have kept hidden until now. We hide them because they are names of shame, deliberately taken. They remind us every day that we are, *hem,* lowly and wretched. Do you know what my last free ancestor was named? Shiningstone Fox. When the Flower-folk took us into captivity they even took away our names, and those of us who worked in their houses they named after small and demeaning things, unimportant objects. But the names we saved for ourselves, Worm, Roach, Carrion, Stain—these are our legacy of despair . . . and, just perhaps, strength. Bug! I am a bug as far as the Flower lords are concerned, a lowly and crawling thing, but on that day they learned that even the lowliest thing can bite."

Anger came off him now like a shimmer of heat—Theo could almost squint his eyes and see it. Paradoxically, as he spoke Button became more and more still, as if he were retreating back into some internal place that Theo could not even imagine. "It was too horrible to watch any longer. I threw myself at the beast from Hydrangea House with only the idea that I might absorb some of the beating and it would give the porter a chance to escape. But he could not rise— many bones broken—and the fairy lordling turned his attention to me. He was astonished by my arrival, but the astonishment quickly became rage and he struck out at me with the stick, damaging my throat. It is still in my speaking to this day. But that first look of surprise he gave me did something to me that the blows only strengthened. He could not believe that anyone, even another goblin, would be so foolhardy as to interfere with him. Do you understand? He felt he had every right to beat that porter to death. And it was true, the bus stop was full of all kinds of fairy-folk, big and small. Some turned away in dismay, but most simply watched. They were not surprised, not outraged.

"I went mad, Theo Vilmos. He struck me and struck me

again while I hung onto his leg—I was too close for him to
hit me as hard as he would have liked—and before he could
immobilize me with some charm or call for help I climbed
up his body and I ripped open his neck so that he bled to
death. Yes, with these teeth."

Theo sat through the long silence, not sure what to think.
Button had certainly ceased to be the charming, cartoonish
character he had thought him to be, but now that he considered it, even with this sick feeling in his stomach he had to
wonder if that Button had ever truly existed. No, he had
been a version that Theo wanted to believe, a sort of Ma-
hatma Gandhi of the fairyland revolution.

Button smiled, but this time kept the sharp ends of his
fangs hidden, perhaps in deference to Theo's troubled expression. "You do not like the Mud Bug Button you see now
so much, eh? Then I should tell you that I have killed again,
twice. Both times to defend myself and avoid capture—and
once captured, Theo, have no doubt that after a few months
as an unhappy guest of Lord Monkshood and his parliamentary constables I would wind up in a lime pit somewhere, or
a furnace. Neither victim was anyone that I think you would
mourn much, but that may not lessen the offense in your
eyes. They were fairies, your kind. I had no right to resist
them, let alone kill them. But I did."

"People like that aren't my kind, whether I think of myself as a fairy or a mortal."

"Ah, but the lines are not so easy to draw, Theo Vilmos,
as I think I told you the other day. You have already, *hem,*
helped me. As a result of that help, people may die. Not the
innocent, I hope, but war is a demon in a box and when the
lid opens it flies where it wishes to fly."

Theo had not come to the bridgehouse with the idea of
exploring Button's background—he was too consumed with
his own problems for that—but he realized that the goblin
had his own agenda and had deliberately set him a sort of
quandary. *More holes,* he thought. He straightened, met the
goblin's melted-butter stare. "If you're asking me if I want

to join you, the answer is still 'not entirely.' I'm sympathetic. I've been here long enough to see that things are wrong, that a change is needed. And your enemies are my enemies, I guess. I don't know—what do you want to hear from me? I still want your help. I'll still do my best to help you, if it makes sense to me . . ."

Button shook his head, amused. "You are no soldier, Theo Vilmos, that is certain. Soldiers are not allowed to make such distinctions. But I *have* soldiers—those who will do what they are told and only think about it afterward, if at all. And I suppose that until we know why you are so important to Hellebore and Thornapple and their minions, you have some bargaining power."

"Speaking of doing what you're told," Theo said, "what exactly were we trying to accomplish with Streedy at Elysium House? I saw something on the screen—well, on the mirror, I guess—about getting permission for one immigrant laborer and one livestock animal."

Button nodded. "Yes. And you and Streedy Nettle and Cumber Sedge and Coathook did your jobs very well."

"But what does it mean? What are you going to accomplish by smuggling one person and one animal into the City—unless it's a giant riding on a dinosaur or something . . ."

"A dinosaur . . . ? Ah, wait, yes, I have heard of those fabled beasts." The goblin laughed, a quiet hissing sound. "You are full of wit, Theo Vilmos. No, that is not quite what I plan, but I think you are best not knowing—after all, we are all liable to capture, and the technicians of Hellebore House in particular are very, very skilled. But you cannot tell what you do not know, no matter how much you might wish to do so."

"But . . ."

The goblin suddenly looked up. Theo turned to see Caradenus Primrose waiting in the doorway, his face a smoothly handsome mask of patience. "Ah, you are returned, my comrade," said Button. "Please, come and sit with us. I will make more tea."

Primrose seated himself cross-legged on one side of the rug. He nodded to Theo in a way that was not unfriendly, but he seemed in no hurry to speak. In fact, both he and Button were quite content to sit in silence while the teapot heated on the brazier. Even though he had not actually talked to Button about what was most important, Theo began to wonder if they were waiting for him to leave so they could talk in private and he was just ignorant of the fairyland social protocols.

"I . . . I did have something else I wanted to discuss with you," he said. *Jesus, man, Applecore's a prisoner, bait to trap you, and you make it sound like you don't think there's enough donuts in the break room at work.* "Something important. Really important."

Button inclined his head. "Of course, Theo Vilmos."

"Should I leave?" asked Primrose.

"No! No, in fact, I'd like to hear what you think about this, too." He sipped his now-cold tea. "But I don't want to hold you two up, either."

Primrose almost smiled. "It is true that I have something I wish to give to Button, and the sooner the better." He raised an eyebrow in inquiry. Button nodded. "Good," Primrose said. "It feels very heavy to me. Not in weight, but in substance, and I have felt that all eyes were on me." He reached into the pocket of his long coat.

"Did you have trouble?"

"Less than I expected—it was quite strange. I would not be able to walk into my own house without being arrested, but I was able to walk into the Parliamentary Museum and not only did no one recognize or question me, I was able to take it out of the case using only the simplest charm to quell the protections." He withdrew something wrapped in dull velvet or fur and held it out to Button. "I suppose it is because the wing dedicated to the Goblin Wars is not often visited these days. The cases were dusty, the room empty."

Button cradled the bundle, apparently in no hurry to unwrap it. Theo felt his heart quicken—was it some legendary goblin weapon? It wasn't big enough to be a sword or an ax—maybe some sacred dagger or a kind of magic gun that could kill Hellebores from a mile away?

The goblin peeled back the black covering.

"It's a stick," said Theo in surprise, and then raised his hand to his mouth, afraid he had insulted a sacred goblin treasure. Treasured or not, it was definitely a stick, a piece of a slender branch about eighteen inches in length. Bark had been peeled from it in a spiral pattern, and signs that could have been writing—but which, unlike normal fairy-writing, Theo could not read—had been carved into the white wood where the bark was gone and then rubbed with something dark to make them visible.

"It is indeed," said Button, almost smiling. His eyes seemed unusually bright. "Small things make all the difference." He contemplated the object for a moment. "Should I do it now? No, perhaps not yet. An audience is what I need, I think." As Theo watched in befuddlement, the goblin carefully wrapped the stick in the covering cloth again and tucked it into his robe. "I thank you, Caradenus Primrose," he said. "You have perhaps changed the world—let us hope it is for the better."

The fairy nodded solemnly. For a long silent moment they just looked at each other; then, as if on cue, they turned their attention to Theo.

He was still struggling to understand what he had just witnessed, especially the air of high seriousness that had surrounded the passing of a piece of wood, but he had already been Button's guest for what must be a couple of hours without mentioning his true purpose. "Shall I start?" he asked. The goblin nodded and poured him more tea.

Button already knew most of what Theo had experienced since coming to Faerie, but Primrose still did not know many of the details so Theo quickly sketched out his recent history, trying to make clear how much Applecore had done for him. Then he told them both about the bit of broadcast news or whatever it was he had seen on the mirrorcases in the display window—Hellebore and the nasty bell jar beside him on the desk.

". . . And don't tell me it's a trap, because I know that. I may not know why they want me, but I'm not an idiot." He stared at Primrose and Button as if daring them to suggest otherwise. "But you both think a lot about honor, so I know you'll understand that I can't just leave her to suffer, even if I know that me trying to rescue her is exactly what they want."

The fairy and the goblin were quiet for some time after he finished. Theo was beginning to wonder what the two of them were like together on their own—did they even talk, or just sit side by side, silent as bookends?

"I am not surprised by much," said Primrose at last, "but I am surprised to learn that Quillius Tansy would do this. Not because I like the fellow—I never have—but because I did not know he coveted anything enough to be bought by Hellebore."

"His life, perhaps," Button offered.

"Perhaps." Primrose did that sinuous thing that among the Flower-folk passed for a shrug, but to Theo looked more like a snake easing an itch in its nonexistent shoulders. "But this does not answer Master Vilmos."

The goblin nodded. "You know, Theo Vilmos, that even were every living creature in this camp to take up arms and march on Hellebore House it would not be enough. Zirus Jonquil is alive and gathering some resistance fighters from the other Flower houses—you met him, I believe—and there are others who might play some part, but even if we all join together our numbers would still be very small compared to what Hellebore and his allies can muster. We hope to throw down that grim place of Hellebore's when our day comes, Theo, but I cannot say how far away that day will be, or whether your sprite friend will be alive to see it—although of course, *hem,* there is always hope. So there is little I can offer you in the way of direct action. We cannot allow our plans to be changed—and thus put at risk—for any one individual, especially at such a critical point.

"I don't care," Theo said, and realized that, in an odd way, that was true. "Well, I do care—of course I do, I don't want to die. But I can't just leave her there, either, so I might as well not think about it too much. Just help me figure out what's going to be least likely to get me caught, even if the odds of failing would only be ninety-nine percent instead of a hundred."

"You must give us more time to think, Theo Vilmos," said Button gently. "You have waited some time to tell us of your problem. Allow us a few moments to think about it."

He sat back, frustrated, but relieved that at least they weren't trying to tell him that Applecore was just a casualty of war and that he should forget about her. Unfortunately, their acceptance of his debt of honor had also made it clearer to him that he really didn't have much choice: he was going to have to do more than talk about it. He was going to have to risk his life—and probably lose it—trying to get her free. The thought of what he was up against made him go cold all over, made his balls try to climb back into his body. Now he understood why the military made sure you had a bunch of other guys with you, so that you'd be ashamed to run. And why there was usually a sergeant with a gun, too . . .

"What about the one who lives down at the waterfront?" Primrose said suddenly. "You know who I mean. The old one."

While Theo was wondering how mind-bogglingly ancient you had to be before a fairy called you "old," Button stirred and said, "You refer to the one often called the Remover of Inconvenient Obstacles? He has shown no sign of being sympathetic to our cause. *Hem.* Rather the reverse."

"Yes, but that is because he is largely mercenary. Certainly in the most recent years he has done little—or so rumor suggests—that was not purely for profit, even if that profit was more often in favors than in gold." Primrose frowned. It hardly even creased his smooth forehead. "It is not a pleasing idea, I know, but unless we can come up with another . . ."

"Hang on, who is this 'Remover of Obstacles'? I mean, it sounds like an old Black Sabbath song title or something." Theo pushed on past his companions' blank looks. "Just tell me what you know. I deserve to be in on the conversation, since I'm the one who's going to be putting his ass on the line."

"The mortal world gives you a very colorful way of talking," noted Primrose. "But you are right, of course. I'll tell you what I know and Button can supply whatever's missing."

"Never, never expect a goblin to fill the gaps in the tale," Button said with a quick smile. "It is against our nature."

Theo thought Primrose looked like he would have liked to appreciate the joke, but hadn't yet had the humor update for his software. "Yes," said the fairy. "Well, what little I know of the one called the Remover is second- or even third-hand. He is very old—nobody I know can remember a time when he was not around, and when I was growing up our nurses used to frighten us by threatening that he would come to take us if we were bad. I am told he is extremely unpleasant to look at."

And in a world full of ogres and trolls, Theo thought, that must mean somebody is pretty damn ugly. "But what does he *do?*"

"Only what he wishes to do, and only for those who can afford his price. He has amassed secrets of science over his centuries of study that no one else can touch. It is said that many a lord thought to be too well-protected to be assassinated has instead found that the Remover's terrible face is the last thing he sees. But these are not the only sorts of obstacles he removes, only the most dramatic. As I said, his command of the scientific arts is broad. Doubtless many things in our society, things we now take for granted, began as a notation in the Remover's diary."

"So he's part wizard, part mercenary killer."

"I will say this for him. I have never heard of him killing an innocent. That proves nothing, though. There are no doubt as many false tales as true, and doubtless far more tales that have never been told at all." The fairy lord turned to Button. "Do you agree?"

The goblin nodded slowly. "You know more than I—he has never had dealings with my folk, to my knowledge. He is powerful. He is without loyalty except to his agreements, as far as anyone can tell. That is perhaps the true sum of what is known about him."

"And how on earth would I persuade this person to do something for me?" Theo asked. "Even assuming he could help me get into Hellebore House."

"Or perhaps he could get your friend out without you having to risk yourself," said Button. "Would that not be the best alternative?"

"Good God, yes—I'm no hero. But why should he help me?"

The goblin tented his long fingers so that the talons clicked against each other. "You are an unusual person, Theo Vilmos, and there are still mysteries around you. Perhaps there is something you know that can buy the Remover's help."

"And maybe he'll just whack me on the head and call Hellebore on the shell phone and make some easy money. But I suppose it's a better risk than me trying to sneak into Hellebore House in a wagon full of guest towels or something." He spoke with a lightness he did not feel. He had more than an inkling now of what it might mean to know your platoon was heading for the front lines at dawn. "So just tell me where it is and I'll go."

Button raised his hand. "I hope you will prepare with a little more caution than that. Also, there are still things in your story I would like to understand better, before you go to see the Remover."

"Before I go get myself killed, is what you mean."

The goblin smoothed the fur on his jaw. "We are none of us promised anything but the last breath we take, Theo Vilmos."

That was so obviously and depressingly true it made Theo want to kill himself now, just to end the suspense.

Part Four

The Lost Child

34

INTERLUDE WITH VAN GOGH STARS

"No, you're not going. It's my problem. I'll deal with it." Cumber looked irritated but spoke calmly. "You'll do nothing of the sort. You're no hero, Theo. Neither am I, but maybe together we might manage to equal one Lord Rose or whatever."

"It's not a battle, Cumber. I'm not going to fight anyone with a sword or anything, just going to ask for some help."

"From the Remover of Inconvenient Obstacles, one of the most dangerous creatures in all the world. You don't even know how to find your way there, do you?"

"I wrote down the directions." It didn't sound very heroic, he had to admit. "I know you like Applecore, Cumber, but you don't owe her the way I do. She saved my life."

The ferisher shook his head. "I'm not demanding to go in your place, Theo, I'm just going with you. We'll have a better chance of making it work, especially if something goes wrong. You don't know the city very well, Theo. No, I'm definitely going with you."

The tent flap opened and Mistress Twinge looked in. "Going where?"

Theo almost told her—misery being the inveterate lover of company—but a look from Cumber seemed to indicate caution. "Nowhere special. Just having an argument."

"Ah." She slouched in and arranged herself in a corner of the tent. "I like arguments. Can I play, too?"

The goblin Coathook came in behind her, dark and quiet as a raincloud slipping across the sky. He nodded to Theo and Cumber as he settled on his bedroll.

"Hey, Coathook, that was a world-class fit you threw in what's-it-called—Elysium House," Theo said. "You really looked like you were dying or something."

"He was," said Mistress Twinge cheerfully. "There's too many people with diagnostic charms around these days. A little poison makes it look good and feel good, no matter what charm you use to read it with. You just have to make sure to take the antidote before the stuff hits—right, Hooky?"

Coathook was wearing his poker face today. He didn't even blink at the nickname.

"Hang on," said Theo. "I'm not sure I'm getting this. Coathook took *real* poison so he could fake that fit in the records office?"

"Had to," the pooka explained. "Most of the guards in places like that have at least some elementary healing training. They've got charms that will tell them what's wrong so they know whether to call for an ambulance or just make the person comfortable. So Coathook had a little sack of iron filings in his pocket and a healing charm to make him right again. Take the first, wait 'til you begin to feel it, then take the other before you forget." She chuckled. "Good, huh?"

"Jeez . . . Wow," Theo said. "So all that screaming and . . . you were really *feeling* that?"

Coathook looked at him with inscrutable yellow eyes. "Yes." He unrolled his bedroll and stretched out. "Sleeping now." He closed his eyes and appeared to begin doing so immediately.

After a long moment's silence Mistress Twinge stood up, pulling a cigar out of the pocket of her red overalls. "Well, I can see you young lovers want to be alone so I think I'll just go for a walk and a smoke—maybe I'll grab Streedy on his way back from Button and teach the boy how to drink or something. That might be amusing." She gave them a jaunty salute. "Have fun, kids!"

"Is that where Streedy is?" Theo asked when the pooka was gone. "With Button? I was just over there and I didn't see him."

Cumber shrugged. "Anything else you want to talk about, now that we're agreed I'm going along to see the Remover? Are you still planning on tomorrow?"

"I guess. Button wouldn't be specific, but I got the feeling things are about to start happening and if something's really up I want to be ready with information on how to get into Hellebore House—if we can get any, that is." Theo rubbed his face. Watching Coathook's placid slumber was making him tired and it was getting late. "What do you think Button has planned, anyway? Do you think he has a hope in hell against the Flower houses?"

Cumber frowned at the unfamiliar expression. "I don't know, Theo. He's awfully smart. Primrose isn't stupid, either, although he's not in Button's league. But if they really think there's a chance they must know something we don't, because even if you gave every able-bodied adult in this camp a weapon they still wouldn't have a chance against the Parliamentary Guard, let alone Hellebore's dragons. It looks quite hopeless to me, but they used to hunt dragons, you know. Goblins did, I mean—Button's people. Perhaps that means he's tough and hard-minded enough to pull it off." Cumber didn't sound very much like he believed it, though.

"The dragons seem to have caught everyone by surprise," said Theo. "I remember Daffodil shouting something about it wasn't fair, or that Hellebore had broken the rules . . ."

"There have always been dragons in Faerie," said Cumber. "But the big ones were killed off a long time ago in the Dragon Campaigns back in the days of the Tree Lords—the first generation of fairies. Everyone agreed the dragons had to go—they were just too dangerous, too big and too smart.

Only a few of the smallest survived, mostly hiding in caves in the high mountains. Every now and then one would carry off few sheep or something, but basically they were scavengers living in remote areas and nobody even knew they were there except the wild goblins. But during the last Gigantine War it was clear to everyone that we were going to have to come up with something new to beat the giants, so Parliament decided to start a breeding program, but only after a lot of very bitter argument—see, the dragons had almost wiped us out early on, and a lot of folk weren't too pleased about bringing them back. All kinds of agreements were signed by all the houses, swearing that these dragons would be kept under control, that they could only be flown by an act of the full Parliament of Blooms, and they could never—never, never, *never*—be used against fairy-folk."

"So Hellebore broke that law."

"Of course, although he got Parliament to rubber-stamp it once the smoke had cleared. Because the winners make the rules, Theo." A depth of bitterness was in Cumber's words Theo hadn't heard since the night in the club named Christmas. "That's how it always works. They make the rules and they write the histories. So if things end the way they're probably going to, Hellebore and Thornapple and those other lizards will be the heroes and Button and Primrose will be the villains—you and me too, if they even remember us. Five hundred years from now there will probably be a public holiday to celebrate the anniversary of our executions."

"Thanks for that pleasant thought," said Theo. "Shit, I just thought of something. Five hundred years—but fairies don't die, do they? I mean, if he wins, Hellebore will probably still be around then, won't he? Celebrating."

"He'll be fairly old by then—nobody lives forever, we just endure a lot longer than mortals—but unless someone kills him, yes, he'll probably be sitting in Strawflower Square watching us being burned in effigy for the five hundredth time."

It was disconcerting that although Coathook was apparently sleeping deeply, he made no noise or movements at all—not a snore, not a fidget. "Answer me one more question," Theo said quietly. "It's purely hypothetical since I'm probably going to get killed tomorrow anyway. I'm a fairy too, or at least that's what you and the others tell me. Does that mean if I didn't do anything stupid, just kept my head down and my nose clean, I might live for a thousand years or so as well?"

Cumber frowned. "It's hard to say, because nobody knows all the effects of being raised in the mortal world. You're not entirely like other fairies—I saw some of the physical differences when we were testing you in Daffodil House. Your facial features and body shape have taken on a little mortal coarsening. Excuse the expression, Theo, but you must know what I mean."

"Yeah. I don't look like an anorexic male model like the rest of these Flower-folk."

"But you're not that different, either, so it's hard to tell. I'm trying to remember—you didn't have children, did you? That makes a big difference."

For a moment that terrible night flashed through Theo's thoughts—Cat in her blood-soaked bathrobe, the over-worked emergency room intern saying in a weary, offhand way, *"It's a miscarriage, of course. There shouldn't be any permanent harm to her ability to conceive, if that's any help at a time like this."* "No," he said. "No kids. But what does that have to do with anything?"

"Nobody knows for certain—by the time people began to want to test these things in a proper, rigorous way there weren't enough mortals crossing over to our side, or fairies to the mortal side, to provide the information necessary for a decent study. But the conventional wisdom is that a changeling—a fairy raised by mortals—will still retain most of the Faerie birthright, whether he or she knows it or not, until the changeling in turn becomes father or mother to a child in the mortal world. Then what remains of the birthright, which can be anything from fairy-nature to some

kinds of fairy talents and innate knowledge, passes to that
child, diminishing a bit with each generation. At least that's
what everyone thinks. There hasn't been a chance to test, as
I said."

Theo sighed. "So there really is a chance I might live to
be a thousand or so. A chance."

Cumber nodded. "I suppose so."

"Well, at least I'll have that to be miserable about when
they're torturing me and killing me—you know, just to keep
me distracted."

"Does being raised as a mortal make everyone strange?"
asked Cumber.

"Do you have the expression here, 'You have to laugh to
keep from crying'? Well, right now it's more like, 'You have
to laugh to keep from throwing up in terror.'"

He slept only fitfully that night, for several reasons.
After falling almost immediately into one of the
worst of the shared-mind dreams yet—One in which he felt
himself helplessly drowning inside his own stolen self,
swallowed up by a terrible cold blackness—he escaped into
a succession of less frightening episodes, although he was
never entirely free of the feeling that he was sharing his
thoughts with something foreign, something *other*. The last
dream was something about delivering flowers to his mother
in the hospital and trying to tell her that it was really him,
her boy Theo, and that he didn't care whether she was his
real mother or not, he still loved her, but in the dream she
was too far gone in her illness and couldn't understand him.
All she could do was stare at the flowers on the bedside table
as if they had her hypnotized.

It was a sad dream, and usually he didn't remember the
sad ones, just the happy ones (making out with some woman
he'd lusted after but would never touch in real life, winning
the lottery) or the really dreadful ones. Lately there had been
quite a few really dreadful ones. But the chances were that
he would not have remembered this one, with his mother's

lost face and the drooping flowers beside the hospital bed, if
he had not woken up in the middle of it to find a hand across
his mouth and another around his throat.

The thing! It's found me! His heart sped from sleep-slow
to terrified in a second, as though someone had pushed the
cardiac pedal to the floorboards. He tried to roll away from
the clutching hands; the one on his throat came away but the
grip on his mouth only tightened. He clawed at the arm and
torso, expecting to find rotting flesh, but his attacker was
distinctly whole . . . and distinctly feminine.

"Theo! Ssshhh! You'll wake everybody!"

"Poppy?" He was stunned. "What are you doing here?
Why are you trying to strangle me?"

"I'm not, you idiot," she whispered. "I was trying to find
your mouth to keep you from shouting and I slipped . . ."
She suddenly let out a little gasp and fell away from him into
a deeper shadow.

"Are you well, Theo Vilmos?" It was Coathook's voice.
The goblin had come out of his bedroll across the tent as
silently as a cat, and now seemed to have Poppy Thornapple
in some kind of chokehold.

"I . . . I think he's going to kill me!" she wheezed. Theo
could barely hear her.

"Don't, Coathook. She's a friend. Let her go."

"Are you certain?"

"Yes! Yes, let her go."

Suddenly Poppy came sprawling into his lap, knocking
him back onto his rumpled blanket. The other three residents
of the tent were beginning to stir now as well. He pushed her
toward the tent flap. "Wait for me outside."

"Theo?" asked Cumber, muzzy with sleep. "What . . . ?"

"It's okay, really. Just someone with a message for me.
Coathook was looking out for all of us but it's a false alarm."
By the thin moonlight leaking in through the flap Theo could
see the yellow eyes staring back at him. It was like being
watched by the Devil himself, but he knew that if the intruder had been anyone other than Poppy he would have

been helplessly grateful for the goblin's vigilance and excellent night vision. "Thanks," he said.

Coathook nodded, blinked, then slithered back across the tent and under his blanket once more. Theo took a moment to catch his breath his hands were still shaking—and then followed Poppy out through the flap.

The Faerie-moon was almost full, a vast white onion sinking toward the horizon, so bright that even the pyrotechnic stars were glared into the background. Washed in its light, Button's bridge loomed above the flat emptiness at the far end of the camp like a phantom castle out of an old folktale making its once-in-a-century appearance on some misty Scottish heath.

Before Theo had even stood all the way upright she had her arms around him. She kissed his face, then pulled back, her dark eyes wide and serious. "Is it too terrible I've come? I was half-afraid I'd find you with some other woman."

He didn't think it was terrible at all—she felt wonderful against him. He kissed her for an answer, then suddenly stopped and leaned back. "But how did you find me?"

"I have a friend who works in the Parliamentary Bureau of Mirror Service. She's having an affair with her boss and she has an access to records that is simply scandalous. It wasn't that hard for her to trace back the call you had your friend make to me the other day."

"But you already knew I was in the camp."

"I didn't trace it back to the camp, I traced it back to your friend." She lifted the small wand she used as a phone. It glowed with the faintest silvery light. "See? I had it charmed to show me when it was getting close to the person who made the call. I was hoping that if you weren't in the same tent he'd at least know where you stayed—but there you were."

He was shocked and disturbed. He'd underestimated the technology of Faerie again. "But that's terrible! That means anyone can trace us . . . !"

"Why, have you been calling a lot of other girls? Because

if you haven't, then you only have to worry about me and I'm obviously not going to turn you in." She gave him a look, half-suspicious, half-amused. "There aren't any other calls, are there?"

"No, no. That was the first time I tried that. But what if your friend in the Whatsit Bureau . . . ?"

"She won't think twice about it. I told her a man with an attractive voice got my shell by accident and I was curious what he looked like. She's so busy agonizing over what's going on with her and her boss she's probably forgotten already. Feel better?"

"Yeah, I guess so. I was just . . . see, I made Streedy do it. I'd feel terrible if something happened to him because of me."

Now she did look amused. "You and your obligations! You may be of fairy blood but it's certainly not from any of the high houses, not if you spend your time worrying about things like that. Even the relatively nice boys like Lander Foxglove would step over their own dying grandmothers to get into an interesting party."

"But you're not like that." Although, remembering how she had spoken about her own brother's murder, he couldn't be sure.

"I don't want to be," she said seriously. "Sometimes I think I'm not, then sometimes I think I can't change it, it's just the world I grew up in." She put her arm through his and pulled him down the path atop the levee, away from the camp. "People like my father and his friends—I'm not talking about the Hellebores, they're *completely* mad, I'm talking about the ones that everyone thinks of as normal Flower types—they don't waste their strength caring much for anyone except themselves. I used to think that was normal, but every now and then one of the servants or one of my more distant relatives would be . . . different. Do something simply because it was nice. Be kind to me just because I was a sad little girl, not because they wanted something from my father. One of my aunts actually stood up to him—told him he treated his children worse than he treated the servants, and he treated the servants like animals. That was almost the only time I'd ever seen him surprised."

"Wow. What happened?"

"He killed her." She gave an angry little laugh. "Oh, not in an obvious way. But he ruined her life. Destroyed her husband's business, spread poison about her all through our social circle. Got her children thrown out of their school. Eventually her husband left her and she went to the Well."

"The Well . . . ?"

"She killed herself. But really he murdered her, my father murdered her. If she'd said those things about him in private he wouldn't have cared—he would have laughed, probably, that she thought it worth mentioning as though it were something bad. But she said it in public, in front of the lower orders who are supposed to worship him, and that he couldn't allow, so he destroyed her. That's when I started hating him." She stopped suddenly. "I don't want to talk about this any more, Theo. I know you're going after your friend. I . . . I don't want to talk about my horrible family when I don't know how much time we have before . . . before . . ."

"Before I head off to get myself killed, too."

"Don't say things like that!" She threw her arms around him and squeezed hard, like a drowning swimmer and Theo suddenly understood how a rescuer could be turned into a victim. He wished he had spoken in a less petty, self-pitying way, but at the moment he felt caught between duty and common sense, neither of which were things he really wanted running his life in the first place—they certainly hadn't been big parts of the Theo Vilmos Master Plan before now.

Poppy still held him. "I couldn't stand it when you walked away the other night. I could just tell you were planning to do something heroic and stupid."

"I was? I mean, you could tell that?"

"Yes, you had this determined air that they always have in the mirror-plays—Lord Rose going off to fight the goblins, kissing his little daughters good-bye, or Memnon Alder on the eve of the Frost War."

Theo hadn't really thought of himself as determined, let alone heroic, but for this instant it was nice to think it might be so. *Maybe all heroes are basically cowards like me,* he thought, *and it's doing whatever you have to do anyway that's important. I mean, if you aren't scared, if you're just completely oblivious to danger, how heroic is that?* Still, he didn't quite feel ready to put himself in the camp of the determined and brave just yet—it went against too many years of self-image. He turned his attention to something much more immediate and much more pleasant.

When he had finished kissing her she took his hand and began to lead him down the levee once more, the moonlight so strong Theo and Poppy even cast shadows. "Where are we going?" he asked.

"I'll show you." She led him on until the camp was just a clot of darkness lit by a few fires huddled along the banks of the river. The big moon was disappearing into the horizon like a leaking balloon. Poppy rucked up her long skirt and sat cross-legged on the damp ground, then beckoned Theo to join her. The wind had picked up. He shivered a little and wished once again that he hadn't been forced to trade away his leather jacket to a troll, however sensible the bargain.

When he was seated she put her cool hands on either side of his face. She seemed to have retreated a little, her face set in that now-familiar Flower mask. "I want you to love me, Theo—but only if you mean it."

He shook his head. "I don't know enough . . . that is, I wouldn't want you to . . ."

"That's not what I mean, whatever you're going to say. I want you to love me with your body. Your heart—well, that will make its own choices. But I don't want you to be my lover because you feel sorry for me or because you think it will make up for something else you did wrong."

He took her hand. "I don't know how much of me there

really is, Poppy, but what there is—well, right now, it's yours."

"Good." And now she let the mask slip a little. "Then come back and kiss me again and let's forget about all the horrible things for a while. Love me."

He got up on his knees to kiss her and found himself shivering again. "But . . . it's so cold. And not very private."

She laughed. "I brought a pavilion."

"A what?"

"Watch." She took something out of the pocket of her pants and held it out to him. It was a small sachet about the size of a tea bag. "A very useful charm. Will you think I'm terrible if I admit I bought it this afternoon, planning to come find you?" She closed it in her hand and broke it open with her fingers, then clambered to her feet, bent over, and began to sprinkle the shimmery dust in a wide circle around them. The air just above the line of powder on the ground seemed to waver; it might have been a trick of the dying moonlight, but Theo felt pretty sure it wasn't. The effect spread and traveled upward with surprising speed, coming together over their heads at a point some six or seven feet above the ground.

"You mean . . . no one can see us now?" He looked around. The walls distorted the light like thick glass, turning the stars wobbly, but they were by no means opaque. He also didn't feel much warmer. The whole experience was exciting but strange; he shivered again, not entirely from the cold.

"Nobody can see in—in fact, unless they're standing right next to it, they won't even see the pavilion at all." She reached out and clasped his hands. "You really are cold, aren't you? I'm sorry, Theo. The store where I got it only had these inexpensive ones. We'll have to warm it with our own body heat—but that shouldn't be too bad, should it?" She shrugged off her coat and pulled her sweater over her head then undid her blouse. She was wearing nothing underneath but a thin silver-white chain around her neck; her pale skin seemed to glow like the moon. He reached out his hand and touched her breast. "It's not warm in here yet, though, is it?" She laughed but she sounded nervous. "Look—goosebumps."

He pulled her to him then and by the time he had puzzled out the strange mechanics of the fastenings on her other clothes (you had to tap on them at least four times) he had forgotten about the temperature, about other eyes, about nearly everything except the black-haired woman he was kissing and the glossy, underwater stars gleaming above them, and he was fast forgetting about the stars as well.

At one point she pulled back from him and said, a little breathlessly, "I have some other charms as well."

"For what?" It was hard to use spoken language after long minutes of nearly perfect silent communication. A thought occurred to him. "Birth control? I mean, for not having babies?"

"Black iron, no!" she said and giggled. "We learn those charms with our first blood and I've already done mine for this moon. No, these are just . . . lovemaking charms. Little ones to make things, I don't know, more interesting. They were in this display at the apothecary." She looked away, suddenly shy. "I just thought you might . . ."

"I don't need anything but you." Whether because of heightened senses or the close space inside the charmed circle, the smells of her skin and hair were as powerful as any drug. "And I don't want anything but you. This is magic . . . pardon . . . science enough for me."

"I'm so glad you said that."

And then they stopped talking again. The Van Gogh stars glittered like snowflakes in the cold sky, but inside the pavilion the air had grown warm as deepest summer.

35

A SORT OF REUNION

Another dream of a lost parent had caught him up. He was surrounded by clouds again, a hospital corridor full of smoke, or perhaps it was Daffodil House—the ghostly shapes in the halls might have been ash-covered victims or only patients in white hospital gowns. He was looking for his father, shouting for him—but not for "Pete" (which Theo had called him in that awkward, twenty-something stage of trying to find some common ground) or even "Dad."

"Daddy! Daddy, where are you?"

He thought he saw him through the haze, turning the corner at the end of the hall, slump-shouldered, balding on top, wearing one of the Hawaiian shirts that he put on every Saturday morning as if to prove to himself that the weekend had really come. As a teenager Theo had been astonished to realize that to the old man a Hawaiian shirt was actually cool, a symbol of some kind of tiny rebellion against the gray suits, white shirts, and ugly ties.

"Daddy?" He realized, or at least the Theo in the dream realized, that he had never said good-bye, not properly. He had clutched his father's hand while he lay in the hospital bed after his stroke, but if Pete Vilmos had been aware of his son and his wife in those last hours he had given no sign.

Theo hurried down the darkening corridor. It seemed increasingly important he tell his father something of what he had learned and done in the years since the old man's death, prove to him that life was worth it, that the mind-numbing years of work Pete Vilmos had endured to put food on the table and toys under the Christmas tree meant something, but he couldn't think of what to say. *There's nothing to tell, is there? I'm nobody, just like he was.* Still, he was desperate to catch up with that shuffling figure.

"Daddy?"

A voice came back to him through the smoke, thinned by distance. *"Theo? Theo, where are you?"*

He struggled toward the sound but something had caught him, hands were pulling at him—the other patients must be trying to hold him back . . . unless they were victims, burned sufferers trying to climb past him and down the stairs to safety. Had the dragon come back? He fought without strength. He could still hear his father's voice but it seemed to be receding.

"Theo, wake up!" It was another voice—a woman's voice. "Theo, someone's looking for you."

He came up shuddering, tangled in his own discarded clothes. Poppy had her arms around him. "There's someone out there," she said.

He shook his head, clumsily trying to assemble the details into a coherent whole and having little luck. Then the voice came again and for an instant he thought it really was his father or his father's unsettled spirit; his heart lurched and his skin tingled.

"Theo? Are you out here?"

"Oh my God—it's Cumber. I completely forgot. I'm supposed to . . ." He sat up and began to drag on his pants. "Where is he? Why can I hear him so clearly?"

"Because he's probably only a few yards away." She was naked and seemed a little shy. It was very distracting to be here with this lovely unclothed near-stranger while someone was searching for him. The filtered light of the stars played unevenly across her milky skin as she sat up.

"Then why doesn't he . . . ?" He remembered. "The charm."

"Just step outside, then he'll see you." She tried to smile.

Still hopping as he pulled up his pants, he passed through the wall of the pavilion without feeling anything until he was suddenly engulfed in the chill of night. Cumber was a few dozen paces down the levee, his back turned until Theo called him.

"By the Grove, you startled me!" the ferisher said. "Where have you been? I was terrified—I thought that dead thing had come and taken you! We have only a little more than an hour until dawn." He squinted. "What are you doing wandering around out here half-naked?"

"I'll explain later. I'm sorry I forgot. I'll meet you back at the tent in a few minutes."

Cumber Sedge shook his head. "Not there. Down by the river at this end of the camp. You'll see why when you get there. You really had me worried—I've been looking for you all over. Are you sure you're all right?"

"Fine. Sorry for the trouble. Go ahead now and I'll catch up with you."

The ferisher gave him a strange look. "Are you sure everything is all right?"

"Really. Go on."

Cumber nodded slowly, then turned and walked back up the levee.

Even though he was only a yard from it, it took Theo a few moments to locate the pavilion again: with the moon down, the slight blurring of the air that marked its presence was hard to distinguish from the mists rising off the river. Crossing the barrier was much different this time, moving from the cold into the warm and back into the scents of their lovemaking.

"You have to go." She had put her blouse back on but stopped there. He wanted to lie down beside her and kiss her smooth leg, the taut skin of her side just above her hip, but knew that if he did he would never be able to make himself get up again.

"I do," he said, "I really do. Button seemed to think it was very important we leave before dawn."

"Who's Button?"

He hesitated. He trusted her now, of course he did, but he did not want to add to her danger, either. What had Button said? *"We cannot tell what we do not know."* "He's a friend of mine from the camp. A goblin."

"I want to make you stay," she said. "Make you want to stay, that is,"—again, the sad smile—"but I know I shouldn't. If you weren't the kind of person who was going to help his friend, you wouldn't be the person I'm . . . that I feel this way about."

Is this how it works? he wondered. The magnitude of what was before him came rushing back, dreams and even Poppy's presence no longer enough to distract him. He felt weak and ill. *Is this how you get less shallow? You do the right thing, no matter how it feels and how much you wish you could run away, then everyone thinks you're a grand guy? Everybody cries at your funeral?* But there was something heartening in it too, even if it was a lesson he was learning too late to be of much use—a path toward reinvention. *She thinks that's who I am, so that's who I am to her.* "I don't want to leave you," was all he could think of to say. "But I have to."

"I know." She had put her mask of control back on, but it was not entirely effective and she could not meet his eye. "I . . . I want you to have something. Well, two things."

"One of your gloves to wear on my lance when I ride into battle?"

She did look up then, puzzled. "Why would you be taking a lance?"

"I'm not, it's just . . . what the knights of my world used to do with gifts from their lady-loves."

"Well, you'd better take more care of these than putting them on some lance." She handed him something about the size and shape of a long lipstick tube. "Use this and call me if you need me. I mean it, Theo. If you need anything, I'll get it for you. If you need *me,* I'll be there—no matter what."

He looked at the small, silvery wand. "I may not get a chance to make any calls for a little while. But thanks. After . . . after whatever happens, it will be nice to be able to reach you without having to give Streedy a headache."

She smiled but her eyes were wet. "You'd better call me, that's all I'll say. And I want you to have this, too." She tugged a thin silver chain and pendant out of the neck of her blouse, the one thing she had kept on all during the night. Now she took it off and held it out to him. What he had thought might be a small coin he now saw was a moon, one crescent of it made of something like polished opal. "It's a chip from my mother's family moundstone. She gave this to me."

"What does it do?"

"Do? It doesn't do anything. It's something she gave me—one of the only things she ever gave me. It's really important to me, Theo, and I'm giving it to you to make sure you come back to me."

He had expected some fairy-charm, some magical talisman to protect against danger, and for a moment he was almost disappointed—he suspected he was going to need all the help he could get. Then he realized the significance of what she was giving to him and he felt something expand inside his chest, a quiet rapture that was bigger and more powerful than even the heights of their lovemaking. "Thank you," he managed to say. He carefully lifted the necklace over his head, let the moon fall onto his chest. "Thank you. I'll do my best to come back to you."

She laughed, but it was raw with pain and anger. "This is so wretched. I knew there was a reason I didn't want to fall in love any more, but I never thought . . ." She struggled for composure. "Kiss me and go, Theo. Hurry."

"Will you be able to get back all right . . . ?"

"Black iron, will you just kiss me and get out of here? My heart is breaking."

"Mine too," he said, and was surprised and frightened to realize it was true.

Cumber was waiting for him on the banks of the dark river, but he was not alone.

"Coathook?" Theo had to look twice to make sure—he was still not entirely adept at telling one goblin from another. "What are you doing here?"

"Button says we shouldn't go through the City to get to . . . to the place we're going," Cumber told Theo. "Even just along the edges. He says it's better to go by water."

"That doesn't explain why you're here," Theo said to Coathook.

"Because I know how to paddle a boat without making as much noise as a drowning troll." The goblin's slot-eyes gleamed with reflected starlight. "You don't."

"Oh. Well . . . thanks."

Coathook pointed to the open boat, which was little more than a canoe. "Come."

"Where's Streedy?" Theo asked as they pushed off and into the sluggish current. "I was kind of hoping he could come with us, in case there were some, I don't know, alarms or magic fences . . ."

"Button says he needs him today," Cumber said. "And that he doesn't think getting *in* will be our biggest problem, anyway."

Theo let that sink in as they made their way silently up the Moonflood to the point where it widened as they met the newer channel of the river. Theo and Cumber ate a breakfast of bread and sweet cheese the ferisher had brought while Coathook guided the boat across the breadth of the flow and up close to the bank on the far side. Theo could see houses on slender stilts looming above them, some with lights burning in the windows. Below them, like barnacles on the pil-

ings of a dock, smaller and far humbler dwellings clustered
on the river shore.

"Who lives there?" Theo asked in a whisper.

"Niskies," said Cumber. Coathook silenced them both
with a motion of his clawed hand.

A few larger boats were anchored in the coves and in
marinas, shiny, many-oared things that looked more like ancient triremes or even upside-down centipedes than like
modern ships, but no other traffic was moving on this section of the river. Theo wondered if that was normal, or if it
was something to do with the Flower War curfew. He
couldn't help wishing there were a few other vessels plying
the channel down toward Ys, if only to make their own boat
less conspicuous. Although Coathook kept to the edge of the
river and, as he had promised, plied his paddle as quietly as
a knife cutting warm butter, Theo could not help feeling terribly exposed.

Finally, as they turned a bend in the Moonflood and saw
the whole expanse of Ys stretching before them, a black immensity barely touched even by Faerie's exuberant starlight,
Coathook took his paddle out of the water. "After this, no
more talking," he said, so quietly it barely carried. "But Button says to tell you, today might be a good day to go on to
Hellebore House."

"What?" Theo had trouble keeping his voice low. "What
does that mean?"

Coathook shrugged. "No more talking now. We are
close."

The word "close," Theo decided, must have a very odd
meaning to goblins, since they paddled on for at least another quarter of an hour. The section of riverbank they could
see through the hanging mists was studded with broken-
down industrial buildings, once-exuberant Faerie versions
of old warehouses and canneries. A few of the structures
were apparently still occupied—signs glowed sputteringly
here and there like dying fireflies, "End of the Rainbow
Storage" or "Grotto-4-U"—but the rest seemed long-

disused, and with the first lightening of the sky Theo could make out painted advertisements, sometimes with one sign flaking off to reveal an earlier message. They were close enough to the bank that he could even read some of them. *"King Kilpie Ocean Goodes,"* proclaimed one, illustrated by a dim, rather frightening picture of a fishy humanoid with a crown and a basket full of fish and shellfish: *"Lawfull Purveyor by Their Majesties' Charter of the Fruites of Ys."*

Something slapped at the water and Theo looked over, startled that Coathook should suddenly lose his touch, but the goblin was looking back at him as though the noise had been Theo's doing. Something in the dark water beside the boat caught Theo's eye: a little sprinkling of pale blue-green lights was moving just below the surface. For a moment he thought it was a parade of glowing fish, but the movement was different than any shoal of fish he had seen on a television nature show. He found himself watching in fascination as the ordered glimmer moved closer to the surface just below him, but it was another long moment before he realized that what he was looking at was a human shape, pacing them in the water with effortless movements. It rolled toward him, the face only inches beneath the surface, glowing like the dial of a watch. The eyes met his—a woman's eyes, he could see now, but huge compared to the rest of the narrow face. Even with all its strangeness, it was a very lovely face. The staring eyes were black, so very black . . . blacker even than the water, and they seemed to be getting larger and larger as he leaned toward them. Larger . . . and larger . . .

Instead of going over into the inviting darkness he was yanked backward into the boat so abruptly that the air whooshed out of his lungs and he bumped his head on the boat's other rail as he fell. The whole craft swayed alarmingly as he struggled onto the bench again. The swift pressure of Coathook's talons still hurt his arm even after the goblin had let go. Cumber had not moved, but was watching with startled eyes. Theo looked at his companions, then back at the glimmering shape beneath the surface. It had slowed its pace and they were beginning to pull away. The lean, predatory features no longer looked quite so human. He thought he could feel a certain disappointment emanate from it that lingered in his mind like a faint odor even after the swimming shape vanished into the depths.

Theo was trembling and breathing hard, as though he had actually been pulled into the water and had been forced to struggle for his life. The nymph-band around his wrist seemed hot and tight, chafing his skin. He nodded at Coathook to show that he was grateful, that he understood. He thought he understood, anyway. He suspected that the thing in the water had been much more interested in him than his two companions.

There's such a fine line here, he thought, *between a useful reminder and getting yourself killed. Or worse.*

Coathook's paddling was so smooth and silent that Theo did not realize for some moments that the goblin had stopped and that the boat was stopping too. They were in among the pilings of a dock, but although what he could see of the dock was made of wood, the posts were cylinders of ancient stone that loomed through the river-mist like a half-submerged Stonehenge. A soaked and deteriorating wooden ladder tied to the nearest one led up through a hatch toward the purpling sky. The goblin drew his hand across his mouth again, reminding them to be silent, then pointed to the ladder. As Theo got unsteadily to his feet and clambered up, moving far enough for Cumber to climb out behind him, Coathook made another sign, this one unrecognizable, and then turned the little boat around; within a few heartbeats he had disappeared into the roil of fog. Theo looked down at Cumber with wide eyes. The ferisher seemed almost as alarmed as Theo was, but only shrugged. Perhaps he had known Coathook was not going to wait for them, but it was strange that the goblin had not even mentioned coming back to pick them up. Theo found it hard not to feel a bit betrayed.

What do you want? he chided himself. *You're not the center of his universe or Button's, either. You wanted to go and*

*get yourself killed trying to help a friend. Well, they helped
you get here. Now you're on your own.*

He climbed the ladder, pausing to gather his courage before thrusting his head through the open hatch. The catwalk
of weathered timbers was empty and the warehouse wall
featureless, a long stretch of salt-stained boards with only
the smallest remnant of its original coat of white paint. He
wanted to ask Cumber how this broken-down barn could
be the headquarters of one of the most dangerous creatures
in Faerie, but if the creaking ladder hadn't already alerted
the occupants that someone was out here, he didn't want to
do its job for it.

The ferisher came up behind him and crouched. Together
they listened to the slap of waves on the pilings below, the
cries of waterbirds, and, briefly, a distant voice rising above
the other noises in a snatch of quaveringly alien song. Theo
took a breath and stood, then followed the catwalk around
toward the side of the building away from the water. They
were at the end of a long stone pier that pushed out at least
a hundred yards into the Moonflood just a short distance
from where it joined Ys. A line of ramshackle buildings in
different shapes and sizes covered the pier all the way to the
end, as though some weird circus train had ground to a shuddering, bumping halt a moment before it would have rolled
off into the water. But if the building they were to enter was
the train's engine, it did not look the part: it was a featureless rectangle with no visible windows. In the pre-dawn light
its high blank sides gave it the look of some ancient stone
slab, the foundations of an antediluvian temple where
screaming victims had once been sacrificed.

Steady, Theo told himself. *Don't make it worse than it is.*
But the windowless walls disturbed him. Who lived like
that? Who would build a long low box like this at the end of
a pier and leave no openings to the ocean breeze, no view of
the estuary and the sea? He suddenly saw the building as
something different, not a temple, not an edifice at all, but
the shell of some immense, angular thing.

Instead of being in character with the rest of the structure, the door set in the side of the building was a small and quite ordinary thing of wind-scoured wood with a single tarnished bronze handle, as though someone had built a storage closet into the base of the Sphinx. Theo looked at Cumber, who seemed one loud noise away from running for his life—not that Theo blamed him: *In fact, I'd be right behind him.* He reached out his trembling hand toward the latch. *This is crazy,* he thought. *It's a warehouse. Even if it's full of monsters or guys with guns or . . . or whatever, on the outside it's just a warehouse and I'm not psychic. Why should I feel like I'm about to walk through the Gates of Hades?*

Before he could touch it, the door silently swung open. Theo gasped and jumped back, half-expecting something slimy and otherworldly to stretch a tentacle out of the darkness and yank him in, but no such appendage appeared. The door remained open. The darkness beyond remained impenetrable.

Whoever, whatever . . . they must know we're here. No use trying to sneak up on them. Still, he didn't feel like shouting "Hello!" either. "Do we have a light?" he whispered.

Cumber, bug-eyed and unable to look away from that dark opening, shook his head several times before he realized what Theo had asked and turned the headshake into a nod. He fumbled out a small witchlight sphere like the one he had produced in the underground garage. He ran his thumb across it and passed it to Theo as it bloomed into a swampy glow.

As Theo stepped through the door the first thing he noticed was that the glow didn't seem to go very far—that it showed him his own legs and arms and a suggestion of a flat vertical surface beside him that might be a wall, but did not illuminate the greater darkness. All he could see for certain was that the dark, carpeted floor seemed to go on for some distance. He was also aware—he couldn't have missed it— of a powerful unpleasant smell. The sour-sweet odor was frighteningly similar to the thing that had found him three different times in three different rotting bodies, but after a moment he realized this smell was more complicated, a combination of scents that had putrefaction in it, but also strange sweet spices and the vigorous essence of growing things, the smell of a fistful of wet mud and spring grass bumping improbably against the reek of burning sulfur, of whiskey and cinnamon and excrement and other far less recognizable things all jumbled together until it made his eyes water.

Strange as it was, he couldn't really waste time considering it, not with his heart thumping like some insanely overhyped click-track as he edged forward through the near-darkness, brandishing what he was beginning to think was a faulty witchlight. He reached out toward the spot where it looked like there might be a wall and was relieved to find something cool, hard, and ever so slightly damp. He slid his foot forward and found that the solid floor continued. He bent, holding the globe at the height of his shoetops, and suddenly the hallway began to grow brighter.

"Theo . . . ?"

"Ssshh!"

It happened quickly but smoothly and had nothing whatsoever to do with the witchlight in his hand. Within a few moments he could see that they were standing at one end of a long hallway with matte-black walls on both sides and a carpet of the same shade beneath their feet. At the far end, basking in a little directionless glow of its own, a door with a golden nameplate waited.

I wonder whose name is on that? But it was only a tiny flick of curiosity in the midst of dread, like a bird flying just ahead of a storm. He looked at Cumber. Cumber looked back. It was pretty clear to Theo that if either one of them suggested turning around instead of walking down that long, black hallway toward the door, the other would agree.

Applecore, he reminded himself. *Applecore with that corkscrew. Fighting with that thing to help someone she didn't even know.*

Despite the carpet which all but silenced their footfalls, by the time they reached the door Theo felt like they were walking across bubblewrap in stone shoes, each step excruciatingly loud. The weird odors were making him lightheaded, but instead of reducing his inhibitions it made him feel like the worst sort of stoned, paranoid teenager stuck at a stoplight next to a cop car.

The nameplate had the word "Enter" scratched on it in a crude, almost childish hand. As he watched, the word ran off the golden rectangle like water; a moment later the word "Push" appeared in its place.

Is that somebody's little joke? Anger gave back a little of his bravery, although it was stretched thinly over a great deal of raw terror. He reached out and shoved the door open, then stepped through.

The room beyond was completely unexpected after the featureless hallway. Jumbled mountains of objects stretched yards above his head on all sides, thousands of unfathomable things scattered seemingly at random, as if someone had crashed an old-fashioned pharmacy into a particularly disturbing toy shop at high speed, then liberally sprinkled the wreckage with the contents of the Library of Alexandria. Pinkish-purple dawn light streamed down from oblong windows high above, illuminating the piles so that it all looked a bit like a stage set or a Disneyland ride.

Dazzled and overwhelmed, Theo did not notice the massive figure in the shadows behind him until it reached an arm around his chest and immobilized him, then pinioned his head with its other huge hand. The arm across his torso was so tight that after he let out his breath in a panicked gust he could get no air back in again. He was lifted up until he dangled helplessly above the floor, struggling unsuccessfully to breathe. Sparks danced before his eyes. Everything turned red, then black.

*   *   *

E ven though someone was speaking to him, he was not at first aware that he was awake, or where he was, or even precisely *who* he was. The voice itself was a strange thing, insubstantial as wind stirring a pile of leaves, but oddly loud, as though the person speaking might be small enough to sit inside his ear.

". . . Your pardon," the breathy voice was saying. "They are not very subtle, I'm afraid. You are awake, aren't you?"

Memory came back, and with it a quickening of his heart, which did not help his pounding head any.

Not good. Something not good happening.

Theo was lying on the floor. Cumber lay beside him, arms at his sides like a toy put neatly back in its box, his face covered by a semitransparent membrane so unexpected and baffling that for a wretched second Theo thought the ferisher had been skinned.

"Don't worry, he's not dead," the invisible presence explained. "It's a caul. He's sleeping. I wanted to speak to you alone."

Theo got up into a crouch, looking from side to side trying to discover the source of the voice.

"I'm in the room with you," his captor told him. "But you really don't want to see me. You'll be happier where you are."

Theo pretended to look for the Remover, if that was indeed who the speaker was, but meanwhile he was getting his feet under him, unobtrusively balancing himself to move quickly. Half his mind was screaming at him just to run for the door and keep running, Cumber Sedge and even Applecore be damned, but he was also wondering how far and how fast he could drag the unconscious ferisher and what it was that had manhandled them both so easily in the first place.

He turned and grabbed at Cumber, but no sooner did his fingers touch his companion's clothes than a pair of pale shapes almost as big as ogres but much stiffer in their movements stepped out of the shadows near the doorway. Theo froze as the things walked slowly toward him and stopped a

few yards away. They looked like living statues, crude ones
at that, their features barely defined in the chalky white
flesh, the eyes black dots that he recognized a startled moment later were nothing more than holes punched into the
heavy, dead faces.

"Please," the voice said, "do not challenge them. They
are not very subtle, the mandragora, and I would prefer not
to have to wait for you to regain consciousness again."

"Mandragora . . . ?" The twinned faces stared at him, unmoving, impassive. They might have just arrived from their
perches atop the cliffs of Easter Island.

"Children of the mandrake. Each slave has been carved
from one of the great roots. Very time-consuming, actually,
and finding the roots is a long and boring and dangerous
process, but once you've got them they're very useful. Incredibly strong and about as much sensitivity to pain as a
steam locomotive. But, as I said, not extremely good with
more complicated tasks like grappling someone without
crushing them to death. I truly did not wish them to be so
rough with you."

"I've seen one of these before." Theo slowly disentan-
gled his hand from Cumber's coat. Keep the Remover talking—that seemed the best bet right now. Maybe it wasn't as
bad as it seemed. Maybe he treated all his guests this way.
"There was one in Daffodil House. Just before . . ."

"Yes." The Remover actually sounded a little regretful.
"A waste of a great root, and really for no purpose except to
allow Hellebore to gloat."

"You . . . you know about that?" He suddenly realized
that not only was he helpless, this person, whoever he was,
might be more of an ally of the Hellebore faction than
Button or Primrose had known. He might already have contacted them. "Did you do it? Did you help them do that?"

The Remover did not sound overly disturbed. "The dragons, you mean? No, no—Nidrus Hellebore is quite capable
of thinking up something like that on his own. Oh, yes, he
certainly is." His voice had an odd note in it. Theo looked

around the room again and saw that the shadows seemed darker in the room's north corner. He even thought he saw a little movement. The Remover must be sitting there watching him from the depths of that insane clutter, like a dragon crouched on its hoard.

"What are you going to do with me?"

To his surprise the Remover laughed, not an archvillain's chortle but an honest wheeze of near-breathless amusement. "You know, I can't really say, at least not in the short term. In the long term . . . well, I'll explain. But at the moment, I'm just trying to appreciate the irony."

"Irony?" It seemed he was going to be allowed to survive for at least another few minutes. Theo began surreptitiously to examine his surroundings. Now that his eyes were adjusting to the dim light, he was even more certain that he had discerned the Remover's position: far back in the corner, half-hidden by a ring of draped statuary, was something that looked a bit like a high-backed chair occupied by a very complicated shadow. Theo took a step toward it.

"Don't!" the voice said. "I told you—you will not like what you see."

"I've seen all kinds of shit since I've been here. How much worse can it be?"

"You'd be surprised," the voice told him. "Besides, it is not entirely your feelings I am concerned with. I am . . . ashamed of what I have become."

Theo retreated a few steps. What little he could see of the thing in the chair was certainly unsettling—a suggestion of sticklike limbs, but also of membranous folds and glistening wetness. "Okay. You said . . . irony."

"Yes. It is ironic that I expended so much effort to bring you to me, and failed so completely, and yet here you are in my place of business. Voluntarily." Again came the whispering laugh.

"What do you mean?"

"The *irrha* that I sent to capture you—that one that is still no doubt hunting you. Do you have any idea what sort of energy it costs to summon such a thing out of the old, dead places? And what mostly forgotten skills are necessary to keep it in the breathing world for such a long time?"

"You sent that *thing* after me?" His panic, which had eased for a moment, came rushing back like a fever chill. "Then . . . then you *are* working for Hellebore." So all this had been for nothing. Not only hadn't he found a way to free Applecore, he had saved the bad guys the trouble of waiting until he reached Hellebore House. "God, I really am an idiot."

"Perhaps. But it's a bit more complicated than that. I had hoped for just this chance, the chance to have you to myself. The *irrha* is a creature of instincts, but it is compelled by the summoning. In this case, it's compelled to do only one thing—to seize you and bring you here, to this place."

"So you can turn me over to Hellebore, get the credit, earn a tidy little commission." Theo looked over to where Cumber lay on the floor, gaul-faced, his chest moving shallowly. "You bastard. I should make you kill me—or make your big old root monsters kill me. Better than letting Hellebore and Thornapple get their hands on me." A thought wiggled up through the anger and fear. "But I'll make a bargain with you. Let him go." He pointed to Cumber. "They don't care about him. Let him go and I'll let them take me quietly."

"Interesting." The tone was flat. "You would do that for a friend? What they plan for you is terrible, you know. And not just for you."

Theo suddenly recalled Lord Hollyhock's speculations on the afternoon that Daffodil House burned. "You're talking about Old Night, aren't you? What they're planning to do to the rest of the mortal world. Some kind of black magic tidal wave . . ." And even as he said it Theo realized that he could not afford to sacrifice himself for Cumber Sedge, for Applecore, for anyone. He had no idea what he was supposed to know but he could not take the risk. He turned abruptly and bolted for the door.

It was a near-miss, or seemed to be. Even as his fingers brushed the latch a huge, doughy hand curled in the back of his shirt, which tore at the seams but held long enough for the thing to enfold him in its grip. He kicked and fought, trying to reach the mandragorum's face with his free hand, to scratch at its eyes and enrage it. He knew it might be his last moment, that he was choosing suicide over being made a tool of the Hellebore faction, but although he sunk his nails deep into the thing's sockets there was nothing there to injure; the damp, fibrous substance just scraped away and spattered down his wrist. The thing pulled him in, wrapped him in its massive arms, held him fast.

Theo's eyes were blurred with tears of rage and desperation. "Fuck you!" he screamed at the watcher in the shadows. "If you won't kill me, I'll make them do it. I won't give them what they want."

"You would not keep that promise very long once they began to work on you," said the dry voice. "But you misunderstand me. The *irrha* was summoned to bring you to me first, not so I could earn Hellebore's commission, but so I can have my own conversation with you. Nidrus Hellebore is not the only one who has waited a long time to gain his heart's desire. You see, I too need your help."

"Help you! You must be joking. I'll die first. You might as well start with the thumbscrews." But it was false, hollow. He knew that even the strongest, most iron-willed people could succumb to torture, and he wasn't one of those. His only hope was to keep this Remover-thing talking and pray for a better chance to escape. He remembered Poppy's phone, and for a moment wondered if he could pretend to be more compliant, then find a chance to signal her with it somehow. But what could she do? Drive here with her school chum? He had already failed his other two closest friends, Cumber and Applecore; he could not drag Poppy into this as well. "So you're double-crossing Hellebore," he said. "So you've found some other client who'll pay more for whatever it is I'm supposed to know."

"I am truly sorry that it has come to this, Theo. I already have enough on my conscience with the suffering I have brought to you and yours, but my need is very great."

"Conscience? Fairies don't have goddamned consciences. All of you people, you're the most self-centered creatures I've ever heard of. Even Hitler wouldn't do what Hellebore wants to do, destroy an entire world just to keep himself in power."

"I rather suspect he would have if he'd had the chance," the Remover said. "But in any case, your accusation isn't entirely fair. You see, I'm not a fairy. Or at least not really."

"So what are you? A monster, obviously."

"Whether I am a monster is open to debate. But I am even less of this world than you are."

Theo's terror had turned into a thick, queasy heaviness. "I don't care. I don't give a damn about your problems or your riddles."

"I had hoped this would go better," the voice in the shadows said after a long pause. "Perhaps I have done a poor job of presenting things. When I anticipated this day, I felt sure we could find some way to speak to each other, since we have so much in common."

"So much in common! Are you joking? You're . . . you're a thing! A murderer, a mercenary kidnapper! You're a traitor even to the bastards who hired you!"

"All those things are probably true, Theo. But I am also the closest thing you have to family and I had hoped we would be able to speak to each other in a civil way."

"What? What are you talking about?"

The Remover cleared his throat with a noise like newspapers blowing in an alleyway. "I am . . . I used to be . . . Eamonn Dowd."

36

CHANGELINGS

"That's a lie! You're dead!" Theo realized what he had just said a moment later. "I mean, Eamonn Dowd is dead."

"In a way, yes. In a way, no." The thing in the shadows shifted itself with a noise halfway between a rustle and a squelch. "Believe me, Theo, this is not the way I imagined it. I had hoped our first conversation could be a bit more . . . familial. See here, if I tell the mandragorum to let you go, will you promise not to try to escape until you hear what I have to say? It won't do you any good, anyway—you've seen how fast and strong they are."

Theo wondered why the thing would make such a claim. It didn't seem possible—life in Fairyland was strange, but surely not that strange—but it couldn't hurt to play for time. "All right. Tell it to quit breaking my ribs. I'll stay put." The root slave, responding to some silent command, set him down and then moved quietly back toward the wall to stand next to its twin. "Okay, look, whoever you are, you can't be Eamonn Dowd. For one thing, everyone here says the Remover is very old—ancient. That he's been around longer than anyone can remember."

"And so he has—or at least he had been, before I took his place. In fact, I've often wondered if it was possible that the

Remover I ousted had once replaced an earlier version. Perhaps the role of Remover is more title than name, and each one who holds that title eventually has it taken away from him by a younger contender . . . as it were." The sad, dry chuckle issued from nowhere and everywhere. "If so, it's a dubious prize, believe me."

"Go ahead, say what you need to say. But I'll only listen if you promise to let my friend go."

"The ferisher? I have no interest in him—I certainly don't want to harm him. But it's in my interests to keep you calm and keep you here, so for now he will remain sleeping peacefully on the floor."

"Why don't you show yourself? I don't like talking to the air."

"Do not presume too much, Theo—you're not in a position to dictate to me, even if I have a certain family-feeling toward you. As I said, I am ashamed of how I look, so keep your distance. I can put on a slightly less disturbing form when I go out into the city—nothing pleasant, but with a long coat and hat on I do not attract too much attention if I keep to shadows and back entrances. However, putting on that semblance takes a great deal of energy, a great deal, and I am very tired today. It's been a busy week." The thing rustled again. "I suppose I can't blame you for doubting me."

"If you want me to believe you, then prove it. Tell me something only Eamonn Dowd would know."

"Now there's an old chestnut—right out of some radio play, it sounds like. What might such a private something be, Theo? It is not as if I shared your childhood, came to visit you like an ordinary great-uncle, brought you sweets and comic books and exchanged little secrets that we could recall together now. Shall I tell you something written in the notebook? It would prove very little, since I know others beside you have had it—including, if I am correct, your ferisher friend lying there." The Remover seemed to consider. "What else would prove it to you? Shall I list the presidents, Washington to Nixon? That's all I know—I'm a bit blank on

American history after the early 1970s, which is understandable when you remember where I've been. Or should we stick with the personal? Do you want me to tell you what was in the letter I sent to your mother, or at least to the woman you thought was your mother? You are eventually going to hear something of why I apologized to her, whether you wish to or not . . ."

He did not want it to be true. "But you . . . but Eamonn Dowd died! I read his obituary!"

"You read an obituary written after Eamonn Dowd's body was discovered. Yes, that particular physical envelope is definitely dead now, dust or near-dust. Do you think if I still had it available to me, however old and infirm, I would choose to live like this? Hiding in the shadows, solitary as a spider, so terrifying that even the children of trolls and goblins run from me, shrieking?" For the first time Theo could hear pain in the voice, real and powerful.

But maybe he's just a good actor. They're tricky, these fairies. Who knows what one of them might do to weasel answers out of me, if what I know is really so damn important? "Just keep talking."

"I presume you read the notebook so I won't bother to reiterate the early part of my story. I came here to New Erewhon and grew attached to the place. I made a sort of life for myself. All well and good, and no different than the story of many other mortals who found their way to Faerie and then never wanted to leave again. I even fell in love.

"Ah. I see that you know something about that. You have heard the gossip, perhaps? Or the propaganda of her family, the lies of the Primrose clan? Because that is who I fell in love with—Erephine Primrose, youngest daughter of that great house."

"They . . . they say you kidnapped her." Whether the story was true or not seemed to make little difference just now: Theo needed his invisible captor to go on talking until he figured out how to free himself. Even if this thing *was* somehow what was left of his great-uncle, he had all but

admitted he was working for Hellebore. Still, Theo's earlier
certainty that the Remover was lying about his true identity
was definitely weakening.

"They say that, do they, that I kidnapped her? Well,
they're right—up to a point. But I am not ready to tell that
part of the story yet. Trust me, Theo, if you are patient the
whole sordid, wretched mess will come out."

"Go on." He stole a glance at Cumber. The film over his
face obscured his features but his chest was still moving regularly. Would he never wake up as long as that caul thing
was on him? What if you had to perform some fairy magic
to get it off? It would be hard enough to escape the two swift
and powerful root slaves on his own, let alone while carrying the dead weight of Cumber Sedge.

"I met her at one of Tertius Stock's house-parties. She
thought I was an amusing freak, at first, but I waited her out
as patiently as one of her own kind, because she was . . . she
was . . ." He made a kind of strangled noise, anger or grief.
"No, there is no use telling you what I felt for Erephine or
trying to describe our time together. If you have been in love
that way, you know. If you haven't, no words will make it
sound like anything but craziness. When her family brow-
beat Parliament into doing what they wanted—the Primroses were one of the Seven Families, you know, the lords of
New Erewhon—and my banishment was proclaimed, my
life was effectively over. They would have done me a kindness simply to kill me. As it turns out, they would have done
themselves a kindness as well." A sudden icy edge in the Remover's voice brought up goose pimples on Theo's skin.
"Instead I was cast out of the Garden of Eden and back into
the world of mortals, alone, miserable . . . no, more than
miserable. Bereft. Insane with grief."

"See? You can't be Eamonn Dowd because you've got
the details wrong. Dowd never left this world—Primrose
told me that his sister was kidnapped *after* Dowd's banishment was supposed to have gone down. So he dodged it
somehow. If there's one thing everyone knows for certain,

it's that, what's it called, Clover Effect. No one can come
here, leave, and then come back again, so if you say you did,
you're not him. *Quid pro quo.*"

The dry laugh gusted through the room again, but there
wasn't much mirth in it. "What you want to say is 'Q.E.D.'—
Quod Erat Demonstrandum, 'to be demonstrated'—not *quid
pro quo,* which basically means 'tit for tat'."

Theo was far too frightened and angry to be embarrassed.
"So sue me. You know what I mean. You say you went to the
mortal world but Eamonn Dowd couldn't have done that."

"Theo, Theo." He could almost imagine the thing in the
dark corner shaking its head, although he saw no motion in
the shadows to indicate it. "Don't wave the Clover Effect at
me of all people. What you don't know about the way Faerie
works—in fact, what most of the fairies themselves don't
know about it is staggering to contemplate. So why don't
you shut your mouth for a while and listen?

"I was sentenced to banishment. I was going to be forcefully removed from New Erewhon. There were three days of
legal formality before the banishment took effect—these
Flower fairies are as bad as the British or even the Russian
apparatchiks when it comes to meaningless paper-stamping
and standing in line for no good reason. Erephine had been
taken away from me and hauled back to her family's country house, which was more or less a fortress. I knew that I
could not reach her there without being killed, and yet I honestly thought about it, considered whether dying on her lawn
might not be a better choice than simply letting her family
and their tame members in Parliament boot me out. I was not
a well man, Theo. I loved her—I would have sold my immortal soul without a moment's thought to be with her . . ."

"Oh, my God." Theo's skin was tingling, and something
tightened inside his gut until he felt quite ill. "Oh, my God,
you really are him. You really are Eamonn Dowd."

"I knew that already," the Remover said. "Why do *you*
suddenly believe me?"

"On top of all the other things, it was the way you just

said you'd have sold your soul. The way a person would, an ordinary human person, even if they didn't believe they had one. The human-type fairies don't think about souls, any of that stuff. It's not just that they don't believe in them, they don't even seem to have considered it. The few times I've asked about it, it was like I'd asked them if they thought they had tentacles—something anyone could see they didn't have."

"Actually, some of the fairy-folk *do* have tentacles. You should see some of the deep-sea nixies. Even if you start out looking more or less like a human here, this is a Lamarckian world and a couple of thousand years of intense pressure will do funny things to you."

"Okay, okay, you win—you really are my great-uncle. I don't need to hear the whole story, I need to help my friend Applecore—and this friend here." He pointed at Cumber. "So what are you going to do? Help me? Or sell me to those murdering creeps Hellebore and Thornapple?"

"I told you, you must listen to . . ."

"No! I have responsibilities!"

There was a long silence. When Dowd broke it, his voice had taken on a new quality, cold and precise, which Theo had not heard before and didn't much like. "You are not to interrupt me, whatever claims you may have on my conscience. I have waited a long time and the situation is complicated. I will tell you my story . . ."

"But . . .

"I will tell you my story. After that, we will see what is to be done."

Theo lowered his head. He might not be related by actual blood to this man, but even with no more of him to judge from than his voice, Theo could recognize a family resemblance to his mother, that chilly disaffection that could sweep down suddenly in the middle of an apparently insignificant argument, transmuting it to something painful, and against which there was no more sense arguing than there was value in waving your arms at a hurricane to turn it aside. "So talk," he said at last.

"Very well." The chill abated a little. "As I said, Theo, I was desperate. I was a condemned man, waiting for something I feared more than death—not merely being sent away from the woman I loved, but being sent across a barrier that I could never cross again. I had appealed to the few allies I had among the high houses, Stocks, Violets, Daffodils, but none of them were willing to support me against Parliament and especially against the Primroses, who were frequently allies of theirs in the fierce struggles among the highest houses for dominance. The Flower war that until recently everyone called 'the last Flower War' was just beginning, so allegiances were even more delicate and crucially important. In fact, things had grown worse than I knew, as I found out later. So I turned instead to the only person I had heard of who might know more about that barrier than the Seven Families and their tame wizards—or 'scientists,' as they are called here. The day before the banishment was to be carried out I went to the one known as the Remover of Inconvenient Obstacles.

"Yes, I came here to this desolate place, just as you did, and probably feeling many of the same things—terror, hopelessness, rage over what had been done to me and those I loved. I was desperate. I was willing to do anything.

"The old Remover was a creature of infinite subtlety and malice, but he never bothered to waste his energies against those who had done him no personal harm unless he stood to gain something from their suffering, so I was safe enough . . . at least at first. Still, he liked to be entertained, so he let me wander for hours in the maze outside this room before he let me in."

"I didn't see a maze."

"No, you didn't. And he was also less reticent than I am about showing himself to supplicants. When I was finally admitted into his presence it was all I could do not to run away again, but my need was greater than any horror or nausea and I forced myself to look at him as I begged for his assistance. I told him I would pay nearly any price for it.

"He could help me, he said at last, but he needed something from me in return—a mortal child to give to one of the most powerful families, who had developed a sudden and serious need for one. Even in my madness and despair I was not so far gone that I was willing to give an infant up to torture or murder, so I demanded to know the purpose and who would get the child. He would not reveal which house, but he swore—invoking certain powers in whose names it is a very bad idea to swear falsely, as he and I knew—that the child would be treated as a member of that family and raised by them, that no hurt would be done to it. This was true, it turned out, but in a rather horrid way . . ."

Theo suddenly thought he felt things fitting together. "Was . . . was that me? Is that what you did—why you apologized to my mother in that letter?" But somehow the details remained confusingly wrong.

"Good lord," Dowd said in disgust. "I can understand not knowing 'Q.E.D.' but can you not use logic at all? What have they done to the schools since I was a boy?" The dark shape rustled and twitched in the corner shadows. Despite the weirdness of the setting, the life or death matters, Theo had a momentary taste of what it would have been like to grow up with a cross old great-uncle. "Think, boy! If you were a mortal child taken from your parents and brought here, then how did you wind up spending your entire life until now in the mortal world? How would that make sense?"

"All right, all right, I didn't work it through—but this does have something to do with me, doesn't it?"

"Of course it does, if you'll let me tell it without interrupting." Dowd took a moment to reorder his thoughts. "So the Remover made a bargain with me. Swearing by the same oaths he used to proclaim the safety of the child I would steal, he promised that if I would secure a mortal child for him before the first sunrise after my return, he would help to bring me back to Faerie, despite the Clover Effect—something that no one but the Remover himself even thought possible. There was more to his scheme, of course, but I hadn't learned that yet.

"So I went away from this place on my last night in Faerie, still miserable—still almost mad with grief, really— but also with a little hope that I might not be separated from my beloved Erephine forever. I returned to my house in Forenoon to pack up those few things I planned to take back with me . . ."

"You mean you can, like, take a suitcase when you leave Faerie?"

Again Dowd did not bother to hide his irritation. "Did the person who went to your world to fetch you arrive naked? Didn't you yourself bring my notebook and whatever you were wearing when you came through? Of course you can take things. Not everything will remain what it seems to be once it leaves Faerie, of course—the legends of what happens to fairy gold are common enough that even your television-dulled generation has probably heard them—but I was certainly able to take a few keepsakes." His voice calmed, but still remained chilly. "Now, where was I? Ah, yes. So I went to my house to pack up. I had made my devil's bargain with the Remover. I would give him a child, a mortal child, and in return he would help me return to Faerie, in secret."

"That's still a horrible thing," Theo said despite his own determination not to interrupt again.

"What is?"

"Stealing a child."

"Even when I was promised that the child would be raised as a member of one of the high families? That it would want for nothing?"

"That's fine for the child, but what about the baby's parents, its real parents? That would ruin their lives, having their baby disappear."

A long moment passed. To Theo's surprise, when Dowd

spoke again there was no anger left, nothing but a bleak emptiness. "Of course. Of course. And I knew that. Knew also that on such short notice I would have little chance to find a child who deserved to be saved, one whose parents were bullying monsters or drunkards or drug addicts—little chance to salve my conscience by stealing a child whose parents, I could tell myself, deserved it. So as I prepared to leave New Erewhon I was on the horns of a terrible dilemma. If the Remover was wrong, or lying, I would never see my love Erephine again. If he was right, I would regain what I had lost only by inflicting a dreadful loss on someone else."

You shouldn't have agreed to it, Theo thought but did not say. *There are some bargains you just can't make.* But he still felt a kind of pity for the thing that had been Eamonn Dowd. He had been hammered by love a few times himself, badly enough that he had done some really idiotic things. He had slept in his car outside one ex-girlfriend's house three freezing nights in a row just so he could torture himself by watching her go in and out with her new boyfriend, compelled against all sense to make himself miserable imagining what they were doing in bed together just inside. He certainly understood being violently, almost criminally love-stupid. *But there are still limits. There have to be limits.*

"As it turned out, the old Remover was far more subtle than I understood," Dowd went on, his whispery voice distant with what might have been grief. "He had many projects in hand and was not going to squander such an opportunity on just one. That very night, as I lay sleepless on my bed, someone knocked at my door. It was a uniformed doonie— you must have met a few of them by now—and he told me I was to accompany him. I was confused, but because I thought it might be something the Remover had arranged to help accomplish our plot, or that the doonie might even have been sent to bring me back here to the Remover's house, I dressed and got into the huge black luxury coach and we sped across New Erewhon.

"We didn't go all the way to the waterfront, but toward the center of town instead, into Eventide. It was only when we suddenly turned in at one of its back entrances that I understood that for some reason I had been summoned to Violet House. I had been there before. The Violets were among the families who were, if not friendly to mortals, reasonably tolerant of them.

"As the bodyguards carefully searched me before allowing me out of the garage and into the main house, I began to realize for the first time how bad things had gotten between the highest Flower houses just during the months of my downfall and my trial in Parliament, when I had been largely oblivious to other events. There were soldiers everywhere in the compound, a private army, and they were all busy. The house seemed to be preparing for some kind of imminent assault, maybe even a full-blown war. Actually, as I found out later, they were preparing for what would happen when they lost that war.

"The doonie chauffeur was left behind and a young, high-handed fairy of the Violet clan inner circle took charge of me with as much enthusiasm as if I were a basket of dirty linen, hurrying me into the heart of the house. I was searched one more time by a quartet of ogre guards, then ushered into the house library. Belleius Violet, the head of the family, was waiting there for me.

"I can probably best describe him if I tell you that he was something like the head of a wealthy old New England family—Boston Brahmins, as we used to call them. As fairy nobility goes he was better than most, reasonably fair-minded, no crueler than average. In fact, by the standards of his people he would have to be called a liberal. This does not mean he treated me well that night. He was angry and heartsick, and it must also have galled him to have to turn in his most desperate need to one such as I—a mortal, an interloper.

" 'You have received a fitting punishment for your presumption, Eamonn Dowd,' he said to me. 'Do not think I feel sympathy for you. But it is not because, as many in the other houses do, I deem my blood above yours, although even among mortals I understand yours is not particularly distinguished. Rather, I object to what you did because we of the ruling families constitute the thin walls that separate our world from the barbarous old days, and we simply cannot afford to let ourselves be diluted with mortal ideas, our daughters taken as wives by mortals, our houses inherited by them. That may not be what you intended but I know well how things happen, how one liberty opens the door for the rest. If such a thing came to pass, we would soon be only an adjunct of your world. That cannot be allowed.' That's what he said to me by way of hello." Dowd allowed himself a sour, wheezing chuckle. "And remember, he was one of the progressive party.

"I asked him if he had brought me all the way across town merely to insult me and my race. He grew angry, but could not afford to lose his temper, as I guessed. I didn't press my advantage. I had also guessed that the hand of the Remover was in this somewhere and I didn't have much time left. Much of the night was already gone and in the morning I was to be taken to Strawflower Square.

"It took a while—he had to call for a stiff drink to nerve himself to be open with someone like me. To be fair, it was a terrible moment for him, one nobody would envy. He began with a rambling explanation of what I had seen outside, which confirmed my guess that not only had things become very bad between the seven ruling houses, they were worse than I could have imagined.

"In short, war was about to break out. All of the other ruling houses were either supporting Hellebore—for he was the instigator, of course—or were unwilling to resist him openly. Only Violet stood against him, and that meant that Violet House would almost certainly lose."

"What were they fighting about?"

"Ah, yes. That is, of course, a significant detail. It wasn't known to me at the time, but it certainly is to you now—and to the point of this story. The leading families had fallen out over a difference of approach. Of management, if you will. At the end of what they call here the Second Gigantine War—you have heard of that?"

"Yes."

"The king and queen of Faerie—not quite Shakespeare's Oberon and Titania, as I have discovered since, but definitely the rulers of this place—had died at the end of that war. Somehow, by means I have never been able to discover, the Seven Families gained control over the channeling of power that had once been a part of the king's and queen's duties . . . no, duties is the wrong word . . . that had once been a part of the king's and queen's very essences. The Seven put themselves in the place of the king and queen, and not incidentally gained power over the lives of all who had been royal subjects—in short, all of Faerie.

"But, and here is the significant part, they might have gained control of the conduit—the pipeline, as it were—but they couldn't insure the continued flow of power, of magic, of whatever you wish to call it that is the lifeblood of this place. Somehow the magic of Faerie had been either controlled by or even generated by the old king and queen, and the Seven Families could not make things work in the same way. They were forced to find cruder substitutes. Instead of tapping a self-renewing source they were forced to use the actual energies of living fairies. A bit like eating your friends instead of eating fruits and vegetables that need only water and sun to grow, I suppose. Certainly it was not very efficient. Also, to their dismay, the leaders of the Seven Families soon discovered that the human-type fairies themselves act as concentrators of the kind of power they need in a way that other people of Faerie do not . . ."

"A friend of mine explained that to me."

"Yes, well, it is a significant fact. The ruthlessness of the families in question is such that if they could have used those they deemed 'lesser races' of Faerie, this crisis could have been averted for thousands of years more, perhaps forever. I have seen the plans commissioned by Hellebore and his allies, curious antiques now, for self-contained power stations that would have bred their own goblins and kobolds, used them up, then essentially thrown them away, like the Nazi camps. But they could not make such a thing work. The cost of use was and still is too high—as much power is expended extracting the essence of one of that kind of fairy as is gained. Even taking power from the 'higher fairies,' so-called, is a bad bargain, although that is what they have been doing for years. And even if it were a better bargain in terms of energy generated, the morality of it has always troubled many folk here.

"That had already become clear on that night, as I stood before Lord Violet. He alone, apparently, had found the courage to stand before the other families and say that he could no longer countenance living off what was essentially the slavery of other fairies. He might have felt differently if the strategy had been an effective one, but it was clearly only a delaying action against inevitable collapse. You see, a fairy city is similar to a human city in at least one important respect. It is an unnatural thing, and the more unnatural a thing is—in this case, a concentration of people in one place, using countless labor-saving devices and altering the very land to cram ever more people in—the more energy it uses. New Erewhon is a kind of reverse solar system, with the City becoming a sun that does not give light and heat to that which surrounds it, but draws it away from everything else.

"In any case, back on that long-ago day, Violet had made his stand and had failed. Things still seemed normal on the surface—very few people on the street would have guessed that another Flower War was about to begin—but Belleius Violet was no fool. He had not swayed the other ruling families to his side, and since he had angered Hellebore and his faction by challenging them in public they would certainly seek revenge. Lord Violet knew he did not have enough powerful allies to win, and he knew that Hellebore would not be content merely to push Violet House out of the inner circle of power. It would be destroyed, its ruling family dev-astated, perhaps even exterminated."

"Like Daffodil House this time."

"Exactly. Now, something else you must understand about Faerie is that its rules may be strange, but they *work*. I have had thirty years to study this place and I have learned a great deal. I still cannot tell you exactly what Faerie *is*, whether it is a place in its own right or a sort of reflection of the mortal world, but although its rules may be incompre-hensible to our way of thinking, they are just as valid as any physics you may have learned back home. If you swear an oath here then you had better fulfill it or you will definitely reap the consequences and they will be unpleasant in some particularly apt way. If you go to a crossroads at midnight, you will meet someone who will offer you a bargain, even if it's only a barrow-troll who's willing to let you have a two-step head start before he catches you and eats the flesh off your bones."

Theo's fear had begun to ebb a little, although he was by no means feeling comfortable. "Does this have something to do with Lord Violet?"

"It does. Don't hurry me. Faerie has its rules and they may seem magical—they *are* magical, or at least so differ-ent as to seem so—but they work. One of them is primo-geniture. Do you know what that means? No? Good God, boy. It means that the firstborn inherits, or in some cases, the oldest living child. And I'm not just talking about land or the family limousine. I mean *everything*—all the powers, con-tracts, charms, and obligations that the head of the family, usually the father, has accumulated during his long, long life. This is one reason that even a progressive like Violet hated me for marrying into a fairy family, and why he was so particularly galled to have to ask for my help. As far as they were concerned, letting mortals into the bloodline of the high houses was more than a social issue, it meant a pos-sible end to one of the most important truths of life in Faerie—namely, that as long as one child survives, the family still exists and can be reconstituted, in a sense, no matter how low they have fallen. The games of power between houses are played over millennia here, Theo, and they are very complicated.

"So this was the situation in which Violet found himself. He faced a war he almost certainly could not win, and in which he feared that not only he might die, but his sons and daughters as well, thus ending his family. Nidrus Hellebore of all people understands that you have not destroyed an enemy until you have destroyed his issue as well—'It is not enough to kill the bloom,' an old expression here goes, 'you must burn the seeds and salt the ground.' And that is what Violet feared would happen. His wife had given birth to a son only a few months earlier, an infant who would normally have had nothing more unusual to look forward to than the life of a seventh child in a powerful family, but now he might be the seed that could let the family live again, no matter the outcome of the next Flower War. Violet wanted to send that child somewhere beyond Hellebore's reach, but there was nowhere in Faerie he could feel confident that would be true. So he had thought of a Faerie tradition from the old days. He would send the child to the mortal world."

An overwhelming idea was knocking like an impatient stranger at the door, but Theo held it at bay for a moment to grapple with something in Dowd's story that was confusing him. "But why send a baby? Why not send one of his older children—someone who would be able to do the family some good if they wound up as the last one?"

"Because although travel to the mortal world has been curtailed by the Clover Effect, it is still possible. Violet knew that if Hellebore ever learned what had happened, or even guessed, he would begin to search the mortal world. One of the other strange things about the overlap between the mortal world and Faerie is that a fairy child raised in the mortal world very quickly begins to resemble a mortal—to smell like a mortal, as it were—while an older child or adult will never fully lose the scent of Faerie. Trained hunters would find it much easier to locate one of Violet's older children."

"So he wanted you to take . . . take this child to the mortal world."

"Well, not precisely—I was going to be banished in public. Violet's plan would not be much of a secret if I was seen to cross back into the human world with an infant in my arms. But in desperation he had gone to the Remover with this problem and that cunning old monstrosity had seen a way to kill two birds with one stone—or rather, to swap birds. The Remover of Inconvenient Obstacles was going to take Lord and Lady Violet's youngest child and pass that child to me once I was back on the mortal side. I was then to take it and keep it, or so Violet intended, and he promised me that if he survived to recover his child—since that would mean he had somewhat improbably triumphed over Hellebore's faction— he would work to revoke my banishment and find a way to bring me back to Faerie. Not a very good bargain for me, he must have thought, but it must have seemed that as a beggar I could not afford to be too choosy.

"What he did not know of course was that the Remover was manipulating everything, most definitely including me, and that I fully intended to return without any help from the obviously doomed Violet House. The Remover had foreseen my ethical dilemma—you know, it makes me wonder if like me, he had once been a mortal—and was providing me with a sop to my conscience. I would take a mortal child from its parents, but now I would have a healthy fairy child to leave in its place. One of the oldest of fairy tales, that is—the changeling child, substituted in the cradle. So I agreed to Violet's bargain, thinking that Violet House's plans would mean little to me—that I would be coming back to Faerie on my own and that the Violet family would never survive to want to claim their offspring. I was right, of course, but not in the ways that I thought that night."

"And that baby, the fairy child . . . that was me."

There was a long pause. "Yes, Theo. That was you. For

what it is worth at this late date, I can confirm that you were born Septimus Violet and that everything your father feared came to pass. You are the last living member of Violet House."

37

THE EBONY BOX

"Septimus? I was named *Septimus?*"

"Not exactly," said Dowd. "You and I seem to perceive first names here as Classical names, mostly Roman—at least among the upper-class fairy families. Septimus is Latin for 'Seventh,' which is what you were called."

"Jesus, that's even worse. I was called 'Number Seven'? They didn't even bother to think up a name for me?"

"They may not have used much imagination in naming you, Theo,"—the whispery voice was as close to kind as it had been—"but your brothers and sisters were all killed in the Flower War, so they gave you something better than a clever name. They gave you a life."

"So that's how I wound up with my mom and dad? You stole your own niece's baby and left me in his place!"

Dowd took a rattling breath. "If it means anything, I am sorry now for all that I did. More sorry than you can guess."

"Just tell me what happened. No, tell me about my real family." He was finding it hard to absorb all that he had learned. To discover that the great-uncle he had thought was dead was alive—a man he had only recently learned wasn't really his great-uncle, after all—would have been strange enough. But to learn of his true family and find that they were all dead at the same time . . . Theo felt as though he had a fever: his head seemed to be floating, but the messages coming through from his body were of illness and discomfort. He turned to look at Cumber and felt a sudden powerful dislike for his unconscious friend, for all the creatures of this world that a month ago he had not believed existed, but which had nevertheless turned his entire life upside-down.

Yeah, but be honest—it wasn't much of a life, was it?

"We have been talking a long time and I am weary," Dowd announced. "I use several unnatural means to keep this crippled body functioning and I have not taken advantage of any of them recently. Also, to be honest with you, I did not sell half my vitality to raise an *irrha* to fetch you here just so I might tell you what nice people your true parents were. In any case, there are things in my own story you must hear first."

Theo didn't have the strength to argue. The weird warehouse room had begun to seem like the setting of some existentialist play in which he would stand forever listening to a disembodied voice telling him about how miserable and pointless the universe was. "Yeah, okay. Go ahead."

"Very well. The morning of my banishment came. The marshals of the Parliamentary Guard came to take me to Strawflower Square, which was almost deserted. Rumors of impending trouble between the ruling houses had inclined some of the more powerful families to stay home, and in any case my so-called crime and trial had been a bit of a nine-day wonder—there was more exciting gossip on the wind now. Only a few ordinary working fairies passing through the square dallied long enough to witness a mortal being sent back to the mortal world.

"My sentence was read by a minor Parliamentary official—he had not even bothered to put on a formal coat. A doorway, a gate, whatever you wish to call it, was opened and I was thrust through the fiery seam with no more ceremony than a bag of rubbish dropped down a chute. I took nothing with me but the clothes in which I had arrived in Faerie, my notebook, and, on a necklace underneath my shirt, a charmed stone given to me by the Remover—a sort of signal beacon, as I understood it. The doorway closed behind me and I found myself back in San Francisco—in Golden Gate Park, in an open meadow where I terrified a pair of tramps by appearing out of nowhere. I imagine the after-effects as having been something from an old newspaper cartoon, with both of them swearing on the spot to give up alcohol forever.

"In any case, I found myself in the middle of a bright California day after how long away I could only guess. Longer than I suspected, as it turned out. I had been gone perhaps three or four years by my own reckoning, but something like twenty had passed in the mortal world. When I had left, the Second World War had only recently ended. Truman was still the president. Now I had returned to an America that was unhappily embroiled in Southeast Asia, at war in a country called Viet Nam. Richard Nixon, a man I only vaguely remembered, was the president. The nineteen-sixties were just ending and the entire world I knew had been reshaped like an image in a carnival mirror.

"I did not know all this at the time, of course, and if things had gone the way I planned I would never have learned any of it.

"A bit overwhelmed, I wandered over to the park bandstand and thought about what I should do next. Every time a couple walked past pushing a baby carriage on their way to the aquarium or the Japanese tea garden I had to fight down the impulse to simply grab the child and run. I didn't have long, you see—I had to accomplish my task before the next sunrise if I wanted the Remover to be able to use the stone around my neck to locate me in the mortal world, or at least that is what he had told me. Perhaps it was a lie—certainly the stone had a darker purpose, as I discovered. But the fact was, I was in a panic, finally coming to realize how difficult this task would be and knowing that if I failed I would lose any chance to see my beloved Erephine again.

"The more I thought about it, the more obvious it became

that I could not simply snatch any child. For one thing, I could not substitute the Violet baby—you, Theo, yes—for the stolen child until the Remover put him into my hands. I had to arrange things so that everything could happen in one place, at one time, and I could not afford to attract attention until that moment for fear I would be arrested and lose any chance of getting back.

"I had not really thought the problem through in all its intricacy during my last distracted hours in Faerie. Now, faced with half a day in which to come up with a solution, I walked across the park and considered my plight. I kept moving—I certainly did not want to wind up in jail as a vagrant—and eventually wandered over to the post office in my old neighborhood in Cole Valley. I knew that after twenty years most of the mail waiting in my box would be meaningless, but I still had no idea of how I was going to proceed with my real errand, so I was more or less killing time. The account I had set up at the Traveler's Bank before crossing over to Faerie had done its work and the post office box was still mine. I had a sack of mail waiting—a very small sack considering it had been twenty years, but the era of junk mail was only beginning—and I went to a diner to read it over a cup of coffee. There were a few letters from fellows I'd sailed with and a few from gals I'd known in various ports. Some business mail as well. And then I found it, three months old but incredibly timely—the birth notice."

"From my mom and dad," Theo said flatly.

"From my niece Anna and her husband, yes," said Dowd. "Your adoptive parents, so to speak. I still remember it. A son, seven pounds, ten ounces, named Theodore Patrick Vilmos.

"I won't draw this out. I can imagine that it's painful for you. I thought simply of calling up, inviting myself to their home down in San Mateo for a visit—what more natural for an uncle only just returned to town than to want to meet his niece and her husband and new baby?—but I was more than a little worried about what could happen if something went wrong. Also, I was close to two decades younger than I should have been, because of the differences between time in Faerie and in the mortal world, and I was afraid that would make them suspicious—make them think I was some impostor. There's irony, eh? I didn't want them to think I was some dangerous stranger because it might hinder me from stealing their child! So instead I took a cab to the Traveler's Bank in Russian Hill, which you must have guessed by now is a place that has long catered to those who travel to Faerie or other strange lands, and withdrew a decent sum of money, then took a taxi all the way down the peninsula to San Mateo at the cost of a small fortune. I located the house and then walked the neighborhood, waiting for it to get dark. When night came I watched Anna and her baby through their back window from a tree in the yard of an absent neighbor. I didn't feel very good about what I was doing, needless to say."

Theo was feeling sick to his stomach again. It was like having someone stick a finger right into his memories and smear them around: nothing was what he had thought it was. "Just . . . tell. Tell what happened."

"You may well despise me, but remember, I was desperate. Besides, I thought little Theodore would be going off to Faerie to be raised by a good family, that my niece would be getting prime fairy stock in return and that she would never know a change had been made. You see, the Remover had explained to me that there is a sort of . . . melding that happens when a changeling is substituted for a human baby. Both take on something of the other's essence. The changeling baby takes on the semblance of the mortal child during the first night as it lies in the crib and the mortal baby, even at a distance, is changed in subtle ways as well. They are linked like Siamese twins despite their separation."

"So I look like what the real baby would have looked like?"

"Not exactly, but quite closely, as far as I have been able to discover."

His mother's sad little deathbed confession floated up
from his memory. "She did know."

"What?"

"My mother knew. That I wasn't real . . . that I wasn't
really hers."

Eamonn Dowd seemed distracted and uneasy, but not because of what Theo was saying; in fact, he hardly seemed to
be listening. "Yes, well, I should finish this explanation.
Time may be shorter than I thought."

"What does that mean?"

Dowd went on as though Theo had not spoken. "At midnight, after I used the charm to make myself visible to the
Remover, a shining gate opened and a shrouded, masked figure appeared at the foot of the tree with the Violet infant—
you—in its arms. It was not the Remover. I still do not know
who or what it was. Some other poor fool tricked into doing
the Remover's will, using his one trip to the mortal world on
a visit that lasted only minutes. Feeling like a murderer, my
heart racing, I went to the basement window that I had noticed was unlocked, crawled through, then brought the Violet baby up the stairs and into the house. I could hear Anna's
husband snoring. I took Anna's child out of the cradle and
put you in—it was most strange, I could already feel you beginning to change even as I laid you down, a kind of . . .
sliding sensation . . . but I was too breathless with anticipation and fear to pay much attention. I hurried out through the
back door with my niece's child. As I stepped out into the
yard a hand reached out and touched the Remover's stone
dangling on my chest. I had time only to shout in pain at
the shock that ran through me before I found myself tumbling helplessly to the ground.

"A terrible coldness overtook me, and something else as
well, a sensation so strange I still cannot describe it except
to say that I found myself rushing away from myself at right
angles. Suddenly I was floating in the air like a soap bubble,
looking down on the scene in your parents' back garden,
which included my own body lying curled on the grass. I

can't tell you how strange it was to realize that I was not inside that body anymore. The masked stranger handed the stolen baby through the gateway to what must have been, I can only presume, the Remover waiting on the far side. Then the stranger came back. He pulled the stone and its chain from the neck of my lifeless body and I found myself drawn after that stone as he headed back to the gateway—the stone was pulling my bodiless essence with it!

"I had been a fool to forget Faerie's natural laws, and especially that they were as literal as in any folktale. The Remover had sworn to bring the baby and me back across the barrier, but he had not promised how he would do it. The Remover clearly meant to fulfill the letter of the contract— it is always perilous not to do that here—in the only way he could, which meant leaving my body behind and dooming me to roam Faerie as an unhomed spirit.

"But chance intervened. Someone had heard my cry of surprise and pain. Peter Vilmos opened the window and shouted at the shadowy figure. I wonder if he saw the doorway to Faerie and if he did, what he made of it. Did he ever mention such a night? Ah, no matter. Startled, the Remover's lackey dropped the stone and its chain in the undergrowth near the shining gate. Your stepfather was shouting about the police now and the doorway to Faerie was already flickering. The masked stranger hesitated for a moment, then abandoned the magical stone and dove through, making his escape back to Faerie. As soon as the gate closed I found myself back in my body again. I managed to drag myself to my feet and locate the stone—in my bodiless form I had seen its fall quite clearly—then pocket it and climb over your stepparents' fence. I was still disoriented by my experience and must have looked like a hapless drunk. Certainly I barely made it over. By the time I had crashed through the hedges into the next street I had recovered my wits enough to know that I would never escape the neighborhood on foot—the police had undoubtedly already been summoned. I found an empty garden shed and shivered there until just before dawn, then headed back to San Francisco, full of despair. I had been double-crossed. I had betrayed my own kin and received nothing for it. I was never going to see my love Erephine Primrose again.

"If I'd been a bit mad before, it was as nothing to what I went through in the days that followed. If I hadn't had money in the bank, I'm sure I would have died in a gutter somewhere, another derelict killed by the cold. But I did have money, so I took a hotel room, then later an apartment, living modestly so that I would not have to find a job and take time away from the obsession that drove me. To my neighbors I must have seemed merely a distracted and solitary man, but truly I was no longer sane. I was consumed with one thought—somehow to return to Faerie and Erephine. Oh, yes, and most definitely to get revenge against the creature who had betrayed me, the Remover of Inconvenient Obstacles, not to mention the master and mistress of Primrose House—and all their lackeys in the Parliament. Such fantasies I had! They made the terrible things that Hellebore has done look tame.

"Other than the books and artifacts I had collected before, which had been waiting for me in storage for all those years, I had only one thing to help me, one very large clue—the charmed stone the Remover had given me, the thing which had brought his henchman so unerringly to me and which had somehow briefly separated my essence from my body. Faerie has very strict natural rules, as I have said, and anything used in that sort of magic—or that sort of science, as they would say—bears some traces of its user.

"It took me several years to discover a way, a very dangerous way, that I could turn the charm-stone to my own use. The search was hard, hard work, particularly because many of the sources I needed to study were scattered widely around the world. So during that time I reasserted my identity somewhat, disguising myself to seem closer to the age I should have been and re-establishing myself as traveler and a student of curiosities who was also a respectable member of the community. Not that all of my sources and contributors cared about such things, of course. Some of them had led far stranger lives than mine. You would be astonished, Theo, to learn the number of people—well, some of them only *look* like people—who hang about on the fringes of the mortal world trying to get back into Faerie or one of the other, less well-known destinations.

"In any case, I had found what seemed to be my only chance to return to New Erewhon. Still, the odds were not good, and when I sent that letter of apology to my niece Anna, the letter you have read, I truly believed I was likely to die. Perhaps it would have been better if I had."

Theo had been standing for too long, shifting from foot to foot. He was tired and, now that the worst of his terror had worn off, even a little hungry. But more than anything else he was beginning to be very angry. His entire life—a life that had seemed a little pointless anyway—was now shown to be largely the outcome of other people's plans, other people's needs. "Yeah, maybe it would have been better," he said. "So what happened? How did you get to be a . . . to be the way you are, where you won't even show yourself? And more important, why am I here at all? Why did you send that zombie-thing after me instead of just allowing me to be a happy thinks-he's-human idiot back in my own world?"

"I am giving you answers, Theo, but only because I wish to do so. You act as though you deserve them—as though it is your right." The voice had gone ice-cold again. "You are a typical American of your time. You believe the universe should have rules, like some board game, that cheating will be punished and virtue rewarded. Nonsense. That is nonsense."

Theo took a few steps into the middle of the room. "I'm tired of talking to the air."

"Come no farther!" There might have been a touch of fear behind the fury. "Your ferisher friend is hostage to your good behavior, Theo. I was never really your uncle, remember, so do not presume too much on family connections. We are not even related."

Theo could not help himself—he laughed out loud in shock and anger. "Family connections? Shit. You took me from my parents, stole my stepparents' real baby, all for your own selfish goddamn plans. I don't think *I'm* really the one who's taking advantage of family connections, am I?"

After a pause, Dowd spoke again in a calmer voice. "I am trying to tell you what you want to know, Theo. Please, just listen. You're not the only one who finds this hard."

Theo waved his hand angrily, directing him to continue. It was pointless to argue, everything was decades in the past.

But it's new to me.

"To be brief, my experiment succeeded, although not the way I had hoped. I crossed the barrier, but in a way completely unlike what I had experienced before . . ." Eamonn Dowd had now begun speaking a bit more quickly. Theo thought he seemed nervous and distracted, and wondered what he had done to make Dowd fretful—certainly he couldn't have expected anyone to take news like this cheerfully.

Actually, all things considered, I've been pretty damn calm so far, and he sure seems like he's holding all the cards, anyway. So what's his trip? What's he afraid of? Theo squinted at the shadowed corner. *Maybe he's like Oz the Great and Terrible. Maybe there's something about how he looks—who he really is—that he doesn't want me to see, and all this "I'm so ugly" stuff is just a cover.* He began to move slowly forward under the guise of restlessly shifting from foot to foot.

"It did not take me long to discover what the strange thing was that had happened to me," Dowd was saying. "I passed over into Faerie—but not all of me made the trip. Just as the Remover had planned for me earlier, I traveled as a disembodied spirit. Whether my actual body died at that moment or only when I had been out of it a certain time, I don't know, but I knew I was leaving it behind forever. I cannot tell you how dreadful that felt and I will not try.

"I found myself here in this place, but not precisely the place that you are seeing now. I can offer no better explanation than to say that in my bodiless state I saw a larger version of the Remover's house—a version that opened out into planes of existence I had only suspected to exist. My God, how little most people guess! And at the center of it all, in the middle of his web of intrigues and experiments, the Remover of Inconvenient Obstacles sat like a multi-dimensional spider. A barely imaginable hatred swept over me. I had no mortal body anymore, so I became that hatred. Here in front of me was the creature that had cheated me and stolen my hope! Like a dog who has long been tortured by a vicious owner, and whose confining chain finally breaks, I could think of only one thing—*Attack. Destroy.*

"I took him by surprise, I think, and that helped. Whatever he truly was, the Remover was certainly powerful and much better schooled than me—even with surprise on my side I would have had no chance except that in the place where we fought my fury was a pure thing, a powerful thing. It is also possible that, in the way peculiar to Faerie, his own breaking of his promise to me weakened him. He had *not* brought me back from the mortal world as he had sworn he would—his lackey had made a mistake. If he had done so and then killed me or left me to roam bodiless I doubt it would have rippled even the quietest side-currents of reality . . . but he had not fulfilled his bargain. In Faerie, such things have a price.

"We struggled a long time. But he had a body, and a strange and crippled one at that—I of all people understand that now. Bound as he was to that malformed shell, he did not have the strength to prevail in a long struggle. When his earliest and deadliest attempts to destroy me failed, I knew that eventually I would win. In that strange place he was like a jellyfish of shadows and lightning, but I burned like a comet—white-hot, blazing with hatred. As he weakened he tried one last time to banish me from his plane of existence, but I had the upper hand and I turned his own power against him. His soul or whatever it might be went shrieking away into the ultimate darkness, leaving me exhausted but victorious. With my last strength I wrapped his empty body around me like a blanket and found myself back in Faerie again. But I was stuck in the Remover's rotting, alien carcass, and despite many attempts, I have not been able to replace it with anything less dreadful, this body that bears the residue of a million horrible thoughts, sights, deeds. If you think I have done bad things, Theo, you should feel comforted to know the hell in which I have trapped myself.

"When I regained my strength I was desperate to see Erephine, to show her that I had returned to her against all odds, even if it was in this grotesque form. I tried to contact her but received no reply. I sent her message after clandestine message without hearing anything back—if I had not seen occasional mention of her on the talking mirrors I would have feared that she had died. After a while I began to consider that her family might somehow have turned her against me. Much had happened during the years I had been absent—the Flower War had come and gone, the Violets had been destroyed as I had supposed they would be and six families now ruled New Erewhon and Faerie instead of seven—but it was still a short time by fairy standards, far too short for a love like ours simply to evaporate. I decided I must have her brought to me, to get her away from her cursed family and show her how I had broken the very laws of time and space to be with her again.

"Things did not go as I planned. My hired hands brought her to me but she was strangely resistant. The woman I had loved and who had loved me beyond all meaning now acted as though the time that had passed in Faerie during my absence had changed everything—impossible in a race that lives for centuries! I could not show myself to her directly, of course, not in the form I was wearing—I was cloaked and masked like the Phantom of the Opera or some other melodramatic nonsense, and this made her suspicious despite all the proofs I offered her. She demanded to know what I

looked like—she said that I might be hiding from her because I was not Eamonn Dowd at all but the infamous Remover trying to embroil her in some scheme! I had my
employees transport her across town to my old house in
Forenoon, which I had reclaimed under a new name. I had
hoped to remind her of what we had together, but it quickly
became clear that something dreadful had happened—that
her parents had found some Faerie magic to brainwash her,
to make her think she didn't love me anymore. And after all
I had been through! It was a terrible night, me demanding
that she admit that it was really me that stood before her, that
she remember our love, and she insisting in turn that I was
trying to trick her, complaining that she was tired and frightened and wanted to go home. Home! To the very people who
had tried to pull us apart!"

My God, Theo thought, *he really is crazy. He can't even
imagine she might just have changed her mind, fallen out of
love.*

"At last, in desperation, I revealed myself to her. 'This is
what I did for you!' I shouted. 'This is the torment I suffer
every day to be in your world!' But I should not have done
it. She was not ready for the truth. She screamed and
screamed and tried to escape and I was forced to restrain
her—not physically, because this body does not have that
sort of strength, but with certain charms I had found in the
Remover's vast library. I suppose I was more hasty than I
should have been—remember, I was also tired, and heartbroken, and much of the Remover's science was new to me.
I silenced her and made her pliable, but only at a terrible
cost."

Theo finally broke the long silence. "What does that
mean?"

Dowd sighed. "Step forward. Now turn to your right. Do
you see that wooden casket?"

Theo stared at the nearest pile of strange objects. The
black chest was a little over a foot long and almost as wide.
"Yes, I see it."

"Open it. Go ahead. Do not fear—there is nothing in it that can harm you."

He picked it up carefully—it was surprisingly heavy—and slowly lifted the lid. Inside, couched on dark gray velvet, lay the stone head of a woman, a white marble mask carved in an attitude of serenity and repose. Whoever the model had been, her beauty was unearthly. "I don't underst . . ."

The stone eyes opened. The lips curled into a rictus of horror and the mask began to shriek. Theo gasped in terror and dropped the box, which thumped down onto the floor and landed on its side, the lid open. The screaming grew louder.

"Close it!" shouted Dowd. "Close the lid!"

It was one of the most terrible sounds Theo had ever heard, an endless shrill of raw terror. He jammed his hands over his ears, almost weeping, and at last managed to kick the ebony box shut.

"She is seldom awake," said Dowd in a shaken voice. "I did not think . . ."

"Jesus Christ, what did you do to her?"

"Nothing, not intentionally. Somehow the charm I used to calm her only paralyzed her body. In an attempt to reach inside her and bring the real Erephine back to the surface, I pulled out her essence but could not reintegrate it. Do not look at me—I did my best! Do you think I wanted this?" His voice shook. "You don't understand. Her family soon tracked us down and I was forced to escape, taking only her essence with me. Her body is still alive, unlike my own mortal form, but it is virtually empty. Her family has installed the shell, for that is what it is, in a sanitarium outside of the city, but she, the real, true Erephine, remains with me." He was quiet for a long moment, as if he'd lost his way in some prepared speech. "I saved her," he said weakly, "and one day I will reunite body and mind again . . ."

"You're a fucking monster, do you know that? Saved her? You drove her mad and then you took her mind and locked it up in some statue!"

"Listen to me, you don't understand . . . !"

"I understand as much as I need to!" Theo strode toward the corner where Dowd hid in shadow. "Is this the kind of help you've got in mind for me, too? No fucking thanks. I was an idiot to stand here listening to you. Come out! Come out of there or I'll drag you out."

"Stay away, boy!" Dowd's voice rose to a hysterical pitch. "I'm warning you!"

Theo made it another few steps forward before the man-dragorum caught up to him. He was close enough to see some of the shape that was Eamonn Dowd trying to struggle away from him and into deeper shadows like a bat with two broken wings. It was incomprehensible, really, at least in that brief instant, something that might have been a mass of slime and dead leaves and chicken bones picked half clean, although even that did not really explain the complex wrongness of what he saw. Worst of all, what stopped him even before the hand of the root slave clamped his shoulder, was the momentary glimpse of the ruin that was Dowd's face, the distorted knob of head whose only clear features were the eyes, the only human things in the glistening, tattered face, eyes that were wide with terror and misery and shame. Theo could not help himself. He recoiled with a cry of disgust.

"I told you not to come near me," Dowd screamed. "I told you! I should kill you."

"For what? For seeing what you've done to yourself?"

"Done to m-m-myself?" Dowd sounded like he was having trouble breathing. "H-how can you say such a thing, boy? Was it me who banished myself from Faerie in the first place? Did I double-cross myself?"

"Oh, God. Yeah, in a way you damn well did." Theo had reached the point where he no longer cared. "The hell with all of it. The hell with you. Just tell me what you're going to do to me."

Dowd calmed himself a little. "The same thing Hellebore and Thornapple and the others would have done if they'd been able to lay their hands on you. As the heir of the Violets you possess some kind of key they think will allow them to access the ultimate source of power, the beliefs of the mortal world. I don't need to destroy the sanity of our old world to achieve my goals—I do not need so much power— but I must find out what that key is and use it to restore Erephine and myself to some semblance of normality. I am sorry, Theo, but unlike Hellebore, I will do my best not to harm you."

"Drop dead, you psycho—there is no key. Everyone's hunting for me but I don't have anything! No key, no magic wand, no one ring to bind them all—nothing!" He writhed uselessly in the grip of the mandragorum.

"We will not know for certain until I have a chance to examine you. Don't you see, it's only fair, after all they did to me, to Erephine. That is why I pretended to search for you on their behalf, even though I knew exactly where you were. Hellebore needed me and I needed him, because I have slowly taken resources and knowledge from him under the guise of doing his bidding, until I think I have discovered much of what I need to know."

"So you're not really any different from Hellebore, are you?" Theo spat on the floor. "Oh, I forgot—you're going to try not to kill me while you're doing whatever you do."

"I am not Hellebore," Dowd said coldly. He had shrunk back into the darkened corner again; Theo could see him only as an irregular shadow. "I have done terrible things, but I did them for love."

"That's one of the most frightening things I've ever heard."

The other mandragorum suddenly stepped out from the shadows by the wall and into one of the pools of light. Theo felt sure that Dowd had suffered more recrimination than he could stomach, that he was going to have the root slave beat Theo unconscious or worse, but then it wobbled and bent forward as if in a bow and just kept bending—collapsing, really in the most surreal, cartoonish way possible. It fell into several huge pale slices that thumped onto the floor and rolled.

"What the hell . . . ?" was all that Theo had time to ask, then half a dozen figures spilled out into the room from the spot where the root slave had stood—armed constables in what looked like riot gear, eyes hidden behind insectoid goggles, beehive guns trained on Theo and the place where Dowd sat hidden by shadow. Two more men dressed in civilian clothes stepped out behind them, one extremely tall and thin and somehow vaguely familiar, holding what looked like a whip made of curling light. The other was of more ordinary size and all too recognizable.

"Tansy." Theo spat on the ground. It was a futile gesture, but it didn't look like he was going to get to make any other kind of gesture in the near future.

"Yes, Master Vilmos—or should I say Master Violet? I am alive, thanks to you. You merely left me to die instead of finishing me off." There was something wrong with the fairy's face, an unnatural gleam. "You are clearly out of touch with your true heritage."

"Shut your hole, Tansy," said the tall, dead-faced one. "Father wants this done quickly."

Doomed, Theo thought as he looked at the array of flaring gun barrels pointed in his direction. His veins seemed to be trying to pump icy water through him instead of blood. He had recognized the tall one, or at least the family resemblance. *He must be Hellebore's kid—the one Poppy said was completely mad.*

38

THE BROKEN STICK

"*This is outrageous!*" Eamonn Dowd's voice boomed so loud out of the empty air that Theo stumbled and even the helmeted constables flinched. Tansy covered his ears as Dowd's voice blared again. *"How dare you break into my sanctuary like this, uninvited?"*

"Spare us," said the tall, pale fairy. "You're a traitor, playing both ends against each other. My father has already heard and decided."

"What are you talking about?" Dowd sounded so alarmed that Theo's spirits, already at rock bottom, began scraping themselves a hole so they could sink even lower. "That's a lie, Anton Hellebore! I have done your father countless favors—your entire family . . ."

Hellebore raised his hand and snapped his fingers. There was a flurry of musical tones like the harmonics at the top end of a guitar neck, then a complicated gleam of light near the ceiling above Hellebore's head slowly became the glinting outline of a spiderweb stretched across the space where two walls met near the door. A curiously mechanical-looking spider crawled out of the dark spaces and into the middle of the web. "You're not the only one who can hide in the shadows," the younger Hellebore said. "We sent this in

here the last time you were out visiting us." He gestured
again and Dowd's voice filled the room.

"... *That is why I pretended to search for you on their
behalf, even though I knew exactly where you were. Hellebore needed me and I needed him, because I have slowly
taken resources and knowledge from him under the guise of
doing his bidding, until I think I have discovered much of
what I need to know.*"

Theo looked around desperately for a way out, but there
were armed constables on all sides and at least two of them
stood between him and Cumber's sleeping form.

"All right, Anton," said Dowd. "You have me, I'll admit
it, although you know perfectly well that your father not
only understands the advantage of playing one's rivals off
against each other, he does it himself. So let's not waste time
arguing when we could be bargaining. You want my more-
or-less grand-nephew, and doubtless you know that I have
lots of other valuable information as well, things gathered
over many centuries by my predecessor. My own needs are
few and I have no illusions about fighting with your father
over ultimate power—all I ask for letting you take the Violet heir without resistance is a day to leave the City . . ."

"You bastard!" Theo shouted.

Anton Hellebore had the disconcerting laugh of an idiot
child. "That's funny, it really is. But it's a bit late to be surprised by anything he does, Violet or Vilmos or whatever
you are. You already know what Dowd did to his own family, not to mention the so-called love of his life. Now ask
him what he did to the baby that was in your woman's
belly."

For a moment, a sharp, panicky moment, Theo believed
the young Hellebore meant Poppy—that they knew about
her somehow, had captured her. Then it sank in.

"The miscarriage?" he asked, turning to the shadowy spot
where Dowd crouched. In a day of bizarre surprises, of terror and revelation, he could barely encompass one more.
"Cat's miscarriage? *You* did that?"

"For Hellebore! I didn't want to. I hated doing it! But if I hadn't he would have pulled you out of the mortal world right then, to keep the birthright from passing on, and I . . . I wasn't ready . . ." A strange, choking sound came from both the air and, for the first time, audibly from the huddled form. "I wasn't ready . . . !"

Theo could not speak.

Hellebore's lips twitched briefly, as though he had learned to smile from a manual. "Well, that was fun, I must say."

"You're a fool, Anton Hellebore." Dowd's anger now sounded like nothing but bluster. "Your father would never make such a mistake. Now Vilmos is angry at me—you've made it even harder for us to put him to use. Not only can't you do it without me, now I will have to work very diligently indeed . . ."

"No, you're the fool, Dowd," said Lord Hellebore's son. "We don't need anything from you at all." He turned to the constables. "Shoot him."

In an instant, before Theo even had time to do more than flinch, two of the armored men stepped forward, goggles darkening as they lowered their weapons. The muzzles flashed and for an instant a whine like a plane's engine filled the room and seemed to suck everything toward it like a tunnel of vacuum. The whole shadowed corner of the room where Dowd had hidden flew apart, bits everywhere, tatters floating down. Theo heard one harsh breath, a raw gurgle, and then the twitching thing in the wreckage stopped moving. Something rattled down between the rafters and fell to the floor, rolled near to Theo's feet. It was a wasp—a spent bullet in the form of a tiny bronze automaton, legs kicking feebly. Theo could only stare at it, stupid with shock.

He's dead. Dowd's gone. Just like that.

"Now bring out the salamanders and burn the place." Anton Hellebore seemed utterly unmoved by what he had just ordered done; he might have been a cadaver jolted just strongly enough to move around in a semblance of life without actually feeling anything. "Oh, and someone put this short-timer in the coach. So you're really one of those weakling Violets," he said, grinning at Theo. "Well, I can't say I'm surprised." He turned back to the beetle-eyed guards. "Don't damage him fatally, but if he resists, hurt him. You, why are you moving so slowly? Take the one with the caul over his face, too. Maybe he knows something useful."

Four constables grabbed Theo and Cumber as the others began to empty sacks they had been carrying onto the floor, spilling out dozens of tiny reddish creatures with bright golden eyes. If they were salamanders, the words didn't mean quite the same thing here—there was something of amphibian shape to them but they also looked a bit like cartoon demons as they fled the center of the room and scuttled toward the nearest dark hiding places, some of them already smoldering into flame.

Tansy was almost jumping in place with anxiety. "My lord, you're not really going to burn this place, are you? The knowledge collected here is invaluable . . ."

"The knowledge here is false." For the first time there was real fury in young Hellebore's voice. "I should have known the Remover was a mortal—he never understood anything I told him, couldn't answer any of my questions. He didn't like the way I performed my experiments, either. I should have known!"

"But there are things here gathered by the original Remover . . . !"

Theo watched, sickly fascinated even as the guards handcuffed his hands behind his back. The surface of the restraints was strangely wet and rubbery, but Theo was distracted by something else: Count Tansy's features seemed almost to flicker and slide, inconstant as an oil slick. *His face—it's held together by some kind of charm,* Theo realized, *like the kind that Poppy was talking about, youth charms, beauty charms. He must have been really messed up in Daffodil House.*

"Enough, Tansy. If you try to tell me what to do here, you will burn with it." Hellebore's sullenness sounded almost

teenaged, but with an edge of something else as well, something truly terrifying. "I don't like this place and I don't believe it. I am a great scientist—greater than my father, even.
I know what's important. I know why my experiments
scream, what they are seeing, what they are feeling. Anything else is wrong. This Dowd person was wrong. I want it
all to go away."

In fact, fires were already springing up wherever the
salamander-demons had hidden themselves, burning as
silvery-hot as magnesium flares. Great billows of flame
began to climb the walls and lick at the ceiling. In other
spots the fires had taken something of the character of their
fuel—weird colors filtered through the blaze and an even
more disturbing set of harsh chemical smells began to fill
the air.

Tansy scuttled toward the exit, too frightened to argue
any more. Anton Hellebore walked backward out of the
room so he could watch the growing blaze, his long arms
held out as though he were conducting the fire like music.
"Old and rotten and wrong," he said, almost to himself. He
turned to look at Theo, flashing that humorless, rictus grin.
"This place will burn for days. They'll be able to see it at
night from the mountains of Alder."

My God, he really is crazy. Psychotic. Theo had little left
but despair—the thing he had most feared had now happened. He managed to get the fingers of one of his cuffed
hands into his pocket and pulled out the phone that Poppy
had given him. While his guards turned to pull him through
the door he dropped it on the floor and kicked it into the
nearest smoldering pile of bric-a-brac, and felt the only kind
of relief he was likely to feel until at some indeterminate
point in the future he escaped these people into death. At
least they weren't going to find a phone on him that would
lead them straight to Poppy. That was something, anyway.

Although the lighting was still inconstant, the hallway
seemed much more normal on the way out than it had

on the way in. A short, squat figure, a brownie with friz-zled hair and an eyepatch, was sitting with a mirrorcase open on his lap just inside the front door. He looked up at their approach. "Something's gone wrong, master," he said. "The scientific envelope has gone all pear-shaped. The defenses are still smothered, but I don't know how much longer I can . . ."

"I'm burning the place down, Squelch," said Anton Hellebore. "So forget about it. Do you want to stay and see what happens when some of the old pockets under the floors and between the walls take fire?"

The brownie paled and scrambled to his feet. One of his legs was shorter than the other and he wore a huge correc-tive boot. "By the Well, there are reserves of pure pyroman-tic vitality in there! It's going to burn like the sun!"

The young Hellebore nodded. "Until it all falls smoking into Ys." He waited as the guards opened the front door of the Remover's storehouse and peered out, then exited in swift military fashion, dragging Theo and Cumber as though they were suitcases. Theo wanted to shriek at the pain in his arms, but he was able to sink down and find a deeper part of himself, numb and distant enough that the pain could touch him but not overcome him.

A pair of huge matte-black utility coaches waited in the alley, motors vibrating silently but so deeply that Theo could feel it in his bones. They were shaped like armored person-nel carriers but were streamlined and shiny as limousines, the bubble-windows opaque blind eyes. A group of people had gathered around the coaches, mostly women and chil-dren whose faint blue skin made them look more like drowning victims than living folks, but as the guards came out the bystanders retreated back down the pier's main road and out of sight, leaving nothing behind but a few webbed handprints on the coaches' polished exteriors.

"Wretched nixies," said Hellebore. "Touching things that aren't theirs. Wait until this whole nasty neighborhood goes up in smoke and lava-blisters." Cumber and Theo were thrown onto the floor of the coach; Hellebore climbed in after them. The interior was rigged for half a dozen people to sit in comfort, with racks overhead to hold luggage—or, presumably, automatic weapons. Tansy, the brownie, and two of the guards got in with the Hellebore heir and ranged themselves in the seats. The coach's back door was open, and for an instant Theo saw the rest of the constables clambering into the other vehicle, helping one of their number who seemed to have been overcome by the growing fumes, then someone slammed the door closed.

Anton Hellebore flicked his fingers to signal the driver, invisible on the other side of one of the compartment's black front windows, and the coach started to move. The exterior windows were big enough that Theo could see a little something of what was behind them and on either side, although from his position on the floor that didn't amount to much more than gray sky and rooftops. He rolled over to check Cumber's breathing, then slowly began to push himself toward the compartment's rear door. No one seemed to be the slightest bit worried that he might somehow get the door open and escape. Theo couldn't help seeing this as a bad sign, but tried not to let it discourage him. Ignoring the pain of his bound hands, he sat up straighter and tried to reach behind his back, searching for the edge of the door. Perhaps he could pop the handle with his head and fall out when it came open. If he hooked a foot through Cumber's handcuffs, he could take the ferisher with him. Roll, get up and run. Scream. He couldn't carry Cumber, not cuffed like this, but maybe the niskies or someone else would help. *Not too goddamn likely, though, is it? Not against armed Flower guards.* Still, he kept feeling for the door. *First things first . . .*

Something bit into his wrists, hard—a thousand hot needles through the skin. He screamed.

A couple of the guards jumped, but Anton Hellebore only looked up lazily. The dead smile appeared again, no more cheering than a crease in a jellyfish. "You really shouldn't move if you can avoid it, Violet. You'll upset the annis. It's a kind of sea-sprite, no brain, all teeth and reflexes—and very amusing reflexes, they are. I bred it into a shape where it could be used as a restraint."

It felt like there was poison burning upward along the veins in Theo's arms; it took all his restraint not to try to smash the things, to scrape them off, but every time he moved the needles closed on his flesh again. He lay as still as he could until the pain began to subside.

The coach was moving slowly; at first Theo thought they must be maneuvering through some of the smaller back streets around the Remover's dockside building, but when he lifted his head high enough he could see through the windows that the streets were unusually crowded, with masses of fairy-folk on the sidewalks and in the intersections, tall and small, winged and unwinged, although an unusually large proportion were long-nosed and hairy.

Theo was not the only one to notice. When the coach rocked to a sudden stop, the young Hellebore made a hissing noise of irritation. "What is going on?"

The driver's voice filled the compartment. *"There are a lot of folk around, master. I can't go very fast."*

"What is it?" Anton Hellebore peered through the thick windows. "Goblins? It looks like lots of goblins. Troublemakers."

"Not just goblins, master."

"Drive over them if you have to."

The chauffeur did not seem in any hurry to do that, but he kept the coach moving forward. Theo heard people shouting outside and some of them thumped on the coach's fenders or doors, but he never heard anyone screaming or sounding really upset. It was strange: they all seemed to be out in the streets without really knowing why they were there—like Mardi Gras, he thought, but a little less cheerful. But as faces pressed in on the windows, trying and failing to see in through the one-way glass, Theo sensed a menacing undertone. It was hard to worry about it too much, and in fact he

was half-hoping the chauffeur would crush someone, that
the crowd would turn seriously ugly, tip the coach over and
drag Hellebore and Tansy out, and—most importantly—that
someone would notice Theo was a handcuffed prisoner before the crowd got down to tearing the rest of the vehicle's
occupants to shreds.

"Why are they all here?" said Tansy. His control over his
rebuilt face seemed to be growing worse. It wobbled and
even seemed to slip a little, although Theo guessed that
might be a trick of the light bouncing off something that was
not quite real. It was disturbing to see both Tansy's ordinary,
coldly handsome features and glimpses of a raw, tattered
something else underneath, but even if his entire face slid off
and onto the carpeted floor of the utility coach Theo knew it
wouldn't help his own cause much.

"Why did you do it?" Theo asked him suddenly. "You
didn't just betray me, you helped betray a lot of others,
too—the Daffodil folk, the Hollyhocks, all of them. Why?"

Tansy's unstable features turned pale and angry but he
wouldn't meet Theo's eye. "Shut your mouth, mortal."

"Count Tansy has a lot of debts." It was clear that Anton
Hellebore was mocking Tansy, not really talking to Theo at
all. "And very few loyalties."

The driver's voice came again. *"Um, pardon me, master,
but . . . well, I think you should see this. It's on every tributary. I'll open the mirror back there."*

What Theo had thought was only a dark window between
their compartment and the driver sparkled alight, displaying
a street scene not that different from what was outside. A
voice was speaking calmly but with a certain breathlessness.

*". . . Made the unexpected and so far inexplicable an-
nouncement an hour ago. The criminals and their leader
managed to insert the bizarre message into every mirror-
stream and tributary, disguised as an emergency bulletin
from First Councillor Thornapple. Much unrest has followed, although so far there has been no violence. Spokes-
men for the leading houses assure the public that there is no*

real danger, but all citizens are commanded to return to their homes as quickly as possible. Parliament is meeting in emergency session later today to consider an earlier curfew and perhaps even the re-imposition of military law. In a moment we will go to the reception room in the Parliament of Blooms, but first, here is that . . . announcement . . . again . . ."

The picture shifted, the crowd scene vanishing to be replaced by an extremely familiar face.

"I speak to my people, and to all good folk." Button was dressed, as always, in a nondescript robe of rough cloth, sitting cross-legged in front of a wall that Theo recognized after a moment as the piled stones of the Fayfort Bridge. *"My name is Mud Bug Button. I am a goblin. Any thinking creature who values freedom and justice is part of my tribe. Any who tries to take those precious things from others is my enemy.*

"People of Faerie, your masters are murderers. Many of you know that, although you are afraid to acknowledge it. But did you know this, also? They have failed. All their repression, all their theft, all their cruelty, and still they have failed to provide the only thing that might overshadow their crimes—a safe, secure life for all Faerie. Their time is over now. Those of you who hear me, you know I speak the truth." He nodded his head as though he had just answered a difficult question. *"To my own goblin people I have something else to say. Long we have let ourselves be mistreated, in large part because our sacred word was given in contract, those long, long centuries ago, by our venerated elders. Had they seen into the future, seen what the Flower lords would do, they would not have given those words, of course. But they did, and we have lived with their promise at terrible cost."*

Slowly, and with unhurried, ritualistic care, Button produced a dull black bundle and began to unfold it.

"What is the little skin-eater *doing?*" Anton Hellebore actually sounded frightened. "Why doesn't someone arrest him, kill him? How did he get control over the mirror-system . . . ?"

Button lifted the decorated stick and held it up to the thousands upon thousands who must have been watching him. When Primrose had first brought it out Theo had been close enough to touch it, this object that almost everyone in Faerie must now be watching. He had wondered then if such an ordinary-looking thing might be a weapon. He had wondered why it had been worth the bother.

"Here is our word," said Button. *"Here is the record, the embodiment of our ancient pledge."* His face, already sober, became even more unreadable. His eyes closed. *"Knowing full well what I do, and doing it willingly—joyfully!—I set my people free of this bargain with their oppressors."* His clawed hands held out the stick. He snapped it in half and dropped the pieces onto the stones in front of him.

"Today our ancestors are smiling." Mud Bug Button opened his yellow eyes again. *"Today you are free. Hem. Today every one of you is free, no matter who you are, no matter what you have been told. Make of that freedom what you will."*

Then he was gone, replaced once more by scenes of the city's streets filled with uneasy people, goblins and many other sorts of fairies, while commentators rushed back to fill the mirror-void with excited analysis.

"A lot of people are going to be tasting iron before this day's over," was all Anton Hellebore said, but he looked surprisingly shaken. He ordered the driver to pick up speed. They moved onto smaller streets so they could avoid the restless crowds that now seemed to be at every major intersection.

Button's strange publicity coup had lifted Theo's spirits a little but the effects were short-lived. The miserable facts remained: Button had admitted earlier that he did not have enough would-be revolutionaries at the bridge to overcome even one of the ruling houses' security forces. If he thought he could inspire others in the City to rise up and join them, then he was reckoning without the terror that just one of Hellebore's tame dragons would bring. How could anyone stand up to something like that, how could they fight it with rocks and sticks and shovels? Hundreds, even thousands would be carbonized on the spot and the uprising would be over.

Still, the streets were unquestionably filling—more with people wanting reassurance and answers than with hot-eyed revolutionaries determined to follow some strange little goblin to an honorable death, Theo felt sure, but it certainly seemed to have the ruling houses worried. The mirror-talkers were reporting anxiously about riots that had broken out in the Barrows district on the outskirts of the City and a workers' action of some kind at the Eastwater docks. Even the fire in Dowd's waterfront storehouse was interpreted as another attack on established order—not surprising because it was burning so fiercely now. The images showed the flames billowing a hundred feet high and a nixie man from the local fire department saying it was so hot his men couldn't approach it, that it was all they could do to keep it from spreading farther and that he couldn't imagine them getting it under control for days.

Aston Hellebore laughed a little at that, but in general he did not seem very happy.

His own brief moment of hope now dissipated, Theo slid back into despair. He saw Hellebore House getting larger and larger before them, jutting against the harsh gray light of the smoky sky, and felt as though he were observing something happening to someone else, an old movie or something on the television news back home, half-seen while walking from room to room. He knew that it was his own death he was approaching, but even so he could only watch the building grow larger and wonder dully how long he would have to wait until all the horror was over.

Dowd helped them kill Cat's baby. Our baby. Whatever

they want from me, they'll get it. Button and the rest will be burned into black cornflakes and blow away on the wind.

Something pushed at his thoughts like a memory trying to assert itself, but it was no memory, just a blank shove against his mind, a pinching ghost. He twitched and the annis nipped him gently, almost playfully. Fire danced again in his veins.

However unlikely the success of Button's revolution might be, Hellebore House was clearly not taking anything lightly. As they drove down the long street in front of the building—little more than a vast driveway, really—Theo could see that the concrete apron around the skyscraper was lined with vehicles like theirs and open coaches full of armed and armored men. Strange shapes like concave butterfly wings dangled from wires strung high overhead, some kind of communication array, perhaps. A grim purposefulness seemed to have hardened the faces of all the constables and other fairies they passed.

Wartime, Theo thought. *Going to the mattresses. Button would need a division of tanks to get anywhere near here.*

A spasm of unreality suddenly gripped him so hard as the vehicle stopped that Theo thought the annis had bitten him again. For a moment he was both inside his body looking at the tusk-shaped skyscraper and looking down on the utility coach from above. That dreadfully familiar, intrusive presence was back inside his head—but he wasn't dreaming now. He was all too terribly awake, and something was rubbing up against his mind, clearly enjoying the way it made his thoughts squirm.

Soon. He felt it rather than heard it, not a word but a communication—a cold, amused promise. *Soon.* Then the presence was gone and he was alone in his own head again, weak and shaking.

Tansy finished talking on his shell. "The guards are holding the third lift for us."

"I didn't need you to tell me that." Hellebore stretched out his long legs. For a fairy, he was quite ungainly. He flicked an uninterested glance at Theo, then down at sleeping Cumber Sedge. "If you want to make yourself useful, Tansy, take that thing off the ferisher. If Father wants to talk to him, he'll need to be awake first. Father doesn't like waiting."

As Tansy began to remove the gluey, clinging mask from Cumber's face, the coach slowed. Theo felt certain that if he went into Hellebore House he would never come out again, that the malign presence he had sensed was waiting there for him, that the tower standing like a stump of broken legbone would be the last place he ever saw. It would swallow him like the sea monster swallowed Jonah—but Theo did not believe that any god would deliver him up again.

He straightened. If there was ever a time to try something, one last chance . . .

But somehow either the mere thought or perhaps the minute tensing of his muscles upset the annis. It clamped its wet, needle-toothed mouth on his wrist again and dropped him screaming to the floor, muscles in spasm.

He was barely conscious when they pulled him out of the back of the van and dragged him across the lobby of Hellebore House into the elevator, aware of little except that he was lost beyond all hope.

39

STEPCHILD

The blurriness of pain began to recede as Theo stumbled out of the elevator with a helmeted guard holding his arms on either side. The long hallway came into focus as though appearing out of the fog. Anton Hellebore slowly leaned down—to Theo's dazed mind the tall fairy seemed twice normal height—and seized his face in a grip that was much more powerful than the pale, soft hands would suggest. He pulled down one of Theo's lower eyelids with a cold finger so he could examine his eyes.

"Look at that," he said cheerfully. "So many of the rootlets of blood are broken that the white of the eye turns quite pink—it's as though they tried to jump out of the sockets. What do you think, Tansy? There must be many undiscovered uses for annis venom in this exciting world of ours. Perhaps we should make that your new project."

Tansy was clutching his own face as though trying to hold broken pieces together. "Certainly, Master Hellebore," he said through clenched teeth. "If you wish." He sounded like he would have agreed to being shot out of a cannon to avoid talking.

Theo heard himself make a very strange noise—a kind of bubbling groan, very distant—and then realized that it was not him at all but Cumber Sedge waking up. Almost coma-

tose for hours, the ferisher had avoided being savaged by his
own annis-cuffs, but from the noises he was making, recov-
ering from a cauling didn't sound very nice either.

"What . . . ?" Cumber looked around blearily. His knees
buckled but he had a pair of personal constable-wardens just
like Theo's and they kept him from falling.

"We're in Hellebore House," Theo said. "Don't move or
the thing around your wrists will bite you. And *don't say
anything.*" It was ultimately pointless, but at least their captors wouldn't get anything blurted out by accident. *Make
them work for it,* he told himself, but that made him consider
what kind of work that might be and his legs went rubbery.
*The hell with it—who am I kidding? I'll tell them anything
they want to know. Nobody stands up to torture forever, so
it's just a question of when you wave the white flag.*

The simple, unmarked door at the end of the hall looked
like nothing so much as the entrance to a janitor's closet—
the type of place people got dragged into for this kind of
thing because there were buckets and tools and concrete
floors with drains. "Look," Theo said suddenly. "I'll tell you
whatever you want to know. Tell your daddy that, Hellebore.
Just let the ferisher and the little sprite go. You don't need
them—you're only after them because of me."

Anton Hellebore flicked him a look of contempt. "My . . .
daddy . . . may not want to talk to you. He may just want to
cut pieces off you because you did something that annoyed
him—your friends too, for all I know. If you think you can
bargain you're as stupid as your uncle, or whatever that Remover creature really was. Your side lost. You are an orphan.
You have no power and you make no deals."

As if to silently illustrate power and access, the door at
the end of the hall swung open. Theo's guards let go of his
wrists and one of them put a boot in his rump and shoved
him through.

His hands annis-wrapped, Theo could not keep his balance; he stumbled and fell, then struggled up onto his knees.
At first it was dark except for a circle of light that touched

the wide desk but illuminated only the single flower at its center. The light grew brighter as a man stood up behind the desk. In person, he was quite strikingly beautiful—a god of the underworld. It was easy to see where Anton Hellebore got his height, but there was none of the son's sullen immaturity in the father's pale face. For a long moment the endlessly black eyes regarded him in silence.

Pleased to meet you, Theo could not help thinking, the old Stones song ringing in his mind. *Hope you guessed my name.* A moment later he wondered, *Is this the one who's been in my head?* He seemed powerful enough, and more than cruel enough, but for some reason Theo didn't think it was so. Out loud, and with his voice only shaking a little, he said, "And you must be Satan, Lord of Darkness."

Nidrus Hellebore actually smiled a little. "And you must be the last of the Violets. What a tiresome family. Like birds—musical, flighty, shrill. But the nest has long since fallen from the tree and nearly all the eggs are shattered." He shook his head, dismissing the tiresome business of the destruction of an entire clan. "The rest of you out there may also come into the office. Do not waste any more of my time than is necessary."

His son and Tansy entered, along with the four constables, two of whom were still propping up Cumber. Nidrus Hellebore raised an eyebrow. "Guards, you are dismissed."

"Are you sure, Lord Hellebore . . . ?" Tansy began and then abruptly fell silent. The constables showed an open-palm salute before marching out.

"They're both bound, Father," said Anton Hellebore with a touch of pride. "Helpless. Something new of mine . . ."

Lord Hellebore came out from behind the desk and moved behind Theo. It was hard to keep still, stinging annis or no stinging annis—just the proximity of the fairy lord brought a deep chill of unease, like knowing Dracula was examining the back of your neck. "I don't think we'll need these anymore," Hellebore said. Something flicked Theo's wrists. A moment later the pressure of the annis cuffs was gone and his wrists were prickling with returning circulation.

"But Father . . . !"

"Don't be petulant, Antoninus. Do you really think that a physical restraint around their arms is better than what I can do?" All of a sudden Lord Hellebore was in front of Theo again. His hand came up so quickly that Theo did not even begin to flinch until after Hellebore's finger had tapped his forehead. He seemed to have put some kind of freezing dot on Theo's skin, something so cold it burned, but before even a second had passed it became less intense and yet somehow wider, spreading across his skin and into the muscles, tangling itself around Theo's spine like a climbing thorn. "You will go wherever I tell you to go," Hellebore said. "You will do whatever I tell you to do. For now, you will stand and listen and speak only when I ask you a question."

"Die, you corpse-faced bastard," was what Theo wanted to say, but as in those nightmares where he tried desperately to scream but couldn't, only a tiny whistle of air escaped his mouth. As he struggled against silence, Hellebore moved in front of Cumber. The ferisher's eyes were wide with terror.

"What does this one know?" he asked.

"Perhaps nothing, Lord Hellebore," said Tansy. "We brought them straight to you."

"I brought them," Anton proclaimed. "I was in charge."

"Yes, and you made some other decisions as well," said his father. "Not very good ones, in fact." He touched Cumber's forehead and repeated the words he had said to Theo, then made a broader gesture. Lights began to gleam against the dark walls, or perhaps even within the walls themselves; Theo could suddenly see that the space was quite large, that the desk was in one corner of an octagonal room some forty yards across.

The walls were windows—a complete circle of windows providing a spectacular penthouse view of the City spreading away on all sides, a view that made Hellebore House appear to be what it had now become in fact, the hub of Faerie.

Staring at the three-hundred-and-sixty-degree cityscape, Theo found that he still had a little freedom of movement, could move his head and arms, even shuffle his feet a bit. He tried to take a small, inconspicuous step backward and discovered that he didn't have *that* much freedom: he was held to the spot where he stood as though magnetized.

Hellebore gazed at a patch of light across town that blazed like a highway flare. "I see a fire in the warehouse district, Antoninus. Why is there a fire?"

"The Remover's place was f-full of traps." The younger Hellebore was suddenly fighting a stammer. "I . . . w-we couldn't . . . I had to . . ."

Hellebore's voice was ice. "We will talk about it later. I am not pleased. Just now, however, we have more important things to do." He looked up at nothing at all for a silent moment. "Ah. The others have arrived and are on their way up." He turned his queerly uninterested stare on Theo. "You are struggling to say something. You may speak. Use the chance wisely."

Theo swallowed the insults he wanted to spit at him. "You've got a friend of mine. In a jar. May I see her?"

Hellebore considered for a moment, then nodded his head at Tansy, who ran to Hellebore's massive desk and lifted out the bell-shaped jar from the place it had been hidden. "You may walk to the desk and have your reunion."

Theo dimly heard Anton Hellebore protesting, heard his father's low, amused voice replying, but he did not care about any of it. He moved toward the desk, feeling altogether normal except when he tried to step more than a little bit out of the way, at which point a kind of numb cramp set in until he turned his foot back in the right direction again.

He stopped in front of the desk, more or less of his own volition. She was standing with her tiny hands pressed against the inside of the bell jar. "Oh, Theo, I am sorry," she said. He could barely hear her.

Tears filled his eyes. "It's my fault, not yours."

She said something else he could not make out.

"What?"

"You may open the jar," Hellebore told him.

"Father, do you think that's wise?"

"Open the jar."

Theo only wished he had done it sooner, so that it felt like his own idea, his own gesture. His hands moved toward the heavy glass vessel and lifted it away from the base. Applecore took a moment to fan her wings and then sprang into the air to hover in front of him. She was crying too, and that upset him more than had any of the pain inflicted on him. "I'm sorry I dragged you into this shite, Theo, really I am."

"What are you talking about? None of this was your fault."

"I was the one who brought you out of your world in the first place." She was pale and bony-thin and had bruised-looking blue circles under her eyes.

"It's good to see you, Applecore," he said quietly. "It really is. I thought . . . Cumber and I thought you were dead."

She darted a pitying look over at Cumber Sedge, then stiffened when she saw who stood beside him. "Tansy," she said slowly. "What in the name of the bloody Trees are you doing here, you traitor? I heard Hellebore talking about you—you sold us all out, you lyin', murderin' . . . !"

Before Theo or anyone else could move she had darted across the room and was buzzing around Quillius Tansy like a maddened hornet. He swatted at her. "Stop her! My face, she's going to . . . Somebody kill her!"

Hellebore spoke in a deep, untroubled voice. "Walk to the window."

Theo wondered who the fairy lord was talking to, and understood only when his own legs began to carry him toward the nearest panel of the City panorama. He tried to fight, but could not—it was as though Hellebore had reached directly into his spine and was manipulating his nerves like the strings of a marionette. The view of the City shimmered and distorted, stretching, bending, then began to dissolve like some ultraslow view of a soap bubble popping. There was another window behind it with an identical City-view spreading below. *Hellebore must have mirror-screens in front of the windows, so he can look at things beside the view,* Theo thought absently. *He's got spiders, dragons, all the modern conveniences . . .* Then the outer window began to open, sliding up like a rising eyelid, and Theo could feel cold air slapping at his face.

"Stop!" Applecore shouted. "All right, Hellebore, I'm off Tansy—just make him stop!"

Theo took three more steps before halting at the frame of the open window. Each time he swayed in the wind he could feel how easy it would be to tilt too far forward and simply tumble into space, go spinning down through the air to the ground many hundred feet below. A few small drops of rain patted against his cheeks and forehead. If Hellebore misjudged how long and how steadily he could stand on his tired, tired legs, there was nowhere to go but down . . .

"Sprite, I allowed you out of the jar because now that we have the last of the Violets in our custody you no longer matter," said Lord Hellebore. "But when you attack one of my employees you become an annoyance. Rather than waste our time and impair our dignity chasing you, I instead remind you who wields the power."

Applecore was still hovering above Tansy, just out of his reach. "But you wouldn't go through all that trouble to get him and then chuck him out a window, now would you?" Her defiance was not entirely convincing.

"There is some truth to that," Hellebore said. "But I could have him pull out one of his own eyes without impairing his usefulness at all. I'd prefer not to have a mess like that in my office, however, so if you irritate me I will simply throw the ferisher out a window instead. Now I am through talking to you."

Applecore looked back at him hard—as hard as a person her size could look at the master of all Faerie, anyway—then zipped across the room and landed on Theo's shoulder. "Get away from there now, Theo," she said. "Please."

"You may step back from the window," said Hellebore, and Theo suddenly found that he could. He took a few steps backward, then his knees finally gave out and he half-sank, half-fell to the floor, clutching the carpet as though at any moment the room might turn sideways and send him tumbling back toward that open window, that leap into nothing.

"Lord Foxglove and Lord Thornapple are in the outer office," announced a crisply inhuman voice.

"They are late. Send them in." Hellebore turned to his sulking son. "For the time being, I think we should find some secure accommodation for Master Violet, or whatever he is to be called."

"Yes, Father." The younger Hellebore seemed to perk up a little.

"But not in the laboratories. Do you understand me? He is not to be experimented upon. I have far more important uses for him."

The outer door opened and two well-dressed fairy men walked in, both lean, both in that indeterminate middle age that, as far as Theo could tell, indicated they had reached at least a few centuries of age. One had reddish-gold hair, straight and hanging to his collar in a way that in any other city would seem intentionally foppish. He wore a huge medallion on the chest of his tailored suit and had a certain watchfulness in his manner that Theo guessed might be the fairy equivalent of nerves. The other, his unnaturally black hair so dark as to seem dyed, but still no blacker than his spidersilk suit, and with bushy white eyebrows in weird contrast, was clearly Poppy's father. Theo did not have much attention left for anything but minute-to-minute survival, but it was still very disturbing to see the face of the woman he had come to care for so much reinterpreted in her father's stony mask.

Thornapple looked Theo over with some interest. "So this is the Violet heir. He does not look like much."

Your daughter likes me a lot more than she likes you, buddy, was what Theo wanted to say, but of course he didn't.

"Your pardon, Nidrus," said the golden-haired one, Lord Foxglove. "We were delayed. The streets are full of troublemakers."

"I know." Hellebore waved a white hand in casual dismissal. "We will find the little goblin soon, I think. A depressing public execution is the best example for the shirkers and ne'er-do-wells blocking our thoroughfares."

Thornapple gave him a curious look. "Have you not heard? It is more than the unemployed and the usual rabble-rousers. The goblins are rioting, Hellebore, rioting! They have set fires all through the Sunlight district and come flooding out of Goblintown. At this moment there are thousands of them surrounding New Mound House and threatening to burn down the Parliament! At least twenty constables have been killed already. By the Grove, have you been ignoring your calls all day?"

Hellebore for the first time seemed surprised. "Because of a broken stick? Are you telling me that the only thing that has kept the goblins orderly was some ancient treaty?" He turned and flicked his fingers at the windows. The cityscape shimmered and vanished as the mirrors came on, the elevated view replaced by street-level perspectives of angry crowds fighting with armored constables. Theo guessed that an ornate, multistory building behind the scene of conflict, a little like a white, gray, and gold wedding cake, must be the place they called New Mound House, the parliamentary building. He was surprised and pleased to see that it was not only goblins who seemed to be fighting against the authorities—many types of fairies were there, including some that, except for their wings, looked not much different from Hellebore and his peers. They had thrown together barricades across the streets and built fires in trash cans. Rocks and other objects were banging off the constables' shields, but for the moment it seemed a bit of a standoff.

"It won't do them or us any good," Applecore whispered

in Theo's ear. "The Flowers are too strong. But it's grand to see, isn't it?"

"Oberon's Blood." Hellebore stared at the scene, his mouth twisted as though he had eaten something very sour. "Set fires in our City, will they? Then I will see Goblintown burned to its foundations and the ground seeded with salt. A whole goblin generation will . . . will . . ." His eyes narrowed. "What . . . is . . . *that?*"

A disturbance was eddying through the crowd of goblins and their allies, a surge as though the mob were some unicellular animal about to divide itself and reproduce. A gap formed and people threw themselves out of the way, barely avoiding the mounted riders who crashed out onto the street of the paved no-man's land in front of the startled police. Theo bit back a shout of surprise. He had seen these riders before, and also their single-horned mounts.

"Grims!" snarled Foxglove. "Where in the name of the Elder Trees did they come from?"

They were weirdly stirring in their bright furs and feathers, something not just out of an earlier, wilder era of Faerie but out of a dream, a full-blown nightmare. Spears and spiral horns flashed and bell mouthed rifles gouted fire as the howling troop surged forward. Theo thought that with their gleaming yellow eyes and painted faces stranger than any mask, the wild goblins looked altogether uncontrollable, like all of Hallowe'en lifted up and flung forward by a hurricane wind. The constables who stood in their way with riot shields locked together did their best to stand up to the hundreds of spear-wielding riders and razor-hooved unicorns, but the grims had the advantage of momentum; within moments they had crashed through the police line, scattering the constables, spearing dozens and crushing as many more under their mounts' kicking, silver-hooved feet. Heartened by the charge, the mob surged forward with a rising, rumbling shout of gleeful bloodlust that even through the mirror-stream lifted the hairs on Theo's neck, and fairy and goblin alike threw themselves on the reeling Parliamentary Guards.

"Where did the grims come from?" Foxglove demanded again. "How could all those cursed hill-country vermin have got into the City?"

Thornapple had one hand on his ear as though he were listening to a headphone, although of course there was no headphone. "It is not just Strawflower Square," he said. "I have reports that they are all over the City. Larkspur's secretary says that they have surrounded his family tower in Longshadow, that wild goblins have destroyed the guardhouse and set the grounds on fire."

"It can't be!" said Foxglove.

Hellebore did not waste his time protesting the obvious. He walked to his desk and touched the side of it. "I want to speak to Snakeroot at the caves," he said. "Tell him this is a Class Four alert. I need all the available animals."

"Black iron," said Thornapple, surprised, "are you really going to use them again?"

"Yes," said Hellebore. "Would you like me to send them to Thornapple House, too? No? Then be silent."

Theo barely listened, staring at the screen with a muted joy. It would be no help to him or his friends, he knew, but it was good to see somebody striking back at Hellebore and his crew, to see them alarmed and forced to scramble. It was Button's work, it had to be. Somehow he had managed to smuggle wild grims into the city . . . wild grims and their unicorns, too . . .

"Oh, my God," he said quietly. "It was us!"

"What?" Applecore leaned in close.

"Nothing. I'll tell you later . . . if there is a later." He didn't want to miss any of what was going on, but he felt sure that, with the help of Streedy Nettle's strange gift, the entrance permit to the City he and Sedge had obtained for one individual and one livestock animal had become multiplied. *My God! Button must have had them coming into the City through every single checkpoint, a dozen here, a dozen there . . .* He felt a quiet glow of pride that he had helped throw this particular monkey wrench into Hellebore's smooth-running machinery.

Indeed, it was turning out to be a fairly good-sized wrench. It was now almost impossible to make complete sense of what was happening on the ring of mirror-screens: several small blazes had sprung up around the edges of New Mound House, a few even on the roof. Theo had no idea how anyone had managed to get fire up there until he saw one of the wild goblins lean back in his saddle and put a flaming arrow through one of the parliament building's up-stairs windows. The protectors and the mounted grims seemed to have control of the field with all the parliamen-tary constables killed, lying wounded, or in retreat. The grims were forming up to ride again, leaving the protectors in a spasm of joyful destruction, uprooting benches and starting to smash in the front doors of New Mound House. A cascade of golden bugs sluiced out of the broken door-frame and skittered away across the steps, following each other in blind compulsion right into a pile of flaming trash. Pale, anxious faces peered down from the upstairs windows. Theo thought he should feel sorry for them—many of them were probably nothing but functionaries, trapped now be-tween fires and an angry mob—but at the moment he had problems of his own.

A word, a horrifying word, yanked his attention back to his captors.

"But if you bring in the dragons," said Thornapple, "the destruction may keep us pinned here for days."

Theo flinched as though he had been punched in the stomach. That big black snake squirming across the sky . . .

"We cannot wait that long, Nidrus, you know that," Thornapple continued. "You said yourself there is only a brief time when the invocation will work. Let Monkshood and his constables handle this. Revenge must wait, I insist."

Hellebore looked at the First Councillor of Faerie with a face so hard and expressionless that Theo saw for the first time how too much rationality could be a form of madness.

"I do not think you can insist, Aulus. You are right that the destruction will interfere with our plans, but that does not mean we will refrain from teaching these skin-eaters a lesson. It merely means we must move up our schedule." He touched his desk again. "Ready three battle-coaches. We are leaving now." He smiled at his co-conspirator, who did not smile back. It was one of the creepiest things Theo had ever seen. If he were Thornapple, Theo thought, he'd be planning to find himself another world to live in as soon as possible, because there was clearly only going to be one big dog in this particular kennel before much longer. "We will proceed to the Cathedral. In fact, if we are lucky, we will not only accomplish our main task, but also pass one or two very fine vantage points along the way where we can pause to watch the punishment being administered to that ungrateful rabble."

A moment later half a dozen armed constables and a pair of ogre guards entered, their appearance so sudden that even Thornapple and Foxglove were visibly startled. Hellebore was still issuing orders to the air.

"And prepare the child. Yes, now. We will be there in moments." He turned and walked toward the door. All the others, even the Flower lords, fell in behind him without protest.

Two constables dragged Cumber toward the door. Two more moved to take Theo's arms, but there was no need: he was already following Lord Hellebore like a dog on an invisible leash. One of the constables swatted half-heartedly at Applecore where she sat on Theo's shoulder, but she pulled herself into the tangle of his hair at the side of his neck. Theo wanted to say something brave and reassuring to her but he couldn't. Even though it appeared they were actually going to leave Hellebore House, something he hadn't believed would happen, it was all still too hopeless. Nidrus Hellebore's spell of control lay on top of him like a lead blanket—something he could carry as he walked, but just barely.

*   *   *

Theo quickly lost track of the twists and turns of the hallways, the doors that appeared from nowhere in empty halls, but although the air had grown notably warmer they had been walking for only a few minutes when a figure in a white cloak appeared in the hallway before them. For a fairy, he was displaying a great deal of emotion, most of it nervousness. "My lord! I did not expect . . . That is, I thought we had until tomorrow at least—the portents were all taken for tomorrow, the scrying, the oneiromantic metering . . ."

Hellebore barely looked at him. "Is he ready?"

"In a moment. He is being dressed to go outside. He was just finishing his meal—we were caught by surprise . . ."

"Then that is all I need from you, weft-Iris. You may return to your other work."

The fairy in white still seemed agitated. "But . . . but my lord, if it is to be today, do you not wish me to accompany you? To accompany the child, that is? There is so much about him . . . that is, I have worked so long and hard . . ."

"If we succeed you will be rewarded. Go now."

Weft-Iris stared for a moment, then ran his hands through his hair, bowed, and stepped away through a door. Nidrus Hellebore stood waiting, patient as a statue, but Foxglove and Thornapple looked a little uncomfortable. Cumber Sedge gave out a quiet whimper of pain and despair.

Theo felt something hovering over his thoughts like a storm cloud, moving nearer each moment. Every cell of his body seemed to contract in fear. Only the guards' firm grip on his arms kept him from dropping bonelessly to the floor. *It's coming.* It was very close now. He felt sick, hopeless. *The thing that's been waiting for me. The thing in my dreams . . .*

The door opened and two fairy women led out a surprisingly small figure in a thick hooded cloak and equally heavy pants and shoes—something that looked for all the world like a child setting out on the fairyland equivalent of an arctic trek. The women's skin gleamed with moisture; their movements were sluggish and their eyes heavy, as though they had been drugged, but as they adjusted the cloak and hood they still seemed to go out of their way to avoid touching the little figure. Theo knew just how they felt—at this moment he wanted nothing more than to put distance between himself and this small, silent thing.

"Is there anything else he needs?" Hellebore asked, betraying impatience. "It is time."

The hood fell back, revealing a pink, childish face and curly brown hair. Despite the enormity of his fear Theo's attention snagged for a moment on a detail, a little spot of blood on the boy's lower lip and the tiny arm and wingtip that protruded from his mouth. The child sucked it in, chewed, swallowed, and then smiled a dreadful, satisfied smile.

"I am ready, Stepfather." The brown eyes turned from Hellebore to Theo. "And here you are at last, my . . . half brother. We meet face to face."

For a dizzying, nauseating moment Theo felt certain the child-creature was in his head again, that he was seeing through two sets of eyes simultaneously, both the child looking at Theo and Theo looking at the child, like two mirrors facing each other. Then he realized he was seeing his own features, his family's features, in the face of this little monstrosity as if it were all the punchline of some dreadful joke. It was like staring at one of his own elementary school pictures on a hit of bad acid, the obscenity of his own nose—his mother's thin nose—with what was still a childish upturn, his father's stolid jaw gleaming beneath the oiled pink skin. But the eyes . . . except for the color, they were nothing to do with his family, or with anything human. They were as dead as something in a mortuary jar.

"Oh, save the Elder Trees . . ." Applecore said in a shocked whisper.

The last piece of Dowd's story suddenly fell into place. *He's the changeling. No, I'm the changeling—he's my parents' . . . he's the real child, the lost child . . .* Theo suddenly jackknifed at the waist and threw up what little there was in his stomach.

"Not such a happy reunion, I fear," said the boy. "I hoped for more, since we shared so many interesting dreams. We are almost twins, after all."

Hellebore made a noise of disgust. "Clean that up," he told the two dazed women. "We are taking the boy with us now." He looked at the Terrible Child for a moment. "Shared dreams?" He barked an angry laugh. "It seems you two have a deeper bond than I have been told."

"I am often bored, Stepfather. It was a small private pleasure."

Hellebore shook his head. "I do not like surprises. This . . . connection makes for uncertainty at a time we cannot afford any."

"He is weak, Stepfather, and I grow stronger by the hour."

"Still." He frowned. "The Remover might have been able to answer some questions about the exact nature of the relationship, but thanks to my eldest son, we have lost that resource."

"But Father!" Anton Hellebore protested, "I did it for you! I did it because . . ."

"Close your mouth—I am tired of your whining. Everyone into the coaches. We have urgent business. Tansy, you will travel with me and our long-lost Violet . . . and the child, of course. I have questions about what happened at the Remover's house on the waterfront."

"*I* can tell you everything you need to know, Father," protested Anton, but was ignored.

"Things have changed, apparently," said the child. "We are leaving early."

"There is resistance." Hellebore turned to the others. "Come, we are wasting time. I am about to make an example of some malcontents."

The group began to move rapidly down the corridor. Theo, still staggering, had to be all but carried by his guards.

The little obscenity reached up and wrapped his hot, wet hand around Theo's, who was too weak to pull free of the surprisingly firm grip.

"I have finally met my true brother." The Terrible Child again showed his perfect teeth, which only made the spot of blood on his mouth harder to ignore. "It is too bad we will be separated again so soon."

40

STRAWFLOWER SQUARE

E ven after all the oddities he had seen in Faerie, the creatures standing at attention outside the three huge battle-
coaches in the garage caught Theo by surprise: with long,
gleaming snouts and bulbous, insectoid eyes they looked
like Hollywood extraterrestrials. They were doonie drivers,
he realized, dressed in some kind of battle-rig, with helmets
over their long equine heads. The vehicles themselves were
even bulkier than the utility coaches that had brought them
into Hellebore House, with heavy leaf-textured armor
around the sides and front and rear bumpers, but with tops
that seemed to be a single dome of black glass.

His guardian constables thrust him into a seat in the middle coach, shoving him so hard that he feared for Applecore,
who was still clinging to his neck. Lord Hellebore and Tansy
and a pair of ogre bodyguards climbed in after them, the
ogres even bulkier than was usual with their massive kind
because they were wearing some kind of flak jackets. The
Terrible Child entered last.

"You will stay where you are until I tell you otherwise,"
Hellebore instructed Theo, who found that to be quite true:
he could move his head, even adjust his position in small
ways, but he sure as hell wasn't going to be getting up and
going anywhere.

At first he couldn't make out anything through the dome that surrounded them except the dim, marsh-gas glow of the lights in the garage ceiling, but as they came up the ramp and out into the filtered sunlight he could see all around with complete clarity, as though they rode in an open-top car and nothing stood between him and the world except a pair of polarized sunglasses. Nothing seemed unusual inside the compound as the lines of Hellebore guards moved quickly and efficiently to the side of the road to let them pass, but when they rode out between the blocky gatehouses Theo could see how things had changed even just during the time they had been indoors. The streets of the Moonlight district were crowded too, now, and the mixture of goblins and other fairy-folk from the lower end of the social ladder looked angry.

Although a little surprised by the appearance of the Hellebore coaches, some of the mob scrambled out into the road to block the way. The battle-coaches simply drove on; Theo saw at least one goat-horned fairy fall and disappear beneath the wheels of the front vehicle. Rather than frightening off the rest of the throng, it made them angry, and brought many more of them surging out from the sidewalks. The lead battle-coach struck a half-dozen more people before it had to stop. The rioters began to press in tightly on all sides, surrounding Theo's coach as well. Faces flattened against the dome, an array as bizarre as a Bosch painting. Fists thumped on the doors. A few bolder members of the crowd were climbing onto the hood.

"There are too many, my lord," the driver announced from the front compartment.

"Drive over them," said Hellebore.

"There are too many," another voice said, stubborn despite obvious fear at contradicting his master. *"This is Coach One. We already have bodies jammed in the wheel wells. A few more and it will slow us down so much we will be undergoing unacceptable risk—they're dragging paving stones out down the street to block the way. We can*

survive a few firebombs, my lord, but if we're stuck in one place, eventually the heat-dispersal charms will lose their effectiveness . . ."

"Use the guns."

"But there are hundreds of bystanders trapped in this street, not just the ones blocking our way . . ."

"Use the guns or I will have you thrown to the mob." Hellebore sat back in his seat. "Now, Tansy, tell me what happened at the Remover's. I have not had time to review the transcripts very thoroughly."

A loud noise like a bandsaw penetrated the bubble of Theo's vehicle as something sprayed from the sides and front of the lead car, turning the closest rioters into little more than a mist of red, knocking down scores of others for what seemed like hundred of yards in each direction. People were fighting to get away now, sliding off the hood of Theo's coach, knocking over the slower wounded in their hurry to escape and stepping on those who had fallen, dozens of fleeing fairies skidding and stumbling on the blood-spattered road. The lead car lurched forward but there were still too many upright bodies in the way and the industrial whine rose again. Something ticked onto the hood of Theo's coach, rolled halfway up the window, then slid down again. It was not just a bullet, he saw in a brief glimpse, but more like a tiny, rigid lamprey, its toothy, circular jaw irising open and closed even as it fell away into the road. Theo's stomach convulsed and hot bile rose into his throat, but he had nothing left in his stomach to vomit. Within moments the convoy was bumping along once more, driving over still-twitching bodies while the crowd ran screaming in front of them. People on the roofs or in upper windows flung down stones that thumped on the coach's hardened dome like a drunk percussionist.

Theo could actually feel the pleasure emanating from the small figure beside him at all this destructive upheaval, waves of glee pushing against his thoughts like buffeting winds.

Hellebore seemed hardly to notice any of it, but Tansy was clearly finding it difficult to talk. The Daisy-lord still had the look of a porcelain doll whose face had been repaired with faulty glue, and it seemed to be giving him pain. His stare flicked from side to side, drawn to the carnage all around. "My lord, please, I . . . I thought your son acted with your express orders . . ."

"He did, up to a point. It is the point where he diverged that I wish to ascertain."

"We . . . we listened with the spider for a while. The Remover said . . . he said . . ." Tansy's voice dropped into a conspiratorial whisper and Theo could no longer hear what he was saying.

Here, Theo. The pull was as strong as Hellebore's spell of command but more subtle, like the compulsion to stare at a terrible accident. *Look here.* Theo turned toward the child.

"Do you know what they call me?" the boy asked out loud. He had pulled his thick cloak around him as though the car were a sled racing across the Russian steppes, only his small round face and the tips of his stubby fingers visible. The eyes held Theo's gaze; his helplessness terrified him. "They call me the Terrible Child. It's a title, really, not a name. Because of course I have a name, even though no one uses it. You know what it is, don't you?"

Theo tried to answer but a nightmare weight was pressing on his chest and he could not breathe deeply enough.

"It's Theo Vilmos." The child laughed, showing the tip of his tongue between his small, shiny teeth. "My name is Theodore Patrick Vilmos. You were given my name and my parents, but they were never truly yours. You are just another Violet child, the last and least of a dead family. You know, I see my parents sometimes in your dreams—Anna and Peter. I make them rise up from your memories just so I can see what they looked like, so I can laugh as I watch you struggling to apologize to them even while you hate them for your own shortcomings."

Sickened to hear their names out of that mouth, Theo finally found the air to make his voice work. "They . . . weren't . . . your parents. You might have been their child to begin with, but . . . but you're not anybody's anything now. You're . . . a freak. A messed-up, inhuman freak."

The boy nodded, not at all displeased. "I am the only one like me, that is true. There are worse things to be, of course—average, or less than average. A failure. A nonentity. Speaking of which, did you know I was with you in Daffodil House as you stumbled around in the smoke and dust? I was watching it all through your eyes, drinking your thoughts. Oh, the poor little fairy-folk! Oh, the destruction! How sad! I drank your fear, too. It was a very pleasant experience, actually, so at least you're good for something."

Theo tried to strike at the child, but could not lift his hand more than a few inches off his lap. Struggling hopelessly, he let out a little moan of frustration and despair.

The boy smiled. "Even now, you are only still alive because of what other people did years ago, not because of anything you have done yourself." He paused for a moment and sniffed. "That sprite is still with you, isn't she, hiding somewhere? I can smell her." He smacked his lips and opened his eyes wide in a grotesque parody of juvenile pleasure. "Yum! It's too bad I've already eaten quite a lot for my afternoon meal—she would be very sweet, I think. And crunchy."

Disgust overcame Theo's exhaustion and horror, even gave him a little strength. "You're proud of not being human, aren't you? You enjoyed it when they killed our child—the baby that Cat was carrying. Eamonn Dowd might have been a bastard, might even have helped, but he didn't enjoy it like you did. Yeah, I can feel it—this thought-drinking thing doesn't just go one way. Jesus Christ, and you think being like you is better than being me?" Theo took a shuddering breath. It was difficult to speak, but he couldn't just let the thing smirk at him.

"I am what I am." The smile flashed like cold bone. "I have lived a thousand lives in my short time, seen a million indescribable things while you have trudged through a single meaningless life and muddled even that. Your pointless span will end today, but mine will go on. I have been in preparation for this since the first hour I was brought into Faerie. One day I will shake the very secrets of the universe down like fruit from a tree."

That it was his parents' faces combined here in this soulless thing, more than it being a younger version of his own face, more than any words it spoke, finally brought tears to Theo's eyes. He had not done any better a job of loving his mother and father than they had him, but there had been some love there, however muted and confused. This abomination made it all a mockery. He summoned up a little more strength. "I'll destroy you."

"Don't talk to it, Theo—oh, by the Trees, don't talk to it," Applecore whispered in his ear. "It'll only poison you."

He grunted, too tired to talk more in any case.

The child laughed and turned back to the window. *Destroy me? I think not.* The stream of alien thought pushed its way into Theo's mind, a cold and painful intruder against which he was helpless. *You are not really Septimus Violet, and you are certainly not Theo Vilmos. In fact, you are nothing.*

They had reached the top of a hill at the edge of the Moonlight district, the street crowds long gone behind them, when Hellebore directed the convoy to stop and the three coaches pulled up onto the grass of a small, manicured park. The City lay below them, threads of smoke rising in many places now, especially down by the waterfront where, true to Anton Hellebore's prediction, the Remover's warehouse seemed still to be burning like the heart of the sun. Another large blaze raged in the center of town near the ivory spike of Hellebore House.

"Why have we stopped, lord?" asked Tansy. "Are we under attack?"

"They are on their way," Hellebore said, although it didn't seem to explain anything. He raised his voice, perhaps talking to the invisible driver of the coach. "Give me my birds. I wish a closer look at Strawflower Square."

The two ogre guards got out—the massive coach rocked as their weight was removed—and made a quick check around the vicinity. Satisfied that the park did not contain an ambush, they stood in the muted sun, stretching their long, slab-muscled gray arms and whispering quietly to each other. The bubble dome of the coach flickered just as the windows of Hellebore's penthouse office had, and suddenly the natural cityscape was gone across one side, replaced by a bizarre street-level view of the riot zone around the Parliament, as though the coach in which Theo sat had suddenly dived down into the City center like a submarine.

"The constables have been reinforced, but I see there is still resistance," said Hellebore. "Too much resistance. I think that when this has ended, Lord Monkshood will no longer hold domain over the constables—this has been a debacle. Well, I will do what his men cannot."

Theo was too distracted by what he was seeing in the actual sky above them to pay much attention to the scenes of constables and mounted grims fighting across the rubble of Strawflower Square's fountains and benches and public walkways. Coming down through the clouds like kites on a single string were three vast serpentine shapes. It was so much like that awful day in Daffodil House that for a moment he found himself plunged into a disassociated near-faint, suspended in a loop of unreality where dragons were always coming down the sky toward him like living missiles.

The huge beasts dropped so fast that it seemed as though they must crash down on the hillside where Theo's coach stood, must smash and destroy the caravan and everything in it, Hellebore and Theo and Applecore and the monstrous, pink-faced child. He found himself half-praying for it as the huge, dark bodies plummeted toward them. Then, just a few hundred feet overhead, three mighty pairs of batlike wings flared out and the dragons' descent suddenly flattened. They swooped over the park, only a couple of hundred feet off the ground, with a crack of air that knocked the ogre bodyguards to their knees, ripped branches from the bending trees and made the coaches rock crazily on their suspensions. Theo could see that the nearest dragon had a rider, a small, humanoid shape crouched in a boxy glass case strapped around the massive neck just in front of the wings. The stink of the monsters, sulfur and a rank, sour odor like the alligator pool at the San Francisco Aquarium on a hot day, lingered in Theo's nostrils even after the dragons themselves were only dwindling shapes against the City skyline.

As horrible as the creatures' passage had been, he still found himself turning with a kind of miserable avidity to the coach window that displayed Strawflower Square, not so much wanting to see what would happen next as unable to avoid looking. There was a feeling of supreme aliveness in witnessing such horror, he knew that now: it sang in the blood. To watch death, no matter how terrible, was to be alive oneself, at least for a few moments longer.

The dragons entered the mirror-picture of the square first as long shadows that whipped across the crowd so quickly that many of the combatants didn't even look up—but terror filled the faces of all who did see them, even the parliamentary constables. Only the grims kept their faces set hard and cold, as if a long-anticipated moment had finally come, although they threw themselves from their unicorns and scrambled for shelter like the rest of the shrieking multitude. The dragons rushed past like stunting jet planes, wrenching tornados of dirt and trash up in their wake, even pieces of clothing ripped from rioters' backs. For a suspended moment all sign of the monsters disappeared from the scene Theo was watching, so that the thousands of people fleeing randomly in all directions seemed conceived of a kind of mass-psychosis, but then the shadows fell across the square once more, followed immediately by the fire.

The first great gout swept across the broad steps in front of New Mound House like a broom of orange flame—a broom that did not merely tumble away that which was in front of it but burned it to black carbon. The flames were so hot that the sudden blooms of ash seemed to hold the shapes of the fleeing victims for an instant before bursting into whirling, sparking fragments.

Applecore was weeping loudly beside Theo's ear, but he had no more tears. He could only watch, limp and numb— the second time he had been forced to witness a horror no one should ever have to see once.

The viewpoint of the mirror-screen was shifting now, moving rapidly away from the destruction and refocusing elsewhere in the square. Jarred by the unsteady movement, Theo found a moment's refuge in wondering what kind of birds these were, magical or mechanical, that acted as Hellebore's eyes at the scene.

The dragons made another pass, sweeping the square with flame, killing all that could not escape, rioters and riot-fighters, civilians and constables. A maddened unicorn ran past the fountain, its mane trailing fire. But Theo saw something else happening, too, something so strange that even Hellebore sat up in his leather seat.

"Blood and iron," growled the fairy lord, "what are they doing?"

The grims, alone of all the living things in Strawflower Square, were not running for their lives—or at least they had not run very far. Knots of them had taken up places where they were shielded from the worst of the inferno by build-ings or statuary, and now were working with a swift econ-omy of movement, unpacking long poles that had hung beside their saddles, bending these staves and stringing them.

"Bows?" Hellebore sounded angry as well as surprised, as though the spectacle were aesthetically displeasing. "They are going to fight dragons with *arrows?*"

As the winged monsters came in on their next pass sev-eral of the grims leaped out from behind their makeshift ramparts and raised their bows. A dripping burst of fire caught two of them and turned them into shrieking, jigging torches, but the others loosed their arrows before running for cover again.

"Are they mad, these skin-eaters?" Hellebore demanded.

"They hunted dragons in the old days, Stepfather." The Terrible Child sounded amused. "They do what they know best. I think it involves some kind of very powerful poison."

As the dragons wheeled and their shadows again dropped onto the square, a full dozen more of the grims darted from cover and fired their shafts; with their long, almost apelike arms, the wild goblins were perfectly suited to draw such tall, heavy bows. The dragons spat death and then wheeled away. The grims kept loosing arrows until the great winged worms turned and came down again, blazing.

Again and again the liquid flame splashed across the square, which was now covered with leaping fires even where there seemed nothing that could burn. Again and again wild goblins were caught and martyred by the spray, but others ran out in the dragons' wake, firing up into the air before the giant creatures could rise out of range. At first it seemed that it was all just some goblin-gesture, a bit of primitive bravery in the face of certain death, but finally on the sixth or seventh pass all the shadows did not disappear as the dragons swung out of range: one shadow grew in size until darkness covered the entire square. The goblins stared up, shouting to each other and pointing before running for cover as the shadow rapidly began to grow smaller and blacker: the monster was falling.

The dragon dropped out of the sky and hit the ground so hard that one of the buildings along the square shuddered and collapsed, adding its own dust to the flume of black blood and gobbets of molten pavement thrown up by the creature's fall. Other facades shook and the few windows left unbroken now shattered. Then all was silence, the square motionless except for the jittering of flames, the monster lying dead in a crater at the center of a spiderweb of cracked stone with a thicket of arrows protruding from its great filming eye and more picketing its long throat, its tail stretched across the smoldering steps of New Mound House like the snapped cable of a suspension bridge.

"It cannot be," said Hellebore. Theo had never imagined he would see the fairy lord so astonished. He almost looked mortal. "It cannot be."

"But it is, Stepfather," said the child. "Look and your eyes will tell you the truth. The goblins have killed one of your big lizards. Do you doubt they will manage to kill the rest, too? They can afford to sacrifice a few dozen to bring down each one—they will think it a good trade. And can you imagine what will happen to Hellebore House when the mob realizes the high families are actually vulnerable? If you had been paying attention to your private line you would have just heard the security force calling out to you, telling you that our house is surrounded." The Terrible Child definitely appeared to be more entertained than upset by what had happened. "And the grims have more weapons than simply bows and arrows, the commander says—they are shooting out the windows of our tower with lightning-throwers and many of the guards are dead."

"We won't be vulnerable long," said Hellebore. "Into the coach!" he shouted at the ogre bodyguards. "Drive! Now! Straight to the Cathedral!"

The ogres did not even have time to climb all the way into their seats before the armored coach spun around on the park lawn, spitting divots of grass and mud; one of the huge gray creatures almost rolled on Theo—which, he couldn't help thinking, would at least be a faster way to die than whatever Hellebore had planned for him.

"They did it," Applecore crowed softly by his ear. "Did you see? It was brilliant!"

He couldn't help feeling pride. What the goblins had done was more than a heroic gesture—Hellebore was set back, even a little scared. And Theo and Cumber Sedge had helped it happen.

Good old Button, he thought. *That will serve the Flower bastards right for underestimating him.*

Within minutes they were driving through a sudden mist into a part of the City he had never seen, a district he did not remember even being described in Dowd's journal. The buildings on either side of the increasingly narrow road were odd conglomerations of stone and earth that looked almost like termite mounds or some ancient archaeological site. The dark, foggy streets were empty, and the strange buildings seemed empty too, doors and unglassed windows gaping like the eyes of skulls piled in a catacomb. Even the mist seemed to be growing thicker as the convoy made its way down the sloping streets between the crude, close-leaning buildings.

No, Theo realized, *it isn't just the mist.* The sky itself was growing darker overhead, as though afternoon was ending and evening coming on fast. *But evening should still be hours away. Can you have a power blackout in the sky?*

Hellebore was snapping orders on his invisible private line, the child was looking calmly out the window, and Tansy seemed lost in some personal realm of pain, but Theo still whispered as he asked Applecore, "Where are we? Why is it getting dark already? Is it the smoke from the fires?"

"We're driving into Midnight," she said in his ear. Her moment of joy had evaporated and her voice trembled. "It's not good, Theo. Ever since the king and queen died, nobody comes here except for funerals. It's . . . it's thick."

"What's thick?"

"Everything. It just is. Faerie—it gets thick here."

The Terrible Child stirred, took a deep ecstatic breath. "It is the heart of the realm, home to the first mound where civilization began—but it was alive long before that." He smiled and nodded. "It is where the edges are, where things come in and go out, are born . . . and die." The Terrible Child pushed his way into Theo's head: *You will find it instructive, my almost-twin—for a little while.*

Applecore moved in even closer to Theo's neck, although she was on the far side from the boy. "Don't talk to him!"

But he could not resist. The grims' killing of the dragon had heartened him. "And this is where you're going to bring on this, what is it called, Eternal Night?"

"Old Night. Ah, yes. But I will not bring it on, as you say. It already is. I will simply open a door so that it can make its way to the mortal world. Not that your world is a stranger to it, to the old ways and the old nightmares. But there are only a few small points of contact now—like tiny holes in an otherwise watertight ship, they are not enough to change things. But I will open a great gash in the side of reality as they know it on your world—a hole too big for patching or bailing. Once Old Night starts pouring in, bringing chaos such as even your troubled world has not known in a thousand years or more, nothing will stop it." He sighed. "It will be lovely. Like bathing in a river of discordant music. A blizzard of dark light. Screams, useless prayers, the unique sound of the very lattices of reality coming apart—I will drink it all in, until I am intoxicated. It was what I have waited my entire life to do."

Theo was sickened, but would not show it. "All, what, seven years?"

"I have had as many moments of life as you, my half brother, my blind and deaf twin, but mine have passed in this world. We age more slowly here, breathing the airs of Faerie, but you know the date of my birth—that was something else of mine that was given to you."

"But you know what I had that you didn't? A real family. A life." Theo wanted to hurt the smiling creature shaped like a child any way he could, as though it were the worst parts of himself that sat beside him, gloating and mocking. "Love. Do you even know what that is?"

The Terrible Child laughed. "Do you?"

Hellebore turned in irritation. "Shut your mouth." Something seized control of Theo and he could no longer speak. The child smiled and looked out the window.

The battle-coaches drove on, the winding road taking them down into what seemed a kind of wooded valley thick with ground fog. Great corridors of uninterrupted darkness yawned between the trees. Empty buildings still stood on either side of the bumpy road, but they had been dug straight into the ground and seemed almost invisible: only dusty openings too regular be animal dens, or here and there a jut of roof protruding from a pile of dirt or tangle of leaves showed that someone had once lived there.

"I don't like this place," Applecore moaned. "It's bad."

Theo could not talk and could barely move. He let his head loll back and stared up through the domed top of the coach at the tips of the tall old trees. The tops of the treeline on either side shimmied up and down as they passed like wave patterns on an oscilloscope. Something was tracking them from high above, a minuscule winged shape barely visible against the darkening sky, and for a heart-freezing moment Theo thought it was another dragon coming down from the heights, but he realized he would never have been able to see anything that far up through the swirling mists. It was a gray bird, passing back and forth only a few dozen yards overhead as though it were keeping the car in sight—an owl, or perhaps a small hawk. Then the mists thickened and the sky seemed to grow darker. As he lost sight of the bird he felt a moment of sadness.

Maybe the last free creature I'll see. I should have told Applecore to fly away while I could still talk. They say they don't care about her, but once they've done whatever it is to me, they might just kill her for spite. A brief image of her back in the jar, but this time in the long-fingered hands of Anton Hellebore—or worse, the hungry child—pulled up a groan of fear and disgust that died somewhere between his lungs and larynx, unable to overcome Lord Hellebore's order of silence.

And it will get better still, the Terrible Child silently mocked him. Theo whimpered. He could not force the voice, the presence out of his head: it was like struggling in a nightmare. *Pain and terror such as is visited on the waking world only once in an entire epoch. Just wait, O my brother. You will see such sublime things . . . !*

The winding road took them over a rise and they emerged for a moment from the endless colonnade of phantom trees. A great forested valley stretched before them, a thick carpet of treetop foliage that rose unexpectedly from the lowlands and ended in a ring of huge trees at the valley's center that stood more than twice the height of the others. He could see something gleaming at the center of that ring, a dull shine like old silver, but then the coach crested the rise and started back down; within moments they were deep in the blind woods again. The trees around him were taller now, vast cylinders of bark whose lowest branches jutted far above the top of the coach, and it made Theo wonder how big the trees in the ring at the center must be—giants. The light was dim here but in some odd way still seemed too bright, like the sideways glare just before sunset. In fact, even through his own fog of weariness and despair he could not help feeling the strangeness of the place: not just the light, but the way that loud noises like the engines seemed unduly muffled yet quiet sounds like the wind through the trees penetrated even the hardened bubble windows. Even the air he breathed was both thinner and headier than it should have been. It all contributed to a growing sense of dislocation like a bad drug trip, as though reality itself were congealing around him, time slowing, everything increasing in density . . .

No, it's not getting more dense, that's too scientific or something, it's just getting . . . He had to hunt through his bruised, exhausted mind until he could come up with Applecore's words. *Thick. Faerie gets thicker here. There's just . . . more of everything.*

The passengers were all silent as the convoy wound through the foggy, light-streaked woodland, Hellebore and his monstrous stepchild perhaps lost in dreams of what was to come, Tansy distracted and still apparently in pain. Only Applecore had anything to say: she crept close to his ear and whispered, "Be brave, Theo," but there was nothing he could have said to that even if he could speak.

At last the armored coach slowed and stopped. The world seemed to have dropped away in front of them, and it took Theo a little while to realize that he was not looking at some kind of interdimensional nothingness but the silvery blankness of a still lake shrouded in fog.

"Get out," said Hellebore.

He was a prisoner in his own clumsy body: all he could do was obey. Outside the protective bubble of the coach, the world felt even stranger. He had often heard or read of silences that were tangible, so thick they could be cut with a knife, but this was the first time he had ever truly experienced such a thing. The quiet was stiflingly heavy, as though the entire world had drawn in its breath and held it.

He wasn't the only one to feel overwhelmed. The ogre guards didn't even waste a glance on him as they got out, but like tourists come to the big city, leaned back and stared up at the immense ring of trees surrounding the lake. Theo found himself doing the same. The trees were as huge as they had looked at a distance, big as office towers, the innermost circle stretching so high that Theo guessed that full daylight only touched the water for a few minutes around noon each day.

The size of them was arresting enough, but although Theo knew little about trees, it was also hard to ignore the fact that no two of them in the ring were quite the same: the tree beneath which they had parked was a skyscraping pine, but it stood between a massive oak and an improbably vast birch whose pale trunk loomed like a moon rocket. This made the ring of giant trees around the lake seem artificial—odd, when in other ways the place seemed so extremely natural, almost throbbing with primordial grandeur and solitude. Also, each tree was rooted in its own grassy mound of earth, each mound as big as a school playing field, so that if it had not been for the brilliance of the colors, the hundreds of different shades of greenery, the splendid diversity of gray, white, and brown trunks, and the way their terrifyingly distant tops swayed in a breeze unfelt at ground level, the giants might almost have been titanic statues of trees instead of real living things, a sort of arboreal museum for young gods, with each display set on its own plinth overlooking the lake.

As the last members of the convoy climbed out to stand beside the lake Theo looked out across the expanse of mirror-still water. The fog had grown a little thinner, and he could now see a bump at the center of it all, a low island several hundred yards from the shore, a bizarrely unassuming lump in the midst of so much majesty, its outlines partially hidden by low, drifting mist. The island had no tall trees: it was covered with grass and underbrush which made it hard to see against the forest on the shore behind it, but even through the mist and in this dim, directionless afternoon light Theo could see something sparkling at the island's center like a pile of diamonds.

Hellebore walked to the edge of the lake and raised his hand, a gesture so imperially casual that any Caesar would have been envious. At first Theo thought that he was summoning one of his bodyguards or his son, but then a long, low boat detached itself from the shadows at the island's waterline and begin to move toward them across the lake, a robed and hooded figure sitting in the stern. It all seemed a little too much, even to Theo's exhausted eye. The legendary Ferryman out of the old myths, coming to take him away? But that had been a river in that story, hadn't it? It was hard to live in the middle of all these old tales, to try to make sense of them. In fact, he felt like he was being eaten by a story . . . a story with teeth . . .

The boat moved swiftly; within what seemed to Theo only a minute or two—he had so few minutes left, and even in this place of clotted time they were racing by so quickly!—the silent craft was sliding up to the bank. The boatman was small and slender, with a handsome longnosed face, ears that would make a bat proud, and a shock of graying hair. He was chained to the bench by a shiny ring around his neck, and—if what protruded from beneath his robe was any indication—had woolly legs and goat's feet.

"Still here, I see," said Hellebore.

"By dint of your chain around my neck, my lord," said the goat-legged man with a slight bow. His voice was high-pitched and extremely musical; Theo thought that in another story, one that was going to have a happier ending than this one, it would be interesting to hear him sing. "The iron in it burns at night and keeps me from sleeping. I think of you during all the lonely hours. You haven't by any chance come to drown yourself in a fit of remorse, have you?"

Hellebore didn't waste the energy on either a smile or frown. "No. We will all cross to the island."

The handsome little man nodded his head. "Nidrus Helle-bore, it shall be done." Now that he was closer, Theo could see that the shape of the ferryman's face was much less human than he had initially thought.

Lord Hellebore glanced back at the small crowd from the coaches that had gathered on the grassy bank behind him—eight or ten constables, half a dozen ogre bodyguards, and Hellebore's son and stepchild and fellow fairy lords (although Tansy for one looked as though he would be happy to stay behind, and even Lord Foxglove appeared a bit nervous), as well as the prisoners Cumber and Theo—then looked at the boat, a small barge made of ancient black wood. "How many trips?" asked Hellebore.

The ferryman smiled. "All will cross together, my lord."

Hellebore ordered Theo onto the boat. It pitched gently as he stepped from the lakeside and Applecore held onto his hair tightly, but even in his exhausted and almost helpless state he found it easy to stay upright. As the constables prodded him toward the stern the rest of Hellebore's little party followed, leaving only the trio of doonie drivers in their buglike riot gear to wait with the battle-coaches. Just as the ferryman had said, there was room for all, although to Theo it seemed no more credible now that it had happened than it had been while everyone was still on the bank: in whichever direction he looked the boat seemed to stretch a little wider than was actually possible.

When Cumber and the last of the constables were on board the craft turned away from the bank, apparently of its own accord, and began a stately progress back toward the island.

The ferryman was looking at Theo with interest. His amber eyes slanted upward, glowing like the gaze of a jack-o'-lantern, but the look of intelligence and the deep laughter lines on his brown skin almost made up for it. "You have something of the smell of mortals about you," the ferryman said. "But not quite. What is your name?"

To his surprise, Theo found he could talk again. "I'm not sure anymore. Theo Vilmos. Septimus Violet. It doesn't seem like it matters much." He could feel the Terrible Child on the edge of his thoughts, although he could not see him, and the cold glow of the child's anticipation for what was to come made it hard to concentrate.

"Robin is my name." The ferryman looked Theo up and down. "Goodfellow is my other name, if not always my true tale, I must regretfully admit. I see you have an appointment with the wet sisterhood."

"What?" Theo glanced over at Hellebore, but if the Flower lord had noticed Theo could speak once more, he didn't seem disturbed by it.

"He means the nymphs," Applecore said quietly. "Your . . . bracelet."

Theo looked down at the knotted band of grass, then at the still water all around them, the surface barely disturbed by the boat's passage. The lake seemed as silent and ancient as the forest; Theo could imagine almost anything living in its depths. "Ah. Yes. Well, they'll have to get in line."

Robin smiled again, showing surprisingly sharp teeth. "In fact, it is one of the oldest and greatest of the sisterhood who lives here, but never doubt she will take you just as quickly if you fall in as her youngest, hungriest sisters. Perhaps you should not sit so close to the edge."

Theo shrugged. If it was hard to concentrate with the rising joy of the child pushing at his mind, it was almost harder to care. "I'm not very good at moving right now unless Lord Hellebore allows me to."

Robin nodded and tapped the ring on his neck. "Our current master is indeed one for bindings and suchlike, isn't he?" He leaned forward and said in a loud, theatrical whisper. "We wonder what sort of games his mama played with him when he was wee, our Nidrus."

"You are alive because you are a curiosity, pooka." Apparently Hellebore had not been ignoring their conversation entirely. "But curiosity is not a very strong emotion, and thus not much of a guarantee of safety."

"I take your excellent point, Lord Hellebore." Despite the ring on his neck and the heavy links that chained him to the bench, Robin Goodfellow contrived a graceful little bow. "And what," he said to Theo, "is the purpose of your visit here, if I may ask? Not that I'm complaining—a little company helps the centuries to inch by a bit faster."

Theo sighed. "I think we're going to destroy the world. Somebody's world, anyway. It used to be my world."

"Ah," said Robin, "another busy day for the Flower lords," but he seemed depressed by the news and did not speak again.

The ferry passed through a last swirl of mist and grounded against the island.

41

THE CATHEDRAL

The island itself was not very big, but even so, as Theo acted out Hellebore's command and disembarked under the utterly unnecessary guns of the guards he found himself having trouble understanding what it looked like. It was not the dying light that made its shape hard to judge, or the shroud of mist that rose from the water's edge, or even the disorienting shimmer at the top of the low hill, although they all added to his confusion. Instead, it was something in the place itself, some intense anomaly that was part of its very nature, as if the primeval silence of the ring of giant trees became something even more concentrated and yet paradoxically also more cloudy here, a pulse of irreducible strangeness at the still heart of Faerie that confused Theo's senses just as the magnetism of the North Pole deranged compasses.

Soon, the avid voice whispered in his head, but it was talking to itself now even more than to him, a child's quiet song of impatience and hunger. *Soon, soon . . .* This was its hour, and Theo could only wonder what horrors had come before this crowning moment, to create something that looked forward so gleefully to madness and destruction being visited on an entire world.

What he could make out through the disorienting nature of the place and his own hopeless misery was that the island sloped up from the water's edge to the top, a long, low hillock covered with uneven grass and gnarled shrubbery. In a depression at the top, hidden from the base of the island by the curve of the land, lay whatever was creating that blur of inconstant, refracted light which hung over the hilltop as though something up there was trying, with some difficulty, to birth a rainbow.

They trooped up the hill, Lord Hellebore first, his flawless white suit a beacon in the gloom. The little monster with Theo's features followed right behind, hurrying along on his short legs, excited even in his physical movements, as though he were a normal child being led through the gates of the zoo. Theo and Cumber followed, prodded along by helmeted constables, then Tansy, Anton Hellebore, Foxglove, and Thornapple, and the rest of the guards. The ogre bodyguards brought up the rear, walking silently, very attentive to the surroundings despite the minuscule size of the landscape they were surveying.

"We're in the real middle of it now," Applecore whispered in a choked voice. "Never . . ." She fell silent for a moment. "I've heard . . ." Again she ran out of words. "It's here, Theo."

"What?" he whispered back, fighting to stay calm, fighting to concentrate his straggling thoughts. "What is this?" Somehow the conversation with Robin Goodfellow seemed to have released him from Hellebore's silence. A momentary flicker of hope—perhaps the ferryman had other powers and could intervene on his behalf or at least interfere with Hellebore's control over him—died when Theo looked back and saw the black boat slipping out of sight around the edge of the island, gliding into a curtain of mist. Goodfellow again sat hunched in the stern, motionless as a stone garden faun, looking at nothing except perhaps his own cloven hooves.

"This is where the old mound was—the first mound." Applecore was struggling to keep her voice under control. It was not just caution or confusion making her speak that way—she was struggling against overwhelming panic. "This is where the king and queen lived!"

"Here?" Theo looked from side to side. Even this small freedom from his lockstepped obedience to Hellebore seemed exhilarating, dangerous. "On this pokey little thing?"

He must have spoken louder than he intended. Cumber Sedge looked over at them, his face gray, his expression hopeless. Just when he had thought he could not feel worse, Theo had a cold squeeze of guilt: *Look what happens to the people who trusted me, who treated me like a friend.*

"There wasn't any water here then," Applecore whispered. "No lake, not like this. Just the mound. Deep into the ground it goes—deeper than the Elder Trees, even. The first place of all the people."

Theo felt something even chillier grab at his vitals. Was Hellebore planning to lead them down into the earth, into some horrible tomb in the wet ground under the lake? He didn't know why it actually made any difference, but if he had to die he wanted to do it under the open sky . . .

Here. The child's voice rang in his head, triumphant, mad. *Here. The waiting is ended.*

Theo reached the top of the crest and saw what was making the air shimmer.

It was not so much a crater as a depression, the grassy earth of the hilltop dented like a piece of dough into which someone had gently pushed a fist. Within it, mostly scattered in gleaming shards, but with enough broken sections still upright to give a ghostly hint of what had once stood there, lay the ruins of some great building that had been made entirely of glass. The ground at the top of the hill seemed to have been badly scorched, and although none of the glass was blackened—Theo wondered if the crystalline stuff might not be glass at all but something else entirely, something burnproof like diamond—many of the pieces on the ground had been melted into smooth, twisting shapes, and the few sections still standing were veined with cracks, so that in his dizzied, loose-minded way, Theo thought they looked like something fractal, the results of some bubble-chamber experiment lovingly photographed and displayed in *Smithsonian Magazine*. Even in their destruction the shards had a power and beauty that held his eye until the bending of the light around them made his head ache.

Here.

In short, the hilltop looked like it had been the site of a small but very powerful and very weird explosion. Something of that actual event seemed to remain, a shifting liquid glow in a pit at the center—a bright smear like magma, but only loosely bound by gravity. It was this, bounced and refracted by the shards of glass, which made the twinkling above the crown of the hill.

Hellebore ordered Theo to walk forward. If his command over his prisoner's speech had grown lax, his command over his body had not. When Theo had marched helplessly to him, Hellebore took him by the arm in a disturbingly familiar way, like an older man about to impart the secrets of life to a younger colleague, then led him along the lip of the depression, a sort of battlefield of broken spikes and blobs of glass. The colors in the shining pit were now vibrating more swiftly and unevenly, as though the hole were a living thing that had sensed their presence. Theo tensed as Hellebore touched his neck, positive he was about to be thrown in, the volcano-virgin of this particular religious ritual, but still unable to resist. Instead, the fairy lord's hand moved with startling swiftness to pluck Applecore out from behind Theo's ear.

"You will interfere with the project if you remain," Hellebore said to the kicking sprite held between finger and thumb. "He cannot do what he is meant to do with you so close to him—even your tiny bit of life-force will confuse the connection."

She reached up, clawing at his finger with her hands. "And you can go and shag yourself, you pasty-faced . . ."

"You will not be able to approach him again." Hellebore flicked her away with surprising force—a slight movement of his hand and she went whizzing away through the air as though shot out of a gun and vanished out over the lake.

Keep flying, Theo silently begged her. *Keep flying. Get yourself out of here . . . !*

"Now," Hellebore told Theo, "you will wait here until I am ready for you." He turned and walked back toward the others.

For once, Theo desperately wanted to follow the fairy lord—proximity to the glowing pit and its vivid, liquid colors was making him feel like he imagined an epileptic did just before a seizure struck—but he could not make his legs move. The smoldering amber and smoky purple-blue bubbled without noise or even substance. From his standing imprisonment at the edge of the pit he heard Hellebore saying something, and from the corner of his eye he saw the Terrible Child taking up a position on the opposite rim, but something even more disturbing had arrested his attention: deep in the pool of light, so faint that at first he thought his eyes were creating patterns out of nothingness, lay two vaguely human shapes.

There are bodies in there. The horror that was making his skin prickle and his breath hitch seemed to be happening at a distance, but he could still feel it, like the screams of someone being murdered a few apartments down coming up through the floorboards. *Bodies. Is it . . . ?*

"The king and queen!" cried Lord Foxglove, who sounded almost as frightened as Theo. "By the Trees, Hellebore, surely we dare not meddle with their resting place . . . !"

"Shut your mouth," Aulus Thornapple said, but there was a hairline crack of fear in his voice as well. "Don't speak about what you don't know, Foxglove."

Now the bodies in the crypt of light seemed to come more strongly into focus, as though they rose toward the surface without getting any nearer, but as Theo stared helplessly he still could make little of them except that one had a more female shape than the other and that both seemed tall—taller than even Anton Hellebore, although it was hard to judge

anything through the distortions of the glowing medium. He
saw hints of other attributes as well—a crown, a curl of dark
hair that wavered in the pulsing light like tide-swept kelp—
but this only confused him, because at the same time he saw
other aspects of the two figures that did not match, contra-
dictory and simultaneous: a hand suddenly became a claw, a
curly-haired head was at the same moment a bald dome with
a crest of stretched flesh like the fin of a sailfish. The sword
lying on the king's breast blurred and became a club, then a
musical instrument almost like something the goblins had
played. The gem cupped in the queen's graceful hands grew
into an egg, then a flower, while the hands themselves also
changed shape like candlewax in a fire, fingers long then
stubby, talons appearing and vanishing, skin changing color,
growing fur like mold that disappeared again in a moment.
It was as though a hundred different figures, a thousand,
floated in the smoldering depths, all reflected in one place,
so that not a single version came to his eye without bearing
traces of all the others.

But although each and every one of these spectral, super-
imposed kings and queens lay arranged as if for ritual burial, they also had one other thing in common: though their
eyes seemed as variable as everything else—round as an
owl's or slitted, some spike-pupiled like a cat's or a snake's,
others covered with some kind of film, or invisible but for a
gleam from beneath lowering, bony brows—all the eyes,
every pair on each and every one of the royal bodies, were
open.

"They're alive." Lord Foxglove's voice was a horrified
whisper. "Oberon and Titania . . . they're still alive!"

"Of course they are, you idiot," said Hellebore. "They are
chained, not dead. They *are* Faerie, they are its embodiment—its heart. If they were dead we would probably not
exist. How could we have survived without them?"

"But . . . but you didn't warn me . . ." Foxglove seemed
on the verge of weeping. "You said we were just going to tap
the mortal world!"

"And where do you think such power will go, once we have it?" Hellebore laughed. "Without using the king and queen, it would be like channeling the Moonflood into a rain barrel."

Foxglove fell into a shaking silence, but someone else spoke up—a halting voice that Theo did not recognize for a moment. "It was *you*, wasn't it? The Seven Families. You did this to them."

Hellebore smiled. Except for the Terrible Child, he seemed the only person not overwhelmed by the weird power of the place. "The little ferisher speaks at last. I seem to remember you worked for Lady Jonquil. Obviously she was wise to see something in you. But you are only half-right. The king and queen were badly weakened by the last Gigantine War, had expended almost all their energy to hold the fabric of the realm together. They were in no position to fight back when we staged our little . . . coup."

"You wouldn't have needed to steal their power if you hadn't been so busy imitating the mortals' ways." Cumber spoke like one who expected at any moment to be silenced. "Is that why you hate mortals—because you recognize that they are alive in a way you are not? That they change and grow, make mistakes, learn—but all we of Faerie can do is mimic them? You spent years among them, they say, studying them. Was it interest, or envy?"

"Mortals have their uses, even perhaps some talents we do not." Hellebore seemed to be enjoying the discourse, as though he wanted to savor every single part of this triumphant hour. "That proves nothing. I cannot give milk. That does not make a cow my equal."

"But, Nidrus!" said Foxglove. "Surely this explains the problems we have been having, the difficulty maintaining energy in our world, if the king and queen have been kept helpless all this time, imprisoned . . ."

"Of course it explains it," snapped Hellebore, but he still did not seem very angry: rather he seemed to be enjoying the playing out of some large and very complicated joke whose full extent was still not obvious to anyone but himself. "It was never meant to be a long-term solution. I argued years ago that if this realm was not eventually to become cold and barren and dark, we had to find a way to tap the old science of the mortal world, but it was the resistance of those sentimentalist idiots like Violet and Lily and Daffodil—not to mention your own craven family, who didn't even have the courage of such convictions, however wrong they might be—that kept us from that solution."

"I can assure you," Foxglove said, "that if I had understood . . ."

"If you had understood, you would have been pissing yourself in fright just as you are now. You are terrified to discover we have usurped the king and queen, aren't you? It was all well and good when you thought we had no choice, that they had died defending the realm—you Coextensives resented their control, too—but since your conscience was clear, you were satisfied. It is always that way. The cowards not only rely on the brave to take the needed actions, they wish to be protected from the truth of those actions as well." Hellebore snorted. "Count Tansy may be from another one of the fence-straddling families, but at least he had the wisdom to recognize early which side of this particular conflict was going to win. In fact, we might not have been able to harness even what power we have had without his help, since I did not trust the Remover with the secret of the king and queen's true state—discretion that has proved well-founded."

Theo yearned to speak but the pull of the smoldering pit and the bubbling thoughts of the Terrible Child were too powerful.

"So you've owned Tansy for a long time." It clearly was not easy for Cumber to talk, and he must have felt, as Theo did, that he would not take what he was learning anywhere but the grave, but even in these last moments the ferisher remained true to himself: he wanted to know the answers. "He had already helped you commit the greatest treason of all."

"He does indeed have a keen eye for both sides of an equation," Hellebore said. "A bit too keen. Quillius Tansy, come forward." Obviously, Tansy did not obey quickly enough: a moment later Theo heard him protesting as the guards dragged him to Hellebore. "It has come to my attention, Tansy, that although you have long professed loyalty to me, even if secretly, you let Hollyhock and the others use you to bring the Violet heir across from the mortal world without telling me until he was here in Faerie. This muddled my plans and caused me a great deal of needless irritation. I suspect you were hedging your bets in case my design should fail, so that you could claim to Hollyhock and the others that you had been on their side all along."

"But, Lord Hellebore!" Tansy shrieked in alarm, his features showing more than a trace now of the terrible damage that had been mostly hidden. "How can you believe such . . . I did my best . . . I never . . ."

"I note your protestations of innocence," Hellebore said. "I am sure the king and queen have noted them also, even in their slumber, although they may take a rather different view of it when you are shortly introduced to them."

"Black iron! Here, just a moment, Hellebore." It was Lord Thornapple, his voice shaky with the fear that seemed to have seized him now as well. He stepped forward to the edge of the depression, looking down with obvious alarm into the pit; bruise-colored light played on his face. "Nidrus, I don't . . . You never said anything about . . . about waking them up."

"No, I did not, *Aulus*,"—he made Thornapple's first name sound like an insult—"and I am not planning to do so. What I said was that Tansy is about to be introduced to them." He turned and waved a hand. Instantly two of the constables stepped forward and seized Tansy by the arms. "You of all people should know there are rules that must be rigidly observed," Hellebore told the struggling prisoner. "That is why it is science. And this sort of process has its rules, however infrequently it is attempted. A blood sacrifice

is necessary." He nodded to the constables. "Slit his throat
and throw him in."

"No!" Tansy screamed. As though he had lost almost all
control of it now, the fairy's face began to shift and slide
beneath the skin as if pieces of his skull had broken free
and were floating loose like pack ice. It was a horrible
sight: Theo wanted to close his eyes, but couldn't. "These
others are expendable, not me! I did everything you asked,
Hellebore!"

"Hurry, Stepfather!" The Terrible Child's eyes were
closed, his face seized in an ecstatic grimace. Perched on the
far rim of the depression, he looked as though he were standing in a kitchen full of wonderful smells. "The moment has
grown ripe."

"Yes, Tansy," said Lord Hellebore, "you did everything I
asked, but you are a traitor by nature—you wake up every
day intent only on doing what is best for Quillius Tansy. Because you wanted the power I promised you and feared my
anger, you betrayed the Hollyhocks and the Daffodils and
your other allies, but at the same time you left a door open
so that you could turn to them again if our enterprise did not
succeed. And one day you may conceive another idea, however wrongly—the idea that doing my bidding is no longer
what is best for you. I will spare us all such a future annoyance." He turned to the constables. "Do it now."

"But, Lord Hellebore . . . !" one of the guards holding
Tansy said. They were all looking at the pit and their terror
was obvious even behind the goggles that covered half their
faces. "Here . . . where the king and queen . . . ?"

"Of course, here. That is the whole point. By the Well, is
there anyone else who wishes to question me? Do it now or
you will go in with him."

"Let me, Father!" cried Anton Hellebore, bounding forward. The younger Hellebore pulled a long, wicked-looking
bladed tool out of his breast pocket and, with startling econ-
omy of motion, grabbed Tansy's long white hair, yanked
back his head, then dragged the blade across his throat.

Tansy's shrieks turned to gurgles, his face becoming an almost unrecognizable puzzle of bruises and healing scars as he lost his grip on the cosmetic charm for once and all. Blood spurted from the wound, and much of it guttered down his front. The guards, their mouths screwed up in expressions of fear and disgust, did their best to hold him without getting splashed.

"Throw him in, curse it!" said Lord Hellebore.

The constables took a few steps down into the depression and flung Tansy away from them. He stayed up for a few staggering steps, knocked down one of the standing shards of broken glass, then tumbled blindly into the pool of light.

Theo flinched, half-expecting some kind of explosion, some great outflaring of heat and light, but although the fairy vanished struggling into the bright depths, within seconds the only sign of what had happened was a reddening of the plasma so that the whole thing glared like a sunset sky.

"Yes," shrieked the Terrible Child, "the blood has opened the door, Stepfather!" He raised his little arms as though asking to be lifted, embraced. "Hurry! Help me reach through!"

Hellebore walked back toward Theo.

This is it. My turn. He struggled until a bolt of pain slammed down his spine but he could not move from the spot. He thought helplessly of Tansy's last moments, lurching down that slope as the life fountained out of him. But what if they were not his last moments? What if Tansy was doomed to live forever, dying forever, in that pool of scarlet light? What if that was going to be Theo's fate, too? He let his eyes flick across the others gathered on the edge of the low hilltop, the lords Thornapple and Foxglove, terror struggling with greed and anticipation on their faces, Cumber Sedge hanging in the grasp of two constables, the Terrible Child already immersed in some paroxysm of joyful discovery. Then something else caught his attention, although he could not have said why—a small movement on the far shore of the lake. For a moment he thought it might be the ferryman Robin Goodfellow, especially when the manlike shape slid over the bank and into the water, but then it was gone and did not come up again.

Too late, whatever it was, if it even mattered. Hellebore stood in front of him now, pale face masked in calm despite an inner furor that only leaked out through his crazily intent eyes. Theo could feel the fairy lord's will like a physical thing. "Your turn, Violet child. We need the key to open the final door."

Theo tried to speak and found he could, although every word hurt coming out, as though he were disgorging a train of objects covered in thorns. "I . . . don't . . . know . . . about . . . any . . . key . . ."

"You *are* the key, fool. Your true father would not let me have control over the powers of the king and queen, even when we had all sworn not to meddle with them. The others backed him and I did not have the strength then to make them do otherwise. We two were given authority over this place, the first place, so that we could only use the powers prisoned here if we agreed, Violet and Hellebore. But of course we did not agree."

"And . . . I . . . still . . . don't . . ."

"It no longer matters. You are not your father. You cannot resist my will, Theo Vilmos—Septimus Violet. Hold out your hands."

Despite every ounce of resistance, even though he fought until the muscles in his arms writhed and cramped, Theo saw his hands slowly rise. Hellebore took them with his own. The fairylord's flesh was cool and dry. Bizarrely, he began to sing, although in a tuneless and hurried way.

"The toil of Death now enwraps feet and hands and head, but does not bind the heart!"

There was poetry in Hellebore's chant, but none in the uninflected way he spoke. Still, Theo could feel something swimming up from inside him as though to a summons, a deep movement without physical substance. If he was the key, he was being fitted into the lock and turned, just like those fail-safe launch systems down in the nuclear bunkers. *That's why he's saying it like that, singing.* The pressure in Theo's head made him feel he was plunging into a miles-deep ocean trench. *Because it's not poetry to him, it's a formula. It's just science. Like the formula for an H-bomb . . .*

> *"Here where all the Great Lords stand, one by the other*
> *Trunk to trunk, brother to brother*
> *Now let the power of the first hill, of the Master and*
> *Mistress of Trees*
> *Open to me!*

> *"The darkness of Between now blinds eye and deafens*
> *ear, but does not shroud the heart!*
> *Here where Time itself first stirs, alone and indivisible*
> *Coil swallowing coil, all invisible*
> *Now let the power of the first hill, of the Master and*
> *Mistress of Air*
> *Open to me!*

> *"The endlessness of Silence now stops every tongue,*
> *but does not mute the heart!*
> *Here where the first bird sings, waking all the stars*
> *Alone in the ash-tree, making what it mars*
> *Now let the power of the first hill, of the Master and*
> *Mistress of Song*
> *Open to me!*

> *"The circle of this charm*
> *Is mine*
> *The breaking of this stick*
> *Is mine*
> *The kindling of this flame*
> *Is mine*
> *The blowing of this cloud*
> *Is mine*

The circle of this charm
Is mine
The circle of
This charm
Is
Mine."

The shift of pressure inside Theo grew stronger, became something else, a feeling of something breaking free that had been moored so long and so firmly that he had thought it a part of himself. Suddenly the Terrible Child was in his head again, but no longer simply as a presence that poked and prodded. Now the cold joy that was the child began to leach Theo's own life and energy away, as though he were on one end of some great conduit with the empty vacuum of space on the other side.

Give it to me, the child crooned as the pressure mounted. *Let go. You are done.*

Theo fought, struggling against the flow, but it was only a fading reflex: whatever the key might be, an idea or a thing, it would not belong to him much longer. He did not feel queasy, but still felt as if he needed to vomit, to void himself of something that was no longer wanted. It was like waiting to give birth, but bleak and hopeless, as if he knew already that any issue would be dead. His mind flashed to Cat and then he could not get free of her again, of her terrible, bloodless face in the hospital, lit only by despair. In some ways he hardly remembered her, but he ached at the thought of what he was helping to release, however unwillingly, on the world and people he had known and even loved. Johnny, Cat, her friends and family, his co-workers at Khasigian's, people Theo hadn't even met, all were going to be plunged into some kind of endless age of horror, and there was nothing he could do to stop it. He wasn't even an integral part, he was just a key—an inanimate appliance as far as Hellebore and the rest were concerned.

No! I won't let them do it! But it was pointless. They *were* doing it, tapping into the sleeping power of the king and queen so that Hellebore and his bonsai demon could open a door into some unimaginably dark place. And even as he thought this, Theo felt the block or barrier finally give way and the thing inside began to stream out of him like water from a wrung cloth.

Hellebore nodded, satisfied, then let go of Theo's hands, turned his back and walked away, leaving Theo to sink slowly to his knees as life ebbed slowly but steadily out of him and into his gleeful twin, the Terrible Child.

The low gleam of red and amber light had flared high now, a huge bonfire of something less substantial than flame, but although it continued to billow upward in an unstable column whose top was invisible in the clouds, the color of it had cooled to a sort of shifting lavender-blue only distinguishable from the twilight sky because it gave off its own light. The Terrible Child stood before it, small hands spread wide, and pulses of a brighter glow jumped and throbbed at the child's nearness. The Terrible Child was chanting something, a spell, a manipulation of the universe, just as Hellebore had done, but the boy was using a language that barely sounded like words, shouting it joyfully, and where Hellebore had hurried through his own invocation like a man trying to get off the phone, the Terrible Child was immersed in his, riding it through some unimaginable experience, laughing, squealing with pleasure, moving toward some hideous climax.

That's it. Theo looked sadly at Cumber Sedge, but his friend was slumped between his guards, head down. Theo hoped he had only been stunned by a punitive blow to the head, not killed, although it didn't seem to matter much now. *That's it. We lose. Button loses. I lose. Hellebore wins.* He could feel the last dregs of whatever made up the magical Violet part of the key leaking out of him and into the child, along with his own vitality, as though he were a sack with a hole ripped in it. The escaping essence was running out swiftly and smoothly, synchronized with the tempo of the child's slow, exultant chant.

No, not just running smoothly, he realized as his head nodded forward and his weary eyes closed. He was falling into something deep and dark, endlessly dark, a slow-motion plummet at right angles from his own self. The outward flow of the key was the only strong thing left now, and impossible to ignore. It didn't just run, it pulsed, and there was a rhythm to it, something as remorselessly steady as a cosmic heartbeat.

Ba-bump. Ba-bump. It might have been his own heart slowly pumping. *Ba-bump. Ba-bump.* The connection between himself and the child pulsed like Tansy's slashed artery, gushing out life. He felt it, floated in it for a long moment. *Always a musician,* a dying part of him thought, distantly amused. *The end of the world has a backbeat . . .*

The remorseless pulse was dragging him ever deeper toward sleep and final darkness, but he did not want to sleep yet. He thought suddenly of the goblin music, its gloriously disordered yet organized tangle, the elliptical rhythms that would tug a plodding beat like this to pieces. *Goblin sounds.* He tried to summon them up, but they seemed as distant as the waking world is from the center of a nightmare. Then a drift, a hint, a fragment of memory came back to him. *Goblins make shapes like . . . like this.* He remembered them, or maybe only imagined them, but they felt right, a sprung rhythm that ran out-of-kilter circles around the slow pulse. *Just that crazy bit off. Yeah, like that.* Astonishingly, he discovered a sort of strength in the memory. For a moment he thought it was only a fleeting relief, the way a candle might flare one last instant in air from the breath that extinguished it, but then the larger pulse quieted. Suddenly he felt an impatient swallowing suction from the child, demanding what Theo was holding back.

Without conscious thought, he felt even more intently for the alternate rhythm. He wasn't really certain now it had anything to do with goblins, but it was a counter-pattern, and

one that he could hold. He grabbed it, worked the changes
with slippery mental fingers that threatened at any moment
to fumble away the complicated cadence. *I should have
worked harder at this stuff,* he thought dizzily, desperately,
from a perch on the edge of a black hole, one mistake away
from a plunge into unbeing. *I was always shit at real jazz.*

Let go. The words that came to him from the child were
not mockery, but a command. *You are too weak to stop me.*
And Theo knew it was true—he *was* too weak. But he also
knew that if the child and Hellebore were to have their victory, he would make them crawl scratched and bleeding
through his coils of barbed-wire polyrhythms to get it.

The pull grew more intense as the angry child fought
harder, and pain suddenly seemed to turn Theo inside out so
that for a moment he lost everything, but he grabbed at the
memory of the goblin song—not just the beat itself, or even
the music, but the feeling of connection and belonging that
it had given him—and pulled himself back up to his perch
above the internal abyss. *Not yet,* he told the child, and despite the certain knowledge that eventually he would lose, it
was Theo who did the taunting now. *Not that easy. First
we're going to make some music, little brother.*

He gave it all he had left, pulling the plodding beat to
pieces and throwing those pieces around, reassembling them
into something that went twice as far sideways at any given
timeless instant as it went forward. He sang, even if it was
only in his own head, and the dark, cold child could only
grab at him without catching him, surround him without
caging him. He sang about the spaces between beats, of the
beats between spaces, about the sounds that came after quiet
and even the sounds that were in quiet itself. He was aware
as he did so, and even a little amused, that it was the greatest performance he would ever give—*could* ever give—but
not only would it be his last, it was utterly, entirely silent.

The rage of the child built and built, but it was coupled
with a growing worry that the peak opportunity would
pass—a worry that was so tangible Theo could almost see it

in his mind's eye, and for a brief moment could almost believe he might actually thwart the Terrible Child. As the child worked harder to encircle his resistance and beat him down, Theo not only glimpsed the child's unprotected and innermost feelings but could even sense for the first time what was on the other side of their complicated transaction—both the endlessly complex energies of the waiting world that Theo had known and something that was both bigger and smaller, a shadow as nebulous as smoke and as real as death.

Old Night. The sudden touch of it surprised him and shocked him to the core of himself—even just this merest hint of it nearly killed him. He faltered at the suggestion of that mad emptiness, fell for a moment into a blank, complete terror, and lost his grip on that thing in him which had been resisting. With a surge of freezing triumph the child drained away all that Theo had been holding back: one moment it was still there and active inside him, the next moment it was gone. Suddenly Theo's eyes were open and the hilltop was around him once more, but he was no longer the center of anything.

Time to die, he thought, but it no longer seemed like such a dreadful thing as it once had. It was almost comfortable lying on the ground, comfortable to know you had done all you could and that nothing else was expected from you, even at the end of the world—*especially* at the end of the world. The others around the rim of the pit were still locked into life, looking on in apprehension and expectation as the Terrible Child's invocation rose to new heights of fervor as it neared the finish, every one of the faces afire with the purplish light, all of them rigidly still, as though they were more afraid of being noticed than of anything else. Nothing moved but the light.

No, that was not quite true: Theo had spotted another hint of motion in the near distance, in the water near the island's shore. It was hard to make out—at first he thought it must be a trick of the mists and the light seething above the low hilltop—but after a moment he was certain: something was coming out the lake. At first it was only a head, but as the neck and shoulders came smoothly, slowly up he realized that whatever it was had not been swimming but walking. It was the thing he had seen go into the water on the far side, and it had walked all the way to the island across the bottom of the lake.

Even before he could make out the empty eye sockets, the ragged, rotting shreds of what had been a constable's uniform, he knew what was coming. Even as a small, dark part of himself felt reassured by this proof that the universe was really as shitty as it seemed, that even after the worst thing imaginable had happened there was still more bad stuff to come, Theo was trying desperately to move, all illusion of comfort gone now, but although he could manage a twitch, even a small shuffling of his feet in place, Hellebore's command and the exhaustion of his struggle with the child still held him.

Eyes fixed on the pit and the Terrible Child, Hellebore and the others had not seen the interloper yet. The *irrha*, Dowd's summoning, breasted the water and made its clumsy way up onto the bottom of the low slope; then, despite the black holes where the dead eyes had once been, it began to lurch up the hill directly toward the spot where Theo lay, its clenched teeth and withered gums like a horrid cartoon of determination.

"Theo!" Astonishingly, it was Applecore's voice at the center of a fierce whirring of wings a few yards away—she looked as though she was trying to fly into a windstorm. "Oh, Theo, get up, Hellebore's charm won't let me get any closer to you. It's that dead thing, coming for you! Run, by the Trees, run!"

He wept as he forced out the words. "Hellebore's . . . too . . . strong . . ." *Oh, why didn't you get out of here when you had the chance, you brave, stupid woman . . . !*

The sprite did not hesitate, but flew away, speeding low across the grass. She headed for Lord Hellebore where he stood behind the Terrible Child, watching with the closest thing to fatherly approval Theo could imagine him showing as the child began to twist the glow of the royal fires into bizarre shapes. The air was thickening around the island— Theo could feel it in his ears, on his skin, a tightening as though all of reality were about to burst like a balloon.

Hellebore suddenly shrieked in surprise and put a hand up to his face. A moment later a line of blood appeared between his fingers as though drawn by some magical, slow-appearing paint. A blur slid around his head and then something poked at his eye. He reeled back, waving angrily at the invisible something. Applecore slowed and hovered for a moment and Theo could see a glint in her arms, the long sliver of Cathedral glass she had snatched up from the ground. Then, as if she had suddenly remembered the greater danger, she turned and flew at the Terrible Child, but skidded off him and his blanket of purple light like water off a hot griddle. Undeterred, she buzzed back toward Helle-bore. The master of Hellebore House swung his hand at her and she dodged, even managing to jab his finger with the bright shard. He drew the hand back in pain, then suddenly seemed to realize his error and snapped the hand back out. Yards away, the hovering sprite suddenly became a tiny knot of flame.

"No!" Theo shrieked, and with a surge of strength he could not have guessed he had, struggled to his feet. He had no time to mourn Applecore's sacrifice: the *irrha* was most of the way up the slope, still headed right for him. Even Hellebore had noticed it now. One of the constables turned and set his hornet-gun against his shoulder, then fired. The whining roar of the gun sawed across the hillside. The un-dead thing's arm whipped back and then fluttered forward, rags of it now stripped away, but it kept trudging grimly upward.

"It wants only the one it was summoned for," shouted Hellebore. He wiped at the blood on his cheek, smearing it across his snow-pale skin. He turned and saw to his satisfaction that the Terrible Child was still actively immersed in the storm of lavender light, still singing and laughing obliviously, still climbing toward conclusion. "Let it have him," Hellebore directed the guards. "They are hard to kill, those things."

You're thick, Vilmos, you really are! Plunged back into reality again, Theo was full of desperation and shame. *Just like she always said!* Applecore had sacrificed her life for this moment, for his freedom, and it was vanishing. He threw himself against the rigid resistance of his own sinews, fighting to move away from the spot where he was held. Hellebore was distracted, still dabbing at his cheek and staring at the thing coming up the slope, but the fairy lord was no longer fighting: Theo could feel the power of Hellebore's will stretch but hold, keeping Theo's feet planted, leaving him helpless.

The *irrha* opened its arms, one of them green-brown with putrefaction, the other wet and tattered, shredded to ribbons by the constable's gun—an embrace without human feeling, only hunger to complete its task. Theo turned away from the relentless horror, not wanting to see that face as it closed on him. His hand climbed to the chain around his neck, Poppy's chain, and clutched it. So many had given so much, risked so much, for him, but in the end it had not been enough. He looked out to the lake, the water dark now, only silvered a little by the light from the island's center. *All ending now.*

The water . . .

He had no more than a few seconds left to act. With an effort that felt as though it tore every nerve in his body loose from its sheath, he tried one last time to throw himself sideways, away from the advancing creature. Scalding pain splashed through him, made him scream until it felt like his lungs were going to come out of his throat, but it was not enough to move his feet.

It was enough, however—just barely enough—to tip him sideways.

For a moment Theo felt the supremely weird sensation of

his overmatched muscles trying independently of his own will to do the impossible, to keep his body upright when it was already falling, then he thumped onto his side and began to roll down the sloping hillside toward the lake. He reached the bottom and teetered there for a moment on a low hummock at the water's edge, everything depending on the minutiae of balance, then his legs went over and the rest of him was tugged behind them, sliding him into the cold gray water.

He bobbed up to the surface, in control of his own exhausted body once more. The water was so shallow that even on his knees he was still only half-submerged.

"Ha!" said Lord Hellebore. "You are stronger than I suspected. But it was pointless, wasn't it? Better to give in gracefully—I do not think a cubit of water is going to keep you out of the hands of your nemesis."

Everything seemed to pause—the Terrible Child still busy in the center of his glow, almost hidden now by its stunning brightness, Hellebore and the others watching the confrontation between Theo and the dead thing. Even the *irrha* itself seemed surprised into immobility for a few seconds. Then it simply turned and came lurching down the slope toward him, as though someone had switched it back on.

Theo felt something vast and cold touch him. He looked down and saw two arms pale almost to the point of translucence encircle him like bars of iron, felt himself pulled back against wet fabric and a hard, flat breast as chill as ice.

"No, nothing else will have him. He is mine." The voice resounded in his ear, ancient, slow. *"He wears our shackle on his arm. He was freed to ransom himself but I smell no gold, no bright jewels for my hair, so now he is reclaimed."*

Theo could only crouch in the belly-high water, held in her unbreakable, clammy grip. Her wet hair lay across his shoulders like seaweed. He did not turn, knew that if he looked into her eyes that would be the last thing he saw. "Please," he said. "Not yet. Just a few moments more."

"You have no right of plea or pardon," the ancient water-nymph told him, but not harshly.

"I know. But I want to see . . . if I was right . . ."

He could feel cold radiating from her, filling him where he lay cradled against her freezing belly, could feel her slow, slow heartbeat. *"A moment, then,"* she said.

And as he watched the *irrha* halted and stood motionless on the hillside, just yards from Theo but suddenly as blind to him as if he had ceased to exist. It slowly pivoted its ruined head from side to side, then turned to the place where Hellebore and his monstrous stepchild stood. It took a hesitant step toward them, then another.

Hellebore watched with wide eyes. "Stop, you idiot thing, stop!" he shouted, but the *irrha* did not stop. Hellebore moved out of its way, waving his arms, screaming, "Shoot it! Destroy it!" Several of the constables began to fire; their guns hissed and snapped and the bronze hornets leaped toward the thing and through it. Gobbets of rotting flesh flew into the air. Much of the *irrha*'s stolen face vanished in a spray of dead tissue, leaving hanging bone and a few teeth, but still it trudged up the hill. Only then did Hellebore realize that the thing was not after him. With Theo now the rightful possession of the ancient water-spirit and out of the *irrha*'s circle of perception, it headed inexorably toward the only thing like him, his almost-twin, the small boy luxuriating in the lavender glow of pure power at the lip of the hill.

Hellebore screamed in rage as he dashed after the *irrha* and was almost shot by his own guards before they saw him and stopped firing. The ogres sprang after their master, but too late: Hellebore leaped and caught the creature's leg even as it stretched out its arms toward the oblivious child. Rotted fabric tore away in Hellebore's fingers, and so did a long strip of putrid flesh. He lost his grip and tumbled backward.

The dead thing waded into the purple gleam and wrapped its arms around the child, who began to writhe and murmur like someone shaken out a beautiful dream. Simultaneously, the light changed color, blooming scarlet and orange, or so it appeared at first; it was a moment before Theo, watching from the nymph's cold embrace, could be certain of what had happened. The *irrha* had opened a gateway like the one that had brought Theo to Faerie, but this gateway led straight into a raging inferno—the blaze that had been the warehouse of the Remover of Inconvenient Obstacles.

"It is compelled to do only one thing," Eamonn Dowd had told him as they had stood in that place, *"—to seize you and bring you here."* Dowd was gone, but it seemed the *irrha*'s compulsion was not.

The Terrible Child awoke to full reality only as the thing stepped through the gateway. He began to scream, a heartrending screech of horror that could have been any child's. The boy's flesh was already smoking, the little body struggling helplessly in the grip of its burning captor, as the doorway in reality closed again.

Straight to hell, Theo thought. *Just like in the old stories.* Then for an instant the severed connection between them returned—just a brief touch, but even that merest hint of what the child was feeling made Theo scream and convulse in the unbending arms of his captor.

Nidrus Hellebore had only time for a single shout of rage before the billowing purple light, uncontrolled in the wake of the Terrible Child's vanishing, or perhaps returned to the control of those who had reason to hate him, suddenly enfolded the fairy lord. Hellebore squealed as the very bones inside his flesh turned white hot and began to burn their way out of his body, howled as light burst from his joints, his belly, his eyes and mouth, then fell silent and collapsed in on himself, although small sounds still came out of the smoking mass. As the light from the pit expanded outward, growing weaker as it spread, the others ran away down the hill in heedless terror, scattering in all directions like startled pigeons.

A chill hand covered Theo's eyes. *"Enough,"* said the strong old voice, and the nymph pulled him down.

As the hand that had temporarily blinded him lifted free,

Theo saw green depths rushing up to meet him, incalculable depths.

So that was it. That was a life. The thoughts were like bubbles, rising and popping. *Goodnight nobody. Say goodnight* . . . Then the water flooded into his startled, open mouth and blackness rushed in behind it.

Part Five

FAIRY-TALE ENDING

42

FAREWELL FEAST

In his dream he floated in thick, cool space, surrounded by streamers of green movement. In fact, almost everything was green—the light, the shadows, his own hands where they drifted slowly in front of his face, stained a sickly color like old lunch meat. Fish, hundreds of them, perhaps thousands, floated amid the rising bubbles just as he himself was floating, watching him with more curiosity in their glassy eyes than seemed decent.

Sometimes the green went away completely, swallowed by darkness, and when it came back he was surrounded by women instead of fish, all of them lovely in a strange sort of way, hair furling and waving, moved by invisible currents. These women watched him as the fish had watched him, smiling (some of them seemed to have very sharp teeth) and whispering among themselves. Through it all, through the green light that came and went, he was aware of nothing about himself except weightlessness and a feeling of unconcern that seemed to make his thoughts as buoyant as his slowly kicking legs.

Only occasionally did it occur to him that he should be drowning, or might even already have done so.

He had been staring at her for a while before he realized her black hair was not drifting, but instead hung down beside her pale, pretty face in what once would have seemed a perfectly ordinary manner. He stared a while longer before he realized he recognized her, although something about her was different and her name was slow in coming.

"His eyes are open!" the dark-haired young woman said. "I think he's waking up!"

Another face, this one less familiar, leaned in. "It is sooner than we would have guessed, but he has a strong constitution. Good breeding."

"Don't say that!" the young woman said. "I hate that."

"Poppy . . . ?" He had the name now, although some of the details were still wrong; his vision remained cloudy, as though he had not entirely left the lake bottom. She seemed to have lost her eyebrows. No, he realized, they were there, but they were so pale as to be almost invisible. It gave her a strangely Japanese look, the face a white oval, like a geisha's. One thing was certain, though—just seeing her made him feel good. "Poppy, is that . . . ? Am I . . . ?"

"You're fine, Theo. You're alive!" She suddenly climbed up on whatever supported him—it had a certain give, and he momentarily feared tumbling back down into whatever green depths he had escaped—and kissed his face. She hugged him and he let out a little huff of pain. "Oh! Sorry!"

"I think . . . did I break a rib?" He was trying to make sense of his surroundings. A tent? Whatever it was, the only light came from one of the glowing witchlight spheres. The other fairy woman had gone somewhere—he could just make out the light of what might be a doorway, but he couldn't lift his head high enough to be certain. "What else did I do? I can hardly move. Everything hurts."

"No one's quite sure. You were bruised all over, but by the time we saw you they were all old bruises. The Duchess treated you well down there."

"Duchess?" His head was quite remarkably empty of any

useful memories, although it felt very full of something else, swollen and aching.

"The one who had you. The nymph. Oh, Theo, I thought we'd never get you back!" She had a tight grip on him again, and he found that the pleasure of it was such that he could even ignore the pain in his side.

"What . . . what happened?" He was starting to remember a little of it now, and the dominant image was a column of billowing lavender light and the terrible shrieking of . . . of . . . "Hellebore, Lord Hellebore. He's dead. And that child-thing, too." He looked up, worried by her expression. "They are dead, aren't they? They have to be. But doesn't that mean . . . we won?" But the memory of Applecore's last brave moments had returned and winning suddenly didn't mean as much as it should have. "Did we win?"

She shrugged. "Yes, I suppose. Everything is a mess, but it's a lot better than it would have been." A noise distracted her and she looked up toward the doorway. "There are people here to see you. They've been waiting as long as I have, hoping that Primrose could make a bargain."

"Primrose? Bargain?"

"Wait. You'll find out everything. And I'll be right here with you."

"What happened to your eyebrows?"

"What do you mean?" But she knew. "Oh, the color? It's nothing—they were always white like this. I decided to stop dyeing them, that's all. To stop pretending I wasn't a Thornapple."

"Ah." He lifted a hand to touch the pale white stripes, although it seemed a long distance to reach. She took the hand before it reached her face and held it, as though it might hurt her to be touched there.

"You do still care about me, don't you, Theo? No, that's not fair, to ask you that right now."

"Just try to leave and you'll find out how I feel." He gave her hand the strongest, most reassuring squeeze he could muster—which in his present state, he guessed, was something

like being humped by a very old starfish. But for all his growing joy at realizing that by some mysterious means he was
back in the world again, and that Poppy was in it and waiting
for him, there was a hole inside him that could not be so easily filled. "Oh, Applecore," he said quietly, speaking to a ghost,
a memory. "I'm sorry. I'm so sorry."

"Sorry for what?" someone said. "Being a great, hulking
eejit? That's not entirely your fault, now is it?"

Cumber Sedge was sitting on the foot of the bed, and unless he had become an amazing ventriloquist, the tiny shape
sitting on his shoulder had to be . . . "Applecore!" Theo tried
to sit up but couldn't manage it. "You're not dead!"

"And neither are you, you daft thing, but not for lack of
trying." She stood and Cumber picked her up and set her
carefully on Theo's chest. She was paler than usual, with
pronounced dark rings under her eyes and some healing
burns on her face and even on parts of her head, as displayed
by her very closely cropped hair, but otherwise she seemed
to have all her limbs and her old personality intact. "What
are you staring at? Have you never seen a good-looking
woman before?"

"Not one I'm as surprised to see. And Cumber, thank
God! I mean, sorry, thank the Trees or whatever. Didn't
mean to make you flinch. We all made it! We're alive!"

Cumber nodded slowly. His smile, too, took a while to
come. "We are. Not everyone was so lucky. There were
many deaths in the City before the end. Zirus Jonquil,
among others, and hundreds upon hundreds more. In fact,
Zirus died trying to save you."

"I'm sorry to hear that. He was nice to me—nicer than almost anybody else of his kind. But what do you mean, trying to save me?"

"He and a bunch of folk from the Flower houses fighting
against Hellebore's lot were following all of you," Applecore said. "The goblins helped them track you, but it
gets very hard in the center of Midnight. I found them in the
woods, trying to get to the lake, but I knew they wouldn't

make it in time. That's why I came back by myself. Then, when they did get there, the rest of the constables and Foxglove and . . . and Poppy's father . . . sorry, Poppy . . ."

"Nothing to apologize for," Poppy said, but her expression had gone stiff and cold.

"Well, they fought back, even though Lord Hellebore was dead. Lord Foxglove was killed, and some of the guards, and Poppy's father was wounded, but Zirus and several of his troops were killed, too." Applecore sighed. "Anton Hellebore threw himself into the Well instead of letting himself be captured, the pig. At least they say it took him a long time to die. And of course, thousands were killed in the City, and there were terrible fires even after the dragons died. So nobody's felt much like celebrating these last few weeks."

It took a moment. "Few weeks . . . ?" Theo tried to sit up but couldn't. "Where . . . ? Have I been unconscious all that time?"

"Perhaps." Cumber too had more than a few healing scars, but there was something else about him that was also different—a gravity he had not possessed before. *He's a survivor,* Theo suddenly realized. *If he were a mortal, I'd say he's grown up now.* "We don't really know what you went through. You were under the water, you see."

"Under the water . . . Yeah, I suppose I knew that—even remembered it a little. But how did I get back here again? Wherever 'here' is."

"We're in the camp at the Old Fayfort Bridge," Cumber said. "Button's tent city has become sort of a temporary headquarters for . . . for the reorganization, I guess you'd call it. You see, the Parliament of Blooms is scattered, a lot of them dead or retreated to their country estates, so there's no one in charge here, really. Also, the big power plants aren't working any more and New Mound House is just a mass of smoking rubble, so this seemed as good a place as any—we never had much generated power to work with out here, anyway. And pretty much everybody knows now that this is where it all started, so they're showing up here from all over Faerie, asking to help. That, or trying to get a piece of whatever's coming next . . ."

"But I still don't know why I'm not living with the water-nymphs or whatever they were. How did I get out again?"

"We should let Primrose tell that story," Cumber began. "I think he'll be coming to see you later . . ."

"I have come now," declared a new voice. This time Theo found he could lift himself enough to see the tall shape silhouetted by daylight in the doorway of the tent.

"This is like the end of Wizard of Oz," Theo said. "You know, 'I had a dream—and you were in it, and you, and you . . .'"

Primrose shook his head. "I do not understand your reference, but this is certainly no dream. I too have been waiting to speak to you, Theo Vilmos. Or would you prefer to be known as Septimus Violet, now?"

"I think it's too late for me to change names," he said. "At least the Theo part. Speaking of which, you must be Lord Primrose now."

Primrose came closer. "I do not know. We may find that in the new world coming there are no longer lords and ladies. The goblins will have much to say about that, and others, too."

"Goblins! How is Button? Did he survive? Jesus, was he smart about everything!"

Primrose hesitated for a moment. "Yes, he is alive. He is well. He has asked to see you later. In the meantime, I will tell you my part of the story, although it is largely uninteresting, even the bargain I made for your freedom. The nymphs, like everyone else, are interested in having a stake in the changes that are to come. I offered them my help and they agreed, more or less."

"More or less?"

"It is nothing for you to concern yourself with. You are free of your nymph-binding, that is what matters."

Theo could not help staring at the band of rivergrass that encircled the fairy's wrist.

"Yes, well." Caradenus Primrose shrugged. "I suspect that even with the world upside down, enough of my family fortune remains intact that I will be able to ransom myself before spring comes and I have the urge to swim in any ponds or lakes. I owed you a debt of honor, Theo. I nearly killed you, after all."

"You didn't owe me anything. Actually, I think it's me who owes you something, now. Some information." The memory had been nagging at him since Primrose had appeared. The thought of Eamonn Dowd's crimes made him feel a bit queasy but he had no right to keep them secret. He reached for Poppy's hand, found it, and squeezed again. She reached across and spread her fingers on his chest as Theo turned back to Caradenus Primrose. "I have to tell you about what happened to your sister."

"But how could you know?" Primrose asked, surprise creasing his forehead.

"Know? Know what?"

"That she is dead. Her heart failed." For a moment even the Flower lord could not hide what was inside him, but then he composed himself again. "It is for the best, I suppose. It was just before we struck back at Hellebore, before the dragons came down on the City. Her nurses say that for a moment she was herself again, but so frightened they could not comfort her. Then she died. I saw her. She looked as though she was at peace at the last."

Theo swallowed. "Let me tell you what I know. In fact, since Cumber was out cold for most of what I heard, there are probably things in all this that none of you know yet."

It was hard to tell when an already grim fairy had become more so, but that certainly seemed to be the case with Primrose. As Theo finished his explanation, the new master of Primrose House rose and bowed.

"I salute you again for your bravery and your honesty. These tidings do not ease my heart much, I must confess— my sister suffered long and terribly, and must have suffered even at the end, when Dowd's spell was broken by his death and her wounded mind returned to its body—but it is better to know, I think, than to be ignorant. Still, after I pass the most important pieces of news along to Button I would be alone for a time."

"I'm sorry for what he did to your family, even if he wasn't my real great-uncle." Theo shook his head. "I liked him, at least from his notebook. It's hard to believe it was the same person."

"We enter a perilous country when we decide that because we mean well, or because we are largely good, that we are thus allowed to do something we know is wrong." The fairy paused in the doorway. "Oh, and Theo, Button would very much like you to come to him in the bridgehouse this evening." Primrose lifted a hand, his face somber, and walked out of the tent.

"I should go, too," Cumber said. "For now, I am nearly the only ferisher here that any of the powerful parties actually know, and decisions are being made in small groups and at surprise meetings that will be laws one day—may even be the stuff of learned books. You would find it most interesting, Theo—you'll be in more than a few pages of those books yourself, by the way. We are building a new Faerie from the ground up."

"When I can actually sit up without puking, I'd love to hear about it. I don't know how big I am on meetings, though."

"It is your future being planned, too." Cumber suddenly flushed. "Oh, I forgot. You'll be going back to your world."

"If it's still there, I guess I will," Theo said. "Did we stop the Terrible Child in time?"

Cumber smiled. "We think so. What scientific tests we have been able to do suggest that your world continues much as it always has, no better and no worse."

Theo noticed that Poppy had suddenly let go of his hand and was staring steadily at the fabric of the tent wall. "Poppy?"

Cumber cleared his throat. "As I said, I should be going. Core, can I carry you someplace, or would you like to stay and talk to Theo and Poppy a bit longer?"

"Core?" Theo saw that Cumber was blushing again. "Hold on, are you two, like . . . an item?"

Applecore gave him her most baleful stare. "Maybe. And what business of yours is it, boyo? You seem to have been keeping yourself occupied." Her face softened. "Meaning no offense, Mistress Thornapple. You make a cute couple."

"None taken," Poppy said, but there was not much life in it.

"But . . ." Theo stared at Applecore, then at Cumber Sedge. "But I still don't get it. I mean . . . how would . . . ?"

"Once the hospitals aren't quite so busy, one of us will probably have the operation," Cumber said, and now the blush was lighting him up like a neon sign. "I mean, me, probably. It's a lot easier to go large-to-small."

"Large-to . . ." Theo couldn't quite wrap his head around it, but he could tell it wasn't going to get any less weird no matter how hard he tried. "Whatever. I wish you both well." He paused for a moment. "That doesn't sound right, but I mean it. You're two of my best friends in the whole world—in any world. That's all I can say. I hope you'll be so happy together you wake up every day singing."

"Thanks." Cumber could not quite meet Theo's eye, but he was grinning.

"Pick me up, Theo," said Applecore, waving her hand at him. "Come on, I want to tell you something private, like."

He had already put his hand down for her to step into before it hit him. "Why . . . why aren't you flying?"

She looked at him in surprise, then her face twisted into a sadness that he now realized had been beneath the surface all along. "Ah, of course, you don't know, poor thing. You've been down with that soggy lot at the bottom of the lake." She hesitated a moment, then turned her back toward him and carefully pulled the top of her dress down over her shoulders, edging it lower until he could see the blackened stumps where her wings had been.

"Oh, Applecore!" His eyes filled with tears. "Oh, my God, I'm so sorry."

"I'm not dead, Theo, and that's what counts. If Hellebore had pointed that finger another few inches to the side, I would have been, so I was bloody lucky." She made herself smile. "Besides, it gives me and Cumber something else in common besides what we already have—both being intellectual types, and both having a lot of practice at putting up with arsehole you."

He laughed even though he knew she meant him to, that she was only trying to get out from under his pity. "You didn't lose your charm, either—or your ladylike demeanor."

"Yeah, and you can shag yourself twice. You better watch your lip, Dolly the ogre's coming out soon for a visit and she still owes you a good thumping. Now lift me up—I told you I want to say something quiet-like." When he had raised her to his ear, she whispered, "Go easy on her, Theo—the Thornapple girl. For some reason no normal person could understand, she really cares about you. Also, she's going to have to help decide whether her father gets put to death or just imprisoned for the rest of his life—and remember, we fairy-folk have long lives. Whether or not she hates him, that can't be much fun. And one last thing. I was so afraid for you, and I'm just blindingly glad you're not dead. But tell anyone I said that and you will be."

When Cumber had carried her out—Applecore effected a ladylike farewell wave as they went through the tent door, like someone at the first-class rail of a departing luxury liner—Theo turned to Poppy. "Applecore told me about your father. That's bad. They shouldn't make you help decide."

She turned on him, surprisingly angry. "Yes, they should. Of course they should. Because I'm part of it—the old way. I'm the daughter of one of the men who destroyed Daffodil House, who murdered all those people and helped start a Flower War that destroyed half the City and plunged civilization back into the Forest Age. They need to see where I stand so they know whether I need to be imprisoned too. Well, I suppose it's more likely they'd just exile me, since I have people like Primrose and Cumber to speak for me. Anyway, it's perfectly reasonable." She softened a little, but still looked weary and unhappy.

"But if that's not what's bothering you . . ."

"What do you *think* is bothering me? You're going to go back to the mortal world, Theo. I heard you. The adventure is over and you're going to hop the first gateway back. That's fine. You have every right, you've suffered terrible things in a world that wasn't really yours for something that wasn't your fault, only the accident of your birth. But you can't expect me to be very happy about it." She stood, dry-eyed and angry. "I have to go now. I've been here all day and I have other things to do."

Just before she reached the door of the tent, Theo found his voice. Poppy. Poppy, wait!"

"What?"

"Come back, please." He patted the bed. "Sit."

She did, like a cat with its fur up.

"First off, here. This is yours." It hurt to raise his arms, but he slipped the chain over his head and held it out to her. "Your mother's family moundstone, I think you said it was."

"I gave it to you."

"And it gave me strength when things were really dark. But it's yours, Poppy—something important from someone else who loved you. Take it." He closed her fingers around it.

"Fine. I'll be going, then."

He held her arm when she tried to stand, but was too weak to hold her. "Hey, maybe I do want to go back home—but did I ever say I wanted to go back without you?"

She looked at him suspiciously. "What does that mean?"

"What it sounds like. You're angry because you think I'm going back to the world where I grew up. Maybe I will. But why are you so certain I won't ask you to go with me?"

She frowned, but it was mainly to cover confusion and a hitch of sudden hope. "Why are you so certain I have my Clover Effect exemption—that I haven't already been there?"

"Have you?"

"No, as it happens, I haven't. But why would I want to go to your world, anyway? To get old and die, probably on my own after you leave me? Anyway, there are plenty of grown-up women in the mortal world who'll be better matches for you—women who know the things you know, the songs, the places, the names."

He laughed. "Grown-up women? Good God, don't you know you've been around long enough to be my great-grandmother?"

"Now you're just making fun."

"Maybe I am, maybe I'm not. Look, Poppy, you have to remember, I just woke up and the world—a world I hadn't really figured out in the first place—is suddenly completely different. I'm trying to sort it all out. I can't even guess at half the things that have happened since . . . since it all went down. Come on. Give me a chance." He extended his hand. At last she took it, then allowed herself to be drawn back onto the edge of the bed. "I do know I want to be with you, wherever we might wind up. You and me, Poppy. I want to . . . to try this thing out, this thing we've started. I don't pretend to know how love works, and I don't know much about these mortal-and-immortal relationships—well, immortal-who-thinks-he's-a-mortal-and-another-immortal-who-thinks-she's-too-young-for-him, to be more exact—but give us a chance to figure it out together, will you?"

"Truly, Theo? I hate pity. I'd kill you before I'd let you pity me." And with her Thornapple mask in place, she looked like she meant it.

"Truly."

She stared at him hard—not the Thornapple mask now, but not a lot warmer and fuzzier than that, either—and then seemed to make up her mind. She let go of his hand, but only long enough to climb into bed beside him and wrap her legs and arms around him. She put her warm mouth against his ear.

"Okay, so how weak *are* you?" she asked. "Really weak? Or just enough that you'll need a long nap afterward?"

He woke up at the sound of Cumber's discreet cough outside the tent. He got up, aching and wobbly-headed but more or less functional, and dressed by the light of the globe in the clean clothes that had been put out for him, a kind of white tunic and pants that to his eye looked something like the dress uniform from a karate academy. He pulled on the feather-light boots, then kissed Poppy on the cheek and left her to sleep.

"It took you long enough," said Applecore, sitting on Cumber's shoulder.

Theo fought an undeniable moment of jealousy at seeing her in her favorite position, but on someone else. "I'm not moving very fast." He looked around at the riverside camp, bright with campfires as a carnival midway. "So, we're going to see Button?"

"You are." Cumber seemed depressed, but with a ferisher it was a bit hard to tell. "It's an honor. Button isn't seeing very many people tonight."

Theo nodded. "Let's walk, then. I'm pretty hungry. And maybe you can tell me a bit more on the way about what happened while I was floating around at the bottom of the lake." He said it lightly, but it was in him still, the languor and green silence, like a dream from which he couldn't quite wake up. "The whole thing, the battle—I still don't quite get it. I know about how we helped Button bring those grims into the City, and I'm guessing they killed the dragons, but still . . ." He looked up, a little startled, as a gang of gnome-like creatures sitting around one of the fires called to him by name, wishing him a fine evening. Other passersby seemed

to recognize him too, smiling shyly or even giving him a
kind of salute. "What's with these people? What did you tell
them, Cumber?"

"The truth, Theo. That without you it all would have
failed. Zirus Jonquil and his troops would have been too late
and definitely too little to stop Hellebore. He and his monster-
child would have been in control of a power as great as that
of the king and queen themselves—greater, perhaps."

"But even so, even with the grims . . . Hellebore and the
others had all those soldiers, the parliamentary constables
with their bee-guns or whatever, guards, armies. Even with
the dragons dead, how is it that one of the other Parliament
bigwigs didn't just take over?"

Cumber walked on for a way without speaking. "I heard
Lord Hollyhock speak once, at a symposium at Daffodil
House," he said at last. "Lady Aemilia brought me along as
her secretary. You remember Hollyhock, don't you, Theo?
He was a good man, very smart. Anyway, I heard him say
that the Flower lords were sitting on top of the people of
Faerie and thought they were riding the population as
though it were a horse, but it was more like an unbroken
dragon. There would come a point, Hollyhock said, that if
the Flower lords didn't mend their ways, the beast beneath
them would realize how strong it was and would simply
shake them off and crush them. That's what happened. Button's revolution, if you want to call it that, made everyone
aware that things could change. You see, not only the goblins were angry."

"But thousands of people must have died!"

"Not as many as you'd think. Hundreds in the first hours,
when the constables still believed they were simply quelling
a riot. But when the dragons fell and the people came out
into the streets in real numbers . . . well, you have to understand that most of the constables aren't Flower nobility,
they're just ordinary fairy-folk, not that different from Core
or me. If you're a century-old shee fresh out of the
Hawthorn suburbs, it's one thing to shoot at troublemakers

who are trying to brain you with rocks or set you on fire with scattershot flame-charms, but another thing entirely to mow down ordinary men and women and even children—your own people—who are standing in front of you, refusing to do what they're told. Especially when you know, as many of the constables must have, that they are right and the people you serve are wrong."

"But if the Flower lords are out, who's going to take over? Who's in charge?"

"That's the question all right, boyo," said Applecore.

Cumber shrugged. "Nobody knows. That's why these are such important days. Come look at something, Theo." They had reached the edge of the bridge, and now Cumber led him up the spiral of stairs from the riverside. A pair of goblins with spears—Theo could not tell if they were grims or simply armed that way—stopped them at the top for a moment's quick examination, then waved them past onto the bridge. "Come over here." Cumber beckoned him to the edge of the bridge.

It took a moment of peering out into the night for Theo to realize that the great haphazard mass of dim lights before him was the City. "It looks so different. Like a dying campfire or something."

"Troops under control of the new council—it's fairies of all sorts now, goblins, even ferishers, working together, at least for the moment—have been sent to free all the slaves from the power plants, to close the places and lock them. There is no longer any power in this city that a person cannot make for himself or herself," Cumber explained. "Those are fires, candles, lanterns. A few radiance-charms, but most people are saving their strength for what is more important, making sure their families are fed and protected. The downtown area is dark, the buildings empty. It's a new world, and nobody knows what kind of world yet."

The last time Theo had seen the City it had glowed like the display in a jewelry store window, diamond and ruby and sapphire gleams, dazzlingly bright. Now it looked like all the gems had been replaced with amber and topaz—an ancient light, murky and mysterious, but somehow also satisfying. "You said the king and queen are gone."

"Vanished from the ruins of the Cathedral on the Old Mound. They might be dead—really dead, this time—but I doubt that could be true. Perhaps they've simply . . . moved on. Changed. Nobody knows. I suspect there will be whole university departments trying to answer these questions for centuries." He took Theo's arm and led him along the bridge. Cumber *had* changed. He had something now, a sort of reserve, an inner weight that made the rest of his traits seem to fit better. "Now go on," the ferisher said, pointing to the bridgehouse. "Button's waiting to see you."

"Pick me up for a minute, Theo," commanded Applecore.

When Theo had her safe, Cumber Sedge retreated a few steps to give them a little privacy. "Are you happy?" Theo asked her.

"With Cumber? He's a fine lad. Gentle and sweet as spring rain. A bit on the quiet side sometimes, but I've got enough to say for both of us." She looked at him, her little face owlish in the torchlight. "Don't worry about me, Theo. Yes, I'm happy. And whatever you do, I think you'll be happy, too. I just wanted to say . . . well, I'm proud of you. You're not anywhere near as much of an eejit as I suspected."

He laughed. "I'd like that in writing."

Applecore snorted. "Like any of your other friends can read." She stood on tiptoe, balancing herself with a hand on his jaw, and kissed him at the corner of his mouth, a touch as light and cool as a snowflake just before it melts. "If you don't come back to us, we won't forget you. And I'm not talking about Cumber's history-book nonsense, either. I'm talking about the ones who care about you."

"Like you?"

"Yeah, like me."

He lifted her up and kissed the top of her head as gently as he could. "I haven't had many real friends, you know."

"Could be your breath." She was scowling, but he knew better. "Now give me back to my boyfriend before he decides to come over and hit you with a grimoire or somethin'."

He had expected to be met at the top of the stairs by Button's ogre bodyguards but there was no sign of them. He was met instead by a trio of goblins he didn't recognize, all dressed in loose, colorful clothing, with knives stuck in their belts and various lines painted or tattooed on their faces. They did not seem delighted to see him, but there was no hostility, either: they bowed in a stiffly formal way, arms at their sides, and then led him into Button's apartment. A group of goblin musicians sat cross-legged in one corner, playing a soft but angular melody, and for a moment Theo was thrown back into that hour when the music was all that had saved him. Might it have saved more than that? Could goblin jazz have spared the entire mortal world from ruin?

What a concept! An overblown rock opera if ever there was one.

One of the instrumentalists nodded as Theo passed. It was Bottlecap, with whom he had shared a night of music and ghostweed, but the hush of the room and the air of ceremony kept him from stopping to converse. Still, Theo thought, it would be interesting to talk to him about what had happened on the little island, even to try to work out in actual music some of what he had experienced. Maybe someday . . .

Yeah, but I'll be going home, so that won't happen.

Theo had also anticipated that Primrose and some of Button's other closest confidants would be there, but other than himself, there were only goblins. He saw Doorlatch and a few others that he recognized from the camp, but there were far more unfamiliar faces, serious, wild-looking goblins in festival colors, many of them armed. At the center of the room, in front of a carpet laid with dishes and tea bowls, sat Mud Bug Button. He was dressed in white, as Theo was; he looked like an Indian holy man holding court in his *ashram*. He stood as Theo approached, reaching out to him with a taloned hand.

"Welcome, Theo Vilmos. It is good of you to come. I had feared you would not be well enough, and this would be a poor farewell feast without the most important guest."

"But . . . well, to be honest, I'm not a hundred percent certain I'm going back."

"Ah." Button sat down and directed one of the goblins next to him to pour tea for Theo. The person in question looked more like a warrior than a servant, but he did as he was asked.

When Theo had taken a few sips for courtesy's sake and allowed his dish to be piled with various savories—he had a quick if covert look to make sure none of them were field mouse-based—he leaned forward. "Where are Primrose and the others?"

"Caradenus is in mourning," Button explained. "He begged to be excused."

"He must have loved his sister very much."

Button looked at him for a long moment, then nodded. "Yes. He did."

Theo said, "I'm amazed to be alive. I'm surprised so many of us are. Did you know it would work this way?"

For the first time, Button showed a little of his old, sly self. "If I told you I did, would you promise to tell that story to all who ask you? Then history will remember me as a genius of tactics—another Lord Rose. But to be truthful, *hem,* no. I hoped. Primrose and I made the best plan we could. We knew the goblins would fight after the stick was broken— that my people's anger was too hot to be contained once the treaty was ended. But did we know for certain that others would come out, that the streets would be full of discontent and rage? No. We could only do what was best and hope."

"But you did know that grims could kill dragons."

Again, Button smiled. "I knew that they could, yes, but even that was what might be called a gamble, and everyone knows that although we goblins love gambling, we are not always good at it." He turned to the goblin on his left, whose costume bristled with feathers and beadwork jewelry. "Otter, when you lived in the hills you killed a dragon, yes?"

The goblin looked at Theo, then rubbed his long nose. "Yes. My people called me 'Wormslayer.'"

"How big was it?" Button asked.

The one called Otter thought for a moment, then spread his arms wide. "Wings like this," he said. "One of the big ones." He went back to his solemn chewing.

"That would mean Otter's famous trophy was . . . *hem* . . . about ten or twelve feet long." Button laughed. "So you see, even the grims had little experience with the great worms. Again, we could only hope that arrows steeped in poison in their eyes and soft throats would have the same effect that they did on the monsters' much smaller cousins."

"My God! They were trying that for the first time?"

"War is often that way," said Button. "Now, eat. I would ask you more questions about what you heard and saw, what happened to you. Particularly of the Remover. The little I have heard is very surprising."

"But you're not eating."

"I am fasting," the goblin explained. "But the food is very good. Eat. You have been a long time asleep and I think you need it."

Theo really was very hungry, and although many of the tastes were unfamiliar, the food was good. As he answered Button's questions, struggling to remember the order in which things had happened, having to backtrack several times when he realized he had left out an important detail, he realized that goblin food and goblin music, just to name two unquestionably foreign things, were beginning to seem almost ordinary to him.

"So you yourself were the key," Button said at last.

"Just a tool."

"No. That was Hellebore's great error. He thought of you that way, but it was your mind and your heart that broke him.

Now I will ask you a question, just as you asked me. Did you
know that the *irrha* would take the child if it could not take
you?"

Theo shrugged. "Like you said yourself—I hoped. I
didn't have much time to think about it, really. I just remembered Dowd saying something about how a changeling
and the mortal child he gets switched with have some kind
of bond. I didn't really understand it, but there weren't a lot
of other options. Also, I suddenly realized that I'd rather
have one of those water-women get me than that thing."

"It would have been a quick death by fire or a slow death
beneath the water," Button said thoughtfully. "They say that
those taken by water-spirits come to love their captors before they die." He went silent for a moment and then shook
his head. "There has been too much talk about death. Tell me
more about your world. This is a feast, after all! I have been
too much in the company of my own people lately, however
much I love them. Tell me tales of your world, which has so
recently escaped a terrible fate that it likely did not even
know existed."

"I hope so—I'd hate to go back and find myself in the middle of the new Dark Ages or something." Theo paused. "Just
one more question for you, if you don't mind—something I
still don't understand. You said the goblins were ready to fight
back, and it seems like the only thing keeping them under the
thumb of those Flower lords was the treaty stick. Why hadn't
anyone broken it before? Why were you the first?"

Button gave him a quizzical look. "Do you really want
another goblin tale? Very well—I cannot refuse you tonight.
I will try to make it a swift one. The answer is deceptively
simple, Theo. First of all, most goblins did not know where
the stick was kept. We supposed it would be hidden in some
deep and well-guarded vault. It did not occur to us that the
Flower lords knew so little about us, or cared so little for the
danger we posed to them, that they did not understand only
our sacred word bound us to them—our ancestors' promise
in the form of the treaty stick. Primrose himself told me

where it was. It was, *hem,* merely a curiosity to him, something he had stumbled across in the dusty back rooms of the Parliamentary Museum as he pursued his studies in justice and history. When he mentioned it to me, years after he had seen it, I realized exactly what it was and began to plan."

"But somebody must have known—there must have been goblin janitors or *somebody.* Why didn't anyone ever take it before? Why were you the one who broke it?"

Button was silent for a moment. "I suppose it is a bit shameful, in a way, that no one before me dared to do this thing. Yes, there may have been some that knew, but it was also true that no one wanted to face the death that would result from breaking that treaty."

Theo didn't understand. The goblins seemed a bit more gung-ho than that: it was hard to imagine them enduring servitude merely out of fear that many of them would die in a rebellion. He would never forget the wild warriors he had seen in Strawflower Square, calmly stringing their bows as the flailing black shadows came down on them from the sky.

"Enough of this," Button said suddenly. "I invoke my privilege as guest of honor. Tell me the tales of your world, Theo. Tell me of your life. Make me laugh."

"I'll do my best." He shrugged off the thoughts of war and worms, tried to think of the things he missed about the world to which it seemed he would soon be returning. He wondered if Button would understand why Johnny Battistini trying to parallel park a stolen ice cream wagon while ripped out of his mind on mushrooms was funny.

He told him the story. Button understood, or seemed to.

It seemed to be nearly midnight when he finally got up to say goodbye. Button also rose, and hugged him, a strange, wiry embrace that was not quite like anything Theo had experienced.

"I will miss you, Theo. It has been good to know you."

"Well, don't change my address in your Rolodex quite yet. I'm still thinking it over."

"Ah." Button took his hand for a moment, fixed him with those slotted yellow eyes. "I feel sure that whatever you do, you will, *hem,* take a little goblin music with you always." He let go of Theo's hand. "Go safely, Theo Vilmos."

"I like that better than what you said to me the last time we were together. What was that? Something like, 'We aren't promised anything but the last breath we took.'"

"Something like, yes. Goodnight."

No one was waiting for him outside the bridgehouse, Cumber and Applecore long since gone off to bed—and that was a personal arrangement Theo still hadn't completely wrapped his head around—but there were enough fires and torches burning in the riverside camp, not to mention the flaring stars, to make finding his way back easy. Something nagged at him as he walked, something about the way Button had spoken, the things he had said. On any other such night Theo would have let it go, but he was stone sober, having drunk nothing but goblin tea, and it was either that or think about his own still very muddled plans.

I'm not a mortal, but I think like one—so where do I belong? And if I don't go home to the mortal world, will they take back the farewell feast? He was full of questions, and found himself almost nostalgic for the old days, for the happy ignorance of going home blasted and blank. *Here's another one—why did Button throw a farewell get-together for me and invite a bunch of wild goblins I don't know?* Perhaps it was only the goblin's odd, semiformal way of speaking, but the theme had come up several times, including Button ending the conversation about the breaking of the treaty stick by invoking his privilege as guest of honor.

But if it's a farewell feast for me, wouldn't I be the guest of honor?

And then it suddenly clicked, the whole strange way that things had gone, everyone's reticence and odd remarks. *It was a goblin story, about the stick—he told me so. And they always have a hole in the middle.* Button had said it himself, but Theo hadn't recognized it. *"No one wanted to face the death that would result from breaking that treaty,"* those had been his exact words. Theo had assumed he meant the death of Button's fellow goblins in a rebellion, but he had been talking about himself. Those white robes—he hadn't been a holy man surrounded by acolytes, but a condemned prisoner, however respected, surrounded by his jailers. By his executioners.

Theo ran back across the camp as fast as he could but the bridgehouse was locked, the upper windows dark. He hammered his fists on the door but no one answered. At last old Doorlatch came out of one of the other buildings on the ramshackle bridge, wiping his eyes—whether because he had been asleep or crying, Theo couldn't tell. When he at last understood Theo's heartbroken ramblings, he tried to lead him back to his tent.

"There is nothing you can do," the goblin said. "Nothing. It is the law. Button knew that. He did what was best. He shall remain in us always—a great hero."

Theo would not be comforted by this and would not go away quietly. It seemed like he had been tricked, although if anyone had fooled him, he had fooled himself. He felt cheated of a final chance to say good-bye. Doorlatch had to summon half a dozen helpers, goblins and fairy-folk and one ogre bodyguard that Theo didn't recognize, to carry him back forcibly to his tent and Poppy.

The only thing he could think about, the only thing that made the pain the tiniest bit less agonizing, was that perhaps it had been easier for Button this way—one less weeping farewell, one less time having to listen to someone demanding the impossible.

Poppy, the child of a cold culture and a cruel family, did not try to make things better; poison was poison, she seemed to know, and had to be sweated out. She held Theo while he wept and groaned and shouted, and kept on holding him until, exhausted, he was taken by sleep at last.

43

THE LIMITS
OF MAGIC

At the first light of morning he went to Caradenus Primrose, who invited him into his tent, which seemed to be
both more sumptuous and more sparse than Theo's own, or
any of the other riverside dwellings he had seen. The simple
life seemed to agree with Flower-folk: like Button, Primrose
could make a carpet seem like a throne.

He listened to Theo's impassioned plea for long minutes,
but at last put up a long-fingered hand to stop him.

"You must listen, Theo Vilmos, please. We owe you
much, but nobody owes you this. And even were it possible
I could not grant it. I have not the power. I have no power
anymore, at least not the sort that comes with privilege and
birth. That may return—we Flower families still have many
resources, and I do not think the world will be so completely
topsy-turvy as some believe—but even if I did, I would not
have stepped in and tried to change things. Button chose this
path, knowing all along what would happen to him, whether
after victory or defeat. It was his will and his wish." Primrose lowered his eyes for a moment. "But most of all,
Theo . . . it is already too late. He is dead. The council of his
tribesmen put him to death him last night."

For long moments, Theo could only sit, wiping tears from
eyes that were already sore with weeping, trying to keep

from losing his wits entirely. "H-he said . . . you were in mourning," Theo managed at last. "I th-thought he meant . . . for your sister."

"For her, too, but she has been lost to me a long time. Button was my brother, although we were from different worlds and peoples. He was my friend."

Theo looked up at Primrose's stiff, expressionless face. The mask of the Flower nobility, he had learned, was not always effective. "He said once that the two of you weren't friends, that you couldn't be. That you were . . . *too* different."

Primrose actually laughed, but it was a sound with a great deal of pain in it. "Then it only proves the goblin was not as wise as he usually appeared."

Theo dried his eyes with his sleeve. He felt empty except for the ache in his chest. "I . . . I don't think I like this world anymore. Can I really go home? Does the magic . . . the science . . . still work?"

Primrose thought for a moment. "I know of no reason why you cannot go back to your world, now that you need no longer fear the undead spirit that pursued you. Any reasonably practiced person can open a gateway for you to use. It is not the power of the generating plants that is needed for that, since no one will be trying to hide the gateway as they did when you were brought here, but the power that each of us in Faerie contain in ourselves. With a little study, I do not doubt you could do it yourself." He brought his hands together in his lap. "We will miss you, Theo. If you go, you will not be able to return—not until such a time as we can undo the Clover Effect, which was a work of great craft performed in an era when power was more freely available."

"To be honest, right now I don't care about returning." But he did care about Poppy, he suddenly realized. He needed her to go with him or it would all be meaningless. What use the memories of heroism, of life-and-death decisions, of beauty and horror, if he left behind the only truly good thing that had happened to him? He would turn into

Eamonn Dowd, sour and bitter and maybe even driven mad by what he had lost. "I'll leave you alone now. I have to go talk to someone."

"Then go in peace, Theo Vilmos."

"You, too." He reached the door of the tent and looked out for a moment at the morning of a day that showed something of the stunning loveliness Faerie could produce. Even the distant City skyline seemed to him again, as it once had, a wondrous, supernatural thing, the tips of the towers not skyscrapers but minarets, elfin castles. He turned back to Primrose. "Will you make things better this time? Here, I mean. In this new age you're starting."

Caradenus Primrose did not quite manage a smile. "I hope so. We can only try."

"Yeah." He lifted a hand, suddenly feeling awkward. "Take it easy."

He had only gone a hundred paces or so when a fairy man he did not recognize emerged from the crowd of passersby and fell into step beside him. The newcomer was dark-haired, and of the same human-type as the Flower lords, but otherwise undistinguished. He kept his eyes down as he walked.

"I wanted to say good-bye," the stranger said. "And that I am sorry. I have done terrible things. I have much to think about."

Theo shook his head. Why did everyone know so much about his business? "I'm sorry, do I know you?"

The stranger smiled, still without looking Theo in the face. He had his shoulders hunched, as though he didn't want anyone to notice him, which was odd because he was already almost completely unremarkable. "You turned out to be quite clever, really—I admired what you did with the water-nymph. I don't think that was all just your true heritage coming out, either. There's something to be said for a mortal upbringing, after all—I'm beginning to think we're tougher than the fairies, in some ways. Are you called Theo Violet now, by the way?"

"Wait a second—who are you?" He grabbed the man by the shoulder, spun him around.

The man looked back at him, but even face-to-face he was still unfamiliar. The stranger's posture was that of someone ready to run away, but a sly little smile flickered around the edges of his mouth. "You haven't figured it out yet? Maybe I've given you too much credit."

"Dowd?" It seemed impossible, but suddenly he could hear the suggestion of that soft, strained voice coming from this far more ordinary throat. "But you're dead! I saw you die!"

"Come, Theo, that could have been a speech out of a Flash Gordon comic. You saw that *body* die. It's happened to me once before, as you know, and I survived it. Since then I've spent years trying to strengthen myself so I could eventually get into another, less . . . unpleasant . . . body than the Remover's. As it turned out, I needed every moment of that practice." He held out his arms like someone who had just performed an impressive conjuring trick—which, obviously, he had. "As my body died, I took refuge in one of Hellebore's guards. He wasn't a particularly nice man but I'm still not proud of forcing him out of his own flesh. The body and I were captured on the hilltop after Hellebore and the Terrible Child died—we were running away, of course—but we were let go after a few days. This fellow's been officially rehabilitated, you see, so I'm in the clear. There's no real guilt attached to being a foot soldier in the losing army, or even one of Nidrus Hellebore's private guard. So here I am. I think I'll head out to Ash or Birch, start over. Erephine is dead now, really dead. I have much to think about."

"I should turn you over to Caradenus Primrose—he's just back there. Or kill you myself!" Theo fought the overwhelming sense of unreality: this was the second time he had spoken with Eamonn Dowd, and both times it was after discovering the man was alive beyond all logic. "You helped to kill our baby. Me and Cat."

"There is nothing I can say except that I am sorry. Yes, I

assisted Hellebore in delivering the spell. It was a madness
that affected all I did, my desperate love and my anger at
having been cheated. I think it has passed now. I certainly
feel I see things more clearly. But perhaps that is just the effect of having a new body."

"I still can't let you walk away."

"Yes, you can, and in fact you will. Because if you don't,
I'll be forced to take someone else's body to escape—not
yours, but some innocent's. You won't stop me, no matter
what you do. I will leap from body to body if I need to and
many will die needlessly."

Theo stared at the stranger's face. He felt weary and sick.
"So I have to let you go?"

"Yes, you do. In fact, I'm going now." The dark-haired
fairy turned and walked away down a narrow street between
rows of ramshackle dwellings, tents, and lean-tos, a small
thoroughfare crowded with fairy-folk of all shapes and sorts,
talking, trading, living their lives. Within moments Eamonn
Dowd was lost from sight among all the other refugees.

Poppy wasn't at the tent when Theo got back. He had
been full of useful arguments, scads of convincing reasons why she should come with him back to the mortal
world, but he suddenly found himself with nothing much to
say and no one to say it to. In fact, he was stunned. Things
had become altogether too strange. Dowd was dead but had
come back. Mud Bug Button was dead and wasn't going to
be making any reappearances. There lay the unfairness of
life in a single nutshell, and it went pretty much the same
way in Faerie as it did in the mortal world.

*There's not much difference between the two when it
comes to the important stuff—not really.*

He sat for a long while in the doorway, staring out at the
clouds and the play of light in the sky, listening to the racket
of the camp's daily life. There seemed to be more children
around than before, or at least they were being allowed to
make more noise. *Children always sound the same,* he

thought. *No matter where they come from, what language they speak, whether they have fox-ears or yellow goat-eyes or whatever, they always sound the same.*

It was a nice sound, he realized.

Good-bye, Button, he thought. *I guess this is your epitaph—the sound of children playing. Goblin children, fairy children. There are worse things to leave behind.*

Someone made a small sound and he looked up to find three faces looking down at him, one from a very great height. It was the nearest face that startled him, the goblin face, since he had been thinking of Button, but he hadn't seen any of them since he had returned from the lake-bottom and it took him a fraction of a moment to put names back on the familiar expressions.

"Streedy Nettle! And Mistress Twinge and Coathook, too. How are you all?"

The tall, shock-haired fairy did not look any better connected to reality than he had been before the downfall of the old order, but at least he looked calm and happy. He extended a long-fingered hand to help Theo up. "Hello, Theo," he said, and his cheeks colored. "Poppy's here. Not just in my head, but she's here. Every day."

"I know. It's good to see you, Streedy."

"She's nice."

"Yes, she is." He turned to the others. "So we all survived, huh?"

"More or less," said the pooka, then leaned toward him and lowered her voice. "Although eedy-Stray here doesn't know about utton-Bay just yet, if you get what I mean, so watch what you say. It's going to upset him and we want to have a wire around his ankle when he finds out so he's grounded and he doesn't set the whole camp on fire or turn us all into butterflies or something." She straightened up again. "Anyway, Coathook had something he needed to talk to you about and me and Streedy thought we'd tag along and say hello. So how's it hangin', roommate? I hear *you've* been pretty busy."

Theo shrugged. "Not by choice. Actually, almost none of it was by choice."

"Even so, the grapevine says you met the Big Guy himself."

"Big Guy . . . ?" For a moment he thought of Button, small slender Button handing him that card at the bus stop, and had to swallow hard. "Sorry, who would that be?"

Mistress Twinge took a moment to reply, applying a flame from her fingertip to an ugly turd-colored cigar. "The Big Guy!" she said through a cloud of foul smoke. "Robin Goodfellow, of course. He's pretty much the hero of my folk. The king's right-hand man, he used to be. Most famous pooka that ever lived. What was he like?"

Theo tried to remember, but much had happened since those moments on the black boat. "Sad. Wise, I guess, as far as I could tell. Kind of funny, too. He didn't like Hellebore much."

Mistress Twinge nodded happily. "A man of the people. I wonder where he is."

"Nobody knows?"

The pooka didn't seem much worried. "Now that Hellebore and the rest are gone, the binding-spells are gone too. He's probably sailing around with the king or queen somewhere. Getting a little well-earned rest."

"You think they're all still alive?"

The pooka leaned forward again, bringing a fog of tobacco fumes with her that would make a hyena squint. "Of *course* they are. You don't kill off any of those folks. They're like the stars, the moon. Like taxes." She stood up and gave Theo a hearty slap on the back that nearly dislocated his scapula. "We gotta get going now. Come on, Streedy, let's go make some of the new arrivals nervous. Theo, sorry to hear you're leaving, fella—I was going to teach you how to play Beetlebout for money, which would be a comfort to your declining years."

Coathook sat silently until Mistress Twinge had vanished whistling down the muddy street between the rows of tents,

Streedy Nettle tagging along after her like a stork following a bulldog pup it had misidentified as its mother. The goblin blinked, then looked at Theo almost shyly. "You saw him last night. What was he like?"

It took a few seconds for Theo to understand, and understanding brought back pain. "I'm not sure I want to talk about it right now."

Coathook's clawed fingers closed on his arm—gently, but with enough force to tell Theo he didn't want the goblin ever to grab him for real. "Please."

He thought of this small fellow writhing on the floor of Elysium House, having taken real poison to facilitate Button's desperate plan. *A desperate plan that actually worked,* Theo reminded himself, marveling. "He was . . . well. Very well, considering . . . considering what was coming. We talked about what happened. He asked me to tell him stories about my world."

Coathook was looking down again. "I would like to hear those stories someday."

But I won't be here to tell them, Theo thought. Out loud, he said, "I hope I get the chance to do it. Did you know him?"

"Not well. Only from a distance. But he was important to me, in a way. He was my father."

Theo could not reply immediately. "You . . . you don't mean he was, like, your spiritual father, do you?" he said at last.

Coathook slowly shook his head. The swing of his long nose as he did so should have been grotesque, even comical, but it only reminded Theo of the strange world in which he found himself, where there was so much he still did not understand. "He fathered me. On my mother. In the usual way."

"My God, and you only knew him from a distance? Didn't you talk to him? Did he know?"

"I do not think he knew, although once or twice he looked at me as though something about me troubled him. But I was

only a child of one of his early matings and so he did not recognize my name—he had never known it. My mother met
him at the goblin academy. She was driven from her nest in
shame when I was born fatherless, and took refuge in the
countryside." He gave an uncomfortable shrug. "It does not
matter now. He is dead. He is a hero. I am Coathook. I am
not more or less because of him."

Theo thought of his own parents, of his lifelong struggle
to make sense of himself by making sense of them, to justify
himself by making them responsible for all they had done
wrong to him, or failed to do for him at all. "That's all?
Don't you care?"

"Of course I care. That is why I wished to hear from you
of his last hours. I am on my way to the funeral ceremony,
as are all the others of my people who are here, and I wish
to think of him in wholeness, but that is all. I am one of
them, one of the living, and he is not. Of course I care, but I
have always lived my life without him."

"May outsiders go to the funeral?"

"It is not for you, only goblins. That is why he said his
good-bye to you on the bridge, last night."

An honor, Cumber had called it, when Theo did not understand what he meant. Now he did. "Did you love him?"

Coathook threw up his hand, touched his forehead in a
gesture Theo did not recognize, but which had the look of
ritual. "As a son or as another goblin, proud of what he did?"

"Either, I guess."

"Then, yes." Coathook stood. "But today the sun came up
again, as it always does. Thank you for your time, Theo. I
must leave now. I have to go and eat my father."

Theo sat and watched him walk away, the small, dark-
furred figure growing smaller and smaller. Even after
Coathook had disappeared Theo still sat in the doorway,
watching clouds and listening to the noises all around.

The three of them looked back at him, Poppy with a look of poorly concealed worry, Cumber curious but reserved, Applecore hiding whatever she was feeling behind one of the world's smallest but most concentrated looks of disdain.

"I suppose you're wondering why I've called you all here," Theo said. "Sorry, that's a joke, and it's not a very good one because I actually *did* call you all here. I'm kind of nervous." He looked down at his hands, clutched together as if both sets of fingers were afraid the other set might sneak off. "I have a question I need to ask you, Cumber. About gateways and going back and forth."

Cumber Sedge nodded. "I had a feeling you might be wondering, Theo. The answer is, no, there's still no way to come back after you've been here and gone. Undoing the Clover Effect has been set back years. There was your uncle's way of returning, but nobody else will ever try anything that horrible and dangerous and the conditions probably won't arise anyway. So, again, no. If you leave, you are almost certainly leaving for good."

Theo smiled despite himself. "That wasn't the question I was going to ask, but thanks. What I was wondering is, can people from the other side—from my old world, the mortal world—still come over here? And can they leave again afterward?"

Cumber looked surprised. It took him a moment to respond. "You mean, are things still the same that way, too? Yes, I suppose so. We haven't had any visitors from there since . . . since everything happened, and you'd still have to get someone with an available trip to go fetch them. But yes, I think so."

"How about you, Cumber? You've always wanted to visit the mortal world. Applecore's used up her exemption but you haven't. Maybe you could take a trip. A short one, since I'm sure you wouldn't want to be away from Core very long,"—he gave the sprite a mocking look as he emphasized the nickname, then turned back to Cumber—"but enough to see a few things first hand that you've only ever read about. It wouldn't have to be right away."

Cumber looked at Applecore, then at Theo. "But why?"

"Because I have a friend back there named Johnny, just about the only real friend I had, who deserves to see this place—he would get a kick out of it like you wouldn't believe. He'd love goblin drumming, too. And if I can have that one friend come for an extended visit—he might even want to stay, who knows? Maybe we could fix him up with Dolly the ogre—then I think I won't really miss my old world all that much."

It was Poppy who understood first, but that was because it meant more to her. "You mean . . . you're going to stay?"

"Unless you're really, really hot to see the Golden Gate Bridge and visit Chinatown, yeah. Maybe someday Cumber and his science-buddies will find out a way to solve the back-and-forth thing, then we can go live there for a while. It actually would be fun to show you around. But I've been thinking about it all day and I realized that I don't have that much left to do back there. My unfinished business is here, learning about my fairy family, learning about the world itself, keeping an eye on . . . on old friends and acquaintances. Not to mention learning more about who and what I really am. And there's a ton of music I still need to hear. I bet there's even ferisher music, right?"

Cumber laughed. "Sort of. If you like that sort of thing. A lot of it is about farming. And sweeping."

"I'll probably love it. And there's probably even wilder stuff I need to hear—giant music, ocean-bottom-living, weird-ass nymph music, all of it waiting for me. What does my old world have to offer that's better? No, I realized I'd be going back just as a sort of, I don't know, way of living up to what my parents wanted. 'You can make it, Theo. You can make something of yourself.' But I *have* made something of myself—I've just done it here. And I have to admit, I'm interested to see what's going to happen next in this new world everyone wants to build."

Poppy had moved over next to him and had his hand tightly in hers. "We'll help, Theo. You and I. We'll help build it."

"Yeah, maybe we will. If I've learned anything, though, it's that I'm a much better musician than I am anything else. I sure as hell ain't a politician."

Applecore chortled. "No, you sure as hell are not, boyo."

"But by far the most important thing is that I have friends here—real friends. I'll miss some things about my old world—the way the sun looks on the trees in October in California, that's almost as good as anything here. And the fog creeping down the hills and stuff like that. But there aren't a lot of people left that I need who aren't here."

He turned and kissed Poppy. She kissed him back, and in the smell of her breath and the scent of her warm skin he knew that wherever he lived could, with a little luck, become the best of all possible places. With an effort of will he pulled back at last and looked over, a bit embarrassed, to where Cumber still sat with Applecore on his shoulder. They were both grinning at him.

"You don't inherit anything, you know," said Cumber, teasing. "Just because you stay here you won't automatically be a hero and you certainly won't be rich. No Violet family fortune left. It's all gone into Hellebore's assets years ago, and any property of his will probably be confiscated by the new council and sold to help pay for rebuilding."

"Didn't want it," Theo said happily. "All I want as an inheritance from my fairy family is some information. Maybe you could help me with libraries or whatever. As far as money and property, well, I've been living in tents practically since I got here. Why change?" He had a sudden thought. "There is one thing I just realized I miss. Cumber, if you do go back to my world to fetch Johnny for a visit, do you think you could get me another leather jacket? Oh, and you might as well bring back my motorcycle, too."

Cumber Sedge rolled his eyes. "It won't work here, Theo. Machinery from the mortal world won't run."

"No. But it sure will look cool."

Applecore had the last word, as usual. "You mean like when you walked into the freezer, fella?"

The four went out under the fierce stars in search of something to teat and drink. None of them had finished mourning and they all had scars of one kind or another, but even without a word spoken about it they shared an understanding now. As they walked, Theo suddenly fell quiet.

"Oh," he said at last. "Wow. I just realized something."

"What?" Poppy leaned into him.

"I couldn't go back to the mortal world anyway—not until they fix the Clover Effect thingie. We've all been talking like that's where I came from in the first place, but I didn't. I came from here. When I was a baby. So I've used up my exemption." He turned to Applecore. "You weren't leading me away from somewhere when you got me out of that cabin. You were bringing me home."

"He's right," said Cumber. "We didn't think of that."

"Ah." Applecore smiled. "See? Even when I don't know what I'm doing, I know what I'm doing."

"I'm glad you made your decision before you figured that out," Poppy told him.

"Home." Theo weighed the word for a moment, then took her arm and began walking again. After a while, he started to sing. Poppy joined him and their voices blended sweetly until the ferisher and the sprite chimed in and made it raucous and lovely and silly.

I think I get it, Theo decided, watching his friends make each other laugh until they couldn't speak. Applecore almost tumbled out of Cumber's pocket and Poppy was clinging to Theo so she didn't fall over either. *You really can find Happily Ever After.*

You just needed luck, then it was up to you to make it happen.

One day at a time.

INDEX
OF PEOPLE, PLACES, AND THINGS

"In the impressive opening installment of his first new high fantasy trilogy in a decade, Williams injects hope and humor into an end-of-the-world conflict. The author's richly detailed world will enchant established fans and win new converts."
—*Publishers Weekly* (Starred Review)

Tad Williams

SHADOWPLAY

The Second Volume of *Shadowmarch*

March 2007

Available in Hardcover
Wherever Books are Sold

DAW 47

TAD
WILLIAMS

Memory, Sorrow & Thorn

"THE FANTASY EQUIVALENT OF *WAR AND PEACE*...
readers who delight in losing themselves in long complex
tales of epic fantasy will be in their element here."
—*Locus*

THE DRAGONBONE CHAIR
0-88677-384-9

STONE OF FAREWELL
0-88677-480-2

TO GREEN ANGEL TOWER (Part One)
0-88677-598-1

TO GREEN ANGEL TOWER (Part Two)
0-88677-606-6

To Order Call: 1-800-788-6262
www.dawbooks.com

DAW 42

OTHERLAND

TAD WILLIAMS

"The Otherland books are a
major accomplishment."
—*Publishers Weekly*

"It will captivate you."
—*Cinescape*

In many ways it is humankind's most stunning
achievement. This most exclusive of places is also
one of the world's best-kept secrets, but somehow,
bit by bit, it is claiming Earth's most valuable
resource: its children.

CITY OF GOLDEN SHADOW (Vol. One)
0-88677-763-1

RIVER OF BLUE FIRE (Vol. Two)
0-88677-844-1

MOUNTAIN OF BLACK GLASS (Vol. Three)
0-88677-906-5

SEA OF SILVER LIGHT (Vol. Four)
0-75640-030-9

To Order Call: 1-800-788-6262
www.dawbooks.com

DAW 44

TAD WILLIAMS

TAILCHASER'S SONG

"Williams' fantasy, in the tradion of WATERSHIP DOWN, captures the nuances and delights of feline behavior in a story that should appeal to both fantasy and cat lovers. Readers will lose their hearts to Tailchaser and his companions."
—*Library Journal*

"TAILCHASER'S SONG is more than just an absorbing adventure, more than just a fanciful tale of cat lore. It is a story of self-discovery...Fritti faces challenges—responsibility, loyalty, and loss—that are universal. His is the story of growing up, of accepting change, of coming of age."
—*Seventeen*

"A wonderfully exciting quest fantasy. Fantasy fans are sure to be enthralled by this remarkable book." —*Booklist*

0-88677-953-7

To Order Call: 1-800-788-6262
www.dawbooks.com

Praise for the novels of
Joan Johnston

"Johnston's characters struggle against seriously deranged foes and face seemingly insurmountable obstacles to true love."
—*Booklist*

"Johnston warms your heart and tickles your fancy."
—*New York Daily News*

"Complex and suspenseful."
—*RT Book Reviews* on *A Stranger's Game*

"Johnston rivets the reader."
—*Bookreporter.com*

"Timely subject matter, strong plotting, and a quick pace."
—*RT Book Reviews* on *Outcast*

"Romance devotees will find Johnston lively and well-written, and her characters perfectly enchanting."
—*Publishers Weekly*

"Joan Johnston continually gives us everything we want…a story that you wish would never end, and lots of tension and sensuality."
—*RT Book Reviews*

"Joan Johnston [creates] unforgettable subplots and characters who make every fine thread weave into a touching tapestry."
—*Affaire de Coeur*

"A guaranteed good read."
—*New York Times* bestselling author Heather Graham

LIBRARY
7117 W. 7 MILE RD.
DETROIT, MI 48221

JOAN JOHNSTON

New York Times *bestselling author of*

OUTCAST

the Bitter Creek novels, which include

THE COWBOY
THE TEXAN
THE LONER
THE PRICE
THE RIVALS
THE NEXT MRS. BLACKTHORNE
A STRANGER'S GAME

and the Hawk's Way series

Please visit her Web site at
www.JoanJohnston.com
*for a complete listing
of her titles and series.*